G000255307

DIED IN TH...

FINAL C...

SWING, BROTHER, SWING

Dame Ngaio Marsh was born in New Zealand in 1895 and died in February 1982. She wrote over 30 detective novels and many of her stories have theatrical settings, for Ngaio Marsh's real passion was the theatre. Both actress and producer, she almost single-handedly revived the New Zealand public's interest in the theatre. It was for this work that she received what she called her 'damery' in 1966.

'The finest writer in the English language of the pure, classical puzzle whodunit. Among the crime queens, Ngaio Marsh stands out as an Empress.'   *The Sun*

'Ngaio Marsh transforms the detective story from a mere puzzle into a novel.'   *Daily Express*

'Her work is as nearly flawless as makes no odds. Character, plot, wit, good writing, and sound technique.'   *Sunday Times*

'She writes better than Christie!'   *New York Times*

'Brilliantly readable . . . first class detection.'   *Observer*

'Still, quite simply, the greatest exponent of the classical English detective story.'   *Daily Telegraph*

'Read just one of Ngaio Marsh's novels and you've got to read them all . . .'   *Daily Mail*

BY THE SAME AUTHOR

A Man Lay Dead
Enter a Murderer
The Nursing Home Murder
Death in Ecstasy
Vintage Murder
Artists in Crime
Death in a White Tie
Overture to Death
Death at the Bar
Surfeit of Lampreys
Death and the Dancing Footman
Colour Scheme
Died in the Wool
Final Curtain
Swing, Brother, Swing
Opening Night
Spinsters in Jeopardy
Scales of Justice
Off With His Head
Singing in the Shrouds
False Scent
Hand in Glove
Dead Water
Death at the Dolphin
Clutch of Constables
When in Rome
Tied up in Tinsel
Black As He's Painted
Last Ditch
Grave Mistake
Photo-Finish
Light Thickens
Black Beech and Honeydew (autobiography)

NGAIO MARSH

Died in the Wool

Final Curtain

Swing, Brother, Swing

AND

I Can Find My Way Out

HARPER

HARPER

an imprint of HarperCollins*Publishers*
1 London Bridge Street
London SE1 9GF
www.harpercollins.co.uk

This omnibus edition 2009

Died in the Wool first published in Great Britain by Collins 1945
Final Curtain first published in Great Britain by Collins 1947
Swing, Brother, Swing first published in Great Britain by Collins 1949
I Can Find My Way Out first published in Great Britain in
Death on the Air and Other Stories by HarperCollins*Publishers* 1995

Ngaio Marsh asserts the moral right to
be identified as the author of these works

Copyright © Ngaio Marsh Ltd 1945, 1947, 1949
I Can Find My Way Out copyright © Ngaio Marsh (Jersey) Ltd 1989

ISBN 978 0 00 732873 4
Printed and bound by CPI Group (UK) Ltd, Croydon, CR0 4YY

MIX
Paper from
responsible sources
FSC™ C007454
www.fsc.org

FSC is a non-profit international organisation established to promote the
responsible management of the world's forests. Products carrying the FSC
label are independently certified to assure consumers that they come
from forests that are managed to meet the social, economic and
ecological needs of present and future generations.

Find out more about HarperCollins and the environment at
www.harpercollins.co.uk/green

CONTENTS

Died in the Wool
1

Final Curtain
229

Swing, Brother, Swing
491

BONUS STORY:
I Can Find My Way Out
735

Died in the Wool

Died in the Wool

Contents

	Prologue – 1939–1942	5
1	Alleyn at Mount Moon	12
2	According to Ursula Harme	32
3	According to Douglas Grace	49
4	According to Fabian Losse	68
5	According to Terence Lynne	85
6	According to the Files	103
7	According to Ben Wilson	126
8	According to Cliff Johns	146
9	Attack	162
10	Night Piece	181
11	According to Arthur Rubrick	203
	Epilogue – According to Alleyn	222

Cast of Characters

Florence Rubrick	*Of Mount Moon*
Arthur Rubrick	*Her husband*
Sammy Joseph	*Wool buyer for Riven Brothers*
Alf	*Storeman at Riven Brothers*
Roderick Alleyn	*Chief Detective-Inspector, CID*
Fabian Losse	*Nephew to Arthur Rubrick*
Douglas Grace	*Nephew to Florence Rubrick*
Ursula Harme	*Her niece*
Terence Lynne	*Her secretary. Later gardener at Mount Moon*
Mrs Aceworthy	*Housekeeper at Mount Moon*
Markins	*Manservant at Mount Moon*
Tommy Johns	*Working manager at Mount Moon*
Mrs Johns	*His wife*
Cliff Johns	*Their son*
Ben Wilson	*Wool sorter*
Jack Merrywether	*Presser*
Albert Black	*Rouseabout*
Percy Gould	*Shearers' cook*

Prologue

1939

'I am Mrs Rubrick of Mount Moon,' said the golden-headed lady. 'And I should like to come in.'

The man at the stage-door looked down into her face. Its nose and eyes thrust out at him, pale, all of them, and flecked with brown. Seen at close quarters these features appeared to be slightly out of perspective. The rest of the face receded from them, fell away to insignificance. Even the mouth with its slightly projecting, its never quite hidden teeth, was forgotten in favour of that acquisitive nose, those protuberant exacting eyes. 'I should like to come in,' Flossie Rubrick repeated.

The man glanced over his shoulder into the hall. 'There are seats at the back,' he said. 'Behind the buyers' benches.'

'I know there are. But I don't want to see the backs of the buyers. I want to watch their faces. I'm Mrs Rubrick of Mount Moon and my wool clip should be coming up in the next half-hour. I want to sit up *here* somewhere.' She looked beyond the man at the door, through a pair of scenic book-wings to the stage where an auctioneer in shirt-sleeves sat at a high rostrum, gabbling. 'Just there,' said Flossie Rubrick, 'on that chair by those painted things. That will do quite well.' She moved past the man at the door. 'How do you do?' she said piercingly as she came face-to-face with a second figure. 'You don't mind if I come in, do you? I'm Mrs Arthur Rubrick. May I sit down?'

She settled herself on a chair she had chosen, pulling it forward until she could look through an open door in the proscenium and down into the front of the house. She was a tiny creature and it was a tall chair. Her feet scarcely reached the floor. The auctioneer's clerks who sat below his rostrum, glanced up curiously from their papers.

'Lot one seven six,' gabbled the auctioneer. 'Mount Silver.'

'Eleven,' a voice shouted.

In the auditorium two men, their arms stretched rigid, sprang to their feet and screamed. 'Three!' Flossie settled her furs and looked at them with interest. 'Eleven-three,' said the auctioneer.

The chairs proper to the front of the hall had been replaced by rows of desks, each of which was labelled with the name of its occupant's firm. Van Huys. Riven Bros. Dubois. Yen. Steiner. James Ogden. Hartz. Ormerod. Rhodes. Markino. James Barnett. Dressed in business men's suits woven from good wool, the buyers had come in from the four corners of the world for the summer wool sales. They might have been carefully selected types, so eloquently did they display their nationality. Van Huys's buyer with his round wooden head and soft hat, Dubois's, sleek, with a thin moustache and heavy grooves running from his nostrils to the corners of his mouth, old Jimmy Ormerod who bought for himself, screamed like a stallion, and turned purple in the face, Hartz with horn-rimmed glasses who barked, and Mr Kurata Kan of Markino's with his falsetto yelp. Each buyer held printed lists before him, and from time to time, like a well-trained chorus-ensemble, they would all turn a page. The auctioneer's recital was uninflected, and monotonous; yet, as if the buyers were marionettes and he their puppet-master, they would twitch into violent action and as suddenly return to their nervously intent immobility. Some holding the papers before their eyes, stood waiting for a particular wool clip to come up. Others wrote at their desks. Each had trained himself to jerk in a flash from watchful relaxation into spreadeagled yelling urgency. Many of them smoked continuously and Flossie Rubrick saw them through drifts of blue tobacco clouds.

In the open doorways and under the gallery stood groups of men whose faces and hands were raddled and creased by the sun and whose clothes were those of the country man in town. They were the wool-growers, the run-holders, the sheep-cockies, the back-countrymen.

Upon the behaviour of the buyers their manner of living for the next twelve months would depend. The wool sale was what it all amounted to; long musters over high country, nights spent by shepherds in tin huts on mountain sides, late snows that came down into lambing paddocks, noisy rituals of dipping, crutching, shearing; the final down-country journey of the wool bales – this was the brief and final comment on the sheep man's working year.

Flossie saw her husband, Arthur Rubrick, standing in a doorway. She waved vigorously. The men who were with Arthur pointed her out. He gave her a dubious nod and began to make his way along a side aisle towards her. As soon as he reached the steps that led from the auditorium up to her doorway she called out in a sprightly manner. 'Look where I've got to! Come up and join me!' He did so but without enthusiasm.

'What are you doing up here, Floss?' he said. 'You ought to have gone down below.'

'Down below wouldn't suit me at all.'

'Everyone's looking at you.'

'That doesn't embarrass me,' she said loudly. 'When will he get to us, darling? Show me.'

'Ssh!' said her husband unhappily and handed her his catalogue. Flossie made play with her lorgnette. She flicked it open modishly with white-gloved hand and looked through it at the lists. There was a simultaneous flutter of white paper throughout the hall. 'Over we go, I see,' said Flossie and turned a page. 'Now, where are we?'

Her husband grunted urgently and jerked up his head.

'Lot one eighty,' gabbled the auctioneer.

'Thirteen.'

'Half!' yelled old Ormerod.

'Three!'

'Fourteen!'

The spectacled Mr Kurata Kan was on his feet, yelping, a fraction of a second quicker than Ormerod.

'Top price,' cried Flossie shrilly. 'Top price! Isn't it, darling? We've got top price, haven't we? That dear little Jap!'

A ripple of laughter ran through the hall. The auctioneer grinned. The two men near the stage-door moved away, their hands over their mouths. Arthur Rubrick's face, habitually cyanosed, deepened to a richer purple. Flossie clapped her white gloves together and rose excitedly. 'Isn't he too sweet,' she demanded. 'Arthur, isn't he a pet?'

'Flossie, for God's sake,' Arthur Rubrick muttered.

But Flossie made a series of crisp little nods in the direction of Mr Kurata Kan and at last succeeded in attracting his attention. His eyelids creased, his upper lip lifted in a crescent over his long teeth and he bowed.

'There!' said Flossie in triumph as she swept out at the stage-door, followed by her discomforted husband. 'Isn't that splendid?'

He piloted her into a narrow yard. 'I wish you wouldn't make me quite so conspicuous, my dear,' he said. 'I mean, waving to that Jap. We don't know him or anything.'

'No,' cried Flossie. 'But we're going to. You're going to call on him, darling, and we shall ask him to Mount Moon for the weekend.'

'Oh, no, Flossie. Why? Why on earth?'

'I'm all for promoting friendly relations. Besides he's paid top price for my wool. He's a sensible man. I want to meet him.'

'Grinning little pip-squeak. I don't like 'em, Floss. Do you in the eye for tuppence, the Japs would. Any day. They're our natural enemies.'

'Darling, you're absolutely antediluvian. Before we know where we are you'll be talking about The Yellow Peril.'

She tossed her head and a lock of hair dyed a brilliant gold slipped down her forehead. 'Do remember this is 1939,' said Flossie.

1942

On a summer's day in February 1942, Mr Sammy Joseph, buyer for Riven Brothers Textile Manufactory, was going through their wool stores with the storeman. The windows had been blacked out with paint, and the storeman, as they entered, switched on a solitary lamp. This had the effect of throwing into strong relief the square hessian bales immediately under the lamp. Farther down the store they dissolved in shadow. The lamp was high and encrusted with dust: the faces of the two men looked cadaverous. Their voices sounded stifled: there is no echo in a building lined with wool. The air was stuffy and smelt of hessian.

'When did we start buying dead wool, Mr Joseph?' asked the storeman.

'We never buy dead wool,' Joseph said sharply. 'What are you talking about?'

'There's a bale of it down at the far end.'

'Not in this store.'

'I'm good for a bet on it.'

'What's biting you? Why d'you say it's dead?'

'Gawd, Mr Joseph, I've been in the game long enough, haven't I? Don't I know dead wool when I smell it? It pongs.'

'Here!' said Sammy Joseph. 'Where is this bale?'

'Come and see.'

They walked down the aisle between ranks of baled wool. The storeman at intervals switched on more lights and the aisle was extended before them. At the far end he paused and jerked his thumb at the last bale. 'Take a sniff, Mr Joseph,' he said.

Sammy Joseph bent towards the bale. His shadow was thrown up on the surface, across stencilled letters, a number and a rough crescent.

'That's from the Mount Moon clip,' he said.

'I know it is.' The storeman's voice rose nervously. 'Stinks, doesn't it?'

'Yes,' said Joseph. 'It does.'

'Dead wool.'

'I've never bought dead wool in my life. Least of all from Mount Moon. And the smell of dead wool goes off after it's plucked. You know that as well as I do. Dead rat, more likely. Have you looked?'

'Yes, I have looked, Mr Joseph. I shifted her out the other day. It's in the bale. You can tell.'

'Split her up,' Mr Joseph commanded.

The storeman pulled out a clasp knife, opened it, and dug the blade into the front of the bale. Sammy Joseph watched him in a silence that was broken only by the uneasy sighing of the rafters above their heads.

'It's hot in here,' said Sammy Joseph. 'There's a nor'west gale blowing outside. I hate a hot wind.'

'Oppressive,' said the storeman. He drew the blade of his knife downwards, sawing at the bale. The strands of sacking parted in a series of tiny explosions. Through the fissure bulged a ridge of white wool.

'Get a lung full of that,' said the storeman, straightening himself. 'It's something chronic. Try.'

Mr Joseph said: 'I get it from here, thanks. I can't understand it. It's not bellies in that pack, either. Bellies smell a bit but nothing to touch this.' He opened his cigarette case. 'Have one?'

'Ta, Mr Joseph. I don't mind if I do. It's not so good, this pong, is it?'

'It's coming from inside, all right. They must have baled up something in the press. A rat.'

'You will have your rat, sir, won't you?'

'Let's have some of that wool out.' Mr Joseph glanced at his neat worsted suit. 'You're in your working clothes,' he added.

The storeman pulled at a tuft of wool. 'Half a sec', Mr Joseph. She's packed too solid.' He moved away to the end wall. Sammy Joseph looked at the rent in the bale, reached out his hand and drew it back again. The storeman returned wearing a gauntleted canvas glove on his right hand and carrying one of the iron hooks used for shifting wool bales. He worked it into the fissure and began to drag out lumps of fleece.

'Phew!' whispered Sammy Joseph.

'I'll have to hand it to you in one respect, sir. She's not dead wool.'

Mr Joseph picked a lock from the floor, looked at it, and dropped it. He turned away and wiped his hand vigorously on a bale. 'It's frightful,' he said. 'It's a godalmighty stench. What the hell's wrong with you?'

The storeman had sworn with violence and extreme obscenity. Joseph turned to look at him. His gloved hand had disappeared inside the fissure. The edge of the gauntlet showed and no more. His face turned towards Joseph. The eyes and mouth were wide open.

'I'm touching something.'

'With the hook?'

The storeman nodded. 'I won't look any more,' he said loudly.

'Why not?'

'I won't look.'

'Why the hell?'

'It's the Mount Moon clip.'

'I know that. What of it?'

'Don't you read the papers?'

Sammy Joseph changed colour. 'You're mad,' he said. 'God, you're crazy.'

'It's three weeks, isn't it, and they can't find her? I was in the last war. I know what that stink reminds me of – Flanders.'

'Go to hell,' said Mr Joseph, incredulous but violent. 'What do you think you are? A radio play or what?'

The storeman plucked his arm from the bale. Locks of fleece were sticking to the canvas glove. With a violent movement he jerked them free and they lay on the floor, rust coloured and wet.

'You've left the hook in the bale.'

' – the hook.'

'Get it out, Alf.'

' – !'

'Come on. What's wrong with you. Get it out.'

The storeman looked at Sammy Joseph as if he hated him. A loose sheet of galvanized iron on the roof rattled in the wind and the store was filled momentarily with a vague soughing.

'Come on,' Sammy Joseph said again. 'It's only a rat.'

The storeman plunged his hand into the fissure. His bare arm twisted and worked. He braced the palm of his left hand against the bale and wrenched out the hook. With an air of incredulity he held the hook out, displaying it.

'Look!' he said. With an imperative gesture he waved Mr Joseph aside. The iron hook fell at Sammy Joseph's feet. A strand of metallic-gold hair was twisted about it.

CHAPTER 1

Alleyn at Mount Moon

May 1943

A service car pulled out of the township below the Pass. It mounted a steep shingled road until its passengers looked down on the iron roof of the pub and upon a child's farm-animal design of tiny horses tethered to veranda posts, upon specks that were sheep dogs and upon a toy sulky with motor car wheels that moved slowly along the road, down country. Beyond this a system of foothills, gorges, and clumps of pinus insignis stepped down into a plain fifty miles wide, a plain that rose slowly as its horizon mounted with the eyes of the mounting passengers.

Though their tops were shrouded by a heavy mask of cloud, the hills about the Pass grew more formidable. The intervals between cloud-roof and earth-floor lessened. The Pass climbed into the sky. A mountain rain now fell.

'Going into bad weather?' suggested the passenger on the front seat.

'Going out of it, you mean,' rejoined the driver.

'Do I?'

'Take a look at the sky, sir.'

The passenger wound down his window for a moment and craned out. 'Jet black and lowering,' he said, 'but there's a good smell in the air.'

'Watch ahead.'

The passenger dutifully peered through the rain-blinded windscreen and saw nothing to justify the driver's prediction but only a

12

confusion of black cones whose peaks were cut off by the curtain of the sky. The head of the Pass was lost in a blur of rain. The road now hung above a gorge through whose bed hurried a stream, its turbulence seen but not heard at that height. The driver changed down and the engine whined and roared. Pieces of shingle banged violently on the underneath of the car.

'Hallo!' said the passenger. 'Is this the top!' And a moment later: 'Good God, how remarkable!'

The mountain tops had marched away to left and right. The head of the Pass was an open square of piercing blue. As they reached it the black cloud drew back like a curtain. In a moment it was behind them and they looked down into another country.

It was a great plateau, high itself, but ringed about with mountains that were crowned in perpetual snow. It was laced with rivers of snow water. Three lakes of a strange milky green lay across its surface. It stretched bare and golden under a sky that was brilliant as a paladin's mantle. Upon the plateau and the foothills, up to the level of perpetual snow, grew giant tussocks, but there were no forests. Many miles apart, patches of pinus radiata or lombardy poplars could be seen and these marked the solitary homesteads of the sheep farmers. The air was clear beyond belief, unbreathed, one would have said, newly poured out from the blue chalice of the sky.

The passenger again lowered the window, which was still wet but steaming now, in the sun. He looked back. The cloud curtain lolled a little way over the mountain barrier and that was all there was to be seen of it.

'It's a new world,' he said.

The driver stretched out his hand to a pigeon-hole in the dashboard where his store of loose cigarettes joggled together. His leather coat smelt unpleasantly of fish oil. The passenger wished that his journey was over and that he could enter into this new world of which, remaining in the car, he was merely a spectator. He looked at the mountain ring that curved sickle-wise to right and left of the plateau. 'Where is Mount Moon?' he asked. The driver pointed sweepingly to the left. 'They'll pick you up at the forks.'

The road, a pale stripe in the landscape, pointed down the centre of the plateau and then, far ahead, forked towards the mountain ramparts. The passenger could see a car, tiny but perfectly clear, standing at the forks. 'That'll be Mr Losse's car,' said the driver. The passenger thought of the letter he carried in his wallet. Phrases returned to his memory. '. . . the situation has become positively Russian, or, if you prefer the allusion, a setting for a modern crime story . . . We continue here together in an atmosphere that twangs with stretched nerves. One expects them to relax with time, but no . . . it's over a year ago . . . I should not have ventured to make the demand upon your time if there had not been this preposterous suggestion of espionage . . . refuse to be subjected any longer to this particular form of torment . . .' And, in a pointed irritable calligraphy the signature: 'Fabian Losse.'

The bus completed its descent and with a following cloud of dust began to travel across the plateau. Against some distant region of cloud a system of mountains revealed, glittering spear upon spear. One would have said that these must be the ultimate expression of loftiness but soon the clouds parted and there, remote from them, was the shining horn of the great peak, the cloud piercer, Aorangi. The passenger was so intent upon this unfolding picture that he had no eyes for the road and they were close upon the forks before he saw the sign post with its two arms at right-angles. The car pulled up beside them and he read their legends: 'Main South Road' and 'Mount Moon'.

The air was lively with the sound of grasshoppers. Its touch was fresh and invigorating. A tall young man wearing a brown jacket and grey trousers, came round the car to meet him. 'Mr Alleyn? I'm Fabian Losse.' He took a mail bag from the driver who had already begun to unload Alleyn's luggage and a large box of stores for Mount Moon. The service car drove away to the south in its attendant cloud of dust. Alleyn and Losse took the road to Mount Moon.

II

'It's a relief to me that you've come, sir,' said Losse after they had driven in silence for some minutes. 'I hope I haven't misled you with my dark hints of espionage. They had to be dark, you know, because they are based entirely on conjecture. Personally I find the whole theory of espionage dubious, indeed I don't believe in it for a moment. But I used it as bait.'

'Does anyone believe in it?'

'My deceased aunt's nephew, Douglas Grace, urges it passionately. He wanted to come and meet you in order to press his case but I thought I'd get in first. After all it was I who wrote to you and not Douglas.'

The road they had taken was rough, little more than a pair of wheel tracks separated by a tussocky ridge. It ran up to the foothills of the eastern mountains and skirted them. Far to the west now, midway across the plateau, Alleyn could still see the service car, a clouded point of movement driving south.

'I didn't expect you to come,' said Fabian Losse.

'No?'

'No. Of course I wouldn't have known anything about you if Flossie herself hadn't told me. That's rather a curious thought, isn't it? Horrible in a way. It was not long before it happened that you met, was it? I remember her returning from her lawful parliamentary occasions (you knew, of course, that she was an MP) full of the meeting and of dark hints about your mission in this country. "Of course I tell you nothing that you shouldn't know but if you imagine there are no fifth columnists in this country . . ." I think she expected to be put on some secret convention but as far as I know that never came off. Did she invite you to Mount Moon?'

'Yes. It was extremely kind of her. Unfortunately, at the moment . . .'

'I know, I know. More pressing business. We pictured you in a false beard, dodging round geysers.'

Alleyn grinned. 'You can eliminate the false beard, at least,' he said.

'But not the geysers? However, curiosity, as Flossie would have said, is the most potent weapon in the fifth-column armoury. Flossie was my aunt by marriage, you know,' Fabian added unexpectedly. 'Her husband, the ever-patient Arthur, was my blood uncle, if that's the correct expression. He survived her by three months: Curious, isn't it? In spite of his chronic endocarditis, Flossie, alive, did him no serious damage. Dead, she polished him off completely. I hope you don't think me very heartless.'

'I was wondering,' Alleyn murmured, 'if Mrs Rubrick's death was a shock only to her husband.'

'Well, hardly that,' Fabian began and then glanced sharply at his guest. 'You mean you think that because I'm suffering from shock, I adopt a gay ruthlessness to mask my lacerated nerves?' He drove for a few moments in silence and then, speaking very rapidly and on a high note, he said: 'If your aunt by marriage turned up in a highly compressed state in the middle of a wool bale, would you be able to pass it off with the most accomplished sang-froid? Or would you? Perhaps, in your profession, you would.' He waited and then said very quickly, as if he uttered an indecency, 'I had to identify her.'

'Don't you think,' Alleyn said, 'that this is a good moment to tell me the whole story, from the beginning?'

'That was my idea, of course. Do forgive me. I'm afraid my instinct is to regard you as omniscience itself. An oracle. To be consulted rather than informed. How much, by the way, do you know?'

Alleyn, who had had his share of precious young moderns, wondered if this particular specimen was habitually so disjointed in speech and manner. He knew that Fabian Losse had seen war service. He wondered what had sent him to New Zealand and whether, as Fabian himself had suggested, he was, in truth, suffering from shock.

'I mean,' Fabian was saying, 'it's no use my filling you up with vain repetitions.'

'When I decided to come,' said Alleyn, 'I naturally looked up the case. On my way here I had an exhaustive session with Sub-Inspector Jackson who, as of course you know, is the officer in charge of the investigation.'

'All he was entitled to do,' said Fabian with some heat, 'was to burst into sobs and turn away his face. Did he, by any chance, show you his notes?'

'I was given full access to the files.'

'I couldn't be more sorry for you. And I must say that in comparison with the files even my account may seem a model of lucidity.'

'At any rate,' said Alleyn placidly, 'let's have it. Pretend I've heard nothing.'

He waited while Fabian, driving at fifty miles an hour, lit a cigarette, striking the match across the windscreen and shaking it out carefully before throwing it into the dry tussock.

'On the evening of the last Thursday in January, 1942,' he began, with the air of repeating something he had memorized, 'my aunt by marriage, Florence Rubrick, together with Arthur Rubrick (her husband and my uncle), Douglas Grace (her own nephew), Miss Terence Lynne (her secretary), Miss Ursula Harme (her ward), and me, sat on the tennis lawn at Mount Moon and made arrangements for a patriotic gathering to be held, ten days later, in the wool-shed. In addition to being our member, Flossie was also president of a local rehabilitation committee, set up by herself to propagate the gospel of turning good soldiers into bewildered farmers. The meeting was to be given tea, beer, and a dance. Flossie, stationed on an improvised rostrum hard by the wool-press, was to address them for three-quarters of an hour. She was a remorseless orator, was Flossie. This she planned, sitting in a deck-chair on the tennis lawn. It may give you some idea of her character when I tell you she began with the announcement that in ten minutes she was going to the wool-shed to try her voice. We were exhausted. The evening was stiflingly hot. Flossie, who was fond of saying she thought best when walking, had marched us up and down the rose garden and had not spared us the glass houses and the raspberry canes. Wan with heat and already exhausted by an after-dinner set of tennis, we had trotted at her heels, unwilling acolytes. During this promenade she had worn a long diaphanous coat garnished with two diamond clips. When we were at last allowed to sit down, Flossie, heated with exercise and embryonic oratory, had peeled off this garment and thrown it over the back of the deck-chair. Some twenty minutes later, when she was about to resume the garment, one of the diamond clips was missing. Douglas, blast him, discovered the loss while he was helping Flossie into her coat and, like a damned officious booby, immediately came over all efficient and said we'd look for it. With fainting hearts we suffered ourselves to be organized into a search party; this one to the rose-beds, that to the cucumber frames. My lot fell among the vegetable marrows. Flossie, encouraged by Douglas, was most insistent that we separate and cover the ground exhaustively. She had the infernal cheek to announce that she was going off to the wool-shed to practise her speech and was not to be disturbed. She marched off down a long path, bordered with lavender, and that, as far as we know, was the last time she was seen alive.'

Fabian paused, looked at Alleyn out of the corners of his eyes, and inhaled a deep draught of smoke. 'I had forgotten the classic exception,' he said. 'The last time she was seen alive, except by her murderer. She turned up some three weeks later at Messrs Riven Brothers' wool store, baled up among the Mount Moon fleeces, poor thing. Did I forget to say we were shearing at the time of her disappearance? But of course you know all that.'

'You followed her instructions about hunting for the clip?'

Fabian did not answer immediately. 'With waning enthusiasm, on my part, at least,' he said. 'But, yes. We hunted for about forty-five minutes. Just as it was getting too dark to continue, the clip was found by Arthur, her husband, in a clump of zinnias that he had already ransacked a dozen times. Faint with our search, we returned to the house and the others drank whiskies and sodas in the dining-room. Unfortunately, I'm not allowed alcohol. Ursula Harme hurried away to return the clip to Flossie. The wool-shed was in darkness. She was not in her drawing-room or her study. When Ursula went up to her bedroom she was confronted by a poisonously arch little notice that Flossie was in the habit of hanging on her door handle when she didn't want to be disturbed:

> *"Please don't knock upon the door,*
> *The only answer is a snore."*

'Disgusted but not altogether surprised, Ursula stole away, but not before she had scribbled the good news on a piece of paper and slipped it under the door. She returned and told us what she had done. We went to our beds believing Flossie to be in hers. Shall I go on, sir?'

'Please do.'

'Flossie was to leave at the crack of dawn for the mail car. Thence by train and ferry she was to travel to the seat of government where normally she would arrive, full of kick and drive, the following morning. On the eve of these departures she always retired early, and woe betide the wretch who disturbed her.'

The track descended into a shingle-bed and the car splashed through a clear race of water. They had drawn nearer to the foothills and now the mountains themselves were close above them. Between desultory boulders and giant tussocks, coloured like torches in sunlight, patches of bare earth lay ruddy in the late afternoon light. In the distance, spires of lombardy poplars appeared above the naked curve of a hill and, beyond them, a twist of blue smoke.

'Nobody got up on the following morning to see Flossie off,' said Fabian. 'The mail car goes through at half-past five. It's a kind of local arrangement. A farmer eight miles up the road from here runs it. He goes down to the forks three times a week and links up with the government mail car that you caught. Tommy Johns, the manager, usually drove her down to the front gate to catch it. She used to ring up his cottage when she was ready to start. When he didn't hear from her, he says, he thought one of us had taken her. That's what he says,' Fabian repeated. 'He thought one of us had taken her and didn't bother. We, of course, never doubted that she had been driven down by him. It was all very neat when you come to think of it. Nobody worried about Flossie. We imagined her happily popping in and out of secret sessions and bobbing up and down at the Speaker. She'd told Arthur she had something to say in open debate. He tuned in to the House of Representatives and appeared to be disappointed when he didn't hear his wife taking her usual energetic part in the interjections of "what about yourself?" and "sit down" which are so characteristic of the parry and riposte of our parliamentary debates. Flossie, we decided, must be holding her fire. On the day she was supposed to have left here, the communal wool-lorry arrived and collected our bales. I watched them load up.'

A shower of pebbles spattered on the windscreen as they lurched through the dry bed of a creek. Fabian dropped his cigarette on the floor and ground it out with his heel. The knuckles of his hands showed white as he changed his grip on the wheel. He spoke more slowly and with less affectation.

'I watched the lorry go down the drive. It's a long stretch. Then I saw it turn into this road, and lurch through this race. There was more water in the race then. It fanned up and shone in the sunlight. Look. You can see the wool-shed now. A long building with an iron roof. The house is out of sight, behind the trees. Can you see the shearing-shed?'

'Yes. How far away is it?'

'About four miles. Everything looks uncannily close in this air. We'll pull up if you don't mind, I'd rather like to get this finished before we arrive.'

'By all means.'

When they stopped, the smell and sounds of the plateau blew freshly in at the windows; the smell of sun-warmed tussock and earth and lichen, the sound of grasshoppers and, far away up the hillside, the multiple drone of a mob of sheep in transit, a dreamlike sound.

'Not,' said Fabian, 'that there's very much more to say. The first inkling we had that anything was wrong came on the fifth evening after she had walked down the lavender path. It took the form of a telegram from one of her brother MPs. He wanted to know why she hadn't come up for the debate. It gave one the most extraordinarily empty and helpless feeling. We thought, at first, that for some reason she'd changed her mind and not left the South Island. Arthur rang up her club and some of her friends in town. Then he rang up her lawyers. She had an appointment with them and hadn't kept it. They understood it was about her will. She was prolific of codicils and was always adding bits about what Douglas was to do with odds and ends of silver and jewellery. Then a little procession of discoveries came along. Terry Lynne found Flossie's suitcase, ready-packed, stowed away at the back of a cupboard. Her purse with her travel pass and money was in a drawer of her dressing-table. Then Tommy Johns said he hadn't taken her to the mail car. Then the search parties, beginning in a desultory sort of way and gradually getting more organized and systematic.

'The Moon River runs through a gorge beyond the homestead. Flossie sometimes walked up there in the evening. She said it helped her, God save the mark, to think. When, finally, the police were brought in, they fastened like limpets upon this bit of information and, after hunting about the cliff for hours at a time, waited for poor Flossie to turn up ten miles downstream where there is a backwash or something. They were still waiting when the foreman at Riven's wool store made his unspeakable discovery. By that time the trail was cold. The wool-shed had been cleaned out, the shearers had moved on, heavy rains had fallen, nobody could remember with any degree of accuracy the events of the fatal evening. Your colleagues of our inspired detective force are still giving an unconvincing impersonation of hounds with nose to ground. They return at intervals and ask us the same questions all over again. That's all, really. Or is it?'

'It's a very neat resumé, at all events,' said Alleyn. 'But I'm afraid I shall have to imitate my detested colleagues and ask a great many questions.'

'I am resigned.'

'Good. First, then, is your household unchanged since Mrs Rubrick's death?'

'Arthur died of heart trouble three months after she disappeared. We've acquired a housekeeper, an elderly cousin of Arthur's called Mrs Aceworthy, who quarrels with the outside men and preserves the proprieties between the two girls, Douglas and myself. Otherwise there's been no change.'

'Yourself,' said Alleyn, counting, 'Captain Grace, who is Mrs Rubrick's nephew, Miss Ursula Harme, her ward, and Miss Terence Lynne, her secretary. What about servants?'

'A cook, Mrs Duck, if you'll believe me, who has been at Mount Moon for fifteen years, and a manservant, Markins, whom Flossie acquired in a fashion to be related hereafter. He's a phenomenon. Menservants are practically non-existent in this country.'

'And what about the outside staff at that time? As far as I can remember there was Mr Thomas Johns, the manager, his wife and his son, Cliff; an odd man – is rouseabout the right word? – called Albert Black, three shepherds, five visiting shearers, a wool-classer, three boys, two gardeners, a cowman, and a station cook. Right?'

'Correct, even to the cowman. I need tell you nothing, I see.'

'On the night of the disappearance, the shearers, the gardeners, the boys, the station cook, the sorter, the shepherds and the cowman were all at an entertainment held some fifteen miles away?'

'Dance at the Social Hall, Lakeside. It's across the flat on the main road,' said Fabian, jerking his head at the vast emptiness of the plateau. 'Arthur let them take the station lorry. We had more petrol in those days.'

'That leaves the house-party, the Johns family, Mrs Duck, the rouseabout, and Markins?'

'Exactly.'

Alleyn clasped his long hands round his knee and turned to his companion. 'Now, Mr Losse,' he said tranquilly, 'will you tell me exactly why you asked me to come?'

Fabian beat his open palm against the driving-wheel. 'I told you in my letter. I'm living in a nightmare. Look at the place. Our nearest neighbour's ten miles up the road. What do you think it feels like? And when in January shearing came round again, there were the same men, the same routine, the same long evenings, the same smell of lavender and honeysuckle and oily wool. We're crutching now and getting it all over again. The shearers talk about it. They stop when any of us come up, but every smoke-oh and every time they knock off it's "the murder". What a beastly soft noise the word makes. They're using the wool-press, of course. The other evening I caught one of the boys that sweep up the crutchings squatting in the press while the other packed a fleece round him. Experimenting. God, I gave them a fright, the little bastards.' He swung round and confronted Alleyn. 'We don't talk about it. We've clamped down on it now for six months. That's bad for all of us. It's interfering with my work. I'm doing nothing.'

'Your work. Yes, I was coming to that.'

'I suppose the police told you.'

'I'd heard already at army headquarters. It overlaps my job out here.'

'I suppose so,' said Fabian. 'Yes, of course.'

'You realize, don't you, that I'm out here on a specific job. I'm here to investigate the possible leakage of information to the enemy. My peace-time job as a CID man has nothing to do with my present employment. But for the suggestion that Mrs Rubrick's death may have some connection with our particular problem I should not have come. It's with the knowledge and at the invitation of my colleagues that I'm here.'

'I got a rise with my bait then,' said Fabian. 'What did you think of my brain-child?'

'They showed me the blueprints. Beyond me, of course. I'm not a gunner. But I could at least appreciate its importance and also the extreme necessity of keeping your work secret. It is from that point of view, I believe, that the suggestion of espionage has cropped up?'

'Yes. To my mind it's an absurd suggestion. We work in a room that's locked when we're not in it, and the papers and gear – any of them that matter – are always shut up in a safe.'

'We?'

'Douglas Grace has worked with me. He's done the practical stuff. My side is purely theoretical. I was at Home when war broke out and took an inglorious part in the now mercifully forgotten Norwegian campaign, I picked up rheumatic fever but, with an extraordinarily bad sense of timing, got back into active service just in time to get a crack on the head at Dunkirk.' Fabian paused for a moment as if he had been about to say something further but now changed his mind. 'Ah, well,' he said. 'There it was. Later on still, when I was supposed to be fairly fit, they put me into a special show in England. That's when I got the germ of the idea. I cracked up again rather thoroughly and they kicked me out for good. While I was still too groggy to defend myself, Flossie, who was Home on a visit, bore down upon me and conceived the idea of bringing her poor English nephew-in-law back with her to recuperate in this country. She said she was used to looking after invalids, meaning poor old Arthur's endocarditis. I started messing about with my notion soon after I got here.'

'And her own nephew? Captain Grace?'

'He was actually taking an engineering course at Heidelberg in 1939 but he left on the advice of some of his German friends and returned to England. May I take this opportunity of assuring you that Douglas is not in the pay of Hitler or any of his myrmidons, a belief ardently nursed, I feel sure, by Sub-Inspector Jackson. He enlisted when he got to England, was transferred to a New Zealand unit, and was subsequently pinked in the bottom by the Luftwaffe in Greece. Flossie hauled him in as soon as he was demobilized. He used to work here as a cadet in his school holidays. He's always been good with his hands. He'd got a small precision lathe and some useful instruments. I pulled him in. It's Douglas who's got this bee in his bonnet. He will insist that in some fantastic way his Auntie Flossie's death is mixed up with our egg-beater, which is what we ambiguously call our magnetic fuse.'

'Why does he think so?'

Fabian did not answer.

'Has he any data – ' Alleyn began.

'Look here, sir,' said Fabian abruptly. 'I've got a notion for your visit. It may not appeal to you. In fact, you may dismiss it as the purest tripe, but here it is. You're full of official information about the whole miserable show, aren't you? All those files! You know, for example, that any one of us could have left the garden and gone to the shearing-shed. You may even have gathered that apart from protracted irritation, which God knows may be sufficient motive, none of us had any reason for killing Flossie. We were a tolerably happy collection of people. Flossie bossed us about but, more or less, we went our own way.' He paused and added unexpectedly, 'Most of us. Very well. It seems to me that as Flossie was murdered there was something about Flossie that only one of us knew. Something monstrous. I mean something monstrously out of character that I, for one, have conceived of as being "Flossie Rubrick"; something murder-worthy. Now that something may not appear in any one of the Flossies that each of us has formed for his or herself but, to a newcomer, an expert, might it not appear in the collective Flossie that emerges from all these units put together? Or am I talking unadulterated bilge?'

Alleyn said carefully, 'Women have been murdered for some chance intrusion upon other people's affairs, some idiotic blunder that has nothing to do with character.'

'Yes. But in the mind of the murderer of such a victim she is forever The Intruder. If he could be persuaded to talk of his victim, don't you feel that something of that aspect of her character in his mind would come out? To a sensitive observer?'

'I'm a policeman in a strange country,' said Alleyn. 'You mustn't try me too high.'

'At any rate,' said Fabian, with an air of relief that was unexpectedly naive, 'you're not laughing at me.'

'Of course not, but I don't fully understand you.'

'The official stuff has been useless. It's a year old. It's just a string of uncorrected details. For what it's worth you've got it in these precious files. It doesn't give you a picture of a Flossie Rubrick who was murder-worthy.'

'You know,' said Alleyn cheerfully, 'that's only another way of saying there was no apparent motive.'

'All right. I'm being too elaborate. Put it this way. If factual evidence doesn't produce a motive, isn't it at least possible that something might come out of our collective idea of Flossie?'

'If it could be discovered.'

'Well, but couldn't it?' Fabian was now earnest and persuasive. Alleyn began to wonder if he had been very profoundly disturbed by his experience and was indeed a little unhinged. 'If we could get them all together and start them talking, couldn't you, an expert, coming fresh to the situation, get something? By the colour of our voices, by our very evasions? Aren't those signs that a man with your training would be able to read? Aren't they?'

'They are signs,' Alleyn replied, trying not to sound too patient, 'that a man with my training learns to treat with extreme reserve. They are not evidence.'

'No, but taken in conjunction with the evidence, such as it is?'

'They can't be disregarded, certainly.'

Fabian said fretfully, 'But I want you to get a picture of Flossie in the round. I don't want you to have only my idea of her which, truth to tell, is of a maddeningly arrogant piece of efficiency, but Ursula's idea of a wonderwoman, Douglas's idea of a manageable and not unprofitable aunt, Terence's idea of an exacting employer – all these. But I didn't mean to give you an inkling. I wanted you to hear for yourself, to start cold.'

'You say you haven't spoken of her for six months. How am I to break the spell?'

'Isn't it part of your job,' Fabian asked impatiently, 'to be a corkscrew?'

'Lord help us,' said Alleyn good-humouredly, 'I suppose it is.'

'Well, then!' cried Fabian triumphantly. 'Here's a fair field with me to back you up. And, you know, I don't believe it's going to be so difficult. I believe they must be in much the same case as I am. It took a Herculean effort to write that letter. If I could have grabbed it back, I would have done so. I can't tell you how much I funked the idea of starting this conversation but, you see, now I have started there's no holding me.'

'Have you warned them about this visitation?'

'I talked grandly about "an expert from a special branch". I said you were a high-up who'd been lent to this country. They know your visit is official and that the police and hush-hush birds have a hand in it. Honestly, I don't think that alarms them much. At first, I suppose, each of us was afraid; personally afraid, I mean, afraid that we should be suspected. But I don't think we four ever suspected each other. In that one thing we are agreed. And would you believe it, as the weeks went on and the police interrogation persisted, we

got just plain bored. Bored to exhaustion. Bored to the last nerve.
Then it stopped, and instead of Flossie's death fading a bit, it grew
into a bogey that none of us talked about. We could see each other
thinking of it and a nightmarish sort of watching game set in. In a
funny kind of way I think they were relieved when I told them what
I'd done. They know, of course, that your visit has something to do
with our X Adjustment, as Douglas pompously calls it.'

'So they also know about your X Adjustment?'

'Only very vaguely, except Douglas. Just that it's rather special.
That couldn't be helped.'

Alleyn stared out at a clear and uncompromising landscape. 'It's a
rum go,' he said, and after a moment: 'Have you thought carefully
about this? Do you realize you're starting something you may want
to stop and – not be able to stop?'

'I've thought about it *ad nauseam*'.

'I think I ought to warn you. I'm a bit of state machinery. Any one
can start me up but only the state can switch me off.'

'OK.'

'Well,' Alleyn said, 'you have been warned.'

'At least,' said Fabian, 'I'll give you a good dinner.'

'Then you're my host?'

'Oh, yes. Didn't you know? Arthur left Mount Moon to me and
Flossie left her money to Douglas. You might say we were joint
hosts,' said Fabian.

III

Mount Moon homestead was eighty years old and that is a great age
for a house in the antipodes. It had been built by Arthur Rubrick's
grandfather, from wood transported over the Pass in bullock wag-
ons. Starting as a four-roomed cottage, room after room had been
added, at a rate about twice as slow as that achieved by the intrepid
Mrs Rubrick of those days in adding child after child to her husband's quiver. The house bore a dim family resemblance to the
Somersetshire seat which Arthur's grandfather had thankfully relinquished to a less adventurous brother. Victorian gables and the
inevitable conservatory, together with lesser family portraits and

surplus pieces of furniture traced unmistakably the family's English origin. The garden had been laid out in a nostalgic mood, at considerable expense, and with a bland disregard for the climate of the plateau. Of the trees old Rubrick had planted, only lombardy poplars, pinus insignis and a few natives had flourished. The tennis lawn, carved out of the tussocky hillside, turned yellow and dusty during summer. The pleached walks of Somerset had been in part realized with hardy ramblers and, where these failed, with clipped hedges of poplar. The dining-room windows looked down upon a queer transformation of what had been originally an essentially English conception of a well-planned garden. But beyond this unconvincing piece of pastiche – what uncompromising vastness! The plateau swam away into an illimitable haze of purple, its boundaries mingled with clouds. Above the cloud, suspended, it seemed, in a tincture of rose, floated the great mountains.

At dinner, that first night, Alleyn witnessed the pageant of nightfall on the plateau. He saw the horn of the Cloud Piercer shine gold and crimson long after the hollows of the lesser Alps, as though a dark wine poured into them, had filled with shadow. He felt the night air of the mountains enter the house and was glad to smell newly-lit wood in the open fireplaces.

He considered once again the inmates of the house.

Seen by candlelight round the dining-room table they seemed, with the exception of the housekeeper-chaperon, extremely young. Terence Lynne, an English girl who had been Florence Rubrick's secretary, was perhaps the oldest, though her way of dressing her hair may have given him this impression. It swept, close-fitting as a cap, in two black wings from a central parting to a knot at the nape of her neck, giving her the look of a coryphée, an impression that was not contradicted by the extreme, the almost complacent neatness of her dress. This was black, with crisp lawn collar and cuffs. Not quite an evening dress, but he felt that, unlike the two young men, Miss Lynne changed punctiliously every night. Her hands were long and white and it was a shock to learn that since her employer's death she had returned to Mount Moon as a kind of landgirl, or more accurately, as he was to learn later, a female gardener. Some hint of her former employment still hung about her. She had an air of responsibility and was, he thought, a trifle mousey.

Ursula Harme was an enchanting girl, slim, copper-haired and extremely talkative. On his arrival Alleyn had encountered her stretched out on the tennis lawn wearing a brief white garment and dark glasses. She at once began to speak of England, sketching modish pre-war gaieties and asking him which of the night clubs had survived the blitz. She had been in England with her guardian, she said, when war broke out. Her uncle, now fighting in the Middle East, had urged her to return with Mrs Rubrick to New Zealand, and Mount Moon.

'I am a New Zealander,' said Miss Harme, 'but all my relations – I haven't any close relations except my uncle – live in England. Aunt Flossie – she wasn't really an aunt but I called her that – was better than any real relation could have been.'

She was swift in her movements and had the silken air of a girl who is, beyond argument, attractive. Alleyn thought her restless and noticed that though she looked gay and brilliant when she talked her face in repose was watchful. Though, during dinner, she spoke most readily to Douglas Grace, her eyes more often were for Fabian Losse.

The two men were well contrasted. Everything about Fabian Losse, his hollow temples and his nervous hands, his lightly waving hair, was drawn delicately with a sharp pencil. But Captain Grace was a magnificent fellow with a fine moustache, a sleek head and large eyes. His accent was slightly antipodean but his manners were formal. He called Alleyn 'sir' each time he spoke to him and was inclined to pin a rather meaningless little laugh on the end of his remarks. He seemed to Alleyn to be an extremely conventional young man.

Mrs Aceworthy, Arthur Rubrick's elderly cousin who had come to Mount Moon on the death of his wife, was a large sandy woman with an air of uncertain authority and a tendency to bridle. Her manner towards Alleyn was cautious. He thought that she disapproved of his visit and he wondered how much Fabian Losse had told her. She spoke playfully and in inverted commas of 'my family', and seemed to show a preference for the two New Zealanders, Douglas Grace and Ursula Harme.

The vast landscape outside darkened and the candles on the dining-room table showed ghostly in the uncurtained window panes. When dinner was over they all moved into a comfortable, conglomerate sort of room hung with faded photographs of past cadets and lit cosily by a kerosene lamp. Mrs Aceworthy, with a vague murmur about 'having to see to things' left them with their coffee.

Above the fireplace hung the full-dress portrait of a woman.

It was a formal painting. The bare arms executed with machine-like precision, flowed wirily from shoulders to clasped hands. The dress was of mustard-coloured satin, very décolleté, and this hue was repeated in the brassy highlights of Mrs Rubrick's incredibly golden coiffure. The painter had dealt remorselessly with a formidable display of jewellery. It was an Academy portrait by an experienced painter but his habit of flattery had met its Waterloo in Florence Rubrick's face. No trick of understatement could soften that large mouth, closed with difficulty over protuberant teeth, or modify the acquisitive glare of the pale goitrous eyes which evidently had been fixed on the artist's and therefore appeared, as laymen will say, to 'follow one about the room'. Upon each of the five persons seated in Arthur Rubrick's study did his wife Florence seem to fix her arrogant and merciless stare.

There was no other picture in the room. Alleyn looked round for a photograph of Arthur Rubrick but could find none that seemed likely.

The flow of talk, which had run continuously if not quite easily throughout dinner, was now checked. The pauses grew longer and their interruptions more forced. Fabian Losse began to stare expectantly at Alleyn. Douglas Grace sang discordantly under his breath. The two girls fidgeted, caught each other's eyes, and looked away again.

Alleyn, sitting in shadow, a little removed from the fireside group, said, 'That's a portrait of Mrs Rubrick, isn't it?'

It was as if he had gathered up the reins of a team of nervously expectant horses. He saw by their startled glances at the portrait that custom had made it invisible to them, a mere piece of furniture of which, for all its ghastly associations, they were normally unaware. They stared at it now rather stupidly, gaping a little.

Fabian said, 'Yes. It was painted ten years ago. I don't need to tell you it's by a determined Academician. Rather a pity, really. John would have made something terrific out of Flossie. Or, better still, Agatha Troy.'

Alleyn, who was married to Agatha Troy, said, 'I only saw Mrs Rubrick for a few minutes. Is it a good likeness?'

Fabian and Ursula Harme said, 'No.' Douglas Grace and Terence Lynne said, 'Yes.'

'Hallo!' said Alleyn. 'A divergence of opinion?'

'It doesn't give you any idea of how tiny she was,' said Douglas Grace, 'but I'd call it a speaking likeness.'

'Oh, it's a conscientious map of her face,' said Fabian.

'It's a caricature,' cried Ursula Harme. Her eyes were fixed indignantly on the portrait.

'I should have called it an unblushing understatement,' said Fabian. He was standing before the fire, his hands on the mantelpiece. Ursula Harme turned to look at him, knitting her brows. Alleyn heard her sigh as if Fabian had wakened some old controversy between them.

'And there's no vitality in it, Fabian,' she said anxiously. 'You must admit that. I mean she was a much more splendid person than that. So marvellously alive.' She caught her breath at the unhappy phrase. 'She made you feel like that about her,' she added. 'The portrait gives you nothing of it.'

'I don't pretend to know anything about painting,' said Douglas Grace, 'but I do know what I like.'

'Would you believe it?' Fabian murmured under his breath. He said aloud, 'Is it so great a merit, Ursy, to be marvellously alive? I find unbounded vitality very unnerving.'

'Not if it's directed into suitable channels,' pronounced Grace.

'But hers was. Look what she did!' said Ursula.

'She was extraordinarily public-spirited, you know,' Grace agreed. 'I must say I took my hat off to her for that. She had a man's grasp of things.' He squared his shoulders and took a cigar case out of his pocket. 'Not that I admire managing women,' he said, sitting down by Miss Lynne. 'But Auntie Floss was a bit of a marvel. You've got to hand it to her, you know.'

'Apart from her work as an MP?' Alleyn suggested.

'Yes, of course,' said Ursula, still watching Fabian Losse. 'I don't know why we're talking about her, Fabian, unless it's for Mr Alleyn's information.'

'You may say it is,' said Fabian.

'Then I think he ought to know what a splendid sort of person she was.'

Fabian did an unexpected thing. He reached out his long arm and touched her lightly on the cheek. 'Go ahead, Ursy,' he said gently. 'I'm all for it.'

'Yes,' she cried out, 'but you don't believe.'

'Never mind. Tell Mr Alleyn.'

'I thought,' said Douglas Grace, 'that Mr Alleyn was here to make an expert investigation. I shouldn't think our ideas of Aunt Florence are likely to be of much help. He wants facts.'

'But you'll all talk to him about her,' said Ursula, 'and you won't be fair.'

Alleyn stirred a little in his chair in the shadows. 'I should be very glad if you'd tell me about her, Miss Harme,' he said. 'Please do.'

'Yes, Ursy,' said Fabian. 'We want you to. Please do.'

She looked brilliantly from one to another of her companions. 'But – it seems so queer. It's months since we spoke of her. I'm not at all good at expressing myself. Are you serious, Fabian? Is it important?'

'I think so.'

'Mr Alleyn?'

'I think so, too, I want to start with the right idea of your guardian. Mrs Rubrick was your guardian, wasn't she?'

'Yes.'

'So you must have known her very well.'

'I think I did. Though we didn't meet until I was thirteen.'

'I should like to hear how that came about.'

Ursula leant forward, resting her bare arms on her knees and clasping her hands. She moved into the region of firelight.

'You see – ' she began.

CHAPTER 2
According to Ursula Harme

Ursula began haltingly with many pauses but with a certain air of championship. At first Fabian helped her, making a conversation rather than a solo performance of the business. Douglas Grace, sitting beside Terence Lynne, sometimes spoke to her in a low voice. She had taken up a piece of knitting and the click of the needles lent a domestic note to the scene, a note much at variance with her sleek and burnished appearance. She did not reply to Grace but once Alleyn saw her mouth flicker in a smile. She had small sharp teeth.

As Ursula grew into her narrative she became less uneasy, less in need of Fabian's support, until presently she could speak strongly, eager to draw her portrait of Florence Rubrick.

A firm picture took shape. A schoolgirl, bewildered and desolated by news of her mother's death, sat in the polished chilliness of a headmistress's drawing-room. 'I'd known ever since the morning. They'd arranged for me to go home by the evening train. They were very kind but they were too tactful, too careful not to say the obvious thing. I didn't want tact and delicacy, I wanted warmth. Literally, I was shivering. I can hear the sound of the horn now. It was the sort that chimes like bells. She brought it out from England. I saw the car slide past the window and then I heard her voice in the hall asking for me. It's years ago but I can see her as clearly as if it were yesterday. She wore a fur cape and smelt lovely and she hugged me and talked loudly and cheerfully and said she was my guardian and had come for me and that she was my mother's greatest friend and had been with her when it happened. Of course I knew all about her. She was my godmother. But she had stayed in England when she married after the last war and when she returned we lived too far away to visit. So I'd never seen her. So I went away with her. My other guardian is an English uncle. He's a soldier and follows the drum and he was very glad when Aunt Florence (that's what I called her) took hold. I stayed with her until it was time to go back to school. She used to come during term and that was marvellous.'

The picture sharpened on a note of adolescent devotion. There had been the year when Auntie Florence returned to England but wrote occasionally and caused sumptuous presents to be sent from London stores. She reappeared when Ursula was sixteen and ready to leave school.

'It was Heaven. She took me Home with her. We had a house in London and she brought me out and presented me and everything. It was wizard. She gave a dance for me.' Ursula hesitated. 'I met Fabian at that dance, didn't I, Fabian?'

'It was a great night,' said Fabian. He had settled on the floor, his back was propped against the side of her chair and his thin knees were drawn up to his chin. He had lit a pipe.

'And then,' said Ursula, 'it was September, 1939, and Uncle Arthur began to say we'd better come out to New Zealand. Auntie Florence wanted us to stay and get war jobs but he kept on cabling for her to come.'

Terence Lynne's composed voice cut across the narrative. 'After all,' she said, 'he was her husband.'

'Hear, hear!' said Douglas Grace and patted her knee.

'Yes, but she'd have been wonderful in a war job,' said Ursula impatiently. 'I always took rather a gloomy view of his insisting like that. I mean, it was a thought selfish. Doing without her would really have been his drop of war work.'

'He'd had three months in a nursing-home,' said Miss Lynne without emphasis.

'I know, Terry, but all the same . . . Well, anyway, soon after Dunkirk he cabled again and out we came. I had rather thought of joining something but she was so depressed about leaving. She said I was too young to be alone and she'd be lost without me, so I came. I loved coming, of course.'

'Of course,' Fabian murmured.

'And there was you to be looked after on the voyage.'

'Yes, I'd staged my collapse by that time. Ursula acted,' Fabian said, turning his head towards Alleyn, 'as a kind of buffer between my defencelessness and Flossie's zeal. Flossie had been a VAD in the last war and the mysteries had lain fallow in her for twenty years. I owe my reason if not my life to Ursula.'

'You're not fair,' she said but with a certain softening of her voice. 'You're ungrateful, Fab.'

'Ungrateful to Flossie for plumping herself down in your affections like an amiable, no, not even an amiable cuttlefish? But go on, Ursy.'

'I don't know how much time Mr Alleyn has to spare for our reminiscences,' began Douglas Grace, 'but I must say I feel deeply sorry for him.'

'I've any amount of time,' said Alleyn, 'and I'm extremely interested. So you all three arrived in New Zealand in 1940? Is that it, Miss Harme?'

'Yes. We came straight here. After London,' said Ursula gaily, 'it did seem rather hearty and primitive but quite soon after we got here the member for the district died and they asked her to stand and everything got exciting. That's when you came in, Terry, isn't it?'

'Yes,' said Miss Lynne, clicking her needles. 'That's where I came in.'

'Auntie Floss was marvellous to me,' Ursula continued. 'You see, she had no children of her own so I suppose I was rather special. Anyway she used to say so. You should have seen her at the meetings, Mr Alleyn. She loved being heckled. She was as quick as lightning and absolutely fearless, wasn't she, Douglas?'

'She certainly could handle them,' agreed Grace. 'She was up to her neck in it when I got back. I remember at one meeting some woman shouted out: "Do you think it's right for you to have cocktails and champagne when I can't afford to give my kiddies eggs?" Aunt Floss came back at her in a flash: "I'll give you a dozen eggs for every alcoholic drink I've consumed."'

'Because,' Ursula explained, 'she didn't drink, ever, and most of the people knew and clapped, and Aunt Florence said at once: "That wasn't fair, was it? You didn't know about my humdrum habits." And she said: "If things are as bad as that you should apply to my Relief Supply Service. We send plenty of eggs in from Mount Moon."'

Ursula's voice ran down on a note of uncertainty. Douglas Grace cut in with his loud laugh. 'And the woman shouted "I'd rather be without eggs," and Aunt Floss said: "Just as well perhaps while I'm on my soap-box," and they roared with laughter.'

'Parry and riposte,' muttered Fabian. 'Parry and riposte!'

'It was damned quick of her, Fabian,' said Douglas Grace.

'And the kids continued eggless.'

'That wasn't Aunt Florence's fault,' said Ursula.

'All right, darling. My sympathies are with the woman but let it pass. I must say,' Fabian added, 'that in a sort of way I rather enjoyed Floss's electioneering campaign.'

'You don't understand the people in this country,' said Grace. 'We like it straight from the shoulder and Aunt Floss gave it to us that way. She had them eating out of her hand, hadn't she, Terry?'

'She was very popular,' said Terence Lynne.

'Did her husband take an active part in her public life?' asked Alleyn.

'It practically killed him,' said Miss Lynne, clicking her needles.

II

There was a flabbergasted silence and she continued sedately. 'He went for long drives and sat on platforms and fagged about from one meeting to another. This house was never quiet. What with Red Cross and Women's Institute and EPS and political parties it was never quiet. Even this room, which was supposed to be his, was invaded.'

'She was always looking after him,' Ursula protested. 'That's unfair, Terry. She looked after him marvellously.'

'It was like being minded by a hurricane.'

Fabian and Douglas laughed. 'You're disloyal and cruel,' Ursula flashed out at them. 'I'm ashamed of you. To make her into a figure of fun! How can you, when you, each of you, owed her so much.'

Douglas Grace at once began to protest that this was unfair, that nobody could have been fonder of his aunt than he was, that he used to pull her leg when she was alive and that she liked it. He was flustered and affronted and the others listened to him in an uncomfortable silence. 'If we've got to talk about her,' Douglas said hotly, 'for God's sake let's be honest. We were all fond of her, weren't we?' Fabian hunched up his shoulders but said nothing. 'We all took a pretty solid knock when she was murdered, didn't we? We all agreed that Fabian should ask Mr Alleyn to come? All right. If we've got to hold a post-mortem on her character which, personally, seems to me to be a waste of time, I suppose we're meant to say what we think.'

'Certainly,' said Fabian. 'Unburden the bosom, work off the inhibitions. But it's Ursy's innings at the moment, isn't it?'

'You interrupted her, Fab.'

'Did I? I'm sorry, Ursy,' said Fabian gently. He slewed round – put his chin on the arm of her chair and looked up comically at her.

'I'm ashamed of you,' she said uncertainly.

'Please go on. You'd got roughly to 1941 with Flossie in the full flush of her parliamentary career, you know. Here we were, Mr Alleyn. Douglas, recovered from his wound but passed unfit for further service, going the rounds of a kind of superior Shepherd's Calendar. Terry, building up Flossie's prestige with copious shorthand notes and cross-references. Ursula –' He broke off for a moment. 'Ursula provided enchantment,' he said lightly, 'and I, comedy. I fell off horses and collapsed at high altitudes, and fainted into sheep-dips. Perhaps these antics brought me *en rapport* with my unfortunate uncle who, at the same time, was fighting his own endocarditic battle. Carry on, Ursy.'

'Carry on with what? What's the good of my trying to give my picture of her when you all – when you all – ' Her voice wavered for a moment. 'All right,' she said more firmly. 'The idea is that we each give our own account of the whole thing, isn't it? The same account that I've bleated out at dictation speed to that monumental bore from the detective's office. All right.'

'One moment,' said Alleyn's voice out of the shadows.

He saw the four heads turn to him in the firelight.

'There's this difference,' he said. 'If I know anything of police routine you were continually stopped by questions. At the moment I don't want to nail you down to an interrogation. I want you, if you can manage to do so, to talk about this tragedy as if you spoke of it for the first time. You realize, don't you, that I've not come here, primarily, to arrest a murderer. I've been sent to try and discover if this particular crime has anything to do with unlawful behaviour in time of war.'

'Exactly,' said Douglas Grace. 'Exactly, sir. And in my humble opinion,' he added, stroking the back of his head, 'it most undoubtedly has. However!'

'All in good time,' said Alleyn. 'Now, Miss Harme, you've given us a clear picture of a rather isolated little community up to, let us say, something over a year ago. At the close of 1941 Mrs Rubrick is much occupied by her public duties, with Miss Lynne as her secretary. Captain Grace is a cadet on this sheep station. Mr Losse is recuperating and has begun, with Captain Grace's help, to do some very specialized work. Mr Rubrick is a confirmed invalid. You are all fed by Mrs Duck, the cook, and attended by Markins, the houseman. What are you doing?'

'Me?' Ursula shook her head impatiently. 'I'm nothing in particular. Auntie Florence called me her ADC. I helped wherever I could and did my VAD training in between. It was fun – something going to happen all the time. I adore that,' cried Ursula. 'To have events waiting for me like little presents in a treasure-hunt. She made everything exciting, all her events were tied up in gala wrappings with red ribbon. It was Heaven.'

'Like the party that was to be held in the wool-shed?' asked Fabian dryly.

'Oh dear!' said Ursula, catching her breath. 'Yes. Like that one. I remember – '

III

The picture of that warm summer evening of fifteen months ago grew as she spoke of it. Alleyn, remembering his view through the dining-room window of a darkling garden, saw the shadowy company move along a lavender path and assemble on the lawn. The light dresses of the women glimmered in the dusk. Lancelike flames burned steadily as they lit cigarettes. They drew deck-chairs together. One of the women threw a coat of some thin texture over the back of her chair. A tall personable young man leant over the back in an attitude of somewhat studied gallantry. The smell of tobacco mingled with that of night-scented stocks and of earth and tussock that had not yet lost all warmth of the sun. It was the hour when sounds take on a significant clearness and the senses are sharpened to receive them. The voices of the party drifted vaguely yet profoundly across the dusk. Ursula could remember it very clearly.

'You must be tired, Aunt Florence,' she had said.

'I don't let myself be tired,' answered that brave voice. 'One mustn't think about fatigue, Ursy, one must nurse a secret store of energy.' And she spoke of Indian ascetics and their mastery of fatigue and of munition workers in England and of air-raid wardens. 'If they can do so much surely I, with my humdrum old routine, can jog along at a decent trot.' She stretched out her bare arms and strong hands to the girls on each side of her: 'And with my Second Brain and my kind little ADC to back me up,' she cried cheerfully, 'what can I not do?'

Ursula slipped down to the warm dry grass and leant her cheek against her guardian's knee. Her guardian's vigorous fingers caressed rather thoroughly the hair which Ursula had been at some expense to have set on a three days' visit down-country.

'Let's make a plan,' said Aunt Florence.

It was a phrase Ursula loved. It was the prelude to adventure. It didn't matter that the plan was concerned with nothing more exciting than a party in the wool-shed which would be attended by back-country men and their womenkind, dressed unhappily in co-operative store clothes, and by a sprinkling of such runholders as had enough enthusiasm and petrol to bring them many miles to Mount Moon. Aunt Florence invested it all in a pink cloud of anticipation. Even Douglas became enthusiastic and, leaning over the back of Flossie's chair, began to make suggestions. Why not a dance? he asked, looking at Terence Lynne. Florence agreed. There would be a dance. Old Jimmy Wyke and his brothers who played accordions must practise together and take turn about with the radio-gramophone.

'You ought to take that old piano over from the annexe,' said Arthur Rubrick in his tired breathless voice, 'and get young Cliff Johns to join forces with the others. He's extraordinarily good. Play anything. Listen to him now.'

It was an unfortunate suggestion and Ursula felt the caressing fingers stiffen. As she recalled this moment, fifteen months later, for Alleyn, he heard her story recede backwards, into the past, and this quality, he realized, would be characteristic of all the stories he was to hear. They would dive backwards from the moment on the lawn into the events that foreshadowed it.

Ursula said she knew that Aunt Florence had been too thoughtful to worry Uncle Arthur with the downfall of young Cliff Johns. It was a story of the basest sort of ingratitude. Young Cliff, son of the manager, Tommy Johns, had been an unusual child. He had thrown his parents into a state of confusion and doubt by his early manifestations of aesthetic preferences, screaming and plugging his ears with his fists when his mother sang, yet listening with complacency for long periods to certain instrumental programmes on the wireless. He had taken a similar line over pictures and books. When he grew older and was collected in a lorry every morning and taken to a minute pink-painted State school out on the plateau, he developed a talent for writing florid compositions which changed their style with each new book he read, and much too fast for the comprehension of his teacher. His passion for music grew precociously and the schoolmistress wrote to his parents saying that his talent was exceptional. Her letter had an air of nervous enthusiasm. The boy, she said bravely, was phenomenal. He was, on the other hand, bad at arithmetic and games and made no attempt to conceal his indifference to both.

Aunt Florence hearing of this took an interest in young Cliff, explaining to his reluctant parents that they were face to face with the Artistic Temperament.

'Now, Mrs Johns,' she said cheerfully, 'you mustn't bully that boy of yours because he's different. He wants special handling and lots of sympathy. I've got my eye on him.'

Soon after that she began to ask Cliff to the big house. She gave him books and a gramophone with carefully-chosen records and she won him completely. When he was thirteen years old, she told his bewildered parents that she wanted to send him to the nearest equivalent in this country of an English Public School. Tommy Johns raised passionate objections. He was an ardent trades unionist, a working manager and a bit of a communist. But his wife, persuaded

by Flossie, overruled him and Cliff went off to boarding-school with
sons of the six runholders scattered over the plateau.

His devotion to Florence, Ursula said, appeared to continue. In
the holidays he spent a great deal of time with her and, having taken
music lessons at her expense, played to her on the Bechstein in the
drawing-room. At this point in Ursula's narrative, Fabian gave a
short laugh.

'He plays very well,' Ursula said. 'Doesn't he?'

'Astonishingly well,' Fabian agreed, and she said quickly: 'She
was very fond of music, Fab.'

'Like Douglas,' Fabian murmured, 'she knew what she liked, but
unlike Douglas she wouldn't own up to it.'

'I don't know what you mean by that,' said Ursula grandly and
went on with her narrative.

Young Cliff continued at school when Florence went to England.
He had full use of the Bechstein in the drawing-room during the
holidays. She returned to find him a big boy but otherwise, it
seemed, still docile under her patronage. But when he came home
for his summer holidays at the end of 1941, he was changed, not,
Ursula said emphatically, for the better. He had had trouble with his
eyes and the school oculist had told him that he would never be
accepted for active service. He had immediately broken bounds and
attempted to enlist. On being turned down he wrote to Florence
saying that he wanted to leave school and, if possible, do a job of war
work on the sheeprun until he was old enough to get into the army,
if only in a C3 capacity. He was now sixteen. This letter was a bombshell for Flossie. She planned a university career, followed, if the war
ended soon enough, by a move to London and the Royal College of
Music. She went to the manager's cottage with the letter in her
hand, only to find that Tommy Johns, also, had heard from his son
and was delighted. 'We're going to need good men on the land as
we've never needed them before, Mrs Rubrick. I'm very very
pleased young Cliff looks at it that way. If you'll excuse me for saying so, I thought this posh education he's been getting would make
a class-conscious snob of the boy but from what he tells me of his
ideas I see it's worked out different.' For young Cliff, it appeared,
was now a communist. Nothing could have been further removed
from Flossie's plans.

When he appeared, she could make no impression on him. He seemed to think that she alone would sympathize with his change of heart and plans and would support him. He couldn't understand her disappointment nor, as he continued in his attitude, her mounting anger. He grew dogmatic and stubborn. The woman of forty-seven and the boy of sixteen quarrelled bitterly and strangely. It was a cruel thing for him to do, Ursula said, cruel and stupid. Aunt Florence was the most patriotic soul alive. Look at her war work. It wasn't as though he was old enough or fit for the army. The least he could do was to complete the education she had so generously planned and in part given him.

After their quarrel they no longer met. Cliff went out with the high-country musterers and continued in their company when they came in from the mountains behind droning mobs of sheep. He became very friendly with Albie Black, the rouseabout. There was a rickety old piano in the bunkhouse annexe and in the evenings Cliff played it for the men. Their voices, singing 'Waltzing Matilda' and strangely Victorian ballads, would drift across the yards and paddocks and reach the lawn where Flossie sat with her assembled forces, every night after dinner. But on the night she disappeared, his mates had gone to the dance and Cliff played alone in the annexe, strange music for that inarticulate old instrument.

'Listen to him, now,' said Arthur Rubrick. 'Remarkable chap, that boy. You wouldn't believe that old hurdy-gurdy over there had as much music in it. Extraordinary. Sounds like a professional.'

'Yes,' Fabian agreed after a pause. 'It's remarkable.'

Ursula wished they wouldn't talk about Cliff. It would have been better to have told Uncle Arthur about the episode of the previous night, she thought, and let him deal with Cliff. Aunt Florence shouldn't have to cope with everything and this had hurt her so deeply.

For the previous night, Markins, the manservant, hearing furtive noises in the old dairy that now served as a cellar, and imagining them to be made by a rat, had crept up and flashed his torch in at the window. Its beam darted mothlike about dusty surfaces of bottles. There was a brief sound of movement. Markins sought it out with his light. Cliff Johns' face sprang out of the dark. His eyes were screwed up blindly and his mouth was open. Markins had described

this very vividly. He had dipped the torch beam until it discovered
Cliff's hands. They were long and flexible hands and they grasped a
bottle of Arthur's twenty-year-old whisky. As the light found them
they opened and the bottle crashed on the stone floor. Markins, a
taciturn man, darted into the dairy, grasped Cliff by his wrist and,
without a word, lugged him unresisting into the kitchen. Mrs Duck,
outraged beyond measure, had instantly bustled off and fetched Mrs
Rubrick. The interview took place in the kitchen. It nearly broke
Florence's heart, Ursula said. Cliff, who of course reeked of priceless
whisky, said repeatedly that he had not been stealing, but would
give no further explanation. In the meantime Markins had discovered four more bottles in a sugar bag, dumped round the corner of
the dairy. Florence, naturally, did not believe Cliff and in a mounting
scene called him a sneak-thief and accused him of depravity and
ingratitude. He broke into a white rage and stammered out an
extraordinary arraignment of Florence, saying that she had tried to
buy him and that he would never rest until he had returned every
penny she had spent on his schooling. At this stage Florence sent
Markins and Mrs Duck out of the kitchen. The scene ended by Cliff
rushing away while Florence, weeping and shaking, sought out
Ursula and poured out the whole story. Arthur Rubrick had been
very unwell and they decided to tell him nothing of this incident.

Next morning – the day of her disappearance – Florence went to
the manager's cottage only to be told that Cliff's bed had not been
slept in and his town clothes were missing. His father had gone off
in their car down the road to the Pass. At midday he returned with
Cliff whom he had overtaken at the crossroads, dead-beat, having
covered sixteen miles on the first stage down-country to the nearest
army depot. Florence would tell Ursula nothing of her subsequent
interview with Tommy Johns.

'So Uncle Arthur's suggestion on that same evening that Cliff
should play at the dance came at rather a grim moment,' said Ursula.

'The boy's a damned conceited pup if he's nothing worse,' said
Douglas Grace.

'And he's still here?' said Alleyn. Fabian looked round at him.

'Oh, yes. They won't have him in the army. He's got something
wrong with his eyes, and anyway he's ranked as doing an essential
job on the place. The police got the whole story out of Markins, of

course,' said Fabian, 'and for want of a better suspect, concentrated on the boy. I expect he looms large in the files, doesn't he?'

'He peters out about halfway through.'

'That's because he's the only member of the household who's got a sort of alibi. We all heard him playing the piano until just before the diamond clip was found, which was at five to nine. When he'd just started, at eight o'clock it was, Markins saw him in the annexe, playing, and he never stopped for longer than half a minute or less. Incidentally, to the best of my belief, that's the last time young Cliff played on the piano in the annexe, or on any other piano, for a matter of that. His mother, who was worried about him, went over to the annexe and persuaded him to return with her to the cottage. There he heard the nine o'clock news bulletin and listened to a programme of classical music.

'You may think that was a bit thick,' said Fabian. 'I mean a bit too much in character with the sensitive young plant, but it's what he did. The previous night you must remember he'd had a snorting row with Flossie, and followed it up with a sixteen-mile hike and no sleep. He was physically and emotionally exhausted and dropped off to sleep in his chair. His mother got him to bed and she and his father sat up until after midnight, talking about him. Before she turned in, Mrs Johns looked at young Cliff and found him fathoms deep. Even the detective-sergeant saw that Flossie would have returned by midnight if she'd been alive. Sorry, Ursy dear, I interrupt continually. We are back on the lawn. Cliff is playing Bach on a piano that misses on six notes and Flossie's talking about the party in the shearing-shed. Carry on.'

Ursula and Florence had steered Arthur Rubrick away from Cliff though the piano in the annexe continued to remind them of him. Flossie began to plan her speech on post-war land settlement for soldiers. 'There'll be no blunders this time,' she declared. 'The bill we're planning will see to that. A committee of experts.' The phrases drifted out over the darkling garden. 'Good country, properly stocked . . . adequate equipment . . . Soldiers Rehabilitation Fund . . . I shall speak for twenty minutes before supper . . .' But from what part of the wool-shed should she speak? Why not from the press itself? There would be a touch of symbolism in that, Flossie cried, taking fire. It would be from the press itself with an improvised platform across the top. She would be a dominant figure there. Perhaps some extra lighting? 'We must go and look!' she cried, jumping to her feet. That had always been her way with everything. No sooner said than done. She had tremendous driving power and enthusiasm. 'I'm going to try my voice there – now. Give me my coat, Douglas darling.' Douglas helped her into the diaphanous coat.

It was then that he discovered the loss of the diamond clip.

It had been a silver wedding present from Arthur, one of a pair. Its mate still twinkled on the left lapel of the coat. Flossie announced simply that it must be found, and Douglas organized the search party. 'You'll see it quite easily,' she told them, 'by the glitter. I shall walk slowly to the shearing-shed, looking as I go. I want to try my voice. Please don't interrupt me, any of you. I shan't get another chance and I must be in bed before ten. An early start in the morning. Look carefully and mind you don't tread on it. Off you go.'

To Ursula's lot had fallen a long path running down the right-hand side of the tennis lawn between hedges of clipped poplars, dense with summer foliage. This path divided the tennis lawn from a farther lawn which extended from the front along the south side of the house. This also was bordered by a hedged walk where Terence Lynne hunted, and, beyond her again, lay the kitchen gardens, allotted to Fabian. To the left of the tennis lawn Douglas Grace moved parallel with Ursula. Beyond him, Arthur Rubrick explored a lavender path that led off at right angles through a flower garden to a farther fence, beyond which lay a cart track leading to the manager's hut, the bunkhouses and the shearing-shed.

'No gossiping, now,' said Flossie. 'Be thorough.'

She turned down the lavender path, moving slowly. Ursula watched her go. The hills beyond her had now darkened to a purple that was almost black and, by the blotting out of nearer forms, Flossie seemed to walk directly into these hills until, reaching the end of the path, she turned to the left and suddenly vanished.

Ursula walked round the top of the tennis court, past the front of the house, to her allotted beat between the two lawns. The path was flanked by scrubby borders of parched annuals amongst which she hunted assiduously. Cliff Johns now played noisily but she was farther away and only heard disjointed passages, strident and angry. She thought it was a Polonaise. TUM, te-tum. Te-tum-te-tum-te TUM, te-tum. Tiddlytumtum. She didn't know how he could proclaim himself like that after what had happened. Across the lawn, on her right, Fabian, making for the kitchen garden, whistled sweetly. Between them Terence Lynne hunted along the companion path to Ursula's. The poplar fences completely hid them from each other but every now and then they would call out: 'Any luck?' 'Not so far.' It was now almost dark. Ursula had worked her way to the bottom of her beat and turned into the connecting path that ran right along the lower end of the garden. Here she found Terence Lynne. 'It's no good looking along here,' Terence had said. 'We didn't come here with Mrs Rubrick. We crossed the lawn to the kitchen garden.' But Ursula reminded her that earlier in the evening while Douglas and Fabian played an after-dinner singles, the girls had come this way with Florence. 'But I'm sure she had the clip then,' Terence objected. 'We should have noticed if one was missing. And in any case, I've looked along here. We'd better not be together. You know what she said.' They argued in a desultory way and then Ursula returned to her beat. She saw a light flash beyond the fence on the right side of the tennis lawn and heard Douglas call out, 'Here's a torch, Uncle Arthur.' It was not long after this that Arthur Rubrick found the clip in a clump of zinnias along the lavender walk.

'He said the beam from the torch caught it and it sent out sparks of blue light. They shouted, "Got it. We've found it!" and we all met on the tennis lawn. I ran out to a place on the drive where you can see the shearing-shed but there was no light there so we all went indoors.' As they did this the music in the annexe stopped abruptly.

They had trailed rather wearily into the dining-room just as the nine o'clock bulletin was beginning on the radio. Fabian had turned it off. Arthur Rubrick had sat at the table, breathing short, his face more congested than usual. Terence Lynne, without consulting him, poured out a stiff nip of whisky. This instantly reminded Ursula of Cliff's performance on the previous night. Arthur thanked Terence in his breathless voice and pushed the diamond clip across the table to Ursula.

'I'll just run up with it. Auntie Floss will like to know it's found.'

It struck her that the house was extraordinarily quiet. This impression deepened as she climbed the stairs. She stood for a moment on the top landing, listening. As in all moments of quietude, undercurrents of sound, generally unheard, became disconcertingly audible. The day had been hot and the old wooden house relaxed with stealthy sighs or sudden cracks. Flossie's room was opposite the stairhead. Ursula, stock-still on the landing, listened intently for any movement in the room. There was none. She moved nearer to the door and stooping down could just see the printed legend. Flossie was adamant about obedience to this notice, but Ursula paused while the inane couplet which she couldn't read jigged through her memory:

> *Please don't knock upon my door,*
> *The only answer is a snore.*

Auntie Flossie, she confessed, was a formidable snorer. Indeed it was mainly on this score that Uncle Arthur, an uneasy sleeper, had removed to an adjoining room. But on this night no energetic counterpoint of intake and expulsion sounded from behind the closed door. Ursula waited in vain and a small trickle of apprehension dropped down her spine. She stole away to her own room and wrote a little note. 'It's found. Happy trip, darling. We'll listen to you.' When she came back and slid it under Flossie's door the room beyond was still quite silent.

Ursula returned to the dining-room. She said the light dazzled her eyes after the dark landing. She stood in the doorway and peered at the group round the table, 'It's odd, isn't it, how, for no particular reason, something you see will stick in your memory? I mean there was no particular significance about my going back to the dining-room. I didn't know then. Terry stood behind Uncle Arthur's chair. Fabian was lighting a cigarette and I remember feeling worried about him – ' Ursula paused unaccountably. 'I thought he'd been overdoing things a bit,' she said. 'Douglas was sitting on the table with his back towards me. They all turned their heads as I came in. Of course they were just wondering if I'd given her the diamond clip but it seems to me now that they asked me where she was. And, really, I answered as if they had done so. I said, "She's in her room. She's asleep!"'

'Did it strike you as odd that she'd made no inquiries about the clip?' Alleyn asked.

'Not very odd. It was her way, to organize things and then leave them, knowing they'd be done. She was rather wonderful like that. She never nagged.'

'There's no need to nag if you're an efficient dictator,' Fabian pointed out. 'I'll admit her efficiency.'

'Masculine jealousy,' said Ursula, without malice, and he grinned and said, 'Perhaps.'

Ursula waited for a moment and then continued her narrative.

'We were all rather quiet. I suppose we were tired. We had a drink each and then we parted for the night. We keep early hours on the plateau, Mr Alleyn. Can you face breakfast at a quarter to six?'

'With gusto.'

'Good. We all went quietly upstairs and said goodnight in whispers on the landing. My room is at the end of the landing and overlooks the side lawn. Terry's is opposite Auntie Florence's and there's a bathroom next door to her that is opposite Uncle Arthur's dressing-room where he was sleeping. He'd once had a bad attack in the night and Auntie always left the communicating door open so that he could call to her. He remembered afterwards that this door was shut and that he'd opened it a crack and listened, thinking, as I had thought, how still she was. The boys' rooms are down the corridor and the servants' quarters at the back. When I came out in my dressing-gown to go to the bathroom, I met Terry. We could hear Uncle Arthur moving about quietly in his room. I glanced down the corridor and saw Douglas there and, farther along, Fabian in the door of his room. We all had candles, of course. We didn't speak. It seemed to me that we were all listening. We've agreed, since, that we felt not exactly uneasy but not quite comfortable. Restless. I didn't go to sleep for some time, and when I did it was to dream that I was searching in rather terrifying places for the diamond clip. It was somewhere in the wool-shed but I couldn't find it because the party had started and Auntie Florence was making a speech on the edge of a precipice. I was late for an appointment and hunted in that horribly thwarted way one does in nightmares. I wouldn't have bored you with my dream if it hadn't turned into the dark staircase with me feeling on the treads for the brooch. The stairs creaked like they do at night, but I knew somebody was crossing the landing and I was terrified and woke up. The point is,' said Ursula, leaning forward and looking directly at Alleyn, 'some-body really was crossing the landing.'

The others stirred. Fabian reached over to the wood box and flung a log on the fire. Douglas muttered impatiently. Terence Lynne put down her knitting and folded her elegant hands together in her lap.

'In what direction?' Alleyn asked.

'I'm not sure. You know how it is. Dream and waking overlap, and by the time you are really alert the sound that came into your dream and woke you has stopped. I simply know that it was real.'

'Mrs Duck returning from the party,' said Terence.

'But it was three o'clock, Terry. I heard the grandfather strike about five minutes later and Duckie says they got back at a quarter to two.'

'They'd hung about, cackling,' said Douglas.

'For an hour and a quarter? And, anyway, Duckie would come up the back stair. I don't suppose it amounts to anything, Mr Alleyn, because we know now that – that it hadn't – that it happened away from the house. It must have. But I don't care what any one says,' Ursula said, lifting her chin, 'somebody was about on the landing at five minutes to three that morning.'

'And we don't know definitely and positively,' said Fabian, 'that it wasn't Flossie herself.'

CHAPTER 3

According to Douglas Grace

Fabian's suggestion raised a storm of protest. The two girls and Douglas Grace began at once to combat it. It seemed to Alleyn that they thrust it from them as an idea that shocked and horrified their emotions rather than offended their reason. In the blaze of firelight that sprang from the fresh log he saw Terence Lynne's hands weave together.

She said sharply, 'That's a beastly thing to suggest, Fabian.'

Alleyn saw Douglas Grace slide his arm along the sofa behind Terence. 'I agree,' Douglas said. 'Not only beastly but idiotic. Why in God's name should Flossie stay out until three in the morning, return to her room, go out again and get murdered?'

'I didn't say it was likely. I said it wasn't impossible. We can't prove it wasn't Flossie.'

'But what possible reason – '

'A rendezvous?' Fabian suggested, and looked out of the corner of his eyes at Terence.

'I consider that's a remark in abominable taste, Fab,' said Ursula.

'Do you, Ursy? I'm sorry. Must we never laugh a little at people after they are dead? But I'm very sorry. Let's go back to our story.'

'I've finished,' said Ursula shortly and there was an uncomfortable silence.

'As far as we're concerned,' said Douglas at last, 'that's the end of the story. Ursula went into Aunt Floss's room the next morning to do it out, and she noticed nothing wrong. The bed was made but that meant nothing because we all do our own beds and Ursy simply thought Flossie had tidied up before she left.'

49

'But it was odd all the same,' said Terence. 'Mrs Rubrick's sheets were always taken off when she went away and the bed made up again the day she returned. She always left it unmade, for that reason.'

'It didn't strike me at the time,' said Ursula. 'I ran the carpet sweeper over the floor and dusted and came away. It was all very tidy. She was a tremendously orderly person.'

'There was another thing that didn't strike you, Ursula,' said Terence Lynne. 'You may remember that you took the carpet sweeper from me and that I came for it when you'd finished. It wanted emptying and I took it down to the rubbish bin. I noticed there was something twisted round one of the axles, between the wheel and the box. I unwound it.' Terence paused, looking at her hands. 'It was a lock of wool,' she said tranquilly. 'Natural wool, I mean, from the fleece.'

'You never told us that,' said Fabian sharply.

'I told the detective. He didn't seem to think it important. He said that was the sort of thing you'd expect to find in the house at shearing-time. He was a town-bred man.'

'It might have been there for ages, Terry,' said Ursula.

'Oh, no. It wasn't there when you borrowed the sweeper from me. I'm very observant of details,' said Terence, 'and I know. And if Mrs Rubrick had seen it she'd have picked it up. She hated bits on the carpet. She had a "thing" about them and always picked them up. I'll swear it wasn't there when she was in the room.'

'How big was it?' Fabian demanded.

'Quite small. Not a lock, really. Just a twist.'

'A teeny-weeny twist,' said Ursula in a ridiculous voice, suddenly gay again. She had a chancy way with her, one moment nervously intent on her memories, the next full of mockery.

'I suppose,' said Alleyn, 'one might pick up a bit of wool in the shed and, being greasy, it might hang about on one's clothes?'

'It might,' said Fabian lightly.

'And being greasy,' Douglas added, 'it might also hang about in one's room.'

'Not in Auntie Floss's room,' Ursula said. 'I always did her room, Douglas, you shan't dare to say I left greasy wool lying squalidly about for days on the carpet. Pig!' she mocked at him.

He turned his head lazily and looked at her. Alleyn saw his arm slip down the back of the sofa to Terence Lynne's shoulders. Ursula laughed and pulled a face at him. 'It's all nonsense,' she said, 'this talk of locks of wool. Moonshine!'

'Personally,' said Terence Lynne, 'I can't think it very amusing. For me, and I'd have thought for all of us, the idea of sheep's wool in her room that morning is perfectly horrible.'

'You're hateful, Terry,' Ursula flashed at her. 'It's bad enough to have to talk about it. I mind more than any of you. You all know that. It's because I mind so much that I can't be too solemn. You know I'm the only one of us that loved her. You're cold as ice, Terry, and I hate you.'

'Now then, Ursy,' Fabian protested. He knelt up and put his hands over hers. 'Behave!' he said. 'Be your age, woman. You astonish me.'

'She was a darling, and I loved her. If it hadn't been for her – '

'All right, all right.'

'You would never even have seen me if it hadn't been for her.'

'Who was it,' Fabian murmured, 'who held the grapes above Tantalus's lips? Could it have been Aunt Florence?'

'All the same,' said Ursula with that curious air, half-rueful, half-obstinate, that seemed to characterize her relationship with Fabian, 'you're beastly to me. I'm sorry, Terry.'

'May we go on?' asked Douglas.

Alleyn, in his chair beyond the firelight, stirred slightly and at once they were attentive and still.

'Captain Grace,' Alleyn said, 'during the hunt for the diamond brooch, you went up to the house for a torch, didn't you?'

'For two torches, sir. I gave one to Uncle Arthur.'

'Did you see any one in the house?'

'No. There was only Markins. Markins says he was in his room. There's no proof of that. The torches are kept on the hall table. The telephone rang while I was there and I answered it. But that only took a few seconds. Somebody wanting to know if Aunt Florence was going north in the morning.'

'From the terrace in front of the house you look down on the fenced paths, don't you? Could you see the other searchers from there?'

'Not Uncle Arthur or Fabian, but I could just see the two girls. It was almost dark. I went straight to my uncle with the torch, he was there all right.'

'Were you with him when he found the brooch?'

'No. I simply gave him the torch and returned to my own beat with mine. I heard him call out a few moments later. He left the brooch where it was for me to see. It looked like a cluster of blue and red sparks in the torchlight. It was half-hidden by zinnia leaves. He said he'd looked there before. It wasn't too good for him to stoop much and his sight wasn't so marvellous. I supposed he'd just missed it.'

'Did you go into the end path, the one that runs parallel with the others and links them?'

'No. He did.'

'Mr Rubrick?'

'Yes. Earlier. Just as I was going to the house and before you went down there, Ursy, and talked to Terry.'

'Then you and Mr Rubrick must have been there together, Miss Lynne,' said Alleyn.

'No,' said Terence Lynne quickly.

'I understood Miss Harme to say that when she met you in the bottom path you told her you had been searching there.'

'I looked about there for a moment. I don't remember seeing Mr Rubrick. I wasn't with him.'

'But – ' Douglas broke off. 'I suppose I made a mistake,' he said. 'I had it in my head that as I was going up to the house for the torches he came out of the lavender walk into my path and then moved on into the bottom path. And then I had the impression that as I returned with the torches he came back from the bottom path. It was just then that I heard you two arguing about whether you'd stop in the bottom path or not. You were there then.'

'I may have seen him,' said Terence. 'I was only there a short time. I don't remember positively, but we didn't speak – I mean we were not together. It was getting dark.'

'Well, but Terry,' said Ursula, 'when I went into the bottom path you came towards me from the far end, the end nearest the lavender walk. If he was there at all, it would have been at that end.'

'I don't remember, Ursula. If he was there we didn't speak and I've simply forgotten.'

'Perhaps I was mistaken,' said Douglas uncertainly. 'But it doesn't matter much, does it? Arthur was somewhere down there and so were both of you. I don't mind admitting that the gentleman whose movements that evening I've always been anxious to trace, is our friend Mr Markins.'

'And away we go,' said Fabian cheerfully. 'We're on your territory now, sir.'

'Good,' said Alleyn; 'what about Markins, Captain Grace? Let's have it.'

'It goes back some way,' said Douglas. 'It goes back, to be exact, to the last wool sale held in this country, which was early in 1939.'

II

' – So Aunt Floss jockeyed poor old Arthur into scraping acquaintance with this Jap. Kurata Kan his name was. They brought him up here for the weekend. I've heard that he took a great interest in everything, grinning like a monkey and asking questions. He'd got a wizard of a camera, a German one, and told them photography was his hobby. Landscape mostly, he said, but he liked doing groups of objects too. He took a photograph in the Pass. He was keen on flying. Uncle Arthur told me he must have spent a whole heap of money on private trips while he was here, taking his camera with him. He bought photographs too, particularly infra-red aerial affairs. He got the names of the photographers from the newspaper offices. We found that out afterwards, though apparently he didn't make any secret of it at the time. It seems he was bloody quaint in his ways and talked like something out of the movies. Flossie fell for it like an avalanche. "My dear little Mr Kan." She was frightfully bucked because he gave top price for her wool clip. The Japs always bought second-rate stuff and anyway it's very unusual for merino wool to fetch top price. I consider the whole thing was damn fishy. When she went to England they kept up a correspondence. Flossie had always said the Japs would weigh in on our side when war came. "My Mr Kan tells me all sorts of things." By God, there's this to say for the totalitarian countries, they wouldn't have had gentlemen like Mr Kurata Kan hanging about for long. I'll hand that to them. They know how to keep the rats out of their houses.' Douglas laughed shortly.

'But not the bats out of their belfries,' said Fabian. 'Please don't deviate into herrenvolk-lore, Douglas.'

'This Kan lived for half the year in Australia,' Douglas continued. 'Remember that. Flossie got back here in '40, bringing Ursy and Fabian with her. Before she went Home she used to run this place on a cook and two housemaids, but the maids had gone and this time she couldn't raise the sight of a help. Mrs Duck was looking after Uncle Arthur singlehanded. She said she couldn't carry on like that. Ursy did what she could but she wasn't used to housework, and anyway it didn't suit Flossie.'

'Ursy seemed to me to wield a very pretty mop,' said Fabian.

'Of course she did, but it was damned hard work scrubbing and so on, and Auntie Floss knew it.'

'I didn't mind,' said Ursula.

'Anyway, when I got back after Greece, I found the marvellous Markins running the show. And where d'you think he'd blown in from? From Sydney, with a letter from Mr Kurata Kan. Can you beat that?'

'A reference, do you mean?'

'Yes. He hadn't actually been with these precious Kans. He says he was valet to an English artillery officer who'd picked him up in America. He says he was friendly with the Kans' servants. He says that when his employer left Australia he applied to Kan for a job. But the Kans were winging their way to Japan. Markins said he'd like to try his luck in New Zealand and Kan remembered Flossie moaning about the servant problem in this country. Hence, the letter. That's Kan's story. The whole thing looks damned fishy to me. Markins, an efficient, well-trained servant, could have taken a job anywhere. Beyond the fact that he was born British but has an American passport we know nothing about him. He gave the name of his American employers but doesn't know their present address.'

'I think I should tell you,' said Alleyn, 'that the American employers have been traced for us and verify the story.'

This produced an impression. Fabian said, 'Not Understood, or The Modest Detective! I take back some of my remarks about him.

Only some,' he added. 'I still maintain that, taking him by and large, our Mr Jackson is almost certifiable.'

'It makes no difference,' Douglas said. 'It proves nothing. My case rests on pretty firm ground, as I think you'll agree, sir, when you've heard it.'

'Do remember, Douglas,' Fabian murmured, 'that Mr Alleyn has seen the files.'

'I realize that, but God knows what sort of a hash they've made of it. Now, I don't want to be unnecessarily hard on the dead,' said Douglas loudly; Fabian grimaced and muttered to himself; 'but I look at it this way. It's my duty to give an honest opinion, and I wouldn't be honest if I didn't say that Aunt Floss liked to know about things. Not to mince matters, she was a very inquisitive woman, and what's more she enjoyed showing people that she was in on everything.'

'I know what you're going to say next,' said Ursula brightly, 'and I disagree with every word of it.'

'My dear girl, you're talking through your hat. Look here, sir. When I got back from Greece and was marched out of the army and came here, I found Fabian doing a certain type of work. I needn't be more explicit than that,' said Douglas portentously and raised his eyebrows.

'You're superb, Douglas,' said Fabian. 'Of course you needn't. Do remember that Mr Alleyn is the man who knows all.'

'Be quiet, Losse,' said Alleyn unexpectedly. Fabian opened his mouth and shut it again. 'You're a mosquito,' Alleyn added mildly.

'I really am sorry,' said Fabian. 'I know.'

'Shall I go on?' asked Douglas huffily.

'Please do.'

'Fabian told me about his work. He called it, for security reasons, the egg-beater. Fabian's idea. I prefer simply the X Adjustment.'

'I see,' said Alleyn. 'The X Adjustment.' Fabian grinned.

'And he asked me if I'd like to have a look at his notes and drawings and so on. As a gunner I was, of course, interested. I satisfied myself there was something in it. I'd taken my electrical engineering degree before I joined up, and was rather keen on the magnetic fuse idea. I need go no further at the moment,' said Douglas with another significant glance.

Alleyn thought, 'He really is superb,' and nodded solemnly.

'Of course,' Douglas continued, 'Auntie Floss had to be told something. I mean, we wanted a room and certain facilities, and so on. She advanced us the cash for our gear. There's no electrical supply this side of the plateau. We built a windmill and got a small dynamo. Later on she was going to have the house wired, but at the moment we've only got the juice in the workroom. She paid for all that. We began to spend more and more time on it. And later on, when we were ready to show something to somebody in the right quarter, she was damned useful. She'd talk anybody into anything, would Flossie, and she got hold of a certain authority at army headquarters and arranged for us to go up north and see him. He sent a report Home and things began to look up. We've now had a very encouraging answer from – however! I need not go into that.'

'Quite,' said Alleyn. Fabian suddenly offered him a cigar which he refused.

'Well, as I say, she was very helpful in many ways, but she did *gimlet* rather and she used to talk jolly indiscreetly at meal times.'

'You should have heard her,' said Fabian. '"Now, what do my two inventors think?" And then, you know, she'd pull an arch face and for all the world like one of the weird sisters in *Macbeth*, she'd lay her rather choppy finger on her lips and say, "But we mustn't be indiscreet, must we?"'

Alleyn glanced up at the picture. The spare, wiry woman stared down at him with the blank inscrutability of all Academy portraits. He was visited by a strange notion. If the painted finger should be raised to those lips, that seemed to be strained with such difficulty over projecting teeth! If she could give him a secret signal: 'Speak now. Ask this question. Be silent here, they are approaching a matter of importance.'

'That's how she carried on,' Douglas agreed. 'It was damned difficult, and of course everybody in the house knew we were doing something hush-hush. Fabian always said, "What of it? We keep our stuff locked up and even if we didn't, nobody could understand it." But I didn't like the way Flossie talked. Later on, her attitude changed.'

'That was after questions had been asked in the House about leakage of information to the enemy,' said Ursula. 'She took that very much to heart, Douglas, you know she did. And then that ship was torpedoed off the North Island. She was terribly upset.'

'Personally,' said Fabian, 'I found her caution much more alarming than her curiosity. You'd have thought we had the Secret Death Ray of fiction on the stocks. She papered the walls with cautionary posters. Go on, Douglas.'

'It was about three weeks before she was killed that it happened,' said Douglas. 'And if you don't find a parallel between my experience and Ursy's, I shall be very much surprised. Fabian and I had worked late on a certain improvement to a crucial part of our gadget, a safety device, let us call it.'

'Why not,' Fabian, 'since it is one?'

'I absolutely fail to understand your attitude, Fabian, and I'm sure Mr Alleyn does. Your bloody English facetiousness – '

'All right. You're perfectly right, old thing, only it's just that all these portentous hints seem to me to be so many fancy touches. You know as well as I do that the idea of a sort of aerial magnetic mine must have occurred to countless schoolboys. The only thing that could possibly be of use to the most sanguinary dirty dog would be either the drawings or the dummy model.'

'Exactly!' Douglas shouted, and then immediately lowered his voice. 'The drawings and the model.'

'And it's all right about Markins. He's spending the evening with the Johns family.'

'So he says,' Douglas retorted. 'Well, now, sir, on this night, three weeks before Aunt Floss was killed, I was worrying about the alteration in the safety device – '

His story did bear a curious resemblance to Ursula's.

On this particular evening, at about nine o'clock, Douglas and Fabian stood outside their workroom door, having locked it up for the night. They were excited by the proposed alteration to the safety device which Fabian now thought could be improved still further. 'We'd talked ourselves silly and decided to chuck it up for the night,' said Douglas. He usually kept the keys of the workroom door and safe but on this occasion each of them said that he might feel inclined to return to the calculations later on that night. It was agreed that Douglas should leave the keys in a box on his dressing-table where Fabian, if he so desired, could get them without disturbing him. It was at this point that they noticed Markins, who had come quietly along the passage from the back stairs. He asked them if they knew where Mrs Rubrick was as a long-distance call had come through for her. He almost certainly overheard the arrangement about the keys. 'And, by God,' said Douglas, 'he tried to make use of it.'

They parted company and Douglas went to bed. But he was over-stimulated and slept restlessly. At last, finding himself broad awake and obsessed with their experiment, he had decided to get up and look through the calculations they had been working on that evening. He had stretched out his hand to his bedside-table when he heard a sound in the passage beyond his door. It was no more than the impression of stealthy pressure, as though someone advanced with exaggerated caution and in slow motion. Douglas listened spellbound, his hand still outstretched. The steps paused outside his door. At that moment he made some involuntary movement of his hand and knocked his candlestick to the floor. The noise seemed to him to be shocking. It was followed by a series of creaks fading in a rapid diminuendo down the passage. He leapt out of bed and pulled open his door.

The passage was almost pitch dark. At the far end it met a shorter passage that ran across it like the head of a T. Here, there was a faint glow that faded while Douglas watched it, as if, he said, somebody with a torch was moving away to the left. The only inhabited room to the left was Markins'. The back stairs were to the right.

At this point in his narrative, Douglas tipped himself back on the sofa and glanced complacently about him. Why, he demanded, was Markins abroad in the passage at a quarter to three in the morning (Douglas had noted the time) unless it was upon some exceedingly dubious errand? And why did he pause outside his, Douglas's door? There was one explanation which, in the light of subsequent events, could scarcely be refuted. Markins had intended to enter Douglas's room and attempt to steal the keys of the workshop.

'Well, well,' said Fabian, 'let's have the subsequent events.'

They were, Alleyn thought, at least suggestive.

After the incident of the night Douglas took his keys to bed with him and lay fuming until daylight when he woke Fabian and told him of his suspicions. Fabian was sceptical. 'A purely gastronomic episode, I bet you anything you like.' But he agreed that they should be more careful with the keys and he himself contrived a heavy shutter which padlocked over the window when the room was not in use. 'There was no satisfying Douglas,' Fabian said plaintively. 'He jeered at my lovely shutter, and didn't believe I went to bed with the keys on a bootlace round my neck. I did, though.'

'I wasn't satisfied to let it go like that,' said Douglas. 'I was damned worried, and next day I kept the tag on Master Markins. Once or twice I caught him watching me with a very funny look in his eye. That was on the Thursday. Flossie had given him the Saturday off and he went down to the Pass with the mail car. He's friendly with the pubkeeper there. I thought things over and decided to do a little investigation and I think you'll agree I was justified, sir. I went to his room. It was locked, but I'd seen a bunch of old keys hanging up in the store-room and after filing one of them I got it to function all right.' Douglas paused, half-smiling. His arm still rested along the back of the sofa behind Terence Lynne. She turned and, clicking her knitting-needles, looked thoughtfully at him.

'I don't know how you could, Douglas,' said Ursula. 'Honestly!'

'My dear child, I had every reason to believe I was up against a very nasty bit of work; a spy, an enemy. Don't you understand?'

'Of course I understand, but I just don't believe Markins is a spy. I rather like him.'

Douglas raised his eyebrows and addressed himself pointedly to Alleyn.

'At first I thought I'd drawn a blank. Every blinking box and case in his room, and there were five all told, was locked. I looked in the cupboard and there, on the floor, I did discover something.'

Douglas cleared his throat, took a wallet from his breast pocket and an envelope from the wallet. This he handed to Alleyn. 'Take a look at it, sir. It's not the original. I handed that over to the police. But it's an exact replica.'

'Yes,' said Alleyn, raising an eyebrow at it. 'A fragment of the covering used on a film package for a Leica or similar camera.'

'That's right, sir. I thought I wasn't mistaken. A bloke in our mess had used those films and I remembered the look of them. Now it seemed pretty funny to me that a man in Markins' position should be able to afford a Leica camera. They cost anything from twenty-five to a hundred pounds out here when you could get them. Of course, I said to myself, it mightn't be his. But there was a suit hanging up in the cupboard and in one of the pockets I found a sale docket from a

photographic supply firm. Markins had spent five pounds there, and
amongst the stuff he'd bought were twelve films for a Leica. I suppose
he was afraid he'd run out. I shifted one of his locked cases and it
rattled and clinked. I bet it had his developing plant in it. When I left
his room I was satisfied I'd hit on something pretty startling. Markins
was probably going to photograph everything he could lay his hands
on in our workroom and send it on to his principals.'

'I see,' said Alleyn. 'So what did you do?'

'Told Fabian,' said Douglas. 'Right away.'

Alleyn looked at Fabian.

'Oh, yes. He told me, and we disagreed completely over the whole
thing. In fact,' said Fabian, 'we had one hell of a flaming row over it,
didn't we, Doug?'

III

'There's no need to exaggerate,' said Douglas. 'We merely took up
different attitudes.'

'Wildly different,' Fabian agreed. 'You see, Mr Alleyn, my idea, for
what it's worth, was this. Suppose Markins was a dirty dog. If questioned about his nightly prowl he had only to say: *(a)* That his tummy
was upset and he didn't feel up to going to the downstairs Usual
Offices so had visited ours, or *(b)* That it wasn't him at all. As for his
photographic zeal, if it existed, he might have been given a Leica camera by a grateful employer or saved up his little dimes and dollars and
bought one second-hand in America. Every photographic zealot is not
a, fifth columnist. If he kept his developing stuff locked up it might be
because he was innately tidy or because he didn't trust us, and I must
say that with Douglas on the premises he wasn't far wrong.'

'So you were for doing nothing about it?'

'No. I thought we should keep our stuff well stowed away and
our eyes open. I suggested that if, on consideration, we thought
Markins was a bit dubious, we should report the whole story to the
people who are dealing with espionage in this country.'

'And did you agree with this plan, Grace?'

Douglas had disagreed most vigorously. He had, he said with a
short laugh, the poorest opinion of the official counter-espionage

system and would greatly prefer to tackle the matter himself. 'That's what we're like, out here, sir,' he told Alleyn. 'We like to go to it on our own and get things done.' He added that he felt, personally, so angry with Markins that he had to do something about it. Fabian's suggestion he dismissed as unrealistic. Why wait? Report the matter certainly, but satisfy themselves first and then go direct to the authority they had seen at army headquarters and get rid of the fellow. They argued for some time and separated without having come to any conclusion. Douglas, on parting from Fabian, encountered his aunt who, as luck would have it, launched out on an encomium upon her manservant. 'What should I do without my Markins? Thank Heaven he comes back this evening. I touch wood,' Flossie had said, tapping a gnarled finger playfully on her forehead, 'every time he says he's happy here. It'd be so unspeakably dreadful if he were lost to us.'

This, Douglas said, was too much for him. He followed his aunt into the study and, as he said, gave her the works. 'I stood no nonsense from Flossie,' said Douglas, brushing up his moustache. 'We understood each other pretty well. I used to pull her leg a bit and she liked it. She was a good scout, taking her all round, only you didn't want to let her ride roughshod over you. I talked pretty straight to her. I told her she'd have to get rid of Markins, and I told her why.'

Terence Lynne said under her breath, 'I never realized you did that.'

Flossie had been very much upset. She was caught. On the one hand there was her extreme reluctance to part with her jewel, as she had so often called Markins; on the other, her noted zeal, backed up by public utterance, in the matter of counter-espionage. Douglas said he reminded her of a speech she had made in open debate in which she had wound up with a particularly stately peroration: 'I say now, and I say it solemnly and advisedly,' Flossie had urged, 'that with our very life blood at stake, it is the duty of us all not only to set a guard upon our own tongue but to make a public example of any one, be he stranger or dearest friend, who, by the slightest deviation from that discretion, which is his duty, endangers in the least degree the safety of our realm. Make no doubt about it,' she had finally shouted, 'there is an enemy in our midst and let each of us beware lest, unknowingly, we give him shelter.' This piece of rhetoric had a wry flavour in regurgitation, and for a moment Flossie stared miserably at her nephew. Then she rallied.

'You've been working too hard, Douglas,' she said. 'You're suffering from nervous strain, dear.'

But Douglas made short work of this objection and indignantly put before her the link with Mr Kurata Kan, at which Flossie winced, the vagueness of Markins' antecedents, the importance of their work, the impossibility of taking the smallest risk and their clear duty in the matter. It would be better, he said, if after further investigation on Douglas's part Markins still looked suspicious, for Flossie and not Douglas or Fabian to report the matter to the highest possible authority.

Poor Flossie wrung her hands. 'Think of what he does,' she wailed. 'And he's so good with Arthur. He's marvellous with Arthur. And he's so obliging, Douglas. Single-handed butler in a house of this size! Everything so nice, always. And there's no help to be got. None.'

'The girls will have to manage.'

'I don't believe it!' she cried, rallying. 'I'm always right in my judgement of people. I never go wrong. I won't believe it.'

But, as Ursula had said, Flossie was an honest woman, and it seemed as if Douglas had done his work effectively. She tramped up and down the room hitting her top teeth with a pencil, a sure sign that she was upset. He waited.

'You're right,' Flossie said at last. 'I can't let it go.' She lowered her chin and looked at Douglas over the tops of her pince-nez. 'You were quite right to tell me, dear,' she said. 'I'll handle it.'

This was disturbing. 'What will you do?' he asked.

'Consider,' said Florence magnificently. 'And act.'

'How?'

'Never you mind.' She patted him rather too vigorously on the cheek. 'Leave it all to your old Floosy,' she said. This was the abominable pet name she had for herself.

'But, Auntie,' he protested, 'we've a right to know. After all – '

'So you shall. At the right moment.' She dumped herself down at her desk. She was a tiny creature but all her movements were heavy and noisy. 'Away with you,' she said. Douglas hung about. She began to write scratchily and in a moment or two tossed another remark at him. 'I'm going to tackle him,' she said.

Douglas was horrified. 'Oh, no, Aunt Floss. Honestly, you must-n't. It'll give the whole show away. Look here, Aunt Floss – '

But she told him sharply that he had chosen to come to her with his story and must allow her to deal with her own servants in the way that seemed best to her. Her pen scratched busily. When in his distress he roared at her, she, too, lost her temper and told him to be quiet. Douglas, unable to make up his mind to leave her, stared despondently through the window and saw Markins, neatly dressed, walk past the window mopping his brow. He had tramped up from the front gate.

'Auntie Floss, please listen to me!'

'I thought I told you – '

Appalled at his own handiwork, he left her.

At this point in his narrative Douglas rose and straddled the hearth-rug.

'I don't mind telling you,' he said, 'that we weren't the same after it. She got the huff and treated me like a kid.'

'We noticed,' Fabian said, 'that your popularity had waned a little. Poor Flossie! You'd hoist her with the petard of her own conscience. A maddening and unforgivable thing to do, of course. Obviously she would hate your guts for it.'

'There's no need to put it like that,' said Douglas grandly.

'With a little enlargement,' Fabian grinned, 'it might work up into quite a pretty motive against you.'

'That's a damned silly thing to say, Fabian,' Douglas shouted.

'Shut up, Fab,' said Ursula. 'You're impossible.'

'Sorry, darling.'

'I still don't see,' Douglas fumed, 'that I could have taken any other line. After all, as she pointed out, it was her house and he was her servant.'

'You didn't think of that when you picked his door lock,' Fabian pointed out.

'I didn't pick the lock, Fabian, and anyhow that was entirely different.'

'Did Mrs Rubrick tackle him?' Alleyn asked.

'I presume so. She said nothing to me, and I wasn't going to ask and be ticked off again.'

Douglas lit a cigarette and inhaled deeply. 'Obviously,' Alleyn thought, 'he still has something up his sleeve.'

'As a matter of fact,' said Douglas lightly, 'I'm quite positive she did tackle him, and I believe it's because of what she said that Markins killed her.'

IV

'And there,' said Fabian cheerfully, 'you have it. Flossie says to Markins, "I understand from my nephew that you're an enemy agent. Take a week's wages in lieu of notice and expect to be arrested and shot when you get to the railway station!" "No, you don't," says Markins to himself. He serves up the soup with murder in his heart, takes a stroll past the wool-shed, hears Flossie in the full spate of her experimental oratory, nips in and – does it. To me it just doesn't make sense.'

'You deliberately make it sound silly,' said Douglas hotly.

'It is silly. Moreover, it's not in her character as I read it, to accuse Markins. It would have been the action of a fool and, bless my soul, Flossie was no fool.'

'It was her deliberately expressed intention.'

'To "tackle Markins". That was her phrase, wasn't it? That is, to tackle l'affaire Markins. She wanted to get rid of you and think. And, upon my soul, I don't blame her.'

'But how would she tackle Markins?' Terence objected, 'except by questioning him?' She spoke so seldom that the sound of her voice, cool and incisive, came as a little shock.

'She was a bit of a Polonius, was Flossie. I think she went round to work. She may even,' said Fabian, giving a curious inflection to the phrase, 'she may even have consulted Uncle Arthur.'

'No,' said Douglas.

'How on earth can you tell?' asked Ursula.

There was a moment's silence.

'It would not have been in her character,' said Douglas.

'Her character, you see,' Fabian said to Alleyn. 'Always her character.'

'Ever since fifth column trouble started in this country,' said Douglas, 'Flossie had been asking questions about it in the House. Markins knew that as well as we did. If she gave him so much as an inkling that she suspected him, how d'you suppose he'd feel?'

'And even if she decided not to accuse him straight out,' Ursula said, 'don't you think he'd notice some change in her manner?'

'Of course he would, Ursy,' Douglas agreed. 'How could she help herself?'

'Quite easily,' said Fabian. 'She was as clever as a bagful of monkeys.'

'I agree,' said Terence.

'Well, now,' said Alleyn, 'did any of you, in fact, notice any change in her manner towards Markins?'

'To be quite honest,' said Fabian slowly, 'we did. But I think we all put it down to her row with Cliff Johns. She was extremely cantankerous with all hands and the cook during that last week, was poor Flossie.'

'She was unhappy,' Ursula declared. 'She was wretchedly unhappy about Cliff. She used to tell me everything. I'm sure if she'd had a row with Markins she'd have told me about it. She used to call me her Safety Valve.'

'Mrs Arthur Rubrick,' said Fabian, 'accompanied by Miss U. Harme, SV, ADC, etc., etc.!'

'She may have waited to talk to him until that night,' said Douglas. 'The night she disappeared, I mean. She may have written for advice to a certain higher authority, and waited for the reply before she tackled Markins. Good Lord, that might have been the very letter she started writing while I was there!'

'I think,' said Alleyn, 'that I should have heard if she'd done that.'

'Yes,' agreed Fabian. 'Yes. After all, you are the higher authority, aren't you?'

Again there was a silence, an awkward one. Alleyn thought: Damn that boy, he's said precisely the wrong thing. He's made them self-conscious again.

'Well, there's my case against Markins,' said Douglas grandly. 'I don't pretend it's complete or anything like that, but I'll swear there's something in it, and you can't deny that after she disappeared his behaviour was suspicious.'

'I can deny it,' said Fabian, 'and what's more I jolly well do. Categorically, whatever that may mean. He was worried and so were all of us.'

'He was jumpy.'

'We were all as jumpy as cats. Why shouldn't he jump with us? It'd have been much more suspicious if he'd remained all suave and imperturbable. You're reasoning backwards, Douglas.'

'I couldn't stand the sight of the chap about the house,' said Douglas. 'I can't now. It's monstrous that he should still be here.'

'Yes,' Alleyn said. 'Why is he still here?'

'You might well ask,' Douglas rejoined. 'You'll scarcely credit it, sir, but he's here because the police asked Uncle Arthur to keep him on. It was like this . . . '

The story moved forward. Out of the narrative grew a theme of mounting dissonance, anxiety and fear. Five days after Florence had walked down the lavender path and turned to the left, the overture opened on the sharp note of a telephone bell. The post office at the Pass had a wire for Mrs Rubrick. Should they read it? Terence took it down. 'Trust you are not indisposed your presence urgently requested at Thursday's meeting.' It was signed by a brother MP. There followed a confused and hurried passage. Florence had not gone north! Where was she? Inquiries, tentative at first but growing hourly less guarded and more frantic, long distance calls, calls to her lawyers, with whom she was known to have made an appointment, to hospitals and police stations, the abandonment of privacy following a dominion-wide SOS on the air; search parties radiating from Mount Moon and culminating in the sudden collapse of Arthur Rubrick; his refusal to have a trained nurse or indeed any one but Terence and Markins to look after him: all these abnormalities followed each other in an ominous crescendo that reached its peak in the dreadful finality of discovery. As this phase unfolded, Alleyn thought he could trace a change of mood in the little company assembled in the study. At first Douglas alone stated the theme. Then, one by one, at first reluctantly, then with increasing freedom the other voices joined in, and it seemed to Alleyn that after their long avoidance of the subject they now found ease in speaking of it. After the impact of the discovery, there followed the slow assembly of official themes: the inquest adjourned, the constant appearance of the police, and the tremendous complications of the public funeral: these events mingled like phrases of a movement until they were interrupted emphatically by Fabian. When Douglas, who had evidently been impressed by it, described Flossie's cortege – 'there were three bands' – Fabian shocked them all by breaking into laughter. Laughter bubbled out of him. He stammered, 'It was so horrible . . . disgusting . . . I'm terribly sorry, but when you think of what had happened to her . . . and then to have three brass bands . . . Oh, God, it's so electrically comic!' He drew in his breath in a shuddering gasp.

'Fabian!' Ursula murmured, and put her arm about him, pressing him against her knees. 'Darling Fabian, don't.'

Douglas stared at Fabian and then looked away in embarrassment. 'You don't want to think of it like that,' he said. 'It was a tribute. She was enormously popular. We had to let them do it. Personally – '

'Go on with the story, Douglas,' said Terence.

'Wait,' said Fabian. 'I've got to explain. It's my turn. I want to explain.'

'No,' cried Ursula. 'Please not.'

'We agreed to tell him everything. I've got to explain why I can't join in this *nil nisi* stuff. It crops up at every turn. Let's clear it up and then get on with the job.'

'No!'

'I've got to, Ursy. Please don't interrupt, it's so deadly important. And, after all, one can't make a fool of oneself without some sort of apology.'

'Mr Alleyn will understand.' Ursula appealed urgently to Alleyn, her hands still pressed down on Fabian's shoulders. 'It's the war,' she said. 'He was dreadfully ill after Dunkirk. You mustn't mind.'

'For pity's sake shut up, darling, and let me tell him,' said Fabian violently.

'But it's crazy. I won't let you, Fabian. I won't let you.'

'You can't stop me,' he said.

'What the hell is this about?' Douglas asked angrily.

'It's about me,' said Fabian. 'It's about whether or not I killed your Aunt Florence. Now, for God's sake, hold your tongue and listen.'

CHAPTER 4

According to Fabian Losse

Sitting on the floor and hugging his knees, Fabian began his narrative. At first he stammered. The phrases tumbled over each other and his lips trembled. As often as this happened he paused, frowning, and, in a level voice, repeated the sentence he had bungled, so that presently he was master of himself and spoke composedly.

'I think I told you,' he said, 'that I got a crack on the head at Dunkirk. I also told you, didn't I, that for some weeks after I was supposed to be more or less patched up, they put me on a specialized job in England. It was then I got the notion of a magnetic fuse for anti-aircraft shells, which is, to make no bones about it, the general idea behind our precious X Adjustment. I suppose, if things had gone normally, I'd have muddled away at it there in England, but they didn't.

'I went to my job one morning with a splitting headache. What an admirably chosen expression that is: "a splitting headache". My head really felt like that. I'd had bad bouts of it before and tried not to pay any attention. I was sitting at my desk looking at a memorandum from my senior officer and thinking I must collect myself and do something about it. I remember pulling a sheet of paper towards me. An age of nothingness followed this and then I came up in horrible waves out of dark into light. I was hanging over a gate in a road a few minutes away from my own billet. It was a very high gate, an eight-barred affair with wire on top, and padlocked. The place beyond was army property. I must have climbed up. I was very sick. After a bit I looked at my watch. I'd missed an hour. It was as if it had been cut out of my mind. I looked at my right hand and saw there was ink on my fingers. Then I went home, feeling filthily ill. I rang up the office and I suppose I sounded peculiar because the army quack came in the next morning and had a look at me. He said it was the crack on my skull. I've got the report he gave me to bring out here. You can see it if you like.

'While he was with me the letter came.

'It was addressed to me by me. That gives one an unpleasant feeling at any time. When I opened it, six sheets of office paper fell out. They were covered in my writing and figures. Nonsense they were, disjointed bits and pieces from my notes and calculations hopelessly jumbled together. I showed them to the doctor. He found it all enthralling and had me marched out of the army. That was when Flossie turned up.'

Fabian paused for a moment, his chin on his knees.

'I only had two other goes of it,' he said at last, rousing himself. 'One was in the ship. I was supposed to be resting in my deck-chair. Ursy says she found me climbing. This time it was up the companion-way to the boat-deck. I don't know if I told you that when I caught my packet at Dunkirk I was climbing up a rope ladder into a rescue ship. I've sometimes wondered if there's a connection. Ursy couldn't get me to come down so she stayed with me. I wandered about, it seems, and generally made a nuisance of myself: I got very angry about something and said I was going to knock hell out of Flossie. A point to remember, Mr Alleyn. I think I've mentioned before that Flossie's ministrations in the ship were very agitating and tiresome. Ursy seems to have kept me quiet. When I came up to the surface she was there and she helped me get back to my cabin. I made her promise not to tell Flossie. The ship's doctor was generally tight so we didn't trouble him either.

'Then the last go. The last go. I suppose you've guessed. It was on what your friend in the force calls the Night In Question. It was, in point of fact, while I was among the vegetable marrows hunting for Flossie's brooch. Unhappily, this time Ursy was not there.

'I suppose,' Fabian said, shifting his position and looking at his hands, 'that I'd walked about, with my nose to the ground, for so long that I'd upset my equilibrium or something. I don't know. All I do know is that I heard the two girls having their argument in the bottom path and then without the slightest warning there was the black-out and, after the usual age of nothingness, that abominable, that disgusting sense of coming up to the surface. There I was at the opposite end of the vegetable garden, under a poplar tree, feeling like death and bruised all over. I heard Uncle Arthur call out, "Here it is. I've found it." I heard the others exclaim and shout to each other and then to me. So I pulled myself together and trotted round to meet them. It was almost dark by then. They couldn't see my face which I dare say was bright green. Anyway, they were all congratulating themselves over the blasted brooch. I trailed indoors after them and genteelly sipped soda water while they drank hock and Uncle Arthur's whisky. He was pretty well knocked up himself, poor old thing. So I escaped notice, except – '

He moved away a little from Ursula and looked up at her with a singularly sweet smile. 'Except by Ursula,' he said. 'She appeared to have noted the resemblance to a dead fish and she tackled me about it the next morning. So I told her that I'd had another of my Turns as poor Flossie called them.'

'It's so silly,' Ursula whispered. 'The whole thing's so silly. Mr Alleyn is going to laugh at you.'

'Is he? I hope he is. I must say it'd be a great relief to me if Mr Alleyn began to rock with professional laughter, but at the moment I see no signs of it. Of course, you know where all this is leading, sir, don't you?'

'I think so,' said Alleyn. 'You wonder, don't you, if in a condition of amnesia or automatism or unconscious behaviour or whatever it should be called, you could have gone to the wool-shed and committed this crime?'

'That's it.'

'You say you heard Miss Harme and Miss Lynne talking in the bottom path?'

'Yes. I heard Terry say, "Why not just do what we're asked. It would be so much simpler."'

'Did you say that, Miss Lynne?'

'Something like it, I believe.'

'Yes,' said Ursula. 'She said that. I remember.'

'And then I blacked out,' said Fabian.

'Soon after you came to yourself again you heard Mr Rubrick call out that he had found the diamond clip?'

'Yes. It's the first thing I was fully aware of. His voice.'

'And how long,' Alleyn asked Terence Lynne, 'was the interval between your remark and the discovery of the brooch?'

'Perhaps ten minutes. No longer.'

'I see. Mr Losse,' said Alleyn, 'you seem to me to be a more than usually intelligent young man.'

'Thank you,' said Fabian, 'for those few unsolicited orchids.'

'So why on earth, I wonder, have you produced this ridiculous tarradiddle?'

II

'There!' cried Ursula. 'There! What did I tell you.'

'All I can say,' said Fabian stiffly, 'is that I am extremely relieved that Mr Alleyn considers pure tarradiddle a statement upon which I found it difficult to embark and which was, in effect, a confession.'

'My dear chap,' said Alleyn, 'I don't doubt for a moment that you've had these beastly experiences. I spoke carelessly and I apologize. What I do suggest is that the inference you have drawn is quite preposterous. I don't say that, pathologically speaking, you were incapable of committing this crime, but I do say that, physically speaking, on the evidence we've got, you couldn't possibly have done so.'

'Ten minutes,' said Fabian.

'Exactly. Ten minutes. Ten minutes in which to travel about a fifth of a mile, strike a blow, and – I'm sorry to be specific over unpleasant details but it's as well to clear this up – suffocate your victim – remove a great deal of wool from the press, bind up the body, dispose of it, and refill the press. You couldn't have done it during the short time you were conscious and I don't imagine you are going to tell me you returned later, master of yourself, to tidy up a crime you didn't remember committing. As you know, those must have been the circumstances. You wore white flannels, I understand? Very well, what sort of state were they in when you came to yourself?'

'Loamy,' said Fabian. 'Don't forget the vegetable marrows. Evidently I'd collapsed into them.'

'But not woolly? Not stained in any other way?'

Ursula got up quickly and walked over to the window.

'Need we?' asked Fabian, watching her.

'Certainly not. It can wait.'

'No,' said Ursula. 'We asked for it; let's get on with it. I'm all right. I'm only getting a cigarette.'

Her back was towards them. Her voice sounded remote and it was impossible to glean from it the colour of her thoughts. 'Let's get on with it,' she repeated.

'You may remember,' said Fabian, 'that the murderer was supposed to have used a suit of overalls, belonging to Tommy Johns and a pair of working gloves out of one of the pockets. The overalls hung on a nail near the press. Next morning when Tommy put them on he found a seam had split and he noticed – other details.'

'If that theory is correct,' said Alleyn, 'and I think that very probably it is, another minute or two is added to the timetable. You know, you must have thought all this out for yourself. You must have thrashed it out a great many times. To reach the wool-shed and escape the notice of the rest of the party in the garden, you would have had to go round about, either through the house or by way of the side lawn and the yards at the back. You couldn't have used the bottom path because Miss Lynne or Miss Harme would have seen you. Now, before dinner I ran by the most direct route from the vegetable garden to the wool-shed and it took me two minutes. In your case the direct route is impossible. By the indirect routes it took three and four minutes respectively. That leaves a margin, at the best, of about four minutes in which to commit the crime. Can you wonder that I described your theory, inaccurately perhaps but with some justification, as a tarradiddle?'

'In England,' Fabian said, 'after I'd had my first lapse, I went rather thoroughly into the whole business of unconscious behaviour following injuries to the head. I was – ' his mouth twisted, ' – rather interested. The condition is quite well known and apparently not even fantastically unusual. Oddly enough it's sometimes accompanied by an increase in physical strength.'

'But not,' Alleyn pointed out mildly, 'by the speed of a scalded cat going off madly in all directions.'

'All right, all right,' said Fabian with a jerk of his head. 'I'm immensely relieved. Naturally.'

'I still don't see – ' Alleyn began, but Fabian, with a spurt of nervous irritation, cut him short: 'Can you see, at least, that a man in my condition might become morbidly apprehensive about his own actions? To have even one minute cut out of my life, leaving an unknown black lane down which you must have wandered, horribly busy! It's a disgusting, an intolerable thing to happen to you. You feel that nothing was impossible during the lost time, nothing!'

'I see,' said Alleyn's voice quietly in the shadow.

'I assure you I'm not burning to persuade you. You say I couldn't have done it. All right. Grand. And now, for God's sake let's get on with it.'

Ursula came back from the window and sat on the arm of the sofa. Fabian got to his feet, and moved restlessly about the room. There was a brief silence.

'I've always thought,' Fabian said abruptly, 'that the Buchmanite habit of public confession was one of the few really indecent practices of modern times but I must say it has its horrid fascination. Once you start on it, it's very difficult to leave off. It's like taking the cap off a steam whistle. I'm afraid there's still a squeak left in me.'

'Well, I don't pretend to understand – ' Douglas began.

'Of course not,' Fabian rejoined. 'How should you? You're not the neurotic sort like me, Douglas, are you? I wasn't that sort before, you know. Before Dunkirk, I mean. You were wounded in the bottom, I was cracked on the head. That's the difference between us.'

'To accuse yourself of murder – '

'War neurosis, my dear Doug. Typical case: Losse, F., first lieut. Subject to attacks of depression. Refusal to discuss condition. Treatment: Murder in the family followed by psychotherapy (police brand) and Buchmanism. Patient evinced marked desire to talk about himself. Sense of guilt strongly manifested. Cure: doubtful.'

'I don't know what the hell you're talking about.'

'Of course not. Sense of guilt aggravated by history of violent antagonism to victim. In fact,' said Fabian, coming to a halt before Alleyn's chair, 'three weeks before she was killed, Flossie and I had one hell of a row!'

Alleyn looked up at Fabian and saw his lips tremble into a sneer. He made a small breathy sound something like laughter. He wore the conceited, defiant air of the neurotic who bitterly despises his own weakness. 'Difficult,' Alleyn thought, 'and damned tiresome. He's going to treat me like an alienist. Blast!' And he said: 'So you had a row?'

Ursula bent forward and put her hand in Fabian's. For a moment his fingers closed tightly about hers and then, with an impatient movement, he jerked away from her.

'Oh, yes,' he said loudly. 'I'm afraid, since I've started on my course of indecent exposure, I've got to tell you about that too. I'm sorry I can't wait until we're alone together. Very boring for the others. Especially Douglas. Douggy always pays. And I apologize to Ursula because she comes into it. Sorry, Ursy, very bad form.'

'If you mean what I think you mean,' said Douglas, 'I most certainly agree. Surely Ursy can be left out of this.'

'Don't be an idiot, Douglas,' Ursula said impatiently. 'It's what he's doing to himself that matters.'

'And to Douglas, of course,' Fabian cut in loudly. 'Don't forget what I'm doing to poor old Douglas. He becomes the traditional figure of fun. Upon my word it's like a *fin de siécle* farce. Flossie was the duenna of course and you, Douglas, her candidate for the *mariage de convenance.* Ursy is the wayward heroine who shakes her curls and looks elsewhere. I, at least, should have the sympathy of the audience if only because I didn't get it from anybody else. There is no hero, I go sour in the part. You ought to be the *confidante*, Terry, but I've an idea you ran a little sub-plot of your own.'

'I told you,' said Terence Lynne, clearly, 'that if we started to talk like this, one, if not all, of us, would regret it.'

Fabian turned on her with extraordinary venom. 'But that one won't be you, will it, Terry? At least, not yet.'

She put her work down in her lap. A thread of scarlet wool trickled over her black dress and fell in a little pool on the floor. 'No,' she said easily, 'it won't be me. Except that I find all this talk rather embarrassing. And I don't know what you mean by your "not yet", Fabian.'

'You will please keep Terry's name . . .' Douglas began.

'Poor Douglas!' said Fabian. 'Popping up all over the place as the little pattern of chivalry. But it's no good, you know. I'm hell-bent on my Buchmanism. And, really, Ursy, you needn't mind. I may have a crack in my skull and seem to be a bit crazy but I did pay you the dubious compliment of asking you to marry me.'

III

'It's as a further sidelight on Flossie,' Fabian said, 'that the story is really significant,' and as he listened to it Alleyn was inclined to agree with him. It was also a sidelight, he thought, on the character of Ursula Harme, who, when she found there was no stopping Fabian, took the surprising and admirable line of discussing their extraordinary courtship objectively and with an air of judicial impartiality.

Fabian, it appeared, had fallen in love with her during the voyage out. He said, jeering at himself, that he had made up his mind to keep his feelings to himself. 'Because, taking me by and large, I was not a suitable claimant for the hand of Mrs Rubrick's ward.' On his arrival in New Zealand he had consulted a specialist and had shown him the official report on his injury and subsequent condition. By that time Fabian was feeling very much better. His headaches were less frequent and there had been no recrudescence of the black-outs. The specialist took fresh X-ray photographs of his head, and comparing them with the English ones, found an improvement at the site of injury. He told Fabian to go slow and said there was no reason why he should not make a complete recovery. Fabian, greatly cheered, returned to Mount Moon. He attempted to take part in the normal activities of a sheep station but found that undue exertion still upset him, and he finally settled down to work seriously on his magnetic fuse.

'All this time,' he said, 'I did not change either in my feeling for Ursy, or in my decision to say nothing about it. She was Heavenly-kind to me, which perhaps made things a little more difficult, but I had no idea, none at all, that she was in the least fond of me. I avoided anything like a declaration, not only because I thought it would be dishonest, but because I believed it would be useless and embarrassing.'

Fabian made this statement with simplicity and firmness and Alleyn thought: he's working his way out of this. Evidently, it was necessary for him to speak.

One afternoon some months after his arrival at Mount Moon, Flossie plunged upstairs and beat excitedly on the workroom door. Fabian opened it and she shook a piece of paper in his face. 'Read that,' she shouted. 'My Favourite Nephew! Isn't it perfectly splendid!'

It was a cable taken down by Markins over the telephone and it announced the imminent return of Douglas Grace. Flossie was delighted. He was, she repeated emphatically, her Favourite Nephew. 'So sweet always to his old aunt. We had such high old times together in London before the war.' Douglas was to come straight to Mount Moon. As a schoolboy he had spent all his holidays there. 'It's his home,' said Flossie emphatically. His father had been killed in 1918 and his mother had died some three years ago when Douglas was taking a post-graduate engineering course at Heidelberg. 'So he's only got his old Auntie,' said Flossie. 'Your uncle says that if he's demobilized he shall stay here as a salaried cadet. We don't know how badly he's been hurt, of course.' Fabian asked where Douglas had been wounded. 'A muscular wound,' said Flossie evasively and then added, 'the gluteus maximus,' and was deeply offended when Fabian laughed. But she was too excited to remain long in a huff and Fabian saw that she hovered on the edge of a confidence. 'Isn't it fun,' she exclaimed, letting her lips fly apart over her prominent teeth, 'that Ursy and Douglas should meet! My little ADC and my Favourite Nephew. And you, of course, Fab. I've told Ursy so much about Douglas that she feels she knows him already.' Here Flossie gave Fabian a very sharp gimlet-like glance. He came out, shut the workroom door and locked it. He felt a cold jolt of apprehension in the pit of his stomach, a dreadful turning over. Flossie took his arm and walked him along the passage. 'You'll call me a silly romantic old thing,' she began and even in his distress he found time to reflect how irritating she was when she playfully assumed octogenarian whimsies. 'It's only a little dream, of course,' she continued, 'but it would make me so happy if they should come together. It's always been a little plot of poor old Floosie's. Now, if I was a French guardian and aunt . . .' She gave Fabian's arm a little squeeze. 'Ah, well,' she said, 'we'll see.' He received another gimlet-like glance. 'He'll be very good for you, Fab,' she said firmly. 'He's so sane and vigorous. Take you out of yourself. Ha!'

So Douglas arrived at Mount Moon and presently the two young men began their partnership in the workroom. Fabian said, wryly, that from the beginning he had watched for an attraction to spring up between Ursula and Douglas. 'Certainly Flossie made every possible effort to promote it. She left no stone unturned. The trips *a deux* to the Pass! The elaborate sorting-out. She displayed the virtuosity of Tommy Johns in the drafting yards. Ursy and Douglas to the right. Terry, Uncle Arthur and me to the left. It was masterly and quite shameless. One evening when, on the eve of one of her trips north, her machinations had been particularly blatant, Uncle Arthur called her Pandora, but she missed the allusion and thought he was making a joke about her luggage.'

For a time Fabian thought her plot was going to work and tried to accustom himself to the notion. He watched, sick with uncertainty, for intimate glances, private jokes, the small change of courtship, to develop between Ursula and Douglas, and thought he saw them where they didn't exist. 'I was even glad to keep Douglas in the workshop because then, at least, I knew they were not together. I was mean and subtle but I tried not to be and I don't think any one noticed.'

'I merely thought he was fed up with me,' Ursula said to Alleyn. 'He treated me with deathly courtesy.'

And then, on a day when Fabian had one of his now very rare headaches, there had been a scene between them. 'A ridiculous scene,' he said, looking gently at Ursula. 'I needn't describe it. We talked at cross-purposes like people in a Victorian novel.'

'And I bawled and wept and said if I irritated him he needn't talk to me at all, and then,' said Ursula, 'we had a magic scene in which everything was sorted out and it all looked as if it was going to be Heaven.'

'But it didn't work out that way,' Fabian said. 'I came to earth and remembered I'd no business making love to anybody and, ten minutes too late, did the little hero number and told Ursy to forget me. She said, no. We had the sort of argument that you might imagine from the context. I weakened, of course. I never was much good at heroics and – well, we agreed I should see the quack again and stand by what he told me. But we'd reckoned without our Floss.'

Fabian turned back to the fireplace and, thrusting his hands in his pockets, looked up at the portrait of his aunt.

'I told you she was as clever as a bagful of monkeys, didn't I? That's what this thing doesn't convey. She was sharp. For example she was wise enough to avoid tackling Ursy about me and, still more remarkable, she had denied herself too many heart-to-heart talks with Ursy about Douglas. I imagine what she did say was indirect, a building up of allusive romantics. She was by no means incapable of subtlety. Just a spot or two of the Beatrice and Benedict stuff and the merest hint that she'd be so, so happy if ever – and then a change of topic. Like that, wasn't it, Ursy?'

'But she would have liked it,' said Ursula unhappily. 'She was so fond of Douglas.'

'And not so fond of me. From what you've heard already, Mr Alleyn, you'll have gathered that my popularity had waned. I wasn't a good enough yes-man for Flossie. I hadn't responded too well to her terrifying ministrations when she nursed me and she didn't really like my friendship with Uncle Arthur.'

'That's nonsense,' Ursula said. 'Honestly, darling, it's the purest bilge. She told me it was so nice for Uncle Arthur having you to talk to.'

'You old innocent,' he said, 'of course she did. She disliked it intensely. It was something outside the Flossie System, something she wasn't in on. I was very fond of my Uncle Arthur,' Fabian said thoughtfully, 'he was a good vintage, dry, with a nice bouquet. Wasn't he, Terry?'

'You're straying from the point,' said Terence.

'Right. After Ursy and I had come to our decision I tried to be very non-committal and unexalted but I suppose I made a poor fist at it. I was – translated. I'm afraid,' said Fabian abruptly, 'that all this is intolerably egotistical but I don't see how that can be avoided. At any rate, Flossie spotted something was up. That eye of hers! You do get a hint of it in the portrait. It was sort of blank and yet the pupils had the looks of drills. Ursy managed better than I did. She rather made up to you, Douglas, didn't she, during lunch?'

The fire had burned low and the glowing ball of the kerosene lamp was behind Douglas but Alleyn thought that he had turned redder in the face. His hand went to his moustache and he said in an easy, jocular voice: 'I think Ursy and I understood each other pretty well, didn't we, Ursy? We both knew our Flossie, what?'

Ursy moved uncomfortably. 'No, Douglas,' she said. 'I won't quite take that. I mean – oh, well, it doesn't matter.'

'Come on, Douglas,' said Fabian with something of his former impishness, 'be a little gent and take your medicine.'

'I've said a dozen times already that I fail to see what we gain by parading matters that are merely personal before Mr Alleyn. Talk about dirty linen!'

'But, my God, isn't it better to wash it, however publicly, than to hide it away, still dirty, in our cupboards? I'm persuaded,' said Fabian vigorously, 'that only by getting the whole story, the whole complicated mix-up of emotions and circumstances, sorted out and related, shall we ever get at the truth. And after all, this particular bit of linen is perfectly clean. Only rather comic, like Mr Robertson Hare's underpants.'

'Honestly!' said Ursula and giggled.

'Come on, now, Douglas. Egged on by Flossie you did make a formal pass at Ursy that very afternoon. Didn't you, now?'

'I only want to spare Ursy – '

'No you don't,' said Fabian. 'Come off it, Doug. You want to spare yourself, old cock. This is how it went, I fancy: Flossie, observing my exaltation, told you that it was high time you made a move. Encouraged by Ursy's carryings on at lunch – you overdid it a bit, Ursy – and gingered up by Flossie, you proposed and were refused.'

'You didn't really mind, though, did you, Douglas?' asked Ursula gently. 'I mean, it was all rather spur-of-the-momentish, wasn't it?'

'Well, yes,' said Douglas. 'Yes, it was. But I don't mean . . . '

'Give it up,' Fabian advised him kindly. 'Or were you by any chance in love with Ursy?'

'Naturally. I wouldn't have asked Ursy to be my wife . . .' Douglas began and then swore softly to himself.

'And with the wealthy aunt's blessing why shouldn't the good little heir speak up like a man? We'll let it go at that,' said Fabian, 'Ursy said her piece, Mr Alleyn, and Douglas took it like a hero and the next thing that happened was me on the mat before Flossie.'

The scene had been formidable and had taken place there, in the study. Flossie, Fabian explained, had contrived to give the whole thing an air of the grossest impropriety. She had spoken in a cold hushed voice. 'Fabian, I'm afraid what I'm going to say to you is very serious and most unpleasant. I am bitterly disappointed and dreadfully grieved. I think you know what it is that has hurt me so much, don't you?'

'I'm afraid I haven't an inkling so far, Aunt Flossie,' Fabian had answered brightly and with profound inward misgivings.

'If you think for a minute, Fabian, I'm sure your conscience will tell you.'

But Fabian refused to play this uncomfortable game and remained obstinately unhelpful. Flossie extended her long upper lip and the corners of her mouth turned down dolorously. 'Oh, Fabian, Fabian!' she said in a wounded voice, and, after an unfruitful pause, she added: 'And I put such trust in you. Such trust!' She bit her lip and shielded her eyes wearily. 'You refuse to help me, then. I had hoped it would be easier than this. What have you been saying to Ursula? What have you done, Fabian?'

This persistent repetition of his name had jarred on his nerves, Fabian said, but he had replied without emphasis. 'I'm afraid I've told Ursula that I'm fond of her.'

'Do you realize how dreadfully wrong that was? What right had you to speak to Ursy?'

There was only one answer to this. 'None,' said Fabian.

'None,' Flossie repeated. 'None! You see? Oh, Fabian.'

'Ursula returns my love,' said Fabian, taking some pleasure in the old-fashioned phrase.

Two brick-red patches appeared over Flossie's cheek bones. She abandoned her martyrdom. 'Nonsense,' she said sharply.

'I know it's incredible, but I have her word for it.'

'She's a child. You've taken advantage of her youth.'

'That's ridiculous, Aunt Florence,' said Fabian.

'She's sorry for you,' said Flossie cruelly. 'It's pity she feels. You've played on her sympathy for your bad health. That's what it is. Pity,' she added with an air of originality, 'may be akin to love but it's not love and you've behaved most unscrupulously in appealing to it.'

'I made no appeal. I agree that I've no business to ask Ursula to marry me and I said as much to her.'

'That was very astute of you,' she said.

'I said there must be no engagement between us unless my doctor could give me a clean bill of health. I assure you, Aunt Florence, I've no intention of asking her to marry a crock.'

'If you were bursting with health,' Flossie shouted, 'you'd still be entirely unsuited to each other.' She elaborated her theme, pointing out to Fabian the weaknesses in his character, his conceit, his cynicism, his absence of ideals. She emphasized the difference in their circumstances. No doubt, she said, Fabian knew very well that Ursula had an income of her own and, on her uncle's death, would be extremely well provided. Fabian said that he agreed with everything Flossie said but that after all it was for Ursula to decide. He added that if the magnetic fuse came up to their expectations he would be in a better position financially and could hope for regular employment in specialized and experimental jobs. Flossie stared at him. Almost, Fabian said, you could see her lay back her ears.

'I shall speak to Ursula,' she said.

This announcement filled him with dismay. He lost his head and implored her to wait until he had seen the doctor. 'You see,' he told Alleyn, 'I knew so well what would happen. Ursy, of course, doesn't agree with me but the truth is that for her Flossie was a purely symbolic figure. You've heard what Flossie did for Ursy. When Ursy was thirteen years old and completely desolate, Flossie came along like a plain but comforting goddess and snatched her up into a system of pink clouds. She still sees her as the beneficent super-mother. Flossie had a complete success with Ursula. She caught her young. She loaded her down with a sense of gratitude and gingered her up with inoculations of heroine-worship. Flossie was, as people say, everything to Ursula. She combined the roles of adored form-mistress, Queen-Mother and lover.'

'I never heard such utter tripe,' said Ursula, quite undisconcerted by this analysis. 'All this talk of Queen-Mothers! Do pipe down, darling.'

'I mean it,' Fabian persisted. 'Instead of having a good healthy giggle about some frightful youth or mooning over a talkie idol or turning violently Anglo-Catholic which is the correct behaviour in female adolescence, you converted all these normal impulses into a blind devotion to Flossie.'

'Shut up, do. We've had it all out a dozen times.'

'It wouldn't have mattered if it had passed off in the normal way but it became a fixation.'

'She was marvellous to me. I owed everything to her. I was discreetly grateful. And I loved her. I'd have been a monster if I didn't. You and your fixations!'

'Would you believe it,' said Fabian, angrily addressing himself to Alleyn. 'This silly girl, although she says she loves me, won't marry

me, not because I'm a bad bargain physically which I admit, but simply because Flossie, who's dead, screwed some sort of undertaking
out of her that she'd give me up.'

'I promised to wait two years and I'm going to keep my promise.'

'There!' cried Fabian triumphantly. 'A promise under duress if
ever there was one. Imagine the interview. All the emotional jig-
gery-pokery that she'd tried on me and then some. "Darling little
Ursy, if I'd had a baby of my own she couldn't have been dearer.
Poor old Floosie knows best. You're making me so unhappy."
Faugh!' said Fabian violently. 'It's enough to make you sick.'

'I didn't think anybody ever said "Faugh" in real life,' Ursula
observed. 'Only Hamlet. "And smelt so. Faugh!"'

'That was "Puh!"' said Alleyn mildly.

IV

'Well, there you have it,' said Fabian after a pause. 'Ursy went off the
day after our respective scenes with Flossie. The Red Cross people
rang up to know if she could do her sixty-hours hospital duty. I've
always considered that Flossie arranged it. Ursula wrote to me from
the hospital and that was the first I knew about this outrageous
promise. And, by the way, Flossie didn't commute the sentence into
two years' probation until afterwards. At first she exacted a straight-
out pledge that Ursy would give me up altogether. The alteration
was due, I fancy, to my uncle.'

'You confided in him?' Alleyn asked.

'He found out for himself. He was extraordinarily perceptive. He
seemed to me,' said Fabian, 'to resemble some instrument. He would
catch and echo in himself, delicately, the coarser sounds made by
other people. I suppose his ill health made for a contemplative habit
of mind. At all events he achieved it. He was very quiet always. One
would almost forget he was in the room sometimes, and then one
would look up and meet his eye and know that he had been with
one all the time; perhaps critically, perhaps sympathetically. That
didn't matter. He was a good companion. It was like that over this
affair with Ursy. Apparently he had known all the time that I was in
love with her. He asked me to come and see him while he was

having his afternoon rest. It was the first time, I believe, that he'd ever asked me a direct question. He said: "Has it reached a climax, then, between you and that child?" You know, he was fond of you, Ursy. He said, once, that since Flossie was not transparent he could hardly expect that you should notice him.'

'I liked him very much,' said Ursula defensively, 'he was just so quiet that somehow one didn't notice him.'

'I told him the whole story. It was one of his bad days. He was breathing short and I was afraid I'd tire him but he made me go on. When I'd finished he asked me what we were going to do if the doctor didn't give me a clean bill. I said I didn't know, but it didn't matter much because Flossie was going to take a stand about it and I was afraid of her influence over Ursy. He said he believed that might be overcome. I thought then that perhaps he meant to tackle Flossie. I still think that he may have been responsible for her suddenly commuting the life sentence into a mere two years, but of course her row with Douglas over Markins may have had something to do with it. You were never quite the same hot favourite after that, were you, Douglas?'

'Not quite,' Douglas agreed sadly.

'Perhaps it was a bit of both,' Fabian continued. 'But I fancy Uncle Arthur did tackle her. Before I left him he said with that wheezy little laugh of his: "It takes a strong man to be a weak husband. Matrimonially speaking, a condition of perpetual apology is difficult to sustain. I've failed signally in the role." I think I know what he meant, don't you, Terry?'

'I,' said Terence. 'Why do you ask me?'

'Because unlike Ursy you were not blinded by Flossie's splendours. You must have been able to look at them both objectively.'

'I don't think so,' she said, but so quietly that perhaps only Alleyn heard her.

'And he must have been attached to you, you know, because when he became ill, you were the one he wanted to see.'

As if answering some implied criticism in this Douglas said: 'I don't know what we'd have done without Terry all through that time. She was marvellous.'

'I know,' said Fabian, still looking at her. 'You see, Terry, I've often thought that of all of us you're best equipped to look at the whole thing in perspective. Or are you?'

'I wasn't a relation,' said Terence, 'if that's what you mean. I was an outsider, a paid employee.'

'Put it that way if you like. What I meant was that in your case there were no emotional complications.' He waited, and then, with a precise repetition of his former inflection, he added: 'Or were there?'

'How could there be? I don't know what you want me to say. I'm no good at this kind of thing.'

'Not much in our line, is it, Terry?' said Douglas, instantly forming an alliance. 'When it comes to all this messing about and holding post-mortems and wondering what everybody was thinking about everybody else, you and I are out of the picture, aren't we?'

'All right,' said Fabian, 'let's put it to the authority. What do you say, Mr Alleyn? Is this admittedly ragged discussion a complete waste of time? Does it leave you precisely where you were with the police files? Or has it, if only in the remotest degree, helped you along the path towards a solution?'

'It's of interest,' Alleyn replied. 'It's given me something that no amount of poring over the files could have produced.'

'And my third question?' Fabian persisted.

'I can't answer it,' Alleyn rejoined gravely. 'But I do hope, very much, that you'll carry on with the discussion.'

'There you are, Terry,' said Fabian, 'it's up to you, you see.'

'To do what?'

'To carry forward the theme, to be sure. To tell us where we were wrong and why. To give us, without prejudice, your portrait of Flossie Rubrick.'

Again Fabian looked up at the painting. 'You said you thought that blank affair up there was like her. Why?'

Without glancing at the portrait, Miss Lynne said: 'It's a stupid looking face in the picture. In my opinion that's what she was. A stupid woman.'

CHAPTER 5
According to Terence Lynne

I

The aspect of Terence Lynne that struck Alleyn most forcibly was her composure. He felt quite sure that, more than any of them, she disliked and resented these interminable discussions. Yet she answered his questions composedly. Unlike her companions, she showed no sign of launching into a continuous narrative and the sense of release which had encouraged them to talk was, he felt certain, absent in Miss Lynne. He had the feeling that unless he was careful he would find himself engaged in something very like routine police interrogation. This, above all things, he was anxious to avoid. He wanted to retain his position as an onlooker before whom the spoil of an indiscriminate rummage was displayed, leaving him free to sort, reject and set aside. Terence Lynne waited for a specific demand, yet her one contribution up to date had been, in its way, sufficiently startling.

'Here at least,' Alleyn said, 'are two completely opposed views. Losse, if I remember him, said Mrs Rubrick was as clever as a bagful of monkeys. You disagree, Miss Lynne?'

'She had a few tricks,' said Terence. 'She could talk.'

'To her electors?'

'Yes, to them. She had the knack. Her speeches sounded rather effective. They didn't read well.'

'I always thought you wrote them for her, Terry,' said Fabian with a grin.

85

'If I'd done that they would have read well and sounded dull. I haven't the knack.'

'But wasn't it pretty hot to know what they'd like?' asked Douglas.

'She used to listen to people on the wireless and then adapt the phrases.'

'By golly, so she did!' cried Fabian delightedly. 'Do you remember, Ursy, the clarion call in the speech on rehabilitation? "We shall settle them on the good ground, in the fallow fields, in the workshops and in the hills. We shall never abandon them!" Good Lord, she had got a nerve.'

'It was utterly unconscious!' Ursy declaimed. 'An instinctive echo.'

'Was it!' said Terence Lynne quietly.

'You're unfair, Terry.'

'I don't think so. She had a very good memory for other people's ideas. But she couldn't reason very well and she used to make the most painful floaters over finance: She hadn't got the dimmest notion of how her rehabilitation scheme would work out financially.'

'Uncle Arthur helped in that department,' said Fabian.

'Of course he did.'

'He played an active part in her public life?' asked Alleyn.

'I told you,' she said. 'I think it killed him. People talked about the shock of her death, but he was worn out before she died. I tried to stop it happening but it was no good. Night after night we would sit up working on the notes she handed over to him. She gave him no credit for that.'

She spoke rapidly and with more colour in her voice. Hallo! Alleyn thought, she's off.

'His own work died of it, too,' she said.

'What on earth do you mean, Terry?' asked Fabian. 'What work?'

'His essays. He'd started a group of six essays on the pastoral element in Elizabethan poetry. Before that, he wrote a descriptive poem treating the plateau in the Elizabethan mode. That was the best thing he did, we thought. He wrote very lucidly.'

'Terry,' said Fabian, 'you bewilder me with these revelations. I knew his taste in reading, of course. It was surprisingly austere. But – essays? I wonder why he never told me.'

'He was sensitive about them. He didn't want to talk about them until they were complete. They were really very good.'

'I should have liked to know,' said Fabian gently. 'I wish he had felt he could tell me.'

'I suppose he had to have a hobby,' said Douglas. 'He couldn't play games, of course. There's nothing much in that, just doing a bit of writing, I mean.'

'"Scribble, scribble, scribble, Mr Gibbon,"' Alleyn muttered. Terence and Fabian looked quickly at him and Fabian grinned.

'They were never finished,' said Terence. 'I tried to help by taking down at his dictation and then by typing, but he got so tired and there were always other things.'

'Terry,' said Fabian suddenly, 'have I by any chance done you rather a bloody injustice?'

Alleyn saw the oval shape of Terence's face lift attentively. It was the colour of a Staffordshire shepherdess, a cool cream. The brows and eyes were dark accents, the mouth a firm red brush stroke. It was an enigmatic face, a mask framed neatly in its sleek cap of black hair.

She said, 'I tried very hard not to complicate things.'

'I'm sorry,' said Fabian. She raised her hands a little way and let them fall into her lap.

'It doesn't matter,' she said, 'in the very least. It's all over. I didn't altogether succeed.'

'You people!' Fabian said, bending a look of tenderness and pain upon Ursula. 'You rather make for complications.'

'We people?' she said. 'Terry and me?'

'Both of you, it seems,' he agreed.

Douglas suddenly raised his cry of, 'I don't know what all this is about.'

'It doesn't matter,' Terence repeated. 'It's over.'

'Poor Terry,' said Fabian, but it seemed that Miss Lynne did not respond easily to sympathy. She took up her work again and the needles clicked.

'Poor Terry,' Douglas echoed playfully, obtusely, and sat beside her again, laying his big muscular hand on her knee.

'Where are the essays?' Fabian asked.

'I've got them.'

'I'd like to read them, Terry. May I?'

'No,' she said coldly.

'Isn't that rather churlish?'

'I'm sorry. He gave them to me.'

'I always thought,' said Douglas out of a clear sky, 'that they were an ideal couple. Awfully fond of each other. Uncle Arthur thought she was the cat's whiskers. Always telling people how marvellous she was.' He slapped Terence's knee. 'Wasn't he?' he persisted.

'Yes.'

'Yes,' said Ursula. 'He was. He admired her tremendously. You can't deny that, Fabian.'

'I don't deny it. It's incredible, but true. He thought a great deal of her.'

'For the things he hadn't got,' said Terence. 'Vitality. Initiative. Drive. Popularity. Nerve.'

'You're prejudiced,' Ursy said fiercely, 'you and Fabian. It's not fair. She was kind, kind and warm and generous. She was never petty or spiteful and how you, both of you, who owed her so much – '

'I owed her nothing whatever,' said Terence. 'I did my job well. She was lucky to have me. I admit she was kind in the way that vain people are kind. She knew how kind she was. She was quite kind.'

'And generous?'

'Yes. Quite.'

'And unsuspicious?'

'Yes,' Terence agreed after a pause. 'I suppose so.'

'Then I think it's poor Florence Rubrick,' said Ursula stoutly. 'I do indeed, Terry.'

'I won't take that,' Terence said, and for the first time Alleyn heard a note of anger in her voice. 'She was too stupid to know, to notice how fortunate she was . . . might have been . . . She didn't even look after her proprietary rights. She was like an absentee landlord.'

'But she didn't ask you to poach on the estates.'

'What are you two arguing about?' demanded the punctual Douglas. 'What's it all in aid of?'

'Nothing,' said Fabian. 'There's no argument. Let it go.'

'But it was you who organized this striptease act, Fabian,' Ursula pointed out. 'The rest of us have had to do our stuff. Why should Terry get off?'

She looked at Terence and frowned. She was a lovely creature, Alleyn thought. Her hair shone in copper tendrils along the nape of her neck. Her eyes were wide and lively, her mouth vivid. She had something of the quality of a Victorian portrait in crayons, a resemblance that was heightened by the extreme delicacy and freshness of her complexion and by the slender grace of her long neck and her elegant hands. She displayed too, something of the waywardness and conscious poise of such a type. These qualities lent her a dignity that was at variance with her modern habit of speech. She looked, Alleyn thought, as though she knew she would inevitably command attention and that much would be forgiven her. She was obstinate, he thought, but he doubted if obstinacy alone was responsible for her persistent defence of Florence Rubrick. He had been watching her closely and, as though she felt his gaze upon her and even caught the tenor of his thoughts, she threw him a brilliant glance and ran impulsively to Terence.

'Terry,' she said, 'am I unfair? I don't want to be unfair but there's no one else but me to speak for her.'

Without looking at him she held out her hand to Fabian, and immediately he was beside her, holding it.

'You're not allowed to snub me, Fabian, or talk over my head or go intellectual at me. I loved her. She was my friend. I can't stand off and look at her and analyse her faults. And when all of you do this, I have to fight for her.'

'I know,' said Fabian, holding her by the hand. 'It's all right. I know.'

'But I don't want to fight with Terry. Terry, I don't want to fight with you, do you hear? I'd rather, after all, that you didn't tell us. I'd rather go on liking you.'

'You won't get me to believe,' said Douglas, 'that Terry's done anything wrong, and I tell you straight, Fabian, that I don't much like the way you're handling this. If you're suggesting that Terry's got anything to be ashamed about – '

'Be quiet!'

Terence was on her feet. She had spoken violently, as if prompted by some unbearable sense of irritation. 'You're talking like a fool, Douglas. "Ashamed" or "not ashamed", what has that got to do with it? I don't want your championship and, Ursula, I promise you

I don't give a damn whether you think you're being fair or unfair or whether, as you put it, you're prepared to "go on liking me". You make too many assumptions. To have dragooned me into going so far and then to talk magnanimously about letting me off! You've all made up your minds, haven't you, that I loved him? Very well, then, it's perfectly true. If Mr Alleyn is to hear the whole story, at least let me tell it, plainly and, if it's not too fantastic a notion, with a little dignity.'

II

It was strange, Alleyn thought, that Terence Lynne, who from the beginning had resented the discussion and all that it implied, should suddenly yield, as the others had yielded, to this urge for self-revelation. As she developed her story, speaking steadily and with a kind of ruthlessness, he regretted more and more that he could form no clear picture in his mind of Florence Rubrick's husband; of how he looked, or how wide a physical disparity there had been between Arthur Rubrick and this girl who must have been twenty years his junior.

Terence had been five years in New Zealand. Equipped with a knowledge of shorthand and typing and six letters of recommendation, including one from the High Commissioner in London to Flossie herself, she had sought her fortune in the antipodes. Flossie immediately engaged her, and she settled down to life at Mount Moon interspersed with frequent visits to Flossie's *pied-à-terre* near Parliament Buildings in Wellington. She must, Alleyn thought, have been lonely in her quiet, contained way, separated by half the world from her own country, her lot fallen among strangers. Fabian and Ursula, he supposed, had already formed an alliance in the ship, Douglas Grace had not yet returned from the Middle East, and she had obviously felt little respect or liking for her employer. Yes, she must have been lonely. And then Flossie began to send her on errands to her husband. 'Those statistics on revaluation, Miss Lynne, I want something I can quote. Something comparative. You might just go over the notes with my husband. Nothing elaborate, tell him. Something that will score a point.' And Arthur Rubrick and Terence

Lynne would work together in the study. She found she could light-
en his task by fetching books from the shelves and by taking notes
at his dictation. Alleyn formed a picture of this exquisitely neat girl
moving quietly about the room or sitting at the desk while the figure in the armchair dictated, a little breathlessly, the verbal bullets
that Flossie was to fire at her political opponents. As they grew to
know each other well, she found that, with a pointer or two from
Arthur Rubrick, she was able to build up most of the statistical
ammunition required by her employer. She had a respect for the
right phrase and for the just fall of good words, each in its true place,
and so, she found, had he. They had a little sober fun together, con-
cocting paragraphs for Flossie, but they never heard themselves
quoted. 'She used to peck over the notes like a magpie,' Terence said,
'and then rehash them with lots of repetition so that she would be
provided with opportunities to thump with her right fist on the palm
of her left hand. "In 1938," she would shout, beating time with her
fist, "in 1938, mark you, in 1938 the revenue from such properties
amounted to three and a quarter million. To three and a quarter million. Three and a quarter million pounds, Mr Speaker, was the sum
realized . . ." And she was quite right. It went down much better than
our austerely balanced phrases would have done if ever she'd been
fool enough to use them. *They* only appeared when she handed in
notes of her speeches for publication. She kept them specially for
that purpose. They looked well in print.'

It had been through this turning of phrases that Flossie's husband
and her secretary came to understand each other more thoroughly.
Flossie was asked by a weekly journal to contribute an article on the
theme of women workers in the back country. She was flattered, said
Terence, but a bit uneasy. She came into the study and talked a good
deal about the beauty of women's work in the home. She said she
thought the cocky-farmer's wife led a supremely beautiful existence
because it was devoted to the basic fundamentals (she occasionally
coined such phrases) of life. 'A noble life,' Flossie said, ringing for
Markins, 'they also serve –' But the quotation faltered before the picture of any cocky-farmer's wife, whose working-day is fourteen hours
long and comparable only to that of a man under a sentence of hard
labour. 'Look up something appropriate, Miss Lynne. Arthur darling,
you'll help her. I want to stress the sanctity of women's work in the

high country. Unaided, alone. You might say matriarchal,' she threw at them as Markins came in with the cup of patent food she took at eleven o'clock. Flossie sipped it and walked up and down the room throwing out unrelated words: 'True sphere . . . splendour . . . heritage . . . fitting mate.' She was called to the telephone but found time to pause in the door and say, 'Away you go, both of you. Quotations, remember, but not too highbrow, Arthur darling. Something sweet and natural and telling.' She waved her hand and was gone.

The article they wrote was frankly heretical. They had stood side by side in the window and looked over the plateau to the ranges, now a clean thin blue in the mid-morning sunshine.

'When I look out there,' Arthur Rubrick had said, 'it always strikes me as being faintly comic that we should talk of "settling" on the plateau and of "bringing in new country". All we do is to move over the surface of a few hills. There is nothing new about them. Primal, yes, and almost unblotted by such new things as men and sheep. Essentially back among the earlier unhuman ages.' He added that perhaps this was the reason why no one had been able to write very well about this country. It had been possible, he said, to write of the human beings moving about parasitically over the skin of the country, but the edge of modern idiom was turned when it was tried against the implacable surface of the plateau. He said that some older and therefore fresher idiom was needed, 'something that has the hard edge of a spring wind in it, something comparable to the Elizabethan mode.' From this conversation was born his idea of writing about the plateau in a prose that smacked of Hakluyt's *Voyages*. 'It sounds affected,' said Terence, 'but he only did it as a kind of game. I thought it really did give one the sensation of this country. But it was only a game.'

'A fascinating game,' said Alleyn. 'What else did he write?'

Five more essays, she said, that were redrafted many times and never really completed. Very often he wasn't up to working on them, and Flossie's odd jobs absorbed his energy when he was well. There were many occasions when he fagged over her speeches and reports, or dragged himself to meetings and parties when he should have been resting. He had a morbid dread of admitting to his wife that he was unwell. 'It's so tiresome for her,' he used to say. 'She's too good about it, too kind.'

'And she was kind,' Ursula declared. 'She took endless trouble.'

'It was the wrong kind of trouble,' Fabian said. 'She oozed long-suffering patronage.'

'I didn't think so. Nor did he.'

'Did he, Terry?' asked Fabian.

'He was extraordinarily loyal. That's all he ever said, "It's too good of her, too kind." But, of course, it wasn't much fun being the object of that sort of compassion. And then – ' Terence paused.

'Then what, Terry?' said Fabian.

'Nothing. That's all.'

'But it isn't quite all, is it? Something happened, didn't it? There was some crisis, wasn't there? What was he worrying about that last fortnight before she died? He was worried, you know. What was it?'

'He was feeling ill. He had an idea things were going wrong in the background. Mrs Rubrick obviously was upset. I see now that it was the trouble with Cliff Johns and Markins that had put her in a diffi-cult mood. She didn't tell him about Cliff and Markins, I'm sure, but she dropped dark hints about ingratitude and disappointment. She was always doing it. She kept saying that she stood alone, that other women in her position had somebody to whom they could turn and that she had nobody. He sat over there in the window, listening, with his hand shading his eyes, just taking it. I could have murdered her.'

This statement was met by a scandalized hush.

'A commonplace exaggeration,' said Fabian at last. 'I've used it repeatedly myself in speaking of Flossie. "I could have murdered her." I suppose she got home with her cracks at Uncle Arthur, didn't she? Every time a coconut?'

'Yes,' said Terence. 'She got home.'

A longer silence followed. Alleyn felt certain that Terence had reached a point in her story where something was to be withheld from her listeners. The suggestion of antagonism, never long absent from her manner, now deepened. She set her lips and, after a quick look into the shadow where he sat, took up her work again with an air of finality.

'Funny,' said Fabian suddenly. 'I thought she seemed to be rather come-hither-ish with Uncle Arthur during that last week. There was a hint of skittishness which I found extremely awe-inspiring. And,

I may say, extremely unusual. You must have noticed it, all of you. What was she up to?'

'Honestly, Fabian darling,' said Ursula, 'you are too difficult. At one moment you find fault with Auntie Floss for neglecting Uncle Arthur and at the next you complain because she was nice to him. What should she have done, poor darling, to please you and Terry?'

'How old was she?' Douglas blurted out. 'Forty-seven, wasn't it? Well, I mean to say, she was jolly spry for her age, wasn't she? I mean to say . . . well, I mean, there it was . . . I suppose – '

'Let it pass, Douglas,' Fabian said kindly. 'We know what you mean. But I can't think that Florence's sudden access of playfulness was entirely due to natural or even pathological causes. There seemed to me to be a distinct suggestion of proprietary rights. What I have I hold. The bitch, if you will excuse the usage, Douglas, in the marital manger.'

'It's entirely inexcusable,' said Ursula, 'and so are you, Fab.'

'I don't mean to show off and be tiresome, darling, I promise you, I don't. You can't deny that she was different during that last week. As sour as a lemon with all of us, and suddenly so, so keen on Uncle Arthur. She watched him too. Indeed she looked at him as if he was some *objet d'art* that she'd forgotten she possessed until someone else came along and saw that it was – well, rare, and in its way rather beautiful. Wasn't it like that?'

'I don't know. I thought she was horrible, baiting him about his illness. That's what it amounted to, and that's what I saw,' said Terence.

'But don't you agree,' Fabian persisted, 'that along with that there was a definite – what shall I call it – why, damn it, she made advances. She was kittenish. She shook her curls and did the little devil number. Didn't she, now?'

'I didn't watch her antics,' said Terence coldly.

'But you did, Terry. You watched. Listen to me, Terry,' said Fabian very earnestly, 'don't get it into your head that I'm an enemy. I'm not. I'm sorry for you and I realize now that I've misjudged you. You see, I thought you were merely doing your line of oomph with Uncle Arthur out of boredom. I thought you just sat round being a cryptic woman at him to keep your hand in. I know this sounds insufferable but he was so very much older and, well, as I thought, so definitely not your cup of tea. It was perfectly obvious that he was losing his heart to you and I resented what I imagined was merely a bit of practice technique on your part. I don't suppose you give two tuppenny damns for what I thought, Terry, but I am sorry. All right. Now, when I suggested that we should ask Mr Alleyn to come, we all agreed that rather than carry on as we were, with this unspeakable business festering in our minds, we would, each of us, risk becoming an object of suspicion. We agreed that none of us suspected any of the other three and, even with the terrifying example of the local detective force to daunt us, we said we didn't believe that the truth, the whole truth, although it might be unpalatable, could do us any harm. Were we right in that, Mr Alleyn?'

Alleyn stirred a little in his armchair and joined his long fingers. 'It's a truism to say that if the whole facts of a case are known there can be no miscarriage of justice. It's very seldom indeed, in homicide investigations, that the police arrive at the whole truth. Sometimes they get enough of the truth to enable them to build up a case and make an arrest. Most often they get a smattering of essential facts, a plethora of inessential facts and a maddening accumulation of lies. If you really do stick to your original plan of thrashing out the whole story here tonight, in this room, you will, I think, bring off a remarkable, indeed a unique performance.'

He saw that they were young enough to be flattered and stimulated by this assurance. 'There, now!' said Fabian triumphantly. 'But,' said Alleyn, 'I don't believe for a moment that you will succeed. How long does it take a psychoanalyst to complete his terrifying course of treatment? Months, isn't it? His aim, as I understand it, is to get to the bottom, to spring-clean completely, to arrive, in fact, at the clinical truths. Aren't you, Losse, attempting something of that sort? If so, I'm sure you cannot succeed, nor, as a policeman, would I want you to do so. As a policeman, I am not concerned with the whole clinical truth. Faced with it, I should probably find myself unable to make any arrest, ever. I am required only to produce facts. If your discussion of Mrs Rubrick's character and that of her husband can throw the smallest ray of light along the path that leads to an unknown murderer who struck her from, behind, suffocated her, bound up her body, and concealed it in a wool-press, then from the official point of view it will have been valuable. If, at the same time, somewhere along that path, there is the trace of an enemy agent, then again from my point of view, as an investigator of espionage in this country, it will have been valuable. If finally, it relieves the burden of secrecy under which you have all suffered, you, also, may profit by it, though, as you have already seen, the process is painful and may be dangerous.'

'We realize that,' Fabian said.

'Do you fully realize it? You told me at first that there was a complete absence of motive among you. Would you still say so? Look what has come out. Captain Grace was Mrs Rubrick's heir. That circumstance, which suggests the most common of all motives, has of course always been recognized by the police and must have occurred to all of you. You, Losse, advanced a theory that you yourself in a condition of amnesia attacked Mrs Rubrick and killed her. What's more, as you developed this theme you also revealed a motive, Mrs Rubrick's opposition to your engagement to Miss Harme. Now, under this same process of self-revelation, Miss Lynne must also be said to have a motive. Most courageously she has told us that she had formed a deep attachment for the murdered woman's husband and you, Losse, say that this attachment obviously was returned. The second most common motive appears in both your case and hers. You have said, bravely, that none of you has anything to fear from this discussion. Are you sure you have the right to make this statement? You are using this room as a sort of confessional, but I am bound by no priestly rule. What you tell me, I shall consider from the practical point of view and may afterwards use in the report I send to your police. I should neglect my duty if, before she goes any further, I didn't remind Miss Lynne of all the circumstances.' Alleyn paused and rubbed his nose. 'That all sounds pompous,' he said. 'But there it is. The whole thing's a departure from the usual procedure. I doubt if any collection of possible suspects has ever before decided to have what Miss Harme has aptly described as a verbal striptease before an investigating officer.' He looked at Terence. 'Well, now, Miss Lynne,' he said, 'if you don't want to go on – '

'It's not because I'm afraid,' she said. 'I didn't do it and any attempt to prove I did would fail. I suppose I ought to be afraid but I'm not. I don't feel in the least anxious for myself.'

'Very well. Losse has suggested that there is some significance in the change during the last week of Mrs Rubrick's life in her manner towards her husband. He has suggested that you can explain this change. Is he right?'

She did not answer. Slowly and, as it seemed, reluctantly, she raised her eyes and looked at the portrait of Florence Rubrick.

'Terry!' said Ursula suddenly, 'did she know? Did she find out?'

Fabian gave a sharp ejaculation and Terence turned, not upon Ursula but upon him.

'You idiot, Fabian,' she said. 'You unutterable fool.'

III

The fire had burnt low, and the room was colder and stale with tobacco smoke.

'I give it up,' said Douglas loudly. 'I never was any good at riddles and I'm damned if I know half the time what you're all getting at. For God's sake let's have some air in this room.'

He went to the far end of the study, jerked back the curtains, and pushed open a french window. The night air came in, not as a wind, but stilly, with a tang of extreme cleanliness. The moon was up and, across the plateau, fifty miles away, it shone on the Cloud Piercer and his attendant peaks. Alleyn joined Douglas at the window. 'If I spoke,' he thought, 'my voice would go out towards those mountains and between my moving lips and that distant snow there would be only clear darkness.' He had noticed, on the drive up to Mount Moon, that the flats in front of the homestead were swampy and studded with a few desultory willows. Now, in the moonlight, he caught a glint of water and he heard the cry of wild duck and the beat of wings. Behind him in the room, someone threw wood upon the fire and Alleyn's shadow flickered across the terrace.

'Need we freeze?' Ursula asked fretfully. Douglas reached out his hand to the french window, but before he shut it or drew the curtain a footfall sounded briskly and a man walked along the terrace towards the north side of the house. As he reached the part of the terrace that was lit from the room he was seen to be wearing a neat black suit and a felt hat. It was Markins, returning from his visit to the manager's cottage. Douglas slammed the french window and pulled the curtain across it.

'And there goes the expert,' he said, 'who runs about the place, scot-free, while we sit yammering a lot of high-falutin bilge about the character of the woman he may have killed. I'm going to bed.'

'He'll bring the drinks in a minute,' said Fabian. 'Why not wait and have one.'

'If he's got wind of this I wouldn't put it past him to monkey with the decanter.'

'Honestly, Douglas!' Fabian and Ursula said together. 'You are – !'

'All right, all right,' Douglas said angrily. 'I'm a fool. Say no more.' He flung himself down on the sofa again, but this time he did not rest his arm along the back behind Terence. Instead he eyed her with an air of discomfort and curiosity.

'So you prefer to leave Miss Harme's question unanswered,' Alleyn said to Terence.

She had picked up her knitting as if hoping by that gesture to recapture something of her lost composure. But her hands turned her work over, rolling the scarlet mesh round the white needles and, as aimlessly, spreading it out again across her knees.

'You force me to speak of it,' she said. 'All of you. You talk about us all agreeing to this discussion, Fabian. When you and Ursula and Douglas planned it, how could I not agree? It's not my business to refuse. I'm an outsider. I was paid to work for Mrs Rubrick, and now you, Fabian, pay me to work for you in your garden. It's not my business to refuse.'

'Nonsense, Terry,' said Fabian.

'You've never been in my position. You don't understand. You're all very kind and informal and treat me, as we say in my class, almost like one of yourselves. Almost, not quite.'

'My dear girl, that's an insult to me, at least. You know quite enough about my views to realize that any such attitude is revolting to me. "Your class." How dare you go class-conscious at me, Terry.'

'You're my boss. You were not too much of a communist to accept Mount Moon when he left it to you.'

'I think,' said Alleyn crisply, 'that we might come back to the question which, believe me, Miss Lynne, you are under no compulsion to answer. This is it. Did Mrs Rubrick, during the last week of her life, become aware of the attachment between you and her husband?'

'And if I don't answer what will you think? What will you do? Go to Mrs Aceworthy, who dislikes me intensely, and get some monstrously distorted story that she's concocted. When he was ill he wanted me to look after him and wouldn't see her or have her here. She's never forgiven me. Better you should hear the truth from me.'

'Very much better,' Alleyn agreed cheerfully. 'Let's have it.'

It would have come as something of an anti-climax if it had not made a little clearer the still nebulous picture of that strange companionship. They had been working together over one of Flossie's articles, he at the table near the windows and Terence moving between him and the bookcases. She had returned to him with a volume of Hansard and had laid it on the table before him, standing behind him and pressing it open with her hand at the passage he had asked for. He leant forward and the rough tweed of his coat sleeve brushed her forearm. They were motionless. She looked down at him but his face was hidden from her. He stooped. Her free hand moved and rested on his shoulder. She described the scene carefully, with precision as if these details were important, as if, having undertaken her story, she was resolved to leave nothing unsaid. She was, Alleyn thought, a remarkable young woman. She said it was the first passage of its kind between them and she supposed they were both too much moved by it to hear the door open. Her right hand was still upon him when she turned and saw her employer. He was even slower to move and her left hand remained, weighed down by his, upon the open pages of the book. It was only when she pulled it away that he too turned, and saw his wife.

Florence remained in the doorway. She had a sheaf of papers in her hand and they crackled as her grip tightened on them. 'Hers was an expressionless face,' Terence said, and Alleyn glanced up at the portrait. 'Her teeth showed a little, as usual. Her eyes always looked rather startled, they looked no more so then. She just stared at us.'

Neither Rubrick nor Terence spoke. Florence said loudly, 'I'm in a hurry for those reports,' and turned on her heel. The door slammed behind her. Rubrick said to Terence, 'My dear, I hope you can forgive me,' and Terence, sure now that he loved her, and feeling nothing but pleasure in her heart, kissed him lightly and moved away. They returned tranquilly to Flossie's interminable reports. It was strange, Terence said, how little troubled they both were at that time by Flossie's entrance. It seemed then to be quite irrelevant, something to be dismissed impatiently, before the certainty of their attachment. They continued with their employment, Terence said, and Alleyn had a picture of the two of them at work there, sometimes exchanging a brief smile, more often turning the pages of Hansard, or making notes of suitable platitudes for Flossie. An odd affair, he thought.

This mood of acceptance sustained them through their morning's work. At luncheon when the party of six assembled, Terence noticed that her employer was less talkative than usual and she realized that she herself was being closely watched by Flossie. This did not greatly disturb her. She thought vaguely, 'I suppose she merely said to herself that it's not much like me to put my hand on any one's shoulder. I suppose she thinks it was a bit of presumption on my part. She's noticing me as a human being.'

At the end of lunch Flossie suddenly announced that she wanted Terence to work with her all the afternoon. She kept Terence hard at it, taking down letters and typing them. It was a perfectly normal routine and at first Terence noticed nothing unusual in Flossie's manner. Presently, however, she became conscious that Flossie, from behind the table, across the room, or by the fireplace was watching her closely. She would deny herself the uncomfortable experience of meeting this scrutiny but sooner or later she would find herself unable to resist and would look up, and there, sure enough, would be that gimlet-like stare that contrived to be at once so penetrating and so expressionless. Terence began to feel that she could not support this behaviour and to wish, in acute discomfort, that Florence would speak to, or even upbraid her. The flood of contentment that had come upon her when she knew that Rubrick loved her now receded and left in its wake a sensation of shame. She began to see herself with Flossie's eyes as a second-rate little typist who flirted with her employer's husband. She felt sick and humiliated and was filled with a kind of impatience for the worst to happen. There must be a climax, she thought, or she would never recover from the self-disgust that Flossie's stare had put upon her. But there was no climax. They plodded on with their work. When at last they had finished and Terence was gathering together her papers, Flossie, as she walked to the door, said over her shoulder, 'I don't think Mr Rubrick's at all

well.' Calling him 'Mr Rubrick', Terence felt, put her very neatly in
her place. 'I don't consider,' Florence added, 'that we should bother
him just now with our silly old statistics. I am rather worried about
him. We'll just leave him quietly to himself, Miss Lynne. Will you
remember that?' And she went out, leaving Terence to draw what
conclusions she chose from this pronouncement.

'And it was after that,' Terence said, 'almost immediately after –
it was the same night, at dinner –when the change you all noticed,
appeared in her manner towards him. To me it was horrible.'

'She decided, in fact,' said Fabian, 'to meet you on your own
ground, Terry, and give battle.' He added awkwardly, 'That doesn't
seem horrible to me; pitiful, rather, and intensely embarrassing. How
like her and how futile.'

'But he was devoted to her,' Ursula protested. And, as if she had
made a discovery that astonished and shocked her, she cried out,
'You cheated, Terry. It happened because you were young. You
shouldn't cheat in that way when you're young. They're all alike –
men of his age. If you'd gone away he'd have forgotten.'

'No!' said Terence strongly.

To Alleyn's discomfiture they both turned to him.

'He'd have forgotten,' Ursula repeated. 'Wouldn't he?'

'My dear child,' Alleyn said, intensely conscious of his age, 'how
can I possibly tell?' But when he thought of Arthur Rubrick, ill and
exhausted by his wife's public activities, he was inclined to believe that
Ursula was partly right. With Terence gone, might not the emotion
that Rubrick had felt for her have faded soon into an only half-
regretful memory?

'You're all the same,' Ursula muttered, and Alleyn felt himself
classed, disagreeably, with Arthur Rubrick, among the senile romantics. 'You go queer.'

'Well, but damn it all,' Fabian protested, 'if it comes to that,
Flossie's behaviour was pretty queer too. To flirt with your husband
after twenty-five years of married life – '

'That was entirely different,' Ursula flashed at him, 'and anyway,
Terry, if she did, it was your fault.'

'I didn't do it,' Terence said, for the first time defending herself. 'It
happened. And until she came into the room it was right. I knew it
was right. I knew it completely with my reason as well as with my

emotion. It was as if I had suddenly been brought into focus, as if I was, for the first time, completely Me. It couldn't possibly be wrong.'

She appealed to Ursula and perhaps, Alleyn thought, to the two young men. She asked them for understanding and succeeded in faintly embarrassing them.

'Yes,' said Ursula uncomfortably, 'but how you could! With Uncle Arthur! He was nearly fifty.'

Silence followed this statement. Alleyn, who was forty-seven, realized with amusement that Douglas and Fabian found Ursula's argument unanswerable.

'I didn't hurt him, Fabian,' Terence said at last. 'I'm certain I didn't. If he was hurt it was by her. She was atrociously possessive.'

'Because of you,' said Ursula.

'But we couldn't help it. You talk as if I planned what happened. It came out of a clear sky. It wasn't of my doing. And there wasn't a sequel, Ursula. You needn't think we had surreptitious scenes. We didn't. We were both of us, I believe, a little happier in our knowledge of each other. That was all.'

'When he was ill,' said Fabian, 'did you talk about it, Terry?'

'A little. Just to say we were glad we knew.'

'If he had lived,' said Ursula harshly, 'would you have married him?'

'How can I tell?'

'Why shouldn't you have married? Auntie Florence, who was such a bore to both of you, was out of the way. Wasn't she?'

'That's an extraordinarily cruel thing to say, Ursula.'

'I agree,' said Douglas, and Fabian muttered, 'Pipe down, Ursy.'

'No,' said Ursula. 'We undertook to finish our thoughts in this discussion. You're all cruel to her memory. Why should any of us get off? Why not say what you all must have thought: with her death they were free to marry.'

A footfall sounded outside in the hall, accompanied by a faint jingle of glasses. It was Markins with the drinks.

CHAPTER 6

According to the Files

With Markins' arrival the discussion ended. It was as if he had opened the door to a wave of self-consciousness. Douglas fussed over the drinks, urging Alleyn to have whisky. Alleyn, who considered himself to be on duty, refused it and wondered regretfully if it was from the same matchless company as the bottle that Cliff Johns had smashed on the dairy floor. Any suggestion that the discussion might be taken up again was dispelled by the entrance of Mrs Aceworthy who, with the two girls, drank tea, and who had many playful remarks to make about the lateness of the hour. It was high time, she said, that all her chickens were in their nests. And she asked Alleyn pointedly if he had brought a hot-water bottle. Upon this hint he bade them all goodnight. Fabian brought in candles and offered to see him to his room.

They went upstairs together, their shadows mounting gigantically beside them. On the landing Fabian said: 'You will realize now, of course, that you're in Flossie's room. It's the best one, really, but we all preferred to stay where we were.'

'Ah, yes.'

'It's got no associations for you, of course.'

'None.'

Fabian led the way through Florence's door. He lit candles on the dressing-table and the room came into being, a large white room with gay curtains, a pretty desk, a fine bed and a number of flower prints on the walls. Alleyn's pyjamas were laid out on the bed, by Markins, he supposed, and his locked dispatch and investigation cases were displayed prominently on the desk. He grinned to himself.

'Got everything you want?' Fabian asked.

'Everything, thanks. Before we say goodnight, though, I wonder if I might take a look at your workroom?'

'Why not? Come on.'

It was the second door on the left along the passage. Fabian detached the key from about his neck. 'On a bootlace, you see,' he said. 'No deception practised. Here we go.'

The strong electric lamp over their working bench dazzled eyes that had become accustomed to candlelight. It shone down on a rack of tools and an orderly collection of drawing materials. A small precision lathe was established on a side bench which was littered with a heterogeneous collection of pieces of metal. A large padlocked cupboard was built into the right-hand wall and beside it Alleyn saw a good modern safe with a combination lock. Three capacious drawers under the bench also were locked.

'The crucial drawings and formulas have always been kept in the safe,' Fabian explained. 'As you can see, everything is stowed away under lock and key. And pray spare a kind thought for my window shutter, so witheringly dismissed by dear old Douglas.'

It was, Alleyn thought, an extremely workmanlike job. 'And, I can assure you,' Fabian added, 'it has not been fiddled with.' He sat on the bench and began to talk about their work. 'It's a magnetic fuse for anti-aircraft shells,' he said. 'The shell is made of non-ferrous metal and contains a magnetically operated fuse which will explode the shell when it approaches an aircraft engine, or other metallic object. It will, we hope, be extremely useful at high altitudes where a direct hit is almost impossible. Originally I got the idea from a magnetic mine which, as of course you know, explodes in the magnetic field surrounding steel ships. Now, even though it contains a good deal of alloy, an aeroplane engine must, of necessity, also contain an appreciable amount of steel and in addition, there's a magnetic field from ignition coils. Our fuse is very different from the fuse in a magnetic mine but it's a kind of second cousin in that it's designed to explode a shell in the aeroplane's magnetic field. As a matter of fact,' said Fabian with a glint in his eye, 'if it comes off, and it will come off, I believe, it'll be a pretty big show.'

'Of course it will. Very big indeed. There's one question I'd like to ask. What about "prematures" by attraction to the gun itself, or explosion in transit?'

'There's a safety device incorporated in the doings, and it sees to it that the fuse won't do its stuff until the shell starts to rotate and after it leaves the gun barrel. The result, in effect, is an aerial magnetic mine. I'll show you the blueprints on presentation of your official card,' Fabian ended, with a grin.

'I should be enormously interested. But not tonight, if you don't mind. I've still a job of work to do.'

'In that case, I'll escort you back to your room, first making sure that no adventuresses lurk under the benches. Shall we go?'

Back in Alleyn's room, Fabian lit a cigarette at a candle, and gave his guest one of his sidelong glances. 'Any good,' he asked, 'or rotten?'

'The discussion?'

'Yes. Post-mortem. Inquest. Was it hopelessly stupid to do it?'

'I don't think so.'

'Tomorrow, I suppose, you'll talk to the Johns family and the men and so on.'

'If I may.'

'We're crutching. You'll be able to see the set-up. It's pretty much the same. All except – '

'Yes?' asked Alleyn, as he paused.

'The press is new. I couldn't stomach that. It's the same kind, though.'

'I'll just turn up there if I may.'

'Yes. OK. I don't know if you're going to keep our unearthly hours. Please don't, if you'd rather not. Breakfast at a quarter to six.'

'Of course.'

'Then I'll take you over to the shed. You'll ask me for anything you want?'

'I just want a free hand to fossick. I'd be grateful if I could be disregarded.'

'Not very easy, I'm afraid. But of course you'll have a free hand. I've told the men and Ducky and everybody, that you'll be talking to them.'

'How did they like that?'

'Quite keen. It's given a fillip to the ever-popular murder story. Damned ghouls! There'll be one or two snags, though. Wilson, the wool-sorter, and Jack Merrywether, the presser, are not at all keen. Your friend Sub-Inspector Jackson got badly offside with both of them. And there's Tommy Johns.'

'The boy's father?'

'Yes. He's a difficult chap, Tommy. I get on with him all right. He thinks for himself, does Tommy, and what's more,' said Fabian, with a grin, 'he thinks much like me politically, so I consider him a grand guy. But he's difficult. He resented Flossie's handling of young Cliff arid small blame to him. And what he thinks of police methods! You won't find him precisely come-toish.'

'And the boy himself?'

'He's all right, really. He's a likely lad, and he thinks for himself, too. We're good friends, young Cliff and I. I lend him the *New Statesman* and he rebuilds the government, social customs and moral standards of mankind on a strictly non-economic basis two or three times a week. His music is really good, I believe, though I'm afraid it's not getting much of a run these days. I've tried to induce him to practise on the Bechstein over here, but he's an obstinate young dog and won't.'

'Why?'

'It was Flossie's.'

'So the quarrel went deep?'

'Yes. It's lucky for young Cliff that he spent the crucial time screwing Bach out of that haggard old mass of wreckage in the outhouse. Everybody knew about the row and his bolt down-country afterwards. Your boyfriend, the Sub-Inspector, fastened on it like a limpet, but fortunately we could all swear to the continuous piano playing. Cliff's all right.'

'What's the explanation of the whisky incident?'

'I've not the slightest idea, but I'm perfectly certain he wasn't pinching it. I've tried to get the story out of him, but he won't come clean, blast him.'

'Does he get on well with the other men?'

'Not too badly. They were inclined at one time to look upon him as a freak. His schooling and tastes aroused their deepest suspicions, of course. In this country, young men are judged almost entirely on their ability to play games and do manual labour. However, Cliff set about his holiday jobs on the station with such energy that they overlooked his other unfortunate interests and even grew to encourage him in playing the piano in the evening. When he came home a good whole-hog Leftist, they were delighted, of course. They're a good lot – most of them.'

'Not all?'

'The shearers' cook is not much use. He only comes at shearing time. Mrs Johns looks after the regular hands at other times. Lots of the shearers wait until they've knocked up a good fat cheque and then go down-country and blue it all at the pub. That's the usual routine and you won't change it until you change the social condition of the shearer. But this expert keeps the stuff in his cookhouse and if we get through the shearing season without a bout of DTs we're lucky. He's a nasty affair is Cookie but he's unavoidable. They don't dislike him, oddly enough. The rouseabout, Albie Black, is rather thick with him. He used to be quite matey with young Cliff, too, but they had a break of some sort. Fortunately, I consider. Albie's a hopeless sort of specimen. Now, if it'd been Albie who pinched the whisky, I shouldn't have been the least surprised. Or Perce. The cook's name is Percy Gould, commonly called Perce. All Christian names are abbreviated in this country.'

'How did Mrs Rubrick get on with the men?'

'She thought she was a riotous success with them. She adopted a pose of easy jocularity that set my teeth on edge. They took it, with a private grin, I fancy. She imagined she had converted them to a sort of antipodean feudal system. She couldn't have been more mistaken, of course. I heard the wool-sorter, a perfectly splendid old boy he is, giving a very spirited imitation of her one evening. I'm glad the men were fifteen miles away from the wool-shed that night. The Sub-Inspector is a very class-conscious man. His suspicions would have gravitated naturally to the lower orders.'

'Nonsense,' said Alleyn cheerfully.

'It's not. He brightened up no end when Douglas started off on his Markins legend. Markins, being a servant, might so much more easily be a murderer than any of us gentry. God, it makes you sick!'

'Tell me,' said Alleyn, 'have you any suspicions?'

'None! I think it's odds on a swagger had strayed up to the wool-shed and decided to doss down for the night. Flossie may have surprised him and had a row with him. In the heat of the argument, he may have lost his temper and gone for her. Then when he found what he'd done, he put on Tommy Johns' overalls, disposed of his mistake in the first place that suggested itself to him, and made off down-country. She hated swaggers. Most stations give them their tucker and a doss-down for the night in exchange for a job of work, but not Flossie. That's my idea. It's the only explanation that seems reasonable. The only type that fits.'

'One of the lower orders, in fact?'

'Yes,' said Fabian, after a pause. 'You got me there, didn't you?'

'It was a cheap score, I'm afraid. Your theory is reasonable enough, but no wandering tramp was seen about the district that day. I understand they stick to the road, and usually make themselves known at the homesteads.'

'Not at Mount Moon with Flossie at home.'

'Perhaps not. Still your swagger remains a figure that as far as the police investigations go, and they seem to have been painstaking and thorough, was seen by nobody, either before or after the night of the disappearance.'

'I've no other contribution to offer, I'm afraid, and I'm keeping you up. Goodnight, sir. I'm still glad you came.'

'I hope you'll continue of that mind,' said Alleyn. 'Before you go, would you tell me how many of you played tennis on the night Mrs Rubrick disappeared?'

'Now, this,' said Fabian, with an air of gratification, 'is the real stuff. Why should you want to know that, I wonder? Only Douglas and I played tennis.'

'You wore rubber-soled shoes during the search, then?'

'Certainly.'

'And the others? Can you remember?'

'Pin heels. They always did in the evenings.'

'When, actually, did Mrs Rubrick first say she was going to the wool-shed?'

'Soon after we sat down. Might have been before. She was all arch about it. "What do you suppose your funny old Floosie's going to do presently?" That kind of thing. Then she developed her theme: the party and whatnot.'

'I see. Thank you very much. Goodnight.'

II

Fabian had gone and Alleyn was alone in the silent room. He stood motionless, a tall thin shape, dark in the candlelight. Presently he moved to the desk and opened one of the locked cases. From this he took a small tuft of cotton-wool and dropped it on the carpet. Even by candlelight it was conspicuous, unavoidable, a white accent on a dark green ground. So must the tuft of wool have looked when Ursula, on the morning after Florence disappeared, caught it up in the carpet sweeper. Yet she hadn't noticed it. Or had she merely forgotten it? They were all agreed that Flossie would never have suffered it to lie there. She had been up to her room after dinner and before the walk through the garden. Presumably, there had been no wool on her carpet then. Alleyn heard again Ursula Harme's voice: 'I don't care what anybody says. Somebody was about on the landing at five minutes to three that morning.'

Alleyn pulled out his pipe, sat down at the desk, and unlocked his dispatch case. Here were the police files. With a sigh he opened them out on the desk. The room grew hazy with tobacco smoke, the pages turned at intervals and the grandfather clock on the landing tolled twelve, half-past twelve and one o'clock.

'. . . on February 19th 1942 at 2.45 p.m. I received instructions to proceed to the wool store of Riven Brothers at 68 Jernighan Avenue. I arrived there in company with PC Wetherbridge at 2.50 p.m. and was met by the storeman, Alfred Clark, and by Mr Samuel Joseph, buyer for Riven Brothers. I was shown a certain wool-pack and noted a strong odour resembling decomposition. I was shown a bale hook which was stained brownish-red. I noted that twisted about the hook there was a hank of hair, reddish-gold in colour. I noted that the pack in question had been partly slit. I instructed PC Wetherbridge to extend the slit and open up the pack. This was done in my presence and that of Alfred Clark. Samuel Joseph was not present, having taken sick for the time being, and retired to the outer premises. In the pack we located a body in an advanced state of decomposition. It was secured, in a sitting position, with the legs doubled up and fastened to the trunk with nineteen turns of cord subsequently identified as twine used for wool bales. The arms were doubled up and secured to the body by twenty-five turns of binder-twine passing round the arms and legs. The chin rested on the knees. The body rested upon a layer of fleece, hard packed and six inches in depth. The body was packed round with wool. Above the body the bale was packed hard with fleece up to the top. The bale measured 28 inches in width both ways, and four feet in height. The body was that of a woman of very slight build. I judged it to be about five feet and three inches in height. I left it as it was and proceeded to . . .'

The pages turned slowly.

' . . . the injury to the back of the head. According to medical evidence it might have been caused by a downward blow from the rear made by a blunt instrument. Three medical men agreed that the injury was consistent with such a blow from the branding iron found in the shearing-shed. A microscopic examination of this iron revealed stains subsequently proved by analysis to be human bloodstains. Post-mortem examination revealed that death had been caused by suffocation. The mouth and nostrils contained quantities of sheep's wool. The injury to the skull would almost certainly have brought about unconsciousness. It is possible that the assailant, after striking the blow, suffocated the deceased while she was unconscious. The medical experts are agreed that death cannot be attributed to accidental causes or to self-inflicted injuries.'

Here followed a detailed report from the police surgeon. Alleyn read on steadily. ' . . . a triangular tear near the hem of the dress, corresponding in position to the outside left ankle bone, the apex of the tear being uppermost . . . subsequent investigation . . . nail in wall of wool-shed beside press . . . thread of material attached . . . lack of evidence after so long an interval.'

'Don't I know it,' Alleyn sighed and turned a page.

'. . . John Merrywether, wool-presser, deposed that on the evening of January 29th at knocking-off time, the press was full in both halves. It had been tramped but not pressed. He left it in this condition. The following morning it appeared to be in the same state. The two halves were ready for pressing as he had left them, the top in position on the bottom half. He pressed the wool, using the ratchet mechanism in the ordinary way. He noticed nothing that was unusual. The wool in the top half was compressed until it was packed down level with the top of the bottom half. The bale was then sewn up and branded. It was stacked alongside the other bales, and the same afternoon was removed with them and trucked down-country . . .

'Sydney Barnes, lorry driver, deposed that on January 29th 1942 he collected the Mount Moon clip and trucked it down-country . . . Alfred Clark, storeman . . . received the Mount Moon clip on February 3rd and stacked it to await assessment. . . James MacBride, government wool-assessor . . . February 9th . . . noticed smell but attributed it to dead rat . . . Slit all packs and pulled out tuft of wool near top . . noticed nothing unusual . . . assessed with rest of clip . . . Samuel Joseph, buyer . . .'

'And back we come, full circle,' Alleyn sighed and refilled his pipe.

'Subsequent investigations,' said the files ominously. In their own language they boiled down, de-humanized and tidied up the long accounts he had listened to that evening. 'It seems certain,' said the files, twenty minutes later, 'that the disposal of the body could not have been effected in under forty-five minutes. Tests have been made. The wool must have been removed from the press; the body bound up in the smallest possible compass, placed in the bottom half of the press, and packed round with wool. The fleeces must then have been replaced and tramped down both in the bottom and the top, and the top half replaced on the bottom half . . . Thomas Johns, working manager, deposed that on the next morning he found that his overalls had been split and were stained. He accused the "fleecies" of having interfered with his overalls. They denied having done so.'

It was getting very cold. Alleyn hunted out a sweater and pulled it on. The house was utterly silent now. So must it have been when Ursula Harme awoke to find her dream continued in the sound of a footfall on the landing, and when Douglas Grace heard retreating steps in the passage outside his room. It would be nice, Alleyn, thought wearily, to know if the nocturnal prowler was the same in each instance.

He rose stiffly and moved to the large wardrobe whose doors were flush with the end wall of the room. He opened them and was confronted with his own clothes neatly arranged on hangers. The invaluable Markins again. It was here, at the back of the wardrobe, hidden under three folded rugs, that Flossie Rubrick's suitcase had been found, ready packed for the journey north that she never took. Terence Lynne had discovered it, three days after the night in the garden. The purse with her travelling money and official passes had been in the drawer of the dressing-table. Had this been the errand of Ursula's nocturnal prowler? To conceal the suitcase and the purse? And had the fragment of wool been dropped then? From a shoe that had tramped down the wool over Flossie Rubrick's head?

This, thought Alleyn, had been a neat and expeditious job. Not too fancy. A blow on the head, solid enough to stun, not savage enough to make a great mess. Suffocation, and then the answer to the one great problem, the disposal of the body. Very cool and bold. Risky, but well-conceived and justified by results. The most difficult part had been done by other people.

And the inevitable speculation arose in his mind. What had been the thoughts of this murderer when the shearers went to work the next morning, when the moment came for the wool-presser to throw his weight on the ratchet-arm and force down the trampled wool from the top half of the press into the pack in the lower half? Could the murderer have been sure that, when the pack was sewn up and the press opened, there would be no bulges, no stains? And when the time came for a bale hook to be jabbed into the top corner of the pack and for it to be hauled and heaved into the waiting lorry? Its weight? She had been a tiny woman and very thin, but how much more did she weigh than her bulk in pressed wool?

He turned back to the files.

'The medical experts are of the opinion that the binding of the body was probably effected within six hours of death, as the onset of rigor mortis after that period would probably have rendered such a process impossible. They add, however, that in the circumstances, i.e., warm temperature, lack of violent exercise before death, the onset would be unlikely to be early.'

'Cautious, as always,' Alleyn thought. 'Now then. Supposing he was a man. Did the murderer of Florence Rubrick, believing that he would be undisturbed, finish his appalling job while the members of the household were still up? The men were away, certainly, but what about the Johns family, and Markins and Albert Black? Might their curiosity not have been aroused by a light in the wool-shed windows? Or were they blacked out in 1942? Probably they were not, as Ursula Harme remarked that the shed was in darkness at five to nine, when she went in search of her guardian. This suggests that she expected to see lights.' The files, he reflected, made no mention of this point. If the step that Ursula had heard was the murderer's, had he returned, having finished his work, to hide away the suitcase and purse and thus preserve the illusion that Florence had gone north? Were the killing and the trussing up and the hiding away of the body done as a continuous operation, or was there an interval? She was killed some time after eight o'clock – nobody can give the exact time when she walked down the lavender path and turned left. It had been her intention to try her voice in the shearing-shed and return. She would have been anxious, surely, to know if the brooch were found. Would she have stayed longer than ten minutes or a quarter of an hour giving an imitation of an MP talking to herself in a deserted shed? Surely not. Surely, then, she was killed before or quite soon after, the search party went indoors. It was five to nine when the brooch was found, and five to nine when, on his mother's entrance in the outhouse, Cliff Johns stopped playing and went home with her. During the period after the people in the house went to bed and before the party returned from the dance at a quarter to two, the wool-shed would be completely deserted. The lorry itself had broken down at the gate, but the revellers would be heard long before they reached the shed. He would still have time to put out the lights, and, if necessary, hide. By that time, almost certainly, the body would have been in the bottom half of the press and probably the top half would be partially packed.

'It boils down to this then,' Alleyn thought. 'If any of the five members of the search party committed this crime, he or she probably did so during the actual hunt for the brooch, since, if she'd been alive after then, Mrs Rubrick would almost certainly have returned to the house.' But as, in the case of the searchers, this allowed only a margin of four minutes or so, the murderer, if one of that party, must have returned later to complete the arduous task of encasing the body with firmly packed wool and re-filling the press exactly as it was before the job was begun. The business of packing round the body would be particularly exacting. The wool must have been forced down into a layer solid enough, for all its thinness, to form a kind of wall and prevent the development of bulges on the surface of the pack.

But suppose it was the murderer whom Ursula heard on the landing at five minutes to three. If his errand was to hide the suitcase and purse, whether he was an inmate of the house or not, he would almost certainly wait until he could be reasonably certain that the household was asleep.

Alleyn himself was sleepy now, and tired. The stale chilliness of extreme exhaustion was creeping about his limbs. 'It's been a long day,' he thought, 'and I'm out of practice.' He changed into pyjamas and washed vigorously in cold water. Then, for warmth's sake, he got into bed, wearing his dressing-gown. His candle, now a stump, guttered, spattered in its own wax, and went out. There was another on the desk, but Alleyn had a torch at his bedside and he did not stir. It was half-past two on a cold morning.

'Can I allow myself a cat-nap?' he muttered, 'or shall I write to Troy?' Troy was his wife, thirteen thousand miles away, doing camouflage and pictorial surveys instead of portraits, at Bossicote in England. He said wistfully: 'She's very easy to think about.' He considered the chilly journey from his bed to the writing-desk and had flung back the bed-clothes when, in a moment, he was completely still.

No night wind sighed about the windows of Mount Moon, no mouse scuttled in the wainscotting. From somewhere far outside the house, by the men's quarters, he supposed, a dog barked, once, very desolately. But the sound that had arrested Alleyn came from within the house. It was the measured creak made by the weight of someone moving up the old stairs. Then, very slow but vivid because of their slowness, sensed rather than heard, footfalls sounded on the landing. Alleyn counted eight of them, reached for his torch and waited for the brush of fingertips against his own door, and the decisive unmuffled click of the latch. His eyes had grown accustomed to the dark and he could make out a faint greyness which was the surface of his white-painted door. It shifted towards him, slowly at first, and remained ajar for some seconds. Then, incisively, candidly as it seemed, the door was pushed wide, and against the swimming blue of the landing he saw the shape of a man. His back was towards Alleyn. He shut the door delicately and turned. Alleyn switched on his torch. As if by trickery, a face appeared, its eyes screwed up in the unexpected light.

It was Markins.

'You've been the hell of a time,' said Alleyn.

III

As seen when the remaining candle had been lighted, he was a spare, bird-like man. His black hair was brushed strongly back, like a coarse wig with no parting. He had small black eyes, a thin nose and a mobile mouth. Above his black trousers he wore a servant's alpaca working jacket. His habit of speech was basic Cockney with an overlay of Americanisms, but neither of these characteristics was very marked and he would have been a difficult man to place. He had an air of naivety and frankness, almost of innocence, but his dark eyes never widened, and he seemed, behind his manner, which was pleasing, to be always extremely alert. He carried the candle he had lit to Alleyn's bedside table and then stood waiting, his arms at his sides, his hands turned outwards at the wrists.

'Sorry I couldn't make it before, sir,' he murmured. 'They're light sleepers, all of them, more's the pity. All four.'

'No more?' Alleyn whispered.

'Five.'

'Five's out.'

'It used to be six.'

'And two from six is four with the odd one out.'

They grinned at each other.

'Right,' said Alleyn. 'I walk in deadly fear of forgetting these rigmaroles. What would you have done if I'd got it wrong?'

'Not much chance of that, sir, and I'd have known you anywhere, Mr Alleyn.'

'I should keep a false beard by me,' said Alleyn gloomily. 'Sit down, for Heaven's sake, and shoot the works. Have a cigarette? How long is it since we met?'

'Back in '37, wasn't it, sir? I joined the Special Branch in '36. I saw you before I went over to the States on that pre-war job.'

'So you did. We fixed you up as a steward in a German liner, didn't we?'

'That's right, sir.'

'By the way, is it safe to speak and not whisper?'

'I think so, sir. There!s nobody in the dressing-room or on this side of the landing. The two young ladies are over the way. Their doors are shut.'

'At least we can risk a mutter. You did very well on that first job, Markins.'

'Not so good this time, I'm afraid, sir. I'm properly up against it.'

'Oh, well,' said Alleyn resignedly, 'let's have the whole story.'

'From the beginning?'

'I'm afraid so.'

'Well, sir,' said Markins, and pulled his chair closer to the bed. They leant towards each other. They resembled some illustration by Cruikshank from Dickens; Alleyn in his dark gown, his long hands folded on the counterpane; Markins, small, cautious, bent forward attentively. The candle glowed like a nimbus behind his head, and Alleyn's shadow, stooping with theatrical exaggeration on the wall beside him, seemed to menace both of them. They spoke in a barely vocal but pedantically articulate mutter.

'I was kept on in the States,' said Markins, 'as of course you know. In May, '38, I got instructions from your people, Mr Alleyn, to get alongside a Japanese wool buyer called Kurata Kan, who was in Chicago. It took a bit of time but I made the grade, finally, through his servant. A half-caste Jap this servant was, and used to go to a sort of night school. I joined up, too, and found that this half-caste was sucking up to another pupil, a janitor at a place where they made hush-hush parts for aeroplane engines. He was on the job, all right, that half-caste. They pay on the nail for information, never mind how small, and he and Kan were in the game together. It took me weeks of geography and American history lessons before I got a lead, and then I sold them a little tale about how I'd been in service at our Embassy in Washington and had been sacked for showing too much interest. After that it was money for jam. I sold Mr Kurata Kan quite a nice little line of bogus information. Then he moved on to Australia. I got instructions from the Special Branch to follow him up. They fixed me up as a gent's valet in Sydney. I was supposed to have been in service with an artillery expert from Home who visited the Governor of New South Wales. He gave me the references himself on Government House notepaper. He was in touch with your people, sir. Well, after a bit I looked up Mr Kan and made the usual offer. He was quite glad to see me and I handed him a little line of stuff the gentleman was supposed to have let out when under the influence. Your office supplied it.'

'I remember.'

'He was trying to get on to some stuff about fortifications at Darwin, and we strung him along quite nicely for a time. Of course he was away a great deal on his wool-buying job. Nothing much happened till August, 1940, when he put it up to me that it might be worth my while to come over here with a letter from him to a lady friend of his, a Mrs Arthur Rubrick, MP, who was keen on English servants. He said a nephew of Mr Rubrick's was doing a job they'd like to get a line on. Very thorough, the Japs, sir.'

'Very.'

'That's right. I cabled in code to the Special Branch and they told me to go ahead. They were very interested in Mr Kan. So I came over and it worked out nicely. Mrs Rubrick took me on, and here I stuck. The first catch in it, though, was what would I tell Kurata Kan? The Special Branch warned me that Mr Losse's work was important and they gave me some phoney stuff I could send on to Kan when he got discontented. That was OK. I even rigged up a bit of an affair with some spare radio parts, all pulled to pieces and done up different. I put it in a bad light and took a bad photograph of it and told him I'd done it through a closed window from the top of a ladder. I've often wondered how far it got before some expert took a look at it and said the Japanese for "Nuts". Kan was pleased enough. He knew nothing. He was only a middle man. Of course it couldn't last. They pulled him in at last on my information, and then there was Pearl Harbor. Finish!'

'Only as far as Kan was concerned.'

'True enough, sir. There was the second catch. But you know all about that, Mr Alleyn.'

'I'd like to hear your end of it.'

'Would you, sir? OK, then. My instructions from your end had been that I was on no account to let Mrs Rubrick or either of the young gentlemen get any idea that I wasn't exactly what I seemed. After a bit your people let me know that there'd been leakage of information – not my phoney dope, but genuine stuff – about this magnetic fuse. Not through Japanese canals but German ones. Now that *was* a facer. So my next job was to turn round after three years working the bogus agent, and look for the genuine article. And that,' said Markins plaintively, 'was where I fluttered to pieces. I hadn't got a thing. Not a bloody inkling, if you'll pardon the expression.'

'So we gathered,' said Alleyn.

'The galling thing, Mr Alleyn, the aspect of the affair that got under my professional skin, as you might say, was this: somebody in this household had been working under my nose for months. What did I feel like when I heard it? Dirt. Kuh! Thinking myself the fly operator, cooking up little fake photographs and all the time – look, Mr Alleyn, I handed myself the raspberry in six different positions. I did indeed.'

'If it's any satisfaction to you,' said Alleyn,. 'one source of transit was stopped. Two months ago a German supply ship was taken off the Argentine coast. Detailed drawings of the magnetic fuse and instructions in code were found aboard her. The only link we could establish between this ship and New Zealand was the story of a freelance journalist who was cruising round the world in a tramp steamer. There are lots of these sportsmen about, harmless eccentrics, no doubt, for the most part. This particular specimen, a native of Portugal, visited most of the ports in this country during last year. Our people have tracked him down to a pub in a neutral port, where he was seen drinking with the skipper of this German ship, and was suddenly very flush with cash. Intensive probing brought to light an involved story that cast a very murky light on the journalist. All the usual stuff. We're pretty certain of him and he won't be given a shore permit next time the wanderlust drives him this way, romantic little chap.'

'I remember when he was about,' said Markins. 'Señor or Don or Something de Something. He was in town during Easter race week last year. The two young gentlemen and Miss Harme and most of the staff went down for three days, I stayed behind. Mr Rubrick was very poorly.'

'And Miss Lynne?'

'She stayed behind, too. Wouldn't leave him.' Markins looked quickly at Alleyn. 'Very sad, that,' he added.

'Very. We've found that this gentleman lived aboard his tramp steamer while he was in port. He showed up at the races wearing a

white beret and clad for comfort rather than smartness; a conspicuous figure. We think this stuff about this gadget of Mr Losse's was
passed to him at this time. It had been folded small. The paper was
of New Zealand manufacture.'

Markins clucked angrily. 'Under my very nose, you might say.'

'Well, your nose was up here and the transaction probably took
place on a racecourse two hundred miles away or more.'

'All the same.'

'So you see, by a stroke of luck, we stopped the hole, and the
information, as far as we know, didn't reach the enemy. Mr Losse
was warned by Headquarters that he should take particular care, and
at the same time was advised to confide in nobody, not even his
partner, about the attempt. Oddly enough he seems to have been
sceptical about the danger of espionage while Captain Grace from
the beginning has taken a very gloomy view of – who do you think?'

'You're asking me, sir,' said Markins, in an indignant whisper.
'Look! If that young man had crawled about after me on his stomach in broad daylight, he wouldn't have given himself away more
than he did. Look, sir. He got into my room and messed about like a
coal heaver. His prints all over everything! Butted his head in among
my suits and left them smelling of his hair oil, and I'm blest if he did-
n't pinch a bill out of my pockets. Well, I mean to say, it was awkward. If he went howling up to Headquarters about me being a spy
or some such, they'd be annoyed with me for putting myself away.
It was comical, too. I was there to watch his blinking plant for him
and he goes and makes up his mind I'm just what I pretended I was
to Kan & Co.'

'You must have done something to arouse his suspicions.'

'I never!' said Markins indignantly. 'Why should I? As far as he
knew, I never went near his blinking workroom but once. That was
when I had an urgent telephone call for Mrs Rubrick. I heard voices
up there and went along. He and Mr Losse were muttering in the
doorway and didn't hear me. When he did see me, he looked at me
like I was the Demon King.'

'He says he heard you prowling about the passage at a quarter to
three in the morning, three weeks before Mrs Rubrick was killed.'

Markins made a faint squeaking noise. 'Like hell he did! I never
heard such a thing! What'd I be doing outside his workroom? Yes,

and what does he do but rush off to Madam and tell her she's got to give me the sack.'

'You heard about that, did you?'

'Madam told me. She said she had something very serious to talk to me about. She as good as said I'd been suspected of prying into the workroom. You could have pulled me to pieces with a pin, I was that taken aback. And riled! I reckon my manner was convincing, because she was satisfied. I ought to explain, Mr Alleyn, that I myself had heard somebody that night. I'm a light sleeper and I heard someone all right and it wasn't either of the young gents. They get spasms of working late but they don't bother to tiptoe into the workroom. I got out of bed, you bet, and had a look, but it was all quiet and after a bit I give up. I told Madam. She was very put about. Naturally. I satisfied her, of course, but it was awkward and what's more I'd evidently missed a bit of funny business. Who was it, anyway, in the passage? I'm a sweet little agent, and that's a fact. But before we parted she says: "Markins," she says, "there's something I don't like about this business and next time I go up to Wellington," she says, "I'm going to speak about it to the authorities. I'm going to suggest that the young gentlemen work under proper protection," she says, "in their own interest, and I shall tell the Captain what I've decided." What I cannot understand,' said Markins, pulling at his thin underlip, 'is why the Captain got it into his head I was an agent.'

'Perhaps you look like one, Markins.'

'I begin to think I must, Mr Alleyn, but I'd prefer it was the British variety.'

'Actually, you know, the circumstances were a bit suspicious. He opened his bedroom door and saw a light disappear in the direction of your room. That afternoon, as you yourself admit, you'd come upon Captain Grace and Mr Losse arranging where they'd leave the key of the workroom. I think he had some cause for alarm.'

Markins darted a very sharp glance at Alleyn. 'She never said a word about that,' he said.

'She didn't?'

'Not a word. Only that the Captain was upset because he thought I'd been poking about the passage late at night. I didn't hear what they were saying that afternoon, They spoke too low and stopped as soon as they saw me.' He gave a thoughtful hiss. 'That's different. It's a whole lot different. Saw something did he?'

'A light,' said Alleyn and repeated Douglas's account of the night prowler.

'The only tangible bit of evidence and I miss it,' said Markins. 'That's the way to get promotion. I'm disgusted.'

Alleyn pointed out that, whoever the night prowler might have been, he didn't gain access to the room that night. But Markins instantly objected that this failure must have been followed by success as copies for the designs had been handed over to the Portuguese journalist at Easter. 'You're disappointed in my work, sir,' he whispered dolorously. 'You're disgusted and I'm sure I don't blame you. Put it bluntly, this expert's been one too many for me. He's got into that room and he's got away with the stuff and I don't know who he is or how he did it. It's disgraceful. I'd be better in the Middle East.'

'Well,' said Alleyn, 'it's a poor show, certainly, but I shan't do any good by rubbing it in and you won't do any good by calling yourself names. I'll look at the room. Losse has rigged a home-made but effective shutter that's padlocked over the window every night. There's a Yale lock on the door and after the scare he wore the key on a bootlace round his neck. You can gain entrance by boring a hole in the door post and using wire. That might have been the prowler's errand on the night Grace heard him. He failed then but brought it off some time before Easter. How about that?'

'No, sir. I kept an eye on that lock. There'd been no interference. While they were away at the races that Easter I took a good look round. The room was sealed all right, Mr Alleyn.'

'Very well, then, the entrance was effected before the scare, when they were not so careful, and the interloper was returning for another look when Grace heard him. Any objections?'

'No,' said Markins slowly. 'No. He'd got enough to work on for the stuff he handed to the Portuguese, and he kept it until the man got to this country. That'll work.'

'All right,' said Alleyn. 'Any suspicions?'

'It might have been the old girl herself,' said Markins, 'for anything I know to the contrary. There!'

'Mrs Rubrick?'

'Well, she was in and out of the room often enough. Always tapping at the door and saying: "Can my busy bees spare me a
moment?"'

Alleyn stirred and his shadow moved on the wall. It might be difficult to interview Markins at great length during the day and he
himself had a formidable programme to face. Four versions of Flossie
already and it must now be half-past two at least. Must he listen to
a fifth? He reached out his hand for his cigarettes.

'What did you think of her?' he asked.

'Peculiar,' said Markins.

IV

'Ambitious,' Markins added, after reflection. 'The ambitious type.
You see them everywhere. Very often they're childless women. She
was successful, too, but I wouldn't say she was satisfied. Capable.
Knew how to get her own way, but once she'd got it, liked everybody else to be comfortable when she remembered them. When
women get to her age,' said Markins, 'they're one of three kinds.
They may be OK. They may go jealous of younger women and peculiar about men, particularly young men, or they may take it out in
work. She took it out in work. She thrashed herself and everybody
round her. She wanted to be the big boss and round here she certainly was. Now, you ask me, sir, would she be an enemy agent? Not
for money, she wouldn't. She'd got plenty of that. For an idea? Now,
what idea in the Nazi book of words would appeal to Madam? The
herrenvolk spiel? I'd say, yes, if she was to be one of the herrenvolk.
But was she the type of lady who'd work against her own folk and
her own country? Now, was she? She was great on talking
Imperialism. You know. The brand that's not taken for granted quite
so much, these days. She talked a lot about patriotism. I don't know
how things are at Home, sir, having been away so long, but it seems
to me we are getting round to thinking more about how we can
improve our country and bragging about it less than we used to.
From what I read and hear, it strikes me that the people who criticize are the ones that work and are most set on winning the war.
Take some of the English people who got away to the States when

the war began. Believe me, a lot of them talked that big and that optimistically you'd wonder how the others got on in the blitz without them. And when there was hints about muddle or hints that before the war we'd got slack and a bit too keen on easy money and a bit too pleased with ourselves – Lord, how they'd perform. Wouldn't have it at any price! I've heard these people say that what was wanted at Home was concentration camps for the critics and that a bit of Gestapo technique wouldn't do any harm. Now, Mrs Rubrick was a little in that line of business herself.'

'Miss Harme says she wanted to stay in England and do a job of work.'

'Yes? Is that so? But she'd have to be the boss or nothing, I'll be bound. My point is this, Mr Alleyn. Suppose she was offered something pretty big in the way of a position, a Reich-something-or-other-ship, when the enemy had beaten us, would she have fallen for the notion? That's what I asked myself.'

'And how did you answer yourself?'

'Doubtful. Not impossible. You see, with her as the only member of the house who had a chance of getting into this workroom I thought quite a lot about Madam. She might have got a key for herself when she had the Yale lock put on the door for the young gentlemen. It wasn't impossible. She had to be considered. And the more she talked about getting rid of enemy agents in this country the more I wondered if she might be one herself. She used to say that we oughtn't to be afraid to use what was good in Nazi methods: their youth training schemes and fostering of nationalistic ideas, and she used to come down very hard on anything like independent critical thinking. It was all right, of course. Lots of people think that way, all the diehards, you might say. She read a lot of their pre-war books, too. And she didn't like Jews. She used to say they were parasites. I'd get to thinking about her this way and then I'd kind of come down with a bump and call myself crazy.'

Alleyn asked him if he had anything more tangible to go on and he shook his head mournfully. Nothing. Beyond her curiosity about the young men's work, and she was by nature curious, there had been nothing. There was, he said, another view to take, and in many ways a more reasonable one. Mrs Rubrick had been appointed to a counter-espionage committee and, in that capacity, may have

threatened the success of an agent. She may even have formed suspicions of a member of her household and have given herself away.
She was not a discreet woman. This, pushed a little further, might
produce a motive for her murder.'

'Yes,' said Alleyn dryly. 'That's why Captain Grace thinks you
killed her, you know.'

Markins said with venom that Captain Grace was not immune from
suspicion himself. 'He's silly enough to do anything,' he whispered
angrily. 'And what about his background anyway? Heidelberg. He
doesn't look so hot. And what about him being a Nazi sympathizer?
I may be dumb but I haven't overlooked that little point.'

'You don't really believe it, though, do you?' Alleyn asked with a
smile.

Markins muttered disconsolately, 'No brains.'

'There's one other point,' Alleyn said. 'We've got to consider
whether this attempt to forward documentary information was the
be-all and end-all of the agent's mission. If, having achieved this
object, no more was expected of him, or if he were to forward other
information as regards, for instance, Mrs Rubrick's counter-espionage
activities, which is the sort of stuff that needs no documentary evidence. That perennial nuisance, the hidden radio transmitter, would
meet the case.'

'Don't I know it,' Markins grumbled. 'And there's a sizable range
of mountains where it could be cached.'

'It'd have to be accessible, though. He would be under instruction
to transmit his stuff every so long, when an enemy craft would edge
far enough into these waters to pick it up. The files say that under
cover of the hunt for Mrs Rubrick an extensive search was made.
They even brought up a radio-locator in a car and bumped up the
riverbed with it. But, of course, you were in that party.'

'Yes,' said Markins, 'I was in with the boys. They expected me to
show them the works, and what could I do? Tag on and look silly.
Me, supposed to be the expert! It's a hard world.'

'It's a weary world,' said Alleyn, swallowing a yawn. 'We're both
supposed to appear in less than four hours, with shining morning
faces. I'm out of training, Markins, and you're a working man. I think
we'll call it a night.'

Markins at once got up and, by standing attentively, his head inclined forward, seemed to reassume the character of a man-servant. 'Shall I open the window, sir?' he asked.

'Do, there's a good chap, and pull back the curtains. You've got a torch, haven't you? I'll put out the candle.'

'We're not as fussy as that about the black-out, Mr Alleyn. Not in these parts.'

The curtain rings jingled. A square, faintly luminous, appeared in the wall. Now the air of the plateau gained entry. Alleyn felt it cold on his face and in his eyes. He pinched out the candle and heard Markins tiptoe to the door.

'Markins,' said Alleyn's voice, quiet in the dark.

'Sir?'

'There's another solution. You've thought of it, of course?'

Quite a long silence followed this.

'He may talk highbrow,' Markins whispered, 'but when you get to know him, he's a nice young gentleman.'

The door creaked and Alleyn was alone. He composed himself for sleep.

CHAPTER 7

According to Ben Wilson

Having left instruction with himself to wake at five, Alleyn did so and was aware of distant stirrings in the house. Outside in the dark a cock crowed and the rumour of his voice echoed into nothingness. Beneath Alleyn's window someone walked firmly along the terrace path and round the corner of the house. He carried a tin bucket that clanked with his stride and he whistled shrilly. From over in the direction of the men's quarters all the Mount Moon sheep dogs broke into a chorus, their voices sounding hollow and cold in the dawn air. There followed the ring of an axe, an abrupt burst of conversation and presently, the smell of wood smoke, aromatic and pleasing. Beyond the still nighted windows there was only a faint promise of light, a vague thinning, but, as he watched, there appeared in the darkness a rosy horn, unearthly clear. It was the Cloud Piercer, far beyond the plateau, receiving the dawn.

Alleyn bathed and shaved by candlelight and when he returned to his room found the vague shapes of trees visible outside his window, patches of blanket mist above the swamp, and the road, lonely and bleached, reaching out across the plateau. Beneath his window the garden waited, straw coloured, frosty and rigid. As he dressed, the sky grew clear behind the mountains and though the plateau was still dusky, they became articulate in remote sunlight.

Breakfast began in artificial light, but before it was over, the lamp had grown wan and ineffectual. It was now full morning. The character of the house had changed. There was an air of preparation for the working day. Douglas and Fabian wore farm clothes; shapeless flannel trousers, faded sweaters pulled over dark shirts, old tweed jackets and heavy boots. Ursula was briskly smocked. Terence Lynne appeared, composed as ever, in a drill coat, woollen stockings and breeches – an English touch, this, Alleyn felt: alone of the four she seemed to be dressed deliberately for a high-country role. Mrs Aceworthy, alternately dubious and arch, presided.

Douglas finished before the rest and, with a word to Fabian, went out, passing in front of the dining-room windows. Presently he appeared, far beyond the lawn, in the ram paddock, a dog at his heels. Five merino rams at the far end of the paddock jerked up their heads and stared at him. Alleyn watched Douglas walk to a gate, open it, and wait. After a minute or two the rams began to cross the paddock towards him, heavily, not hurrying. He let them through the gate and they disappeared together, a portentous company.

'When you're ready,' said Fabian, 'shall we go over to the wool-shed?'

'If there's anything you would like – ' Mrs Aceworthy said. 'I mean, I'm sure we all want to be helpful – so dreadful – so many inquiries. One might almost feel – but of course this is quite different, I'm sure.' She drifted unhappily away.

'The Acepot's a bit scattered this morning,' Ursula said. 'You'll tell us, won't you, Mr Alleyn, if there's anything we can do?'

Alleyn thanked her and said there was nothing. He and Fabian went out of doors.

The sun had not yet reached Mount Moon. The air was cold and the ground crisp under their feet. From the direction of the yards came the authentic voice of the high country, a dreamlike and conglomerate drone, the voice of a mob of sheep. Fabian led the way along the left-hand walk between clipped poplar hedges, already flame coloured. They turned down the lavender path and through a gate, making a long stride over an icy little water race, and then walked uphill in the direction of the wool-shed and cottages.

The sound increased in volume. Individual bleatings, persistent and almost human, separated out from the multiple drone. A long galvanized iron shed appeared, flanked with drafting yards, beyond which lay a paddock so full of sheep that at a distance it looked like a shifting greyish lake. The sheep were driven up to the yards by men and dogs: the men yelled and the dogs barked remorselessly and without rhythm. A continual flood of sheep poured through a series of yards, each smaller than the last, into a narrow runway or race and was forced and harried towards a two-way gate which a short, mon-key-faced man shoved now this way, now that, drafting them into separate pens. This progress was assisted by a youth outside the rails who continually ran towards the sheep, waving his hat and crying out in a falsetto voice. At each of these sallies the sheep, harried from the rear by dogs, would dart past the youth towards the drafting gate. The acrid smell of greasy wool was strong on the cold air.

'That's Tommy Johns,' said Fabian, jerking his head at the man at the drafting gate. 'The boy's young Cliff.'

He was rather a nice-looking lad, Alleyn thought. He had a well-shaped head and a thatch of light-brown hair that overhung his forehead. His face was thin. There was an agreeable sharpness and del-icacy in the bony structures of the eyes and cheek bones. The mouth was obstinate. He still had a lean, gangling air about him, the last char-acteristic of adolescence. His hands were broad and nervous. His grey sweater and dirty flannel trousers had a schoolboyish look that con-trasted strongly with the clothes of the older men. When he saw Fabian he gave him a sidelong grin and then with a whoop and a flourish ran again at the oncoming sheep. They streamed past him to the drafting gate and huddled together, clambering on each other's backs.

Now that he had drawn closer Alleyn could resolve the babel into its component parts, the complaint of the sheep, the patter of their hooves on frozen earth and their humanlike coughing and breath-ing; the yelp of dogs and men and, within the shed, the burr of an engine and intermittent bumping and thuds.

'There'll be a smoke-oh in ten minutes,' said Fabian. 'Would you like to see inside?'

'Right,' said Alleyn.

Tommy Johns didn't raise his eyes as they passed him. The gate bumped to and fro against worn posts and the sheep darted through. 'He's counting,' Fabian said.

II

The wool-shed seemed dark when they first went in and the reek of sheep was almost tangible. The greatest area of light fell where the shearers were at work. It came through a doorless opening from which a sacking curtain had been pulled back and through the open portholes that were exits for the sheep. From where Alleyn stood the shearers themselves were outlined with light and each sheep's woolly coat had a bright nimbus. This strangely dramatic illumination focused attention on the shearing-board. The rest of the interior seemed at first to be lost in a swimming dusk. But presently a wool-sorter's bench, ranked packs, and pens filled with waiting sheep took shape in the shadows and Alleyn was able to form a comprehensive picture of the whole scene.

For a time he watched only the shearers. He saw them lug sheep out of the pens by their hind legs and handle them with dexterity so that they became quiescent, voluptuously quiescent almost, lolling back against the shearers' legs in a ridiculous sitting posture, or suffering their necks to be held between the shearers' knees while the mechanically-propelled blades, hanging from long arms with flexible joints, rolled away their wool.

'Is this crutching?' he asked.

'That's it. De-bagging, you might call it.'

Alleyn saw the dirty wool turn back in a wave that was cream inside and watched the quarter-denuded sheep shoved away through the portholes. He saw the broomies, two silent boys, sweep the dirty crutchings up to the sorter and fling them out on his rack. He saw the wool sorted and tossed into bins and finally he followed it to the press.

The press was in a central position, some distance from the shearing-board. It faced the main portion of the shed and actually looked, Alleyn thought, a little like an improvised rostrum. Here Flossie Rubrick was to have stood on the night of her wool-shed party. From here she was to harangue a mob of friends, voters, and fellow-high-countrymen, almost as quiescent as the shorn sheep. Alleyn sharpened his memory until it could encompass the figure of the woman with whom he had spoken for a few minutes. A tiny woman with a clear and insistent voice and an ugly face. A woman who wished to acquire him as a guest and from whom he had escaped with difficulty. He remembered her sharp stare and her rather too-self-confident manner. These recollections remained unchanged by last night's spate of conflicting impressions and it was the wraith of the persistent little woman he had met whom he now conjured up in the dark

end of the wool-shed. Where had she stood? From what direction
had her assailant come?

'She was going to try her voice, you know,' said Fabian at his elbow.

'Yes, but from where? The press? It was full of unpressed wool
and open, when the men stopped work the previous night. Did she
clamp down the pressing-lid or whatever it's called and climb up?'

'That's what we've always supposed.'

'Is the new press in exactly the same place?'

'Yes. Under that red show ticket nailed up on the post.'

Alleyn walked past the shearing-board or floor. The wall opposite was a five-foot-high partition separating the indoor pens from
the rest of the shed. Further along, behind the press, this wall was
extended up towards the roof. At some time a nail had been driven
through it from the other side and the point, now rusty, projected
close to the wool-press. He stopped to look at it. The machines still
thrummed and the sheep plunged and skidded as they were hauled
out of the pens. The work went on but Alleyn thought that the
men knew exactly what he was doing. He straightened up. Above
the rusty nail there ran a cross beam in the wall on which anybody
intending to mount the press might find foothold. Round the nail
they had found a thread of Flossie's dress material. The apex of the
tear in her dress had been uppermost, so it had been caused by an
upward pull. 'As she climbed the press,' thought Alleyn, 'not when
her assailant disposed of the body. It was too securely bound and
the press opens from the front. He would truss the body, then
clear the tramped wool out of the pack, leaving only the bottom
layer, then open the front of the press and get the body into the
bale, then would begin the repacking. But where was she when
he struck her? A downward blow from behind near the base of the
skull and grazing the back of the neck. Was she bent forward, her
hands on the press? Stooping to free her dress? Was she in the act
of climbing down from the press to speak to him, her feet already
on the floor, her back towards him? That seemed most likely,' he
thought.

Near the wool-press a hurricane lantern hung from a nail in the
wall. Further along, to the left, a rough candlestick hammered out of
tin was nailed high up on a joist. It held a guttered stump of candle.
A box of matches stood beside it. These appointments had been

there at the time of the tragedy. Had Flossie lit the lantern or the candle? Surely. It was dusk outside and the wool-shed must have been in darkness. How strange, he thought, as the image of a tiny indomitable woman, lit fantastically, grew in his imagination. There she must have stood, in semi-darkness, shouting out the phrases of which Terence Lynne and Fabian Losse had grown weary, while her sharp voice echoed in the emptiness. 'Ladies and gentlemen!' How far had she got? What did her assailant hear as he approached? Was he – or she – actually an audience, stationed by Flossie at the far end of the shed, to mark the resonant phrases? Or did he creep in under cover of the darkness and wait until she descended? With the branding iron grasped in his right hand? Behind her and to her right, the inside pens had been crowded with sheep waiting for the next day's shearing, too closely packed to do more than shift a little and tap with their small hooves on the slatted floor. Did they bleat at all, Alleyn wondered, when Flossie tried her voice? 'Ladies and gentlemen.' 'Ba-a-a.' From where he stood Alleyn could see slantwise through the five portholes and the open doorway at the end of the shearing-board. The sun was bright on the sheep-pens outside. But when Florence Rubrick stood on the wool-press it had been almost dark outside, the portholes must have been shut and the sacking curtain dropped over the doorway. The main doors of the shed had been shut that night and a heap of folded wool bales that had fallen across the floor, inside the main entrance, had not been disturbed; The murderer, then, had come in by this sacking door. Did Flossie see the sacking drawn aside and a black silhouette against the dusk? Or did he, perhaps, crawl in through one of the portholes, unobserved. 'Ladies and gentlemen. It gives me great pleasure . . .'

A whistle tooted. Each shearer finished crutching the sheep in hand and loosed it through a porthole. The engine stopped and the wool-shed was suddenly quiet. The noise from outside became dominant again.

'Smoke-oh,' Fabian explained. 'Come and meet Ben Wilson.'

Ben Wilson was the sorter, boss of the shed, an elderly mild man who shook hands solemnly with Alleyn and said nothing. Fabian explained why Alleyn was there and Wilson looked at the floor and still said nothing. 'Shall we move away a bit,' Alleyn suggested, and they walked to the double doors at the far end of the shed and stood there, enveloped in sunshine and the silence of Ben Wilson. Alleyn offered his cigarette case. Mr Wilson said, 'Ta,' and took one.

'It's the same old story, Ben,' said Fabian, 'but we're hoping Mr Alleyn may get a bit further than the other experts. We're lucky to have him.'

Mr Wilson glanced at Alleyn and then at the floor. He smoked cautiously, sheltering his cigarette with the palm of his hand. He had the air of a man whose life's object was to avoid making the slightest advance to anybody.

'You were here for the January shearing when Mrs Rubrick was killed, weren't you, Mr Wilson?' asked Alleyn.

'That's right,' said Mr Wilson.

'I'm afraid you must be completely fed up with policemen and their questions.'

'That's right.'

'And I'm afraid mine will be precisely the same set of questions all over again.' Alleyn waited and Mr Wilson with an extremely smug expression, compounded, it seemed, of mistrust, complacency and resignation said, 'You're telling me.'

'All right,' said Alleyn. 'Here goes, then. On the night of January 29th, 1942, when Mrs Rubrick was stunned, suffocated, bound, and packed into a wool bale in the replica of the press over there, you were in charge of the shed as usual, I suppose?'

'I was over at Lakeside,' Mr Wilson muttered as if the statement was an obscenity.

'At the time she was murdered? Yes, you probably were. At a dance, wasn't it? But (you must forgive me if I've got it wrong) the wool-shed is under your management during the shearing, isn't it?'

'Manner of speaking.'

'Yes. And I suppose you have a look round after knock-off time?'

'Not much to look at.'

'Those trap doors or portholes by the shearing-board for instance. Were they shut?'

'That's right.'

'But the traps could be raised from outside?'

'That's right.'

'And the sacking over the door at the end of the board. Was that dropped?'

'That's right.'

'Was it fastened in any way?'

'Fastened?'

'Fastened, yes.'

'She's nailed to a bit of three-by-two and we drop it.'

'I see. And the pile of sacks or empty bales inside these rolling double doors; were they lying in such a way that anybody coming in or going out would disturb them?'

'I'll say.'

'But in the morning, did they look as if they'd been disturbed?'

Mr Wilson shook his head very slightly.

'Did you notice them particularly?'

'That's right.'

'How was that?'

'I'd told the boys to shift them and they never.'

'Could the doors have been rolled open from outside?'

'Not a chance.'

'Were they fastened inside?'

'That's right.'

'Is it remotely possible that there was somebody hiding in here when you knocked off?'

'Not a chance.'

'Mrs Rubrick must have come in by the sacking door?'

Mr Wilson grunted.

'She was very short. She couldn't reach up to fit the baton on the cross beam where it now rests. So she probably pushed it in a little way. Is that right, should you say?'

'Might be.'

'And her murderer must have gained entrance by the same means, if we wash out the possibility of shoving up one of the traps and coming in that way?'

'Looks like it.'

'Where was the branding iron left, when you knocked off?'

'Inside the door, on the floor.'

'The sacking door, that is. And the pot of paint was there too, wasn't it?'

'That's right.'

'Was the iron in its right place next morning?'

'Young Cliff says it was shifted,' said Mr Wilson in a sudden burst of loquacity.

'Had he put it away?'

'That's right. He says it was shifted. It was him first drew attention to the thing. He put the police on to it.'

'Did you notice anything unusual that morning, Mr Wilson? Anything at all, however trivial?'

Mr Wilson fixed his pale blue gaze upon a cluster of ewes at the far end of the paddock and said, 'Look.' Alleyn looked at the ewes. 'Listen,' Mr Wilson continued, 'I told Sergeant Clark what I seen when I come in and I told Sub-Inspector Jackson and they both wrote it down. The men told them what they seen and they wrote that down too, although it was the same as what I seen.'

'I know,' said Alleyn, 'I know. It seems silly but I would rather like to hear it for myself now I've seen the place. You see, there was nothing new or confusing about a wool-shed to Clark and Jackson. They're New Zealanders, dyed in the wool, and they understand.'

Mr Wilson laughed surprisingly and with unexampled contempt. 'Them?' he said. 'They were as much at home in the shed as a couple of ruddy giraffes, those two jokers.'

'In that case,' said Alleyn with a mental apology to his colleagues, 'I should certainly prefer to hear the story from you.'

'There isn't a story,' said Mr Wilson piteously. 'That's what I keep telling you. There isn't a ruddy story.'

'Just give Mr Alleyn an account of the way you opened up the shed and got going, Ben,' said Fabian.

'That's it,' Alleyn agreed hurriedly. 'I only want to know the routine as you went through with it that morning, step by step. So that I can get an idea of how things went. Step by step,' he repeated. 'Put yourself in my position, Mr Wilson. Suppose you had to find out, all of a sudden, exactly what took place at dawn in a – in a pickle factory or a young ladies' boarding school, or a maternity hospital. I mean – ' Alleyn thrust his cigarettes at Mr Wilson and clapped him nervously on the shoulder. 'Be a good chap, for God's sake,' he said, 'and spit it out.'

'Ta,' said Mr Wilson, lighting the new cigarette at the butt of the old one. 'Oh, well,' he said resignedly, and Alleyn sat down on a wool-pack.

Once embarked Mr Wilson made better showing than might have been hoped for. There was a tendency to skip and become cryptic but Fabian acted as a sort of interpreter and on the whole he did not too badly. A picture of the working day in a wool-shed began to take shape. Everybody had been short-tempered that morning, it seemed. Mr Wilson himself had a bad attack of some gastric complaint to which he was prone and which had developed during the night on the journey back from the dance. At a quarter to two that morning, when they reached Mount Moon, he was, he said, proper crook, and he had spent the remainder of the night in acute discomfort. No, he said wearily, they'd noticed nothing funny in the wool-shed when they came home. They were not in the mood, Alleyn gathered, to notice anything. The farm lorry had sprung a puncture down by the front gate, and they decided to leave it there until morning. They walked the half-mile up to the homestead, with the liquor dying out in them as they did so. They hadn't talked much until they got level with the yards, and there a violent political argument had suddenly developed between two of the shearers, 'I told them to pass it up,' said Mr Wilson, 'and we all turned in.'

They were up again at dawn. The sky was overcast and when Albie Black went down to open up the shed a very light drizzle had set in. If this continued, it meant that when the sheep under cover were shorn, the men would have to knock off until the next batch had dried. This was the last day's shearing and the lorry was to call in the afternoon for the clip which should have been ready before noon. Albie Black went to light the hurricane lantern and found that the boys hadn't filled it with kerosene as he had instructed. He cursed and turned to the candle, only to find it had burnt down to a stump and been squashed out so firmly that the wick had sunk into the wax. He got a fresh piece of candle from another part of the shed, gouged the old stump out and tossed it into the pens. By this time it was light enough to do without it. When Mr Wilson arrived, Albie poured out his complaints and Mr Wilson, himself enraged by gastric disorder, gave the boys the sharp edge of his tongue. He was further incensed by finding, as he put it, 'a dump of wool in my number two bin that hadn't been there when we knocked off the night before. All mucked up, it was, as if someone had been messing it about and then tried to roll it up proper.'

'The wool is put into bins according to its grade?' Alleyn asked.

'That's right. This was number two stuff, all right. I reckoned the fleecies had got into the shed when we was over at the dance and started mucking round with the stuff in the press.'

The boys, however, had vigorously denied these accusations. They swore that they had filled the lamp and had not meddled with the candle which had been fully five inches long. Tommy Johns arrived and pulled on his overalls, which hung on a nail near the shearing-board. His foot caught in an open seam in the trousers and tore it wider. He instantly accused Albie Black of having used the overalls, which were new. Albie hotly denied this. Mr Johns pointed out several dark stains on the front of the overalls and muttered incredulously.

The men started shearing. Damp sheep were crammed under cover to dry off as the already dry sheep thinned out. Fabian and Douglas arrived, anxious about the weather. By this time almost everybody on the place was in an evil temper. One of the shearers, in running across the belly of a sheep, cut it badly, and Douglas, who happened to be standing by, trod in a pool of blood. 'And did he go crook!' Mr Wilson ruminated appreciatively.

Arthur Rubrick arrived at this juncture, walking slowly and very short of breath. 'And,' said Mr Wilson, 'the boss picked things was not too pleasant and asked Tommy Johns what was wrong. Tommy started moaning about nobody being any good on the place. They were standing near the sorting-table and I heard what was said.'

'Can you remember it?' Alleyn asked.

'I can remember all right, but there was nothing in it.'

'May I hear about it? I'm enormously grateful for all this, Mr Wilson.'

'It didn't amount to anything. Tommy's a funny joker. He goes crook sometimes. He said the men were a lot of lazy bastards.'

'Anything else?'

'Young Cliff was in trouble about a bottle of booze. Mrs Rubrick had told him off a couple of nights before. Tommy didn't like it. He was complaining about it.'

'What did Mr Rubrick say?'

'He wasn't too good that morning. He was bad, you could see that. His face was a terrible colour. He was very quiet, and kept saying it was unfortunate. He seemed to think it was very very hot in the shed, and kept moving as if he'd like to clear out. His hands were shaky, too. He was bad, all right.'

'How did it end?'

'Young Doug came up – the Captain,' Mr Wilson explained with a hint of irony. 'He was in a bit of a mess. Bloody. It seemed to upset the boss and he said quite violent, "What the devil have you been doing?" and Doug didn't like it and turned his back on him and walked out.'

'Now, that's an incident that we haven't got in the files,' Alleyn said.

'I never mentioned it. This Sub-Inspector Jackson comes into my shed and throws his weight about, treating us from the word go as if we're holding back on him. Very inconsiderate, he was. "I don't want to know what you think. I want you to answer my questions." All right. We answered his questions.'

'Oh, well,' said Alleyn pacifically.

'We don't want to hold back on it,' Mr Wilson continued with warmth. 'We were as much put out as any one else when we heard. It's not very nice to think about. When they told Jack Merryweather – he's the presser – what he must of done that morning, he vomited. All over my shearing-board before any one could take any steps about it. It was nearly a month afterwards but that made no difference to Jack.'

'Quite,' said Alleyn. 'How did this visit of Mr Rubrick's end?'

'It finished up by the boss taking a bad turn. We helped him out into the open. You wasn't about just then, Mr Losse, and he asked us not to say anything. He carried some kind of medicine on him that he sniffed up and it seemed to fix him. Tommy sent young Cliff for the station car and he drove the boss back to the house. He was very particular we shouldn't mention it. Anxious to avoid trouble. He was a gentleman, was Mr Rubrick.'

'Yes. Now, then, Mr Wilson, about the press. When you knocked off on the previous night it was full of wool, wasn't it? The top half was on the bottom half and the wool had been tramped down but not pressed. Is that right?'

'That's right.'

'And that, to all intents and purposes, was what it looked like in the morning?'

'So far as I noticed, but I did no more than glance at it, if that. Jack Merryweather never noticed anything.'

'When did you finish shearing?'

'Not till six that evening. We cleaned up the sheep that'd been brought in overnight and then there was a hold up. That was at eleven. The fresh ones we'd brought in hadn't dried off. Then it come up sunny and we turned them out again. Everyone was snakey. Young Doug says the sheep are dry and I say they're not and Tommy Johns says they're not. The lorry turns up and Syd Barnes, he's the driver, he has to shove in his oar and reckon they're dry because he wants to get on with it and make the pub at the Pass before dark. So I tell the whole gang where they get off and by that time the sheep have dried and we start up again. Young Cliff was hanging round the shed doing nothing, and then he slopes off, and his father goes crook when he can't find him. It was lovely.'

The whistle tooted and the shed was at once active. Five plunging sheep were dragged in by their hind legs from the pens, machinery whirred, a raw-boned man moved over to the press, spat on his hands, and bore down on the ratchet lever. Mr Wilson pinched out his cigarette, nodded and walked back to the sorter's table.

Alleyn watched the presser complete his work. The bale was sewn up, removed, and shoved along the floor towards the double doors where he and Fabian still waited. This process was assisted by the use of a short hook which was caught into the corners of the bale. 'The lorry backs in here,' Fabian said, 'and the packs are dumped on board. The floor's the same height as the lorry, or a little higher. There's no lifting. It's the same sort of business in the wool store at the other end.'

'Is that the same presser? Jack Merrywether?'

'Yes,' said Fabian, 'that's Jack. He who was so acutely inconvenienced by the absence of a vomitorium in the wool-shed.'

'Is he apt to be sick again, do you imagine, if I put a few simple questions to him?'

'Who can tell? What do you want to ask him?'

'Whether he used one of those hooks when he shifted the crucial bale.'

'Ticklish!' Fabian said. 'It makes even me a little queasy to think of it. Hi, Jack!'

Merrywether's reaction to his summons was disquieting. No sooner had Fabian spoken his introductory phrases than the presser turned pale and stared at Alleyn with an expression of panic.

'Look,' he said. 'I wouldn't of come back on this job if it hadn't of been for the war. That's how it affected me. I'd have turned it up only for the war and there being a shortage. "Look," I said to Mr Johns and Ben Wilson, I said: "not if it's the same outfit," I said. "You don't get me coming at the Mount Moon job if it's the same press again," I said. Then they told me it was a new press and I give in. I come to oblige. Not willing, though. I didn't fancy it and I don't yet. Call me soft if you like, but that's how I am. If anybody starts asking me about you know what, it catches me smack in the belly. I feel shocking. I don't reckon I'll ever shake it off. Now!'

Alleyn murmured sympathetically.

'Look at it whatever way you like,' Merrywether continued argumentatively, 'and it's still a fair cow. You think you're mastering the sensation and then somebody comes along and starts asking you a lot of silly questions and you feel terrible again.'

'As far as I'm concerned,' Alleyn said hurriedly, 'there's only one detail I'd like to check.' He glanced at the bale hook which Merrywether still grasped in his pink freckled hand. Merrywether followed his glance. His fingers opened and the hook crashed on the floor. With clairvoyant accuracy he roared out: 'I know what you mean and I never! It wasn't there. I never touched it with the hook. Now!' And before Alleyn could reply, he added: 'You ask me why. All right. They'd dumped the hook on me. There you are! Deliberate, I reckon.'

'Dumped it on you? The hook? Hid it?'

'That's right. Deliberate. Stuck it up on a beam over there.' He gestured excitedly at the far wall of the shed. 'There's two of those hooks and that's what they done with them. In that dark corner and high up, where I couldn't see them. So what do I do? Go crook at the fleecies. Naturally. I get the idea they done it to swing one across me. They're boys and they act like boys. Cheeky. I'd told them off the day before, and I reckoned they'd come back at me with this one. "You come to light with them two hooks," I said, "or I'll knock your blocks off for you." Well, of course, they says they don't know anything about it, and I don't believe them and away we go. And by this time the bins are full and me and my mate are behind on our job.'

Alleyn walked over to the wall and reached up. He could just get his hand on the beam.

'So you moved the bales without using hooks?'

'That's right. Now don't ask me if we noticed anything. If we'd noticed anything we'd have said something, wouldn't we? All right.'

'When did you find the hooks?'

'That night when we was clearing up, Albie Black starts in again on the boys, saying they never done their job, not filling up the kerosene lamps and fooling round with the candle. So we all look over where the lantern and the candle are on the wall and my mate says they've been swarming up the wall like a couple of blasted monkeys. "What's that up there," he howls. He's a tall joker, and he walks across and yanks down the bale hooks off of the top beam. The boys reckon they don't know how the hooks got up there, and we argue round the point till Tommy Johns has to bring up the matter of who the hell put his foot through his overall pants. Oh, it was a lovely day.'

'When the bales were finally loaded on the lorry – ' Alleyn began, but at once Merrywether took fright. 'Now, don't you start in on me about that,' he scolded, 'I never noticed nothing. How would I? I never handled it.'

'All right, my dear man,' said Alleyn pacifically, 'you didn't. That disposes of that. Don't be so damned touchy; I never knew such a chap.'

'I got to consider my stomach,' said Merrywether darkly.

'Your stomach'll have to lump it, I'm afraid. Who stencilled the Mount Moon mark on the bales?'

'Young Cliff.'

'And who sewed up the bales?'

'I did. Now!'

'All right. Now the bale with which I'm concerned was the first one you handled that morning. When you started work, it was full of wool that apparently had been trampled down but not pressed. You pressed it. You told the police you noticed no change whatever, nothing remarkable or unusual in the condition of the bale. It was exactly as you'd left it the night before.'

'So it was the same. Wouldn't I of noticed if it hadn't been?'

'I should have thought so, certainly. The floor, for instance, round the press.'

'What about it?' Merrywether began on a high note. Alleyn saw his hands contract. He blinked, his sandy lashes moving like shutters over his light eyes. 'What about the floor?' he said, less truculently.

'I notice how smooth the surface is. Would that be the natural grease in the fleeces? It's particularly noticeable on the shearing-board and round the press where the bales may act as polishing agents when they are shoved across the floor.' He glanced at Merrywether's feet. 'You wear ordinary boots. The soles must get quite glassy in here, I should have thought.'

'Not to notice,' he said uncomfortably.

'The floor was in its normal condition that morning, was it? No odd pieces of wool lying about?'

'I told you – ' Merrywether began, but Alleyn interrupted him. 'And as smooth as ever?' he said. Merrywether was silent. 'Come now,' said Alleyn, 'haven't you remembered something that escaped your memory before, when Sub-Inspector Jackson talked to you?'

'I couldn't be expected – I was crook. The way he kept asking me how could I of shifted a pack with you-know-what inside it. It turned my stomach on me.'

'I know. But the floor. Thinking back, now. Was there anything about the floor, round the press, when you arrived here that morning? Was it swept and polished as usual?'

'It was swept.'

'And polished?'

'All right, all right, it wasn't. How was I to remember, three weeks later? The way I'd got churned up over what, in all innocence, I done? It never crossed me mind till just now when you brought it up. I noticed it and yet I never noticed it if you can understand.'

'I know,' said Alleyn.

'But, in pity's name, Jack,' cried Fabian, who had been silent throughout the entire interview, 'what did you not notice?'

'The floor was kind of smudged,' said Merrywether.

III

In the men's midday dinner hour, Fabian brought Cliff Johns to the study. Alleyn felt curious about this boy who had so unexpectedly refused the patronage of Florence Rubrick. He had asked Fabian to leave them alone together and now, as he watched the unco-ordinated movements of the youth's hands, he wondered if Cliff knew that, in defiance of his alibi, he was Sub-Inspector Jackson's pet among the suspects.

He got the boy to sit down and asked him if he understood the reason for the interview. Cliff nodded and clenched and unclenched his wide mobile hands. Behind him, beyond open windows, glared a noonday garden, the plateau, blank with sunshine, and the mountains, etherealized now by an intensity of light. Shadows on those ranges appeared translucent as though the sky beyond shone through. Their snows dazzled the eyes and seemed to be composed of light without substance. A nimbus of light rimmed Cliff's hair. Alleyn thought that his wife would have liked to paint the boy, and would have found pleasure in reflected colour that swam in the hollow of his temples and beneath the sharp arches of his brows. He said: 'Are you interested in painting as well as music?'

Cliff blinked at him and shuffled his feet. 'Yes,' he said. 'A friend of mine is keen. Anything that – I mean – there aren't so many people – I mean – '

'I only asked you,' Alleyn said, 'because I wondered if it would be as difficult to express this extraordinary landscape in terms of music as it would be to do so in terms of paint.' Cliff looked sharply at him. 'I don't understand music, you see,' Alleyn went on. 'But paint does say something to me. When I heard that music was your particular thing, I felt rather lost. The technique of approach through channels of interest wouldn't work. So I thought I'd try a switch-over. Any good or rotten?'

'I'd rather do without a channel of approach, I think,' Cliff said. 'I'd rather get it over, if you don't mind.' But, instead of allowing Alleyn to follow this suggestion, he added, half-shamefaced: 'That's what I wanted to do. With music, I mean. Say something about this.' He jerked his head at the vastness beyond the window and added with an air of defiance, 'And I don't mean the introduction of native bird song and Maori hakas into an ersatz symphony.' Alleyn heard an echo of Fabian Losse in this speech.

'It seems to me,' he said, 'that the forcible injection of local colour is the catch in any aesthetic treatment of this country. There is no forcing the growth of an art, is there, and, happily, no denying it when the moment is ripe. Is your music good?'

Cliff sank his head between his shoulders and, with the profundity of the very young, said: 'It might have been. I've chucked it.'

'Why?'

Cliff muttered undistinguishably, caught Alleyn's eye and blurted out: 'The kind of things that have happened to me.'

'I see. You mean, of course, the difference of opinion with Mrs Rubrick, and her murder. Do you really believe that you'll be worse off for these horrors? I've always had a notion that, if his craft has a sound core, an artist should ripen with experience, however beastly the experience may be at the time. But perhaps that's a layman's idea. Perhaps you had two remedies: your music and' – he looked out of the windows – 'all this. You chose the landscape. Is that it?'

'They wouldn't have me for the army.'

'You aren't yet eighteen, are you?'

'They wouldn't have me. Eyes and feet,' said Cliff, as if the naming of these members was an offence against decency. 'I can see as well as anybody, and I can muster the high country for three days without noticing my feet. That's the army for you.'

'So you mean to carry on mustering the high country and seeing as far through a brick wall as the next fellow?'

'I suppose so.'

'Do you ever lend a hand at wool-sorting, or try to learn about it?'

'I keep outside the shed. Always have.'

'It's a profitable job, isn't it?'

'Doesn't appeal to me. I'd rather go up the hill on a muster.'

'And – no music?'

Cliff shuffled his feet.

'Why?' Alleyn persisted. Cliff rubbed his hands across his face and shook his head. 'I can't,' he said. 'I told you I can't.'

'Not since the evening in the annexe? When you played for an hour or more on a very disreputable old instrument. That was the night following the incident over the bottle of whisky, wasn't it?'

More than at anything else, Alleyn thought, more than at the reminder of Florence Rubrick's death, even, Cliff sickened at the memory of this incident. It had been a serio-comic episode. Markins indignant at the window, the crash of a bursting bottle and the reek of spirits. Alleyn remembered that the tragedies of adolescence were felt most often in the self-esteem, and he said: 'I want you to explain this whisky story, but, before you do, you might just remind yourself that there isn't a creature living who doesn't carry within him the memory of some particular shabbiness of which he's much more ashamed than he would be of a major crime. Also that there's probably not a boy in the world who hasn't at some time or other committed petty larceny. I may add that I personally don't give a damn whether you were silly enough to pinch Mr Rubrick's whisky or not. But I am concerned to find out whether you told the truth when you said you didn't pinch it, and why, if this was so, you wouldn't explain what you were up to in the cellarage.'

'I wasn't taking it,' Cliff muttered. 'I hadn't taken it.'

'Bible oath before a beak?'

'Yes. Before anybody.' Cliff looked quickly at him. 'I don't know how to make it sound true. I don't expect you to believe me.'

'I'm doing my best, but it would be a hell of a lot easier if you'd tell me what in the world you were up to.'

Cliff was silent.

'Not anything in the heroic line?' Alleyn asked mildly.

Cliff opened his mouth and shut it again.

'Because,' Alleyn went on, 'there are moments when the heroic line is no more than a spanner in the works of justice. I mean, if you didn't kill Mrs Rubrick, you're deliberately, for some fetish of your own, muddling the trail. The whisky may be completely irrelevant but we can't tell. It's a question of tidying up. Of course, if you did kill her, you may be wise to hold your tongue. I don't know.'

'But you know I didn't,' Cliff said, and his voice faded on a note of bewilderment. 'I've got an alibi. I played.'

'What was it you played?'

'Bach's Art of Fugue.'

'Difficult?' Alleyn asked and had to wait for a long time for his answer. Cliff made two false starts, checking his voice before it was articulate. 'I'd worked at it,' he said at last. 'Now why,' Alleyn wondered, 'does he jib at telling me it was difficult?'

'It must be disheartening work, slogging away at a bad instrument,' he said. 'It is bad, isn't it?'

Again Cliff was unaccountably reluctant. 'Not as bad as all that,' he muttered and, with a sudden spurt: 'A friend of mine in a music shop in town came out for a couple of days and tuned it for me. It wasn't so bad.'

'But nothing like the Bechstein in the drawing-room, for instance?'

'It wasn't so bad,' he persisted. 'It's a good make. It used to be in the house here before – before she got the Bechstein.'

'You must have missed playing the Bechstein.'

'You can't have everything,' Cliff said.

'Honour?' Alleyn suggested lightly, 'or concert grands? Is that it?'

He grinned unexpectedly. 'Something of the sort,' he said.

'See here,' said Alleyn. 'Will you, without further ado and without me plodding round the by-ways of indirect attack – will you tell me the whole story of your falling out with Mrs Rubrick? You needn't, of course. You can refuse to speak, as you did with my colleagues, and force me to behave as they did: listen to other people's versions of the quarrel. Do you know that the police files devote two foolscap pages to hearsay accounts of the relationship between you and Mrs Rubrick?'

'I can imagine it,' said Cliff savagely. 'Gestapo methods.'

'Do you really think so?' Alleyn said with such gravity that Cliff looked fixedly at him and turned red. 'If you can spare the time,' Alleyn went on, 'I'd like to lend you a manual on police law. It would give you an immense feeling of security. You would learn from it that I am forbidden to quote in a court of law anything that you tell me about your relationship with Mrs Rubrick unless it is to read aloud a statement that you've signed before witnesses. And I'm not asking you to do that. I'm asking you to give me the facts of the case, so that I can make up my mind whether they have any bearing on her death.'

'They haven't.'

'Very good. What are they?'

Cliff bent forward, driving his fingers through his hair. Alleyn felt suddenly impatient. 'But it is the impatience,' he thought, 'of a middle-aged man,' and he reminded himself of the enclosed tragedies of youth. 'Like green figs,' he said to himself, 'closed in upon themselves. He is not yet eighteen,' he thought, growing more tolerant, 'and I bring a code to bear upon him.' Then, since the habit was habitual with him, he disciplined his thoughts and prepared himself for another assault upon Cliff's over-tragic silence. Before he could speak, Cliff raised his head and spoke with simplicity. 'I'll tell you,' he said. 'In a way, it'll be a relief. But I'm afraid it's a long story. You see, it all hangs on her. The kind of woman she was.'

CHAPTER 8

According to Cliff Johns

'You didn't know her,' Cliff said. 'That's what makes everything so impossible. You don't know what she was like.'

'I'm learning,' Alleyn said.

'But it doesn't make sense. I've read about that sort of thing, of course, but somehow I never dropped to it when it was happening to me – I mean not until it was too late to avoid a row. I was only a kid, of course. In the beginning.'

'Yes,' said Alleyn and waited.

Cliff turned his foot sideways and looked at the sole of his boot. Alleyn was surprised to see that he was blushing. 'I suppose I'd better explain,' he said at last, 'that I'm not absolutely positive what the Oedipus Complex exactly is.'

'And I'm not at all sure that I can help you. Let's just have the whole story, clinical or otherwise, may we?'

'Right-oh, then. You see, when I was a kid she started taking an interest in me. What they said when I used to go to the Lake School over there on the flat,' he jerked his head at the plateau, 'about my liking music and so on. I was scared of her at first. You may have the idea that in this country there's no class consciousness but it's there, all right, don't you worry. The station-holder's wife taking an interest in the working manager's kid. Accent on "working". I felt the condescension, all right. Her voice sounded funny to me at first too, but after a bit when I got used to it I liked the way she talked. A bit of an English accent. Crisp and clear and not afraid to say straight out what she thought without drawling "You know" after every other word. The first time she had me over here, I was only about ten and I'd never been inside the drawing-room. It seemed very big and white and smelt of flowers and the fire. She played for me. Chopin. Very badly, but I thought it was marvellous. Then she told me to play. I wouldn't at first, but she went out of the room, and then I touched the keyboard. I felt guilty and silly, but nobody came in and I went on striking one note after another, then chords, and then picking out a phrase but nobody came in and I went on striking one note of the Chopin melody. She left me alone for quite a long time and then she brought me in here for tea. I had ginger beer and cake. That was the beginning.'

'You were good friends in those days?'

'Yes. I thought so. You can imagine what it was like for me, coming here. She gave me books and bought new records for the gramophone and there was always the piano. She used to talk a lot about music; terrible stuff, of course, bogus and soulful, but I lapped it up. She began teaching me to "speak nicely" too. Dad and my mother used to sling off at me for it, but Mum half-liked it all the same. Mum used to buck at Women's Institute meetings about the interest Mrs Rubrick took in me. Even Dad, for all his views, was a bit tickled at first. Parental vanity. They never saw how socially unsound the whole thing was; that I was just a sort of highbrow hobby and that every penny she spent on me was so much purchase money. Dad must have known, of course, but I suppose Mum talked him out of it.'

'How did you feel about it?'

'What do you think? It seemed to me that everything I wanted was inside this house. I'd have lived here if I could. But she was very clever. Only one hour every other day, so that the gilt never wore off the gingerbread. She never forced me to do anything too long. I never tired of anything. I can see now what a lot of self-restraint she must have used because by nature she was a slave-driver.' He paused, tracing back his memories. 'Gosh!' he said suddenly, 'what a nasty little bit of work I must have been.'

'Why?'

'Sucking up to her. Wallowing in second-rate ideas about second-rate music. Telling her what Tchaikowsky made me feel like and slobbering out "Chanson Triste" on the Bechstein with plenty of soul and wrong notes. Kidding myself as well as her that I didn't like the Donkey Serenade.'

'At the age of ten?' Alleyn murmured incredulously.

'Up to thirteen. I used to write poems, too, all about nature and high ideals. "We must be nothing weak, valleys and hills are ours, from the last lone rocky peak to where the rata flowers." I set that one to music: "Tiddely tum te tum. Tiddely tum te-te" and wrote it all out and gave it to her for Christmas with a lovely picture in water colour under the dedication. Gosh, I was awful.'

'Well,' said Alleyn peaceably, 'you certainly seem to have been a full-sized *enfant prodigé*. At thirteen you went to boarding-school, didn't you?'

'Yes. At her expense. I was hell-bent on it, of course.'

'Was it a success?' Alleyn asked, and to his surprise Cliff said: 'Not bad. I don't approve of the system, of course. Education ought to be the business of the state; not of a lot of desiccated failures whose real object is to bolster up class consciousness. The teaching on the whole was merely comic, but there were one or two exceptions.' He saw Alleyn raise an eyebrow and reddened. 'I suppose you're thinking I'm an insufferable young puppy, aren't you?'

'I'm merely reminding myself rather strenuously that you are probably giving me an honest answer and that you are not yet eighteen. But do go on. Why, after all, was it not so bad?'

'There were things they couldn't spoil. I was bullied at first, of course, and miserable. It's so bracing for one, being made to feel suicidal at the age of thirteen. But I turned out to be a slow bowler and naturally that saved me. I got a bit of kudos at school concerts and I developed a turn for writing mildly indecent limericks. That helped. And I went to a good man for music. I am grateful to her for that. Honestly grateful. He made music clear for me. He taught me what music is about. And I did make some real friends. People I could talk to,' said Cliff with relish. The phrase carried Alleyn back thirty years to a dark study and the sound of bells. 'In our way,' he told himself, 'we were just another clutch of little egoists.'

'While you were still at school,' he said, 'Mrs Rubrick went to England, didn't she?'

'Yes. That was when it happened.'

'When what happened?'

The story developed slowly. Before Florence Rubrick left for England, she visited young Cliff at his school, bearing down on him, Alleyn thought, as, a few years earlier, she had borne down on Ursula Harme. With less success, however. She seemed, in the extraordinarily critical eyes of a schoolboy, to make every possible *gaffe*. She spoke too loudly. She tipped too lavishly and in the wrong direction. She asked to be introduced to Cliff's seniors and talked about him, in front of his contemporaries, to his house-master. Worst of all she insisted on an interview with his music teacher, a fastidious and austere man, at whom she talked dreadfully about playing with soul and the works of Mendelssohn. Cliff became morbidly sensitive about her patronage, and imagined that those boys in his house who came from the plateau laughed about them both behind his back. He had committed, he felt, the appalling crime of being different. He had a private interview with Flossie, who spoke in an embarrassing manner about his forthcoming confirmation and even, with a formidable use of botanical parallels, of his approaching adolescence. In the course of this interview, she told him that her great sorrow was the tragedy of having been denied (she almost suggested it was by Arthur Rubrick) a son. She took his face between her sharp large hands and looked at it until it turned purple. She then reminded him of all that she had done for him; kindly, breezily, but unmistakably, and said she knew that he would repay her just as much as if he really were her own son. 'We're real pals, aren't we?' she said. 'Real chums. Cobbers?' His blood ran cold.

She wrote him long letters from England and brought him back a marvellous gramophone and a great many records. He was now fifteen. The unpleasant memory of their last meeting had been thrust away at the back of his mind. He had found his feet at school and worked hard at his music. At first his encounters with his patron after her return from England were happy enough. Alleyn gathered that he talked about himself and that Flossie listened.

In the last term of 1940, Cliff formed a friendship with an English boy who had been evacuated to New Zealand by his parents; evidently communistic intellectuals. Their son, delicate, vehement and sardonic, seemed to Cliff extraordinarily mature, a man among children. He devoured everything his friend had to say, became an enthusiastic leftist, argued with his masters and thought himself,

Alleyn suspected, a good deal more of a bombshell than they did. He and his friend gathered round them an ardently iconoclastic group all of whom decided to fight 'without prejudice' against Fascism, reserving the right to revolt when the war was over. The friend, it seemed, had always been of this mind. 'But,' said Cliff ingenuously, 'of course it made a big difference when Russia came in. I suppose,' he added, 'you are horrified.'

'Do you?' said Alleyn. 'Then I mustn't disappoint you. The thing is, was Mrs Rubrick horrified?'

'I'll say she was! That was when the awful row happened. It started first of all with us trying to enlist. This chap and I suddenly felt we couldn't stick it just hanging on at school and – well, anyway, that's what we did. We were turned down, of course. The episode was very sourly received by all hands. That was at the end of 1941. I came home for the Christmas holidays. By that time I realized pretty thoroughly how hopelessly wrong it was for me to play at being a little gentleman at her expense. I realized that if I couldn't get as my right, equally with other chaps, the things she'd given me, then I shouldn't take them at all. I was admitting the right of one class to patronize another. They were short of men all over the high country, and I felt that, if I couldn't get into the army, I'd better work on the place.'

He paused, and, with a very shamefaced air, muttered: 'I'm not trying to make out a flattering case for myself. It wasn't as if I was army-minded. I loathed the prospect. Muddle, boredom, idiotic routine and then carnage. It was just – well, I did honestly feel I ought to.'

'Right,' said Alleyn. 'I take the point.'

'She didn't. She'd got it all taped out. I was to go Home to the Royal College of Music. At her expense. She was delighted when they said I'd never pass fit. When I tried to explain, she treated me like a silly kid. Then, when I stuck to it, she accused me of ingratitude. She had no right,' said Cliff passionately. 'Nobody has the right to take a kid of ten and teach him to accept everything without knowing what it means, and then use that generosity as a weapon against him. She'd always talked about the right of artists to be free. Free! She'd got vested interests in me and she meant to use them. It was horrible.'

'What was the upshot of the discussion?'

Cliff had turned in his chair. His face was dark against the glare of the plateau, and it was by the posture of his body and the tilt of his head that Alleyn first realized he was staring at the portrait of Florence Rubrick.

'She sat, just like that,' he said. 'Her hands were like that and her mouth, not quite shut. She hadn't got much expression, ever, and you couldn't believe, looking at her, that she could say the things she said. What everything had cost and how she'd thought I was fond of her. I couldn't stand it. I walked out.'

'When was this?'

'The night I got home for the summer holidays. I didn't see her again until – until – '

'We're back at the broken bottle of whisky, aren't we?'

Cliff was silent.

'Come,' said Alleyn, 'you've been very frank up to now. Why do you jib at this one point?'

Cliff shuffled his feet and began mumbling. 'All very well, but how do I know . . . not a free agent . . . Gestapo methods . . . Taken down and used against you . . .'

'Nonsense,' said Alleyn, 'I've taken nothing down and I've no witness. Don't let's go over all that again. If you won't tell me what you were doing with the whisky, you won't, but really you can't blame Sub-Inspector Jackson for taking a gloomy view of your reticence. Let's get back to the bare bones of fact. You were in the dairy-cum-cellar with the bottle in your hand. Markins looked through the window, you dropped the bottle, he hauled you into the kitchen. Mrs Duck fetched Mrs Rubrick. There was a scene in the middle of which she dismissed Mrs Duck and Markins. We have their several accounts of the scene up to the point when they left. I should now like to have yours of the whole affair.'

Cliff stared at the portrait. Alleyn saw him wet his lips and, a moment later, give the uncanny little half-yawn of nervous expectancy. Alleyn was familiar with this grimace. He had seen it made by prisoners awaiting sentence and by men under suspicion when the investigating officer carried the interrogation towards danger point.

'Will it help,' he said, 'if I tell you this? Anything that is not relevant to my inquiry will not appear in any subsequent report. I can give you my word, if you'll take it, that I'll never repeat or use such statements if, in fact, they are irrelevant.' He waited for a moment. 'Well,' he said at last, 'what about this scene with Mrs Rubrick in the kitchen? Was it so very bad?'

'You've been told what they heard. The other two. It was bad enough then. Before they went. Almost as if she was glad to be able to go for me. It's as real now as if it had happened last night. Only it's a queer kind of reality. Like the memory of a nightmare.'

'Have you ever spoken to anybody about it?'

'Never.'

'Then bring the monster out into the light of day and let's have a look at it.'

He saw that Cliff half-welcomed, half-resisted this insistence. 'After all,' Alleyn said, 'was it so terrible?'

'Not terrible exactly,' Cliff said. 'Disgusting.'

'Well?'

'I suppose I had a kind of respect for her. Partly bogus, I know that. An acceptance of the feudal idea. But partly genuine too. Partly based on the honest gratitude I'd have felt for her if she hadn't demanded gratitude. I don't know. I only know it made me feel sick to see her lips shake and to hear her voice tremble. There was a master at school who used to get like that before he caned us. He got the sack. She seemed to be acting too. Acting the lady of the house who controlled herself before the servants. It'd have been better if she'd yelled at me. When they'd gone, she did – once. When I said I wasn't stealing it. Then she sort of took hold of herself and dropped back into a whisper. All the same, even then, in a way, I thought she was putting it on. Acting. Really it was almost as if she enjoyed herself. That was what was so particularly beastly.'

'I know,' said Alleyn.

'Do you? And her being old. That made it worse. I started by being furious because she wouldn't believe me. Then I began to be sorry for her. Then I simply wanted to get away and get clean. She began to – to cry. She looked ghastly. I felt as if I could never bear to look at her again. She held out her hand and I couldn't touch it. I was furious with her for making me feel so ashamed, and I turned round and cleared out of it. I suppose you know about the next part.'

'I know you spent the rest of that night and a good bit of the next day, walking towards the Pass.'

'That's right. It sounds silly. An hysterical kid, you'll think. I couldn't help it. I made a pretty good fool of myself. I was out of training and my feet gave out. I'd have gone on, though, if Dad hadn't come after me.'

'You didn't make a second attempt.'

Cliff shook his head.

'Why?'

'They got on to me at home. Mum got me to promise. There was a pretty ghastly scene, when I got home.'

'And in the evening you worked it off with Bach on the outhouse piano? That's how it was, isn't it?' Alleyn insisted, but Cliff was monosyllabic again. 'That's right,' he mumbled, rubbing the arm of his chair. Alleyn tried to get him to talk about the music he played that night in the darkling room while Florence Rubrick and her household sat in deck-chairs on the lawn. All through their conversation it had persisted, and through the search for the brooch. Florence Rubrick must have heard it as she climbed up her improvised rostrum. Her murderer must have heard it when he struck her down and stuffed her mouth and nostrils with wool. Murder to Music, thought Alleyn, and saw the words splashed across a news bill. Was it because of these associations that Cliff would not speak of his music? Was it because this, theatrically enough, had been, the last time he played? Or was it merely that he was reluctant to speak of music with a Philistine? Alleyn found himself satisfied with none of these theories.

'Losse,' he said, 'tells me you played extremely well that night.'

'*What's he mean!*' Cliff stopped dead, as if horrified at his own vehemence. 'I'd worked at it,' he said indistinctly. 'I told you.'

'It's strange to me,' Alleyn said, 'that you don't go on with your music. I should have thought that not to go on would be intolerable.'

'Would you,' he muttered.

'Are you sure you are not a little bit proud of your abstinence?'

This seemed to astonish Cliff. 'Proud!' he repeated. 'If you only realized . . .' He got up. 'If you've finished with me,' he said.

'Almost, yes. You never saw her again?'

Cliff seemed to take this question as a statement of fact. He moved towards the french window. 'Is that right?' Alleyn said and he nodded. 'And you won't tell me what you were doing with the whisky?'

'I can't.'

'All right. I think I'll just take a look at this outhouse. I can find my way. Thank you for being so nearly frank.'

Cliff blinked at him and went out.

II

The annexe proved to be grander than its name suggested. Fabian had told Alleyn that it had been added to the bunkhouse by Arthur Rubrick as a sort of common-room for the men. Florence, in a spurt of solicitude and public-spiritedness, had urged this upon her husband, and, on acquiring the Bechstein, had given the men her old piano and a radio set, and had turned the house out for odd pieces of furniture. 'It was when she stood for parliament,' Fabian explained acidly. 'She had a photograph taken with the station hands sitting about in exquisitely self-conscious attitudes and sent it to the papers. You'll find a framed enlargement above the mantelpiece.'

The room had an unkempt look. There was a bloom of dust on the table, the radio and the piano. A heap of old radio magazines had been stacked untidily in a corner of the room and yellowing newspapers lay about the floor. The top of the piano was piled with music; ballads, student song-books and dance tunes. Underneath these he found a number of classical works with Cliff's name written across the top. Here at the bottom was Bach's Art of Fugue.

Alleyn opened the piano and picked out a phrase from Cliff's music. Two of the notes jammed. Had the Bach been full of hiatuses, then, or had the piano deteriorated so much in fifteen months? Alleyn replaced the Art of Fugue under a pile of song sheets, brushed his hands together absently, closed the door and squatted down by the heap of radio magazines in the corner.

He waded back through sixty-five weeks of wireless programmes that had been pumped into the air from all the broadcasting stations in the country. The magazines were not stacked in order and it was a tedious business. Back to February 1942: laying them down in their sequence. The second week in February, the first week in February. Alleyn's hands were poised over the work. There were only half a dozen left. He sorted them quickly. The last week in January 1942 was missing.

Mechanically he stacked the magazines up in their corner and, after a moment's hesitation, disordered them again. He walked up and down the room whistling a phrase of Cliff's music. 'Oh, well!' he thought. 'It's a long shot and I may be off the mark.' But he stared dolefully at the piano and presently began again to pick out the same phrase, first in the treble and then, very dejectedly, in the bass, swearing when the keys jammed. He shut the lid at last, sat in a rakish old chair and began to fill his pipe. 'I shall be obliged to send them all away on ludicrous errands,' he muttered, 'and get a toll call through to Jackson. Is this high fantasy, or is it murder?' The door opened. A woman stood on the threshold.

She looked dark against the brilliance of sunshine outside. He could see that the hand with which she had opened the door was now pressed against her lips. She was a middle-aged woman, plainly dressed. She was still for a moment and then stepped back. The strong sunshine fell across her face, which was heavy and pale for a countrywoman's. She said breathlessly: 'I heard the piano. I thought it was Cliff.'

'I'm afraid Cliff would not be flattered,' Alleyn said. 'I lack technique!' He moved towards her.

She backed away. 'It was the piano,' she said again. 'Hearing it after so long.'

'Do the men never play it?'

'Not in the daytime,' she said hurriedly. 'And I kind of remember the tune.' She tidied her hair nervously. 'I'm sure I didn't mean to intrude,' she said. 'Excuse me.' She was moving away when Alleyn stopped her.

'Please don't go,' he said. 'You're Cliff's mother, aren't you?'

'That's right.'

'I'd be grateful if you would spare me a moment. It won't be much more than a moment. Really. My name, by the way, is Alleyn.'

'Pleased to meet you,' she said woodenly.

He stood aside, holding back the door. After a little hesitation she went into the room and stood there, staring straight before her, her fingers still moving against her lips. Alleyn left the door open. 'Will you sit down?' he said.

'I won't bother, thanks.'

He moved the chair forward and waited. She sat on the edge of it, unwillingly.

'I expect you've heard why I'm here,' Alleyn said gently. 'Or have you?'

She nodded, still not looking at him.

'I want you to help me, if you will.'

'I can't help you,' she said. 'I don't know the first thing about it. None of us do. Not me, or Mr Johns or my boy.' He voice shook. She added rapidly with an air of desperation, 'You leave my boy alone, Mr Alleyn.'

'Well,' said Alleyn, 'I've got to talk to people, you know. That's my job.'

'It's no use talking to Cliff. I tell you straight, it's no use. It's something cruel what those others done to Cliff. Pestering him, day after day, and him proved to be innocent. They proved it themselves with what they found put and even then they couldn't let him alone. He's not like other lads. Not tough. Different.'

'Yes,' Alleyn agreed, 'he's an exceptional chap, isn't he?'

'They broke his spirit,' she said, frowning, refusing to look at him. 'He's a different boy. I'm his mother and I know what they done. It's wicked. Getting on to a bit of a kid when it was proved he was innocent.'

'The piano?' Alleyn said.

'Mrs Duck saw him. Mrs Duck who cooks for them down there. She was out for a stroll, not having gone to the dance, and she saw him sit down and commence to play. They all heard him and they said they heard him, and me and his Dad heard him too. On and on, and him dead beat, till I couldn't stand it any longer and come over myself and fetched him home. What more do they want?'

'Mrs Johns,' Alleyn began, 'what sort – ' He stopped short, feeling that he could not repeat once more the too-familiar phrase. 'Did you like Mrs Rubrick?' he said.

For the first time she looked sharply at him. 'Like her?' she said unwillingly. 'Yes, I suppose I did. She was kind. Always the same to everyone. She made mistakes as I well know. Things didn't pan out the way she'd reckoned.'

'With Cliff?'

'That's right. There's been a lot of rubbish talked about the inter-est she took in my boy. People are funny like that. Jealous.' She passed her roughened hand over her face with a movement that suggested the wiping away of a cobweb. 'I don't say I wasn't a bit jealous myself,' she said grudgingly. 'I don't say I didn't think it might make him discontented like with his own home. But I saw what a big thing it was for my boy and I wouldn't stand in his light. But there it is. I won't say I didn't feel it.'

She said all this with the same air of antagonism, but Alleyn felt a sudden respect for her. He said: 'But this feeling didn't persist?'

'Persist? Not when he grew older. He grew away from her, if you can understand. Nobody knows a boy like his mother and I know you can't drive Cliff. She tried to drive him and in the finish she set him against her. He's a good boy,' said Mrs Johns coldly, 'though I say it, but he's very unusual. And sensitive.'

'Did you regret taking her offer to send him to school?'

'Regret it?' she repeated, examining the word. 'Seeing what's hap-pened, and the cruel way it's changed him – ' She pressed her lips together and her hands jerked stiffly in her lap. 'I wish she'd never seen my boy,' she said with extraordinary vehemence and then caught her breath and looked frightened. 'It's none of his doing or of hers, poor lady. They were devoted to each other. When it happened there was nobody felt it more than Cliff. Don't let anyone tell you different. It's wicked, the way an innocent boy's been made to suffer. Wicked.'

Her eyes were still fixed on the wall, beyond Alleyn and above his head. They were wet, but so wooden was her face that her tears seemed to be accidental and quite inexpressive of sorrow. She ended each of her speeches with such an air of finality that he felt surprised when she embarked on a new one.

'Mrs Johns,' he said, 'what do you make of this story about the whisky?'

'Anybody who says my boy's a thief is a liar,' she said. 'That's what I make of it. Lies! He never touched a drop in his life.'

'Then what do you think he was doing?'

At last she looked full at him. 'You ask the station cook what he was doing. Ask Albert Black. Cliff won't tell you anything, and he won't tell me. It's my idea and he'd never forgive me if he knew I'd spoken of it.' She got up and walked to the door, staring out into the sunshine. 'Ask them,' she said. 'That's all.'

'Thank you,' said Alleyn, looking thoughtfully at her. 'I believe I shall.'

III

Alleyn's first view of the station cook was dramatic and incredible. It took place that evening, the second of his stay at Mount Moon. After their early dinner, a silent meal at which the members of the household seemed to be suffering from a carry-over from last night's confidences, Fabian suggested that he and Alleyn should walk up to the men's quarters. They did so but, before they left, Alleyn asked Ursula to lend him the diamond clip that Florence Rubrick had lost on the night she was murdered. He and Fabian walked down the lavender path as the evening light faded and the mountains began their nightly pageant of violet and gold. The lavender stalks were grey sticks, now, and the zinnias behind them isolated mummies crowned with friable heads. 'Were they much the same then,' Alleyn asked, 'as far as visibility goes?'

'The lavender was green and bushy,' Fabian replied, 'but the thing was under one of the zinnias and had no better cover than there would be now. They don't flourish up here and were spindly-looking apologies even when they did their stuff.'

Alleyn dropped the clip, first in one place and then in another. It glittered like a monstrously artificial flower on the dry earth. 'Oh, well,' he said, 'let's go and see Cookie.'

They passed through the gate that Florence had used that night and, like her, turned up the main track that led to the men's quarters.

Long before they came within sight of their objective, they heard a high-pitched, raucous voice raised in the unmistakable periods of oratory. They passed the wool-shed and came within full view of the bunkhouse and annexe.

A group of a dozen men, some squatting on their heels, others leaning, relaxed, against the wall of the building, listened in silence to an empurpled man, dressed in dirty white, who stood on an over-turned box and loudly exhorted them.

'I howled unto the Lord,' the orator bawled angrily. 'That's what I done. I howled unto the Lord.'

'That's Cookie,' Fabian murmured, 'in the penultimate stage of his cups. The third and last stage is delirium tremens. It's a regular progression.'

'. . . and the Lord said unto me: "What's biting you, Perce?" And I answered and said: "Me sins lie bitter in me belly," I says, "I've backslid," I says, "and the grade's too hot for me." And the Lord said: "Give it another pop, Perce." And I give it another pop and the Lord backed me up and I'm saved.'

Here the cook paused and, with extreme difficulty, executed a peculiar gesture, as if writing on the air. 'The judgement's writ clear on the wall,' he shouted, 'for them as aren't too shickered to read it. It's writ clear as it might be on that bloody bunk'ouse be'ind yer. And what does it say? It says in letters of flame: "Give it another pop." Hallelujah.'

'Hallelujah,' echoed a small man who sat in an attitude of profound dejection on the annexe step. This was Albie Black, the rouseabout.

'A couple more brands to be snatched from the burning,' the cook continued, catching sight of Alleyn and Fabian, and gesturing wildly towards them. 'A couple more sheep to be cut out from the mob and baled up in the pens of salvation. A couple more dirty two-tooths for the Lord to shear. Shall we gather at the river?' He and the rouseabout broke into a hymn, the melody of which was taken up by an accordion player inside the bunkhouse. Fabian indicated to the men that he and Alleyn would like to be left alone with the cook and Albie Black. Ben Wilson, who was quietly smoking his pipe and looking at the cook with an air of detached disapproval, jerked his head at him and said, 'He's fixed all right.' He led the way into the bunkhouse, the accordion stopped abruptly, and Alleyn was left face to face with the cook, who was still singing, but half-heartedly and in a melancholy key.

'Pretty hopeless, isn't it?' Alleyn muttered, eyeing him dubiously.

'It's now or never,' Fabian rejoined. 'He'll be dead to the world tomorrow and we're supposed to ship him down-country the next day. Unless, of course, you exercise your authority and keep him here. Perce!' he said loudly, placing himself in front of the cook. 'Come down off that. Here's somebody wants to speak to you.'

The cook stepped incontinently off his box into mid-air and was caught like an unwieldy ballerina by Alleyn.

'Open up your bowels of compassion,' he said mildly and allowed them to seat him on the box.

'Shall I leave you?' asked Fabian.

'You stay where you are,' said Alleyn. 'I want a witness.'

The cook was a large man with pale eyes, an unctuous mouth and bad teeth. 'Bare your bosom,' he invited Alleyn. 'Though it's as black as pitch it shall be as white as snow. What's your trouble?'

'Whisky,' said Alleyn.

The cook laid hold of his coat lapels and peered very earnestly into his face. 'You're a pal,' he said. 'I don't mind if I do.'

'But I haven't got any,' Alleyn said. 'Have you?'

The cook shook his head mournfully and, having begun to shake it, seemed unable to leave off. His eyes filled with tears. His breath smelt of beer and of something that at the moment Alleyn was unable to place.

'It's not so easily come by these days, is it?' Alleyn said.

'I ain't seen a drop,' the cook whispered, 'not since . . .' he wiped his mouth and gave Alleyn a look of extraordinary cunning, 'not since you know when.'

'When was that?'

'Ah,' said the cook profoundly, 'that's telling.' He looked out of the corners of his eyes at Fabian, leered, and with a ridiculously Victorian gesture laid his finger alongside his nose. Albie Black burst into loud meaningless laughter. 'Oh, dear!' he said and buried his head in his arms. Fabian moved behind the cook and pointed suggestively in the direction of the house.

'Haven't they got some of the right stuff down there?' Alleyn suggested.

'Ah,' said the cook.

'How about it?'

The cook began to shake his head again.

Alleyn took a deep breath and fired point-blank. 'How about young Cliff,' he suggested. 'Any good?'

'Him!' said the cook, and with startling precision uttered a stream of obscenities.

'What's the matter with Cliff?' Alleyn asked.

'Ask him,' the cook said and looked indignantly at Albie Black. 'They're cobbers, them two – '

'You shut your face,' said Albie Black, suddenly furious. He broke into a storm of abuse to which the cook listened sadly. 'You shut your face, or I'll knock your bloody block off. Didn't I tell you to forget it? Haven't you got any sense?' He pointed a shaking finger at Alleyn. 'Don't you pick what he is? D'you want to land us both in the cooler?'

The cook sighed heavily. 'I thought you said you'd got the fine work in with young Cliff,' he said. 'You know. What you seen that night. I thought you'd fixed him. You know.'

'You come away,' said Albie in great alarm, 'I'm not as sozzled as what you are and I'm telling you. You come away.'

'Wait a minute,' said Alleyn, but the cook had taken fright. 'Change and decay in all around I see,' he said, and rising with some difficulty flung one arm about the neck of his friend. 'See the hosts of Midian,' he shouted, waving the other arm at Alleyn. 'How they prowl around. It's a lousy life. Let's have a little wee drink, Albie.'

'No, you don't!' Alleyn began, but the cook turned until his face was pressed into the bosom of his friend, and by slow degrees slid to the ground.

'Now see what you done,' said Albie Black.

CHAPTER 9

Attack

The cook being insensible and, according to Fabian, certain to remain so for many hours, Alleyn suffered him to be moved and concentrated on Albert Black.

There had been a certain spaciousness about the cook but Albert, he decided, was an abominable specimen. He disseminated meanness and low cunning. He was drunk enough to be truculent and sober enough to look after himself. The only method, Alleyn decided, was that of intimidation. He and Fabian withdrew with Albert into the annexe.

'Have you ever been mixed up in a murder charge before?' Alleyn began, with the nearest approach to police station truculence of which he was capable.

'I'm not mixed up in one now,' said Albert, showing the whites of his eyes. 'Choose your words.'

'You're withholding information in a homicidal investigation, aren't you? D'you know what that means?'

'Here!' said Albert. 'You can't swing that across me.'

'You'll be lucky if you don't get a pair of bracelets swung across you. Haven't you been in trouble before?' Albert looked at him indignantly. 'Come on, now,' Alleyn persisted. 'How about a charge of theft?'

'Me?' said Albert. 'Me, with a clean sheet all the years I bin 'ere! Accusing me of stealing! 'Ow dare yer?'

'What about Mr Rubrick's whisky? Come on, Black, you'd better make a clean breast of it.'

Albert looked at the piano. His dirty fingers pulled at his underlip.
He moved closer to Alleyn and peered into his face. 'It's methylated
spirits they stink of,' Alleyn thought.

'Got a fag on yer?' Albert said ingratiatingly and grasped him by
the coat.

Alleyn freed himself, took out his case and offered it, open, to
Albert.

'You're a pal,' said Albert and took the case. He helped himself
fumblingly to six cigarettes and put them in his pocket. He looked
closely at the case. 'Posh,' he said. 'Not gold, though, d'you reckon,
Mr Losse?'

'Well,' Alleyn said. 'How about this whisky?'

Albert jerked his head at the piano. 'So he got chatty after all, did
he?' he said. 'The little bastard. OK. That lets me out.' He again grasped
Alleyn by the coat with one hand and with the other pointed behind
him at the piano. 'What a pal,' he said. 'Comes the holy Jo over a drop
of Johnny Walker and the next night he's fixing the big job.'

'What the hell are you talking about!' Fabian said violently.

'Can – you – tell – me,' Albert said, swaying and clinging to
Alleyn, 'how a little bastard like that can be playing the ruddy piano
and at the same time run into me round the corner of the wool-
shed? There's a mystery for you, if you like.'

Fabian took a step forward. 'Be quiet, Losse,' said Alleyn.

'It's a very funny thing,' Albert continued, 'how an individual can
be in two places at oncst. And he knew he oughtn't to be there, the
ruddy little twister. Because all the time I sees him by the wool-shed
he keeps on thumping that blasted pianna. Now then!'

'Very strange,' said Alleyn.

'Isn't it. I knew you'd say that.'

'Why haven't you talked about this before?'

Albert freed himself, spat, and wiped his mouth with the back of
his hand. 'Bargain's a bargain, isn't it? Fair dos. Wait till I get me
hands on the little twister. Put me away, has he? Good oh! And what
does he get? Anywhere else he'd swing for it.'

'Did you hear Mrs Rubrick speaking in the wool-shed?'

'How could she speak when he'd fixed her? That was earlier:
"Ladies and gentlemen." Gawd, what a go!'

'Where was he?'

'Alleyn, for God's sake – ' Fabian began, and Alleyn turned on him. 'If you can't be quiet, Losse, you'll have to clear out. Now, Black, where was Cliff?'

'Aren't I telling you? Coming out of the shed.'

Alleyn looked through the annexe window. He saw a rough track running downhill, past the yards, past a side road to the wool-shed, down to a narrow water race above the gate that Florence Rubrick came through when she left the lavender path and struck uphill to the wool-shed.

'Was it then that you asked him to say nothing about the previous night when he caught you stealing the whisky?' Alleyn held his breath. It was a long shot and almost in the dark.

'Not then,' said Albert.

'Did you speak to him?'

'Not then.'

'Had you already spoken about the whisky?'

'I'm not saying anything about that. I'm telling you what he done.'

'And I'm telling you what *you* did. That was the bargain, wasn't it? He found you making away with the bottles. He ordered you off and was caught trying to put them back. He didn't give you away. Later, when the murder came out and the police investigation started, you struck your bargain. If Cliff said nothing about the whisky, you'd say nothing about seeing him come out of the shed?'

Albert was considerably sobered. He looked furtively from Alleyn to Fabian. 'I got to protect myself,' he said. 'Asking a bloke to put himself away.'

'Very good. You'd rather I tell him you've blown the gaff and get the whole story from him. The police will be interested to know you've withheld important information.'

'All right, all right,' said Albert shrilly. 'Have it your own way, you blasted cow,' and burst into tears.

II

Fabian and Alleyn groped their way down the hill in silence. They turned off to the wool-shed, where Alleyn paused and looked at the sacking-covered door. Fabian watched him miserably.

'It must have been in about this light,' Alleyn said. 'Just after dark.'

'You can't do it!' Fabian said. 'You can't believe a drunken sneak-thie's story. I know young Cliff. He's a good chap. You've talked to him. You can't believe it.'

'A year ago,' Alleyn said, 'he was an over-emotionalized, slightly hysterical and extremely unhappy adolescent.'

'I don't give a damn! Oh, God!' Fabian muttered, 'why the hell did I start this?'

'I did warn you,' Alleyn said with something like compassion in his voice.

'It's impossible, I swear – I formally swear to you that the piano never stopped for more than a few seconds. You know what it's like on a still night. The cessation of a noise like that hits your ears. Albie was probably half-tight. Good Lord, he said himself that the piano went on all the time. Of course it wasn't Cliff that he saw. I'm amazed that you pay the smallest attention to his meanderings.' Fabian paused. 'If he saw any one,' he added, and his voice changed, 'I admit that it was probably the murderer. It wasn't Cliff. You yourself pointed out that it was almost dark.'

'Then why did Cliff refuse to talk about the whisky?'

'Schoolboy honour. He'd struck up a friendship with the wretched creature.'

'Yes,' said Alleyn. 'That's tenable.'

'Then why don't you accept it?'

'My dear chap, I'll accept it if it fits. See here. I want you to do two things for me. The first is easy. When you go indoors, help me to get a toll call through in privacy. Will you?'

'Of course.'

'The second is troublesome. You know the pens inside the shearing-shed? With the slatted floor where the unshorn sheep are huddled together?'

'Well?'

'You've finished crutching today, haven't you?'

'Yes.'

'I'm afraid I want to take that slatted floor up.'

Fabian stared at him. 'Why on earth?'

'There may be something underneath.'

'There are the sheep droppings of thirty years underneath.'

'So I feared. Those of the last year are all that concern me. I'll want a sieve and a spade and if you can lay your hands on a pair of rejected overalls, I'd be grateful.'

Fabian looked at Alleyn's hands. 'And gloves if it could be managed,' Alleyn said. 'I'm very sorry about taking up the floor. The police department will pay the damage, of course. It may only be one section – the one nearest the press. I think you might warn the others when we go in.'

'May I ask what you hope to find?'

'A light that failed,' said Alleyn.

'Am I supposed to understand that?'

'I don't see why you shouldn't.' They had reached the gate into the lavender walk. Alleyn turned and looked back at the track. He could see the open door into the annexe where they had left Albie Black weeping off the combined effects of confession, betrayal and the hangover from wood alcohol.

'Was it methylated spirit they'd been drinking?' he asked. 'He and the cook?'

'I wouldn't put it past them. Or Hokanui.'

'What's that?'

'The local equivalent of potheen.'

'Why do you keep him?'

'He doesn't break out very often. We can't pick our men in war-time.'

'I'd love to lock him up,' Alleyn said. 'He stinks. He's a toad.'

'Then why do you listen to him?'

'Do you suppose policemen only take statements from people they fall in love with? Come in. I want to get that call through before the bureau shuts.'

They found the members of the household assembled in the pleasant colonial-Victorian drawing-room, overlooking the lawn on the wool-shed side of the house.

'We rather felt we couldn't face the study again,' Ursula said. 'After last night, you know. We felt it could do with an airing. And I'm going to bed at eight. If Mr Alleyn lets me, of course. Does every one realize we got exactly five and a half hours of sleep last night?'

'I should certainly prefer that Flossie's portrait did not preside over another session,' Fabian agreed. 'If there was to be another session, of course. Having never looked at it for three years I've suddenly become exquisitely self-conscious in its presence. I suppose, Ursy darling, you wouldn't care to have it in your room?'

'If that's meant to be a joke, Fabian,' said Ursula, 'I'm not joining in it.'

'You're very touchy. Mr Alleyn is going to dash off a monograph on one of the less delicious aspects of the merino sheep, Douglas. We are to take up the floor of the wool-shed pens.'

Alleyn, standing in the doorway, watched the group round the fire. Mrs Aceworthy wore her almost habitual expression of half-affronted gentility. Terence Lynne, flashing the needles in her scarlet knitting, stared at him, and drew her thin brows together. Ursula Harme, arrested in the duelling mood she kept for Fabian, paused, her lips parted. Douglas dropped his newspaper and began his usual indignant expostulation: 'What in Heaven's name are you talking about, Fab? Good Lord – '

'Yes, Douglas, my dear,.' said Fabian, 'we know how agitating you find your present condition of perpetual astonishment, but there it is. Up with the slats and down goes poor Mr Alleyn.'

Douglas retired angrily behind his newspaper. 'The whole thing's a farce,' he muttered obscurely. 'I always said so.' He crackled his paper. 'Who's going to do it?'

'If you'll trust me,' said Alleyn, 'I will.'

'I don't envy you your job, sir.'

'The policeman's lot,' Alleyn said lightly.

'I'll tell the men to do it,' Douglas grunted ungraciously from behind his paper. He peeped round the corner of it at Alleyn. The solitary, rather prominent eye he displayed was reminiscent of Florence Rubrick's in her portrait. 'I'll give you a hand, if you like,' he added.

'That's the spirit that forged the empire,' said Fabian. 'Good old Duggie.'

'If you'll excuse me,' Alleyn said and moved into the hall. Fabian joined him there.

'The telephone's switched through to the study,' he said. 'I promise not to eavesdrop.' He paused reflectively. 'Eavesdrop!' he muttered.

'What a curious word! To drop from eaves. Reminds one of the swallows and, by a not too extravagant flight of fancy, of your job for the morrow. Give one long ring and the exchange at the Pass may feel moved to answer you.'

When Alleyn lifted the receiver it was to cut in on a cross-plateau conversation. A voice angrily admonished him: 'Working!' He hung up and waited. He could hear Fabian whistling in the hall. The telephone gave a brief tinkle and he tried again, this time with success. The operator at the Pass came through. Alleyn asked for a police station two hundred miles away, where he hoped Sub-Inspector Jackson might possibly be on duty. 'I'll call you,' said the operator coldly. 'This is a police call,' said Alleyn, 'I'll hold the line.' 'Aren't you Mount Moon?' said the operator sharply. 'Yes, and it's still a police call, if you'll believe me.' 'Not in trouble up there, are you, Mr Losse?' 'I'm as happy as a lark,' said Alleyn, 'but in a bit of a hurry,' 'Hold the line,' giggled the operator. A vast buzzing set up in his ear, threaded with ghost voices. 'That'll be good-oh, then, Bob.' 'Eh?' 'I said, that'll be jake.' The operator's voice cut in omnipotently. 'There you are, Mr Losse. They're waiting.'

Sub-Inspector Jackson was not there but PC Wetherbridge, who had been detailed to the case in town, answered the telephone and was helpful. 'The radio programmes for the second week in January, '42, Mr Alleyn? I think we can do that for you.'

'For the evening of Thursday the 29th,' Alleyn said, 'between eight and nine o'clock. Only stations with good reception in this district.'

'It may take us a wee while, Mr Alleyn.'

'Of course. Would you tell the exchange at the Pass to keep itself open and call me back?'

'That'll be OK, sir.'

'And Wetherbridge. I want you to get hold of Mr Jackson. Tell him it's a very long chance, but I may want to bring someone in to the station. I'd very much like a word with him. I think it would be advisable for him to come up here. He asked me to let him know if there were developments. There are. If you can find him, he might come in on the line when you call me back.'

'He's at home, sir. I'll ring him. I don't think I'll have much trouble over the other call.'

The voice faded, and Alleyn caught only the end of the sentence
. . . 'a cobber of mine . . . all the back numbers . . . quick as I can
make it.'

'Three minutes, Mr Losse,' said the operator. 'Will I extend the call?'

'Yes – No! All right, Wetherbridge. Splendid. I'll wait.'

'Working?' demanded a new voice.

'Like a black,' said Alleyn crossly, and hung up.

He found Fabian sitting on the bottom step of the stairs, a cigarette in his mouth. He hummed a dreary little air to himself.

'Get through?' he asked.

'They're going to call me back.'

'If you're very very lucky. It'll be some considerable time, at the
best, if I know Toll. I'm going up to the workroom. Would you care
to join me? You can hear the telephone from there.'

'Right.' Alleyn felt in his breast pocket. 'Damn!' he said.

'What's up?'

'My cigarette case.'

'Did you leave it in the drawing-room?'

'I don't think so.' He returned to the drawing-room. Its four occu-
pants who seemed to be about to go to bed, broke off what appeared
to be a lively discussion and watched him. The case was not there.
Douglas hunted about politely, and Mrs Aceworthy clucked. While
they were at this employment there was a tap on the door and Cliff
came in with a rolled periodical in his hand.

'Yes?' said Douglas.

'Dad asked me to bring this in,' said Cliff. 'It came up with our
mail by mistake. He says he's sorry.'

'Thank you, Cliff,' they murmured. He shuffled his feet and said
awkwardly, 'Goodnight, then.'

'Goodnight, Cliff,' they said, and he went out.

'Oh Lord!' Alleyn said. 'I've remembered. I left it in the annexe.
I'll run up there and fetch it.'

He saw Terence Lynne's hands check at their work.

'Shall I dodge up and get it?' Douglas offered.

'Not a bit of it, thanks, Grace. I'll do my own tedious job. I'm sorry
to have disturbed you. I'll get a coat and run up there.'

He returned to the hall. Cliff was in the passage leading to the
kitchen. Fabian had gone. Alleyn ran upstairs. A flashlight bobbed in

the long passage and came to rest on the workroom door. Fabian's hand reached out to the lock. 'Hi!' Alleyn called down the passage, 'you had it.' The light shone in his eyes.

'What?'

'My cigarette case. You took it away from the unspeakable Albert.'

'Oh, help! I put it on the piano. It'll be all right.'

'I think I'll get it. It's rather special. Troy – my wife – gave it to me.'

'I'll get it,' Fabian said.

'No, you're going to work. It won't take me a moment.'

He got his overcoat from his room. When he came out he found Fabian hovering uncertainly on the landing. 'Look here,' he said, 'you'd better let me – I mean – '

The telephone in the study gave two long rings. 'There's your call,' Fabian said. 'Away with you. Lend me your coat, will you, it's perishing cold.'

Alleyn threw his coat to him and ran downstairs. As he shut the study door he heard the rest of the party come out of the drawing-room. A moment later the front door banged.

The telephone repeated its double ring.

'There you are, Mr Losse,' said the operator. 'We've kept open for you. They're waiting.'

It was PC Wetherbridge. 'Message from the Sub-Inspector, sir. He's left by car and ought to make it in four hours.'

'Gemini!'

'I beg pardon, Mr Alleyn?'

'Great work, Wetherbridge. Hope I haven't cried Wolf.'

'I don't get you too clear, sir. We've done that little job for you. I've got it noted down here. There are three likely stations.'

'Good for you,' said Alleyn warmly.

'Do you want to write the programmes out, Mr Alleyn?'

'No, no. Just read them to me.'

Wetherbridge cleared his throat and began: 'Starting at 7.30, sir, and continuing till nine.' His voice droned on through a list of items. '. . . Syd Bando and The Rhythm Kids . . . I got a Big Pink Momma . . . Garden Notes and Queries . . . Racing Commentary . . . News Summary . . . Half an Hour with the Jitterbugs . . . Anything there, Mr Alleyn?'

'Nothing like it so far, but carry on. We're looking for something a bit highbrow, Wetherbridge.'

'Old Melodies Made New?'

'Not quite. Carry on.'

'There's only one other station that's likely to come through clearly, up where you are.'

Alleyn thought: 'I hope to God we've drawn a blank.'

'Here we go, sir. 7.30, Twenty-first instalment of: "The Vampire". 7.45, Reading from Old Favourites. 8.5, An Hour with the Masters.'

Alleyn's hand tightened on the receiver. 'Yes?' he said, 'any details?'

'There's a lot of stuff in small print. Wait a jiffy, sir, if you don't mind. I'm putting on my glasses.' Alleyn waited. 'Here we are,' said Wetherbridge, and two hundred miles away a paper crackled. '8.25,' said Wetherbridge, 'Polonaise by Chopping but there's a lot more. Back,' said Wetherbridge uncertainly, 'or would it be Bark? The initials are J.S. It's a pianna solo.'

'Go on, please.'

'The Art of Fewje,' said Wetherbridge. 'I'd better spell that, Mr Alleyn. F for Freddy, U for Uncle, G for George, U for Uncle, E for Edward. Any good?'

'Yes.'

'It seems to have knocked off at 8.57,'

'Yes.'

'Last on the list,' said Wetherbridge. 'Will that be the article we're looking for, sir?'

'I'm afraid so,' said Alleyn.

III

After they'd rung off he sat on for a minute or two, whistling dolefully. His hand went automatically to the pocket where he kept his cigarette case. It was quite ten minutes since Fabian went out. Perhaps he was waiting in the hall.

But the hall was empty and very still. An oil lamp, turned low, burnt on the table. Alleyn saw that only two candles remained from the nightly muster of six. The drawing-room party had evidently gone to bed. Fabian must be upstairs. Using his torch, Alleyn went quietly up to the landing. Light showed under the doors of the girls' rooms and, farther down the passage, under Douglas's. There was none under Fabian's door. Alleyn moved softly down the passage to the workroom. No light in there. He waited, listening, and then moved back towards the landing. A board creaked under his feet.

'Hallo!' called Douglas. 'That you, Fab?'

'It's me,' said Alleyn quietly.

Douglas's door opened and he looked out. 'Well, I wondered who it was,' he said, eyeing Alleyn dubiously. 'I mean it seemed funny.'

'Another night prowler? Up to no good?'

'Well, I must say you sounded a bit stealthy. Anything you want, sir?'

'No,' said Alleyn. 'Just sleuthing. Go to bed.'

Douglas grinned and withdrew his head. 'Enjoy yourself,' Alleyn heard him say cheekily, and the door was shut.

Perhaps Fabian had left the cigarette case in his room and was already asleep. Odd, though, that he didn't wait.

There was no cigarette case in his room. 'Blast!' Alleyn muttered. 'He can't find it! The miserable Albert's pinched it. Blast!'

He crept downstairs again. A faint glimmer of light showed at the end of the hall. A door into the kitchen passage was open. He went through it, and met Markins in the silver pantry, candle in hand.

'Just locking up, sir,' said Markins. 'Were you wanting me?'

'I'm looking for Mr Losse.'

'Wasn't he up by the men's quarters with you, Mr Alleyn? About ten minutes ago.'

'He was probably there, but I wasn't.'

'That's funny,' Markins said, staring at him. 'I'd 'ave sworn it was you.'

'He was wearing my coat.'

'Is that the case? Who was the other gentleman, then?'

'Not me. What other gentleman?'

Markins set his candle down and shut the door. 'I was going up to the manager's cottage,' he said. 'I wanted to have a word with Mr Johns. Cliff had just gone back there. The cottage is up the hill at the back of the annexe, you know. When I came out of the back door here, I thought I saw you on the main track to the men's quarters, going towards the annexe. I thought I'd cut across and see you, and I started up the path from the back door. You lose sight of the other track for a bit. I heard you call out something, and I sung out, "Hallo, sir?" Then I heard you run downhill. When I came up to where you can see the track, you weren't in sight.'

Alleyn took the tip of his nose between thumb and forefinger. 'Not me,' he said. 'Mr Losse.'

'It sounded like you, sir. I thought you must have been talking to someone else.'

'And apparently, on the telephone, I sounded like Mr Losse. Damn it then,' Alleyn said irritably, 'where is he? If he ran downhill, why didn't he come in? And who was he singing out to? Young Cliff?'

'No, sir. Cliff was home by then. When I got up to the cottage, I asked him if he'd seen you, and he said he hadn't seen anybody. What was Mr Losse doing, sir?'

Alleyn told him. 'Come on,' he said. 'I don't like this. Let's hunt him out.'

'There's half a dozen things he might be doing, Mr Alleyn.'

'What sort of things? We'll go through your kitchen, Markins. Lead the way. I've got a torch.'

'Well,' said Markins, moving off, 'letting water out of the truck radiator. It's going to be a hard frost.'

'Would he run downhill to do that?'

'Well, no. The garage is up by the sheds.'

'What was it he called out?' asked Alleyn, following Markins into a dark warm kitchen that smelt of pine wood and fat.

'I couldn't say, really. He just shouted. He sounded surprised. Just a moment, if you please, Mr Alleyn. I've bolted the door. Ever since that young Cliff played up with the whisky, I've shut up careful.'

'Cliff didn't play up. It was the unspeakable Albie.'

'I caught him with the bottle in his hand!'

'He was putting it back.'

'He never was!' Markins cried out, with almost ladylike incredulity.

'Albie's admitted it. The boy was saving his disgusting face for him.'

'Then why the hell couldn't he say so?' Markins demanded in a high voice. 'I'd better stick to valeting and cut out the special stuff,' he added disgustedly. 'I can't pick petty larceny when it's under my nose. Come on, sir.'

It was pitch dark outside and bitingly cold. Markins, using Alleyn's torch, led the way up a steep path. Grass was crisp under their feet and frost scented the air. Ice seemed to move against their faces as they climbed. The sky was clear and full of winking stars.

'Where are we going, Mr Alleyn?'

'To the annexe.'

'This path comes out above the buildings, but we can cut across to the track. It's not too rough, but it's steepish.'

Clods of earth broke icily under Alleyn's shoes. He and Markins skated and slithered. 'Kick your heels in,' Markins said. A sense of urgency, illogically insistent, plagued Alleyn. 'Where's this cursed track?' he grunted.

They mounted a rise and a dim rectangular blackness showed against a hillside that must be white with frost. 'Here we are,' Markins said. "There's a wire fence, sir. No barbs.' The wire clanged as they climbed through. The flashlight played on frozen cart tracks.

'There's no light in the annexe,' Alleyn said.

'Shall we call out, sir?'

'No. If he was about he'd have heard us. We don't want the men roused up. Is this where the branch track goes down to the shearing-shed? Yes, there it goes. Downhill. *Wait a moment.*"

Markins turned quickly, flashing his light on Alleyn, who stood facing towards the shearing-shed. 'Give me the torch, Markins, will you?'

He reached out his hand, took the torch, and flashed it down the branch track. Points of frost glittered like tinsel. The circle of light moved on and came to rest on a sprawling mound.

'My God!' Markins said loudly. 'What's he bin and done to 'imself?'

'Keep off the track.' Alleyn stepped on the frozen turf beside it and moved quickly down towards the wool-shed. The torchlight now showed him the grey shepherd's plaid of his own overcoat with Fabian's legs, spreadeagled, sticking out from under the skirts, Fabian's head, rumpled and pressed face downwards in a frozen rut, and his arms stretched out beyond it as if they had been raised to shield it as he fell.

Alleyn knelt beside him, giving the torch to Markins.

Fabian's hair grew thick over the base of his head, which, like the nape of his thin and delicately grooved neck, looked boyish and vulnerable. Alleyn parted the hair delicately.

Behind him, holding the torch very steadily, Markins whispered a thin stream of blasphemy.

'A downward blow,' said Alleyn. He thrust one hand swiftly under the hidden face, raised the head, and with the other hand, like a macabre conjurer, pulled out of Fabian's mouth a gaily coloured silk handkerchief.

IV

'He's not – ?'

'No, no, of course not.' Alleyn's hands were busy. 'But we must get him out of this damnable cold. It's not more than twelve yards to the wool-shed. There are no other injuries, I fancy. Think we can do it? We mustn't go falling about with him.'

'OK, OK.'

'Steady then. I'll get that sacking door opened first.'

When they lifted him, Fabian's breathing was thick and stertorous. Little jets of vapour came from his mouth. When they reached the open door and Alleyn lifted his shoulders to the level of the raised floor, he groaned deeply.

'Gently, gently,' Alleyn said. 'That's the way, Markins. Good. I've got his head. Slide him in. The floor's like glass. Now, drop the door and I'll get some of those bales.'

The light darted about the wool-shed, on the press, the packed bales, and the heap of empty ones. They bedded Fabian down in strong-smelling sacking.

'Now the hurricane lamp and that candle. I've a notion,' said Alleyn grimly, as he hunted for them, 'that they'll be in order this time. Wrap his feet up, won't you?'

'This place is as cold as a morgue,' Markins complained. 'Not meaning anything unpleasant by the comparison.'

The lantern and home-made candlestick were in their places on the wall. Alleyn took them down, lit them, and brought them over to Fabian. Markins built a stack of bales over him and slid a folded sack under his head.

'He's not losing blood,' he said. 'What about his breathing, Mr Alleyn?'

'All right, I think. The handkerchief, my handkerchief it is, was only a preliminary measure, I imagine. You saved his life, Markins.'

'I did?'

'I hope so. If you hadn't called out – perhaps not, though. Perhaps when this expert fetched the bag in here and had a look at – It all depends on whether Losse recognized his assailant.'

'By God, I hope he did, Mr Alleyn.'

'And, by God, I'm afraid he didn't.'

Alleyn pushed his hand under the bales and groped for Fabian's wrist. 'His pulse seems not too bad,' he said presently, and a moment later, 'He'd been to the annexe.'

'How do you get that, sir?'

Alleyn drew out his hand and held up a flat cigarette case. 'Mine. He went up there to fetch it. It was in the pocket.'

'What's our next move?'

Alleyn stared at Fabian's face. The eyes were not quite closed. Fabian knitted his brows. His lips moved as if to articulate, but no sound came from them. 'Yes,' Alleyn muttered, 'what's best to do?'

'Fetch the Captain?'

'If I was sure he'd be all right, we'd fetch nobody. But we can't be sure of that. We can't risk it. No, don't rouse them yet, down at the house. Go first of all to the men's hut and check their numbers. What they are doing and how long they've been at it. Be quick about this. They'll probably be in bed. Then go on up to the cottage and tell them there's been an accident. No more than that. Ask them for hot-water bottles and blankets, and something that will do as a stretcher. Ask Mr Johns – and Cliff – to come here. Then use their telephone and try to get through somehow to Mr Losse's doctor for instructions.'

'The bureau won't open till the morning, Mr Alleyn.'

'Damn. Then we'll have to use our common sense. Away you go, Markins. And' – Alleyn raised his head and looked at Markins – 'just say an accident. I want Cliff to come with his father and with you. And if he's there when you go in, watch him.'

Markins slipped out of the door.

Alleyn waited in a silence that seemed to be compounded of extreme cold and of the smells of the wool-shed. He sat on his heels and watched Fabian, whose head, emerging like a kernel from its husk of sacking, lay in a pool of yellow light. Portentously he frowned and moved his lips. Sometimes he would turn his head and then he would make a little prosaic grunting sound. Alleyn took a clean handkerchief from his pocket and slid it under the base of Fabian's skull. The frosty air outside moved and a soughing crept among the rafters. Alleyn turned his torch on the press. It was empty, but near it were ranged bales packed with the day's crutchings. 'Was there to be a complete repetition?' he wondered. 'Was one of them to be unpacked, and was I to take Florence Rubrick's journey down-country tomorrow?' He looked at Fabian. 'Or rather you,' he added, 'if you'd been so inconsiderate as to die?' Fabian turned his head. The swelling under his dark thatch was now visible. Very delicately, Alleyn parted and drew back the strands of hair. He shone his torch light on a thick indented mark behind the swelling. He rose and hunted along the pens. Near the door, in its accustomed niche, was the branding iron, a bar with the Mount Moon brand raised on its base. Alleyn squatted down and looked closely at it. He had a second handkerchief in his pocket, and he wrapped it round the shaft of the iron before carrying it over to Fabian.

'I think so,' he said, looking from the iron to Fabian's scalp. He shifted the lantern along the floor and, groping under the bales that covered Fabian, pulled out the skirts of his own overcoat, first on one side, then on the other. On the left-hand skirt he found a kind of scar, a longish mark with the rough tweed puckered about it. He took out his pocket lens. The surface of the tweed was burred and stained brown.

'And where the devil,' said Alleyn, addressing the branding iron, 'am I going to stow you away?'

Still muffling his hand, he carried the iron farther along the shed, spread his handkerchief over it and dropped a sack across the whole. He stood in the dark, looking absently at the pool of light round Fabian's head. It seemed a long way away, an isolated island, without animation, in a sea of dark. Alleyn's gaze turned from it and wandered among the shadows, seeing, not them, but the fork in the track, where it branched off to the wool-shed, the frosty bank that overhung it, the scrubby bush that cast so black a shadow behind it.

'That's funny,' someone said loudly.

Alleyn's skin jumped galvanically. He stood motionless, waiting.

'And what the devil are you up to? Running like a scalded cat.'

There was a movement inside the island of yellow light. The heap of bales shifted.

'Hurry! Hurry!' An arm was flung up. 'All right when I'm up. Sleep,' said the voice, dragging on the word. 'To die. To sleep. Go on, blast you. Up. Oh, dear. Oh, God,' it whispered very drearily. 'So *bloody* tired.'

Alleyn began to move quietly towards Fabian.

'You would butt in,' Fabian chuckled. 'You won't be popular.' Alleyn stopped. 'Funny old thing,' said Fabian affectionately. 'Must have found the damned object. Hal-lo,' he added a moment later and then with disgust and astonishment, 'Terry! Oh, Lord! I do wish I hadn't got up here. Silly old man.'

He sat up. Alleyn moved quickly to him and knelt down.

'It's all right,' he said, 'you can go to sleep now, you know.'

'Yes, but why run like that? Something must have happened up there.'

'Up where?'

'Well, you heard what she said. You will be unpopular. Where was it?'

'In the lavender walk,' Alleyn said. Fabian's eyes were open, staring past Alleyn under scowling brows.

'Who found it?'

'Uncle Arthur.'

'Well, you must be pretty fit. I couldn't . . . I'm so hellish tired. I swear I'll drop off into the sea. It's that damned piano. If only he'd shut up. Excelsibloodyor! Up!'

He fought Alleyn off, his eyes on the wall with its cross beams. 'Come on, chaps,' he said. 'It's easy. I'll give you a lead.'

Alleyn tried to quieten him, but he became so frenzied that to hold him Alleyn himself would have been obliged to use violence, and indeed, stood in some danger of being knocked out.

'I'm trying to help you, you goat,' Alleyn grumbled. 'Think I don't know a Jerry when I get one,' Fabian panted. 'Not yet, Fritzy darling. I'm for Home.' He lashed out, caught Alleyn on the jaw, flung himself forward and, clawing at the beams on the wall, tried to climb it. Alleyn wrapped his arms round his knees. Without warning, Fabian collapsed. They fell together on the floor, Fabian uppermost.

'Thank God,' Alleyn thought, 'his head didn't get another rap,' and crawled out. Fabian lay still, breathing heavily. Alleyn, himself rather groggy, began to cover him up again.

'Oh, Ursy, you celestial imbecile,' Fabian said miserably and, after a moment, sighed deeply and, turning on his side, fell sound asleep.

'If this is amnesia,' Alleyn muttered, nursing his jaw, 'yet, there's method in it.'

He went to the doorway and, pulling aside the sacking, looked out into the cold. His head buzzed. 'Damn the fellow,' he thought irritably and then: 'Not altogether, though. Do they hark back to a former bout? And is it evidence? Up the side of a ship. Up a gate. Up a companion way. But up *what* in the vegetable garden?' He stared down at the dark bulk of the house. Beyond it, out to the right, a giant lombardy poplar made a spearlike pattern against the stars. 'That can't be far from the marrow patch,' Alleyn thought. 'He said his pants were dirty. He was under a tree. Oh, Lord, what's the good of a pair of pants that were dirty over a year ago?'

The thrumming in his head cleared. He shivered violently. 'I'll catch the thick end of a cold before the night's out,' he muttered, and the next second had shrunk back into the shadow of the doorway.

The night was so quiet that the voice of the Moon river, boiling out of its gorge beyond a shoulder of the mountain and sweeping south to a lake out on the plateau, moved like a vague rumour behind the silence and was felt in the ear drums rather than heard. Alleyn had been aware of it once or twice that night, and he heard it now as he listened for the nearer sound that had caught his attention. Down the main track it had been, a tiny rustle, a slipping noise, followed by a faint thud. He remembered how he and Markins had skidded and fallen on the icy ground. He waited and heard a faint

metallic clang. 'That's the fence,' he thought. 'A moment, and whoever it is will come up the track. Now what?'

At that moment, above the men's quarters, there was a rattle of
chains. The Mount Moon dogs, plunging by their kennels, broke into
clamorous barking. A man's voice cursed them: 'Lie down, Jock! By
God, I'll warm your hide!' The chains rattled and a faint metallic
echo, the wire fence down the track twanged again. A light came
bobbing round the annexe.

'Hell and damnation!' said Alleyn violently. 'Am I never to get a
clear run!'

CHAPTER 10

Night Piece

Tommy Johns and his son Cliff followed Markins through the sacking door and stood blinking in the lamplight. Tommy nodded morosely at Alleyn. 'What's the trouble?' he said.

'There it is.'

He moved forward. Cliff said loudly: 'It's Fabian.'

'Yes,' said Alleyn.

'What's happened to him?' He turned on Markins. 'Why didn't you say it was Fabian? What's wrong with you?'

'Orders,' said Markins, and Tommy Johns looked sharply at Alleyn.

'Whose orders?' Cliff demanded. 'Has he had another of his queer turns?' His voice rose shrilly. 'Is he dead?'

'No,' said Alleyn. Cliff strode forward and knelt by Fabian.

'You keep clear of this,' said his father.

'I want to know what's happened to him. I want to know if he's been hurt.'

'He's been hit over the head,' said Alleyn, 'with the branding iron.'

Cliff cried out incoherently and his father put his hand on his shoulder.

'I don't want to say so when he's conscious again,' Alleyn went on. 'Remember that please, it's important. He's had a nasty shock and for the moment he's to be left to his own interpretation on it. Tell nobody.'

'The branding iron,' said Tommy Johns. 'Is that so?' He looked across to the corner where the iron was usually kept. Cliff said quickly, 'it wasn't there. It was left over by the press.'

'Where is it now?' Johns demanded.

'Safely stowed,' said Alleyn.

'Who done it?' In reply to this classic, Alleyn merely shook his head.

'I checked up on the men, sir,' said Markins. 'They're all in their bunks. Ben Wilson was awake and says nobody's gone or come in for over an hour. Albie's dead to the world. Soaked.'

'Right. Have you got a stretcher?'

'Yes, sir,' said Markins. 'It's the one Mrs R had for her first-aid classes.'

'Have you been down to the house?' Alleyn asked sharply.

'No. It was stowed away up above. Come on, Tommy.'

They had dumped a pile of grey blankets inside the door. Markins brought in the stretcher. The three men covered it, moved Fabian on to it, and laid the remaining blankets over him. Cliff, working the palms of his hands together, looked on unhappily.

'What about this damned icy track,' Alleyn muttered. 'You've got nails in your boots, Johns. So's the boy. Markins and I are smooth-soled.'

'It's not so bad on the track, sir,' said Markins.

'Did you come up the kitchen path?' Tommy Johns demanded.

'Ready?' asked Alleyn before Markins could reply.

They took their places at the corners of the stretcher. Fabian opened his eyes and looked at Cliff.

'Hallo,' he said clearly. 'The Infant Phenomenon.'

'That's me,' said Cliff unevenly. 'You'll be all right, Mr Losse.'

'Oh Lord,' Fabian whispered, 'have I been at it again?'

'You've taken a bit of a toss,' said Alleyn. 'We'll get you into bed in a minute.'

'My head.'

'I know. Nasty crack you got. Ready?'

'I can walk,' Fabian protested. 'What's all this nonsense? I've always walked before.'

'You're riding this time, damn your eyes,' said Alleyn cheerfully. 'Up we go, chaps. Keep on the grass if you can.'

'Easier going on the track,' Tommy Johns protested.

'Nevertheless, we'll try the grass. On the left. Keep to the left.'

And as they crept along, flashing their torches, he thought, 'If only I could have been sure he'd be all right for a bit in the wool-shed. A nice set of prints there'll be with this frost and here we go, all over Tom Tiddler's ground tramping out gold and silver.'

It was less slippery on the verge than it had been on the steep hill-side, and when they reached the main track the going was still easier. The french windows into the drawing-room were unlocked and they took Fabian in that way, letting the stretcher down on the floor while Markins lit the lamps. Fabian was so quiet that Alleyn waited anxiously to see him, wondering if he had fainted. But when the lamplight shone on his face his eyes were open and he was frowning.

'All right?' Alleyn asked gently. Fabian turned his head aside and muttered, 'Oh, yes. Yes.'

'I'll go upstairs and tell Grace what you've been up to. Markins, you might get a kettle to boil. You others wait, will you?'

He ran upstairs to be confronted on the landing by Ursula in her dressing-gown, holding a candle above her head and peering into the well.

'What's happened?' she said.

'A bit of an accident. Your young man's given himself a crack on the head, but he's doing nicely.'

'Fabian?' Her eyes widened. 'Where is he?'

'Now, don't go haring off, there's a good child. He's in the drawing-room and we're putting him to bed. Before you go down to him, put a couple of hot-water bottles in his bed and repeat to yourself some appropriate tune from your first-aid manual. He'll do, I fancy.'

They were standing outside Terence Lynne's door and now it opened. She too came out with a candle. She looked very sleek and pale in her ruby silk dressing-gown.

'Fabian's hurt,' said Ursula, and darted back into her own room.

Miss Lynne had left her door open. Alleyn could see where a second candle burnt on her bedside-table above an open book, a fat notebook it seemed to be, its pages covered in a fine script. She followed the direction of his gaze, and with a swift movement shut her door. Ursula returned with a hot-water bag and hurried down the passage to Fabian's room.

Miss Lynne examined Alleyn by the light of her own candle.

'You've been fighting,' she said.

He touched his jaw. 'I ran into something in the shed.'

'It's bleeding.'

'So it is. Can you give me a bit of cotton-wool or something?'

She hesitated. 'Wait here a moment,' she said and slipped through the door, shutting it behind her.

Alleyn tapped and entered. She was beside her dressing-table, but in a flash had moved to the bed and shut the book. 'I asked you to wait,' she said.

'I'm extremely sorry. Would you lend your hot bottle? Take it along to his room, would you? Ah, there's the cotton-wool. Thanks so much.'

He took it from her and turned to her glass. As he dabbed the wool on his jaw he watched her reflection. Her back was towards him. She stooped over the bed. When she moved aside, the bed-clothes had been pulled up and the book was no longer on the table.

'Here's the bottle,' she said, holding it out.

'Will you be an angel and take it yourself? I'm just fixing this blasted cut.'

'Mr Alleyn,' she said loudly, and he turned to face her. 'I'd rather you staunched your wounds in your own room,' said Miss Lynne.

'Please forgive me, I was trying to save my collar. Of course.'

He went to the door. 'Terry!' Ursula called quietly down the passage.

'I'm off,' said Alleyn. He crossed the landing to his own room. 'Terry!' Ursula called again. 'Yes, coming,' said Miss Lynne, and carrying the candle and her hot-water bottle she moved swiftly down the passage, observed by Alleyn through the crack of his own door.

'Every blasted move in the game goes wrong,' he thought and darted back to her room.

The book, a stoutly-bound squat affair, had been thrust well down between the sheets. It fell open in his hands and he read a single long sentence.

'February 1st, 1942.

'Since I am now assured of her affection towards me I must con-fess that the constant unrest of this house and (if I am to be honest in these pages, of Florence herself) under which I have for so long been complaisant, is now quite intolerable to me.'

Alleyn hesitated for a moment. A card folder slipped from between the pages. He opened it and saw the photograph of a man with veiled eyes, painfully compressed lips, and deep grooves running from his nostrils to beyond the corners of his mouth. The initials AR were written at the bottom in the same fine strokes that characterized the script in the book.

'So that was Arthur Rubrick,' Alleyn thought, and returned the photograph and the diary to their hiding-place.

II

Before he left Miss Lynne's room, Alleyn took an extremely rapid look at her shoes. All except one pair were perfectly neat and clean. Her gardening brogues, brushed, but unpolished, were dry. He closed the door behind him as the voices of the two girls sounded in the passage. He found them at the head of the stairs in conference with Mrs Aceworthy, a formidable figure in mottled flannel, which she drew unhappily about her when she saw Alleyn. He persuaded her, with some difficulty, to return to her room.

'I am going to Fabian,' said Ursula. 'How are we going to carry him upstairs?'

'I think he will be able to walk up,' Alleyn said. 'Take him gently. I'll get Grace to help put him to bed. Is he awake, do you know?'

'Not Douglas,' said Terence Lynne. 'He sleeps like a log.'

Ursula said, 'Has Fabian had another black-out, Mr Alleyn?'

'I think so. Wait for me before you bring him.'

'Damn!' said Ursula, 'now, of course, he'll think he can't marry me. Come on, Terry.'

Terence went; not, Alleyn thought, over willingly.

He knocked on Douglas Grace's door and receiving no answer walked in and flashed his torch on a tousled head.

'Grace!'

'Wha-aa?' The clothes were flung back with a convulsive jerk and Douglas stared at him. 'What d'you want to make me jump like that for?' he asked angrily, and then blinked. 'Sorry, sir. I was back at an advanced gun-post. What's up now?'

'Losse has had another black-out.'

Douglas gazed at Alleyn with his familiar air of affronted incredulity. 'He will now,' Alleyn thought crossly, 'repeat the last word I have uttered whenever I pause to draw breath.'

'Black-out,' said Douglas faithfully. 'Oh, hell! How? When? Where?'

'Oh, near the annexe. Half an hour ago. He went up there to collect my cigarette case.'

'I remember that,' cried Douglas triumphantly. 'Is he still all out? Poor old Fab.'

'He's conscious again but he's had a nasty crack on the head. Come and help me get him upstairs, will you?'

'Get him upstairs?' Douglas repeated, looking very startled. He reached for his dressing-gown. 'I say,' he said. 'This is pretty tough luck, isn't it? I mean, what he said about Ursy and him?'

'Yes.'

'Half an hour ago,' said Douglas, thrusting his feet into his slippers. 'That must have been just after we came up. I went out to the side lawn to have a look at the weather. He must have been up there then, good Lord.'

'Did you hear anything?'

Douglas gaped at him with his mouth open. 'I heard the river,' he said. 'That means there's a southerly hanging round. Sure sign. You wouldn't know.'

'No. Did you hear anything else?'

'Hear anything? What sort of thing?'

'Voices or footsteps.'

'Voices? Was he talking? Footsteps?'

'Let it pass,' said Alleyn. 'Come on.'

They went down to the drawing-room.

Fabian was lying on the sofa with Ursula on a low stool beside him. Tommy Johns and Cliff stood awkwardly by the french windows looking at their boots. Markins, with precisely the correct shade of deferential concern, was setting out a tea-tray with drinks. Terence Lynne stood composedly before the fire, which had been mended and flickered its light richly in the folds of her crimson gown.

'Here, I say,' said Douglas. 'This is no good, Fab. Damn bad luck.'

'Extremely tiresome,' Fabian murmured, looking at Ursula. He was still covered by grey blankets and Ursula had slid her hand beneath them. 'Give the stretcher-bearers a drink, Douglas. They must need it.'

'You mustn't,' said Ursula.

'See section four. Alcohol after cerebral injuries, abstain from.'

Markins moved away with decorum. 'You must have a drink, Markins,' said Fabian weakly. Douglas looked scandalized.

'Thank you very much, sir,' said Markins primly.

'You'll have whisky, won't you, Tommy? Cliff?'

'I don't mind,' said Tommy Johns. 'The boy won't take it, thank you.'

'He looks as if he wants it,' said Fabian, and indeed Cliff was very white.

'He doesn't take whisky, thank you,' said his father, with uncomfortable emphasis.

'I think you ought to get to bed, Fab,' fussed Douglas. 'Don't you agree, Mr Alleyn?'

'We'll drink to your recovery when we've finished the job,' Alleyn said.

'I'm not going to be carried upstairs and don't you think it.'

'Well, then, you shall walk, and Grace and I will see you up.'

'OK,' said Douglas amiably.

'One's enough,' Fabian said peevishly. 'I tell you, I'm all right. You give these poor swine a drink, Douglas. Mr Alleyn started the rescue squad, didn't he? He may like to finish the job.'

He sat up and grimaced. He was very white and his hands trembled.

'Please, Fab, go slow,' said Ursula. 'I'll come and see you.'

'Come on,' Fabian said to Alleyn. He grinned at Ursula. 'Thank you, darling,' he said. 'I'd like you to come, but not just yet, please.'

When they were outside in the hall, Fabian took Alleyn's arm. 'Sorry to appear churlish,' he said. 'I wanted to talk to you. God, I do feel sick.'

Alleyn got him to bed. He was very docile. Remembering Markins' story of the medicine cupboard in the bathroom, Alleyn raided it and found dressings. He clipped away the thick hair. The wound, a depression, swollen at the margin and broken only at the top, was seen to be clearly defined. He cleaned it and was about to put on a dressing when Fabian, who was lying face downwards on his pillow, said, 'I didn't get that by falling, did I? Some expert's had a crack at me, hasn't he?'

'What makes you think so?' said Alleyn, pausing with the lint in his fingers.

'After a fashion, I can remember. I was on my feet when I got it. Where the main track branches off to the wool-shed. It felt just like the bump I got at Dunkirk, only, thank the Lord, it's not on the same spot. I think I called out. You needn't bother to deny it. Somebody cracked me.'

'Any more ideas?'

'It was where that bank with a bit of scrub on it overhangs the track. I was coming back from the annexe. There's always water or ice lying about on the far side so I walked close into the bank. Whoever it was must have been lying up there, waiting. But why? Why me?'

Alleyn dropped the lint over the wound and took up a length of strapping. 'You were wearing my coat,' he said.

'Stay me with flagons!' Fabian whispered. 'So I was.' And he was silent while Alleyn finished his dressing. He was comfortable enough lying on his side with a thick pad of cotton-wool under his head. Alleyn tidied his room and when he turned back to the bed Fabian was already dozing. He slipped out.

Before going downstairs he visited the other bedrooms. There were no damp shoes in any of them. Douglas's and Fabian's working boots were evidently kept downstairs. 'But it was something quieter than working boots,' Alleyn muttered, and returned to the drawing-room.

He found the two Johns on the point of departure and Markins about to remove the tray. Douglas, lying back in an armchair with his feet in the hearth and a pipe in his mouth, glanced up with evident relief. Terence Lynne had unearthed her inevitable knitting and, erect on the sofa, her feet to the tire, flashed her needles composedly. Ursula, who was speaking to Tommy Johns, went quickly to Alleyn.

'Is he all right? May I go up?'

'He's comfortably asleep. I think it will be best to leave him. You may listen at his door presently.'

'We'll be going,' said Tommy Johns. 'Goodnight, all.'

'Just a moment,' said Alleyn.

'Hallo!' Douglas looked up quickly. 'What's up now?' And before Alleyn could answer, he added sharply, 'He is all right, isn't he? I mean, shall I go down-country for a doctor? I could get back inside four hours if I stepped on it. We don't want to take any risks with an injury to the head.'

'No,' Alleyn agreed, 'we don't. If you feel you want to do something of the sort, of course you may, but I fancy he'll do very well. I'm sure his skull is not injured. It seems to have been a glancing blow.'

'A blow?' Terence Lynne's voice struck harshly. Her mouth was open. The muscle of the upper lip was contracted, showing her teeth in the parody of a smile.

'But didn't he fall on his head?' Douglas shouted.

'He fell on his face because he'd been struck on the back of the skull.'

'D'you mean someone attacked him?'

'I do.'

'Good God,' Douglas whispered.

Ursula stood before Alleyn, her hands jammed down in the pockets of her dressing-gown. Her voice shook, but she held her chin up and looked squarely at him. 'Does that mean somebody wanted to kill Fabian?' she said.

'It was a dangerous assault,' Alleyn said.

'But – ' She moved quickly to the door. 'I'm going to him,' she said. 'He mustn't be left alone.'

'Please stay here, Miss Harme. The house is locked up and I have the key of his door in my pocket. You see,' Alleyn said, 'we are all in here, so he is quite safe.'

It was at this point that Terence Lynne, winding her hands in her scarlet knitting, broke into a fit of screaming hysteria.

III

Police officers are not unfamiliar with hysteria. Alleyn dealt crisply with Miss Lynne. While Tommy Johns and Douglas turned their backs, Cliff looked sick, and Markins interested; Ursula, with considerable aplomb, offered to fetch a jug of cold water and pour it over the patient. This suggestion, combined with Alleyn's less drastic treatment, had its effect. Miss Lynne grew quieter, rose, and walking to the far end of the room, seemed to fight down savagely her own incontinence.

'Really, Terry!' Ursula said, 'you of all people!'

'Shut up, Ursy,' said Douglas.

'Well, after all, Douglas darling, he's my young man.'

Douglas glared at her and, after a moment's hesitation, went to Terence Lynne and spoke to her in a low voice. Alleyn heard her say, 'No! Please leave me alone. I'm all right. Please go away.' He returned, looking discomforted and portentous.

'I think Terence should be let off,' he said to Alleyn.

'I'm extremely sorry,' Alleyn returned, 'but I'm afraid that's impossible.' He moved to the fireplace and stood with his back to it, collecting their attention. It was an unpleasantly familiar moment and he was struck by the resemblance of all frightened people to each other. There was always a kind of blankness in their faces. They always watched him carefully, yet turned aside their gaze when he looked directly at them. There was always a tendency to draw together, to make a wary little mob of themselves, leaving him isolated.

He was isolated now, a tall figure, authoritative and watchful, unaware of himself, closely attentive to their self-consciousness.

'I'm afraid,' he said, 'that I can't let anybody off. I should tell you that at the moment it seems unlikely that this attack was made by one of the outside men. Each of you, therefore, will be well advised, in your own interest, to give an account of your movements since I left this room to go up to the annexe for my cigarette case.'

'I can't believe this is true,' said Ursula. 'You sound exactly like a detective. For the first time.'

'I'm afraid I must behave like one. Will you all sit down? Suppose we start with you, Captain Grace.'

'Me? I say, look here, sir . . .'

'What did you do when I left the room?'

'Yes, well, what did I do? I was sitting here reading the paper when you came in, wasn't I? Yes, well, you went out and I said, "D'you think I ought to go up with him," meaning you, "and help him look for his blasted case," and nobody answered, and I said, "Oh, well, how about a bit of shut-eye," and I wound up my watch and everybody pushed off. I went out on the side lawn here and had a squint at the sky. I always do that, last thing. Freshens you up. I think I heard you bang the back door.' Douglas paused and looked baffled. 'At least, I suppose it was really Fabian, wasn't it, because you say he went. Well, I mean he must have gone if you found him up there, mustn't he? Someone was moving up the track beyond the side fence. I thought it was probably one of the men. I called out, "Goodnight," but they didn't answer. Well, I just came in and the others had gone, so I put the screen in front of the fire, got my candle and went upstairs. I tapped on Terry's door and said goodnight. I had a bath and went to my room, and then I heard you snooping about the passage and I wondered what was up because I've been a bit jumpy about people in the passage ever since . . .' Here Douglas paused and glanced at Markins. 'However!' he said. 'I called out, "Is that you, Fab?" and you answered, you'll remember, and I went to bed.'

'Any witnesses?' asked Alleyn.

'Terence. I told you I tapped on her door.'

'Did you hear him?' Alleyn asked Ursula.

'Yes. I heard,' she said. 'I heard other people come upstairs, too, and move about after I went to bed, but I didn't take any particular notice. I heard the pipes gurgle. I went to sleep almost at once. I was awakened by the sound of voices and boots downstairs, and I sort of knew something was wrong and came out on the landing where I met you.'

'Did you all go up together? You and Miss Lynne and Mrs Aceworthy?'

'No, we straggled. The Acepot went first, and I know she had a bath because she was in it when I wanted to brush my teeth. I remember hearing the telephone give our ring just before I came out of this room and I was going to answer it when I heard Fabian speaking. At least, I thought it was Fabian. You see, I saw – I thought I saw you whisk out-of-doors.'

'You saw my overcoat whisk out.'

'Well,' said Ursula, 'it's very dark in the hall.'

She looked fixedly at Alleyn. 'You swear he's all right?'

'He was perfectly comfortable and sound asleep when I left him and he's safe from any further assault. You can ring up a doctor when the bureau opens in the morning, indeed I should like to get a medical opinion myself, or – is there any one near the Pass on your party line?'

'Four miles,' said Douglas.

'If you're anxious, couldn't you get these people to drive over the Pass and ring up a doctor? I don't think it's necessary, but isn't it possible?'

'Yes, I suppose it is,' said Ursula. 'If I could just see him,' she added.

'Very well. When I've finished, you may go in with me, wake him up, and ask him if he's all right.'

'You can be rather a pig,' said Ursula, 'can't you?'

'This is a serious matter,' said Alleyn without emphasis.

She flushed delicately and he thought she was startled and bewildered by his disregard of her small attempt at lightness. 'I know it is,' she said.

'You heard me answer the telephone, didn't you, and thought I was Losse? You caught sight of him going out and mistook him for me. What did you do then?'

'I called out, "Goodnight" to Terry, lit my candle, and went upstairs. I undressed and when the Acepot came out of the bathroom I washed and brushed my teeth and went to bed.'

'Seeing nobody?'

'Only her – Mrs Aceworthy.'

'And you, Miss Lynne? You were after Miss Harme?'

She had moved forward and stood behind Ursula. Douglas was close beside her but she seemed to be unaware of him. When he slipped his hand under her arm she freed herself, but with a slight movement as if she loosed a sleeve that had caught on a piece of furniture. She answered Alleyn rapidly, looking straight before her, 'It was cold. Douglas had left the french window open. He was on the lawn. I said goodnight to him and asked him to put the screen in front of the fire. He called out that he would. I went into the hall and lit my candle. I heard a voice in the study and was not sure if it was yours or Fabian's. I went up to my room. Douglas came upstairs and tapped on my door. He said goodnight. I put away some things I had been mending and then undressed. I heard someone come out of the bathroom, it was Mrs Aceworthy's step. Ursula said something to her. I – I read for a minute or two and then I went to the bathroom and returned and got into bed.'

'Did you go to sleep?'

'Not at once.'

'You read, perhaps?'

'Yes. For a – yes, I read.'

'What was your book?'

'Really,' said Ursula impatiently, 'can it possibly matter?'

'It was some novel,' said Terence. 'I've forgotten the title. Some spy story, I think it is.'

'And you were still awake when I came upstairs and spoke to Miss Harme?'

'I was still awake.'

'Yes, your candles were alight. Were you still reading?'

'Yes,' she said, after a pause.

'The spy story must have had some merit,' Alleyn said with a smile. She ran her tongue over her lips.

'Did you hear any one other than Mrs Aceworthy and Miss Harme come upstairs?'

'Yes. More than one person. I thought I heard you speaking to Fabian or Douglas. Or it might have been Fabian speaking to Douglas. Your voices are alike.'

'Any one on the back stairs?'

'I couldn't hear from my room.'

'Did you use the back stairs at all, during this period, Markins?'

'No, sir,' said Markins woodenly.

'I'd like to hear what Markins was doing,' said Douglas suddenly.

'He has already given me an account of his movements,' Alleyn rejoined. 'He was on his way up the back path to the track, when he thought he saw me. Later he heard a voice which he mistook for mine. He continued on his way and met nobody. He visited the manager's cottage and returned. I met him. Together we explored the track and discovered Losse, lying unconscious on the branch track near the wool-shed.'

'So,' said Douglas, raising an extremely obvious eyebrow at Alleyn, 'Markins was almost on the spot at the critical time.' Alleyn heard Markins sigh windily. Tommy Johns said quickly: 'He was up at our place, Captain, and I talked to him. There's nothing funny about that.'

'Supposing we take you next, Mr Johns,' said Alleyn. 'Were you at home all the evening?'

'I went down to the ram paddock after tea – about half-past six, it was, and I looked in at the men's quarters on my way back. That lovely cook of theirs has made a job of it this time, Captain. Him and Albert are both packed up. Singing hymns and heading for the willies.'

'Tcha!' said Douglas.

'And then?' Alleyn asked.

'I went home. The half-past seven programme started up on the radio just after I got in. I didn't go out again.'

'And Markins arrived – when?'

'Round about a quarter to eight. The eight o'clock programme came on just as he left.'

'It was a quarter to eight by radio when I left here, sir,' said Markins, 'and five past when I got back and wound the kitchen clock.'

'You seem to have taken an interest in the time,' said Douglas, staring at him.

'I always do, sir. Yes.'

'Mr Johns,' said Alleyn, 'have you witnesses that you stayed at home from half-past seven onwards?'

Tommy Johns drew down his brows and stuck out his upper lip. 'He *is* like a monkey,' Alleyn thought.

'The wife was about,' said Tommy. 'Her and Mrs Duck. Mrs Duck dropped in after she'd finished here.'

'Ah, yes,' Alleyn thought. 'The wife!' And aloud he said:

'They were in the room with you?'

'They were in the front room. Some of the time. I was in the kitchen.'

'With Cliff?'

'That's right,' said Tommy Johns quickly.

'Except for the time when you sent Cliff down here with the paper?'

Cliff made a brusque movement with his hands.

'Oh, that!' said Tommy loudly, too easily. 'Yes, that's right, he ran down with it, didn't he? That's right. Only away a minute or two. I'd forgotten.'

'You came here,' Alleyn said to Cliff, 'while I was in the room. You went away as I was saying I'd left my cigarette case in the annexe and would go and fetch it.'

'I never heard that,' said Cliff. He cleared his throat and added hurriedly, as if the words were irrelevant, 'I went straight back. I went out by the kitchen door. Mr Markins saw me. I was home when he came up a few minutes later. I never heard anything about anybody going out from here.'

'Did you hear or see Mr Losse, or any one at all as you went back?'

'How could I? He left after me. I mean,' said Cliff, turning very white, 'he must have left after me because he was here when I went away.'

'No. He was upstairs.'

'I mean upstairs. He was going upstairs when I came out.'

'I see. Which way did you take going home?'

'The kitchen path. Then I cut across the hill and through the fence. That brings you out on the main track, just below the fork off to the wool-shed.'

'And you heard nothing of any one else?'

'When I got above the annexe I heard a door slam down below. That would be Mr Markins coming out. He turned up at our place a couple of minutes after I got in. He followed me up.'

'Was it to you that Captain Grace called "goodnight" from the lawn?' Cliff looked at Douglas and away again.

'Not at me,' he said. 'Anyway I didn't think so.'

'But you heard him?'

'I did just hear.'

'Why didn't you answer?'

'I didn't reckon it was me he called out to. I was away up on the kitchen path.'

'Did you hear any one on the track?'

'I didn't notice.'

'Someone was there,' said Douglas positively, and stared at Markins.

'Well, I didn't hear them,' Cliff insisted.

His father scowled anxiously. 'You want to be sure of that,' he said. 'Look, could you swear you didn't hear somebody on the track? Put it that way. Could you swear?'

'You'd make a good barrister, Mr Johns,' said Alleyn, with a smile.

'I don't know anything about that,' said Johns angrily, 'but I reckon Cliff needs a lawyer to stand by before he says anything else. You close down, and don't talk, son.'

'I haven't done anything, Dad.'

'Never mind that. Keep quiet. They'll trip you into making a fool of yourself.'

'I've only one more question in any case, Cliff,' said Alleyn. 'Once at home, did you go out again?'

'No. I sat in the kitchen with Dad and Mr Markins. I was still there when Mr Markins. came back the second time to say there'd been an accident.'

'All right.' Alleyn moved away from the fireplace and sat on the arm of the sofa. His audience also shifted a little, like sheep, he thought, keeping an eye on the dog.

'Well,' he said. 'That about covers the collective questions. I'd like to see some of you individually. I think, Grace, that you and I had better have a consultation, hadn't we?'

'By all means,' said Douglas, looking a little as if he had been summoned to preside over a court-martial. 'I quite agree, sir.'

'Perhaps we could move into the study for a moment. I'd like you all to stay here, if you don't mind. We shan't be long.'

The study was piercingly cold. Douglas lit a lamp and the fire, and they sat together on the wooden fender while, above them, Florence Rubrick's portrait stared at nothing.

'I don't think Losse ought to be bothered with a plan of action just yet,' Alleyn said. 'Do you?'

'Oh, no. Good Lord, no.'

'I wanted to consult you about our next move. I'll have to report this business to the police, you know.'

'Oh, God!'

'Well, I'll have to.'

'They're such hopeless chaps, sir. And to have them mucking about again with notebooks! However! I quite see. It's not altogether your affair, is it?'

'Only in so far as I was the intended victim,' said Alleyn dryly.

'You know,' Douglas muttered with owlish concern, 'I'd come to that conclusion myself. Disgraceful, you know.'

Alleyn disregarded this quaint reflection on the ethics of attempted murder.

'They may,' he said, 'ask me to carry on for a bit, or they may come fuming up here themselves, but the decision rests with them.'

'Quite. Well, I jolly well hope they do leave it to you. I'm sure we all feel like that about it.'

'Including the assailant, do you suppose?'

Douglas pulled his moustache. 'Hardly,' he said. 'That joker would be quite a lot happier without you, I imagine.' He laughed heartily.

'Evidently. But of course he may choose to have another whack at me.'

'Don't you worry, sir,' said Douglas kindly. 'We'll look after that.'

His complacency irritated Alleyn. 'Who's we?' he asked.

'I'll make it my personal responsibility – '

'You,' said Alleyn warmly. 'My dear man, you're a suspect. How do I know you won't come after me with a bludgeon?'

Douglas turned scarlet, 'I don't know if you're serious, Mr Alleyn,' he began, but Alleyn interrupted him. 'Of course I'm serious.'

'In that case,' said Douglas grandly, 'there's no more to be said.'

'There's this much to be said. If you'll prove to me that you couldn't have dodged up that blasted track and had a whack at poor Losse, I'll be profoundly grateful to you. There are too many suspects in this case. The house is littered with them.'

'I've told you,' said Douglas, who seemed to hover between alarm and disapproval. 'I've told you what I did. I went out on the lawn, and I came upstairs and knocked at Terry's door. I said goodnight.'

'Most unnecessary. You'd already said goodnight to her. You might have been establishing an alibi.'

'Good God, you saw me yourself when you came upstairs!'

'Fully ten minutes later. Longer.'

'I was in my pyjamas,' Douglas shouted.

'I saw you. Your pyjamas prove nothing. I'm completely unmoved by your pyjamas.'

'Look here, this is too much. Why would I want to go for Fabian? I'm fond of him. We're partners. Good Lord!' Douglas fumed, 'you can't mean what you're saying. Haven't I urged him to be careful over the work? Why should I go for old Fab?'

'For me.'

'Damn! For you, then. You're supposed to be the blasted expert.'

'And as an expert, God save the mark, I'm keeping my eye on the whole boiling of you, and that's flat.'

'Well, I don't think you put it very nicely,' said Douglas, staring at him, and he added angrily, 'What's the matter with your face?'

'Somebody hit it. It's very stiff and has probably turned purple.'

Douglas gaped at him. 'Hit you!' he repeated.

'Yes, but it's of the smallest consequence, now you've appointed yourself my guardian.'

'Who hit you?'

'It's a secret at the moment.'

'Here!' said Douglas loudly, 'are you pulling my leg?' He looked anxiously at Alleyn. 'It's a funny sort of way to behave,' he said dubiously. 'Oh, well,' he added, 'I'm sorry if I got my rag out, sir.'

'Not a bit,' said Alleyn. 'It's always irritating to be a suspect.'

'I wish you wouldn't keep on like that,' said Douglas fretfully. 'It's damned unpleasant. I hoped I might be allowed to help. I'd like to help.'

'We're talking in circles. Beat me up a respectable alibi, with witnesses, for the murder of your aunt and the attack on Losse and I'll take you to my professional bosom with alacrity.'

'By God,' said Douglas with feeling, 'I wish I could.'

'In the meantime, will you, without prejudice, undertake to do three things for me?'

'Of course!' he said stiffly. 'Anything at all. Naturally.'

'The first is to see I get a fair field and no interference in the wool-shed, from daybreak tomorrow until I let you know I've finished. I can't do any good there at night, by the light of a farthing dip.'

'Right-oh, sir. Can do.'

'The second is to tell the others in confidence that I propose to spend the night in the wool-shed. That'll prevent any unlawful espials up there, and give me a chance to get the tag end of a night's sleep in my room. Actually, I can't start work until daybreak, but they're not to know that. After daybreak we'll keep the shed, the track and the precincts generally, clear of intruders, but you need say nothing about that. Let them suppose I'm going up there now and that you oughtn't to tell them. Let them suppose that I want them to believe I'm going to my room.'

'They won't think that kind of thing very like me,' said Douglas solemnly. 'I'm not the sort to cackle, you know.'

'You'll have to do a bit of acting. Make them understand that you're not supposed to tell them. That's most important.'

'OK. What's the third duty?'

'Oh,' said Alleyn wearily, 'to lend me an alarm clock or knock me up before the household's astir. Unless somebody shakes me up, I'll miss the bus. I wish to Heaven you'd carried your electricity over to the shed. There's important evidence lying there for the taking, but I must have light. Are you sure you follow me? Actually I'm going to my room. They are to suppose I'm going to the wool-shed, but want to be thought in bed.'

'Yes,' said Douglas. 'I've got that. Jolly subtle.'

'Will you give me an alarm clock, or call me?'

'I'll call you,' said Douglas, who had begun to look important and tolerably happy again.

'Good. And now ask Miss Lynne to come in here, will you?'

'Terry? I say, couldn't you . . . I mean . . . well, she's had a pretty rough spin tonight. Couldn't you . . .'

'No,' said Alleyn very firmly. 'With homicide waiting to be served up cold on a plate, I'm afraid I couldn't. Get her, like a good chap, and deliver your illicit information. Don't forget Markins.'

Douglas moved unhappily to the door. Here he paused and a faint glint of complacency appeared on his face.

'Markins, what?' he said. His eyes travelled to Alleyn's jaw. 'I'm not one to ask questions out of my turn,' he said, 'but I bet it was Markins.'

IV

Terence was some time coming. Alleyn built up the fire and thawed himself out. He was caught on a wave of nostalgia; for Troy, his wife, for London, for Inspector Fox with whom he was accustomed to

work, for his own country and his own people. If this had been a routine case from the Yard, he and Fox would, at its present stage, have
gone into one of their huddles, staring at each other meditatively
over their pipes. He could see old Fox now; his large unspeaking face,
his grave attentiveness, his huge passive fists. And when it was over,
there would be Troy, hugging her knees on the hearthrug and bringing him a sense of peace and communion. 'She *is* nice,' he thought.
'I do like my wife,' and he felt a kind of panic that he was so far away
from her. With a sigh, he dismissed his mood and returned to the
house on the slopes of Mount Moon, and felt again the silence of the
plateau beyond the windows and the austerity of the night.

A door banged and someone crossed the hall. It was Terence
Lynne.

She made a sedate entrance, holding herself very erect, looking
straight before her. He noticed that she had powdered her face and
done her lips. Evidently she had visited her room. He wondered if
the book was still tucked down between the sheets.

'All right now?' he asked, and pushed a chair up to the fire.

'Quite, thank you.'

'Sit down, won't you? We'll get it over quickly.'

She did as he suggested, at once, stiffly, as if she obeyed an order.

'Miss Lynne,' Alleyn said, 'I'm afraid I must ask you to let me read
that diary.'

He felt her hatred, as if it was something physical that she
secreted and used against him. 'I wasn't mistaken after all,' she said.
'I was right to think you would go back to my room. That's what
you're like. That's the sort of thing you do.'

'Yes, that's the sort of thing I do. I could have taken it away with
me, you know.'

'I can't imagine why you didn't.'

'Will you please wait here, now, while I get it?'

'I refuse to let you see it.'

'In that case, I must lock your room and report to the police in the
morning. They will come up with a search warrant and take the
whole thing over themselves.'

Her hands trembled. She looked at them irritably and pressed
them together in the fold of her gown. 'Wait a minute,' she said.
'There's something I must say to you. Wait.'

'Of course,' he said and turned away.

After perhaps a minute she began to speak slowly and carefully. 'What I am going to tell you is the exact truth. Until an hour ago I would have been afraid to let you see it. There is something written there that you would have misinterpreted. Now, you would not mis-interpret it. There is nothing in it that could help you. It is because the thought of your reading it is distasteful to me that I want to keep it from you. I swear that is all. I solemnly swear it.'

'You must know,' he said, 'that I can't act on an assurance of that sort. Surely you must know.' She leant forward, resting her forehead on her hand and pushing her hair back from it. 'If it is as you say,' Alleyn continued, 'you must try to think of me as something quite impersonal, as indeed I am. I have read many scores of such docu-ments, written for one reader only, and have laid them aside and put them from my mind. But I must see it or, if I don't, the police must do so. Which is it to be?'

'Does it matter?' she said harshly. 'You then. You know where it is. Go and get it, but don't let me see it in your hands.'

'Before I go, there is one question. Why, when we discussed the search for the brooch, did you tell us you didn't meet Arthur Rubrick in the long walk below the tennis court?'

'I still say so.'

'No, no. You're an intelligent person. You heard what Losse and Grace said about the search. It was obvious you must have met him.' He paused, and the memory returned to him of Fabian muttering: 'Terry! Oh Lord, I do wish I hadn't got up here. Silly old man!' He sat on the wooden fender, facing Terence Lynne. 'Come,' he said, 'there was an encounter, wasn't there? A significant encounter? Something happened that would speak for itself to an observer at some distance.'

'Who was it? Was it Douglas? Ursula?'

'Tell me what happened.'

'If you know as much as this,' she said, 'you know, unless you're trying to trap me, that he – he put his arms about me and kissed me. There's nothing left. Everything has been coarsened now, and made common.'

'Isn't there something unsound in a happiness that fades in the light? I know this particular light is harsh and painful for you, but it

is a passing thing. When it's gone you will have your remembrances – '
He broke off for a moment and then added deliberately, 'Whatever
happens.'

She said impatiently: 'Within the last hour, everything has
altered. I told you. You don't understand.'

'I've got an inkling,' he said. 'Within the last hour there has been
an attempt at a second murder. You think, don't you, that I'm saying to myself: "This attempt follows, in character, the attack on Mrs
Rubrick. Therefore it has been made by Mrs Rubrick's assailant".'

Terence looked attentively at him, a wary sidelong glance. She
seemed to take alarm and rose quickly, facing him. 'What do you
mean . . . ?'

'You think,' said Alleyn, 'that because Arthur Rubrick is dead, I
cannot suspect him of the murder of his wife.'

CHAPTER 11

According to Arthur Rubrick

There was nothing further to be got from Terence Lynne. Alleyn went upstairs with her and stood in the open doorway while she fetched Arthur Rubrick's diary from its hiding-place. She gave it to him without a word, and the last glimpse he had of her was of an inimical face, pale, framed in its loosened wings of black hair. She shut the door on him. He went downstairs and called Cliff Johns and Markins into the study. It was now ten o'clock.

Cliff was nervous, truculent, and inclined to give battle.

'I don't know why you want to pick on me again,' he said. 'I don't know anything, I couldn't have done anything, and I've had just about enough of these sessions. If this is the Scotland Yard method, I don't wonder at what modern psychiatrists say about British justice.'

'Don't you talk silly,' Markins admonished him and added hurriedly: 'Beg pardon, sir, I'm sure.'

'It's absolutely medieval,' Cliff mumbled.

'Now, see here,' Alleyn said. 'I heartily agree that you and I have had more than enough of these interviews. In the course of them, you have refused to give me certain information. I have now got that information from another source. I am going to repeat it to you and ask for your confirmation or denial. You're in a difficult position. Indeed, it is my duty to tell you that what you say will be taken down and may be used in evidence.'

Cliff wetted his lips. 'But that's what they say when – that means – '

'It means that you'll be well advised either to tell the truth or to say nothing at all.'

'I didn't kill her. I didn't touch her.'

'Let us start with this business of the whisky. Is it true that you caught Albert Black in the act of stealing it, and were yourself in the act of replacing it when Markins found you?'

Markins had moved behind Cliff to the desk. He sat at it, opened his pocket book and produced a stump of pencil from his waistcoat.

'Anything to say about that?' Alleyn asked Cliff. 'True or untrue?'

'Did he tell you?'

Alleyn raised an eyebrow. 'I extracted it from his general manner. He admitted it. Why did you refuse to give this story to Mrs Rubrick?'

'He wouldn't hand it over until I promised. He'd have got the sack and might have got gaoled. A year before, one of the chaps on the place pinched some liquor. They searched his room and found it. She got the police on to him and he did a week in gaol. Albie was a bit tight when he took it. I told him he was crazy.'

'I see.'

'I told you it hadn't anything to do with the case,' Cliff muttered.

'But hasn't it? We'll go on to the following night, the night Mrs Rubrick was murdered, the night when you, dog-tired after your sixteen-mile tramp, were supposed to have played difficult music very well for an hour on a wreck of a piano.'

'They all heard me,' Cliff cried out. 'I can show you the music'

'What happened to that week's instalment of the published radio programmes?'

As Cliff's agitation mounted, he seemed to grow younger. His eyes widened and his lips trembled like a small boy's.

'Did you burn it?' Alleyn asked.

Cliff did not answer.

'You knew, of course, that the Art of Fugue was to be broadcast, followed by a Chopin Polonaise. You had started to work at the Bach and perhaps, while you waited for the programme to begin at 8.5 p.m., played the opening passages. You saw him playing, Markins, didn't you?'

'Yes sir,' said Markins, still writing. Cliff started violently at the sound of his voice.

'But at 8.5 you stopped and turned up the radio which was probably already tuned to the station you wanted. From then, until just before your mother came, when you began to play again, the radio didn't stop. But at some time during that fifty minutes you went to the wool-shed. It was almost dark when you came out. Albert Black saw you. He was drunk, but he remembered and when three weeks later Mrs Rubrick's body was found and the police inquiry began, he used his knowledge for blackmail. He was afraid that when the whisky incident came to light, you would speak the truth. He drove a bargain with you. Now. Why did you go down to the wool-shed?'

'I didn't touch her. I didn't plan anything. I didn't know she was going to the shed. It just happened.'

'You sat in the annexe with the door open. If, after you stopped playing and the radio took up the theme, you sat on the piano chair, you would be able to see down the track. You would be able to see Mrs Rubrick come through the gate at the end of the lavender path and walk up the track towards you. You'd see her turn off to the wool-shed and then she would disappear. I don't for a moment suggest that you expected to see her. You couldn't possibly do so. I merely suggest that you did see her. The door was open, otherwise they would not have been able to hear the Bach from the tennis lawn. Why did you leave the Art of Fugue and follow her to the wool-shed?'

Watching Cliff, Alleyn thought: 'When people are afraid, how little their faces express. They become wooden, dead almost. There's only a change of colour and a kind of stiffness in the mouth.'

'Is there to be an answer?' he asked.

'I am innocent,' said Cliff, and this gracious phrase came straight from his lips.

'If that's true, wouldn't it be wise to tell me the facts? Do you want the murderer to be found?'

'I haven't got the hunter's nose,' said Cliff harshly.

'At least, if you're innocent, you want to clear yourself.'

'How can I? How can I clear myself when there's only me to say what happened! She's dead, isn't she?' His voice rose shrilly. 'And even if the dead could talk, she might still bear witness against me. If she had a moment to think, to realize she'd been hit, she may have thought it was me that did it. That may have been the last thought that flashed up in her mind before she died – that I was killing her.'

As if drawn by an intolerable restlessness, he moved aimlessly about the room, blundering short-sightedly against chairs. 'That's a pretty ghastly idea to get into your head, isn't it? Isn't it?' he demanded, his back to Alleyn.

'Then she was alive when you went into the shed? Did you speak to her?'

Cliff turned on him. 'Alive? You must be crazy. Alive! Would I feel like this if I'd been able to speak to her?' His hands were closed on the back of a chair and he took in a shuddering breath. 'Now,' Alleyn thought, 'it's coming.'

'Wouldn't it have been different,' Cliff said rapidly, 'if I could have told her I was sorry, and tried to make her believe I wasn't a thief? That's what I wanted to do. I didn't know she was going to the shed. How could I? I just wanted to hear the Bach. I started off thinking I might try playing in unison with the radio, but it didn't work, so I stopped and listened. Then I saw her come up the track and turn off to the shed. I wanted suddenly to tell her I was sorry. I sat by the radio for a long time listening and thinking about what I could say to her. I couldn't make up my mind to go. Then, almost without properly willing it, I got up and walked out, leaving the music still going. I went down the hill, turning the phrases over in my mind. And then . . . to go in – into the dark – expecting to find her there and . . . I actually called out to her, you know. I wondered what she could be doing, standing so quiet somewhere in the dark. I could hear the music quite clearly. I called out: "Mrs Rubrick, are you there?" and my voice cracked. It hadn't broken properly then, and it cracked and sounded rotten. I walked on, deeper into the shadow.'

He rubbed his face with a shaking hand.

'Yes?' Alleyn said. 'You went on?'

'There was a heap of empty bales beyond the press. I was quite close to it by then. It was so queer, her not being there. I don't know what I thought about. I don't know really if I'd any sort of idea about what was coming, but it seems to me now that I had got a kind of intuition. Like one of those nightmares, when something's waiting for you and you have to go on to meet it. But I don't know. That may not be true. It may not have happened till my foot touched hers.'

'Under the empty bales?'

'Yes, yes. Between the press and the wall. They were heaped up. I think I wondered what they were doing there. I suppose it was that. And then, in the dark, I stumbled into them. It's very queer, but I knew at once that it was Mrs Rubrick and that she was dead.'

'What did you do?' Alleyn said gently.

'I jumped back and bumped into the press. Then I didn't move for a long time. I wanted to but I couldn't. I kept thinking: "I ought to look at her." But it was dark. I stooped down and grabbed up an armful of bales. I could just see something bright. It was that diamond thing. The other one was lost. Then I listened and there wasn't any sound. And then, I put down my hand and it touched soft dead skin. My arms threw the bales down without my knowing what they did. I swear I meant to go and tell them, I swear I never thought, then, of anything else. It wasn't till I was outside and he called out that I had any other idea.'

'Albert Black called out?'

'He was up the track a bit. He was drunk and stumbling. He called out: "Hey, Cliff, what have you been up to?" Then I felt suddenly like − well, as if I'd turned to water inside. It's a lie to say people think when things like this happen to them. They don't. And you don't control your body either. It acts by itself. Mine did. I didn't reason out anything, or tell myself what to do. It wasn't really me that ran uphill, away from the track and round the back of the bunkhouse. It was me, afterwards, thawing back into my body, going to the annexe and beginning to think with the radio still playing. It was me remembering the row we'd had and what I'd said to her. It was me switching off the radio and playing, when I heard the door of our house bang and the dogs start barking. It was me, next day, when nobody said anything, and the next and the next. And the next three weeks, wondering where they'd put it, and whether it was somewhere near. I thought about that much more often than I thought about who had done it. Albie had the wind up, he thought I'd say he'd taken the whisky, and they'd start wondering if he had a grudge against her. She'd wanted Mr Rubrick to sack him. When he was drunk he used to talk as if he'd give her the works. Then, when they found her, he talked to me just like you said. He thought I did it, he still thinks I did it, and he was afraid I'd try and put it across him and say he was tight and went for her.'

He lurched round the chair and flung himself clumsily into it. His agitation, until now precariously under control, suddenly mastered him and he began to sob, angrily, beating his hands on the chair arm. it's gone,' he stammered. 'It's gone. I can't even listen now. There isn't any music'.

Markins eyed him dubiously. Alleyn, after a moment's hesitation, went to him and touched him lightly on the shoulder. 'Come,' he said, 'it's not as bad as all that. There will be music again.'

II

'There's as neat a case against that boy as you'd wish to see,' said Markins. 'Isn't that right, sir? He's signed a statement admitting he did go into the shed, and we've only his word for it that the rest of the yarn's not a tarradiddle. D'you think they'll take his youth into consideration and send him to a reformatory?'

Alleyn was prevented from answering this question by the entrance of Tommy Johns, white to the lips and shaking with rage.

'I'm that boy's father,' he began, standing before Alleyn and lowering his head like an angry monkey, 'and I won't stand for this third degree business. You've had him in here and grilled him till he's broke down and said anything you liked to put into his mouth. They may be your ways, wherever you come from, but they're not ours in this country and we won't take it. I'll make a public example of you. He's out there, poor kid, all broke up and that weak and queer he's not responsible for himself. I told him to keep his trap shut, silly young tyke, and as soon as he gets out of my sight this is what you do to him. Has anything been took down against him? Has he put his name to anything? By God, if he has, I'll bring an action against you.'

'Cliff has made a statement,' Alleyn said, 'and has signed it. In my opinion it's a true statement.'

'You've no right to make him do it. What's your standing? You've no bloody right.'

'On the contrary I am fully authorized by your police. Cliff has taken the only possible course to protect himself. I repeat that I believe him to have told the truth. When he's got over the effects of the experiment he may want to talk to you about it. Until then, if I may advise you, I should leave him to himself.'

'You're trying to swing one across me.'

'No.'

'You reckon he done it. You're looking for a case against him.'

'Without much looking, there is already a tenable case against him. At the moment, however, I don't think he committed either of these assaults. But, as you are here, Mr Johns – '

'You're lying,' Tommy Johns interjected with great energy.

' – I feel I should point out that your own alibis are in both instances extremely sketchy.'

Tommy Johns was at once very still. He leant forward, his arms flexed and hanging free of his body, his chin lowered. 'I'd got no call to do it,' he said. 'Why would I want to do it? She treated me fair enough according to her ideas. I've got no motive.'

'I imagine,' Alleyn said, 'it's a fairly open secret on the place that the work Captain Grace and Mr Losse have been doing together is of military importance. That it is, in fact, an experimental war job and, as such, has been carried out in secrecy. You also know that Mrs Rubrick was particularly interested in anti-espionage precautions.'

'I don't know anything about that,' Tommy Johns began, but Alleyn interrupted him. 'You don't see a windmill put up at a considerable expense to provide an electric supply for one room only, and that a closely-guarded workroom, without wondering what it's in aid of. Mrs Rubrick herself seems to have adopted a somewhat obvious attitude of precaution and mystery. The police investigation was along unmistakable lines. You can't have failed to see that they were making strenuous efforts to link up murder with possible espionage. To put it bluntly, your name appears in the list of persons who might turn out to be agents in the pay of an enemy power, and therefore suspects in the murder of Mrs Rubrick. Of course, there's a far more obvious motive: anger at Mrs Rubrick's attitude towards your son in the matter of the stolen whisky, and fear of any further steps she might take.'

Tommy Johns uttered an extremely raw expletive.

'I only mention it,' said Alleyn, 'to remind you that Cliff's "grilling" as you call it, was in no way peculiar to him. Your turn may come, but not tonight. I've got to start work at five, and I must get some sleep. You pipe down like a sensible chap. If you and your boy had no hand in these assaults, you've nothing to worry about.'

'I'm not so sure,' he said, blinking. 'The wife's had about as much as she can take,' he added indistinctly, and looked at Alleyn from under his jutting brows. 'Oh, well,' he said.

'Murder takes it out of all hands,' Alleyn murmured, piloting him to the door. Johns halted in front of Markins. 'What's he doing in here?' he demanded.

'I'm OK, Tommy,' said Markins. 'Don't start in on me now.'

'I haven't forgot it was you that put the boy away with her in the first instance,' said Johns. 'The boy asked us not to let it make an unpleasantness, so we didn't. But I haven't forgot. You're the fancy witness in this outfit, aren't you? What's he pay you for it?'

'He's not in the least fancy,' said Alleyn. 'He's going to see you and the boy home in about ten minutes. In the meantime I want you all to wait in the drawing-room.'

'What d'you mean, see us home?'

'In case there are any more murders and you're littered about the place without alibis.' He nodded to Markins who opened the door. 'You might ask Miss Harme to come in,' Alleyn said, and they went away.

III

'I wanted to see you by yourself,' said Ursula; 'I never have, you know.'

'I'm afraid there'll be no marked improvement,' said Alleyn.

'Well, I rather like you,' she said, 'and so does Fab. Of course, I'm terribly pleased that the murderer didn't kill you, and so will Fab be when he's better, but I must say I do wish he could have missed altogether and not caught my poor boyfriend on his already very tricky head.'

'It may all turn out for the best,' Alleyn said.

'I don't quite see how. Fabian will almost certainly consider himself well below C3 as a marrying man and turn me down flat.'

'You'll have to insist.'

'Well, so I will if I can, but it's a poor prospect. I wanted to ask you. Was he at all peculiar while he was unconscious? Did he want to go swarming up the walls or anything?'

Alleyn hesitated before answering this startlingly accurate description. 'I see he did,' said Ursula quickly. 'Then it did get to the old spot. I'd hoped not. Because, you know, he was hit behind the ear when he was climbing up into the boat at Dunkirk, and this is at the back of his head.'

'Perhaps it's just because he was unconscious.'

'Perhaps,' she said doubtfully. 'Did he talk about dropping into the sea, and did he do the sort of gallant young leader number for the men who were with him? "Come on, you chaps. Excelsibloodyor."'

'Exactly that.'

'Isn't it difficult!' Ursula said gloomily. 'I had a frightful set-to with him in the ship. Up the companion-way like greased lightning and then all for shinning up the rigging, only fortunately there was no rigging very handy. But to do him justice, I must say he didn't fight me. Although concussed, I suppose he knew a lady when he saw one, and remained the little gent.'

'Does he ever call you "funny old thing"?'

'Never. That's not at all his line. Why?'

'He called somebody that when he was talking.'

'You, perhaps?'

'Positively not. He merely hit me.'

'Well, it would be a man.'

'Are you at all interested in the shearing process?'

Ursula stared at him. 'Me?' she said. 'What do you mean?'

'Do you ever help in the shed? Pick up the fleeces or anything?'

'Good heavens, no. Women don't, though I suppose we'll have to if the war goes on much longer. Why?'

'Then you couldn't tell me anything about sorting?'

'Of course not. Ask Douglas or Fab or Tommy Johns. Or why not Ben Wilson? It's frightfully technical.'

'Yes. Do you suppose Fabian tried to climb anything when he blacked out on the night of the search?'

'I'm quite sure he did,' said Ursula soberly.

'You are? Why?'

'I had a good look at him, you know. You remember I guessed he'd had another go. The palms of his hands were stained, as if he'd held on to things like branches. I sent his white trousers to the wash. They had green lines on them.'

'You're a very good sensible girl,' said Alleyn warmly, 'and if you want to marry him, you shall.'

'I don't see what you can do about it, but it's nice of you, all the same. Why are you so excited about Fabian climbing the tree?'

'Because if he did he had a view of the lay-out.'

'Did he say anything?'

'Yes. Scarcely evidence, I'm afraid. The only way to get that would be to knock him neatly over the head in the witness-box, and I don't suppose you'd allow that. He'll have forgotten all about his black-outs, as usual, when he comes round. It seems that when they happen he is at once aware of the previous experiences and returns in memory to them.'

'Isn't it rum?' said Ursula.

'Very. I think you may go to bed now. Here is the key of Losse's room. You may open the door and look at him if you like. If he wakes, whisper some pacific reassurance and come away.'

'I suppose I couldn't sit with him for a bit?'

'It's half-past ten. I thought it was to be an early night?'

'I'd like to. I'd be as still as a mouse.'

'Very well. I'll leave the key in your charge. What did you decide about a doctor?'

'We're going to nip up when the bureau opens.'

'Very sensible. Goodnight to you.'

'Goodnight,' said Ursula. She took hold of his coat lapels. 'You're terribly attractive,' she said, 'and you're a darling because you don't think it was us. Any of us. I'm sorry he hit you.' She kissed him and walked soberly out of the room.

'A baggage!' Alleyn said to himself, meditatively stroking the side of his face. 'A very notable baggage.'

Markins came in. 'That's the lot, sir,' he said. 'Unless you want me to wake up Mrs Aceworthy and Mrs Duck.'

'They can wait till the morning. Send the others to bed, Markins. Escort the Johns brace to their cottage and then join me in the wool-shed.'

'So you are going.'

'I'm afraid so. We can't wait now. I've told Captain Grace.'

'And he told us. 'Streuth, he's a beauty, that young fellow. "Officially," he says, "Mr Alleyn's going to bed. Between ourselves, he's not letting the grass grow under his feet. You needn't say I said so, but he's going up to the wool-shed to work on the scene of the crime!" Could you beat it? Goes and lets it out.'

'He was under orders to do so.'

Markins looked thoughtfully at his superior. 'Inviting them to come and have another pop at you, sir? Is that the lay? Taking a risk, aren't you?'

'You go and do your stuff. Make sure nobody sees you go into the wool-shed. I shan't be long.'

'Very good, sir.' Markins went out but reopened the door and put his head round it. 'Excuse me, Mr Alleyn,' he said, wrinkling up his face, 'but it's nice to be working with someone – after all these years on me pat – especially you.'

'I'm delighted to have you, Markins,' said Alleyn, and when the little man had gone, he thought, 'He's not old Fox, but he's somebody. He's a nice little bloke.'

He heard the others come out of the drawing-room. Douglas called out importantly, 'Goodnight, Tommy; goodnight, Cliff. Report to me first thing in the morning, remember. You, too, Markins.'

'Certainly, sir,' said Markins briskly. 'I'll lock up, sir.'

'Right.'

Alleyn went into the hall. Douglas and Terence were lighting their candles. The two Johns and Markins were in the back passage.

'Captain Grace,' Alleyn said not too loudly, 'is there such a thing as a paraffin heater on the premises? Sorry to be a nuisance, but I'd be glad of one – for my room.'

'Yes, yes, of course,' said Douglas. 'I quite understand, sir. There's one somewhere about, isn't there, Markins?'

'I'll get it out for Mr Alleyn, sir, and take it up.'

'No. Just leave it in the hall here, will you? When you come back.'

Alleyn looked at Douglas who instantly winked at him. Terence Lynne stood at the foot of the stairs, shielding her candle with her hand. She was an impressive figure in her ruby-red gown. The flame glowed through her thin fingers, turning them blood-red. Her face, lit from below, took on the strangely dramatic air induced by upward-thrown shadows. Her eyes, sunk in black rings above the brilliant points of her cheek bones, seemed to fix their gaze on

Alleyn. She turned stiffly and began to mount the stairs, a dark figure. The glow of her candle died out on the landing.

Alleyn lit one of the candles. 'Don't wait for me,' he said to Douglas. 'I want to see that Markins comes in. I'll lock my door. Don't forget to batter on it at four-thirty, will you?'

'Not I, sir.' Douglas jerked his head complacently. 'I think they're quite satisfied that you're spending the night in the shed,' he whispered. 'Markins and Tommy and Co. Rather amusing.'

'Very,' said Alleyn dryly, 'but please remember that Miss Lynne and Miss Harme are both included in the deception.'

'Oh – er, yes. Yes. All right.'

'It's important.'

'Quite.'

'Thanks very much, Grace,' said Alleyn. 'See you, alas, at four-thirty.'

Douglas lowered his voice, 'Sleep well, sir,' he chuckled.

'Thank you. I've a job of writing to do first.'

'And don't forget to lock your door.'

'No, no. I'll come up quietly in a moment.'

'Goodnight, Mr Alleyn.'

'Goodnight.'

'I'm sorry,' Douglas muttered, 'that I didn't take it better in there. Bad show.'

'Not a bit. Goodnight.'

Alleyn waited until he heard a door bang distantly upstairs and then went up to his room. He brought two sweaters and a cardigan out of his wardrobe, put them all on, and then wedged himself into a tweed jacket. The candle he had used the previous night was burned down to less than a quarter of an inch. 'Good for twenty minutes,' he thought, and lit it. He heard Douglas come along the passage to the landing, go into the bathroom, emerge, and tap on Terence Lynne's door. 'Damn the fellow!' thought Alleyn, 'are we never to be rid of his amatory gambits?' He heard Douglas say, 'Are you all right, Terry? . . . Sure? Promise? Goodnight again, then, bless you.' He creaked away down the passage. Here, it seemed, he ran into Ursula Harme emerging from Fabian's room. Alleyn watched the encounter through the crack between the hinges of his open door. Ursula whispered and nodded, Douglas whispered and smiled.

He patted her on the head. She put her hand lightly on his and came tiptoe with her candle past Alleyn's door to her own room. Douglas went into his and in a minute or two all was quiet. Alleyn put his torch in one pocket and Arthur Rubrick's diary in the other. He then went quietly downstairs. A paraffin heater was set out in the hall. He left it behind him with regret and once more went out into the cold. It was now five minutes to eleven.

IV

Alleyn shone his torch on Markins. Sitting on a heap of empty bales with one pulled about his shoulders, he looked like some chilly kobold. Alleyn squatted beside him and switched off his torch.

'It'll be nice when we can converse in a normal manner with no more stage whispers,' he muttered.

'I've been thinking things over, sir. I take it your idea is to lay a trap for our joker. Whoever he is – say "he" for argument's sake – he thinks the captain's let the cat out of the bag about you coming up here and that you'd be off your guard and wide open to another welt on the napper? I'm to lie low, cut in at the last moment, and catch him hot.'

'Just a second,' said Alleyn. He pulled off his shoes and thudded to the press. 'We've got to stow ourselves away.'

'Both of us?'

'Yes. It may be soon and it may be a hellish long wait. You'll get in the wool-press. Into that half. The one with the door. Be ready to open the front a crack for a view. I'm going to lie alongside it. I'll get you to cover me with these foul sacks. It sounds idiotic, but I think it's going to work. Don't disturb the sacks that Mr Losse was lying on. Now, then.'

Alleyn, remembering Cliff's narrative, spread three empty sacks on the floor behind the press. He lay on them with Arthur Rubrick's diary open under his chin. Markins dropped several more sacks over him. 'I'll put my torch on,' Alleyn whispered. 'Can you see any light?'

'Wait a bit, sir.' A further weight fell across Alleyn's shoulders and head. 'OK now, sir.' Alleyn stretched himself like a cat and relaxed his muscles systematically until his body lay slack and resistless on its hard bed. It was abominably stuffy and there was some danger of the dusty hessian inducing a sneeze. If his nose began to tickle he'd have to plug it. Close beside him the press creaked. Markins' foot rapped against the side. He thudded down into his nest.

'Any good?' Alleyn whispered.

'I'm tying a bit of string to the side,' said a tiny voice. 'I can let it open then.'

'Good. Don't move unless I do.'

After a silence of perhaps a minute, Alleyn said, 'Markins?'

'Sir?'

'Shall I tell you my bet for our visitor?'

'If you please.'

Alleyn told him. He heard Markins give a thin ghost of a whistle. 'Fancy!' he whispered.

Alleyn turned his torch on the open pages of Arthur Rubrick's diary. On closer inspection it proved to be a well-made, expensively-bound affair, with his initials stamped on the cover. On the fly-leaf was an enormous inscription: 'Arthur with fondest love from Florence, Christmas, 1941.'

Alleyn read with some difficulty. The book was no more than five inches from his nose, and Rubrick had written a tiny and delicate script. His curiously formal style appeared in the first line and continued for many pages without interruption or any excursions into modernity. It was in this style or one more antique, Alleyn supposed, that he had written his essays.

'December 28th, 1941,' Alleyn read. 'I cannot but think it a curious circumstance that I should devote these pages, the gift of my wife, to a purpose I have long had in mind, but have been too languid or too idle to pursue. Like an unstudious urchin I am beguiled by the smoothness of paper and the invitation of pale-blue lines, to accomplish a task to which a common ledger or exercise book could not beguile me. In short, I intend to keep a journal. In my judgement there is but one virtue in such a practice: the writer must consider himself free; nay, rather, bound to set down impartially those thoughts, hopes, and secret burdens of the heart which, at all other times, he may not disclose. This, then, I propose to do, and I believe those persons who study the ailments of the mind would applaud my intention as salutary and wise.'

Alleyn paused in his stuffy confinement and listened for a moment. He heard only the sound of his pulse and when he moved his head the scratch of hessian against his shoulders.

'. . . that I had been mistaken in my choice was too soon apparent. We had not been married a year before I wondered at the impulse that had led me into such an unhappy union, and it seemed to me that some other than I had acted so precipitately. Let me be just. The qualities that had invoked the admiration I so rashly mistook for affection were real. All those qualities, indeed, which I am lacking are hers in abundance: energy, intelligence, determination and, above all, vitality . . .'

A rat scuttled in the rafters.

'Markins?'

'Sir?'

'Remember, no move until you get your cue.'

'Quite so, sir.'

Alleyn turned a page.

'. . . is it not a strange circumstance that admiration should go hand in hand with faded love? Those qualities for which I most applaud her have most often diminished, indeed prevented altogether, my affection. Yet I believed my indifference to be caused, not so much by a fault in her or in myself, as by the natural and unhappy consequence of my declining health. Had I been more robust, I thought, I would, in turn, have responded more easily to her energy. In this belief I might have well continued for the remainder of our life together, had not Terence Lynne come upon me in my solitude.'

Alleyn rested his hand upon the open book and called to his mind the photograph of Arthur Rubrick. 'Poor devil!' he thought. 'What bad luck!' He looked at his watch. Twenty minutes past eleven. The candle in his bedroom would soon gutter and go out.

'. . . it is over a fortnight now since I engaged to keep this journal. How can I describe my emotions during this time? "I attempt from love's sickness to fly," and (how true): "I cannot raise forces enough to rebel." Is it not pitiful that a man of my age and sad health should fall a victim of this other distemper? Indeed, I am now become an antic, a classical figure of fun, old Sir Ague who languishes upon a pretty wench. At least she is ignorant of my dotage and in her divine kindness finds nothing but gratitude in me.'

Alleyn thought, 'If, after all, the diary gives no inkling, I shall think myself a toad for having read it.'

'January 10th: Florence came to me today with a tale of espionage at which I am greatly disquieted, the more so that her suspicions are at war with her inclining. I cannot, I will not believe what my judgement tells me is possible. Her very astuteness (I have never known her at fault in appraisement of character), and her great distress, combine to persuade me of that which I cannot bring myself to set down in detail. I am the more uneasy that she is determined to engage herself in the affair. I have entreated her to leave it in the hands of authority, and can only hope that she will pursue this course and that they will be removed from Mount Moon and placed under a more careful guard, as indeed would sort well with their work. I am pledged to say nothing of this and, truth to tell, am glad to be so confined. My health is so poor a thing nowadays, that I have no stomach for responsibility and would be rid, if I might, of all emotions, yet am not so, but rather the more engaged. Yet I must ponder the case and find myself, upon consideration, woefully persuaded. Circumstance, fact, and his views and character all point to it.'

Alleyn read this passage through again. Markins, inside the press, gave a hollow little cough and shifted his position.

'January 13th: I cannot yet believe in my good fortune. My emotion is rather one of humility and wonder than of exaltation. I cannot but think I have made too much of her singular kindness, yet when I recollect, as I do continually, her sweetness and her agitation, I must believe she loves me. It is very strange, for what a poor thing I am, creeping about with my heart my enemy: her equal in nothing but my devotion, and even in that confused and uncertain. I mistrust Florence. She interpreted very shrewdly the scene she interrupted, and I fear she may conclude it to be the latest of many; she cannot believe it to be, as in fact it is, the first of its kind . . . Her strange and most unwelcome attentiveness, the watch she keeps upon me, her removal of Terence; these are signs that cannot be misread.'

Alleyn read on quickly, reaching the sentence he had lighted upon when he first opened the book. Behind the formal phrases he saw Arthur Rubrick, confused and desperately ill, moved and agitated by the discovery of Terence Lynne's attachment to him, irked and repelled by his wife's determined attentions. Less stylized phrases began to appear at the end of the day's record. 'A bad night.' 'Two bad turns today.' A few days before his wife was killed, he had written: 'I have been reading a book called "Famous Trials". I used to think such creatures as Crippen must be monsters, unbalanced and quite without the habit of endurance by which custom inoculates the normal man against intolerance, but am now of a different opinion. I sometimes think that if I could be alone with her and at peace I might recover my health . . .' On the night of Florence's death, he had written: 'It cannot go on like this. I must not see her alone. Tonight, when we met by chance, I was unable to obey the rule I had set myself. It is too much for me.'

There were no other entries.

Alleyn closed the book, shifted his position a little and switched off his torch. Cautiously he adjusted the covering over his head to leave a peephole for his right eye and, like a trained actor, dismissed all senses but one from his mind. He listened. Markins, a few inches away, whispered, 'Now then, sir.'

V

The person who moved across the frozen ground towards the wool-shed did so very slowly. Alleyn was aware, not so much of footsteps as of interruptions in the silence, interruptions that might have been mistaken for some faint disturbance of his own eardrums. They grew more definite and were presently accompanied by a crisp undertone when occasionally the advancing feet brushed against stivered grass. Alleyn directed his gaze through his peephole towards that part of the darkness where the sacking should be.

The steps halted and were followed, after a pause, by a brushing sound. A patch of luminous blue appeared and widened until a star burned in it. It opened still wider and there hung a patch of glittering night sky and the shape of a hill. Into this, sidelong, edged a human form, a dark silhouette that bent forward, seeming to listen. The visitor's feet were still on the ground below, but, after perhaps a minute, the form rose quickly, mounting the high step, and showed complete for a moment before the sacking door fell back and blotted out the picture. Now there were three inhabitants of the wool-shed.

How still and how patient was this visitor to wait so long! No
movement, no sound but quiet breathing. Alleyn became aware of
muscles in his own body that asked for release, of a loose thread in
the packing that crept down and tickled his ear.

At last a movement. Something had been laid down on the floor.
Then two soft thuds. A disc of light appeared, travelled to and fro
across the shearing-board and halted. The reflection from its beam
showed stockinged feet and the dim outline of a coat. The visitor
squatted and the light fanned out as the torch was laid on the floor.
A soft rhythmic noise began. Gloved hands moved in and out of the
regions of light. The visitor was polishing the shearing-board.

It was thoroughly done, backwards and forwards with occasional
shiftings of the torch, always in the direction of the press. There was
a long pause. Torch light found and played steadily upon the heap of
packs where Fabian had rested. It moved on.

It found a single empty pack that Alleyn had dropped over the
branding iron. This was pulled aside by a gloved hand, the iron was
lifted and a cloth was rubbed vigorously over the head and shaft. It
was replaced and its covering restored. For a blinding second the
light shone full in Alleyn's right eye. He wondered how quickly he
could collect himself and dive. It moved on and the press hid it.

Holding his breath, Alleyn writhed forward an inch. He could
make out the visitor's shape, motionless in the shadow beyond the
press. The light now shone on a tin candlestick nailed to a joist, high
up on the wall.

Alleyn had many times used the method of reconstruction, but
this was the first time it had been staged for him by an actor who
was unaware of an audience. The visitor reached up to the candle.
The torch moved and for a brief space Alleyn saw a clear silhouette.
Gloved fingers worked, a hand was drawn back. The figure moved
over to the pens. Presently there was the sound of a sharp impact, a
rattle and a soft plop. Then silence.

'This is going to be our cue,' thought Alleyn.

The visitor had returned to the shearing-board. Suddenly and
quite clearly a long thin object was revealed, lying near the doorway.
It was taken up and Alleyn saw that it was a green branch. The visitor padded back to the sheep pens. The light jogged and wavered
over the barrier and was finally directed inside. Alleyn began to

slough his covering. Now he squatted on his heels with the press between himself and the light. Now he rose until he crouched behind it and could look with his left eye round the corner. The visitor fumbled and thumped softly. The light darted eccentrically about the walls and, for a brief flash, revealed its owner astride the barrier. A movement and the figure disappeared. Alleyn looked over the edge of the press into blackness. He could hear Markins breathing. He reached down and his fingers touched short coarse hair.

'When you hear me,' he breathed, and a tiny voice replied, 'OK.'

He slipped off his too tight jacket and moving sideways glided across the shed and along the wall, until his back was against the portholes. He peered across the shearing-board towards the pens, now faintly lit by reflected light from the visitor's torch. A curious sound came from them, a mixture of rattle and scuffle.

Alleyn drew in his breath. He was about to discover whether the post-mortem on Florence Rubrick's character, the deduction he had drawn from it, and the light it had seemed to cast on her associates, were true or false. The case had closed in upon a point of light still hidden from him. He felt an extraordinary reluctance to take the final step. For a moment time stood still. 'Get it over,' he thought, and lightly crossed the shearing-board. He rested his hand on the partition and switched on his torch.

It shone full in the eyes of Douglas Grace.

EPILOGUE

According to Alleyn

Part of a letter from Chief Detective-Inspector Alleyn to Detective Inspector Fox.

. . . you asked for the works, Br'er Fox, and you'll get them. I enclose a copy of my report, but it may amuse you to have the pointers as I saw them. All right. First pointer. The leakage of information through the Portuguese journalist.

Not being a believer in fairies or in stories of access to sealed rooms, you'll have decided that Fabian Losse, Douglas Grace, and, possibly, Florence Rubrick, were the only persons who had a hope of extracting blueprints and handing them on. Remembering they were copies, not originals, you'll see that Florence Rubrick is ruled out. She hadn't the ability to make copies or the apparatus to photograph originals.

So our enemy agent, murderer or not, looked like Douglas Grace or Fabian Losse. Both had free access to the stuff and the means of passing it on. My job was to find the agent. As a working proposition I supposed he was also the murderer. If, then, the murderer was the agent, the two likeliest bets for the agent were Losse and Grace. Which of them shaped up best as the murderer? Grace. Grace put the coat with the diamond clips over Mrs Rubrick's shoulders and leant over her chair on the tennis lawn. Grace, therefore, could most easily remove one of the clips. It was obvious that the thing would have been

found if it had lain glittering on bare earth under a scraggy
zinnia. I tried it and it showed up like a lighthouse.

Grace egged on his aunt to organize a search-party and take
herself off to the wool-shed. I wondered if he'd pinched the
clip in order to bring about this situation and dropped it among
the zinnias for Arthur Rubrick to find when Grace himself had
finished the job in the wool-shed. If so, he was a quick thinker
and a bold customer altogether. He'd hatched the whole proj-
ect between the time Mrs Rubrick said she was going to the
wool-shed and the moment when she actually left.

Grace had gone up to the house during the search and had
answered the telephone and fetched two torches. This would
give him a chance to bolt out by the dining-room windows and
up the track to the wool-shed. On his return he could hang out
the placard on Mrs Rubrick's bedroom door. This placard is
important. You'll have noticed that he was the only member of
the party who had the opportunity to do this.

You'll notice too, that the disposal of the body must, unless
our expert was Markins, Albert Black, or the quite impossible
Mrs Duck, have been interrupted by a period, not shorter than
the interval between the end of the search and the going to
bed of the household and the cottage; and not longer than that
between the assault and the onset of rigor mortis. Now, the
abominable Black gouged out the candle stump which had
been pressed down, almost certainly by the murderer, and
chucked it into the pens. If he were guilty he would hardly
have volunteered this information.

But suppose Grace was our man?

The pressing out of the light suggests a hurried movement.
The men returning from the dance came quietly up the hill
until they reached the shed, when they broke into a violent
altercation. If you want to put out a candle quietly and quickly,
you don't blow, you press. When I told these people I wanted
to yank up the slatted floor, Grace hid behind his paper and
said he'd give orders to the men to do the job and that he himself would help. I'd have prevented this, of course, but the
offer was suggestive. All right.

You remember the presser told me that the floor round the press was smudged. With what? Florence Rubrick, poor thing, had lost no blood. Grace and Losse wore tennis shoes. If you tramp about on a glassy surface on rubber soles it gets smudged.

The bale hooks were hidden on a very high beam. It was just within my reach and certainly not within the reach of any suspect but Grace. There's no easily movable object, in the shed, by which a shorter person could have gained access to this hiding-place, but Douglas was as tall as I.

Next, Br'er Fox, we come to the wool that was found in number two bin next morning. It hadn't been there overnight. It was tangled and bitty and not in the least like the neatly rolled fleece in the sorter's rack. But it was in the correct bin. Had it been put there by someone who knew about wool-sorting? Fabian Losse, Douglas Grace or possibly Arthur Rubrick? It was, of course, the wool that the body had replaced. A piece of it dropped from the murderer when, late that night, he returned to Florence Rubrick's room to hide away her suitcase. The notice was already on the door and, remember, only Grace could have put it there.

Next, there was his character. There was his legend. He was accepted by the two girls on Fabian's estimate. Fabian thought him an amiable goat with a knack for mechanics.

But Grace was no fool. He'd got a resourceful and a bold mind. He was determined and inventive. Look at his handling of poor old Markins. Without a doubt he guessed that Markins was watching him and, with a flourish, struck first. You've got to admire his cheek. Of course it was Grace himself who was abroad on the night when Markins heard something in the passage. Again, he coolly nipped in the complaint to his aunt that Markins was up to no good and she ought to get rid of him. But he reckoned without his Flossie. Flossie didn't behave according to pattern. The woman who emerged from our post-mortem was nothing if not shrewd. Even Terence Lynne, whose opinion, poor girl, was distorted by jealousy, admitted her astuteness. I fancy Mrs Rubrick was brisk enough to have her doubts about Douglas Grace. His popularity waned; after their quarrel over Markins and again, since they were bound to tell me of this, Grace got in first with his version. It is in his under-estimation of Florence Rubrick that we see, for the first time, that brittle, cast-iron habit of thinking that his earlier German training probably bred in him. He was one of the clutch of young foreign Herrenvolk, small, thank God, but infernal, who did their worst to raise Cain when they returned, bloated with Fascism, to their own countries.

At this point, Br'er Fox, you'll raise your eyebrows and begin to look puffy. You will say that so far I've presented a very scrubby case against this young man. I agree. If he had come to trial we'd have been on tenterhooks, but as you have seen by the report, Grace did not come to trial.

It was with the object of forcing an exposure that I laid for him. I let him know that I proposed to hunt for the candle which Albert Black threw into the pens. This evidently shook Master Douglas. We've found the candle and it has got his prints, but of course they wouldn't have been conclusive evidence. However, he'd probably decided I was a nuisance on general grounds, and that my liquidation would be to the greater glory of the Fatherland.

When I said I'd go to the annexe for my cigarette case, he made one of his snap decisions. He would follow me, get the branding iron from the wool-shed, apply the proved method, and send me down country with the crutchings. Losse, wearing my overcoat, came in for the cosh.

I was now pretty sure of Grace. By dint of a rigmarole so involved that I myself nearly got bogged in it, I induced him to tell the others that I'd be working in the shed all night, and, at the same time, to believe himself that I was going to do no such thing. He had been interrupted by the stretcher party in his first attempt to return and tidy up any prints he'd left. And he must have left some when he fetched and replaced the branding iron. Persuaded that the shed would be deserted, and alarmed by my elephantine hints of clues to be discovered at daybreak, he made his fatal slip. He waited until he thought I was asleep, and then up he came to go over the ground himself. He took off his slippers; he'd dried them at the drawing-room fire after the assault on Losse; and polished the wool-shed floor. He had another go at the branding iron which he'd already wiped on my overcoat. Then, harking back to his earlier intention, he gouged out the existing candle stump, leaving no prints on it, and dropped it into the pens. He then climbed into the pens and scuffled a branch between the slats until he'd covered the new candle end. It was odds on we'd find it before the one that Albert Black had chucked into the pens nearly two years ago.

I'd counted on a show-down and got more than I bargained for.

It all happened quickly and, until the last moment, very quietly. It was a rum scene. I flashed the torch on him and he blinked and peered at me over the partition, while Markins scudded across the shed looking for a fight. There wasn't one. Boxed up in there, he hadn't a hope. The whole affair suddenly became very formal. Grace drew himself up to attention and waited for me to make the first move. He didn't speak. I was never to hear him speak again. I gave him the official warning, told him the police would arrive in two hours, and said that if he liked to give his parole under temporary arrest we'd all move to warmer quarters.

He bowed. He bent stiffly from the waist. This made an extraordinary impression on me because in that moment, when he was queerly lit by two torches, Markins and I having turned both ours upon him, I saw him as a Nazi. He would now, I thought, play the role to which he was naturally suited. He would be formal and courageous, a figure from a recognizable pattern. He would exhibit correct manners because these are the coachwork of the Nazi machine. He would betray nothing.

Then I saw his hand move to his side pocket.

His eyes widened and his lips were compressed. I yelled out: 'Stop that!'

If he'd been slower I'd have gone with him. As it was I'd got my foot in the partition, but it was still between us. It seemed to belly out and hit me amidships in a flare of white light. The last sensation I had was of an appalling noise and of my body hurtling through space and striking itself crazily against a wall. I was, in effect, blown into the middle of next week. He went considerably farther and is now among the eternal Herrenvolk.

There wasn't much left. However, we did find enough to show how he'd provided for the last emergency. His work on shells may have given him the idea, but I fancy he was under orders, in event of a final exit, to take me with him. We found the wreck of a cigarette case showing traces of an explosive and a detonator that had been wired to a torch cell. The cigarette case, we think, was in his breast pocket and the cell in his side pocket.

We shall never hear the story of his engineering days in Germany, of his association with other correct and terrible youths. We shall never know what oaths he took or to what intensive training he submitted himself before he was sent back to await the end of 1939 and the moment when he would enlist with our forces and begin to be useful.

Fabian Losse talks of building a new wool-shed.

II

Part of a letter from Chief Detective-Inspector Alleyn to his wife.

. . . almost midnight and I am in the study with only poor Flossie Rubrick's portrait for company. I'm afraid, my love, that you would be very much put out by this painting and, indeed, it is a dreadfully slick and glossy piece of work. Yet, with its baleful assistance and the post-mortem on her character I feel as if I had known her very well. In a sense, Fabian Losse was right when he said the secret of her end lay in her own character. Who but Florence Rubrick would have practised a speech in the dark to a handful of sheep during a search for her own diamonds? Who but she, having made up her mind that her nephew was an enemy agent, would have informed her husband, bound him over to secrecy, and decided to tackle the job herself? That it was Douglas Grace she suspected, and not Markins, is clear enough when one remembers that Rubrick clung to Markins after her death, and that, after her interview with Grace, her manner towards him altered and she subsequently climbed down over Fabian Losse's engagement to Ursula Harme. She said nothing of her precise suspicions to any one else. She played a lone hand and she hadn't a chance. Down she went, that ugly little woman, with all her obstinacy, arrogance, generosity, shrewdness and energy, down she went before an idea that was too strong for her.

It's all over. Already the inhabitants of Mount Moon are beginning to readjust themselves. Fabian Losse, who is fast recovering from the whack on his head, is naturally shocked and horrified by the discovery that his partner gave it to him, and appalled to think that for years he has been confiding his dearest secret to his country's enemy. Grace's death is no more than an additional cause for bewilderment. It's poor consolation for Fabian that the Portuguese journalist was intercepted. He feels he's criminally blind and stupid. He doesn't think Grace managed to get any information away. I'm not so sure, but at all events there's no sign of the enemy using the Losse aerial magnetic fuse. Fabian will recover. Ursula Harme will make nonsense of his scruples. They will be married and he will become an important but unknown expert, one of the 'boys in the back room'. Miss Lynne will composedly follow her neat destiny and will never forgive herself or me for her one outburst. Young Cliff, who, of the entire set-up, would interest you, will, I hope, grow out of his megrim and return to his music. He was suffering from chronic fear, and psychological constipation. The cause has been removed. His father will doubtless continue to draft sheep and eat fire with perfect virtuosity. I've persuaded Losse to get rid of the abominable Albert.

I almost dare to say I may soon come home. I've just taken my pen again after stopping to ruminate and fill my pipe. When you pause at midnight in this house, the landscape comes in through the windows and sends something exciting down your spinal column. Out there are the plateau, the cincture of mountains, the empty sparkling air. To the north, more mountains, a plain, turbulent straits, another island, thirteen thousand miles of sea and at the far end, you.

The case is wound up but, as I stretch my cold fingers and look once again at the portrait of Florence Rubrick, I regret very much that I didn't accept her invitation and come, before she was dead, for a weekend at Mount Moon.

Final Curtain

For Joan and Cecil
with my love

Contents

1	Siege of Troy	233
2	Departure	244
3	Ancreton	255
4	Sir Henry	272
5	The Bloody Child	285
6	Paint	304
7	Fiesta	318
8	Big Exit	335
9	Alleyn	346
10	Bombshell from Thomas	360
11	Alleyn at Ancreton	369
12	The Bell and the Book	384
13	Spotlight on Cedric	401
14	Psychiatry and a Churchyard	418
15	New System	432
16	Positively the Last Appearance of Sir Henry Ancred	446
17	Escape of Miss O.	463
18	The Last Appearance of Miss O.	476
19	Final Curtain	485

Cast of Characters

Agatha Troy Alleyn
Katti Bostock
Nigel Bathgate
Sir Henry Ancred, Bart
Claude Ancred — *His elder son (absent)*
Thomas Ancred — *His younger son*
Pauline Kentish — *His elder daughter*
Paul Kentish
Patricia Kentish (Panty) — *His grandchildren*
Desdemona Ancred — *His younger daughter*
Millamant Ancred — *His daughter-in-law (wife to Henry Irving Ancred, deceased)*

Cedric Ancred — *His heir apparent (Millamant's son)*

The Hon Mrs Claude Ancred (Jenetta) — *His daughter-in-law (wife to Claude Ancred)*

Fenella Ancred — *Her daughter*
Miss Sonia Orrincourt
Miss Caroline Able
Barker — *Butler at Ancreton Manor*
Dr Withers — *GP at Ancreton*
Mr Juniper — *Chemist*
Mr Rattisbon — *Solicitor*
Mr Mortimer — *Of Mortimer & Loame, Undertakers and Embalmers*

Roderick Alleyn, Chief Detective-Inspector
Detective-Inspector Fox
Detective-Sergeant Bailey
Dr Curtis, Police Surgeon — *Of the Criminal Investigation Department, New Scotland Yard.*
Detective-Sergeant Thompson
Village Constable

CHAPTER 1

Siege of Troy

'Considered severally,' said Troy, coming angrily into the studio, 'a carbuncle, a month's furlough and a husband returning from the antipodes don't sound like the ingredients of a hell-brew. Collectively, they amount to precisely that.'

Katti Bostock stepped heavily back from her easel, screwed up her eyes, and squinting dispassionately at her work said: 'Why?'

They've telephoned from C1. Rory's on his way. He'll probably get here in about three weeks. By which time I shall have returned, cured of my carbuncle, to the girls in the back room.'

'At least,' said Miss Bostock, scowling hideously at her work, 'he won't have to face the carbuncle. There is that.'

'It's on my hip.'

'I know that, you owl.'

'Well – but, Katti,' Troy argued, standing beside her friend, 'you will allow and must admit, it's a stinker. You *are* going it,' she added, squinting at Miss Bostock's canvas.

'You'll have to move into the London flat a bit earlier, that's all.'

'But if only the carbuncle, and Rory and my leave had come together – well, the carbuncle a bit earlier, certainly – we'd have had a fortnight down here together. The AC promised us that. Rory's letters have been full of it. It *is* tough, Katti, you can't deny it. And if you so much as look like saying there are worse things in Europe – '

'All right, all right,' said Miss Bostock, pacifically. 'I was only going to point out that it's reasonably lucky your particular back room and Roderick's job both happen to be in London. Look for the

233

silver lining, dear,' she added unkindly. 'What's that letter you keep taking in and out of your pocket?'

Troy opened her thin hand and disclosed a crushed sheet of notepaper. 'That?' she murmured. 'Oh, yes, there's that. You never heard anything so dotty. Read it.'

'It's got cadmium red all over it.'

'I know. I dropped it on my palette. It's on the back, luckily.'

Miss Bostock spread out the letter on her painting-table, adding several cobalt finger-prints in the process. It was a single sheet of pre-war notepaper, thick, white, with an engraved heading surmounted by a crest – a cross with fluted extremities.

'Cricky!' said Miss Bostock. 'Ancreton Manor. That's the – Cricky!' Being one of those people who invariably read letters aloud she began to mutter:

> Miss Agatha Troy (Mrs Roderick Alleyn)
> Tatlers End House
> Bossicot, Bucks.

Dear Madam,

My father-in-law, Sir Henry Ancred, asks me to write to you in reference to a portrait of himself in the character of Macbeth, for which he would be pleased to engage your services. The picture is to hang in the entrance hall at Ancreton Manor, and will occupy a space six by four feet in dimension. As he is in poor health, he wishes the painting to be done here, and will be pleased if you can arrange to stay with us from Saturday, November 17th, until such time as the portrait is completed. He presumes this will be in about a week. He will be glad to know, by telegram, whether this arrangement will suit you, and also your fee for such a commission.

I am,

Yours faithfully,
MILLAMANT ANCRED.

'Well,' said Miss Bostock, 'of all the cheek!'

Troy grinned. 'You'll notice I'm to dodge up a canvas six by four in seven days. I wonder if he expects me to throw in the three witches and the Bloody Child.'

'Have you answered it?'

'Not yet,' Troy mumbled.

'It was written six days ago,' scolded Miss Bostock.

'I know. I must. How shall I word the telegram: "Deeply regret am not house painter"?'

Katti Bostock paused, her square fingers still planted under the crest. 'I thought only peers had those things peppered about on their notepaper,' she said.

'You'll notice it's a cross, with ends like an anchor. Hence Ancred, one supposes.'

'Oh! I say!' said Katti, rubbing her nose with her blue finger. 'That's funny.'

'What is?'

'Didn't you do a set of designs for that production of *Macbeth*?'

'I did. That may have given them the idea.'

'Good Lord! Do you remember,' said Miss Bostock, 'we saw him in the play. You and Roderick, and I? The Bathgates took us. Before the war.'

'Of course I do,' said Troy. 'He was magnificent, wasn't he?'

'What's more, he looked magnificent. *What* a head. Troy, do you remember, we said – '

'So we did. Katti,' said Troy, 'you're *not* by any chance going to suggest – '

'No, no, of course not. Good Lord, no! But it's rum that we did say it would be fun to have a go at him in the grand manner. Against the backcloth they did from your design; lolloping clouds and a black simplified castle form. The figure cloaked and dim.'

'He wouldn't thank you for that, I dare say. The old gentleman probably wishes to appear in a flash of lightning, making faces. Well, I'd better send the telegram. Oh, damn!' Troy sighed. 'I wish I could settle down to something.'

Miss Bostock glowered thoughtfully at Troy. Four years of intensive work at pictorial surveys for the army, followed by similar and even more exacting work for UNRRA, had, she thought, tried her friend rather high. She was thin and a bit jumpy. She'd be better if she could do more painting, thought Katti, who did not regard the making of pictorial maps, however exquisite, as full compensation for the loss of pure art. Four years' work with little painting and no husband. 'Thank God,' Katti thought, 'I'm different. I get along nicely.'

'If he gets here in three weeks,' Troy was saying, 'where do you suppose he is now? He might be in New York. But he'd cable if he was in New York. The last letter was still from New Zealand, of course. And the cable.'

'Why don't you get on with your work?'

'Work?' said Troy vaguely. 'Oh, well. I'll send off that telegram.' She wandered to the door and came back for the letter. 'Six by four,' she said. 'Imagine it!'

II

'Mr Thomas Ancred?' said Troy, looking at the card in her hand. 'My dear Katti, he's actually *here* on the spot.'

Katti, who had almost completed her vigorous canvas, laid down her brushes and said: 'This is in answer to your telegram. He's come to badger you. Who is he?'

'A son of Sir Henry Ancred's, I fancy. Isn't he a theatrical producer? I seem to remember seeing: "Produced by Thomas Ancred" under casts of characters? Yes, of course he is. That production of *Macbeth* we were talking about at the Unicorn. He was in the picture somewhere then. Look, there's Unicorn Theatre scribbled on the card. We'll have to ask him to dinner, Katti. There's not a train before nine. That'll mean opening another tin. *What* a bore.'

'I don't see why he need stay. There's a pub in the village. If he chooses to come on a fool's errand!'

'I'll see what he's like.'

'Aren't you going to take off that painting smock?'

'I don't suppose so,' Troy said vaguely, and walked up the path from her studio to her house. It was a cold afternoon. Naked trees rattled in a north wind and leaden clouds hurried across the sky. 'Suppose,' Troy pretended, 'I was to walk in and find it was Rory. Suppose he'd kept it a secret and there he was waiting in the library. He'd have lit the fire so that it should be there for us to meet by. His face would be looking like it did the first time he stood there, a bit white with excitement. Suppose – ' She had a lively imagination and she built up her fantasy quickly, warming her thoughts at it. So clear was her picture that it brought a physical reaction; her heart knocked, her hand, even, trembled a little as she opened the library door.

The man who stood before the unkindled hearth was tall and stooped a little. His hair, which had the appearance of floss, stood up thinly like a child's. He wore glasses and blinked behind them at Troy.

'Good afternoon,' he said. 'I'm Thomas Ancred, but of course you know that because of the card. I hope you don't mind my coming. I didn't really want to, but the family insisted.'

He held out his hand, but didn't do anything with it when Troy took it, so that she was obliged to give it a slight squeeze and let it go. 'The whole thing's silly,' he said. 'About Papa's portrait, I mean, of course. We call him "Papa," you know. Some people think it sounds affected, but there it is. About Papa's portrait. I must tell you they all got a great shock when your telegram came. They rang me up. They said you couldn't have understood, and I was to come and explain.'

Troy lit the fire. 'Do sit down,' she said, 'you must be frozen. What did they think I hadn't understood?'

'Well, first of all, that it was an honour to paint Papa. I told them that it would have been the other way round, if anything, supposing you'd consented. Thank you, I will sit down. It's quite a long walk from the station and I think I've blistered my heel. Do you mind if I have a look? I can feel through my sock, you know.'

'Look away,' said Troy.

'Yes,' said Thomas after a pause, 'it is a blister. I'll just keep my toe in my shoe for manners and I dare say the blister will go down. About my father. Of course you know he's the Grand Old Man of the British stage so I needn't go into all that. Do you admire his acting at all?'

'A great deal,' said Troy. She was glad that the statement was truthful. This curious man, she felt, would have recognized a polite evasion.

'*Do you*?' he said. 'That's nice. He is quite good, of course, though a little creaky at times, don't you feel? And then, all those mannerisms! He can't play an emotional bit, you know, without sucking in his breath rather loudly. But he really is good in a magnificent Mrs Beeton sort of way. A recipe for everything and only the best ingredients used.'

'Mr Ancred,' Troy said, 'what is all this about?'

'Well, it's part of the build-up. It's supposed to make you see things in a different light. The great British actor painted by the great British artist, don't you know? And although I don't suppose you'd *like* Ancreton much it might amuse you to see it. It's very baronial. The portrait would hang under the minstrels' gallery with special lighting. He doesn't mind what he pays. It's to commemorate his seventy-fifth birthday. His own idea is that the nation ought to have given it to him, but as the nation doesn't seem to have thought of that he's giving it to himself. And to posterity, of course,' Thomas added as an afterthought, cautiously slipping his finger inside his loosened shoe.

'If you'd like me to suggest one or two painters who might – '

'Some people prick blisters,' said Thomas, 'but I don't. No, thank you, they've made a second-best list. I was telling you about Ancreton. You know those steel engravings of castles and halls in Victorian books? All turrets and an owl flying across the moon? That's Ancreton. It was built by my great-grandfather. He pulled down a nice Queen Anne house and erected Ancreton. There was a moat but people got diphtheria so it was let go and they're growing vegetables in it. The food is quite good, because there are lots of vegetables, and Papa cut down the Great East Spinney during the war and stored the wood, so there are still fires.'

Thomas smiled at his hostess. He had a tentative sidelong smile. 'Yes,' he said, 'that's Ancreton. I expect you'd hate it, but you could-n't help laughing.'

'As I'm not going, however – ' Troy began with a rising sense of panic.

But Thomas continued unmoved. 'And then, of course, there's the family. Well! Papa and Millamant and Pauline and Panty to begin with. Are you at all keen on the emotions?'

'I haven't an idea what you mean.'

'My family is very emotional. They feel everything most deeply. The funny thing about *that*,' said Thomas, 'is that they really do feel deeply. They really are sensitive, only people are inclined to think nobody could really be as sensitive as they seem to be, so that's hard luck on the family.' Thomas took off his spectacles and gazed at Troy with short-sighted innocence. 'Except,' he added, 'that they have the satisfaction of knowing that they are so much more sensitive than any one else. That's a point that might interest you.'

'Mr Ancred,' Troy said patiently, 'I am on leave because I've not been well – '

'Indeed? You look all right. What's the matter with you?'

'A carbuncle,' said Troy angrily.

'Really?' said Thomas clucking his tongue. 'How sickening for you.'

' – and in consequence I'm not at the top of my form. A commission of the sort mentioned in your sister-in-law's letter would take at least three weeks' intensive work. The letter gives me a week.'

'How long is your leave?'

Troy bit her lips. 'That's not the point,' she said. 'The point is – '

'I had a carbuncle once. You feel better if you keep on with your job. Less depressed. Mine,' said Thomas proudly, 'was on my bottom. Now that *is* awkward.' He looked inquiringly at Troy, who by this time, according to her custom, was sitting on the hearth-rug. 'Obviously,' Thomas continued, 'yours – '

'It's on my hip. It's very much better – '

'Well, then – '

' – but that's not the point. Mr Ancred, I can't accept this commission. My husband is coming home after three years' absence – '

'When?' Thomas asked instantly.

'As far as we know in three weeks,' said Troy, wishing she could bring herself to lie freely to her visitor. 'But one can never tell. It might be sooner.'

'Well, of course Scotland Yard will let you know about that, won't they. Because, I mean, he's pretty high up, isn't he? Supposing you did go to Ancreton, they could ring you up there just as well as here.'

'The point is,' Troy almost shouted, 'I don't want to paint your father as Macbeth. I'm sorry to put it so bluntly, but I just don't.'

'I told them you wouldn't,' said Thomas complacently. 'The Bathgates thought they knew better.'

'The Bathgates? Do you mean Nigel and Angela Bathgate?'

'Who else? Nigel and I are old friends. When the family started all this business I went to see him and asked if he thought you'd do it. Nigel said he knew you were on leave, and he thought it would be nice for you.'

'He knows nothing whatever about it.'

'He said you liked meeting queer people. He said you'd revel in Papa as a subject and gloat over his conversation. It only shows you how little we understand our friends, doesn't it?'

'Yes,' said Troy, 'it does.'

'But I can't help wondering what you'd make of Panty.'

Troy had by this time determined to ask Thomas Ancred no questions whatever, and it was with a sense of impotent fury that she heard her own voice: 'Did you say "Panty"?'

'She's my niece, you know. My sister Pauline's youngest. We call her Panty because her bloomers are always coming down. She's a Difficult Child. Her school, which is a school for Difficult Children, was evacuated to Ancreton. They are quartered in the west wing under a *very* nice person called Caroline Able. Panty is frightful.'

'Oh,' said Troy, as he seemed to expect some comment.

'Yes, indeed. She's so awful that I rather like her. She's a little girl with two pigtails and a devilish face. This sort of thing.'

Thomas put his long forefingers at right angles to his head, scowled abominably and blew out his cheeks. His eyes glittered. Much against her will, Troy was suddenly confronted with the face of a bad child. She laughed shortly. Thomas rubbed his hands. 'If I were to tell you,' he said, 'of the things that little girl does, you would open your eyes. Well, a cactus, for instance, in Sonia's bed! Unfortunately she's Papa's favourite, which makes control almost impossible. And, of course, one mustn't beat her except in anger, because that's not proper child psychology.'

He stared thoughtfully into the fire. 'Then there's Pauline, my eldest sister; she's the important type. And Milly, my sister-in-law, who perpetually laughs at nothing and housekeeps for Papa, since her husband, my eldest brother, Henry Irving, died.'

'*Henry Irving!*' Troy ejaculated, thinking with alarm: 'Evidently he's mad.'

'Henry Irving Ancred, of course. Papa had a great admiration for Irving, and regards himself as his spiritual successor, so he called Hal after him. And then there's Sonia. Sonia is Papa's mistress.' Thomas cleared his throat old-maidishly. 'Rather a Biblical situation really. You remember David and Abishag the Shunammite? They all dislike Sonia. I must say she's a *very* bad actress. Am I boring you?'

Troy, though not bored, was extremely reluctant to say so. She muttered: 'Not at all,' and offered Thomas a drink. He replied: 'Yes, thank you, if you've got plenty.' She went off to fetch it, hoping in the interim to sort out her reactions to her visitor. She found Katti Bostock in the dining-room.

'For pity's sake, Katti,' said Troy, 'come back with me. I've got a sort of monster in there.'

'Is it staying to dinner?'

'I haven't asked it, but I should think so. So we shall have to open one of Rory's tins.'

'Hadn't you better go back to this bloke?'

'Do come too. I'm afraid of him. He tells me about his family, presenting each member of it in a repellent light, and yet expecting me to desire nothing more than their acquaintance. And the alarming thing is, Katti, that the narrative has its horrid fascination. Important Pauline, acquisitive Sonia; dreadful little Panty, and Milly, who laughs perpetually at nothing; that's Millamant, of course, who wrote the letter. And Papa, larger than life, and presenting himself with his own portrait because the Nation hasn't come up to scratch – '

'You aren't going to tell me you've accepted!'

'Not I. Good Lord, no! I'd be demented. But – keep an eye on me, Katti,' said Troy.

III

Thomas accepted the invitation to dinner, expressing himself as delighted with his share of tinned New Zealand crayfish. 'We've got friends in New Zealand and America too,' he said, 'but unfortunately tinned fish brings on an attack of Papa's gastroenteritis. If we have it he can't resist it, and so Milly doesn't let us have it. Next time I go to Ancreton she's giving me several tins to take back to my flat.'

'You don't live at Ancreton?' Troy asked.

'How could I when my job's in London? I go there sometimes for weekends to give them all an opportunity of confiding in me. Papa likes us to go. He's having quite a party for his birthday. Pauline's son, Paul, who has a wounded leg, will be there, and Millamant's son, Cedric, who is a dress-designer. I don't think you'd care for Cedric. And my sister Desdemona, who is at liberty just now, though she hopes to be cast for a part in a new play at the Crescent.

My other sister-in-law, Jenetta, will be there too, I hope, with her daughter, Fenella. Her husband, my eldest brother Claude, is a Colonel in the occupation forces and hasn't come home yet.'

'Rather a large party,' said Katti. 'Fun for you.'

'There'll be a good many rows, of course,' Thomas replied. 'When you get two or three Ancreds gathered together they are certain to hurt each other's feelings. That's where I come in handy, because I'm the insensitive one and they talk to me about each other. And about Sonia, I needn't say. We shall all talk about Sonia. We'd hoped to unveil your portrait of Papa on this occasion,' he said, looking wistfully at Troy. 'Indeed, that's really what the party's for.'

Troy mumbled something indistinguishable.

'Papa had a lovely time last week looking out the Macbeth clothes,' Thomas continued. 'I wonder if you remember his costume. Motley did it for us. It's red, a Paul Veroniseish red, dark but clear, with a smoky overcloak. We've got a miniature theatre at Ancreton, you know. I brought down the original backdrop for one of the inset scenes and hung it. It's quite a coincidence, isn't it,' Thomas went on innocently, 'that you did the original designs for that production? Of course, you remember the one I mean. It's very simple. A boldly distorted castle form seen in silhouette. He dressed himself and stood in front of it, resting on his claymore with his head stooped, as if listening. "Good things of day begin to droop and drowse," do you remember?'

Troy remembered that line very well. It was strange that he should have recalled it; for Alleyn was fond of telling her how, in the small hours of a stormy morning, a constable on night duty had once quoted it to him. Thomas, speaking the line, with an actor's sense of its value, sounded like an echo of her husband, and her thoughts were filled with memories of his voice.

' – He's been ill off and on for some time,' Thomas was saying, 'and gets very depressed. But the idea of the portrait bucked him up no end, and he's set his heart on you to paint it. You see, you did his hated rival.'

'Sir Benjamin Corporal?' Troy muttered, eyeing Katti.

'Yes. And old Ben makes a great story about how you only paint subjects that you take a fancy to – pictorially, I mean. He told us you took a great fancy to him pictorially. He said he was the only actor you'd ever wanted to paint.'

'On the contrary,' Troy said angrily. 'It was a commission from his native town – Huddersfield. Old popinjay!'

'He told Papa he'd only be snubbed if he approached you. Actually, Papa was dressed as Macbeth when your telegram arrived. He said: "Ah! This is propitious. Do you think, my dear, that Miss Troy – should he have said 'Mrs Alleyn?' – will care for this pose?" He was quite young-looking when he said it. And then he opened your telegram. He took it rather well, really. He just gave it to Milly, and said: "I shouldn't have put on these garments. It was always an unlucky piece. I'm a vain old fool." And he went away and changed and had an attack of gastroenteritis, poor thing. It must almost be time I thought of walking back to the station, mustn't it?'

'I'll drive you,' Troy said.

Thomas protested mildly, but Troy overruled him brusquely when the time came, and went off to start her car. Thomas said goodbye politely to Katti Bostock.

'You're a clever chap, Mr Ancred,' said Katti grimly.

'Oh, do you think so?' asked Thomas, blinking modestly. 'Oh, no! Clever? Me? Goodness, no. Goodnight. It's been nice to meet you.'

Katti waited for half an hour before she heard the sound of the returning car. Presently the door opened and Troy came in. She wore a white overcoat. A lock of her short dark hair hung over her forehead. Her hands were jammed in her pockets. She walked self-consciously down the room looking at Katti out of the corners of her eyes.

'Got rid of your rum friend?' asked Miss Bostock.

Troy cleared her throat. 'Yes. He's talked himself off.'

'Well,' said Miss Bostock, after a long silence, 'when do you leave for Ancreton?'

'Tomorrow,' said Troy shortly.

CHAPTER 2

Departure

Troy wished that Thomas Ancred would say goodbye and leave her to savour the moment of departure. She enjoyed train journeys enormously, and, in these days, not a second of the precious discomfort should be left unrelished. But there stood Thomas on the Euston platform with nothing to say, and filled, no doubt, with the sense of tediousness that is inseparable from these occasions. 'Why doesn't he take off his hat and walk away,' Troy thought fretfully. But when she caught his eye, he gave her such an anxious smile that she instantly felt obliged to reassure him.

'I have been wondering,' Thomas said, 'if, after all, you will merely loathe my family.'

'In any case I shall be working.'

'Yes,' he agreed, looking immensely relieved, 'there *is* that. I can't tell you how much I dislike many actors, and yet, when I begin to work with them, sometimes I quite love them. If they do what I tell them, of course.'

'Are you working this morning?' And she thought: how unreal the activities seem of people one leaves behind on railway stations.

'Yes,' said Thomas, 'a first rehearsal.'

'Please don't wait,' she said for the fourth time, and for the fourth time he replied: 'I'll just see you off,' and looked at his watch. Doors were slammed farther down the train. Troy leant out of the window. At last she was off. A man in uniform, peering frenziedly into carriage after carriage, was working his way towards her. 'Nigel!' Troy shouted. 'Nigel!'

'Oh, God, there you are!' cried Nigel Bathgate. 'Hallo, Thomas! Here! Troy! I knew I wouldn't have time to talk so I've written.' He thrust a fat envelope at her. A whistle blew. The train clunked, and Thomas said: 'Well, goodbye; they *will* be pleased;' raised his hat and slid out of view. Nigel walked rapidly along beside the window. 'What a go! You will laugh,' he said. 'Is this a novel?' Troy asked, holding up the envelope. 'Almost! You'll see.' Nigel broke into a run. 'I've always wanted to – you'll see – when's Roderick – ?' 'Soon!' Troy cried. 'In three weeks!' 'Goodbye! I can't run any more.' He had gone.

Troy settled down. A young man appeared in the corridor. He peered in at the door and finally entered the already crowded carriage. With a slight twittering noise he settled himself on his upturned suitcase, with his back to the door, and opened an illustrated paper. Troy noticed that he wore a jade ring on his first finger, a particularly bright green hat and suede shoes. The other passengers looked dull and were also preoccupied with their papers. Rows of backyards and occasional heaps of rubble would continue for some time in the world outside the window pane. She sighed luxuriously, thought how much easier it would be to wait for her husband now that she was forced to paint, fell into a brief day-dream, and finally opened Nigel's letter.

Three sheets of closely typed reporter's paper fell out, together with a note written in green ink.

'13 hours, GMT,' Nigel had written. 'Troy, my dear, two hours ago Thomas Ancred, back from his visit to you, rang me up in a triumph. You're in for a party but the GOM will be grand to paint. I've always died to write up the Ancreds but can't afford the inevitable libel action. So I've amused myself by dodging up the enclosed *jeu d'esprit*. It may serve to fill in your journey. NB.'

The typescript was headed: 'Note on Sir Henry Ancred, Bart, and his Immediate Circle.' 'Do I want to read it?' Troy wondered. 'It was charming of Nigel to write it, but I'm in for two weeks of the Ancreds and Thomas's commentary was exhaustive.' And she let the pages fall in her lap. At the same time the young man on the suitcase lowered his modish periodical, and stared fixedly at her. He impressed her disagreeably. His eyes suggested a kind of dull impertinence. Under the line of hair on his lip his mouth was too fresh, and projected too

far above a small white chin. Everything about him was over-elegant,
Troy thought, and dismissed him as an all-too-clearly-defined type.
He continued to stare at her. 'If he was opposite,' she thought, 'he
would begin to ask questions about the windows. What does he
want?' She lifted the sheets of Nigel's typescript and began to read.

II

'Collectively and severally,' Nigel had written, 'the Ancreds, all but
one, are over-emotionalized. Any one attempting to describe or
explain their behaviour must keep this characteristic firmly in mind,
for without it they would scarcely exist. Sir Henry Ancred is perhaps
the worst of the lot, but, because he is an actor, his friends accept his
behaviour as part of his stock-in-trade, and apart from an occasional
feeling of shyness in his presence, seldom make the mistake of
worrying about him. Whether he was drawn to his wife (now
deceased) by the discovery of a similar trait in her character, or
whether, by the phenomenon of marital acclimatization, Lady
Ancred learnt to exhibit emotion with a virtuosity equal to that of
her husband, cannot be discovered. It can only be recorded that she
did so; and died.

'Their elder daughters, Pauline (Ancred played in *The Lady of Lyons*
in '96) and Desdemona *(Othello*, 1909), and their sons, Henry Irving
(Ancred played a bit-part in *The Bells)* and Claude (Pauline's twin) in
their several modes, have inherited or acquired the emotional habit.
Only Thomas (Ancred was resting in 1904 when Thomas was born)
is free of it. Thomas, indeed, is uncommonly placid. Perhaps for this
reason his parent, sisters, and brothers appeal to him when they hurt
each other's feelings, which they do punctually, two or three times a
week, and always with an air of tragic astonishment.

'Pauline, Claude, and Desdemona, in turn, followed their father's
profession. Pauline joined a northern repertory company, married
John Kentish, a local man of property, retired upon provincial glories
more enduring than those she was likely to enjoy as an actress, and
gave birth to Paul and, twelve years later, Patricia (born 1936 and
known as Panty). Like all Ancred's children, except Thomas, Pauline
was extremely handsome, and has retained her looks.

'Claude, her twin, drifted from Oriel into the OUDS, and thence, on his father's back, into romantic juveniles. He married the Hon Miss Jenetta Cairnes, who had a fortune, but never, he is fond of saying, has understood him. She is an intelligent woman. They have one daughter, Fenella.

'Desdemona, Sir Henry's fourth child (aged thirty-six at the time of this narrative), has become a good emotional actress, difficult to place, as she has a knack of cracking the seams of the brittle slickly drawn roles for which West-End managements, addled by her beauty, occasionally cast her. She has become attached to a Group, and appears in pieces written by two surrealists, uttering her lines in such a heartrending manner that they seem, even to Desdemona herself, to be fraught with significance. She is unmarried and has suffered a great deal from two unhappy love affairs.

'The eldest son, Henry Irving Ancred, became a small-part actor and married Mildred Cooper, whom his father promptly re-christened Millamant, as at that time he was engaged upon a revival of *The Way of the World*. Millamant she has remained, and, before her husband died, gave birth to a son, Cedric, about whom the less said the better.

'Your friend, Thomas, is unmarried. Having discovered, after two or three colourless ventures, that he was a bad actor, he set about teaching himself to become a good producer. In this, after a struggle, he succeeded, and is now established as director for Incorporated Playhouses, Limited, Unicorn Theatre. He has never been known to lose his temper at rehearsals, but may sometimes be observed, alone in the stalls, rocking to and fro with his head in his hands. He lives in a bachelor's flat in Westminster.

'All these offspring, Pauline, Claude, Desdemona and Thomas, their sister-in-law, Millamant, and their children, are like details in a design, the central motive of which is Sir Henry himself. Sir Henry, known to his associates as the GOM of the Stage, is believed to be deeply attached to his family. That is part of his legend, and the belief may be founded in fact. He sees a great deal of his family, and perhaps it would be accurate to say that he loves best those particular members of it of whom, at any given moment, he sees least. His wife he presumably loved. They never quarrelled and always sided together against whichever of their young had wounded the feelings of one or the other of them. Thomas was the exception to this, as he is to most other generalities one might apply to the Ancreds.

' "Old Tommy!" Sir Henry will say. "Funny chap! Never quite know where you are with him. T'uh!" This scarcely articulated noise, "T'uh," is used by all the Ancreds (except, of course, Thomas) to express a kind of disillusioned resignation. It's uttered on a high note and is particularly characteristic.

'Sir Henry is not a theatrical knight but a baronet, having inherited his title, late in life, from an enormously wealthy second cousin. It's a completely obscure baronetcy, and, although perfectly genuine, difficult to believe in. Perhaps this is because he himself is so obviously impressed by it and likes to talk about Norman ancestors with names that sound as if they'd been chosen from the dramatis personæ in a Lyceum programme, the Sieur D'Ancred, and so on. His crest is on everything. He looks, as his dresser is fond of saying, every inch the aristocrat – silver hair, hook nose, blue eyes. Up to a few years ago he still appeared in drawing-room comedies, giving exquisite performances of charming or irascible buffers. Sometimes he forgot his lines, but, by the use of a number of famous mannerisms, diddled his audiences into believing it was a lesser actor who had slipped. His last Shakespearian appearance was as Macbeth on the Bard's birthday, at the age of sixty-eight. He then developed a chronic gastric disorder and retired from the stage to his family seat, Ancreton, which in its architectural extravagances may possibly remind him of Dunsinane.

'There he remains, guarded by Millamant, who, since the death of her husband, has house-kept for her father-in-law, and who is supposed by the rest of her family to be feathering a nest for her son, the egregious Cedric, who is delicate. The family (excepting Thomas) is inclined to laugh with bitter emphasis when Cedric is mentioned, and to criticize poor Milly's treatment of the GOM. Milly is a jolly woman and laughs at them. She once told Thomas that if either of his sisters cared to take on her job she'd be delighted to relinquish it. She had them there, for though they all visit Ancreton a great deal, they invariably leave after a few days in a tempest of wounded feelings.

'Occasionally they close their ranks. They have done so at the moment, being at war, as a family, with Miss Sonia Orrincourt, an indifferent actress, with whom, at the age of seventy-five, their father is having a fling. This astounding old man has brought the lady to

Ancreton, and there, it appears, she intends to remain. She is an erst-while member of the chorus and was selected as a type to understudy a small part in a piece at the Unicorn. This was a shattering innovation. The Unicorn, in the theatre world, is as Boodles in clubland. No musical comedy artist, before Miss Orrincourt, had enlivened its stage-door. Sir Henry watched a rehearsal. In three weeks Miss Orrincourt, having proved a complete washout as an understudy, was given the sack by Thomas. She then sought out his father, wept on his waistcoat, and reappeared in her present unmistakable role at Ancreton. She is a blonde. Pauline and Desdemona say that she is holding out on the Old Man with a view to matrimony. Thomas believes her to have taken the more complaisant attitude. Claude, in the Middle East, has sent a cable so guarded in its phrases that the only thing it makes clear is his rage. Claude's wife, Jenetta, a shrewd and amusing woman, who maintains a detached attitude to her relations-by-marriage, has been summoned, in Claude's absence, to a conclave. It is possible that her only child, Fenella, hitherto a second favourite with Sir Henry after Pauline's child Panty, might lose ground if he married. Even jolly Millamant is shaken. Her appalling Cedric is the senior grandson, and Sir Henry has of late begun to drop disconcerting hints that there is life in the old dog yet.

'This, then, is the set-up at Ancreton. My information has come by way of occasional visits and Thomas, who, as you will have discovered, is a talkative chap and doesn't know the meaning of the word reticence.

"In some such fashion as this, dear Troy, would I begin the novel that I dare not attempt. One word more. I understand you are to paint Sir Henry in the character of Macbeth. May I assure you that with Pauline's child Panty on the premises you will find yourself also furnished with a Bloody Child.'

III

Troy folded the typescript, and replaced it in its envelope across which Nigel had written her name in bold characters. The young man on the suitcase stared fixedly at the envelope. She turned it face downwards on her lap. His illustrated paper hung open across his knee. She saw, with annoyance, her own photograph.

So that was what he was up to. He'd recognized her. Probably, she thought, he potters about doing fancy little drawings. He looks like it. If the other people get out before we reach Ancreton Halt, he'll introduce himself and my lovely train journey will be ruined. Damn!

The country outside the window changed to a hurrying tapestry of hedgerows, curving downs and naked trees. Troy watched it contentedly. Having allowed herself to be bamboozled into taking this commission, she had entered into a state of emotional suspension. It was deeply satisfactory to know that her husband would soon return. She no longer experienced moments of something like terror lest his three years absence should drop like a curtain between their understanding of each other. The Commissioner had promised she should know two days beforehand of Alleyn's arrival, and in the meantime the train carried her to a job among strangers who at least would not be commonplace. But I hope, Troy thought, that their family upheaval won't interfere with the old boy's sittings. That *would* be a bore.

The train drew into a junction, and the other passengers, with the exception of the young man on the suitcase, began to collect themselves. Just what she'd feared, thought Troy. She opened her lunch-basket and a book. If I eat and read at him, she thought, that may keep him off; and she remembered Guy de Maupassant's strictures upon people who eat in the train.

Now they were off again. Troy munched her sandwiches and read the opening scene of *Macbeth*. She had decided to revisit that terrible country whose only counterpart, she thought, was to be found in Emily Brontë. This fancy pleased her, and she paused to transport the wraiths of Heathcliff and Cathy to the blasted heath or to follow Fleance over the moors to Wuthering Heights. But, if I am to paint Macbeth, she thought, I must read. And as the first inflexions in the voice of a friend who is re-met after a long absence instantly prepare us for tones that we are yet to hear, so with its opening phrases, the play, which she thought she had forgotten, returned wholly to her memory.

'Do forgive me for interrupting,' said a high-pitched voice, 'but I've been madly anxious to talk to you, and this is such a *magical* opportunity.'

The young man had slid along the seat and was now opposite. His head was tilted ingratiatingly to one side and he smiled at Troy. '*Please* don't think I'm seething with sinister intentions,' he said. 'Honestly, there's *no* need to pull the communication cord.'

'I didn't for a moment suppose there was,' said Troy.

'You are Agatha Troy, aren't you?' he continued anxiously. 'I couldn't be mistaken. I mean, it's too shatteringly coincidental, isn't it? Here I am, reading my little journal, and what should I see but a perfectly blissful photograph of you. *So* exciting and so miraculously *you*. And if I'd had the weeniest doubt left, that alarming affair you're reading would have settled it.'

Troy looked from her book to the young man. 'Macbeth?' she said. 'I'm afraid I don't understand.'

'Oh, but it was too conclusive,' he said. 'But, of course, I haven't introduced myself, have I? I'm Cedric Ancred.'

'Oh,' said Troy after a pause. 'Oh, yes. I see.'

'And then to clinch it, there was your name on that envelope. I'm afraid I peered shamelessly. But it's too exciting that you're actually going to make a picture of the Old Person in all his tatts and bobs. You can't imagine what that costume is like! And the toque! Some terrifically powerful man beat it out of solid steel for him. He's my Grandpa, you know. My mother is Millamant Ancred. My father, only promise you won't tell anyone, was Henry Irving Ancred. Imagine!'

Troy could think of nothing to say in reply to this recital and took another bite out of her sandwich.

'So, you see, I had to make myself known,' he continued with an air that Troy thought of as 'winsome'. 'I'm so burnt up always about your work, and the prospect of meeting you was absolutely tonic.'

'But how did you know,' Troy asked, 'that I was going to paint Sir Henry?'

'I rang up Uncle Thomas last night and he told me. I'd been commanded to the presence, and had decided that I couldn't face it, but immediately changed my plans. You see,' said Cedric with a boyish frankness which Troy found intolerable, 'you see, I actually try to paint. I'm with Pont et Cie and I do the designs. Of course everything's too austerity and grim nowadays, but we keep toddling.'

His suit was silver grey. His shirt was pale green, his pullover was dark green, and his tie was orange. He had rather small eyes, and in the middle of his soft round chin there was a dimple.

'If I may talk about your work,' he was saying, 'there's a quality in it that appeals to me enormously. It – how can I describe it? – its design is always consistent with its subject matter. I mean, the actual *pattern* is not something arbitrarily imposed on the subject but an inevitable consequence of it. Such integrity, always. Or am I talking nonsense?'

He was not talking complete nonsense and Troy grudgingly admitted it. There were few people with whom she cared to discuss her work. Cedric Ancred watched her for a few seconds. She had the unpleasant feeling that he sensed her distaste for him. His next move was unexpected. He ran his fingers through his hair, which was damply blond and wavy. 'God!' he said. 'People! The things they say! If only one could break through, as you have. God! Why is life so perpetually bloody?'

'Oh, *dear!*' Troy thought and shut her luncheon basket. Cedric was gazing at her fixedly. Evidently she was expected to reply.

'I'm not much good,' she said, 'at generalities about life.'

'No!' he muttered and nodded his head profoundly. 'Of course not. I so agree. You are perfectly right, of course.'

Troy looked furtively at her watch. A full half-hour, she thought, before we get to Ancreton Halt and then, he's coming too.

'I'm boring you,' Cedric said loudly. 'No, don't deny it. God! I'm boring you. T'uh!'

'I just don't know how to carry on this sort of conversation, that's all.'

Cedric began to nod again.

'You were reading,' he said. 'I stopped you. One should never do that. It's an offence against the Holy Ghost.'

'I never heard such nonsense,' said Troy with spirit.

Cedric laughed gloomily. 'Go on!' he said. 'Please go on. Return to your "Blasted Heath". It's an atrociously bad play, in my opinion, but go on reading it.'

But it was not easy to read, knowing that a few inches away he was glaring at her over his folded arms. She turned a page. In a minute or two he began to sigh. 'He sighs,' thought Troy, 'like the Mock Turtle, and I think he must be mad.' Presently he laughed shortly, and, in spite of herself, Troy looked up. He was still glaring at her. He had a jade cigarette case open in his hand.

'You smoke?' he asked.

She felt certain that if she refused he would make some further peculiar scene, so she took one of his cigarettes. He lit it in silence and flung himself back in his corner.

After all, Troy thought, I've got to get on with him, somehow, and she said: 'Don't you find it extraordinarily tricky hitting on exactly the right note in fashion drawings? When one thinks of what they used to be like! There's no doubt that commercial art – '

'Prostitution!' Cedric interrupted. 'Just that. If you don't mind the initial sin it's quite amusing.'

'Do you work at all for the theatre?'

'So sweet of you to take an interest,' Cedric answered rather acidly. 'Oh, yes. My Uncle Thomas occasionally uses me. Actually I'm madly keen on it. One would have thought that with the Old Person behind one there would have been an opening. Unfortunately he is not behind me, which is *so* sickening. I've been cut out by the Infant Monstrosity.' He brightened a little. 'It's some comfort to know I'm the eldest grandson, of course. In my more optimistic moments I tell myself he can't leave me *completely* out of his will. My worst nightmare is the one when I dream I've inherited Ancreton. I always wake screaming. Of course, with Sonia on the tapis, almost anything may happen. You've heard about Sonia?'

Troy hesitated and he went on: 'She's the Old Person's little bit of nonsense. Immensely decorative. I can't make up my mind whether she's incredibly stupid or not, but I fear not. The others are all for fighting her, tooth and claw, but I rather think of ingratiating myself in case he does marry her. What do you think?'

Troy was wondering if it was a characteristic of all male Ancreds to take utter strangers into their confidence. But they couldn't all be as bad as Cedric. After all, Nigel Bathgate had said Cedric was frightful, and even Thomas – she thought suddenly how nice Thomas seemed in retrospect when one compared him with his nephew.

'But *do* tell me,' Cedric was saying, 'how do you mean to paint him? All beetling and black? But whatever you decide it will be marvellous. You will let me creep in and see, or are you dreadfully fierce about that?'

'Rather fierce, I'm afraid,' said Troy.

'I suspected so.' Cedric looked out of the window and immediately clasped his forehead. 'It's coming,' he said. 'Every time I brace

myself for the encounter and every time, if there was a train to take
me, I would rush screaming back to London. In a moment we shall
see it. I can't bear it. God! That one should have to face such
horrors.'

'What in the world's the matter?'

'Look!' cried Cedric, covering his eyes. 'Look! Katzenjammer
Castle!'

Troy looked through the window. Some two miles away, on the
crest of a hill, fully displayed, stood Ancreton.

CHAPTER 3

Ancreton

It was an astonishing building. A Victorian architect, fortified and encouraged by the Ancred of his day, had pulled down a Queen Anne house and, from its rubble, caused to rise up a sublimation of his most exotic day-dreams. To no one style or period did Ancreton adhere. Its façade bulged impartially with Norman, Gothic, Baroque and Rococo excrescences. Turrets sprouted like wens from every corner. Towers rose up from a multiplicity of battlements. Arrow slits peered furtively at exopthalmic bay-windows, and out of a kaleidoscope field of tiles rose a forest of variegated chimney-stacks. The whole was presented, not against the sky, but against a dense forest of evergreen trees, for behind Ancreton crest rose another and steeper hillside, richly planted in conifers. Perhaps the imagination of this earlier Ancred was exhausted by the begetting of his monster, for he was content to leave, almost unmolested, the terraced gardens and well-planted spinneys that had been laid out in the tradition of John Evelyn. These, maintaining their integrity, still gently led the eye of the observer towards the site of the house and had an air of blind acquiescence in its iniquities.

Intervening trees soon obliterated Troy's first view of Ancreton. In a minute or two the train paused magnanimously at the tiny station of Ancreton Halt.

'One must face these moments, of course,' Cedric muttered, and they stepped out into a flood of wintry sunshine.

There were only two people on the platform – a young man in second lieutenant's uniform and a tall girl. They were a good-looking pair and somewhat alike – blue-eyed, dark and thin. They came forward, the young man limping and using his stick.

'Oh, lud!' Cedric complained. 'Ancreds by the shoal. Greetings, you two.'

'Hallo, Cedric,' they said without much show of enthusiasm, and the girl turned quickly and cordially towards Troy.

'This is my cousin, Fenella Ancred,' Cedric explained languidly. 'And the warrior is another cousin, Paul Kentish. Miss Agatha Troy, or should it be Mrs Alleyn? *So* difficult.'

'It's splendid that you've come,' said Fenella Ancred. 'Grandfather's terribly excited and easily ten years younger. Have you got lots of luggage? If so, we'll either make two journeys or would you mind walking up the hill? We've only brought the governess-cart and Rosinante's a bit elderly.'

'Walk!' Cedric screamed faintly. 'My dear Fenella, you must be demented! Me? Rosinante (and may I say in parentheses I consider the naming of this animal an insufferable piece of whimsy), Rosinante shall bear me up the hill though it be its last conscious act.'

'I've got two suitcases and my painting gear,' said Troy, 'which is pretty heavy.'

'We'll see what can be done about it,' said Paul Kentish, eyeing Cedric with distaste. 'Come on, Fen.'

Troy's studio easel and heavy luggage had to be left at a cottage, to be sent up later in the evening by carrier, but they packed her worn hand luggage and Cedric's green shade suitcases into the governess-cart and got on top of them. The fat white pony strolled away with them down a narrow lane.

'It's a mile to the gates,' Paul Kentish said, 'and another mile up to the house. We'll get out at the gates, Fen.'

'I should like to walk,' said Troy.

'Then Cedric,' said Fenella with satisfaction, 'can drive.'

'But I'm not a horsy boy,' Cedric protested. 'The creature might sit down or turn round and bite me. Don't you think you're being rather beastly?'

'Don't be an ass,' said Fenella. 'He'll just go on walking home.'

'Who's in residence?' Cedric demanded.

'The usual,' she said. 'Mummy's coming for the weekend after this. I'm on leave for a fortnight. Otherwise, Aunt Milly and Aunt

Pauline. That's Cedric's mother and Paul's mother,' Fenella explained to Troy. 'I expect you'll find us rather muddling to begin with. Aunt Pauline's Mrs Kentish and Mummy's Mrs Claude Ancred, and Aunt Millamant's Mrs Henry Ancred.'

'Henry *Irving* Ancred, don't forget,' Cedric cut in, 'deceased. My papa, you know.'

That's all,' said Fenella, 'in our part. Of course there's Panty' (Cedric moaned), 'Caroline Able and the school in the West Wing. Aunt Pauline's helping them, you know. They're terribly short staffed. That's all.'

'All?' cried Cedric. 'You don't mean to tell me Sonia's gone?'

'No, she's there. I'd forgotten her,' said Fenella shortly.

'Well, Fenella, all I can say is you've an enviable faculty for forgetting. You'll be saying next that everyone's reconciled to Sonia.'

'Is there any point in discussing it?' said Paul Kentish very coldly.

'It's the only topic of any interest at Ancreton,' Cedric rejoined. 'Personally I find it vastly intriguing. I've been telling Mrs Alleyn all about it in the train.'

'Honestly, Cedric,' said Paul and Fenella together, 'you *are!*'

Cedric gave a crowing laugh and they drove on in an uncomfortable silence. Feeling a little desperate, Troy at last began to talk to Paul Kentish. He was a pleasant fellow, she thought, serious-minded, but friendly and ready to speak about his war service. He had been wounded in the leg during the Italian campaign and was still having treatment. Troy asked him what he was going to do when he was discharged, and was surprised to see him turn rather pink.

'As a matter of fact I rather thought – well, actually I had wondered about the police,' said Paul.

'My dear, how terrifying,' Cedric interposed.

'Paul's the only one of us,' Fenella explained, 'who really doesn't want to have anything to do with the theatre.'

'I would have liked to go on in the army,' Paul added, 'only now I'm no good for that. Perhaps, I don't know, but perhaps I'd be no good for the police either.'

'You'd better talk to my husband when he comes back,' Troy said, wondering if Alleyn would mind very much if he did.

'I say!' said Paul. 'That would be perfectly marvellous if you really mean it.'

'Well, I mean he could just tell you whether your limp would make any difference.'

'How glad I am,' Cedric remarked, 'about my duodenal ulcer! I mean I needn't even pretend I want to be brave or strenuous. No doubt I've inherited the Old Person's guts.'

'Are you going on the stage?' Troy asked Fenella.

'I expect so now the war's over. I've been a chauffeur for the duration.'

'You will play exotic roles, Fenella, and I shall design wonderful clothes for you. It would be rather fun,' Cedric went on, 'when and if I inherit Ancreton, to turn it into a frightfully exclusive theatre. The only catch in that is that Sonia might be there as the dowager baronetess, in which case she would insist on playing all the leading roles. Oh, dear, I *do* want some money so badly. What do you suppose is the best technique, Fenella? Shall I woo the Old Person or suck up to Sonia? Paul, you know all about the strategy of indirect approach. Advise me, my dear.'

'Considering you're supposed to earn about twice as much as any of the rest of us!'

'Pure legend. A pittance, I assure you.'

The white pony had sauntered into a lane that ran directly up to the gates of Ancreton, which was now displayed to its greatest advantage. A broad walk ran straight from the gates across a series of terraces, and by way of flights of steps up to a platform before the house. The carriage-drive swept away to the left and was hidden by woods. They must be an extremely rich family, Troy decided, to have kept all this going, and as if in answer to her thoughts, Fenella said: 'You wouldn't guess from here how much the flower gardens have gone back, would you?'

'Are the problem children still digging for a Freudian victory?' asked Cedric.

'They're doing a jolly good job of work,' Paul rejoined. 'All the second terrace was down in potatoes this year. You can see them up there now.' Troy had already noticed a swarm of minute figures on the second terrace.

'The potato!' Cedric murmured. 'A pregnant sublimation, I feel sure.'

'You enjoy eating them, anyway,' Fenella said bluntly.

'Here we are, Mrs Alleyn. Do you honestly feel like walking? If so, we'll go up the Middle Walk and Cedric can drive.'

They climbed out. Paul opened the elaborate and becrested iron gates, explaining that the lodge was now used as a storehouse for vegetables. Cedric, holding the reins with a great show of distaste, was borne slowly off to the left. The other three began the ascent of the terraces.

The curiously metallic sound of children's singing quavered threadily in the autumn air.

> 'Then sing a yeo-heave ho,
> Across the seas we'll go;
> There's many a girl that I know well
> On the banks of the Sacramento.'

As they climbed the second flight of steps a woman's crisp voice could be heard, dominating the rest.

> 'And *Down*, and *Kick*, and *Hee-ee-eeve*. Back.
> I And *Down*, and *Kick* and *Hee-ee-ve*.'

On the second terrace some thirty little girls and boys were digging in time to their own singing. A red-haired young woman, clad in breeches and sweater, shouted the rhythmic orders. Troy was just in time to see a little boy in the back row deliberately heave a spadeful of soil down the neck of a near-by little girl. Singing shrilly, she retaliated by catching him a swinging smack across the rump with the flat of her spade.

'And *Down* and *Kick* and *Heave*. Back,' shouted the young woman, waving cheerfully to Paul and Fenella.

'Come over here!' Fenella screamed. The young woman left her charges and strode towards them. The singing continued, but with less vigour. She was extremely pretty. Fenella introduced her: Miss Caroline Able. She shook hands firmly with Troy, who noticed that the little girl, having downed the little boy, now sat on his face and had begun methodically to plaster his head with soil. In order to do this she had been obliged first to remove a curious white cap. Several of the other children, Troy noticed, wore similar caps.

'You're keeping them hard at it, aren't you, Carol?' said Fenella.

'We stop in five minutes. It's extraordinarily helpful, you know. They feel they're doing something constructive. Something socially worth while,' said Miss Able glowingly. 'And once you can get these children, especially the introverted types, to do that, you've gone quite a bit of the way.'

Fenella and Paul, who had their backs to the children, nodded gravely. The little boy, having unseated the little girl, was making a brave attempt to bite the calf of her left leg.

'How are their heads?' Paul asked solemnly. Miss Able shrugged her shoulders. 'Taking its course,' she said. 'The doctor's coming again tomorrow.'

Troy gave an involuntary exclamation, and at the same moment the little girl screamed so piercingly that her voice rang out above the singing, which instantly stopped.

'It's – perhaps you ought to look,' said Troy, and Miss Able turned in rime to see the little girl attempting strenuously to kick her opponent, who nevertheless maintained his hold on her leg. 'Let go, you cow,' screamed the little girl.

'*Patricia! David!*' cried Miss Able firmly and strode towards them. The other children stopped work and listened in silence. The two principals, maintaining their hold on each other, broke into mutual accusations.

'Now, I wonder,' said Miss Able brightly, and with an air of interest, 'just what made you two feel you'd like to have a fight.' Confused recriminations followed immediately. Miss Able seemed to understand them, and, to Troy's astonishment, actually jotted down one or two notes in a little book, glancing at her watch as she did so.

'And now,' she said, still more brightly, 'you feel ever so much better. You were just angry, and you had to work it off, didn't you? But you know I can think of something that would be much better fun than fighting.'

'No, you can't,' said the little girl instantly, and turned savagely on her opponent. 'I'll kill you,' she said, and fell upon him.

'Suppose,' shouted Miss Able with determined gaiety above the shrieks of the contestants, 'we all shoulder spades and have a jolly good marching song.'

The little girl rolled clear of her opponent, scooped up a handful of earth, and flung it madly and accurately at Miss Able. The little boy and several of the other children laughed very loudly at this exploit. Miss Able, after a second's pause, joined in their laughter.

'Little devil,' said Paul. 'Honestly, Fenella, I really do think a damn good hiding – '

'No, no,' said Fenella, 'it's the method. Listen.'

The ever-jolly Miss Able was saying: 'Well, I expect I do look pretty funny, don't I? Now, come on, let's all have a good rowdy game. Twos and threes. Choose your partners.'

The children split up into pairs, and Miss Able, wiping the earth off her face, joined the three onlookers.

'How you can put up with Panty,' Paul began.

'Oh, but she really is responding, splendidly,' Miss Able interrupted. 'That's the first fight in seven and a half hours, and David began it. He's rather a bad case of maladjustment, I'm afraid. Now, Patricia,' she shouted. 'Into the middle with you. And David, you see if you can catch her. One tries as far as possible,' she explained, 'to divert the anger impulse into less emotional channels.'

They left her, briskly conducting the game, and continued their ascent. On the fourth terrace they encountered a tall and extremely good-looking woman dressed in tweeds and a felt hat, and wearing heavy gauntleted gloves.

'This is my mother,' said Paul Kentish.

Mrs Kentish greeted Troy rather uncertainly: 'You've come to paint Father, haven't you?' she said, inclining her head in the manner of a stage dowager. 'Very nice. I do hope you'll be comfortable. In these days – one can't quite' – she brightened a little – 'but perhaps as an artist you won't mind rather a Bohemian – ' Her voice trailed away and she turned to her son: 'Paul, *darling*,' she said richly, 'you should-n't have walked up all those steps. Your poor leg. Fenella, dear, you shouldn't have let him.'

'It's good for my leg, Mother.'

Mrs Kentish shook her head and gazed mistily at her glowering son. 'Such a brave old boy,' she said. Her voice, which was a warm one, shook a little, and Troy saw with embarrassment that her eyes had filled with tears. 'Such an old Trojan,' she murmured, 'Isn't he, Fenella?'

Fenella laughed uncomfortably and Paul hastily backed away. 'Where are you off to?' he asked loudly.

'To remind Miss Able it's time to come in. Those poor children work so hard. I can't feel – however. I'm afraid I'm rather old-fashioned, Mrs Alleyn. I still feel a mother knows best.'

'Well, but Mother,' Paul objected, 'something had to be done about Panty, didn't it? I mean, she really was pretty frightful.'

'Poor old Panty!' said Mrs Kentish bitterly.

'We'd better move on, Aunt Pauline,' Fenella said. 'Cedric is driving up. He won't do anything about unloading if I know him.'

'Cedric!' Mrs Kentish repeated. 'T'uh!'

She smiled rather grandly at Troy and left them.

'My mother,' Paul said uncomfortably, 'gets in a bit of a flap about things. Doesn't she, Fen?'

'Actually,' said Fenella, 'they all do. That generation, I mean. Daddy rather wallows in emotion and Aunt Dessy's a snorter at it. They get it from Grandfather, don't you think?'

'All except Thomas.'

'Yes, all except Thomas. Don't you think,' Fenella asked Troy, 'that if one generation comes in rather hot and strong emotionally, the next generation swings very much the other way? Paul and I are as hard as nails, aren't we, Paul?'

Troy turned to the young man. He was staring fixedly at his cousin. His dark brows were knitted and his lips were pressed together. He looked preternaturally solemn and did not answer Fenella. 'Why,' thought Troy, 'he's in love with her.'

II

The interior of Ancreton amply sustained the promise of its monstrous façade. Troy was to learn that 'great' was the stock adjective at Ancreton. There was the Great West Spinney, the Great Gallery and the Great Tower. Having crossed the Great Drawbridge over the now dry and cultivated moat, Troy, Fenella, and Paul entered the Great Hall.

Here the tireless ingenuity of the architect had flirted with a number of Elizabethan conceits. There was a plethora of fancy carving, a display of stained-glass windows bearing the Ancred arms, and a number of presumably collateral quarterings. Between these romped occasional mythical animals, and, when mythology and heraldry had run short, the Church had not been forgotten, for crosslets-ancred stood cheek-by-jowl in mild confusion with the keys of St Peter and the Cross of St John of Jerusalem.

Across the back of the hall, facing the entrance, ran a minstrels' gallery, energetically chiselled and hung at intervals with banners. Beneath this, on a wall whose surface was a mass of scrolls and bosses, the portrait, Fenella explained, was to hang. By day, as Troy at once noticed, it would be chequered all over with the reflected colours of a stained-glass heraldry and would take on the aspect of a jig-saw puzzle. By night, according to Paul, it would be floodlit by four lamps specially installed under the gallery.

There were a good many portraits already in the hall, and Troy's attention was caught by an enormous canvas above the fireplace depicting a nautical Ancred of the eighteenth century, who pointed his cutlass at a streak of forked lightning with an air of having made it himself. Underneath this work, in a huge armchair, warming himself at the fire, was Cedric.

'People are seeing about the luggage,' he said, struggling to his feet, 'and one of the minor ancients has led away the horse. Someone has carried dearest Mrs Alleyn's paints up to her inaccessible eyrie. *Do* sit down, Mrs Alleyn. You must be madly exhausted. My Mama is on her way. The Old Person's entrance is timed for eight-thirty. We have a nice long time in which to relax. The Ancient of Days, at my suggestion, is about to serve drinks. In the name of my ridiculous family, in fact, welcome to Katzenjammer Castle.'

'Would you like to see your room first?' asked Fenella.

'Let me warn you,' Cedric added, 'that the visit will entail another arduous climb and a long tramp. Where have they put her, Fenella?'

'The *Siddons* room.'

'I couldn't sympathize more deeply, but of course the choice is appropriate. A steel engraving of that abnormally muscular actress in the role of Lady Macbeth hangs over the washhand-stand, doesn't it, Fenella? I'm in the *Garrick,* which is comparatively lively, especially in the rat season. Here comes the Ancient of Days. *Do* have a stirrup-cup before you set out on your polar expedition.'

An extremely old man-servant was coming across the hall with a tray of drinks. 'Barker,' said Cedric faintly. 'You are welcome as flowers in spring.'

'Thank you, Mr Cedric,' said the old man. 'Sir Henry's compliments, Miss Fenella, and he hopes to have the pleasure of joining you at dinner. Sir Henry hopes Mrs Alleyn has had a pleasant journey.'

Troy said that she had, and wondered if she should return a formal message. Cedric, with the nearest approach to energy that he had yet displayed, began to mix drinks. 'There is one department of Katzenjammer Castle to which one can find *no* objection, and that is the cellar,' he said. 'Thank you, Barker, from my heart. Ganymede himself couldn't foot it more featly.'

'I must say, Cedric,' Paul muttered when the old butler had gone, 'that I don't think your line of comedy with Barker is screamingly funny.'

'Dear Paul! Don't you? I'm completely shattered.'

'Well, he's old,' said Fenella quickly, 'and he's a great friend.'

Cedric darted an extraordinarily malicious glance at his cousins. 'How very feudal,' he said. '*Noblesse oblige*. Dear me!'

At this juncture, rather to Troy's relief, a stout smiling woman came in from one of the side doors. Behind her, Troy caught a glimpse of a vast formal drawing-room.

'This is my Mama,' Cedric explained, faintly waving his hand.

Mrs Henry Ancred was a firmly built, white-skinned woman. Her faded hair was scrupulously groomed into a rather wig-like coiffure. She looked, Troy thought, a little as if she managed some quiet but extremely expensive boarding-house or perhaps a school. Her voice was unusually deep, and her hands and feet unusually large. Unlike her son, she had a wide mouth, but there was a resemblance to Cedric about the eyes and chin. She wore a sensible blouse, a cardigan, and a dark skirt, and she shook hands heartily with Troy. A capable woman.

'So glad you've decided to come,' she said. 'My father-in-law's quite excited. It will take him out of himself and fill in his day nicely.'

Cedric gave a little shriek: 'Milly, *darling!*' he cried. 'How – you can!' He made an agonized face at Troy.

'Have I said something I shouldn't?' asked his mother. 'So like me!' And she laughed heartily.

'Of course you haven't,' Troy said hurriedly, ignoring Cedric. 'I only hope the sittings won't tire Sir Henry.'

'Oh, he'll tell you at once if he's tired,' Millamant Ancred assured her, and Troy had an unpleasant picture of a canvas six by four feet, to be completed in a fortnight, with a sitter who had no hesitation in telling her when he felt tired.

'Well, anyway,' Cedric cried shrilly. 'Drinks!'

They sat round the fire, Paul and Fenella on a sofa, Troy opposite them, and Millamant Ancred, squarely, on a high chair. Cedric pulled a humpty up to his mother, curled himself on it, and rested an arm on her knees. Paul and Fenella glanced at him with ill-concealed distaste.

'What have you been doing, dear?' Millamant asked her son, and put her square white hand on his shoulder.

'Such a lot of tiresome jobs,' he sighed, rubbing his cheek on the hand. 'Tell us what's going to happen here. I want something gay and exciting. A party for Mrs Alleyn. Please! You'd like a party, wouldn't you?' he persisted, appealing to Troy. 'Say you would.'

'But I've come to work,' said Troy, and because he made her feel uncomfortable she spoke abruptly. 'Damn!' she thought. 'Even that sounds as if I expected her to take him seriously.'

But Millamant laughed indulgently. 'Mrs Alleyn will be with us for The Birthday,' she said, 'and so will you, dear, if you really can stay for ten days. Can you?'

'Oh, yes,' he said fretfully. 'The office-place is being tatted up. I've brought my dreary work with me. But The Birthday! How abysmally depressing! Darling Milly, I don't think, really, that I can face another Birthday.'

'Don't be naughty,' said Millamant in her gruff voice.

'Let's have another drink,' said Paul loudly.

'Is somebody talking about drink?' cried a disembodied voice in the minstrels' gallery. 'Goody! Goody! Goody!'

'Oh, God!' Cedric whispered. 'Sonia!'

III

It had grown dark in the hall, and Troy's first impression of Miss Sonia Orrincourt was of a whitish apparition that fluttered down the stairs from the far side of the gallery. Her progress was accompanied by a number of chirruping noises. As she reached the hall and crossed it, Troy saw that she wore a garment which even in the second act of a musical extravaganza would still have been remarkable. Troy supposed it was a negligee.

'Well, for heaven's sake,' squeaked Miss Orrincourt, 'look who's here! Ceddie!' She held out both her hands and Cedric took them.

'You look too marvellous, Sonia,' he cried. 'Where did it come from?'

'Darling, it's a million years old. Oh, pardon me,' said Miss Orrincourt, inclining towards Troy, 'I didn't see – '

Millamant stonily introduced her. Fenella and Paul, having moved away from the sofa, Miss Orrincourt sank into it. She extended her arms and wriggled her fingers. 'Quick! Quick! Quick!' she cried babyishly. 'Sonia wants a d'ink.'

Her hair was almost white. It fell in a fringe across her forehead and in a silk curtain to her shoulders, and reminded Troy vaguely of the inside of an aquarium. Her eyes were as round as saucers, with curving black lashes. When she smiled, her short upper lip flattened, the corners of her mouth turned down, and the shadow of grooves-to-come ran away to her chin. Her skin was white and thick like the petals of a camellia. She was a startling young woman to look at, and she made Troy feel exceedingly dumb. 'But she'd probably be pretty good to paint in the nude,' she reflected. 'I wonder if she's ever been a model. She looks like it.'

Miss Orrincourt and Cedric were conducting an extraordinarily unreal little conversation. Fenella and Paul had moved away, and Troy was left with Millamant Ancred, who began to talk about the difficulties of housekeeping. As she talked, she stitched at an enormous piece of embroidery, which hypnotized Troy by its monstrous colour scheme and tortuous design. Intricate worms and scrolls strangled each other in Millamant's fancy work. No area was left undecorated, no motive was uninterrupted. At times she would pause and eye it with complacency. Her voice was monotonous.

'I suppose I'm lucky,' she said. 'I've got a cook and five maids and Barker, but they're all very old, and have been collected from different branches of the family. My sister-in-law, Pauline, Mrs Claude Ancred, you know, gave up her own house in the evacuation time and has recently joined us with two of her maids. Desdemona did the same thing, and she makes Ancreton her headquarters now. She brought her old Nanny. Barker and the others have always been with us. But even with the West Wing turned into a school it's difficult. In the old days of course,' said Millamant with a certain air of complacency, 'there was a swarm.'

'Do they get on together?' Troy asked vaguely. She was watching Cedric and Miss Orrincourt. Evidently he had decided to adopt ingratiating tactics, and a lively but completely synthetic flirtation had developed. They whispered together.

'Oh, no,' Millamant was saying. 'They fight.' And most unexpectedly she added: 'Like master like man, they say, don't they?' Troy looked at her. She was smiling broadly and blankly. It is a characteristic of these people, Troy reflected, that they constantly make remarks to which there is no answer.

Pauline Ancred came in and joined her son and Fenella. She did this with a certain air of determination, and the smile she gave Fenella was a dismissal. 'Darling,' she said to Paul, 'I've been looking for you.' Fenella at once moved away. Pauline, using a gesture that was Congrevian in its accomplishment, raised a pair of lorgnettes and stared through them at Miss Orrincourt, who now reclined at full length on the sofa. Cedric was perched on the arm at her feet.

'I'll get you a chair, Mother,' said Paul hastily.

'Thank you, dear,' she said, exchanging a glance with her sister-in-law. 'I should like to sit down. No, *please*, Mrs Alleyn, don't move. So sweet of you. Thank you, Paul.'

'Noddy and I,' said Miss Orrincourt brightly, 'have been having such fun. We've been looking at some of that old jewellery.' She stretched her arms above her head and yawned delicately.

'Noddy?' Troy wondered. 'But who is Noddy?' Miss Orrincourt's remark was followed by a rather deadly little pause. 'He's all burnt up about having his picture taken,' Miss Orrincourt added. 'Isn't it killing?'

Pauline Ancred, with a dignified shifting of her torso, brought her sister-in-law into her field of vision. 'Have you seen Papa this afternoon, Millamant?' she asked, not quite cordially, but with an air of joining forces against a common enemy.

'I went up as usual at four o'clock,' Millamant rejoined, 'to see if there was anything I could do for him.' She glanced at Miss Orrincourt. 'He was engaged, however.'

'T'uh!' said Pauline lightly, and she began to revolve her thumbs one around the other. Millamant gave the merest sketch of a significant laugh and turned to Troy.

'We don't quite know,' she said cheerfully, 'if Thomas explained about my father-in-law's portrait. He wishes to be painted in his own little theatre here. The backcloth has been hung and Paul knows about the lights. Papa would like to begin at eleven tomorrow morning, and if he is feeling up to it he will sit for an hour every morning and afternoon.'

'I thought,' said Miss Orrincourt, 'it would be ever so thrilling if Noddy was on a horse in the picture.'

'Sir Henry,' said Millamant, without looking at her, 'will, of course, have decided on the pose.'

'But Aunt Milly,' said Paul, very red in the face, 'Mrs Alleyn might like – I mean – don't you think – '

'Yes, Aunt Milly,' said Fenella.

'Yes, indeed, Milly,' said Cedric. 'I *so* agree. Please, *please* Milly and Aunt Pauline, and please Sonia, angel, *do* consider that Mrs Alleyn is the one to – oh, my goodness,' Cedric implored them, 'pray do consider.'

'I shall be very interested,' said Troy, 'to hear about Sir Henry's plans.'

'That,' said Pauline, 'will be very nice. I forgot to tell you, Millamant, that I heard from Dessy. She's coming for The Birthday.'

'I'm glad you let me know,' said Millamant, looking rather put out.

'And so's Mummy, Aunt Milly,' said Fenella. 'I forgot to say.'

'Well,' said Millamant, with a short laugh, 'I *am* learning about things, aren't I?'

'Jenetta coming? Fancy!' said Pauline. 'It must be two years since Jenetta was at Ancreton. I hope she'll be able to put up with our rough and ready ways.'

'Considering she's been living in a two-roomed flat,' Fenella began rather hotly and checked herself. 'She asked me to say she hoped it wouldn't be too many.'

'I'll move out of *Bernhardt* into *Bracegirdle*,' Pauline offered. 'Of course.'

'You'll do nothing of the sort, Pauline,' said Millamant. '*Bracegirdle* is piercingly cold, the ceiling leaks, and there are rats. Desdemona complained bitterly about the rats last time she was here. I asked Barker to lay poison for them, but he's lost the poison. Until he finds it, *Bracegirdle* is uninhabitable.'

'Mummy could share *Duse* with me,' said Fenella quickly. 'We'd love it and it'd save fires.'

'Oh, we couldn't dream of *that*,' said Pauline and Millamant together.

'Mrs Alleyn,' said Fenella loudly, 'I'm going up to change. Would you like to see your room?'

'Thank you,' said Troy, trying not to sound too eager. 'Thank you, I would.'

IV

Having climbed the stairs and walked with a completely silent Fenella down an interminable picture gallery and two long passages, followed by a break-neck ascent up a winding stair, Troy found herself at a door upon which hung a wooden plaque bearing the word '*Siddons*.' Fenella opened the door, and Troy was pleasantly welcomed by the reflection of leaping flames on white painted walls. White damask curtains with small garlands, a sheepskin rug, a low bed, and there, above a Victorian wash-stand, sure enough, hung Mrs Siddons. Troy's painting gear was stacked in a corner.

'What a nice room,' said Troy.

'I'm glad you like it,' said Fenella in a suppressed voice. Troy saw with astonishment that she was in a rage.

'I apologize,' said Fenella shakily, 'for my beastly family.'

'Hallo,' said Troy, 'what's all this?'

'As if they weren't damned lucky to get you! As if they wouldn't still be damned lucky if you decided to paint Grandpa standing on his head with garlic growing out of the soles of his boots. It's *such* cheek. Even that frightful twirp Cedric was ashamed.'

'Good Lord!' said Troy. 'That's nothing unusual. You've no conception how funny people can be about portraits.'

'I hate them! And you heard how catty they were about Mummy coming. I do think old women are *foul*. And that bitch Sonia lying there lapping it all up. How they can, in front of her! Paul and I were so ashamed.'

Fenella stamped, dropped on her knees in front of the fire and burst into tears. 'I'm sorry,' she stammered. 'I'm worse than they are, but I'm so sick of it all. I wish I hadn't come to Ancreton. I loathe Ancreton. If you only knew what it's like.'

'Look here,' Troy said gently, 'are you sure you want to talk to me like this?'

'I know it's frightful, but I can't help it. How would you feel if *your* grandfather brought a loathsome blonde into the house? How would you feel?'

Troy had a momentary vision of her grandfather, now deceased. He had been an austere and somewhat finicky don.

'Everybody's laughing at him,' Fenella sobbed. 'And I used to like him so much. Now he's just *silly*. A silly amorous old man. He behaves like that himself and then when I – when I went to – it doesn't matter. I'm terribly sorry. It's awful, boring you like this.'

Troy sat on a low chair by the fire and looked thoughtfully at Fenella. The child really is upset, she thought, and realized that already she had begun to question the authenticity of the Ancreds' emotions. She said: 'You needn't think it's awful, and you're not boring me. Only don't say things you'll feel inclined to kick yourself for when you've got under way again.'

'All right.' Fenella got to her feet. She had the fortunate knack, Troy noticed, of looking charming when she cried. She now tossed her head, bit her lips, and gained mastery of herself. 'She'll make a good actress,' Troy thought, and instantly checked herself. 'Because,' she thought, 'the child manages to be so prettily distressed, why should I jump to the conclusion that she's not as distressed as she seems? I'm not sympathetic enough.' She touched Fenella's arm, and although it was quite foreign to her habit, returned the squeeze Fenella instantly gave to her hand.

'Come,' said Troy, 'I thought you said this afternoon that your generation of Ancreds was as hard as nails.'

'Well, we try,' Fenella said. 'It's only because you're so nice that I let go. I won't again.'

'Help!' Troy thought, and said aloud: 'I'm not much use really, I'm afraid. My husband says I shy away from emotion like a nervous mare. But let off steam if you want to.'

Fenella said soberly: 'This'll do for a bit, I expect. You're an angel. Dinner's at half-past eight. You'll hear a warning gong.' She turned at the door. 'All the same,' she said, 'there's something pretty ghastly going on at Ancreton just now. You'll see.'

With an inherited instinct for a good exit line, Fenella stepped backwards and gracefully closed the door.

CHAPTER 4

Sir Henry

In her agitation Fenella had neglected to give Troy the usual host-esses' tips on internal topography. Troy wondered if the nearest bathroom was at the top of another tower or at the end of some interminable corridor. Impossible to tug the embroidered bell-pull and cause one of those aged maids to climb the stairs! She decided to give up her bath in favour of Mrs Siddons, the wash-stand and a Victorian can of warm water which had been left beside it.

She had an hour before dinner. It was pleasant, after the severely rationed fires of Tatler's End, to dress leisurely before this sumptuous blaze. She made the most of it, turning over in her mind the events of the day and sorting out her impressions of the Ancreds. Queer Thomas, she decided, was, so far, the best of the bunch, though the two young things were pleasant enough. Was there an understand-ing between them and had Sir Henry objected? Was that the reason for Fenella's outburst? For the rest: Pauline appeared to be suffering from a general sense of personal affront, Millamant was an unknown quantity, while her Cedric was frankly awful. And then, Sonia! Troy giggled. Sonia really was a bit thick.

Somewhere outside in the cold, a deep-toned clock struck eight. The fire had died down. She might as well begin her journey to the hall. Down the winding stair she went, wondering whose room lay beyond a door on the landing. Troy had no sense of direction. When she reached the first long corridor she couldn't for the life of her remember whether she should turn left or right. A perspective of dark crimson carpet stretched away on each hand, and at intervals the corridor was lit by pseudo-antique candelabra. 'Oh, well,' thought Troy and turned to the right. She passed four doors and read their legends: *'Duse'* (that was Fenella's room), *'Bernhardt'* (Pauline's), *'Terry,'* *'Lady Bancroft,'* and, near the end of the passage, the despised *'Bracegirdle'*. Troy did not remember seeing any of these names on her way up to her tower. 'Blast!' she thought, 'I've gone wrong.' But she went on uncertainly. The corridor led at right-angles into another, at the far end of which she saw the foot of a flight of stairs like those of her own tower. Poor Troy was certain that she had looked down just such a vista on her way up. 'But I suppose,' she thought, 'it must have been its opposite number. From outside, the damn place looked as if it was built round a sort of quadrangle, with a tower at the middle and ends of each wing. In that case, if I keep on turning left, oughtn't I to come back to the picture gallery?'

As she hesitated, a door near the foot of the stairs opened slightly, and a magnificent cat walked out into the passage.

He was white, with a tabby saddle on his back, long haired and amber eyed. He paused and stared at Troy. Then, wafting his tail slightly, he paced slowly towards her. She stooped and waited for him. After some deliberation he approached, examined her hand, bestowed upon it a brief cold thrust of his nose, and continued on his way, walking in the centre of the crimson carpet and still elegantly wafting his tail.

'And one other thing,' said a shrill voice beyond the open door, 'if you think I'm going to hang round here like a bloody extra with the family handing me out the bird in fourteen different positions you've got another think coming.'

A deep voice rumbled unintelligibly.

'I know all about that, and it makes no difference. Nobody's going to tell me I lack refinement and get away with it. They treat me as if I had one of those things in the strip ads. I kept my temper down there because I wasn't going to let them see I minded. What do they think they are? My God, do they think it's any catch living in a mausoleum with a couple of old tats and a kid that ought to be labelled "Crazy Gang"?'

Again the expostulatory rumble.

'I know, I know, I know. It's so merry and bright in this dump it's a wonder we don't all die of laughing. If you're as crazy as all that about me, you ought to put me in a position where I'd keep my

self-respect . . . You owe it to me . . . After all I've done for you. I'm
just miserable . . . And when I get like this, I'm warning you, Noddy,
look out.' The door opened a little further.

Troy, who had stood transfixed, picked up her skirts, turned back
on her tracks, and fairly ran away down the long corridor.

II

This time she reached the gallery and went downstairs. In the hall she
encountered Barker, who showed her into an enormous drawing-
room which looked, she thought, as if it was the setting for a scene in
'Victoria Regina'. Crimson, white, and gold were the predominant
colours, damask and velvet the prevailing textures. Vast canvases by
Leader and MacWhirter occupied the walls. On each occasional table
or cabinet stood a silver-framed photograph of Royalty or Drama.
There were three of Sir Henry at different stages of his career, and
there was one of Sir Henry in Court dress. In this last portrait, the
customary air of a man who can't help feeling he looks a bit of an ass
was completely absent, and for a moment Troy thought Sir Henry had
been taken in yet another of his professional roles. The unmistakable
authenticity of his Windsor coat undeceived her. 'Golly,' she thought,
staring at the photograph, 'it's a good head and no mistake.'

She began a tour of the room and found much to entertain her.
Under the glass lid of a curio table were set out a number of orders,
miniatures and decorations, several *objets d'art*, a signed programme
from a command performance, and, surprisingly, a small book of
antique style, bound in half-calf and heavily tooled. Troy was one of
those people who, when they see a book lying apart, must handle it.
The lid was unlocked. She raised it and opened the little book. The
tide was much faded, and Troy stooped to make it out.

'The Antient Arte of the Embalming of Corpfes,' she read.
'To which is added a Difcourfe on the Concoction of Fluids for the
Purpofe of Preferving Dead Bodies.
   By William Hurfte, Profeffor of Phyfic, London.
   Printed by Robert White for John Crampe at the Sign of the
Three Bibles in St Paul's Churchyard. 1678.'

It was horribly explicit. Here, in the first chapter, were various recipes 'For the Confumation of the Arte of Preferving the Dead in perfect Verifimilitude of Life. It will be remarked,' the author continued, 'that in fpite of their diverfity the chimical of Arfenic is Common to All.' There was a particularly macabre passage on 'The ufe of Cofmetics to Difguife the ghaftly Pallor of Death.'

'But what sort of mind,' Troy wondered, 'could picture with equanimity, even with pleasure, these manipulations upon the body from which it must some day, perhaps soon, be parted?' And she wondered if Sir Henry Ancred had read this book and if he had no imagination or too much. 'And why,' she thought, 'do I go on reading this horrid little book?'

She heard a voice in the hall, and with an illogical feeling of guilt hurriedly closed the book and the glass lid. Millamant came in, wearing a tidy but nondescript evening dress.

'I've been exploring,' Troy said.

'Exploring?' Millamant repeated with her vague laugh.

'That grisly little book in the case. I can't resist a book and I'm afraid I opened the case. I do hope it's allowed.'

'Oh,' said Millamant. 'Yes, of course.' She glanced at the case. 'What book is it?'

'It's about embalming, of all things. It's very old. I should think it might be rather valuable.'

'Perhaps,' said Millamant, 'that's why Miss Orrincourt was so interested in it.'

She moved to the fireplace, looking smugly resentful.

'Miss Orrincourt?' Troy repeated.

'I found her reading a small book when I came in the other day. She put it in the case and dropped the lid. Such a bang! It's a wonder it didn't break, really. I suppose it must have been that book, mustn't it?'

'Yes,' said Troy, hurriedly rearranging her already chaotic ideas of Miss Sonia Orrincourt. 'I suppose it must.'

'Papa,' said Millamant, 'is not quite at his best this evening but he's coming down. On his bad days he dines in his own rooms.'

'I hope,' said Troy, 'that the sittings won't tire him too much.'

'Well, he's so looking forward to them that I'm sure he'll try to keep them up. He's really been much better lately, only sometimes,' said Millamant ambiguously, 'he gets a little upset. He's very highly strung and sensitive, you know. I always think that all the Ancreds are like that. Except Thomas. My poor Cedric, unfortunately, has inherited their temperament.'

Troy had nothing to say to this, and was relieved when Paul Kentish and his mother came in, followed in a moment by Fenella. Barker brought a tray with sherry. Presently an extraordinarily ominous gong sounded in the hall.

'Did anyone see Cedric?' asked his mother. 'I do hope he's not going to be late.'

'He was still in his bath when I tried to get in ten minutes ago,' said Paul.

'Oh, dear,' said Millamant.

Miss Orrincourt, amazingly dressed, and looking at once sulky, triumphant and defiant, drifted into the room. Troy heard a stifled exclamation behind her, and turned to see the assembled Ancreds with their gaze riveted to Miss Orrincourt's bosom.

It was adorned with a large diamond star.

'Milly,' Pauline muttered.

'Do you see what I see?' Millamant replied with a faint hiss.

Miss Orrincourt moved to the fire and laid one arm along the mantelpiece. 'I hope Noddy's not going to be late,' she said. 'I'm starving.' She looked critically at her crimson nails and touched the diamond star. 'I'd like a drink,' she said.

Nobody made any response to this statement, though Paul uncomfortably cleared his throat. The tap of a stick sounded in the hall.

'Here *is* Papa,' said Pauline nervously, and they all moved slightly. Really, thought Troy, they might be waiting to dine with some minor royalty. There was precisely the same air of wary expectation.

Barker opened the door, and the original of all the photographs walked slowly into the room, followed by the white cat.

III

The first thing to be said about Sir Henry Ancred was that he filled his rôle with almost embarrassing virtuosity. He was unbelievably handsome. His hair was silver, his eyes, under heavy brows, were fiercely blue. His nose was ducal in its prominence. Beneath it sprouted a fine snowy moustache, brushed up to lend accent to his actor's mouth. His chin jutted out squarely and was adorned with an ambassadorial tuft. He looked as if he had been specially designed for exhibition. He wore a velvet dinner-jacket, an old-fashioned collar, a wide cravat and a monocle on a broad ribbon. You could hardly believe, Troy thought, that he was true. He came in slowly, using a black and silver stick, but not leaning on it overmuch. It was, Troy felt, more of an adjunct than an aid. He was exceeding tall and still upright.

'Mrs Alleyn, Papa,' said Pauline.

'Ah,' said Sir Henry.

Troy went to meet him. 'Restraining myself,' as she afterwards told Alleyn, 'from curtsying, but with difficulty.'

'So this is our distinguished painter?' said Sir Henry, taking her hand. 'I am delighted.'

He kept her hand in his and looked down at her. Behind him, Troy saw in fancy a young Henry Ancred bending his gaze upon the women in his heyday and imagined how pleasurably they must have melted before it. 'Delighted,' he repeated, and his voice underlined adroitly his pleasure not only in her arrival but in her looks. 'Hold your horses, chaps,' thought Troy and removed her hand. 'I hope you continue of that mind,' she said politely.

Sir Henry bowed. 'I believe I shall,' he said. 'I believe I shall.' She was to learn that he had a habit of repeating himself.

Paul had moved a chair forward. Sir Henry sat in it facing the fire, with the guest and family disposed in arcs on either side of him.

He crossed his knees and rested his left forearm along the arm of his chair, letting his beautifully kept hand dangle elegantly. It was a sort of Charles II pose, and, in lieu of the traditional spaniel, the white cat leapt gracefully on his lap, kneaded it briefly and reclined there.

'Ah, Carabbas!' said Sir Henry, and stroked it, looking graciously awhile upon his family and guest. 'This is pleasant,' he said, including them in a beautiful gesture. For a moment his gaze rested on Miss Orrincourt's bosom. 'Charming,' he said. 'A conversation piece. Ah! A glass of sherry.'

Paul and Fenella dispensed the sherry, which was extremely good. Rather elaborate conversation was made, Sir Henry conducting it with the air of giving an audition. 'But I thought,' he said, 'that Cedric was to join us. Didn't you tell me, Millamant – '

'I'm so sorry he's late, Papa,' said Millamant. 'He had an important letter to write, I know. I think perhaps he didn't hear the gong.'

'Indeed? Where have you put him?'

'In Garrick, Papa.'

'Then he certainly must have heard the gong.'

Barker came in and announced dinner.

'We shall not, I think, wait for Cedric,' Sir Henry continued. He removed the cat, Carabbas, from his knees and rose. His family rose with him. 'Mrs Alleyn, may I have the pleasure of taking you in?' he said.

'It's a pity,' Troy thought as she took the arm he curved for her, 'that there isn't an orchestra.' And as if she had recaptured the lines from some drawing-room comedy of her childhood, she made processional conversation as they moved towards the door. Before they reached it, however, there was a sound of running footsteps in the hall. Cedric, flushed with exertion and wearing a white flower in his dinner-jacket, darted into the room.

'Dearest Grandpapa,' he cried, waving his hands, 'I creep, I grovel. So sorry, truly. Couldn't be more contrite. Find me some sackcloth and ashes somebody, quickly.'

'Good evening, Cedric,' said Sir Henry icily. 'You must make your apologies to Mrs Alleyn, who will perhaps be very kind and forgive you.'

Troy smiled like a duchess at Cedric and inwardly grinned like a Cheshire cat at herself.

'Too heavenly of you,' said Cedric quickly. He slipped in behind them. The procession had splayed out a little on his entrance. He came face to face with Miss Orrincourt. Troy heard him give a curious, half-articulate exclamation. It sounded involuntary and unaffected. This was so unusual from Cedric that Troy turned to look at him. His small mouth was open. His pale eyes stared blankly at the diamond star on Miss Orrincourt's bosom, and then turned incredulously from one member of his family to another.

'But' – he stammered – 'but, I say – I say.'

'Cedric,' whispered his mother.

'Cedric,' said his grandfather imperatively.

But Cedric, still speaking in that strangely natural voice, pointed a white finger at the diamond star and said loudly: 'But, my God, it's Great-Great-Grandmama Ancred's sunburst!'

'Nice, isn't it?' said Miss Orrincourt equally loudly. 'I'm ever so thrilled.'

'In these unhappy times, alas,' said Sir Henry blandly, arming Troy through the door, 'one may not make those gestures with which one would wish to honour a distinguished visitor! "A poor small banquet," as old Capulet had it. Shall we go in?'

IV

The poor small banquet was, if nothing else, a tribute to the zeal of Sir Henry's admirers in the Dominions and the United States of America. Troy had not seen its like for years. He himself, she noticed, ate a mess of something that had been put through a sieve. Conversation was general, innocuous, and sounded a little as if it had been carefully memorized beforehand. It was difficult not to look at Miss Orrincourt's diamonds. They were a sort of visual *faux pas* which no amount of blameless small-talk could shout down. Troy observed that the Ancreds themselves constantly darted furtive glances at them. Sir Henry continued bland, urbane, and, to Troy, excessively gracious. She found his compliments, which were adroit, rather hard to counter. He spoke of her work and asked if she had done a self-portrait. 'Only in my student days when I couldn't afford a model,' said Troy. 'But that's very naughty of you,' he said. 'It is now that you should give us the perfect painting of the perfect subject.'

'Crikey!' thought Troy.

They drank Rudesheimer. When Barker hovered beside him, Sir Henry, announcing that it was a special occasion, said he would take half a glass. Millamant and Pauline looked anxiously at him.

'Papa, darling,' said Pauline. 'Do you think –?' And Millamant murmured: 'Yes, Papa. *Do* you think –?'

'Do I think what?' he replied, glaring at them.

'Wine,' they murmured disjointedly. 'Dr Withers . . . not really advisable . . . however.'

'Fill it up, Barker,' Sir Henry commanded loudly, 'fill it up.'

Troy heard Pauline and Millamant sigh windily.

Dinner proceeded with circumspection but uneasily. Paul and Fenella were silent. Cedric, on Troy's right hand, conversed in feverish spasms with anybody who would listen to him. Sir Henry's flow of compliments continued unabated through three courses, and to Troy's dismay, Miss Orrincourt began to show signs of marked hostility. She was on Sir Henry's left, with Paul on her other side. She began an extremely grand conversation with Paul, and though he responded with every sign of discomfort she lowered her voice, cast significant glances at him, and laughed immoderately at his monosyllabic replies. Troy, who was beginning to find her host very heavy weather indeed, seized an opportunity to speak to Cedric.

'Noddy,' said Miss Orrincourt at once, 'what are we going to do tomorrow?'

'Do?' he repeated, and after a moment's hesitation became playful. 'What does a little girl want to do?'

Miss Orrincourt stretched her arms above her head. 'She wants things to *happen!*' she cried ecstatically. 'Lovely things.'

'Well, if she's very, *very* good perhaps we'll let her have a tiny peep at a great big picture.'

Troy heard this with dismay.

'What else?' Miss Orrincourt persisted babyishly but with an extremely unenthusiastic glance at Troy.

'We'll see,' said Sir Henry uneasily.

'But Noddy – '

'Mrs Alleyn,' said Millamant from the foot of the table, 'shall we – ?'

And she marshalled her ladies out of the dining-room.

The rest of the evening passed uneventfully. Sir Henry led Troy through the pages of three albums of theatrical photographs. This she rather enjoyed. It was strange, she thought, to see how the fashion in Elizabethan garments changed in the world of theatre. Here was a young Victorian Henry Ancred very much be-pointed, be-ruffed, encased and furbished, in a perfect welter of velvet, ribbon and leather; here a modern elderly Henry Ancred in a stylized and simplified costume that had apparently been made of painted scenic canvas. Yet both were the Duke of Buckingham.

Miss Orrincourt joined a little fretfully in this pastime. Perched on the arm of Sir Henry's chair and disseminating an aura of black market scent, she giggled tactlessly over the earlier photographs and yawned over the later ones. 'My dear,' she ejaculated, 'look at you! You've got everything on but the kitchen sink!' This was in reference to a picture of Sir Henry as Richard II. Cedric tittered and immediately looked frightened. Pauline said: 'I must say, Papa, I don't think anyone else has ever approached your flair for exactly the right costume.'

'My dear,' her father rejoined, 'it's the way you wear 'em.' He patted Miss Orrincourt's hand. 'You do very well, my child,' he said, 'in your easy modern dresses. How would you manage if, like Ellen Terry, you had two feet of heavy velvet in front of you on the stage and were asked to move like a queen down a flight of stairs? You'd fall on your nice little nose.'

He was obviously a vain man. It was extraordinary, Troy thought, that he remained unmoved by Miss Orrincourt's lack of reverence, and remembering Thomas's remark about David and Abishag the Shunammite, Troy was forced to the disagreeable conclusion that Sir Henry was in his dotage about Miss Orrincourt.

At ten o'clock a grog-tray was brought in. Sir Henry drank barley water, suffered the women of his family to kiss him goodnight, nodded to Paul and Cedric, and, to her intense embarrassment, kissed Troy's hand. '*A demain*,' he said in his deepest voice. 'We meet at eleven. I am fortunate.'

He made a magnificent exit, and ten minutes later, Miss Orrincourt, yawning extensively, also retired.

Her disappearance was the signal for an outbreak among the Ancreds.

'Honestly, Milly! Honestly, Aunt Pauline. Can we believe our *eyes!*' cried Cedric. 'The Sunburst! I mean *actually!*'

'Well, Millamant,' said Pauline, 'I now see for myself how things stand at Ancreton.'

'You wouldn't believe me when I told you, Pauline,' Millamant rejoined. 'You've been here a month, but you wouldn't – '

'Has he *given* it to her, will somebody tell me?' Cedric demanded.

'He can't,' said Pauline. 'He can't. And what's more, I don't believe he would. Unless – ' She stopped short and turned to Paul. 'If he's given it to her,' she said, 'he's going to marry her. That's all.'

Poor Troy, who had been making completely ineffectual efforts to go, seized upon the silence that followed Pauline's announcement to murmur: 'If I may, I think I shall – '

'*Dear* Mrs Alleyn,' said Cedric, 'I implore you not to be tactful. Do stay and listen.'

'I don't see,' Paul began, 'why poor Mrs Alleyn should be inflicted – '

'She knows,' said Fenella. 'I'm afraid I've already told her, Paul.'

Pauline suddenly made a gracious dive at Troy. 'Isn't it disturbing?' she said with an air of drawing Troy into her confidence. 'You see how things are? Really, it's too naughty of Papa. We're all so dreadfully worried. It's not what's happening so much as what might happen that terrifies one. And now the Sunburst. A little too much. In its way it's a historic jewel.'

'It was a little *cadeau d'estime* from the Regent to Great-Great-Grandmama Honoria Ancred,' Cedric cut in. 'Not only historical, but history repeating itself. And *may* I point out, Aunt Pauline, that I personally am rocked to the foundations. I've always understood that the Sunburst was to come to me.'

'To your daughter,' said Paul. 'The point is academic.'

'I'm sure I don't know why you think so,' said Cedric, bridling. 'Anything might happen.'

Paul raised his eyebrows.

'Really, Pauline,' said Millamant. 'Really, Paul!'

'Paul, darling,' said Pauline offensively, 'don't tease poor Cedric.'

'Anyway,' said Fenella, 'I think Aunt Pauline's right. I think he means to marry, and if he does, I'm never coming to Ancreton again. Never!'

'What shall you call her, Aunt Pauline?' Cedric asked impertinently. 'Mummy, or a pet name?'

'There's only one thing to be done,' said Pauline. 'We must tackle him. I've told Jenetta and I've told Dessy. They're both coming. Thomas will have to come too. In Claude's absence he should take the lead. It's his duty.'

'Do you mean, dearest Aunt Pauline, that we are to lie in ambush for the Old Person and make an altogether-boys bounce at him?'

'I propose, Cedric, that we ask him to meet us all and that we simply – we simply – '

'And a fat lot of good, if you'll forgive me for saying so, Pauline, that is likely to do,' said Millamant, with a chuckle.

'Not being an Ancred, Millamant, you can't be expected to feel this terrible thing as painfully as we do. How Papa, with his deep sense of pride in an old name – we go back to the Conquest, Mrs Alleyn – how Papa can have allowed himself to be entangled! It's too humiliating.'

'Not being an Ancred, as you point out, Pauline, I realize Papa, as well as being blue-blooded, is extremely hot-blooded. Moreover, he's as obstinate and vain as a peacock. He likes the idea of himself with a dashing young wife.'

'Comparatively young,' said Cedric.

Pauline clasped her hands, and turning from one member of her family to another, said, 'I've thought of something! Now listen all of you. I'm going to be perfectly frank and impersonal about this. I know I'm the child's mother, but that needn't prevent me. Panty!'

'What about Panty, Mother?' asked Paul nervously.

'Your grandfather adores the child. Now, suppose Panty were just to drop a childish hint.'

'If you suggest,' said Cedric, 'that Panty should wind her little arms round his neck and whisper: "Grandpapa, when will the howwid lady wun away?" I can only say I don't think she'd get into the skin of the part.'

'He adores her,' Pauline repeated angrily. 'He's like a great big boy with her. It brings the tears into my eyes to see them together. You can't deny it, Millamant.'

'I dare say it does, Pauline.'

'Well, but Mother, Panty plays up to Grandpapa,' said Paul bluntly.

'And in any case,' Cedric pointed out, 'isn't Panty as thick as thieves with Sonia?'

'I happen to know,' said Millamant, 'that Miss Orrincourt encouraged Panty to play a very silly trick on me last Sunday.'

'What did she do?' asked Cedric.

Fenella giggled.

'She pinned a very silly notice on the back of my coat when I was going to church,' said Millamant stuffily.

'What did it say, Milly, darling?' Cedric asked greedily.

'Roll out the Barrel,' said Fenella.

'This is getting us nowhere,' said Millamant.

'And now,' said Troy hurriedly, 'I really think if you'll excuse me – '

This time she was able to get away. The Ancreds distractedly bade her goodnight. She refused an escort to her room, and left them barely waiting, she felt, for her to shut the door before they fell to again.

Only a solitary lamp burned in the hall, which was completely silent, and since the fire had died out, very cold. While Troy climbed the stairs she felt as she had not felt before in this enormous house, that it had its own individuality. It stretched out on all sides of her, an undiscovered territory. It housed, as well as the eccentricities of the Ancreds, their deeper thoughts and the thoughts of their predecessors. When she reached the gallery, which was also dim, she felt that the drawing-room was now profoundly distant, a subterranean island. The rows of mediocre portraits and murky landscapes that she now passed had a life of their own in this half-light and seemed to be indifferently aware of her progress. Here, at last, was her own passage with the tower steps at the end. She halted for a moment before climbing them. Was it imagination, or had the door, out of sight on the half-landing above her, been softly closed? 'Perhaps,' she thought, 'somebody lives in the room below me,' and for some reason the notion affected her unpleasantly. 'Ridiculous!' thought Troy, and turned on a switch at the foot of the stairs. A lamp, out of sight beyond the first spiral, brought the curved wall rather stealthily to life.

Troy mounted briskly, hoping there would still be a fire in her white room. As she turned the spiral, she gathered up her long dress with her right hand and with her left reached out for the narrow rail.

The rail was sticky.

She snatched her hand away with some violence and looked at it. The palm and the under-surface were dark. Troy stood in the shadow of the inner wall, but she now moved up into light. By the single lamps she saw that the stain on her hand was red.

Five seconds must have gone by before she realized that the stuff on her hand was paint.

CHAPTER 5

The Bloody Child

At half past ten the following morning Troy, hung with paint boxes and carrying a roll of canvas and stretchers, made her way to the little theatre. Guided by Paul and Cedric, who carried her studio easel between them, she went down a long passage that led out of the hall, turned right at a green baize door, 'beyond which,' Cedric panted, 'the Difficult Children ravage at will,' and continued towards the rear of that tortuous house. Their journey was not without incident, for as they passed the door of what, as Troy later discovered, was a small sitting-room, it was flung open and a short plumpish man appeared, his back towards them, shouting angrily: 'If you've no faith in my treatment, Sir Henry, you have an obvious remedy. I shall be glad to be relieved of the thankless task of prescribing for a damned obstinate patient and his granddaughter.' Troy made a valiant effort to forge ahead, but was blocked by Cedric, who stopped short, holding the easel diagonally across the passage and listening with an air of the liveliest interest. 'Now, now, keep your temper,' rumbled the invisible Sir Henry. 'I wash my hands of you,' the other proclaimed. 'No, you don't. You keep a civil tongue in your head, Withers. You'd much better look after me and take a bit of honest criticism in the way it's intended.' 'This is outrageous,' the visitor said, but with a note of something like despair in his voice. 'I formally relinquish the case. You will take this as final.' There was a pause, during which Paul attempted, without success, to drag Cedric away. 'I won't accept it,' Sir Henry said at last. 'Come, now, Withers, keep your temper. You ought to understand. I've a great deal to try me. A great deal. Bear with an old fellow's tantrums, won't you?

You shan't regret it. See here, now. Shut that door and listen to me.'
Without turning, the visitor slowly shut the door.

'And *now,*' Cedric whispered, 'he'll tell poor Dr Withers he's
going to be remembered in the Will.'

'Come on, for God's sake,' said Paul, and they made their way to
the little theatre.

Half an hour later Troy had set up her easel, stretched her canvas,
and prepared paper and boards for preliminary studies. The theatre was
a complete little affair with a deepish stage. The *Macbeth* backcloth was
simple and brilliantly conceived. The scenic painter had carried out
Troy's original sketch very well indeed. Before it stood three-dimension-
al monolithic forms that composed well and broke across the cloth in
the right places. She saw where she would place her figure. There would
be no attempt to present the background in terms of actuality. It would
be frankly a stage set. 'A dangling rope would come rather nicely,' she
thought, 'but I suppose they wouldn't like that. If only he'll stand!'

Cedric and Paul now began to show her what could be done with
the lights. Troy was enjoying herself. She liked the smell of canvas and
glue and the feeling that this was a place where people worked. In the
little theatre even Cedric improved. He was knowledgeable and quickly
responsive to her suggestions, checking Paul's desire to flood the set
with a startling display of lighting and getting him to stand in position
while he himself focussed a single spot. 'We must find the backcloth
discreetly,' he cried. 'Try the ground row.' And presently a luminous
glow appeared, delighting Troy.

'But how are you going to *see?*' cried Cedric distractedly. 'Oh,
lawks! How *are* you going to see?'

'I can bring down a standard spot on an extension,' Paul offered.
'Or we could uncover a window.'

Cedric gazed in an agony of inquiry at Troy. 'But the window light
would infiltrate,' he said. 'Or wouldn't it?'

'We could try.'

At last by an ingenious arrangement of screens Troy was able to
get daylight on her canvas and a fair view of the stage.

The clock – it was, of course, known as the Great Clock – in the
central tower struck eleven. A door somewhere backstage opened
and shut, and dead on his cue Sir Henry, in the character of Macbeth,
walked onto the lighted set.

'Golly!' Troy whispered. 'Oh, Golly!'

'Devastatingly fancy dress,' said Cedric in her ear, 'but in its ridiculous way rather exciting. Or not? Too fancy?'

'It's not too fancy for me,' Troy said roundly, and walked down the aisle to greet her sitter.

II

At midday Troy drove her fingers through her hair, propped a large charcoal drawing against the front of the stage and backed away from it down the aisle. Sir Henry took off his helmet, groaned a little, and moved cautiously to a chair in the wings.

'I suppose you want to stop,' said Troy absently, biting her thumb and peering at her drawing.

'One grows a trifle stiff,' he replied. She then noticed that he was looking more than a trifle tired. He had made up for her sitting, painting heavy shadows round his eyes and staining his moustache and the tuft on his chin with water-dye. To this he had added long strands of crêpe hair. But beneath the greasepaint and hair his face sagged a little and his head drooped.

'I must let you go,' said Troy. 'I hope I haven't been too exacting. One forgets.'

'One also remembers,' said Sir Henry. 'I have been remembering my lines. I played the part first in 1904.'

Troy looked up quickly, suddenly liking him.

'It's a wonderful rôle,' he said. 'Wonderful.'

'I was very much moved by it when I saw you five years ago.'

'I've played it six times and always to enormous business. It hasn't been an unlucky piece for me.'

'I've heard about the Macbeth superstition. One mustn't quote from the play, must one?' Troy made a sudden pounce at her drawing and wiped her thumb down a too dominant line. 'Do you believe it's unlucky?' she asked vaguely.

'It has been for other actors,' he said, quite seriously. 'There's always a heavy feeling offstage during performance. People are nervy.'

'Isn't that perhaps because they remember the superstition?'

'It's there,' he said. 'You can't escape the feeling. But the piece has never been unlucky for me.' His voice, which had sounded tired, lifted again. 'If it were otherwise, should I have chosen this role for my portrait? Assuredly not. And now,' he said with a return of his arch and over-gallant manner, 'am I to be allowed a peep before I go?'

Troy was not very keen for him to have his peep, but she took the drawing a little way down the aisle and turned it towards him. 'I'm afraid it won't explain itself,' she said. 'It's merely a sort of plot of what I hope to do.'

'Ah, yes!' He put his hand in his tunic and drew out a pair of gold-rimmed pince-nez and there, in a moment, was Macbeth, with glasses perched on his nose, staring solemnly at his own portrait. 'Such a clever lady,' he said. 'Very clever!' Troy put the drawing away and he got up slowly. 'Off, ye lendings!' he said. 'I must change.' He adjusted his cloak with a practised hand, drew himself up, and, moving into the spot-light, pointed his dirk at the great naked canvas. His voice, as though husbanded for this one flourish, boomed through the empty theatre.

' "Well, may you see things well done there: adieu!
Lest our old robes sit easier than our new!" '

' "God's benison go with you!" ' said Troy, luckily remembering the line. He crossed himself, chuckled and strode off between the monoliths to the door behind the stage. It slammed and Troy was alone.

She had made up her mind to start at once with the laying out of her subject on the big canvas. There would be no more preliminary studies. Time pressed and she knew now what she wanted. There is no other moment, she thought, to compare with this, when you face the tautly stretched surface and raise your hand to make the first touch upon it. And, drawing in her breath, she swept her charcoal across the canvas. It gave a faint drumlike note of response. 'We're off,' thought Troy.

Fifty minutes went by and a rhythm of line and mass grew under her hand. Back and forward she walked, making sharp accents with the end of her charcoal or sweeping it flat across the grain of the canvas. All that was Troy was now poured into her thin blackened hand. At last she stood motionless, ten paces back from her work,

and, after an interval, lit a cigarette, took up her duster and began to
flick her drawing. Showers of charcoal fell down the surface.

'Don't you like it?' asked a sharp voice.

Troy jumped galvanically and turned. The little girl she had seen
fighting on the terrace stood in the aisle, her hands jammed in the
pockets of her pinafore and her feet planted apart.

'Where did you come from?' Troy demanded.

'Through the end door. I came quietly because I'm not allowed.
Why are you rubbing it out? Don't you like it?'

'I'm not rubbing it out. It's still there.' And indeed the ghost of
her drawing remained. 'You take the surplus charcoal off,' she said
curtly. 'Otherwise it messes the paints.'

is it going to be Noddy dressed up funny?'

Troy started at this use of a name she had imagined to be Miss
Orrincourt's prerogative and invention.

'I call him Noddy,' said the child, as if guessing at her thought,
'and so does Sonia. She got it from me. I'm going to be like Sonia
when I'm grown up.'

'Oh,' said Troy, opening her paint box and rummaging in it.

'Are those your paints?'

'Yes,' said Troy, looking fixedly at her. 'They are. Mine.'

'I'm Patricia Claudia Ellen Ancred Kentish.'

'So I'd gathered.'

'You couldn't have gathered all of that, because nobody except
Miss Able ever calls me anything but Panty. Not that I care,' added
Panty, suddenly climbing onto the back of one of the stools and locking her feet in the arms, 'I'm double jointed,' she said, throwing herself back and hanging head downwards.

'That won't help you if you break your neck,' said Troy.

Panty made an offensive gargling noise.

'As you're not allowed here,' Troy continued, 'hadn't you better
run off?'

'No,' said Panty.

Troy squeezed a fat serpent of Flake White out on her palette. 'If
I ignore this child,' she thought, 'perhaps she will get bored and go.'

Now the yellows, next the reds. How beautiful was her palette!

'I'm going to paint with those paints,' said Panty at her elbow.

'You haven't a hope,' said Troy.

'I'm going to.' She made a sudden grab at the tray of long brushes. Troy anticipated this move by a split second.

'Now, see here, Panty,' she said, shutting the box and facing the child, 'if you don't pipe down I shall pick you up by the slack of your breeches and carry you straight back to where you belong. You don't like people butting in on your games, do you? Well, this is my game, and I can't get on with it if you butt in.'

'I'll kill you,' said Panty.

'Don't be an ass,' said Troy mildly.

Panty scooped up a dollop of vermilion on three of her fingers and flung it wildly at Troy's face. She then burst into peals of shrill laughter.

'You can't whack me,' she shrieked. 'I'm being brought up on a system.'

'Can't I!' Troy rejoined. 'System or no system – ' And indeed there was nothing she desired more at the moment than to beat Panty. The child confronted her with an expression of concentrated malevolence. Her cheeks were blown out with such determination that her nose wrinkled and turned up. Her mouth was so tightly shut that lines resembling a cat's whiskers radiated from it. She scowled hideously. Her pigtails stuck out at right angles to her head. Altogether she looked like an infuriated infant Boreas.

Troy sat down and reached for a piece of rag to clean her face. 'Oh, Panty,' she said, 'you do look so exactly like your Uncle Thomas.'

Panty drew back her arm again. 'No, don't,' said Troy. 'Don't do any more damage with red paint, I implore you. Look here, I'll strike a bargain with you. If you'll promise not to take any more paint without asking, I'll give you a board and some brushes and let you make a proper picture.'

Panty glared at her. 'When?' she said warily.

'When we've asked your mother or Miss Able. I'll ask. But no more nonsense. And especially,' Troy added, taking a shot in the dark, 'no more going to my room and squeezing paint on the stair rail.'

Panty stared blankly at her. 'I don't know what you're talking about,' she said flatly. 'When can I paint? I want to. Now.'

'Yes, but let's get this cleared up. What did you do before dinner last night?'

'I don't know. Yes, I do. Dr Withers came. He weighed us all. He's going to make me bald because I've got ringworm. That's why I've got this cap on. Would you like to see my ringworm?'

'No.'

'I got it first. I've given it to sixteen of the others.'

'Did you go up to my room and mess about with my paints?'

'No.'

'Honestly, Panty?'

'Honestly what? I don't know where your room is. When can I paint?'

'Do you promise you didn't put paint . . . '

'You are *silly!*' said Panty furiously. 'Can't you see a person's telling the truth.'

And Troy, greatly bewildered, thought that she could.

While she was still digesting this queer little scene, the door at the back of the stalls opened and Cedric peered round it.

'*So* humble and timid,' he lisped. 'Just a mouse-like squeak to tell you luncheon is almost on the table. *Panty!*' he cried shrilly, catching sight of his cousin. 'You gross child! Back to the West Wing, miss! How dare you muscle your hideous way in here?'

Panty grinned savagely at him. 'Hallo, Sissy,' she said.

'Wait,' said Cedric, 'just wait till the Old Person catches you. What he won't do to you!'

'Why?' Panty demanded.

'Why! You ask me why. Infamy! With the grease-paint fresh on your fingers.'

Both Panty and Troy gaped at this. Panty glanced at her hand. 'That's her paint,' she said, jerking her head at Troy. 'That's not grease-paint.'

'Do you deny,' Cedric pursued, shaking his finger at her, 'do you deny, you toxic child, that you went into your grandfather's dressing-room while he was sitting for Mrs Alleyn, and scrawled some pothouse insult in lake-liner on his looking-glass? Do you deny, moreover, that you painted a red moustache on the cat, Carabbas?'

With an air of bewilderment that Troy could have sworn was genuine, Panty repeated her former statement. 'I don't know what you're talking about. I didn't.'

'Tell that,' said Cedric with relish, 'to your grandpapa and see if he believes you.'

'Noddy likes me,' said Panty, rallying. 'He likes me best in the family. He thinks you're awful. He said you're a simpering popinjay.'

'See here,' said Troy hastily. 'Let's get this straight. You say Panty's written something in grease-paint on Sir Henry's looking-glass. What's she supposed to have written?'

Cedric coughed. 'Dearest Mrs Alleyn, we mustn't allow you for a second to be disturbed . . . '

'I'm not disturbed,' said Troy. 'What was written on the glass?'

'My mama would have wiped it off. She was in his room tidying, and saw it. She hunted madly for a rag but the Old Person, at that moment, walked in and saw it. He's roaring about the house like a major prophet.'

'But what was it, for pity's sake?'

' "Grandfather's a bloody old fool," ' said Cedric. Panty giggled. 'There!' said Cedric. 'You see? Obviously she wrote it. Obviously she made up the cat.'

'I didn't. I *didn't*.' And with one of those emotional *volte-faces* by which children bewilder us, Panty wrinkled up her face, kicked Cedric suddenly but half-heartedly on the shin, and burst into a storm of tears.

'You odious child!' he ejaculated, skipping out of her way.

Panty flung herself on her face, screamed industriously and beat the floor with her fists. 'You all hate me,' she sobbed. 'Wicked beasts! I wish I was dead.'

'Oh, la,' said Cedric, 'how tedious! Now, she'll have a fit or something.'

Upon this scene came Paul Kentish. He limped rapidly down the aisle, seized his sister by the slack of her garments and, picking her up very much as if she was a kitten, attempted to stand her on her feet. Panty drew up her legs and hung from his grasp, in some danger, Troy felt, of suffocation. 'Stop it at once, Panty,' he said. 'You've been a very naughty girl.'

'Wait a minute,' said Troy. 'I don't think she has, honestly. I mean, not in the way you think. There's a muddle, I'm certain of it.'

Paul relinquished his hold. Panty sat on the floor, sobbing harshly, a most desolate child.

'It's all right,' said Troy, 'I'll explain. You didn't do it, Panty, and you shall paint if you still want to.'

'She's not allowed to come out of school,' said Paul. 'Caroline Able will be here in a minute.'

'Thank God for that,' said Cedric.

Miss Able arrived almost immediately, cast a professionally breezy glance at her charge and said it was dinner-time. Panty with a look at Troy which she was unable to interpret, got to her feet.

'Look here. . .' said Troy.

'Yes?' said Miss Able cheerfully.

'About this looking-glass business. I don't think that Panty . . .'

'Next time she feels like that we'll think of something much more sensible to do, won't we, Patricia?'

'Yes, but I don't think she did it.'

'We're getting very good at just facing up to these funny old things we do when we're silly, aren't we, Patricia? It's best just to find out why and then forget about them.'

'But . . .'

'Dinner!' cried Miss Able brightly and firmly. She removed the child without any great ado.

'Dearest Mrs Alleyn,' said Cedric, waving his hands. 'Why are you so sure Panty is not the author of the insult on the Old Person's mirror?'

'Has she ever called him "Grandfather"?'

'Well, no,' said Paul. 'No, actually she hasn't.'

'And what's more . . .' Troy stopped short. Cedric had moved to her painting table. He had taken up a piece of rag and was using it to clean a finger-nail. Only then did Troy realize that the first finger of the right hand he had waved at her had been stained dark crimson under the nail.

He caught her eye and dropped the rag.

'Such a Paul Pry!' he said. 'Dipping my fingers in your paint.'

But there had been no dark crimson laid out on her palette.

'Well,' said Cedric shrilly, 'shall we lunch?'

III

By the light of her flash-lamp Troy was examining the stair rail in her tower. The paint had not been cleaned away and was now in the condition known as tacky. She could see clearly the mark left by her own hand. Above this, the paint was untouched. It had not been squeezed out and left, but brushed over the surface. At one point only, on the stone wall above the rail, someone had left the faint red print of two fingers. 'How Rory would laugh at me,' she thought, peering at them. They were small, but not small enough, she thought, to have been made by a child. Could one of the maids have touched the rail and then the wall? But beyond the mark left by her own grip there were no other prints on the rail. 'Rory,' she thought, 'would take photographs, but how could one ever get anything from these things? They're all broken up by the rough surface. I couldn't even make a drawing of them.' She was about to move away when the light from her torch fell on an object that seemed to be wedged in the gap between a step and the stone wall. Looking more closely she discovered it to be one of her own brushes. She worked it out, and found that the bristles were thick with half-dry Rose Madder.

She went down to the half-landing. There was the door that she had fancied she heard closing last night when she went to bed. It was not quite shut now and she gave it a tentative shove. It swung inwards, and Troy was confronted with a Victorian bathroom.

'Well,' she thought crossly, remembering her long tramp that morning in search of a bath, 'Fenella might have told me I'd got one of my own.'

She had dirtied her fingers on the brush and went in to wash them. The soap in the marble hand-basin was already stained with Rose Madder. 'This is a mad-house,' thought Troy.

IV

Sir Henry posed for an hour that afternoon. The next morning, Sunday, was marked by a massive attendance of the entire family (with Troy) at Ancreton church. In the afternoon, however, he gave her an hour. Troy had decided to go straight for the head. She had laid in a general scheme for her work, an exciting affair of wet shadows and sharp accents. This could be completed without him. She was painting well. The touch of flamboyancy that she had dreaded was absent. She had returned often to the play. Its threat of horror was now a factor in her approach to her work. She was strongly aware of that sense of a directive power which comes only when all is well with painters. With any luck, she thought, I'll be able to say: 'Did the fool that is me, make this?'

At the fourth sitting, Sir Henry returning perhaps to some bygone performance, broke the silence by speaking without warning the lines she had many times read:

> 'Light thickens, and the crow
> Makes wing to the rooky wood. . .'

He startled Troy so much that her hand jerked and she waited motionless until he had finished the speech, resenting the genuine twist of apprehension that had shaken her. She could find nothing to say in response to this unexpected and oddly impersonal performance, but she had the feeling that the old man knew very well how much it had moved her.

After a moment she returned to her work and still it went well. Troy was a deliberate painter, but the head grew with almost frightening rapidity. In an hour she knew that she must not touch it again. She was suddenly exhausted. 'I think we'll stop for today,' she said, and again felt that he was not surprised.

Instead of going away, he came down into the front of the theatre and looked at what she had done. She had that feeling of gratitude to her subject that sometimes follows a sitting that has gone well, but she did not want him to speak of the portrait and began hurriedly to talk of Panty.

'She's doing a most spirited painting of red cows and a green aeroplane.'

'T'uh!' said Sir Henry on a melancholy note.

'She wants to show it to you herself.'

'I have been deeply hurt,' said Sir Henry, 'by Patricia. Deeply hurt.'

'Do you mean,' said Troy uncomfortably, 'because of something she's supposed to have written on – on your looking-glass?'

'Supposed! The thing was flagrant. Not only that, but she opened
the drawers of my dressing-table and pulled out my papers. I may tell
you, that if she were capable of reading the two documents that she
found there, she would perhaps feel some misgivings. I may tell you
that they closely concerned herself, and that if there are any more of
these damnable tricks – ' He paused and scowled portentously. 'Well,
we shall see. We shall see. Let her mother realize that I cannot endure
for ever. And my cat!' he exclaimed. 'She has made a fool of my cat.
There are still marks of grease-paint in his whiskers,' said Sir Henry
angrily. 'Butter has not altogether removed them. As for the insult to
me – '

'But I'm sure she didn't. I was here when they scolded her about
it. Honestly, I'm sure she knew nothing whatever about it.'

'T'uh!'

'No, but really – ' Should she say anything about the dark red stain
under Cedric's finger-nail? No, she'd meddled enough. She went on
quickly: 'Panty brags about her naughtiness. She's told me about all her
practical jokes. She never calls you grandfather and I happen to know
she spells it "farther," because she showed me a story she had written,
and the word occurs frequently. I'm sure Panty's too fond of you,' Troy
continued, wondering if she spoke the truth, 'to do anything so silly
and unkind.'

'I've loved that child,' said Sir Henry with the appallingly rich
display of sentiment so readily commanded by the Ancreds, 'as if she
was my own. My little Best-Beloved, I've always called her. I've never
made any secret of my preference. After I'm Gone,' he went on to
Troy's embarrassment, 'she would have known – however.' He sighed
windily. Troy could think of nothing to say and cleaned her palette.
The light from the single uncovered window had faded. Sir Henry had
switched off the stage lamps and the little theatre was now filled with
shadows. A draught somewhere in the borders caused them to move
uneasily and a rope-end tapped against the canvas backcloth.

'Do you know anything about embalming?' Sir Henry asked in
his deepest voice. Troy jumped.

'No, indeed,' she said.

'I have studied the subject,' said Sir Henry, 'deeply.'

'Oddly enough,' said Troy after a pause, 'I did look at that queer
little book in the drawing-room. The one in the glass case.'

'Ah, yes. It belonged to my ancestor who rebuilt Ancreton. He himself was embalmed and his fathers before him. It has been the custom with the Ancreds. The family vault,' he rambled on depressingly, 'is remarkable for that reason. If I lie there – the Nation may have other wishes: it is not for me to speculate – but if I lie there, it will be after their fashion. I have given explicit directions.'

'I *do* wish,' Troy thought, '*how* I do wish he wouldn't go on like this.' She made a small ambiguous murmuring.

'Ah, well!' said Sir Henry heavily and began to move away. He paused before mounting the steps up to the stage. Troy thought that he was on the edge of some further confidence, and hoped that it would be of a more cheerful character.

'What,' said Sir Henry, 'is your view on the matter of marriage between first cousins?'

'I – really, I don't know,' Troy replied, furiously collecting her wits. 'I fancy I've heard that modern medical opinion doesn't condemn it. But I really haven't the smallest knowledge – '

'I am against it,' he said loudly. 'I cannot approve. Look at the Hapsburgs! The House of Spain! The Romanoffs!' His voice died away in an inarticulate rumble.

Hoping to divert his attention Troy began: 'Panty – '

'Hah!' said Sir Henry. 'These doctors don't know anything. Patricia's scalp! A common childish ailment, and Withers, having pottered about with it for weeks without doing any good, is now going to dose the child with a depilatory. Disgusting! I have spoken to the child's mother, but I'd have done better to hold my tongue. Who,' Sir Henry demanded, 'pays any attention to the old man? Nobody. Ours is an Ancient House, Mrs Alleyn. We have borne arms since my ancestor, the Sieur d'Ancred, fought beside the Conqueror. And before that. Before that. A proud house. Perhaps in my own humble way I have not disgraced it. But what will happen when I am Gone? I look for my Heir and what do I find? A Thing! An emasculated Popinjay!'

He evidently expected some reply to this pronouncement on Cedric, but Troy was quite unable to think of one.

'The last of the Ancreds!' he said, glaring at her. 'A family that came in with the Conqueror to go out with a – '

'But,' said Troy, 'he may marry and . . .'

'And have kittens! P'shaw!'

'Perhaps Mr Thomas Ancred . . .'

'Old Tommy! No! I've talked to old Tommy. He doesn't see it. He'll die a bachelor. And Claude's wife is past it. Well, it was my hope to know the line was secure before I went. I shan't.'

'But, bless my soul,' said Troy, 'you're taking far too gloomy a view of all this. There's not much wrong with a man who can pose for an hour with a helmet weighing half a hundredweight on his head. You may see all sorts of exciting things happen.'

It was astonishing, it was almost alarming, to see how promptly he squared his shoulders, how quickly gallantry made its reappearance. 'Do you think so?' he said, and Troy noticed how his hand went to his cloak, giving it an adroit hitch. 'Well, perhaps, after all, you're right. Clever lady! Yes, *yes*. I *may* see something exciting and what's more – ' he paused and gave a very queer little giggle – 'what's more, my dear, so may other people.'

Troy was never to know if Sir Henry would have elaborated on this strange prophecy, as at that moment a side door in the auditorium was flung open and Miss Orrincourt burst into the little theatre.

'Noddy!' she shouted angrily. 'You've got to come. Get out of that funny costume and protect me. I've had as much of your bloody family as I can stand. It's them or me. Now!'

She strode down the aisle and confronted him, her hands on her hips, a virago.

Sir Henry eyed her with more apprehension, Troy thought, than astonishment, and began a placatory rumbling.

'No you don't,' she said. 'Come off it and *do* something. They're in the library, sitting round a table. Plotting against me. I walked in, and there was Pauline giving an imitation of a cat-fight and telling them how I'd have to be got rid of.'

'My dear, please, I can't allow . . . Surely you're mistaken.'

'Am I dopey? I tell you I *heard* her. They're all against me. I warned you before and I'm warning you again and it's the last time. They're going to frame me. I know what I'm talking about. It's a frame-up. I tell you they've got me all jittery, Noddy. I can't stand it. You can either come and tell them where they get off or it's thanks for the buggy-ride and me for Town in the morning.'

He looked at her disconsolately, hesitated, and took her by the elbow. Her mouth drooped, she gazed at him dolorously. 'It's lonely here, Noddy,' she said. 'Noddy, I'm scared.'

It was strange to watch the expression of extreme tenderness that this instantly evoked; strange, and to Troy, painfully touching.

'Come,' Sir Henry said, stooping over her in his terrifying costume. 'Come along. I'll speak to these children.'

V

The little theatre was on the northern corner of the East Wing. When Troy had tidied up she looked out of doors and found a wintry sun still glinting feebly on Ancreton. She felt stuffed-up with her work. The carriage drive, sweeping downhill through stiffly naked trees, invited her. She fetched a coat and set out bare-headed. The frosty air stung her eyes with tears, the ground rang hard under her feet. Suddenly exhilarated she began to run. Her hair lifted, cold air ran over her scalp and her ears burned icily. 'How ridiculous to run and feel happy,' thought Troy, breathless. And slowing down, she began to make plans. She would leave the head. In two days, perhaps, it would be dry. Tomorrow, the hands and their surrounding drape, and, when he had gone, another hour or so through the background. Touch after touch and for each one the mustering of thought and muscle and the inward remembrance of the scheme.

The drive curved down between banks of dead leaves, and, over-head, frozen branches rattled in a brief visitation of wind, and she thought: 'I'm walking under the scaffolding of summer.' There, beneath her, were the gates. The sun had gone, and already fields of mist had begun to rise from the hollows. 'As far as the gates,' thought Troy, 'and then back up the terraces.' She heard the sound of hooves behind her in the woods and the faint rumbling of wheels. Out of the trees came the governess-cart and Rosinante, and there, gloved and furred and apparently recovered from her fury, sat Miss Orrincourt, flapping the reins.

Troy waited for her and she pulled up. 'I'm going to the village,' she said. 'Do you want to come? Do, like a sweet, because I've got to go to the chemist, and this brute might walk away if nobody watched it.'

Troy got in. 'Can you drive?' said Miss Orrincourt. 'Do, like a ducks. I hate it.' She handed the reins to Troy and at once groped among her magnificent furs for her cigarette case. 'I got the willies up there,' she continued. 'They've all gone out to dinner at the next-door morgue. Well, next door! It's God knows how far away. Cedric and Paul and old Pauline. What a bunch! With their tails *well* down, dear. Well, I mean to say, you saw how upset I was, didn't you? So did Noddy.' She giggled. 'Look, dear, you should have seen him. With that tin toque on his head and everything. Made the big entrance into the library and called them for everything. "This lady," he says, "is my guest and you'll be good enough to remember it." And quite a lot more. Was I tickled! Pauline and Milly looking blue murder and poor little Cedric bleating and waving his hands. He made them apologize. Oh, well,' she said, with a sigh, 'it was something happening anyway. That's the worst of life in this dump. Nothing ever happens. Nothing to do and all day to do it in. God, what a flop! If anybody'd told me a month ago I'd be that fed up I'd get round to crawling about the place in a prehistoric prop like this I'd have thought they'd gone hay-wire. Oh, well, I suppose it'd have been worse in the army.'

'Were you ever in the army?'

'I'm delicate,' said Miss Orrincourt with an air of satisfaction. 'Bronchial asthma. I was fixed up with ENSA but my chest began a rival show. The boys in the orchestra said they couldn't hear themselves play. So I got out. I got an understudy at the Unicorn. It was that West End you barked your shins on the ice. Then,' said Miss Orrincourt simply, 'Noddy noticed me.'

'Was that an improvement?' asked Troy.

'Wouldn't you have thought so? I mean, ask yourself. Well, you know. A man in his position. Top of the tree. Mind, I think he's sweet. I'm crazy about him, in a way. But I've got to look after myself, haven't I? If you don't look after yourself in this old world nobody's going to look after you. Well, between you and I, Mrs Alleyn, things were a bit tricky. Till yesterday. Look, a girl doesn't stick it out in an atmosphere like this, unless there's a future in it, does she? Not if she's still conscious, she doesn't.'

Miss Orrincourt inhaled deeply and then made a petulant little sound. 'Well, I *am* fed up,' she said as if Troy had offered some word of criticism. 'I don't say he hasn't given me things. This coat's rather nice, don't you think? It belonged to a lady who was in the Wrens. I saw it advertised. She'd never worn it. Two hundred and dirt cheap, really.'

They jogged on in a silence broken only by the clop of Rosinante's hooves. There was the little railway Halt and there, beyond a curve in the low hills, the roofs of Ancreton village.

'Well, I mean to say,' said Miss Orrincourt, 'when I fixed up with Noddy to come here I didn't know what I was letting myself in for. I'll say I didn't! Well, *you* know. On the surface it looked like a win. It's high up, and my doctor says my chest ought to be high up, and there wasn't much doing in the business. My voice isn't so hot, and I haven't got the wind for dancing like I had, and the "legitimate" gives me a pain in the neck. So what have you?'

Stumped for an answer, as she had so often been since her arrival at Ancreton, Troy said: 'I suppose the country does feel a bit queer when you're used to bricks and mortar.'

'It feels, to be frank, like death warmed up. Not that I don't say you could do something with that Jack's-come-home up there. You know. Weekend parties, with the old bunch coming down and all the fun and games. And no Ancreds. Well, I wouldn't mind Ceddie. He's one-of-those, of course, but I always think they're good mixers in their own way. I've got it all worked out. Something to do, isn't it, making plans? It may come up in the lift one of these days; you never know. But no Ancreds when I throw a party in the Baronial Hall. You bet, no Ancreds.'

'Sir Henry?' Troy ventured.

'Well,' said Miss Orrincourt, 'I was thinking of later on, if you know what I mean.'

'Good Lord!' Troy ejaculated involuntarily.

'Mind, as I say, I'm fond of Noddy. But it's a funny old world, and there you have it. I must say it's nice having someone to talk to. Someone who isn't an Ancred. I can't exactly *confide* in Ceddie, because he's the heir, and he mightn't quite see things my way.'

'Possibly not.'

'No. Although he's quite nice to me.' The thin voice hardened. 'And, don't you worry, I know why,' Miss Orrincourt added. 'He's stuck for cash, silly kid, and he wants me to use my influence. He'd got the burns on his doorstep when the jitterbugs cleaned up his place, and then he went to the Jews and now he doesn't know where to go. He's scared to turn up at the flat. He'll have to wait till I'm fixed up myself. Then we'll see. I don't mind much,' she said, moving restlessly, 'which way it goes, so long as I'm fixed up.'

They faced each other across the bucket-cart. Troy looked at her companion's beautifully painted face. Behind it stood wraithlike trees, motionless, threaded with mist. It might have been a sharp mask, by a surrealist, hung on that darkling background, thought Troy.

A tiny rhythmic sound grew out of the freezing air. 'I can hear a cat mewing somewhere,' said Troy, pulling Rosinante up.

'That's a good one!' said Miss Orrincourt, laughing and coughing. 'A cat mewing! It's my chest, dear. This damn night air's catching me. Can you hurry that brute up?'

Troy stirred him up, and presently they clopped sedately down the one street of Ancreton village and pulled up outside a small chemist's shop, that seemed also to be a sort of general store.

'Shall I get whatever it is?' Troy offered.

'All right. I don't suppose there's anything worth looking at in the shop. No perfume. Thanks, dear. It's the stuff for the kid's ringworm. The doctor's ordered it. It's meant to be ready.'

The elderly rubicund chemist handed Troy two bottles tied together. One had an envelope attached. 'For the children up at the Manor?' he said. 'Quite so. And the small bottle is for Sir Henry.' When she had climbed back into the governess-cart, she found that he had followed her and stood blinking on the pavement. 'They're labelled,' he said fussily. 'If you'd be good enough to point out the enclosed instructions. The dosage varies, you know. It's determined by the patient's weight. Dr Withers particularly asked me to draw Miss Able's attention. Quite an unusual prescription, actually. Thallium Acetate. Yes. Both labelled. Thank you. One should exercise care . . . So sorry we're out of wrapping paper. Good evening.' He gave a little whooping chuckle and darted back into his shop. Troy was about to turn Rosinate when Miss Orrincourt, asking her to wait, scrambled out and went into the shop, returning in a few minutes with a bulge in her pocket.

'Just something that caught my eye,' she said. 'Righty ho, dear! Home John and don't spare the horses.' On their return journey she exclaimed repeatedly on the subject of the children's ringworm. She held the collar of her fur coat across her mouth and her voice sounded unreal behind it. 'Is it tough, or is it tough? That poor kid Panty. All over her head, and her hair's her one beauty, you might say.'

'You and Panty are rather by way of being friends, aren't you?' said Troy.

'She's a terrible kiddy, really. You know. The things she does! Well! Scribbling across Noddy's mirror with a lake-liner and such a common way to put it, whatever she thought. A few more little cracks like that and she'll cook her goose if she only knew it. The mother's wild about it, naturally. Did you know the kid's favourite in the Will? She won't hold that rôle down much longer if she lets her sense of comedy run away with her. And then the way she put that paint on your bannister! I call it the limit.'

Troy stared at her. 'How did you know about that?'

A spasm of coughing shook her companion, 'I was crazy,' gasped the muffled voice, 'to come out in this lousy fog. Might have known. Pardon me, like a ducks, if I don't talk.'

'Did Panty tell you?' Troy persisted. '*I* haven't told anyone. Did she actually tell you she did it?'

A violent paroxysm prevented Miss Orrincourt from speaking, but with her lovely and enormous eyes fixed on Troy and still clasping her fur collar over the lower part of her face, she nodded three times.

'I'd never have believed it,' said Troy slowly. 'Never.'

Miss Orrincourt's shoulders quivered and shook. 'For all the world,' Troy thought suddenly, 'as if she was laughing.'

CHAPTER 6

Paint

It was on that same night that there was an open flaring row
between Paul and Fenella on the one hand and Sir Henry Ancred on
the other. It occurred at the climax of a game of backgammon
between Troy and Sir Henry. He had insisted upon teaching her this
complicated and maddening game. She would have enjoyed it more
if she hadn't discovered very early in the contest that her opponent
disliked losing so intensely that her own run of beginner's luck had
plunged him into the profoundest melancholy. He had attempted to
explain to her the chances of the possible combinations of a pair of
dice, adding, with some complacency, that he himself had completely
mastered this problem. Troy had found his explanation utterly
incomprehensible, and began by happily moving her pieces with
more regard for the pattern they made on the board than for her
chances of winning the game. She met with uncanny success. Sir
Henry, who had entered the game with an air of gallantry, finding
pretty frequent occasions to pat Troy's fingers, became thoughtful,
then pained, and at last gloomy. The members of his family, aware
of his mortification, watched in nervous silence. Troy moved with
reckless abandon. Sir Henry savagely rattled his dice. Greatly to her
relief the tide turned. She gave herself a 'blot' and looked up, to find
Fenella and Paul watching her with an extraordinary expression of
anxiety. Sir Henry prospered and soon began to 'bear', Paul and
Fenella exchanged a glance. Fenella nodded and turned pale.

'Aha!' cried Sir Henry in triumph. 'The winning throw, I think!
The winning throw!'

He cast himself back in his chair, gazed about him and laughed delightedly. It was at this juncture that Paul, who was standing on the hearthrug with Fenella, put his arm round her and kissed her with extreme heartiness and unmistakable intention. 'Fenella and I,' he said loudly, 'are going to be married.'

There followed an electrified silence, lasting perhaps for ten seconds.

Sir Henry then picked up the backgammon board and threw it a surprising distance across the drawing-room.

'And temper,' Paul added, turning rather pale, 'never got anybody anywhere.'

Miss Orrincourt gave a long whistle. Millamant dropped on her knees and began to pick up backgammon pieces.

Pauline Kentish, gazing with something like terror at her son, gabbled incoherently: 'No darling! No, please! No, Paul, don't be naughty. No! Fenella!'

Cedric, his mouth open, his eyes glistening, rubbed his hands and made his crowing noise. But he, too, looked frightened.

And all the Ancreds, out of the corners of their eyes, watched Sir Henry.

He was the first man Troy had ever seen completely given over to rage. She found the exhibition formidable. If he had not been an old man his passion would have been less disquieting because less pitiable. Old lips, shaking with rage; old eyes, whose fierceness was glazed by rheum; old hands, that jerked in unco-ordinated fury; these were intolerable manifestations of emotion.

Troy got up and attempted an inconspicuous retreat to the door.

'*Come back,*' said her host violently. Troy returned. 'Hear how these people conspire to humiliate me. Come back, I say.' Troy sat on the nearest chair.

'Papa!' whispered Pauline, weaving her hands together, and 'Papa!' Millamant echoed, fumbling with the dice. 'Please! So bad for you. Upsetting yourself! Please!'

He silenced them with a gesture and struggled to his feet. Paul, holding Fenella by the arm, waited until his grandfather stood before him and then said rapidly: 'We're sorry to make a scene. I persuaded Fen that this was the only way to handle the business. We've discussed it with you in private, Grandfather, and you've told us what you feel about it. We don't agree. It's our show, after all, and we've made up our minds. We could have gone off and got married without saying anything about it, but neither of us wanted to do that. So we thought – '

'We thought,' said Fenella rather breathlessly, 'we'd just make a general announcement.'

'Because,' Paul added, 'I've sent one already to the papers and we wanted to tell you before you read it.'

'But, Paul darling – ' his mother faintly began.

'You damned young puppy,' Sir Henry roared out, 'what do you mean by standing up with that god-damned conceited look on your face and talking poppycock to ME?'

'Aunt Pauline,' said Fenella, 'I'm sorry if you're not pleased, but – '

'Ssh!' said Pauline.

'Mother *is* pleased,' said Paul. 'Aren't you, Mother?'

'Ssh!' Pauline repeated distractedly.

'Be silent!' Sir Henry shouted. He was now in the centre of the hearth-rug. It seemed to Troy that his first violence was being rapidly transmuted into something more histrionic and much less disturbing. He rested an elbow on the mantelpiece. He pressed two fingers and a thumb against his eyelids, removed his hand slowly, kept his eyes closed, frowned as if in pain, and finally sighed deeply and opened his eyes very wide indeed.

'I'm an old fellow,' he said in a broken voice. 'An old fellow. It's easy to hurt me. Very easy. You have dealt me a shrewd blow. Never mind. Let me suffer. Why not? It won't be for long. Not for long, now.'

'Papa, *dearest*,' cried Pauline, sweeping up to him and clasping her hands. 'You make us utterly miserable. Don't speak like that, don't. Not for the world would my boy cause you a moment's unhappiness. Let me talk quietly to these children. Papa, I implore you.'

'This,' a voice whispered in Troy's ear, 'is perfect Pinero.' She jumped violently. Cedric had slipped round behind his agitated relations and now leant over the back of her chair. 'She played the name part, you know, in a revival of *The Second Mrs Tanqueray.*'

'It's no use, Pauline. Let them go. They knew my wishes. They have chosen the cruellest way. Let them,' said Sir Henry with relish, 'dree their weird.'

'Thank you, Grandfather,' said Fenella brightly, but with a shake in her voice. 'It's our weird and we shall be delighted to dree it.'

Sir Henry's face turned an uneven crimson. 'This is insufferable,' he shouted, and his teeth, unable to cope with the violence of his diction, leapt precariously from their anchorage and were clamped angrily home. Fenella giggled nervously. 'You are under age,' Sir Henry pronounced suddenly. 'Under age, both of you. Pauline, if you have the smallest regard for your old father's wishes, you will forbid this lunacy. I shall speak to your mother, miss. I shall cable to your father.'

'Mother won't mind,' said Fenella.

'You know well, you know perfectly well, why I cannot countenance this nonsense.'

'You think, don't you, Grandfather,' said Fenella, 'that because we're cousins we'll have loopy young. Well, we've asked about that and it's most unlikely. Modern medical opinion – '

'Be silent! At least let some semblance of decency – '

'I *won't* be silent,' said Fenella, performing with dexterity the feat known by actors as topping the other man's lines. 'And if we're to talk about decency, Grandfather, I should have thought it was a damn sight more decent for two people who are young and in love to say they're going to marry each other than for an old man to make an exhibition of himself – '

'*Fenella!*' shouted Pauline and Millamant in unison.

' – doting on a peroxide blonde fifty years younger than himself, and a brazen gold-digger into the bargain.'

Fenella then burst into tears and ran out of the room, followed rigidly by Paul.

Troy, who had once more determined to make her escape, heard Fenella weeping stormily outside the door and stayed where she was. The remaining Ancreds were all talking at once. Sir Henry beat his fist on the mantelpiece until the ornaments danced again, and roared out: 'My God, I'll not have her under my roof another hour! My God – !' Millamant and Pauline, on either side of him like a distracted chorus, wrung their hands and uttered plaintive cries. Cedric chattered noisily behind the sofa, where Miss Orrincourt still lay. It was she who put a stop to this ensemble by rising and confronting them with her hands on her hips.

'I am not remaining here,' said Miss Orrincourt piercingly, 'to be insulted. Remarks have been passed in this room that no self-respecting girl in my delicate position can be expected to endure. Noddy!'

Sir Henry, who had continued his beating of the mantelpiece during this speech, stopped short and looked at her with a kind of nervousness.

'Since announcements,' said Miss Orrincourt, 'are in the air, Noddy, haven't we got something to say ourselves in that line? Or,' she added ominously, 'have we?'

She looked lovely standing there. It was an entirely plastic loveliness, an affair of colour and shape, of line and texture. It was so complete in its kind, Troy thought, that to bring a consideration of character or vulgarity to bear upon it would be to labour at an irrelevant synthesis. In her kind she was perfect. 'What about it, Noddy?' she said.

Sir Henry stared at her, pulled down his waistcoat, straightened his back and took her hand. 'Whenever you wish, my dear,' he said, 'whenever you wish.'

Pauline and Millamant fell back from them, Cedric drew in his breath and touched his moustache. Troy saw, with astonishment, that his hand was shaking.

'I had intended,' Sir Henry said, 'to make this announcement at The Birthday. Now, however, when I realize only too bitterly that my family cares little, cares nothing for my happiness' ('*Papa*!' Pauline wailed), 'I turn, in my hour of sorrow, to One who does Care.'

'Uh-huh!' Miss Orrincourt assented. 'But keep it sunny-side-up, Petty-pie.'

Sir Henry, less disconcerted than one would have thought possible by this interjection, gathered himself together.

'This lady,' he said loudly, 'has graciously consented to become my wife.'

Considering the intensity of their emotions, Troy felt that the Ancreds really behaved with great aplomb. It was true that Pauline and Millamant were, for a moment, blankly silent, but Cedric almost immediately ran out from cover and seized his grandfather by the hand.

'Dearest Grandpapa – couldn't be more delighted – too marvellous. Sonia, *darling*,' he babbled, '*such* fun,' and he kissed her.

'Well, Papa,' said Millamant, following her son's lead but not kissing Miss Orrincourt, 'we can't say that it's altogether a surprise, can we? I'm sure we all hope you'll be very happy.'

Pauline was more emotional. 'Dearest,' she said, taking her father's hands and gazing with wet eyes into his face, 'dearest, dearest Papa. Please, please believe my only desire is for your happiness.'

Sir Henry inclined his head. Pauline made an upward pounce at his moustache. 'Oh, Pauline,' he said with an air of tragic resignation, 'I have been wounded, Pauline! Deeply wounded!'

'No,' cried Pauline. 'No!'

'Yes,' sighed Sir Henry. 'Yes.'

Pauline turned blindly from him and offered her hand to Miss Orrincourt. 'Be good to him,' she said brokenly. 'It's all we ask. Be good to him.'

With an eloquent gesture, Sir Henry turned aside, crossed the room, and flung himself into a hitherto unoccupied armchair.

It made a loud and extremely vulgar noise.

Sir Henry, scarlet in the face, leapt to his feet and snatched up the loose cushioned seat. He exposed a still partially inflated bladder-like object, across which was printed a legend, 'The Raspberry. Makes your Party go off with a Bang.' He seized it, and again, through some concealed orifice, it emitted its dreadful sound. He hurled it accurately into the fire and the stench of burning rubber filled the room.

'Well, I mean to say,' said Miss Orrincourt, 'fun's fun, but I think that kid's getting common in her ways.'

Sir Henry walked in silence to the door, where, inevitably, he turned to deliver an exit line. 'Millamant,' he said, 'in the morning you will be good enough to send for my solicitor.'

The door banged. After a minute's complete silence Troy was at last able to escape from the drawing-room.

II

Troy was not much surprised in the morning to learn that Sir Henry was too unwell to appear, though he hoped in the afternoon to resume the usual sitting. A note on her early tea-tray informed her that Cedric would be delighted to pose in the costume if this would be of any service. She thought it might. There was the scarlet cloak to be attended to. She had half-expected a disintegration of the family forces, at least the disappearance, possibly in opposite directions, of Fenella and Paul. She had yet to learn of the Ancreds' resilience in inter-tribal warfare. At breakfast they both appeared – Fenella, white and silent; Paul, red and silent. Pauline arrived a little later. Her attitude to her son suggested that he was ill of some not entirely respectable disease. With Fenella she adopted an air of pained antipathy and would scarcely speak to her. Millamant presided. She was less jolly than usual, but behind her anxiety, if she was indeed anxious, Troy detected a hint of complacency. There was more than a touch of condolence in her manner towards her sister-in-law, and this, Troy felt, Pauline deeply resented.

'Well, Milly,' said Pauline after a long silence, 'do you propose to continue your rôle under new management?'

'I'm always rather lost, Pauline, when you adopt theatrical figures of speech.'

'Are you going to house-keep, then, for the new châtelaine?'

'I hardly expect to do so.'

'Poor Milly,' said Pauline. 'It's going to be difficult for you, I'm afraid.'

'I don't think so. Cedric and I have always thought we'd like to have a little *pied-à-terre* together in London.'

'Yes,' Pauline agreed much too readily, 'Cedric will have to draw in his horns a bit too, one supposes.'

'Perhaps Paul and Fenella would consider allowing me to house-keep for them,' said Millamant, with her first laugh that morning. And with an air of genuine interest she turned to them. 'How *are* you going to manage, both of you?' she asked.

'Like any other husband and wife without money,' said Fenella. 'Paul's got his pension and I've got my profession. We'll both get jobs.'

'Oh, well,' said Millamant comfortably, 'perhaps after all, your grandfather – '

'We don't want Grandfather to do anything, Aunt Milly,' said Paul quickly. 'He wouldn't anyway, of course, but we don't want him to.'

'Dearest!' said his mother. 'So hard! So bitter! I don't know you, Paul, when you talk like that. Something' – she glanced with extraordinary distaste at Fenella – 'has changed you so dreadfully.'

'Where,' asked Millamant brightly, 'is Panty?'

'Where should she be if not in school?' Pauline countered with dignity. 'She is not in the habit of breakfasting with us, Milly.'

'Well, you never know,' said Millamant. 'She seems to get about quite a lot, doesn't she? And, by the way, Pauline, I've a bone to pick with Panty myself. Someone has interfered with My Work. A large section of embroidery has been deliberately unpicked. I'd left it in the drawing-room and – '

'Panty never goes there,' cried Pauline.

'Well, I don't know about that. She must, for instance, have been in the drawing-room last evening during dinner.'

'Why?'

'Because Sonia, as I suppose we must call her, says she sat in that chair before dinner, Pauline. She says it was perfectly normal.'

'I can't help that, Milly. Panty did not come into the drawing-room last night at dinner-time for the very good reason that she and the other children were given their medicine then and sent early to bed. You told me yourself, Milly, that Miss Able found the medicine in the flower-room and took it straight in for Dr Withers to give the children.'

'Oh, yes,' said Millamant. 'Would you believe it, the extraordinary Sonia didn't trouble to take it in to Miss Able, or to give Papa's bottle to me. She merely went to the flower-room, where it seems,' said Millamant with a sniff, 'orchids had been brought in for her; and dumped the lot. Miss Able hunted everywhere before she found it, and so did I.'

'T'uh,' said Pauline.

'All the same,' said Paul. 'I don't mind betting that Panty – '

'It has yet to be proved,' Pauline interrupted with spirit rather than conviction, 'that Panty had anything to do with – with – '

'With the Raspberry?' said Paul, grinning. 'Mother, of course she did.'

'I have reason to believe – ' Pauline began.

'No, really, Mother. It's Panty all over. Look at her record.'

'Where did she get it? I've never given her such a thing.'

'Another kid, I suppose, if she didn't buy it. I've seen them in one of the village shops; haven't you, Fen? I remember thinking to myself that they ought to have been sent to a rubber dump.'

'I've had a little talk with Panty,' said Panty's mother obstinately, 'and she promised me on her word of honour she didn't know anything about it. I know when that child is speaking the truth, Milly. A mother always knows.'

'*Honestly*, Mother!' said Paul.

'I don't care what anyone says – ' Pauline began, but was interrupted by the entrance of Cedric, very smooth and elegant, and with more than a touch of smugness in his general aspect.

'Good morning, dearest Mrs Alleyn. Good morning, my sweets,' he said. 'Planning how to lay out the proverbial shilling to advantage, Paul dear? I've been so excited thinking up a scheme for a double wedding. It's a teeny bit involved. The Old Person, you see, in Uncle Claude's absence, must give Fenella away and then whisk over to the other side as First Bridegroom. I thought I might be joint Best Man and Paul could double Second Bridegroom and Sonia's papa. It's like a rather intricate ballet. Uncle Thomas is to be a page and Panty a flower-girl, which will give her wonderful opportunities for throwing things. And you, dearest Mama, and all the aunts shall be Dowagers-in-Waiting. I've invented such marvellously intimidating gowns for you.'

'Don't be naughty,' said Millamant.

'No, but truly,' Cedric went on, bringing his plate to the table. 'I *do* feel, you two, that you've managed your affairs the least bit clumsily.'

'It's not given to all of us,' said Paul dryly, 'to be quite as nimble after the main chance as you.'

'Well, I do rather flatter myself I've exhibited a pretty turn of low cunning,' Cedric agreed readily. 'Sonia's going to let me do her trousseau, and the Old Person said that I at least showed some family feeling. But I'm afraid, dearest Auntie Pauline, that Panty has lost ground almost irretrievably. Such a very robust sense of comedy.'

'I have already told your mother, Cedric, that I have reason to believe that Panty was not responsible for that incident.'

'Oh, Gracious!' said Cedric. 'So touching. Such faith.'

'Or for the writing on your grandfather's looking-glass.'

Cedric made one of his ingratiating wriggles at Troy. 'Panty has another champion,' he said.

Pauline turned quickly to Troy, who, with a sense of stepping from the stalls up to the stage, murmured: 'I didn't think Panty wrote on the glass. I thought her protests rang true.'

'There!' cried Pauline emotionally, and stretched out her hand to Troy. 'There, all of you! *Thank* you, Mrs Alleyn. *Someone* has faith in *my poor old Panty.*'

But Troy's faith in Panty Kentish, already slightly undermined, was to suffer a further jolt.

She went from the dining-room to the little theatre. Her canvas was leaning, face to the wall, where she had left it. She dragged it out, tipped it up on one corner, set it on the lowered tray of her easel and stepped back to look at it.

Across the nose and eyes of the completed head somebody had drawn in black paint an enormous pair of spectacles.

III

For perhaps five seconds alternate lumps of ice and red-hot coal chased each other down her spine and round her stomach. She then touched the face. It was hard dry. The black spectacles were still wet. With a sense of relief that was so violent that it came upon her like an attack of nausea, Troy dipped a rag in oil and gingerly wiped off the addition. She then sat down and pressed her shaking hands together. Not a stain, not a blur on the bluish shadows that she had twisted under the eyes, not a trace of dirt across the strange pink veil that was the flesh under his frontal bone. 'Oh, Golly!' Troy whispered. 'Oh, Golly! Thank God! Oh, Golly!'

'Good morning,' said Panty, coming in by the side door. 'I'm allowed to do another picture. I want some more board and lots more paint. Look, I've finished the cows and the aeroplane. Aren't they good?'

She dumped her board on the floor against the foot of the easel, and, with a stocky imitation of Troy, fell back a pace and looked at it, her hands clasped behind her back. Her picture was of three vermilion cows in an emerald meadow. Above them, against a sky for which Panty had used neat New Blue, flew an emerald aeroplane in the act of secreting a black bomb.

'Damn good,' said Panty, 'isn't it?' She tore her gaze away from her picture and allowed it to rest on Troy's.

'That's good too,' she said. 'It's nice. It gives me a nice feeling inside. I think you paint good pictures.'

'Somebody,' said Troy, watching her, 'thought it would be better if I put in a pair of spectacles.'

'Well, they must have been pretty silly,' said Panty. 'Kings don't wear spectacles. That's a king.'

'Whoever it was, painted them on the face.'

if anybody puts spectacles on my cows,' Panty said, 'I'll kill them.'

'Who do you think could have done it?'

'I dunno,' said Panty without interest. 'Did Noddy?'

'I hardly think so.'

'I suppose it was whoever put whatever it was on Noddy's glass. Not me, anyway. Now can I have another board and more paint? Miss Able likes me to paint.'

'You may go up to my room and get yourself one of the small boards in the cupboard.'

'I don't know where your room is.'

Troy explained as best she could. 'Oh, well,' said Panty, 'if I can't find it I'll just yell till somebody comes.'

She stumped away to the side door. 'By the way,' Troy called after her, 'would you know a Raspberry if you saw one?'

'You bet,' said Panty with interest.

'I mean a rubber thing that makes a noise if you sit on it.'

'What sort of noise?'

'Never mind,' said Troy wearily. 'Forget about it.'

'You're mad,' said Panty flatly and went out.

'If I'm not,' Troy muttered, 'there's somebody in this house who is.'

IV

All that morning she painted solidly through the background. In the afternoon Sir Henry posed for an hour and a half with two rests. He said nothing, but sighed a great deal. Troy worked at the hands, but he was restless, and kept making small nervous movements so that she did little more than lay down the general tone and shape of them. Millamant came in just before the end of the sitting, and, with a word of apology, went to him and murmured something indistinguishable. 'No, no,' he said angrily. 'It must be tomorrow. Ring up again and tell them so.'

'He says it's very inconvenient.'

'That be damned. Ring up again.'

'Very well, Papa,' said the obedient Millamant.

She went away, and Troy, seeing that he was growing still more restless, called an end to the sitting, telling him that Cedric had offered to pose for the cloak. He left with evident relief. Troy grunted disconsolately, scraped down the hands, and turned again to the background. It was a formalized picture of a picture. The rooky wood, a wet mass, rimmed with boldly stated strokes of her brush, struck sharply across a coldly luminous night sky. The monolithic forms in the middle distance were broadly set down as interlocking masses. Troy had dragged a giant brush down the canvas, each stroke the summing-up of painful thinking that suddenly resolved itself in form. The background was right, and the Ancreds, she reflected, would think it very queer and unfinished. All of them, except, perhaps, Cedric and Panty. She had arrived at this conclusion when on to the stage pranced Cedric himself, heavily and most unnecessarily made-up, moving with a sort of bouncing stride, and making much of his grandfather's red cloak.

'Here I am,' he cried, 'feeling *so* keyed up with the mantle of high tragedy across my puny shoulders. Now, what *precisely* is the pose?'

There was no need to show him, however. He swept up his drape, placed himself, and, with an expert wriggle, flung it into precisely the right sweep. Troy eyed it, and, with a sense of rising excitement, spread unctuous bands of brilliant colour across her palette.

Cedric was an admirable model. The drape was frozen in its sculptured folds. Troy worked in silence for an hour, holding her breath so often that she became quite stuffy in the nose.

'Dearest Mrs Alleyn,' said a faint voice, 'I have a tiny cramp in my leg.'

'Lord, I'm sorry!' said Troy. 'You've been wonderful. Do have a rest.'

He came down into the auditorium, limping a little but still with an air, and stood before her canvas.

'It's so piercingly *right*,' he said. 'Too exciting! I mean, it really *is* theatre, and the Old Person and that devastating Bard all synthesized and made eloquent and everything. It terrifies me.'

He sank into a near-by stall, first spreading his cloak over the back, and fanned himself. 'I can't tell you how I've died to prattle,' he went on, 'all the time I was up there. This house is simply *seething* with intrigue.'

Troy, who was herself rather exhausted, lit a cigarette, sat down, and eyed her work. She also listened with considerable interest to Cedric.

'First I must tell you,' he began, 'the Old Person has positively sent for his solicitor. Imagine! Such lobbyings and whisperings! One is reminded of Papal elections in the seventeenth century. First the marriage settlement, of course. What do you suppose darling Sonia will have laid down as the minimum? I've tried *piteously* hard to wheedle it out of her, but she's turned rather secretive and *grande dame.* But, of course, however much it is it's got to come from *somewhere.* Panty was known to be first favourite. He's left her some fabulous sum to make her a *parti* when she grows up. But we all feel her little pranks will have swept her right out of the running. So perhaps darling Sonia will have that lot. Then there's Paul and Fenella, who have undoubtedly polished themselves off. I rather *hope,*' said Cedric with a modest titter and a very sharp look in his eye, 'that I *may* reap something there. I *think* I'm all right, but you never know. He simply detests me, really, and the entail is quite ridiculous. Somebody broke it up or something ages ago, and I *may* only get this awful house and nothing whatever to keep it up with. Still, I really have got Sonia on my side.'

He touched his moustache and pulled a small pellet of cosmetic off his eyelashes. 'I made up,' he explained in parentheses, 'because I felt it was so essential to get the feeling of the Macsoforth *seeping* through into every fold of the mantle. And partly because it's such fun painting one's face.'

He hummed a little air for a moment or two and then continued: 'Thomas and Dessy and the Honourable Mrs A. are all pouring in on Friday night. The Birthday is on Saturday, did you realize? The Old Person and the Ancient of Days will spend Sunday in bed, the one suffering from gastronomic excess, the other from his exertions as Ganymede. The family will no doubt pass the day in mutual recrimination. The general feeling is that the *piece-de-résistance* for the Birthday will be an announcement of the new Will.'

'But, good Lord – !' Troy ejaculated. Cedric talked her down.

'Almost certain, I assure you. He has always made public each new draft. He can't resist the dramatic *mise-en-scène.*'

'But how often does he change his Will?'

'I've never kept count,' Cedric confessed after a pause, 'but on an average I should say once every two years, though for the last three years Panty has held firm as first favourite. While she was still doing baby-talk and only came here occasionally he adored her, and she, most unfortunately, was crazy about him. Pauline must curse the day when she manœuvred the school to Ancreton. Last time I was *grossly* unpopular and down to the bare bones of the entail. Uncle Thomas was second to Panty with the general hope that he would marry and have a son, and I remain a celibate with Ancreton as a millstone round my poor little neck. *Isn't* it all too tricky?'

There was scarcely a thing that Cedric did or said of which Troy did not wholeheartedly disapprove, but it was impossible to be altogether bored by him. She found herself listening quite attentively to his recital, though after a time his gloating delight in Panty's fall from grace began to irritate her.

'I still think,' she said, 'that Panty didn't play these tricks on her grandfather.' Cedric, with extraordinary vehemence, began to protest, but Troy insisted. 'I've talked to her about it. Her manner, to my mind, was conclusive. Obviously she didn't know anything about last night's affair. She'd never heard of the squeaking cushion.'

'That child,' Cedric announced malevolently, 'is incredibly, terrifyingly subtle. She is not an Ancred for nothing. She was acting. Depend upon it, she was acting.'

'I don't believe it. And what's more, she didn't know her way to my room.'

Cedric, who was biting his nails, paused and stared at her. After a long pause he said: 'Didn't know her way to your room? But, dearest Mrs Alleyn, what has that got to do with it?'

It was on the tip of her tongue to relate the incident of the painted banister. She had even begun: 'Well, if you promise – ' And then, catching sight of his face with its full pouting mouth and pale eyes, she suddenly changed her mind. 'It doesn't matter,' Troy said, 'it wouldn't convince you. Never mind.'

'Dearest Mrs Alleyn,' Cedric tittered, pulling at his cloak, 'you are mysterious. Any one would suppose you didn't trust me.'

CHAPTER 7

Fiesta

On Friday, a week after her arrival at Ancreton, Troy dragged her canvas out of the property room, where she now kept it locked up, and stared at it with mixed sensations of which the predominant was one of astonishment. How in the world had she managed it? Another two days would see its completion. Tomorrow night Sir Henry would lead his warring celebrants into the little theatre and she would stand awkwardly in the background while they talked about it. Would they be very disappointed? Would they see at once that the background was not the waste before Forres Castle but a theatrical cloth presenting this, that Troy had painted, not Macbeth himself, but an old actor looking backwards into his realization of the part? Would they see that the mood was one of relinquishment?

Well, the figure was completed. There were some further places she must attend to – a careful balancing stroke here and here. She was filled with a great desire that her husband should see it. It was satisfactory, Troy thought, that of the few people to whom she wished to show her work her husband came first. Perhaps this was because he said so little yet was not embarrassed by his own silence.

As the end of her work drew near her restlessness increased and her fears for their reunion. She remembered phrases spoken by other women: 'The first relationship is never repeated.' 'We were strangers again when we met.' it wasn't the same.' 'It feels extraordinary. We were shy and had nothing to say to each other.' Would her reunion also be inarticulate? 'I've no technique,' Troy thought, 'to see me through. I've no marital technique at all. Any native adroitness I possess has gone into my painting. But perhaps Roderick will know what to say. Shall I tell him at once about the Ancreds?'

She was cleaning her palette when Fenella ran in to say a call had come through for her from London.

It was the Assistant Commissioner at the Yard. Troy listened to him with a hammer knocking at her throat. He thought, he said with arch obscurity, that she might enjoy a run up to London on Monday. If she stayed the night, the Yard might have something of interest to show her on Tuesday morning. A police car would be coming in by way of Ancreton Halt early on Monday and would be delighted to give her a lift. 'Thank you,' said Troy in an unrecognizable voice. 'Yes, I see. Yes, of course. Yes, very exciting: Thank you.'

She fled to her room, realizing as she sat breathless on her bed that she had run like a madwoman up three flights of stairs. 'It's as well,' she thought, 'that the portrait's finished. In this frame of mind I'd be lucky if I reached Panty's form.'

She began distractedly to imagine their meeting. 'But I can't see his face,' she thought in a panic. 'I can't remember his voice. I've forgotten my husband.'

She felt by turns an unreasonable urge for activity and a sense of helpless inertia. Ridiculous incidents from the Ancred repertoire flashed up in her mind. 'I must remember to tell him that,' she would think, and then wonder if, after all, the Ancreds in retrospect would sound funny. She remembered with a jolt that she must let Katti Bostock know about Tuesday. They had arranged for Alleyn's old servant to go to London and open the flat.

'I should have done it at once,' she cried, and returned downstairs. While she waited, fuming, in a little telephone-room near the front doors, for her call to go through, she heard wheels on the drive, the sound of voices, and finally the unmistakable rumpus of arrival in the hall. A charming voice called gaily: 'Milly, where are you? Come down. It's Dessy and Thomas and me. Dessy found a Colonel, and the Colonel had a car, and we've all arrived together.'

'Jenetta!' Millamant's disembodied voice floated down from the gallery. Still more distantly Pauline's echoed her: 'Jenetta!'

Was there an overtone of disapproval, not quite of dismay, in this greeting, Troy wondered, as she quietly shut the door?

II

Jenetta, the Hon Mrs Claude Ancred, unlike Millamant, had caught none of the overtones of her relations-in-law. She was a nice-looking woman, with a gay voice, good clothes, an intelligent face, and an air of quietly enjoying herself. Her conversation was unstressed and crisp. If she sensed internecine warfare she gave no hint of doing so, and seemed to be equally pleased with, and equally remote from, each member of that unlikely clan.

Desdemona, on the other hand, was, of all the Ancreds after Sir Henry, most obviously of the theatre. She was startlingly good looking, of voluptuous build, and had a warm ringing voice that seemed to be perpetually uttering important lines of climax from a West-End success. She ought really, Troy thought, to be surrounded by attendant figures: a secretary, an author, an agent, perhaps a doting producer. She had an aura of richness and warmth, and a knack of causing everybody else to subscribe to the larger-than-life atmosphere in which she herself moved so easily. Her Colonel, after a drink, drove away to his lawful destination, with Dessy's magnificent thanks no doubt ringing in his ears. Troy, emerging from the telephone-room, found herself confronted by the new arrivals. She was glad to see Thomas: already she thought of him as 'old Thomas', with his crest of faded hair and his bland smile. 'Oh, hallo,' he said, blinking at her, 'so here you are! I hope your carbuncle is better.'

'It's gone,' said Troy.

'We're all talking about Papa's engagement,' said Thomas. 'This is my sister-in-law, Mrs Claude Ancred, and this is my sister, Desdemona. Milly and Pauline are seeing about rooms. Have you painted a nice picture?'

'Not bad. Are you producing a nice play?'

'It's quite good, thank you,' said Thomas primly.

'Darling Tommy,' said Desdemona, 'how *can* it be quite good with that woman? What were you thinking about when you cast it!'

'Well, Dessy, I told the management you wanted the part.'

'I didn't want it. I could play it, but I didn't want it, thank you.'

'Then everybody ought to be pleased,' said Thomas mildly. 'I suppose, Jenetta,' he continued, 'you are anxious to see Fenella and Paul. Papa's engagement has rather swamped theirs, you may feel. Are you as angry as he is about them?'

'I'm not a bit angry,' she said, catching Troy's eye and smiling at her. 'I'm fond of Paul and want to talk to him.'

'That's all very nice,' said Dessy restlessly, 'but Milly says it was Paul and Fenella who exploded the bomb.'

'Oh, well,' said Thomas comfortably, 'I expect it would have gone off anyway. Did you know Mr Rattisbon has been sent for to make a new Will? I suppose Papa'll tell us all about it at the Birthday Dinner tomorrow. Do you expect to be cut out this time, Dessy?'

'My dear,' cried his sister, sinking magnificently into the sofa and laying her arms along the back of it, 'I've said so often exactly what I think of the Orrincourt that he can't possibly do anything else. I don't give a damn, Tommy. If Papa expects me to purr round congratulating them, he's never been more mistaken. I can't do it. It's been a hideous shock to me. It hurts me, *here,*' she added, beating a white fist on her striking bosom. 'All my respect, my love, my *ideal* – shattered.' She flashed her eyes at her sister-in-law. 'You think I exaggerate, Jen. You're lucky. You're not easily upset.'

'Well,' said Jenetta lightly, 'I've yet to meet Miss Orrincourt.'

'He's not your father,' Dessy pointed out with emotion.

'No more he is,' she agreed.

'T'uh!' said Dessy bitterly.

This conversation was interrupted by Fenella, who ran downstairs, flew across the hall, and, with an inarticulate cry, flung herself into her mother's arms.

'Now, then,' said Jenetta softly, holding her daughter for a moment, 'no high strikes.'

'Mummy, you're not furious? Say you're not furious!'

'Do I look furious, you goat? Where's Paul?'

'In the library. Will you come? Mummy, you're Heaven. You're an angel.'

'Do pipe down, darling. And what about Aunt Dessy and Uncle Thomas?'

Fenella turned to greet them. Thomas kissed her carefully. 'I hope you'll be happy,' he said. 'It ought to be all right, really. I looked up genetics in a medical encyclopedia after I read the announcement. The chap said the issue of first cousins was generally quite normal, unless there was any marked insanity in the family which was common to both.'

'Tommy!' said his sister. 'Honestly, you *are*!'

'Well,' said Jenetta Ancred, 'with that assurance to fortify us, Fen, suppose you take me to see Paul.'

They went off together. Millamant and Pauline came downstairs. 'Such a nuisance,' Millamant was saying, 'I really don't quite know how to arrange it.'

'If you're talking about rooms, Milly,' said Desdemona, 'I tell you flatly that unless something has been done about the rats I won't go into *Bracegirdle.*'

'Well, but Dessy – ' Pauline began.

'Has something been done about the rats?'

'Barker,' said Millamant unhappily, 'has lost the arsenic. I think he did Miss Orrincourt's rooms some time ago, and after that the tin disappeared.'

'Good God!' said Thomas quietly.

'Pity he didn't put some in her tooth-glass,' said Desdemona vindictively.

'What about *Ellen Terry?*'

'I was putting Jenetta into *Terry.*'

'Come into *Bernhardt* with me, Dess,' Pauline suggested richly. 'I'd love to have you. We can talk. Let's.'

'The only thing against that,' said Millamant, knitting her brows, 'is that since Papa had all those large Jacobean pieces put in *Bernhardt*, there really isn't anywhere for a second bed. I can put one in my room, Desdemona. I wondered if you'd mind . . . *Lady Bancroft*, you know. Quite spacious and plenty of hanging room.'

'Well, Milly, if it isn't turning you upside down.'

'Not at all,' said Millamant coldly.

'And you can still talk to me,' said Pauline. 'I'll be next door.'

III

On Friday night the weather broke and a deluge of rain beat down on the tortuous roofs of Ancreton. On Saturday morning Troy was awakened by a regular sequence of sharp percussionlike notes: Ping, ping, ping.

On going to her bath she nearly fell into a basin that had been placed on the landing. Into it fell a continuous progression of water-drops from a spreading patch in the roof. All day it rained. At three o'clock it had grown too dark to paint in the little theatre, but she had worked through the morning, and, having laid her last touch against the canvas, walked away from it and sat down. She felt that curious blankness which follows the completion of a painting. It was over. Her house was untenanted. It did not long remain so, for now, unchecked by the discipline of her work, Troy's thoughts were filled with the anticipation of reunion. 'The day after tomorrow I shall be saying: "Tomorrow." ' The Ancreds and their machinations now seemed unreal. They were two-dimensional figures gesticulating on a ridiculously magnificent stage. This reaction was to colour all memories of her last two days at Ancreton, blurring their edges, lending a tinge of fantasy to commonplace events, and causing her to doubt the integrity of her recollections when, in a little while, it would be imperative for her to recount them accurately.

She was to remember that Sir Henry was invisible all day, resting in preparation for his Birthday Dinner; that there was an air of anticipation in his enormous house, that his presents were set out in the library, a dark no-man's-land in the east wing, and that the members of his family visited this Mecca frequently, eyeing each other's gifts with intense partiality. Troy herself, in readiness for The Birthday, had made a lively and diverting sketch of Panty, which she had mounted and placed among the other gifts, wondering if, in view of Panty's fall from grace, it was too preposterously inept. The sketch was viewed with wholehearted favour by Panty herself and her mother, and by nobody else except Cedric, who chose to regard it as an acid comment on the child's character, which it was not.

Troy remembered afterwards how she had looked at the long dresses she had brought with her and decided that they were nothing like grand enough for the occasion. She remembered how the air of festivity had deepened as evening came, and how Barker and his retinue of elderly maids were in a continuous state of controlled bustle. Most often, though still with a feeling of incredulity, would it seem to her that there had been a sense of impending climax in the house, an impression of something drawing to its close. At the time Troy said to herself: 'It's because Rory's coming. It's because I've finished an intensive bit of work done at concert pitch.' But in retrospect these answers sounded unconvincing, and she wondered if the thoughts of one malevolent creature could have sent out a thin mist of apprehension.

Troy had cleaned her palette, shut her paint-box on ranks of depleted tubes, and washed her brushes for the last time at Ancreton. The portrait had been set up on the stage and framed in crimson velvet curtains that did their best to kill it. 'If it was spring-time,' Troy thought, 'I believe they'd have festooned it in garlands.' The act-drop had been lowered in front of the portrait and there it waited on a dark stage for the evening's ceremony. She couldn't glower at it. She couldn't walk in that deluge. She was unendurably restless. The dinner itself was at nine; she had three hours to fill in. Taking a book with her, she wandered uncertainly from one vast room to another, and wherever she went there seemed to be two Ancreds in private conversation. Having disclosed Paul and Fenella tightly embraced in the study, disturbed Desdemona and Pauline hissing together in the drawing-room, and interrupted Millamant in what appeared to be angry parley with Barker under the stairs, she made her way to a room next the library, known as the Great Boudoir (the Little Boudoir was upstairs). Unnerved by her previous encounters, Troy paused outside the door and listened. All was still. She pushed open the door, and was confronted by Cedric and Miss Orrincourt side by side on a sofa, doubled up in an ecstasy of silent laughter.

She was well into the room before they saw her. Their behaviour was extraordinary. They stared at her with their mouths open, the laughter drying out on their faces as if she had scorched it. Cedric turned an ugly red, Miss Orrincourt's eyes were as hard as blue glass marbles. She was the first to speak.

'Well, for crying out loud,' she said in a flat voice, 'look who's here.'

'Dearest Mrs Alleyn,' said Cedric breathlessly, 'do come in. We've been having a dreadfully naughty giggle over everything. The Birthday, you know, and all the wheels within wheels and so on. Do join us. Or are you too grand and upright? Dear me, that sounds as if you were a piano, doesn't it?'

'It's all right,' said Troy, 'I won't come in, thank you. I'm on my way upstairs.'

She went out, closing the door on their silence.

In the hall she found a completely strange elderly gentleman reading a newspaper before the fire. He wore London clothes, an old-fashioned wing collar and a narrow black tie. His face was thin and his hands blue-veined and knotty. When he saw Troy he dropped his newspaper, snatched off his pince-nez, and ejaculating 'M-m-m-mah!' rose nimbly to his feet.

'Are you waiting to see somebody?' Troy asked.

'Thank yer, thank yer, no thank-yer,' said the elderly gentleman rapidly. 'Make myself known. Haven't had the pleasure – Introduce myself. M-mah. Rattisbon.'

'Oh, yes, of course,' said Troy. 'I knew you were coming. How do you do?' She introduced herself.

Mr Rattisbon vibrated the tip of his tongue between his lips and wrung his hands. 'How d'do,' he gabbled. 'Delighted. Take it, fellow-guests. If I may so designate myself. Professional visit.'

'So's mine,' said Troy, picking the sense out of this collection of phrases. 'I've been doing a job here.'

He glanced at the painting-smock she had not yet removed. 'Surely,' he clattered, 'Mrs Roderick Alleyn? Née Troy?'

'That's it.'

'Pleasure of your husband's acquaintance,' Mr Rattisbon explained. 'Professional association. Twice. Admirable.'

'Really?' said Troy, at once delighted. 'You know Roderick? Do let's sit down.'

Mr Rattisbon sucked in his breath and made a crowing sound. They sat before the fire. He crossed his knees and joined his gnarled fingers. 'He's a drawing by Cruikshank,' Troy thought. She began to talk to him about Alleyn, and he listened exactly as if she was making a series of statements which he would presently require his clerk to come in and witness. Troy was to remember vividly this quiet encounter, and how in the middle of her recital she broke off apologetically to say: 'But I don't know why I should bore you with these stories about Roderick.'

'Bore?' he said. 'On the contrary. Entirely so. May I add, strictly *in camera*, that I – ah – had contemplated this call with some misgivings as – ah – a not altogether propitious necessity. I find myself unexpectedly received, and most charmingly so, by a lady for whose remarkable talents I have long entertained the highest regard. M-m-mah!' Mr Rattisbon added, dipping like a sparrow towards Troy. 'Entirely so.'

At this juncture Pauline and Desdemona appeared in the hall and bore down rapidly upon Mr Rattisbon.

'We are so sorry,' Pauline began. 'Leaving you so long. Papa's only just been told – a little upset. The great day, of course. He will be ready for you in a few minutes, dear Mr Rattisbon. Until then Dessy and I would be so glad if you – we feel we'd like to – '

Troy was already on her way out. They were waiting for her to get out of earshot.

She heard Desdemona's rich voice: 'Just a tiny talk, Mr Rattisbon. Just to warn you.' And Mr Rattisbon suddenly very dry and brittle: 'If you desire it, certainly.'

'But,' thought Troy, plodding along the passage, 'they won't get much change out of Mr Rattisbon.'

IV

'It's the big scene from a film script,' thought Troy, looking down the table, 'and I'm the bit-part lady.' The analogy was unavoidable. How often had one not seen Sir Aubrey Smith at the head of such a table? Where else but on the screen was such opulence to be found? Where else such a welter of flowers, such sumptuously Edwardian epergnes, or such incredibly appropriate conversation? Never out of a film studio had characters been so well typed. Even the neighbouring squire and the parson, the one lean and monocled, the other rubicund and sleek, who apparently were annual fixtures for the event; even they were carefully selected cameo parts, too like themselves to be credible. And Mr Rattisbon? The absolute in family solicitors. As for the Ancreds themselves, to glance at them or to hear their carefully modulated laughter, their beautifully articulated small-talk, was to realize at once that this was an all-star vehicle. Troy began to make up titles. 'Homage to Sir Henry.' 'The Astonishing Ancreds.'

'Going quite nicely, so far, don't you consider?' said Thomas at her left elbow. She had forgotten Thomas, although he had taken her in. Cedric, on her right hand, had directed at her and at his partner, Desdemona, a number of rather spasmodic and intensely artificial remarks, all of which sounded as if they were designed for the ears of his grandfather. Thomas, presumably, had been silent until now.

'Very nicely,' Troy agreed hurriedly.

'I mean,' Thomas continued, lowering his voice, 'you wouldn't think, if you didn't know, how terrified everyone is about the Will, would you? Everybody except me, that is, and perhaps Cedric.'

'Ssh!' said Troy. 'No, you wouldn't.'

'It's because we're putting on the great Family Act, you know. It's the same on the stage. People that hate each other's guts make love like angels. You'd be surprised, I dare say. Outsiders think it very queer. Well,' Thomas continued, laying down his soup-spoon and gazing mildly at her. 'What, after all, *do* you think of Ancreton?'

'I've found it absorbing.'

'I'm so glad. You've come in for a set-piece, haven't you? All the intrigues and fights. Do you know what will happen after dinner?' And without waiting for her reply he told her. 'Papa will propose the King's health and then I shall propose Papa's. I'm the eldest son present so I shall have to, but it's a pity. Claude would be much better. Last year Panty was brought in to do it. I coached her in the "business" and she managed very nicely. Papa cried. This year, because of ringworm and the practical jokes, she hasn't been invited. Gracious,' Thomas continued, as Troy helped herself from a dish that had appeared over her shoulder, 'that's never New Zealand crayfish! I thought Millamant had decided against it. Has Papa noticed? There'll be trouble if he has.'

Thomas was right. Sir Henry, when offered this dish, glanced truculently at his daughter-in-law and helped himself to it. An instant silence fell upon the table, and Troy, who was opposite Millamant, saw her make a helpless deprecating grimace at Pauline, who, from the foot of the table, responded by raising her eyebrows.

'He insisted,' Millamant whispered to Paul on her left hand.

'What?' asked Sir Henry loudly.

'Nothing, Papa,' said Millamant.

'They call this,' said Sir Henry, addressing himself to Mr Rattisbon, 'rock lobster. No more like a lobster than my foot. It's some antipodean shell-fish.'

Furtively watched by his family, he took a large mouthful and at the same time pointed to his glass and added: 'One must drink something with it. I shall break my rule, Barker. Champagne.'

Barker, with his lips very slightly pursed, filled the glass.

'That's a big boy,' said Miss Orrincourt approvingly. The Ancreds, after a frightened second or two, burst simultaneously into feverish conversation.

'There,' said Thomas with an air of sober triumph. 'What did I tell you? Champagne and hot crayfish. We shall hear more of this, you may depend upon it.'

'Do be careful,' Troy murmured nervously, and then, seeing that Sir Henry was in gallant conversation with Jenetta on his left, she added cautiously: 'Is it so very bad for him?'

'I promise you,' said Thomas, 'disastrous. I don't think it tastes very nice, anyway,' he continued after a pause. 'What do you think?' Troy had already come to this conclusion. The crayfish, she decided, were dubious.

'Hide it under your toast,' said Thomas, 'I'm going to. It's the Birthday turkey next, from the home farm. We can fill up on that, can't we?'

But Sir Henry, Troy noticed, ate all his crayfish.

Apart from this incident, the dinner continued in the same elevated key up to the moment when Sir Henry, with the air of a Field-Marshal in Glorious Technicolor, rose and proposed the King.

A few minutes later Thomas, coughing modestly, embarked upon his speech.

'Well, Papa,' said Thomas, 'I expect you know what I'm going to say, because, after all, this is your Birthday dinner, and we all know it's a great occasion and how splendid it is for us to be here again as usual in spite of everything. Except Claude, of course, which is a pity, because he would think of a lot of new things to say, and I can't.' At this point a slight breeze of discomfort seemed to stir among the Ancreds. 'So I shall only say,' Thomas battled on, 'how proud we are to be gathered here, remembering your past achievements and wishing you many more Birthday dinners in the time that is to come. Yes,' said Thomas, after a thoughtful pause, 'that's all, I think. Oh, I almost forgot! We all, of course, hope that you will be very happy in your married life. I shall now ask everybody to drink Papa's health, please.'

The guests, evidently accustomed to a very much longer speech and taken unawares by the rapidity of Thomas's peroration, hurriedly got to their feet.

'Papa,' said Thomas.

'Papa,' echoed Jenetta, Millamant, Pauline and Desdemona.

'Grandpapa,' murmured Fenella, Cedric and Paul.

'Sir Henry,' said the Rector loudly, followed by Mr Rattisbon, the Squire and Troy.

'Noddy!' said Miss Orrincourt, shrilly. 'Cheers. Oodles of juice in your tank.'

Sir Henry received all this in the traditional manner. He fingered his glass, stared deeply at his plate, glanced up at Thomas, and, towards the end, raised his hand deprecatingly and let it fall. There was evidence of intense but restrained feeling. When they had all settled down he rose to reply. Troy had settled herself for resounding periods and a great display of rhetoric. She was not prepared, in view of the current family atmosphere, for touching simplicity and poignant emotion. These, however, were the characteristics of Sir Henry's speech. It was also intensely manly. He had, he said, taken a good many calls in the course of his life as a busker, and made a good many little speeches of gratitude to a good many audiences. But moving as some of these occasions had been, there was no audience as near and dear to an old fellow as his own kith and kin and his few tried and proven friends. He and his dear old Tommy were alike in this: they had few words in which to express their dearest thoughts. Perhaps they were none the worse for it. (Pauline, Desdemona and the Rector made sounds of fervent acquiescence.) Sir Henry paused and glanced first at Paul and then at Fenella. He had intended, he said, to keep for this occasion the announcement of the happy change he now contemplated. But domestic events had, should he say, a little forced his hand, and they were now all aware of his good fortune. (Apparently the Squire and Rector were not aware of it, as they looked exceedingly startled.) There was however, one little ceremony to be observed.

He took a small morocco box from his pocket, opened it, extracted a dazzling ring, and, raising Miss Orrincourt, placed it on her engagement finger and kissed the finger. Miss Orrincourt responded by casting one practised glance at the ring and embracing him with the liveliest enthusiasm. His hearers broke into agitated applause, under cover of which Cedric muttered: 'That's the Ranee's Solitaire re-set. I swear it is. Stay me with flagons, playmates.'

Sir Henry, with some firmness, reseated his fiancée and resumed his speech. It was, he said, a tradition in his family that the head of it should be twice married. The Sieur d'Ancred – he rambled on genealogically for some time. Troy felt embarrassment give place to boredom. Her attention was caught, however, by a new development. It had also been the custom, Sir Henry was saying, on these occasions, for the fortunate Ancred to reveal to his family the manner in which he had set his house in order. (Mr Rattisbon raised his eyebrows very high and made a little quavering noise in his throat.) Such frankness was perhaps out of fashion nowadays, but it had an appropriate Shakespearian precedent. King Lear – But glancing at his agonized daughters Sir Henry did not pursue the analogy. He said that he proposed to uphold this traditional frankness. 'I have today,' he said, 'executed – my old friend Rattisbon will correct me if this is not the term' – ('M-m-mah!' said Mr Rattisbon confusedly) – 'thank you – executed My Will. It is a simple little document, conceived in the spirit that actuated my ancestor, the Sieur d'Ancred when – ' A fretful sigh eddied round the table. This time, however, Sir Henry's excursion into antiquity was comparatively brief. Clearing his throat, and speaking on a note so solemn that it had an almost ecclesiastical timbre, he fired point-blank and gave them a resumé of his Will.

Troy's major concern was to avoid the eyes of everybody else seated at that table. To this end she stared zealously at a detail of the epergne immediately in front of her. For the rest of her life, any mention of Sir Henry Ancred's last Will and Testament will immediately call up for her the image of a fat silver cupid who, in a pose at once energetic and insouciant, lunged out from a central globe, to which he was affixed only by his great toe, and, curving his right arm, supported on the extreme tip of his first finger a cornucopia three times his own size, dripping with orchids.

Sir Henry was speaking of legacies. Five thousand pounds to his devoted daughter-in-law, Millamant, five thousand pounds to his ewe lamb, Desdemona. To his doctor and his servants, to the hunt club, to the Church there were grand seigneurial legacies. Her attention wandered, and was again arrested by a compassion he seemed to be making between himself and some pentateuchal patriarch. 'Into three parts. The residue divided into three parts.' This, then, was the climax. To his bride-to-be, to Thomas, and to Cedric, he would leave, severally, a life interest in a third of the residue of his estate. The capital of this fund to be held in trust and ultimately devoted to the preservation and endowment of Ancreton as a historical museum of drama to be known as The Henry Ancred Memorial.

'Tra-hippit!' Cedric murmured at her elbow. 'Honestly, I exult. It might have been so much worse.'

Sir Henry was now making a brief summary of the rest of the field. His son, Claude, he thanked God, turning slightly towards Jenetta, had inherited a sufficient portion from his maternal grandmother, and was therefore able through this and through his own talents to make provision for his wife and (he momentarily eyed Fenella) daughter. His daughter Pauline (Troy heard her make an incoherent noise) had been suitably endowed at the time of her marriage and generously provided for by her late husband. She had her own ideas in the bringing up of her children and was able to carry them out. 'Which,' Cedric muttered with relish, 'is a particularly dirty crack at Paul and Panty, don't you feel?'

'Ssh!' said Desdemona on the other side of him.

Sir Henry drifted into a somewhat vague and ambiguous diatribe on the virtues of family unity and the impossibility, however great the temptation, of ever entirely forgetting them. For the last time her attention wandered, and was jerked sharply back by the sound of her own name: 'Mrs Agatha Troy Alleyn. . . her dramatic and, if I as the subject may so call it, magnificent canvas, which you are presently to see – '

Troy, greatly startled, learned that the portrait was to be left to the Nation.

V

'It's not the money, Milly. It's not the money, Dessy,' wailed Pauline in the drawing-room. 'I don't mind about the money, Jen. It's the cruel, *cruel* wound to my love. That's what hurts me, girls. That's what hurts.'

'If I were you,' said Millamant with her laugh, 'I think I should feel a bit hipped about the money, too.'

Miss Orrincourt, according to her custom, had gone away to do her face. The ladies were divided into two parties – the haves and the have-nots. Dessy, a not altogether delighted legatee, had a foot in each camp. 'It's damn mean,' she said; 'but after the things I've said about the Orrincourt, I suppose I'm lucky to get anything. What do you think of her, Jen?'

'I suppose,' said Jenetta Ancred thoughtfully, 'she *is* real, isn't she? I mean, I catch myself wondering, quite seriously, if she could be somebody who has dressed up and is putting on the language and everything as a colossal practical joke. I didn't think people ever were so shatteringly true to type. But she's much too lovely, of course, to be a leg-pull.'

'Lovely!' cried Desdemona. 'Jen! Straight out of the third row of the chorus and appallingly common at that.'

'I dare say, but they *are* generally rather lovely in the chorus nowadays, aren't they, Fenella?'

Fenella had withdrawn entirely from the discussion. Now, when they all turned to her, she faced them rigidly, two bright red spots burning over her cheek-bones.

'I want to say,' she began in a loud, shaky voice, 'that I'm very sorry, Aunt Pauline and Mummy, that because of Paul and me you've been treated so disgracefully. We don't mind for ourselves. We'd neither of us, after the things he's said, touch a penny of his money. But we are sorry about you and Panty.'

'Well, darling,' said her mother, putting an arm through hers, 'That's very handsome of you and Paul, but don't let's have any more speeches, shall we?'

'Yes, but Mummy – '

'Your two families are very anxious for both of you to be happy. It's like that, isn't it, Pauline?'

'Well, Jenetta, that, of course, goes without saying, but – '

'There you are, Fen,' said Jenetta. 'It goes, and without saying, which is such a blessing.'

Pauline, looking extremely vexed, retired into a corner with Desdemona.

Jenetta offered Troy a cigarette. 'I suppose,' she muttered in a friendly manner, 'that was not a very good remark for me to make, but, to tell you the truth, I take a pretty gloomy view of all these naked wounds. Mr Rattisbon tells me your husband's coming back. What fun for you.'

'Yes,' said Troy, 'it's all of that.'

'Does everything else seem vague and two-dimensional? It would to me.'

'It does with me, too. I find it very muddling.'

'Of course the Ancreds are on the two-dimensional side anyway, if it comes to that. Especially my father-in-law. Did it make painting him easier or more difficult?'

Before Troy could answer this entertaining question, Cedric, flushed and smirking, opened the door, and stood against it in a romantic attitude waving his handkerchief.

'Darlings,' he said, '*Allez-houp*! The great moment. I am to bid you to the little theatre. Dearest Mrs Alleyn, you and the Old Person should be jointly feted. A cloud of little doves with gilded wings should be lowered by an ingenious device from the flies, and, with pretty gestures, crown you with laurels. Uncle Thomas could have arranged it. I should so adore to see Panty as an aerial coryphée. Will you all come?'

They found the men assembled in the little theatre. It was brilliantly lit, and had an air of hopefully waiting for a much larger audience. Soft music rumbled synthetically behind the front curtain, which (an inevitable detail) was emblazoned with the arms of Ancred. Troy found herself suddenly projected into a star rôle. Sir Henry led her up the aisle to a seat beside himself. The rest of the party settled behind them. Cedric, with a kind of consequential flutter, hurried backstage.

Sir Henry was smoking a cigar. When he inclined gallantly towards Troy she perceived that he had taken brandy. This circumstance was accompanied by a formidable internal rumbling.

'I shall,' he murmured gustily, 'just say a few words.'

They were actually few, but as usual they were intensely embarrassing. Her reluctance to undertake the portrait was playfully outlined. His own pleasure in the sittings was remorselessly sketched.

Some rather naïve quotations on art from *Timon of Athens* were introduced, and then: 'But I must not tantalize my audience any longer,'
said Sir Henry richly. 'Curtain, my boy. Curtain!'

The house lights went down: the front drop slid upwards.
Simultaneously four powerful floodlamps poured down their beams
from the flies. The scarlet tabs were drawn apart, and there, in a
blaze of highly unsuitable light, the portrait was revealed.

Above the sombre head and flying against a clear patch of night
sky, somebody had painted an emerald green cow with vermilion
wings. It was in the act of secreting an object that might or might not
have been a black bomb.

CHAPTER 8

Big Exit

This time Troy felt only a momentary sensation of panic. That particular area of background was hard-dry, and almost at once she remembered this circumstance. She did, however, feel overwhelmingly irritated. Above the automatic burst of applause that greeted the unveiling and only petered out when the detail of the flying cow was observed, she heard her own voice saying loudly: 'No, really, this is too much.'

At the same moment Cedric, who had evidently operated the curtains, stuck his head round the proscenium, stared blindly into the front of the house, turned, saw the portrait, clapped his hand over his mouth and ejaculated: 'Oh, God! Oh, Dynamite!'

'*Darling*!' said his mother from the back row. 'Ceddie, *dear*! What's the matter?'

Sir Henry, on Troy's left, breathed stertorously, and contrived to let out a sort of hoarse roaring noise.

'It's all right,' said Troy. 'Please don't say anything. Wait.'

She strode furiously down the aisle and up the steps. Sacrificing her best evening handkerchief, she reduced the cow to a green smear. 'I think there's a bottle of turpentine somewhere,' she said loudly. 'Please give it to me.'

Paul ran up with it, offering his own handkerchief. Cedric flew out with a handful of rag. The blemish was removed. Meantime the auditorium rang with Miss Orrincourt's hysterical laughter and buzzed with the sound of bewildered Ancreds. Troy threw the handkerchief and rag into the wings, and, with hot cheeks, returned to her seat. 'I wouldn't have been so cross,' she thought grimly, 'if the damn thing hadn't looked so funny.'

'I *demand*,' Sir Henry was shouting, 'I *demand* to know the author of this outrage.'

He was answered by a minor uproar topped by Pauline: 'It was *not* Panty. I tell you, Millamant, once and for all, that Panty is in bed, and has been there since five o'clock. Papa, I protest. It was *not* Panty.'

'Nuts!' said Miss Orrincourt. 'She's been painting green cows for days. I've seen them. Come off it, dear.'

'Papa, I give you my solemn word – '

'Mother, wait a minute – '

'I shall not wait a second. Papa, I have reason to believe – '

'Look here, *do* wait,' Troy shouted, and at once they were silent. 'It's gone,' she said. 'No harm's been done. But there's one thing I must tell you. Just before dinner I came in here. I was worrying about the red curtains. I thought they might touch the canvas where it's still wet. It was all right then. If Panty's been in bed and is known to have been there since ten to nine, she didn't do it.'

Pauline instantly began to babble. 'Thank you, thank you, Mrs Alleyn. You hear that, Papa. Send for Miss Able. I insist that Miss Able be sent for. My child shall be vindicated.'

'I'll go and ask Caroline,' said Thomas unexpectedly. 'One doesn't send for Caroline, you know. I'll go and ask.'

He went out. The Ancreds were silent. Suddenly Millamant remarked: 'I thought perhaps it was just the modern style. What do they call it? Surrealism?'

'Milly!' screamed her son.

Jenetta Ancred said: 'What particular symbolism, Milly, did you read into the introduction of a flying cow behaving like a rude sea-gull over Papa's head?'

'You never know,' Millamant said, 'in these days,' and laughed uncertainly.

'Papa,' said Desdemona, who had been bending over him, 'is dreadfully upset. Papa, dearest, may I suggest – '

'I'm going to bed,' said Sir Henry. 'I am indeed upset. I am unwell. I am going to bed.'

They all rose. He checked them with a gesture. 'I am going alone,' he said, 'to bed.'

Cedric ran to the door. Sir Henry, without a backward glance, walked down the aisle, a shadowy figure looking larger than life against the glowing stage, and passing magnificently from the theatre.

The Ancreds at once began to chatter. Troy felt that she couldn't endure the inevitable revival of Panty's former misdemeanours, Pauline's indignant denials, Cedric's giggles, Millamant's stolid recital of the obvious. She was profoundly relieved when Thomas, slightly ruffled, returned with Caroline Able.

'I've asked Caroline to come,' he said, 'because I thought you mightn't exactly believe me. Panty's been in the sick-bay with all the other ringworms. Dr Withers wanted them to be kept under observation because of the medicine he's given them, so Caroline has been sitting there reading since half-past seven. So Panty, you see, didn't do it.'

'Certainly she didn't do it,' said Miss Able brightly. 'How could she? It's quite impossible.'

'So you see,' Thomas added mildly.

II

Troy stayed behind in the little theatre with Paul and Fenella. Paul switched on the working lights, and together they examined Troy's painting gear, which had been stacked away behind the wings.

The paint-box had been opened. A dollop of Emerald Oxide of Chromium and one of Ivory Black had been squeezed out on the protective under-lid that separated the paints from a compartment designed to hold sketching-boards. A large brush had been used, and had been dipped first in the green and then in the black.

'You know,' said Paul, 'this brush ought to have finger-prints on it.' He looked rather shyly at Troy. 'Oughtn't it?' he added.

'Well, I suppose Roderick would say so,' she agreed.

'I mean, if it has and if we could get everybody's to compare, that would be pretty conclusive, wouldn't it? What's more, it'd be damned interesting.'

'Yes, but I've a notion fingerprints are not as easy as all that.'

'I know. The hand would move about and so on. But look! There *is* some green paint smeared up the handle. I've read about it.

Suppose we asked them to let us take their prints. They couldn't very well refuse.'

'Oh, Paul, *let's*!' cried Fenella.

'What do you think, Mrs Alleyn?'

'My dear chap, you mustn't imagine I know anything about it. But I agree it would be interesting. I *do* know more or less how they take official prints.'

'I've read it up quite a bit,' said Paul. 'I say. Suppose we did get them to do it, and suppose we kept the brush and the box intact – well – well, would – do you think – ?'

'I'd show them to him like a shot,' said Troy.

'I say, that's perfectly splendid,' said Paul. 'Look here, I'll damn well put it to them in the morning. It ought to be cleared up. It's all bloody rum, the whole show, isn't it? What d'you say, Mrs Alleyn?'

'I'm on,' said Troy.

'Glory!' said Fenella. 'So'm I. Let's.'

'OK,' said Paul, gingerly wrapping the brush in rag. 'We'll lock up the brush and box.'

'I'll take them up with me.'

'Will you? That's grand.'

They locked the portrait in the property-room, and said goodnight conspiratorially. Troy felt she could not face another session with the Ancreds, and sending her excuses, went upstairs to her room.

She could not sleep. Outside, in the night, rain drove solidly against the wall of her tower. The wind seemed to have got into the chimney and be trying uneasily to find its way out again. A bucket had replaced the basin on the landing, and a maddening and irregular progression of taps compelled her attention and played like castanets on her nerves. Only one more night here, she thought, and then the comfort of her familiar things in the London flat and the sharing of them with her husband. Illogically she felt a kind of regret for the tower-room, and in this mood fell to revising in their order the eccentricities of her days and nights at Ancreton. The paint on the banister. The spectacles on the portrait. The legend in grease-paint on Sir Henry's looking-glass. The incident of the inflated bladder. The flying cow.

If Panty was not the authoress of these inane facetiae, who was? If one person only was responsible for them all, then Panty was exonerated. But might not Panty have instituted them with the smearing of paint on the banister and somebody else have carried them on? Undoubtedly Panty's legend and past record included many such antics. Troy wished that she knew something of modern views on child psychology. Was such behaviour characteristic of a child who wished to become a dominant figure and who felt herself to be obstructed and repressed? But Troy was positive that Panty had spoken the truth when she denied having any hand in the tricks with paint. And unless Miss Able had told a lie, Panty, quite definitely, had not been the authoress of the flying cow, though she undoubtedly had a predilection for cows and bombs. Troy turned uneasily in her bed, and fancied that beyond the sound of wind and rain she heard the voice of the Great Clock. Was there any significance in the fact that in each instance the additions to her canvas had been made on a dry area and so had done no harm? Which of the adults in the house would realize this? Cedric. Cedric painted, though probably in water-colours. She fancied his aesthetic fervour was, in its antic way, authentic. He would, she thought, instinctively recoil from this particular kind of vandalism. But suppose he knew that no harm would be done? And where was a motive for Cedric? He appeared to have a kind of liking for her; why should he disfigure her work? Bleakly Troy surveyed the rest of the field, and one by one dismissed them until she came to Miss Orrincourt.

The robust vulgarity of these goings-on was not out of character if Miss Orrincourt was considered. Was it, Troy wondered with an uneasy grin, remotely possible that Miss Orrincourt resented the somewhat florid attentions Sir Henry had lavished upon his guest? Could she have imagined that the sittings had been made occasions for even more marked advances, more ardent pattings of the hand, closer pilotings by the elbow? 'Crikey,' Troy muttered, writhing uncomfortably, *'what* an idea to get in the middle of the night!' No, it was too far-fetched. Perhaps one of the elderly maids had lost her wits and taken to this nonsense. 'Or Barker,' thought the now sleepy Troy. In the drumming of rain and wind about her room she began to hear fantastical things. Presently she dreamed of flying bombs that came out of the night, converging on her tower. When they were almost upon her they changed into green cows, that winked broadly, and with a Cedric-like flirt dropped soft bombs, at the same time saying very distinctly: 'Plop, plop, *dearest* Mrs Alleyn.'

'*Mrs Alleyn. Dearest Mrs Alleyn, do please wake up.*'

Troy opened her eyes. Fenella, fully dressed, stood at her bedside. In the thin light of dawn her face looked cold and very white. Her hands opened and shut aimlessly. The corners of her mouth turned down like those of a child about to cry. 'What now, for pity's sake?' cried Troy.

'I thought I'd better come and tell you. Nobody else would. They're all frantic. Paul can't leave his mother, and Mummy's trying to stop Aunt Dessy having hysterics. I feel so ghastly, I had to talk to someone.'

'But why? What is it? What's happened?'

'Grandfather. When Barker went in with his tea. He found him. Lying there. Dead.'

III

There is no more wretched lot than that of the comparative stranger in a house of grief. The sense of loneliness, the feeling that one constantly trespasses on other people's sorrow, that they would thankfully be rid of one; all these circumstances reduce the unwilling intruder to a condition of perpetual apology that must remain unexpressed. If there is nothing useful to be done this misery is the more acute, and Troy was not altogether sorry that Fenella seemed to find some comfort in staying with her. She hurriedly made a fire on top of last night's embers, set Fenella, who shivered like a puppy, to blow it up while she herself bathed and dressed, and, when at last the child broke down, listened to a confused recital which harked back continually to the break between herself and her grandfather. 'It's so *awful* that Paul and I should have made him miserable. We'll never be able to forgive ourselves – never,' Fenella sobbed.

'Now, look here,' said Troy, 'that just doesn't make sense. You and Paul did what you have every right to do.'

'But we did it brutally. You can't say we didn't. We grieved him frightfully. He said so.'

Sir Henry had said so a great many times and with extreme emphasis. It was impossible to suggest that anger rather than grief had moved him. Troy went off on another tack. 'He seemed to have got over it,' she said.

'Last night!' Fenella wailed. 'When I think of what we said about him last night. In the drawing-room after you'd gone up. Everybody except Mummy and Paul. Aunt Milly said he'd probably have an attack, and I said I didn't care if it was fatal. Actually! And he *did* feel it. He cut Aunt Pauline and Mummy and me and Paul out of his Will because of our engagement and the way we announced it. So he did feel it deeply.'

'The Will,' thought Troy. 'Good heavens, yes. The Will!' She said: 'He was an old man, Fenella. I don't think, do you, that the future was exactly propitious? Isn't it perhaps not so very bad that he should go now when everything seemed to him to be perfectly arranged. He'd had his splendid party.'

'And look how it ended.'

'Oh, dear!' said Troy. 'That. Well, yes.'

'And it was probably the party that killed him,' Fenella continued. 'That hot crayfish. It's what everybody thinks. Dr Withers had warned him. And nobody was there. He just went up to his room and died.'

'Has Dr Withers – ?'

'Yes. He's been. Barker got Aunt Milly and she rang up. He says it was a severe attack of gastro-enteritis. He says it – it happened – it must have been – soon after he went up to bed. It's so awful when you think of all the frightful things we were saying about him down there in the drawing-room. All of us except Cedric, and he was simply gloating over us. Little beast, he's still gloating, if it comes to that.'

The gong rumbled distantly. 'You go down to breakfast,' said Fenella. 'I can't face it.'

'That won't do at all. You can at least choke down some coffee.'

Fenella took Troy's arm in a nervous grip. 'I think I like you so much,' she said, 'because you're so unlike all of us. All right, I'll come.'

The Ancreds in sorrow were a formidable assembly. Pauline, Desdemona and Millamant, who were already in the dining-room, had all found black dresses to wear, and Troy was suddenly conscious that she had without thinking pulled on a scarlet sweater. She uttered those phrases of sympathy that are always inadequate. Desdemona silently gripped her hand and turned aside. Pauline dumbfounded her by bursting into tears and giving her an impulsive kiss. And it was strange to find an unsmiling and pallid Millamant. Thomas came in, looking bewildered. 'Good morning,' he said to Troy. 'Isn't it awful? I really can't realize it a bit, you know. Everybody seems to realize it. They're all crying and everything, but

I don't. Poor Papa.' He looked at his sisters. 'You're not eating anything,' he said. 'What can I get you, Pauline?'

Pauline said: 'Oh, Thomas!' and made an eloquent gesture. 'I suppose,' Thomas continued, 'that later on I shan't want to eat anything, but at the moment I am hungry.'

He sat down beside Troy. 'It's lucky you finished the portrait, isn't it?' he said. 'Poor Papa!'

'*Tommy*!' breathed his sister.

'Well, but it is,' he insisted gently. 'Papa would have been pleased too.'

Paul came in, and, a moment later, Jenetta Ancred, wearing tweeds. It was a relief to Troy that, like Thomas, neither of them spoke in special voices.

Presently Millamant began to speak of the manner in which Barker had discovered Sir Henry. At eight o'clock, it appeared, he had gone in as usual with Sir Henry's cup of milk and water. As he approached the room he heard the cat Carabbas wailing inside, and when he opened the door it darted out and fled down the passage. Barker supposed that Sir Henry had forgotten to let his cat out, and wondered that Carabbas had not waked him.

He entered the room. It was still very dark. Barker was shortsighted, but he could make out the figure lying across the bed.

He turned on the lights, and after one horrified glance, rushed down the corridor and beat on the door of Millamant's room. When she and Pauline answered together, he kept his head, remained outside, and, in an agitated whisper, asked Millamant if he might speak to her. She put on her dressing-gown and went out into the cold passage.

'And I knew,' Pauline interjected at this point. 'Something told me. I knew at once that something had happened.'

'Naturally,' said Millamant. 'Barker doesn't go on like that every morning.'

'I knew it was The Great Visitor,' Pauline insisted firmly. 'I knew.'

Millamant had gone with Barker to the room. She sent Barker to rouse Thomas and herself telephoned Dr Withers. He was out, but finally arrived in about an hour. It had been, he said, a severe attack of gastro-enteritis, probably brought on by his indiscretions at dinner. Sir Henry's heart had been unable to survive the attack and he had collapsed and died.

'What I can't understand,' said Pauline, 'is why he didn't ring. He always rang if he felt ill in the night. There was a special bell in the corridor, Dessy. The cord hung beside his bed.'

'He tried,' said Thomas. 'He must have grasped at it across the bed, we think, and fallen. It had come away from the cord. And I don't think, after all, I want very much to eat.'

IV

Troy spent most of that last day between her room and the little theatre, lingering over her packing, which in any case was considerable. Carabbas, the cat, elected to spend the day in her room. Remembering where he had spent the night, she felt a little shudder at the touch of his fur. But they had become friendly, and after a time she was glad of his company. At first he watched her with some interest, occasionally sitting on such garments as she had laid out on the bed and floor. When she removed him he purred briefly, and at last, with a faint mew, touched her hand with his nose. It was hot. She noticed that his fur was staring. Was he, she wondered, actually distressed by the loss of his master? He grew restless and she opened the door. After a fixed look at her he went out, his tail drooping. She thought she heard him cry again on the stairs. She returned uneasily to her packing, broke off from time to time to wander restlessly about the room or stare out of the tower window at the rain-laced landscape. She came across a sketch-book and found herself absently making drawings of the Ancreds. Half an hour went past, and there they all were, like antics on the page, for her to show her husband. Guiltily she completed her packing.

Thomas had undertaken to send by rail such heavy baggage as the Yard car could not accommodate.

She was oppressed by the sensation of unreality. She felt more strongly than ever that she was held in suspension between two phases of experience. She was out of touch, not only with her surroundings, but with herself. While her hands folded and bestowed garment after garment, her thoughts ranged aimlessly between the events of the past twenty-four hours and those that were to come. 'It is I,' she thought in dismay, 'who will resemble the traveller who can speak of nothing but his fellow-passengers and the little events of his voyage, and it is Rory who will listen unhappily to anecdotes of these Ancreds whom he is never likely to meet.'

Lunch seemed to be an uncanny extension of breakfast. There, again, were the Ancreds, still using their special voices, still expressing so eloquently that sorrow whose authenticity Troy was not quite willing to discredit. She was half-aware of their conversation, catching only desultory pieces of information: Mr Rattisbon had been transferred to the rectory. Thomas had been dictating obituary notices over the telephone. The funeral would be held on Tuesday. The voices murmured on. Momentarily she was consulted, drawn in. A weekly paper had got wind of the portrait ('Nigel Bathgate,' thought Troy), and would like to send down a photographer. She made suitable rejoinders and suggestions. Cedric, whose manner was fretfully subdued, brightened a little over this subject, and then, unaccountably, reverted to a kind of nervous acquiescence. The conversation drifted towards Miss Orrincourt, who had expressed her inability to make a public appearance and was having her meals in her own rooms. 'I saw her breakfast-tray,' said Millamant with a ghost of her usual laugh. 'Her appetite doesn't seem to have suffered.'

'T'uh!' said the Ancreds softly.

'Are we to be told,' Pauline asked, 'how long she proposes to – ?'

'I should imagine,' said Desdemona, 'no longer than it takes for the Will to become effective.'

'Well, but I mean to say,' Cedric began, and they all turned their heads towards him. 'If it's not *too* inappropriate and premature, one wonders rather, or doesn't one, if darling Sonia is in *quite* the same position *unmarried* as she would have been as the Old – as dearest Grandpapa's widow? Or not?'

An attentive stillness fell upon the table. It was broken by Thomas: 'Yes – well, of course,' he said, looking blandly about him, 'won't that depend on how the Will is made out. Whether her share is left to "Sonia Orrincourt," you know, or to "my wife, Sonia," and all that.'

Pauline and Desdemona stared for a moment at Thomas. Cedric smoothed his hair with two unsteady fingers. Fenella and Paul looked stolidly at their plates. Millamant, with a muffled attempt at easiness, said: 'There's no need to jump *that* fence, surely, till we meet it.' Pauline and Desdemona exchanged glances. Millamant had used the sacred 'we'.

'I think it's pretty ghastly,' said Fenella abruptly, 'to begin talking about Grandfather's Will when he's up there – lying there – ' She broke off, biting her lip. Troy saw Paul reach for her hand. Jenetta Ancred, who had been silent throughout luncheon, gave her daughter a smile, half-deprecating, half-anxious. 'How she dislikes it,' Troy thought, 'when Fenella behaves like an Ancred.'

'Darling Fen,' Cedric murmured, 'you, of course, can afford to be grand and virtuous over the Will. I mean, you are so definitely *out* of that party, aren't you?'

'That's a pretty offensive remark, Cedric,' said Paul.

'Has everyone finished?' asked Pauline in a hurry. 'If so, Mrs Alleyn, shall we – ?'

Troy excused herself from the post-prandial gathering in the drawing-room.

As she entered the hall a car drew up outside. Barker, who seemed to have been expecting it, was already in the outer porch. He admitted three pale men, dressed in London clothes of a particularly black character. They wore wide black ties. Two of them carried black cases. The third, glancing at Troy, spoke in a muted and inaudible voice.

'This way, if you please,' said Barker, ushering them into a small waiting-room across the hall. 'I will inform Sir Cedric.'

After the newcomers had been shut away and Barker had gone on his errand, Troy stood digesting the official recognition of Cedric's ascendancy. Her glance strayed to a table where, as she had observed, the senior of the three men, with a practised modesty, suggestive almost of sleight of hand, had dropped or slid a card. He had, indeed, given it a little push with his forefinger, so that it lay, partly concealed, under a book which Troy herself had brought from the library to solace her afternoon. The card was engraved in a type slightly heavier and more black than that of a normal visiting card:

'MORTIMER, SON & LOAME
Undertakers – '

Troy lifted her book, exposing the hidden corner of the card, ' – and Embalmers,' she read.

CHAPTER 9

Alleyn

By an alteration in the rhythm of the ship's progress, suggestive almost of a physiological change, her passengers became aware of the end of their long voyage. Her pulse died. It was replaced by sounds of blind waves washing along her sides; of gulls, of voices, of chains, and, beyond these, of movement along the wharves and in the city beyond them.

At early dawn the Port of London looked as wan and expectant as an invalid already preparing for a return to vigour. Thin mist still hung about sheds and warehouses. Muffled lights were strung like a dim necklace along the waterfront. Frost glinted on roofs and bollards and ropes. Alleyn had gripped the rail for so long that its cold had bitten through his gloves into the palms of his hands. Groups of people stood about the wharves, outward signs of a life from which the passengers were, for a rapidly diminishing period, still remote. These groups, befogged by their own breath, were composed for the main part of men.

There were three women, and one wore a scarlet cap. Inspector Fox had come out in the pilot's boat. Alleyn had not hoped for this, and had been touched and delighted to meet him; but now it was impossible to talk to Fox.

'Mrs Alleyn,' said Fox, behind him, 'is wearing a red cap. If you'll excuse me, Mr Alleyn, I ought to have a word with a chap – The car's just behind the Customs shed. I'll meet you there.'

When Alleyn turned to thank him, he was already walking away, squarely overcoated, tidy, looking just like his job.

Now only a dark channel, a ditch, a gutter lay between the ship and the wharf. Bells rang sharply. Men moved forward to the bollards and stared up at the ship. One raised his hand and shouted a greeting in a clear voice. Ropes were flung out, and a moment later the final stoppage was felt dully throughout the ship.

That was Troy down there. She walked forward. Her hands were jammed down in the pockets of her overcoat. She looked along the deck, scowling a little, her gaze moving towards him. In these last seconds, while he waited for her to discover him, Alleyn knew that, like himself, she was nervous. He lifted his hand. They looked at each other, and a smile of extraordinary intimacy broke across her face.

II

'Three years seven months and twenty-four days,' said Alleyn that afternoon. 'It's a hell of a time to be without your wife.' He looked at Troy sitting on the hearth-rug hugging her knees. 'Or rather,' he added, 'to be away from you, Troy. From you, who, so astonishingly happens to be my wife. I've been getting myself into such a hullabaloo about it.'

'Wondering,' Troy asked, 'if we'd run short of conversation and feel shy?'

'You too, then?'

'It does happen, they say. It might easily happen.'

'I even considered the advisability of quoting Othello on his arrival at Cyprus. How would you have reacted, my darling, if I had laid hold upon you under letter A in the Customs shed and begun: "Oh, my fair warrior!" '

'I should probably have made a snappy come-back with something from *Macbeth*:

'Why *Macbeth*?'

'To explain that would be to use up all the conversation I'd saved up on my own account. Rory – '

'My love?'

'I've been having a very queer time with Macbeth.'

She was looking doubtfully at him from under her ruffled forelock. 'You may not care to hear about it,' she mumbled. 'It's a long story.'

'It won't be too long,' Alleyn said, 'if it's you who tells it.'

Watching her, he thought: 'That's made her shy again. We are to re-learn each other.' Alleyn's habit of mind was accurate and exhaustive. He had recognized and examined in himself thoughts that another man might have preferred to ignore. During the long voyage home, he had many times asked himself if, when they met again, he and Troy might not find that the years had dropped between them a transparent barrier through which they would stare without love, at each other. The possibility had occurred to him, strangely enough, at moments when he most desired and missed her. When she had moved forward on the quay, without at first seeing him, his physical reaction had been so sharp that it had blotted out his thoughts. It was only when she gave him the look of intimacy, which so far had not been repeated, that he knew, without question, he was to love her again.

Now, when she was before him in the room whose very familiarity was a little strange, his delight was of a virgin kind that anticipates a trial of its temper. Were Troy's thoughts at this moment comparable with his own? Could he be as certain of her as he was of himself? She had entered into an entirely different mode of life during his absence. He knew nothing of her new associates beyond the rather sparse phrases she had allowed them in her letters. Now, evidently, he was to hear a little more.

'Come over here,' he said, 'and tell me.'

She moved into her old place, leaning against his chair, and he looked down at her with a more tranquil mind, yet with such intense pleasure that the beginning of her story escaped him. But he had been ruthlessly trained to listen to statements and the habit asserted itself. The saga of Ancreton was unfolded.

Troy's account was at first tentative, but his interest stimulated her. She began to enjoy herself, and presently hunted out her sketch-book with the drawings she had made in her tower-room. Alleyn chuckled over the small lively figures with their enormous heads. 'Like the old-fashioned Happy Families cards,' he said, and she agreed that there was something Victorian and fantastic about the originals. After the eccentricities of the Ancreds themselves, the practical jokes turned out to be a dominant theme in her story. Alleyn heard of this with growing concern. 'Here,' he interrupted, 'did this blasted kid ruin your thing in the end or didn't she?'

'No, no! But it wasn't the blasted kid at all. Listen.'

He did, with a chuckle for her deductive methods. 'She might conceivably, you know, write "grandfarther" at one moment and "grandfather" the next, but it's a point of course.'

'It was her manner more than anything. I'm quite positive she didn't do it. I know she's got a record for practical jokes – but wait till I get to the end. Don't fluster the witness.'

'Why not?' said Alleyn, stooping his head.

'To continue,' said Troy after a moment or two, and this time he let her go on to the end. It was an odd story. He wondered if she realized quite how odd it was.

'I don't know whether I've conveyed the general dottiness of that monstrous house,' she said. 'I mean, the queer little things that turned up. Like the book on embalming amongst the *objets d'art* and the missing rat bane.'

'Why do you put them together?'

'I dunno. I suppose because there's arsenic in both of them.'

'You are *not* by any chance, my angel, attempting to land me with a suspected poisoning case on my return to your arms?'

'Well,' said Troy after a pause, 'you would think that one up, wouldn't you?' She screwed round and looked at him. 'And he's been embalmed, you know. By the Messrs Mortimer and Loame. I met them in the hall with their black bags. The only catch in it is the impossibility of regarding any of the Ancreds in the light of a slow poisoner. But it would fit.'

'A little too neatly, I fancy.' With a trace of reluctance he added: 'What were some of the other queer little things that happened?'

'I'd like to know what Cedric and the Orrincourt were giggling about on the sofa, and whether the Orrincourt was coughing or laughing in the governess-cart. I'd even like to know what it was she bought in the chemist's shop. And I'd like to know more about Millamant. One never knew what Millamant was thinking, except that she doted perpetually on her ghastly Cedric. It would have been in her Cedric's interest, of course, to sicken Sir Henry of poor old Panty, who, by the way, has a complete alibi for the flying cow. Her alibi's a dangerous drug. For ringworm.'

'Has this odious child been taking thallium?'

'Do you know about thallium?'

'I've heard of it.'

'It establishes her alibi for the flying cow,' said Troy. 'I'd better explain.'

'Yes,' Alleyn agreed when she had finished, 'that lets her out for the flying cow.'

'She didn't do any of them,' said Troy firmly. 'I wish now that Paul and Fenella and I had gone on with our experiment.'

'What was that to be?'

'It involved your collaboration,' said Troy, looking at him out of the corners of her eyes.

'Like hell it did!'

'Yes. We wrapped up the paint-brush that had been used for the flying cow and we were going to ask all of them to let us take their finger-prints for you to compare with it. Would you have minded?'

'My darling heart, I'd compare them with the Grand Cham of Tartary's if it would give you any fun.'

'But we never got them. Death, as you and Mr Fox would say, intervened. Sir Henry's death. By the way, the person who painted my banister left finger-prints on the stone wall above it. Perhaps after a decent interval I could hint for an invitation to Ancreton and you could come down with your insufflator and black ink. But honestly, it *is* a queer story, don't you think?'

'Yes,' he agreed, rubbing his nose. 'It's queer enough. We heard about Ancred's death on the ship's wireless. Little did I imagine you were in at it.'

'I liked him,' said Troy after a pause. 'He was a terrific old exhibitionist, and he made one feel dreadfully shy at times, but I did like him. And he was grand to paint.'

'The portrait went well?'

'I think so.'

'I'd like to see it.'

'Well, so you shall one of these days. He said he was leaving it to the Nation. What does the Nation do under those circumstances? Hang it in a dark corner of the Tate, do you imagine? Some paper or another, I suspect Nigel Bathgate's, is going to photograph it. We might get a print.'

But Alleyn was not to wait long for the photograph. It appeared that evening in Nigel's paper over a notice of Sir Henry's funeral. He

had been buried in the family vault at Ancreton with as much ceremony as the times allowed.

'He hoped,' said Troy, 'that the Nation would wish otherwise.'

'The Abbey?'

'I'm afraid so. Poor Sir Henry, I wish it had. Ah, well,' said Troy,
dropping the newspaper, 'that's the end of the Ancreds as far as I'm
concerned.'

'You never know,' Alleyn said, vaguely. Then, suddenly impatient
of the Ancreds and of anything that prolonged beyond this moment
the first tentative phase of their reunion, he stretched out his hands
towards Troy.

This story is concerned with Alleyn and Troy's reunion only in so
far as it affected his attitude towards her account of the Ancreds. If he
had heard it at any other time it is possible that, however unwillingly, he might have dwelt longer on its peculiarities. As it was, he welcomed it as a kind of interlude between their first meeting and its
consummation, and then dismissed it from his conscious thoughts.

They had three days together, broken only by a somewhat prolonged interview between Alleyn and his chief at the Special Branch.
He was to resume, for the time being at least, his normal job at the
Yard. On the Thursday morning when Troy returned to her job, he
walked part of the way with her, watched her turn off, and with an
odd feeling of anxiety, himself set out for the familiar room and the
old associates.

It was pleasant, after all, to cross that barren back hall, smelling
of linoleum and coal, to revisit an undistinguished office where the
superintendent of CI, against a background of crossed swords, com-
memorative photographs and a horseshoe, greeted him with unmistakable satisfaction. It was oddly pleasant to sit again at his old desk
in the chief inspectors' room and contemplate the formidable task of
taking up the threads of routine.

He had looked forward to a preliminary gossip with Fox, but Fox
had gone out on a job somewhere in the country and would not be
back before the evening. In the meantime here was an old acquaintance of Alleyn's, one Squinty Donovan, who, having survived two
courts-martial, six months' confinement in Broadmoor, and a near-
miss from a flying bomb, had left unmistakable signs of his ingenuity
upon a lock-up antique shop in Beachamp Place, Chelsea. Alleyn set

in motion the elaborate police machinery by which Squinty might be hunted home to a receiver. He then turned again to his file.

There was nothing exciting; a series of routine jobs. This pleased him. There had been enough of excursions and alarums, the Lord knew, in his three years' hunting for the Special Branch. He had wanted his return to CI to be uneventful.

Presently Nigel Bathgate rang up. 'I say,' he said, 'has Troy seen about the Will?'

'Whose Will?'

'Old Ancred's. She's told you about the Ancreds, of course.'

'Of course.'

'It's in this morning's *Times*. Have a look at it. It'll rock them considerably.'

'What's he done?' Alleyn asked. But for some reason he was unwilling to hear more about the Ancreds.

He heard Nigel chuckling. 'Well, out with it,' he said. 'What's he done?'

'Handed them the works.'

'In what way?'

'Left the whole caboosh to the Orrincourt.'

III

Nigel's statement was an over-simplification of the facts, as Alleyn discovered when, still with that sense of reluctance, he looked up the Will. Sir Henry had cut Cedric down to the bare bones of the entail, and had left a legacy of one thousand pounds to Millamant, to each of his children and to Dr Withers. The residue he had willed to Sonia Orrincourt.

'But – what about the dinner speech and the other Will!' Troy cried when he showed her the evening paper. 'Was that just a complete have, do you suppose? If so, Mr Rattisbon must have known. Or – Rory,' she said, 'I believe it was the flying cow that did it! I believe he was so utterly fed up with his family he marched upstairs, sent for Mr Rattisbon and made a new Will there and then.'

'But didn't he think the *enfant terrible* had done the flying cow? Why take it out of the whole family?'

'Thomas or somebody may have gone up and told him about Panty's alibi. He wouldn't know who to suspect, and would end up by damning the whole crew.'

'Not Miss Orrincourt, however.'

'She'd see to that,' said Troy with conviction.

She was, he saw, immensely taken up with this news, and at intervals during the evening returned to the Ancreds and their fresh dilemma. 'What will Cedric do, can you imagine? Probably the entail is hopelessly below the cost of keeping up Katzenjammer Castle. That's what he called it, you know. Perhaps he'll give it to the Nation. Then they could hang my portrait in its alloted place, chequered all over with coloured lights and everybody would be satisfied. *How* the Orrincourt will gloat.'

Troy's voice faded on a note of uncertainty. Alleyn saw her hands move nervously together. She caught his eye and turned away. 'Let's not talk about the poor Ancreds,' she said.

'What are you munching over in the back of your mind?' he asked uneasily.

'It's nothing,' she said quickly. He waited, and after a moment she came to him. 'It's only that I'd like you to tell me: Suppose you'd heard from somebody else, or read, about the Ancreds and all the unaccountable odds and ends – what would you think? I mean – ' Troy frowned and looked at her clasped hands. 'Doesn't it sound rather horribly like the beginning of a chapter in *Famous Trials?*

'Are you really worried about this?' he said after a pause.

'Oddly enough,' said Troy, 'I am.'

Alleyn got up and stood with his back turned to her. When he spoke again his voice had changed.

'Well,' he said, 'we'd better tackle it, then.'

'What's the matter?' he heard Troy saying doubtfully. 'What's happened?'

'Something quite ridiculous and we'll get rid of it. A fetish I nurse. I've never fancied coming home and having a nice cosy chat about the current homicide with my wife. I've never talked about such cases when they did crop up.'

'I wouldn't have minded, Rory.'

'It's a kind of fastidiousness. No, that's praising it. It's illogical and indefensible. If my job's not fit for you, it shouldn't be my job.'

'You're being too fancy. I've got over my squeamishness.'

'I didn't want you to get over it,' he said. 'I tell you I'm a fool about this.'

She said the phrase he had hoped to hear. 'Then do you think there's something in it – about the Ancreds?'

'Blast the Ancreds! Here, this won't do. Come on, let's tackle the thing and scotch it. You're thinking like this, aren't you? There's a book about embalming in their ghastly drawing-room. It stresses the use of arsenic. Old Ancred went about bragging that he was going to have himself mummified. Any one might have read the book. Sonia Orrincourt was seen doing so. Arsenic, used for rat poison, disappeared in the house. Old Ancred died immediately after altering his Will in the Orrincourt's favour. There wasn't an autopsy. If one were made now, the presence of arsenic would be accounted for by the embalming. That's the colour of the nigger in the woodpile, isn't it?'

'Yes,' said Troy, 'that's it.'

'And you've been wondering whether the practical jokes and all the rest of the fun and games can be fitted in?'

'It sounds less possible as you say it.'

'Good!' he said quickly turning to her. 'That's better. Come on, then. You've wondered if the practical jokes were organized by the Orrincourt to put the old man off his favourite grandchild?'

'Yes. Or by Cedric, with the same motive. You see, Panty was hot favourite before the Raspberry and Flying Cow Period set in.'

'Yes. So, in short, you're wondering if one of the Ancreds, particularly Cedric, or Miss Orrincourt, murdered old Ancred, having previously, in effect, hamstrung the favourite.'

'This is like talking about a nightmare. It leaves off being horrid and turns silly.'

'All the better,' he said vigorously. 'All right. Now, if the lost arsenic was the lethal weapon, the murder was planned long before the party. You understood Millamant to say it had been missing for some time?'

'Yes. Unless – '

'Unless Millamant herself is a murderess and was doing an elaborate cover-up.'

'Because I said one didn't know what Millamant thought about it, it doesn't follow that she thought about murder.'

'Of course it doesn't, bless your heart. Now, if any one of the Ancreds murdered Sir Henry, it was on the strength of the announcement made at the dinner-party and without any knowledge of the effective Will he made that night. If he made it that night.'

'Unless one of the legatees thought they'd been cheated and did it out of pure fury.'

'Or Fenella and Paul, who got nothing? Yes. There's that.'

'Fenella and Paul,' said Troy firmly, 'are not like that.'

'And if Desdemona or Thomas or Jenetta – '

'Jenetta and Thomas are out of the question – '

' – did it, the practical jokes don't fit in, because they weren't there for the earlier ones.'

'Which leaves the Orrincourt, Cedric, Millamant and Pauline.'

'I can see it's the Orrincourt and Cedric who are really bothering you.'

'More particularly,' said Troy unhappily, 'the Orrincourt.'

'Well, darling, what's she like? Has she got the brains to think it up? Would she work out the idea from reading the book on embalming that arsenic would be found in the body anyway?'

'I shouldn't have thought,' said Troy cheerfully, 'that she'd make head or tail of the book. It was printed in very dim italics with the long "s" like an "f". She's not at all the type to pore over literary curiosa unless she thought they were curious in the specialized sense.'

'Feeling better?' he asked.

'Yes, thank you. I'm thinking of other things for myself. Arsenic takes effect pretty quickly, doesn't it? And tastes beastly? He couldn't have had it at dinner, because, apart from being in a foul rage, he was still all right when he left the little theatre. And – if Sonia Orrincourt had put it in his Ovaltine, or whatever he has in his bedside Thermos, could he have sipped down enough to kill him without noticing the taste?'

'Unlikely,' Alleyn said. Another silence fell between them. Alleyn thought: 'I've never been able to make up my mind about telepathy. Think of something else. Is she listening to my thoughts?'

'Rory,' said Troy. 'It is all right, isn't it?'

The telephone rang and he was glad to answer it. Inspector Fox was speaking from the Yard.

'Where have you been, you old devil?' said Alleyn, and his voice held that cordiality with which we greet a rescuer.

'Good evening, Mr Alleyn,' said Fox. 'I was wondering if it would inconvenience you and Mrs Alleyn very much if – '

'Come along!' Alleyn interrupted. 'Of course it won't. Troy will be delighted; won't you, darling? It's Fox.'

'Of course I shall,' said Troy loudly. 'Tell him to come.'

'Very kind, I'm sure,' Fox was saying in his deliberate way.

'Perhaps I ought to explain though. It's Yard business. You might say very unusual circumstances, really. Quite a contretemps.'

'The accent's improving, Fox.'

'I don't get the practice. About this business, though. In a manner of speaking, sir, I fancy you'll want to consult Mrs Alleyn. She's with you, evidently.'

'What is it?' Troy asked quickly. 'I can hear him. What is it?'

'Well, Fox,' said Alleyn after a pause, 'what is it?'

'Concerning the late Sir Henry Ancred, sir. I'll explain when I see you. There's been an Anonymous Letter.'

IV

'Coincidence,' said Fox, putting on his spectacles and flattening out a sheet of paper on his knee, 'is one of the things you get accustomed to in our line of business, as I think you'll agree, sir. Look at the way one of our chaps asked for a lift in the Gutteridge case. Look at the Thompson-Bywaters case – '

'For the love of heaven!' Alleyn cried, 'let us admit coincidence without further parley. It's staring us in the face. It's a bloody quaint coincidence that my wife should have been staying in this wretched dump, and there's an end of it.'

He glanced at Fox's respectable, grave, and attentive face. 'I'm sorry,' he said. 'It's no good expecting me to be reasonable over this business. Troy's had one bad enough experience of the nastiest end of our job. She'll never altogether forget it, and – well, there you are. One doesn't welcome anything like a reminder.'

'I'm sure it's very upsetting, Mr Alleyn. If I could have – '

'I know, I know.' And looking at Fox, Alleyn felt a spasm of self-distaste.

'Fox,' he said suddenly, 'I'm up against a silly complexity in my own attitude to my job. I've tried to shut it off from my private life. I've adopted what I suppose the Russians would call an unrealistic approach: Troy in one compartment, the detection of crime in another. And now, by way of dotting me one on the wind, the fates have handed Troy this little affair on a platter. If there's anything in it she'll be a witness.'

'There may not be anything in it, Mr Alleyn.'

'True enough. That's precisely the remark I've been making to her for the last hour or so.'

Fox opened his eyes very wide. 'Oh, yes,' said Alleyn, 'she's already thought there was something off-colour about the festivities at Ancreton.'

'Is that so?' Fox said slowly. 'Is that the case?'

'It is indeed. She's left us alone to talk it over. I can give you the story when you want it and so can she. But I'd better have your end first. What's that paper you've got there?'

Fox handed it to him. 'It came in to us yesterday, went through the usual channels, and finally the Chief got on to it and sent for me this evening. You'd gone by then, sir, but he asked me to have a word with you about it. White envelope to match, addressed in block capitals "CID, Scotland Yard, London." Postmark, Victoria.'

Alleyn took the paper. It appeared to be a sheet from a block of faintly ruled notepaper. The lines were, unusually, a pale yellow, and a margin was ruled down the side. The message it contained was flatly explicit:

THE WRITER HAS REASON TO BELIEVE THAT SIR HENRY ANCRED'S DEATH WAS BROUGHT ABOUT BY THE PERSON WHO HAS RECEIVED THE MOST BENEFIT FROM IT.

'Water-mark, "Crescent Script". People write these things,' said Fox. 'You know yourself there may be nothing in it. But we've got to take the usual notice. Talk to the super at the local station, I suppose. And the doctor who attended the old gentleman. He may be able to put the matter beyond doubt. There's an end of it.'

'He will if he can,' said Alleyn grimly. 'You may depend upon that.'

'In the meantime, the AC suggested I should report to you and see about a chat with Mrs Alleyn. He remembered Mrs Alleyn had been at Ancreton before you came back.'

'*Report* to me? If anything comes of this, does he want me to take over?'

'Well, sir, I fancy he will. He mentioned, jokingly-like, that it'd be quite unusual if the investigating officer got his first statement on a case from his wife.'

'Facetious ass!' said Alleyn with improper emphasis.

Fox looked demurely down his nose.

'Oh, well,' said Alleyn, 'let's find Troy and we'll hag over the whole blasted set up. She's in the studio. Come on.'

Troy received Fox cheerfully. 'I know what it's all about, Mr Fox,' she said, shaking hands with him.

'I'm sure I'm very sorry – ' Fox began.

'But you needn't be,' Troy said quickly, linking her arm through Alleyn's. 'Why on earth should you be? If I'm wanted, here I am. What happens?'

'We sit down,' Alleyn said, 'and I go over the whole story as you've told it to me. When I go wrong, you stop me, and when you think of anything extra, you put it in. That's all, so far. The whole thing may be a complete washout, darling. Anonymous letter writers have the same affection for the Yard that elderly naturalists have for *The Times*. Now then. Here, Fox, to the best of my ability, is the Ancred saga.'

He went methodically through Troy's account, correlating the events, tracing the several threads in and out of the texture of the narrative and gathering them together at the end.

'How's that?' he asked her when he had finished. He was surprised to find her staring at him as if he had brought off a feat of sleight of hand.

'Amazingly complete and tidy,' she said.

'Well, Fox? What's it amount to?'

Fox wiped his hand over his jaw. 'I've been asking myself, sir,' he said, 'whether you mightn't find quite a lot of circumstances behind quite a lot of sudden demises that might sound funny if you strung them together. What I mean to say, a lot of big houses keep rat-bane on the premises, and a lot of people can't lay their hands on it when they want it. Things get mislaid.'

'Very true, Foxkin.'

'And as far as this old-fashioned book on embalming goes, Mr Alleyn, I ask myself if perhaps somebody mightn't have picked it up since the funeral and got round to wondering about it like Mrs Alleyn has. You say these good people weren't very keen on Miss Sonia Orrincourt and are probably feeling rather sore about the late old gentleman's Will. They seem to be a highly-strung, excitable lot.'

'But I don't think I'm a particularly highly-strung, excitable lot, Mr Fox,' said Troy. 'And I got the idea too.'

'There!' said Fox, clicking his tongue. 'Putting my foot in it as usual, aren't I, sir?'

'Tell us what else you ask yourself,' said Alleyn.

'Why, whether one of these disappointed angry people hasn't let his imagination, or more likely hers, get the upper hand, and written this letter on the spur of the moment.'

'But what about the practical jokes, Mr Fox?' said Troy.

'Very silly, mischievous behaviour. Committing a nuisance. If the little girl didn't do them, and it looks as if she *couldn't* have done them at all, then somebody's brought off an unpleasant trick. Spiteful,' Fox added severely. 'Trying to prejudice the old gentleman against her, as you suggest, I dare say. But that doesn't necessarily mean murder. Why should it?'

'Why, indeed!' said Alleyn, taking him by the arm. 'You're exactly what we needed in this house, Br'er Fox. Let's all have a drink.' He took his wife on his other arm, and together they returned to the sitting-room. The telephone rang as Troy entered and she answered it. Alleyn held Fox back and they stared at each other.

'Very convincing performance, Fox. Thank you.'

'Rum go, sir, all the same, don't you reckon?'

'Too bloody rum by half. Come on.'

When they went into the room Troy put her hand over the mouthpiece of the telephone and turned to them. Her face was white.

'Rory,' she said, 'it's Thomas Ancred. He wants to come and see you. He says they've all had letters. He says he's made a discovery. He wants to come. What shall I say?'

'I'll speak to him,' said Alleyn. 'He can see me at the Yard in the morning, damn him.'

CHAPTER 10

Bombshell from Thomas

Thomas Ancred arrived punctually at nine o'clock, the hour Alleyn had appointed. Fox was present at the interview, which took place in Alleyn's room.

Troy had the painter's trick of accurate description, and she had been particularly good on Thomas. Alleyn felt he was already familiar with that crest of fine hair, those eyes wide open and palely astonished, that rather tight, small mouth, and the mild meandering voice.

'Thank you very much,' said Thomas, 'for letting me come. I didn't much want to, of course, but it's nice of you to have me. It was knowing Mrs Alleyn that put it into their heads.'

'Whose heads?' asked Alleyn.

'Well, Pauline's and Dessy's, principally. Paul and Fenella were quite keen too. I suppose Mrs Alleyn has told you about my people?'

'I think,' said Alleyn, 'that it might be best if we adopt the idea that I know nothing about anybody.'

'Oh, dear!' said Thomas, sighing. 'That means a lot of talking, doesn't it?'

'What about these letters?'

'Yes, to be sure,' said Thomas, beginning to pat himself all over. 'The letters. I've got them somewhere. Anonymous, you know. Of course I've had them before in the theatre from disappointed patrons and angry actresses, but this is different – really. Now, where?' He picked up one corner of his jacket, looked suspiciously at a bulging pocket, and finally pulled out a number of papers, two pencils and a box of matches. Thomas beamed at Alleyn. 'And there, after all, they are,' he said. In mild triumph he laid them out on the desk – eight copies of the letter Alleyn had already seen, all printed with the same type of pen on the same type of paper.

'What about the envelopes?' Alleyn asked.

'Oh,' said Thomas, 'we didn't keep them. I wasn't going to say anything about mine,' Thomas continued after a pause, 'and nor were Jenetta and Milly, but of course everybody noticed everybody else had the same sort of letter, and Pauline (my sister, Pauline Kentish) made a great hallabaloo over hers, and there we were, you know.'

'Eight,' said Alleyn. 'And there are nine in the party at Ancreton?'

'Sonia didn't get one, so everybody says she's the person meant.'

'Do you take that view, Mr Ancred?'

'Oh, yes,' said Thomas, opening his eyes very wide. 'It seems obvious, doesn't it? With the Will and everything. Sonia's meant, of course, but for my part,' said Thomas with a diffident cough, 'I don't fancy she murdered Papa.'

He gave Alleyn a rather anxious smile. 'It would be such a beastly thing to do, you know,' he said. 'Somehow one can't quite – however. Pauline actually almost leapt at the idea. Dessy, in a way, too. They're both dreadfully upset. Pauline fainted at the funeral anyway, and then with those letters on top of it all she's in a great state of emotional upheaval. You can't imagine what it's like at Ancreton.'

'It was Mrs Kentish, wasn't it, who suggested you should come to the Yard?'

'And Dessy. My unmarried sister, Desdemona. We all opened our letters yesterday morning at breakfast. Can you imagine? I got down first and really – such a shock! I was going to throw it on the fire, but just then Fenella came in, so I folded it up very small under the table. You can see which is mine by the creases. Paul's is the one that looks as if it had been chewed. He crunched it up, don't you know, in his agitation. Well, then I noticed that there were the same kind of envelopes in front of everybody's plate. Sonia has breakfast in her room, but I asked Barker if there were any letters for her. Fenella was by that time looking rather odd, having opened hers. Pauline said: "What an extraordinary looking letter I've got. Written by a child, I should think," and Milly said: "Panty again, perhaps," and there was a row, because Pauline and Milly don't see eye to eye over Panty. And then everybody said: "I've got one too," and then you know they opened them. Well, Pauline swooned away, of course, and Dessy said: "O, my prophetic soul," and began to get very excitable, and Milly said: "I think people who write anonymous letters are the *end,*" and Jenetta (my sister-in-law), Fenella's mother (who is married to my brother Claude), said: "I agree, Milly." Then the next thing was, let me see – the next thing was everybody suspecting everybody else of writing the letter, until Paul got the idea – you must excuse me – that perhaps Mrs Alleyn being married to – '

Alleyn, catching sight of Fox's scandalized countenance, didn't answer, and Thomas, rather pink in the face, hurried on. 'Of course,' he said, 'the rest of us pooh-poohed the notion; quite howled it down, in fact. "The very idea," Fenella, for instance, said, "of Mrs Alleyn writing anonymous letters is just *so* bloody silly that we needn't discuss it," which led directly into another row, because Pauline made the suggestion and Fenella and Paul are engaged against her wish. It ended by my nephew Cedric, who is now the head of the family, saying that he thought the letter sounded like Pauline herself. He mentioned that a favourite phrase of Pauline's is: "I have reason to believe." Milly, Cedric's mother, you know, laughed rather pointedly, so naturally there was another row.'

'Last night,' Alleyn said, "you told me you had made a discovery at Ancreton. What was it?'

'Oh, yes. I was coming to that some time. Now, actually, because it happened after lunch. I really don't care at all for this part of the story. Indeed, I quite forgot myself, and said I would *not* go back to Ancreton until I was assured of not having to get involved in any more goings on.'

'I'm afraid – ' Alleyn began, but Thomas at once interrupted him. 'You don't follow? Well, of course you wouldn't, would you, because I haven't told you? Still, I suppose I'd better.'

Alleyn waited without comment.

'Well,' said Thomas at last. 'Here, after all, we go.'

II

'All yesterday morning,' Thomas said, 'after reading the letters, the battle, as you might put it, raged. Nobody really on anybody else's side except Paul and Fenella and Jenetta wanting to burn the letters and Pauline and Desdemona thinking there was something in it and we ought to keep them. And by lunch-time, you may depend on it, feeling ran very high indeed. And then, you know – '

Here Thomas paused and stared meditatively at a spot on the wall somewhere behind Fox's head. He had this odd trick of stopping short in his narratives. It was as if a gramophone needle was abruptly and unreasonably lifted from the disc. It was impossible to discover whether Thomas was suddenly bereft of the right word or smitten by the intervention of a new train of thought, or whether he had merely forgotten what he was talking about. Apart from a slight glazing of his eyes, his facial expression remained uncannily fixed.

'And then,' Alleyn prompted after a long pause.

'Because, when you come to think of it,' Thomas's voice began, 'it's the last thing one expects to find in the cheese-dish. It was New Zealand cheese, of course. Papa was fortunate in his friends.'

'What,' Alleyn asked temperately, 'is the last thing, Fox, that one would expect to find in the cheese-dish?'

Before Fox could reply Thomas began again.

'It's an old piece of Devonport. Rather nice, really. Blue, with white swans sailing round it. Very large. In times of plenty we used to have a whole Stilton in it, but now, of course, only a tiny packet. Rather ridiculous, really, but it meant there was plenty of room.'

'For what?'

'It was Cedric who lifted the lid and discovered it. He gave one of his little screams, but beyond feeling rather irritated, I dare say nobody paid much attention. Then he brought it over to the table – did I forget to say it's always left on the sideboard? – and dropped it in front of Pauline, who is in a very nervous condition anyway, and nearly shrieked the place down.'

'Dropped the cheese-dish? Or the cheese?'

'The cheese? Good heavens,' cried the scandalized Thomas, 'what an idea! The book, to be sure.'

'What book?' Alleyn said automatically.

'*The* book, you know. The one out of the glass thing in the drawing-room.'

'Oh,' said Alleyn after a pause. 'That book. On embalming?'

'And arsenic and all the rest of it. Too awkward and beastly, because, you know, Papa, by special arrangement, *was*. It upset everybody frightfully. In such very bad taste, everybody thought, and, of course, the cry of "Panty" went up immediately on all sides, and there was Pauline practically in a dead faint for the second time in three days.'

'Yes?'

'Yes, and then Milly remembered seeing Sonia look at the book, and Sonia said she had never seen it before, and then Cedric read out some rather beastly bits about arsenic, and everybody began to remember how Barker couldn't find the rat poison when it was wanted for Bracegirdle. Then Pauline and Desdemona looked at each other in such a meaning sort of way that Sonia became quite frantic with rage, and said she'd leave Ancreton there and then, only she couldn't, because there wasn't a train, so she went out in the rain and the governess-cart, and is now in bed with bronchitis, to which she is subject.'

'Still at Ancreton?'

'Yes, still there. Quite,' said Thomas. His expression became dazed, and he went off into another of his silences.

'And that,' Alleyn said, 'is, of course, the discovery you mentioned on the telephone?'

'That? Discovery? What discovery? Oh, no!' cried Thomas. 'I see what you mean. Oh, no, indeed, *that* was nothing compared to what we found afterwards in her room!'

'What did you find, Mr Ancred, and in whose room?'

'Sonia's,' said Thomas. 'Arsenic.'

III

'It was Cedric and the girls' idea,' Thomas said. 'After Sonia had gone out in the governess-cart they talked and talked. Nobody quite liked to say outright that perhaps Sonia had put rat poison in Papa's hot drink, but even Milly remarked that Sonia had recently got into the way of making it. Papa said she made it better than any of the servants or even than Milly herself. She used to take it in and leave it at his bedside. Cedric remembered seeing Sonia with the Thermos flask in her hands. He passed her in the passage on his way to bed that very night.

'It was at about this stage,' Thomas continued, 'that somebody – I've forgotten quite whom – said that they thought Sonia's room ought to be searched. Jenetta and Fenella and Paul jibbed at this, but Dessy and Cedric and Pauline were as keen as mustard. I had promised to lend Caroline Able a book so I went away rather gladly. Caroline Able teaches the Difficult Children, including Panty, and she is very worried because of Panty not going bald enough. So it might have been an hour later that I went back to our part of the house. And there was Cedric lying in wait for me. Well, he's the head of the house now, so I suppose I mustn't be beastly about him. All mysterious and whispering, he was.

' "Ssh," he said. "Come upstairs."

'He wouldn't say anything more. I felt awfully bored with all this, but I followed him up.'

'To Miss Orrincourt's room?' Alleyn suggested as Thomas's eyes had glazed again.

'That's it. How did you guess? And there were Pauline and Milly and Dessy. I must tell you,' said Thomas delicately, 'that Sonia has a little sort of suite of rooms near Papa's for convenience. It wasn't called anything, because Papa had run out of famous actresses' names. So he had a new label done with *Orrincourt* on it, and that really infuriated everybody, because Sonia, whatever anybody may care to say to the contrary, is a very naughty actress. Well, not an actress at all, really. Absolutely dire, you might say.'

'You found your sisters and Mrs Henry Ancred in these rooms?'

'Yes. I must tell you that Sonia's suite is in a tower. Like the tower your wife had, only Sonia's tower is higher, because the architect who build Ancreton believed in quaintness. So Sonia has got a bedroom on top and then a bathroom, and at the bottom a boudoir. The bedroom's particularly quaint, with a little door and steps up into the pepper-pot roof which makes a box-room. They are milling about in this box-room and Dessy had found the rat poison in one of Sonia's boxes. It's a preparation of arsenic. It says so on the label. Well!'

'What have you done with it?'

'So awkward!' said Thomas crossly. 'They made me take it. To keep, they said, in case of evidence being needed. Cedric was very particular about it, having read detective books, and he wrapped it up in one of my handkerchiefs. So I've got it in my rooms here in London if you really want to see it.'

'We'll take possession of it, I think,' said Alleyn with a glance at Fox. Fox made a slight affirmative rumble. 'If it's convenient, Mr Ancred,' Alleyn went on, 'Fox or I will drop you at your rooms and collect this tin.'

'I hope I can find it,' Thomas said gloomily.

'Find it?'

'One does mislay things so. Only the other day – ' Thomas fell into one of his trances and this time Alleyn waited for something to break through. 'I was just thinking, you know,' Thomas began rather loudly. 'There we all were in her room and I looked out of the window. It was raining. And away down below, like something out of a Noah's Ark, was the governess-cart creeping up the drive, and Sonia, in her fur coat, flapping the reins, I suppose, in the way she has. And when you come to think of it, there, according to Pauline and Dessy and Cedric and Milly, went Papa's murderess.'

'But not according to you?' said Alleyn. He was putting away the eight anonymous letters. Fox had risen, and now stared down at their visitor as if Thomas was some large unopened parcel left by mistake in the room.

'To *me?*' Thomas repeated, opening his eyes very wide. 'I don't know. How should I? But you wouldn't believe how uncomfortable it makes one feel.'

IV

To enter Thomas's room was to walk into a sort of cross between a wastepaper basket and a workshop. Its principal feature was a large round table entirely covered with stacks of paper, paints, photographs, models for stage sets, designs for costumes, and books. In the window was an apparently unused desk. On the walls were portraits of distinguished players, chief among them Sir Henry himself.

'Sit down,' invited Thomas, sweeping sheafs of papers from two chair on to the floor. 'I'll just think where – ' He began to walk round his table, staring rather vacantly at it. 'I came in with my suitcase, of course, and then, you know, the telephone rang. It was *much* later than that when I wanted to find the letters, and I had put them carefully away because of showing them to you. And I *found* them. So I must have unpacked. And I can remember thinking: "It's poison, and I'd better be careful of my handkerchief in case – " '

He walked suddenly to a wall cupboard and opened it. A great quantity of papers instantly fell out. Thomas stared indignantly at them. 'I distinctly remember,' he said, turning to Alleyn and Fox with his mouth slightly open. 'I *distinctly* remember saying to myself – ' But this sentence was also fated to remain unfinished, for Thomas pounced unexpectedly upon some fragment from the cupboard. 'I've been looking for that all over the place,' he said. 'It's *most* important. A cheque, in fact.'

He sat on the floor and began scuffling absently among the papers. Alleyn, who for some minutes had been inspecting the chaos that reigned upon the table, lifted a pile of drawings and discovered a white bundle. He loosened the knot at the top and a stained tin was disclosed. It bore a bright red label with the legend: 'Rat-X-it! Poison,' and, in slightly smaller print, the antidote for arsenical poisoning.

'Here it is, Mr Ancred,' said Alleyn.

'What?' asked Thomas. He glanced up. 'Oh, *that*,' he said. 'I *thought* I'd put it on the table.'

Fox came forward with a bag. Alleyn, muttering something about futile gestures, lifted the tin by the handkerchief. 'You don't mind,' he said to Thomas, 'if we take charge of this? We'll give you a receipt for it.'

'Oh, will you?' asked Thomas mildly. 'Thanks awfully.' He watched them stow away the tin, and then, seeing that they were about to go, scrambled to his feet. 'You must have a drink,' he said. 'There's a bottle of Papa's whisky – I think.'

Alleyn and Fox managed to head him off a further search. He sat down, and listened with an air of helplessness to Alleyn's parting exposition.

'Now, Mr Ancred,' Alleyn said, 'I think I ought to make as clear as possible the usual procedure following the sort of information you have brought to us. Before any definite step can be taken, the police make what are known as "further inquiries". They do this as inconspicuously as possible, since neither their original informant, nor they, enjoy the public exploration of a mare's nest. If these inquiries seem to point to a suspicion of ill practice, the police then get permission from the Home Secretary for the next step to be taken. You know what that is, I expect?'

'I say,' said Thomas, 'that *would* be beastly, wouldn't it?' A sudden thought seemed to strike him. 'I say,' he repeated, 'would I have to be there?'

'We'd probably ask for formal identification by a member of his family.'

'Oh, Lor'!' Thomas whispered dismally. He pinched his lower lip between his thumb and forefinger. A gleam of consolation appeared to visit him.

'I say,' he said, 'it's a good job after all, isn't it, that the Nation *didn't* plump for the Abbey?'

CHAPTER 11

Alleyn at Ancreton

'In our game,' said Fox as they drove back to the Yard, 'you get some funny glimpses into what you might call human nature. I dare say I've said that before, but it's a fact.'

'I believe you,' said Alleyn.

'Look at this chap we've just left,' Fox continued with an air of controversy. 'Vague! And yet he must be good at his job, wouldn't you say, sir?'

'Indisputably.'

'There! Good at his job, and yet to meet him you'd say he'd lose his play, and his actors, and his way to the theatre. In view of which,' Fox summed up, 'I ask myself if this chap's as muddle-headed as he lets on.'

'A pose, you think, do you, Fox?'

'You never know with some jokers,' Fox muttered, and, wiping his great hand over his face, seemed by that gesture to dispose of Thomas Ancred's vagaries. 'I suppose,' he said, 'it'll be a matter of seeing the doctor, won't it?'

'I'm afraid so. I've looked out trains. There's one in an hour. Get us there by midday. We may have to spend the night in Ancreton village. We can pick up our emergency bags at the Yard. I'll talk to the AC and telephone Troy. What a hell of a thing to turn up.'

'It doesn't look as if we'll be able to let it alone, do you reckon, Mr Alleyn?'

'I still have hopes. As it stands, there's not a case in Thomas's story to hang a dead dog on. They lose a tin of rat poison and find it in a garret. Somebody reads a book about embalming, and thinks up an elaborate theme based on an arbitrary supposition. Counsel could play skittles with it – as it stands.'

'Suppose we *did* get an order for exhumation. Suppose they found arsenic in the body. With this embalming business it'd seem as if it would prove nothing.'

'On the contrary,' said Alleyn, 'I rather think, Fox, that if they did find arsenic in the body it would prove everything.'

Fox turned slowly and looked at him. 'I don't get that one, Mr Alleyn,' he said.

'I'm not at all sure that I'm right. We'll have to look it up. Here we are. I'll explain on the way down to this accursed village. Come on.'

He saw his Assistant Commissioner, who, with the air of a connoisseur, discussed the propriety of an investigator handling a case in which his wife might be called as a witness. 'Of course, my dear Rory, if by any chance the thing should come into court and your wife be subpœnaed, we would have to reconsider our position. We've no precedent, so far as I know. But for the time being I imagine it's more reasonable for you to discuss it with her than for anybody else to do so – Fox, for instance. Now, you go down to this place, talk to the indigenous GP, and come back and tell us what you think about it. Tiresome, if it comes to anything. Good luck.'

As they left, Alleyn took from his desk the second volume of a work on medical jurisprudence. It dealt principally with poisons. In the train he commended certain passages to Fox's notice. He watched his old friend put on his spectacles, raise his eyebrows, and develop the slightly catarrhal breathing that invariably accompanied his reading.

'Yes,' said Fox, removing his spectacles as the train drew into Ancreton Halt, 'that's different, of course.'

II

Doctor Herbert Withers was a short, tolerably plump man, with little of the air of wellbeing normally associated with plumpness. He came out into his hall as they arrived, admitting from some inner room the sound of a racing broadcast. After a glance at Alleyn's professional card he took them to his consulting-room, and sat at his desk with a movement whose briskness seemed to overlie a controlled fatigue.

'What's the trouble?' he asked.

It was the conventional opening. Alleyn thought it had slipped involuntarily from Dr Withers's lips.

'We hope there's no trouble,' he said. 'Would you mind if I asked you to clear up a few points about Sir Henry Ancred's death?'

The mechanical attentiveness of Dr Withers's glance sharpened. He made an abrupt movement and looked from Alleyn to Fox.

'Certainly,' he said, 'if there's any necessity. But why?' He still held Alleyn's card in his hand and he glanced at it again. 'You don't mean to say – ' he began, and stopped short. 'Well, what are these few points?'

'I think I'd better tell you exactly what's happened,' Alleyn said. He took a copy of the anonymous letter from his pocket and handed it to Dr Withers. 'Mr Thomas Ancred brought eight of these to us this morning,' he said.

'Damn disgusting piffle,' said Dr Withers and handed it back.

'I hope so. But when we're shown these wretched things we have to do something about them.'

'Well?'

'You signed the death certificate, Dr Withers, and – '

'And I shouldn't have done so if I hadn't been perfectly satisfied as to the cause.'

'Exactly. Now will you, like a good chap, help us to dispose of these letters by giving us, in non-scientific words, the cause of Sir Henry's death?'

Dr Withers fretted a little, but at last went to his files and pulled out a card.

'There you are,' he said. 'That's the last of his cards. I made routine calls at Ancreton. It covers about six weeks.'

Alleyn looked at it. It bore the usual list of dates with appropriate notes. Much of it was illegible and almost all obscure to the lay mind. The final note, however, was flatly lucid. It read: 'Deceased. Between twelve-thirty and two a.m., Nov. 25th.'

'Yes,' said Alleyn. 'Thank you. Now will you translate some of this?'

'He suffered,' said Dr Withers angrily, 'from gastric ulcers and degeneration of the heart. He was exceedingly indiscriminate in his diet. He'd eaten a disastrous meal, had drunk champagne, and had flown into one of his rages. From the look of the room, I diagnosed a severe gastric attack followed by heart failure. I may add that if I had heard about the manner in which he'd spent the evening I should have expected some such development.'

'You'd have expected him to die?'

'That would be an extremely unprofessional prognostication. I would have anticipated grave trouble,' said Dr Withers stuffily.

'Was he in the habit of playing up with his diet?'

'He was. Not continuously, but in bouts.'

'Yet survived?'

'The not unusual tale of "once too often".'

'Yes,' said Alleyn, looking down at the card. 'Would you mind describing the room and the body?'

'Would you, in your turn, Chief Inspector, mind telling me if you have any reason for this interview beyond these utterly preposterous anonymous letters?'

'Some of the family suspect arsenical poisoning.'

'Oh, my God and the little starfish!' Dr Withers shouted and shook his fists above his head. 'That *bloody* family!'

He appeared to wrestle obscurely with his feelings. 'I'm sorry about that,' he said at last, 'inexcusable outburst. I've been busy lately and worried, and there you are. The Ancreds, collectively, have tried me rather high. Why, may one ask, do they suspect arsenical poisoning?'

'It's a long story,' said Alleyn carefully, 'and it involves a tin of rat poison. May I add also, very unprofessionally, that I shall be enormously glad if you can tell me that the condition of the room and the body precludes the smallest likelihood of arsenical poisoning?'

'I can't tell you anything of the sort. Why? *(a)* Because the room had been cleaned up when I got there. And *(b)* because the evidence as described to me, and the appearance of the body were entirely consistent with a severe gastric attack, and therefore *not* inconsistent with arsenical poisoning.'

'Damn!' Alleyn grunted. 'I thought it'd be like that.'

'How the hell could the old fool have got at any rat poison? Will you tell me that?' He jabbed his finger at Alleyn.

'They don't think,' Alleyn explained, 'that he got at it. They think it was introduced to him.'

The well-kept hand closed so strongly that the knuckles whitened. For a moment he held it clenched, and then, as if to cancel this gesture, opened the palm and examined his fingernails.

'That,' he said, 'is implicit in the letter, of course. Even that I can believe of the Ancreds. Who is supposed to have murdered Sir Henry? Am I, by any pleasant chance?'

'Not that I know,' said Alleyn comfortably. Fox cleared his throat and added primly: 'What an idea!'

'Are they going to press for an exhumation? Or are you?'

'Not without more reason than we've got at the moment,' Alleyn said. 'You didn't hold a post-mortem?'

'One doesn't hold a PM on a patient who was liable to go off in precisely this fashion at any moment.'

'True enough. Dr Withers, may I make our position quite clear? We've had a queer set of circumstances placed before us and we've got to take stock of them. Contrary to popular belief, the police do not, in such cases, burn to get a pile of evidence that points unavoidably to exhumation. If the whole thing turns out to be so much nonsense they are, as a general rule, delighted to write it off. Give us a sound argument against arsenical poisoning and we'll be extremely grateful to you.'

Dr Withers waved his hands. 'I can't give you, at a moment's notice, absolute proof that he didn't get arsenic. You couldn't do it for ninety-nine deaths out of a hundred, when there was gastric trouble with vomiting and purging and no analysis was taken of anything. As a matter of fact – '

'Yes?' Alleyn prompted as he paused.

'As a matter of fact, I dare say if there'd been anything left I might have done an analysis simply as a routine measure and to satisfy a somewhat pedantic medical conscience. But the whole place had been washed up.'

'By whose orders?'

'My dear man, by Barker's orders or Mrs Kentish's, or Mrs Henry Ancred's, or whoever happened to think of it. They didn't like to move him. Couldn't very well. Rigor was pretty well established, which gave me, by the way, a lead about the time of his death. When

I saw him later in the day they'd fixed him up, of course, and a nice time Mrs Ancred must have had of it with all of them milling about the house in an advanced condition of hysteria and Mrs Kentish "insisting on taking a hand in the laying-out".'

'Good Lord!'

'Oh, they're like that. Well, as I was saying, there he was when they found him, hunched up on the bed, and the room in a pretty nauseating state. When I got there, two of those old housemaids were waddling off with their buckets and the whole place stank of carbolic. They'd even managed to change the bedclothes. I didn't get there, by the way, for an hour after they telephoned. Confinement.'

'About the children's ringworm – ' Alleyn began.

'You know about them, do you? Yes. Worrying business. Glad to say young Panty's cleared up at last.'

'I understand,' Alleyn said pleasantly, 'that you are bold in your use of drugs.'

There was a long silence. 'And how, may I ask,' said Dr Withers very quietly, 'did you hear details of my treatment?'

'Why, from Thomas Ancred,' said Alleyn, and watched the colour return to Dr Withers's face. 'Why not?'

'I dislike gossip about my patients. As a matter of fact I wondered if you'd been talking to our local pharmacist. I'm not at all pleased with him at the moment, however.'

'Do you remember the evening the children were dosed – Monday, the nineteenth, I think it was?'

Dr Withers stared at him. 'Now, why – ?' he began, and seemed to change his mind. 'I do,' he said. 'Why?'

'Simply because that evening a practical joke was played on Sir Henry and the child Panty has been accused of it. It's too elaborate a story to bother you about, but I'd like to know if she was capable of it. In the physical sense. Mentally, it seems, she certainly is.'

'What time?'

'During dinner. She would have visited the drawing-room.'

'Out of the question. I arrived at seven-thirty – Wait a moment.' He searched his filing cabinet and pulled out another card. 'Here! I superintended the weighing and dosing of these kids and noted the time. Panty got her quota at eight and was put to bed. I stayed on in the ante-room to their dormitory during the rest of the business and talked to Miss Able. I left her my visiting list for the next twenty-four hours so that she could get me quickly if anything cropped up. It was after nine when I left and this wretched kid certainly hadn't budged. I had a look at the lot of them. She was asleep with a normal pulse and so on.'

'That settles Panty, then,' Alleyn muttered.

'Look here, has this any bearing on the other business?'

'I'm not sure. It's a preposterous story. If you've the time and inclination to listen I'll tell it to you.'

'I've got,' said Dr Withers, glancing at his watch, 'twenty-three minutes. Case in half an hour, and I want to hear the racing results before I go out.'

'I shan't be more than ten minutes.'

'Go ahead, then. I should be glad to hear any story, however fantastic, that can connect a practical joke on Monday the nineteenth with the death of Sir Henry Ancred from gastro-enteritis after midnight on Saturday the twenty-fourth.'

Alleyn related all the stories of the practical jokes. Dr Withers punctuated this recital with occasional sounds of incredulity or irritation. When Alleyn reached the incident of the flying cow he interrupted him.

'The child Panty,' he said, 'is capable of every iniquity, but, as I have pointed out, she could not have perpetrated this offence with the blown-up bladder, nor could she have painted the flying cow on Mrs –' He stopped short. 'Is this lady – ?' he began.

'My wife, as it happens,' said Alleyn, 'but let it pass.'

'Good Lord! Unusual that, isn't it?'

'Both unusual and bothering in this context. You were saying?'

'That the child was too seedy that night for it to be conceivable. And you tell me Miss Able (sensible girl that) vouches for her anyway.'

'Yes.'

'All right. Well, some other fool, the egregious Cedric in all likelihood, performed these idiocies. I fail to see how they can possibly be linked up with Sir Henry's death.'

'You have not,' Alleyn said, 'heard of the incident of the book on embalming in the cheese-dish.'

Dr Withers's mouth opened slightly, but he made no comment, and Alleyn continued his narrative. 'You see,' he added, 'this final

trick does bear a sort of family likeness to the others, and, considering the subject matter of the book, and the fact that Sir Henry was
embalmed – '

'Quite so. Because the damned book talks about arsenic they
jump to this imbecile conclusion – '

'Fortified, we must remember, by the discovery of a tin of arsenical rat poison in Miss Orrincourt's luggage.'

'Planted there by the practical joker,' cried Dr Withers. 'I bet you.
Planted!'.

'That's a possibility,' Alleyn agreed, 'that we can't overlook.'

Fox suddenly said: 'Quite so.'

'Well,' said Dr Withers, 'I'm damned if I know what to say. No
medical man enjoys the suggestion that he's been careless or made a
mistake, and this would be a very awkward mistake. Mind, I don't
for a split second believe there's a fragment of truth in the tale, but
if the whole boiling of Ancreds are going to talk arsenic – Here! Have
you seen the embalmers?'

'Not yet. We shall do so, of course.'

'I don't know anything about embalming,' Dr Withers muttered.
'This fossil book may not amount to a row of beans.'

'Taylor,' said Alleyn, 'has a note on it. He says that in such manipulations of a body, antiseptic substances are used (commonly
arsenic), and might prevent detection of poison as the cause of death.'

'So, if we have an exhumation, where are we? Precisely
nowhere.'

'I'm not sure of my ground,' said Alleyn, 'but I fancy that an
exhumation should definitely show whether or not Sir Henry
Ancred was poisoned. I'll explain.'

III

Fox and Alleyn lunched at the Ancreton Arms, on jugged hare, well
cooked, and a tankard each of the local draught beer. It was a pleasant enough little pub, and the landlady, on Alleyn's inquiry, said she
could, if requested, put them up for the night.

'I'm not at all sure we shan't be taking her at her word,' said
Alleyn as they walked out into the village street. It was thinly bright

with winter sunshine, and contained, beside the pub and Dr Withers's house, a post office shop, a chapel, a draper's, a stationer's, a meeting-hall, a chemist-cum-fancy-goods shop, and a row of cottages. Over the brow of intervening hills, the gothic windows, multiple towers and indefatigably varied chimney-pots of Ancreton Manor glinted against their background of conifers, and brooded, with an air of grand seigneury, faintly bogus, over the little village.

'And here,' said Alleyn, pausing at the chemist's window, 'is Mr Juniper's pharmacy. That's a pleasant name, Fox. E.M. Juniper. This is where Troy and Miss Orrincourt came in their governess-cart on a nasty evening. Let's call on Mr Juniper, shall we?'

But he seemed to be in no hurry to go in, and began to mutter to himself before the side window. 'A tidy window, Fox. I like the old-fashioned coloured bottles, don't you? Writing paper, you see, and combs and ink (that brand went off the market in the war) cheek-by-jowel with cough-lozenges and trusses in their modest boxes. Even some children's card games. Happy Families. That's how Troy drew the Ancreds. Let's give them a pack. Mr Juniper the chemist's window. Come on.'

He led the way in. The shop was divided into two sections. One counter was devoted to fancy goods, and one, severe and isolated, to Mr Juniper's professional activities. Alleyn rang a little bell, a door opened, and Mr Juniper, fresh and rosy in his white coat, came out, together with the cleanly smell of drugs.

'*Yes*, sir?' Mr Juniper inquired, placing himself behind his professional counter.

'Good morning,' said Alleyn. 'I wonder if by any chance you've got anything to amuse a small girl who's on the sick list?'

Mr Juniper removed to the fancy-goods department. 'Happy Families? Bubble-blowing?' he suggested.

'Actually,' Alleyn lied pleasantly. 'I've been told I must bring back some form of practical joke. Designed, I'm afraid, for Dr Withers.'

'Really? T't. Ha-ha!' said Mr Juniper. 'Well, now. I'm afraid we haven't anything much in that line. There were some dummy ink-spots, but I'm afraid – No. I know exactly the type of thing you mean, mind, but I'm just afraid – '

'Somebody said something about a thing you blow up and sit on,' Alleyn murmured vaguely. 'It sounded disgusting.'

'Ah! The Raspberry?'

'That's it.'

Mr Juniper shook his head sadly and made a gesture of resignation.

'I thought,' said Alleyn, 'I saw a box in your window that looked – '

'Empty!' Mr Juniper sighed. 'The customer didn't require the box, so I'm afraid I've just left it there. Now isn't that a pity,' Mr Juniper lamented. 'Only last week, or would it be a fortnight ago, I sold the last of that little line to a customer for exactly the same purpose. A sick little girl. Yes. One would almost think,' he hazarded, 'that the same little lady – '

'I expect so. Patricia Kentish,' said Alleyn.

'Ah, quite so. So the customer said! Up at the Manor. Quite a little tinker,' said Mr Juniper. 'Well, sir, I think you'll find that Miss Pant – Miss Pat – has already got a Raspberry.'

'In that case,' said Alleyn, 'I'll take a Happy Families. You want some toothpaste, don't you, Fox?'

'Happy Families,' said Mr Juniper, snatching a packet from the shelf. 'Dentifrice? Any particular make, sir?'

'For a plate,' said Fox stolidly.

'For the denture. Quite,' said Mr Juniper, and darted into the professional side of his shop.

'I wouldn't mind betting,' said Alleyn cheerfully to Fox, 'that it was Sonia Orrincourt who got in first with that thing.'

'Ah,' said Fox. Mr Juniper smiled archly. 'Well, now,' he said, 'I oughtn't to give the young lady away, ought I? Professional secrets. Ha-ha!'

'Ha-ha!' Alleyn agreed, putting Happy Families in his pocket. 'Thank you, Mr Juniper.'

'Thank *you*, sir. All well up at the Manor, I hope? Great loss, that. Loss to the Nation, you might say. Little trouble with the children clearing up, I hope?'

'On its way. Lovely afternoon, isn't it? Goodbye.'

'I didn't want any toothpaste,' said Fox, as they continued up the street.

'I didn't see why I should make all the purchases and you were looking rather too portentous. Put it down to expenses. It was worth it.'

'I don't say it wasn't that,' Fox agreed. 'Now, sir, if this woman Orrincourt took the Raspberry, I suppose we look to her for all the other pranks, don't we?'

'I hardly think so, Fox. Not all. We know, at least, that this ghastly kid tied a notice to the tail of her Aunt Millamant's coat. She's got a reputation for practical jokes. On the other hand, she definitely, it seems, did not perpetrate the Raspberry and the flying cow, and my wife is convinced she's innocent of the spectacles, the painted stair rail and the rude writing on Sir Henry's looking-glass. As for the book in the cheese-dish, I don't think either Panty or Miss Orrincourt is guilty of that flight of fancy.'

'So that if you count out the little girl for anything that matters, we've got Miss Orrincourt and another.'

'That's the cry.'

'And this other is trying to fix something on Miss Orrincourt in the way of arsenic and the old gentleman?'

'It's a reasonable thesis, but Lord knows.'

'Where are we going, Mr Alleyn?'

'Are you good for a two-mile walk? I think we'll call on the Ancreds.'

IV

'It isn't,' said Alleyn as they toiled up the second flight of terraces, 'as if we can hope to keep ourselves dark, supposing that were advisable. Thomas will have rung up his family and told them that we have at least taken notice. We may as well announce ourselves and see what we can see. More especially, this wretched old fellow's bedroom.'

'By this time,' said Fox sourly, 'they'll probably have had it repapered.'

'I wonder if Paul Kentish is handy with electrical gadgets. I'll wager Cedric Ancred isn't.'

'What's that?' Fox demanded.

'What's what?'

'I can hear something. A child crying, isn't it, sir?'

They had reached the second terrace. At each end of this terrace, between the potato-field and the woods, were shrubberies and young copses. From the bushes on their left hand came a thin inter-mittent wailing; very dolorous. They paused uncertainly, staring at each other. The wailing stopped, and into the silence welled the accustomed sounds of the countryside – the wintry chittering of birds and the faint click of naked branches.

'Would it be some kind of bird, should you say?' Fox speculated.

'No bird!' Alleyn began and stopped short. 'There it is again.'

It was a thin piping sound, waving and irregular and the effect of it was peculiarly distressing. Without further speculation they set off across the rough and still frost-encrusted ground. As they drew nearer to it the sound became, not articulate, but more complex, and present-ly, when they had drawn quite close, developed a new character.

'It's mixed up,' Fox whispered, 'with a kind of singing.'

> *'Goodbye poor pussy your coat was so warm,*
> *And even if you did moult you did me no harm.*
> *Goodbye poor pussy for ever and ever*
> *And make me a good girl, amen.*

'For ever and ever,' the thin voice repeated, and drifted off again into its former desolate wail. As they brushed against the first low bush-es it ceased, and there followed a wary silence disrupted by harsh sobbing.

Between the bushes and the copse they came upon a little girl in a white cap, sitting by a newly-turned mound of earth. A child's spade was beside her. Stuck irregularly in the mound of earth were a few heads of geraniums. A piece of paper threaded on a twig stood crookedly at the head of the mound. The little girl's hands were earthy, and she had knuckled her eyes so that black streaks ran down her face. She crouched there scowling at them, rather like an animal that flattens itself near the ground, unable to obey its own instinct for flight.

'Hallo,' said Alleyn, 'this is a bad job!' And unable to think of a more satisfactory opening, he heard himself repeating Dr Withers's phrase. 'What's the trouble?' he asked.

The little girl was convulsed, briefly, by a sob. Alleyn squatted beside her and examined the writing on the paper. It had been exe-cuted in large shaky capitals.

'KARABAS,
R.S.V.P.
LOVE FROM PANTY.'

'Was Carabbas,' Alleyn ventured, 'your own cat?'

Panty glared at him and slowly shook her head.

Alleyn said quickly: 'How stupid of me; he was your grandfather's cat, wasn't he?'

'He loved me,' said Panty on a high note. 'Better than he loved Noddy. He loved me better than he loved anybody. I was his friend.' Her voice rose piercingly like the whistle of a small engine. 'And I didn't,' she screamed, 'I didn't, I didn't, I didn't give him the ring-worms. I hate my Auntie Milly. I wish she was dead. I wish they were all dead. I'll kill my Auntie Milly.' She beat on the ground with her fists, and, catching sight of Fox, screamed at him: 'Get out of here, will you? This is my place.'

Fox stepped back hastily.

'I've heard,' said Alleyn, cautiously, 'about Carabbas and about you. You paint pictures, don't you? Have you painted any more pictures lately?'

'I don't want to paint any more pictures,' said Panty.

'That's a pity, because we rather thought of sending you a box of paints for yourself from London.'

Panty sobbed dryly. 'Who did?' she said.

'Troy Alleyn,' said Alleyn. 'Mrs Alleyn, you know. She's my wife.'

'If I painted a picture of my Auntie Milly,' said Panty, 'I'd give her pig's whiskers, and she'd look like Judas Iscariot. They said my cat Carabbas had the ringworms, and they said I'd given them to him, and they're all, *all* liars. He hadn't, and I didn't. It was only his poor fur coming out.'

With the abandon which Troy had witnessed in the little theatre, Panty flung herself face forward on the ground and kicked. Tentatively Alleyn bent over her, and after a moment's hesitation picked her up. For a moment or two she fought violently, but suddenly, with an air of desolation, let her arms fall and hung limply in his hands.

'Never mind, Panty,' Alleyn muttered helplessly. 'Here, let's mop up your face.' He felt in his pocket and his fingers closed round a hard object. 'Look here,' he said. 'Look what I've got,' and pulled out a small packet. 'Do you ever play Happy Families?' he said. He pushed the box of cards into her hands and not very successfully mopped her face with his handkerchief. 'Let's move on,' he said to Fox.

He carried the now inert Panty across to the third flight of steps. Here she began to wriggle, and he put her down.

'I want to play Happy Families,' said Panty thickly. 'Here,' she added. She squatted down, and, still interrupting herself from time to time with a hiccuping sob, opened her pack of picture cards, and with filthy fingers began to deal them into three heaps.

'Sit down, Fox,' said Alleyn. 'You're going to play Happy Families.'

Fox sat uneasily on the second step.

Panty was a slow dealer, principally because she examined the face of each card before she put it down.

'Do you know the rules?' Alleyn asked Fox.

'I can't say I do,' he replied, putting on his spectacles. 'Would it be anything like euchre?'

'Not much, but you'll pick it up. The object is to collect a family. Would you be good enough,' he said, turning to Panty, 'to oblige me with Mrs Snips the Tailor's Wife?'

'You didn't say "Please," so it's my turn,' said Panty. 'Give me Mr Snips, the Tailor, and Master Snips and Miss Snips, please.'

'Damn,' said Alleyn. 'Here you are,' and handed over the cards, each with its cut of an antic who might have walked out of a Victorian volume of *Punch*.

Panty pushed these cards underneath her and sat on them. Her bloomers, true to her legend, were conspicuous. 'Now,' she said, turning a bleary glance on Fox, 'you give me – '

'Don't I get a turn?' asked Fox.

'Not unless she goes wrong,' said Alleyn. 'You'll learn.'

'Give me,' said Panty, 'Master Grit, the Grocer's Son.'

'Doesn't she have to say "please"?'

'Please,' yelled Panty. 'I said "please". Please.'

Fox handed over the card.

'And Mrs Grit,' Panty went on.

'It beats me,' said Fox, 'how she knows.'

'She knows,' said Alleyn, 'because she looked.'

Panty laughed raucously. 'And you give me Mr Bull, the Butcher,' she demanded, turning on Alleyn. 'Please.'

'Not at home,' said Alleyn triumphantly. 'And now, you see, Fox, it's my turn.'

'The game seems crook to me,' said Fox, gloomily.

'Master Bun,' Panty remarked presently, 'is azzakerly like my Uncle Thomas.' Alleyn, in imagination, changed the grotesque faces on all the cards to those of the Ancreds as Troy had drawn them in her notebook. 'So he is,' he said. 'And now I know you've got him. Please give me Master Ancred, the Actor's Son.' This sally afforded Panty exquisite amusement. With primitive guffaws she began to demand cards under the names of her immediate relations and to the utter confusion of the game.

'There now,' said Alleyn at last, in a voice that struck him as being odiously complacent. 'That was a lovely game. Suppose you take us up to see the – ah – '

'The Happy Family,' Fox prompted in a wooden voice.

'Certainly,' said Alleyn.

'Why?' Panty demanded.

'That's what we've come for.'

Panty stood squarely facing him. Upon her stained face there grew, almost furtively, a strange expression. It was compounded, he thought, of the look of a normal child about to impart a secret and of something less familiar, more disquieting.

'Here!' she said. 'I want to tell you something. Not him. You.'

She drew Alleyn away, and with a sidelong glance pulled him down until she could hook her arm about his neck. He waited, feeling her breath uncomfortably in his ear.

'What is it?'

The whispering was disembodied but unexpectedly clear.

'We've got,' it said, 'a murderer in our family.'

When he drew back and looked at her she was smiling nervously.

CHAPTER 12

The Bell and the Book

So accurate and lively were Troy's drawings that Alleyn recognized Desdemona Ancred as soon as she appeared on the top step of the third terrace and looked down upon the group, doubtless a curious one, made by himself, Panty and Fox. Indeed, as she paused, she struck precisely the attitude, histrionic and grandiose, with which Troy had invested her caricature.

'Ah!' said Dessy richly. 'Panty! At last!'

She held out her hand towards Panty and at the same time looked frankly at Alleyn. 'How do you do?' she said. 'Are you on your way up? Has this terrible young person waylaid you? Shall I introduce myself?'

'Miss Ancred?' Alleyn said.

'He's Mrs Alleyn's husband,' Panty said. 'We don't much want you, thank you, Aunt Dessy.'

Dessy was in the act of advancing with poise down the steps. Her smile remained fixed on her face. Perhaps she halted for a fraction of time in her stride. The next second her hand was in his, and she was gazing with embarrassing intensity into his eyes.

'I'm so glad you've come,' she said in her deepest voice. 'So glad! We are terribly, terribly distressed. My brother has told you, I know.' She pressed his hand, released it, and looked at Fox.

'Inspector Fox,' said Alleyn. Desdemona was tragically gracious.

They turned to climb the steps. Panty gave a threatening wail.

'You,' said her aunt, 'had better run home as fast as you can. Miss Abie's been looking everywhere for you. What *have* you been doing, Panty? You're covered in earth.'

Immediately they were confronted with another scene. Panty repeated her former performance, roaring out strange threats against her family, lamenting the cat Carabbas, and protesting that she had not infected him.

'Really, it's *too* ridiculous,' Dessy said in a loud aside to Alleyn. 'Not that we didn't all feel it. Poor Carabbas! And my father so attached always. But honestly, it was a menace to all our healths. Ringworm, beyond a shadow of doubt. Fur coming out in handfuls. Obviously it had given them the disease in the first instance. We did perfectly right to have it destroyed. Come *on*, Panty.'

By this time they had reached the top terrace, with Panty waddling lamentably behind them. Here they were met by Miss Caroline Able, who brightly ejaculated: 'Goodness, what a noise!' cast a clear sensible glance at Alleyn and Fox, and removed her still bellowing charge.

'I'm so distressed,' Desdemona cried, 'that you should have had this reception. Honestly, poor Panty is simply beyond everything. Nobody loves children more than I do, but she's got such a *difficult* nature. And in a house of tragedy, when one's nerves and emotions are lacerated – '

She gazed into his eyes, made a small helpless gesture, and finally ushered them into the hall. Alleyn glanced quickly at the space under the gallery, but it was still untenanted.

'I'll tell my sister and my sister-in-law,' Dessy began, but Alleyn interrupted her. 'If we might just have a word with you first,' he said. And by Dessy's manner, at once portentous and dignified, he knew that this suggestion was not unpleasing to her. She led them to the small sitting-room where Troy had found Sonia Orrincourt and Cedric giggling together on the sofa. Desdemona placed herself on this sofa. She sat down, Alleyn noticed, quite beautifully; not glancing at her objective, but sinking on it in one movement and then elegantly disposing her arms.

'I expect,' he began, 'that your brother has explained the official attitude to this kind of situation. We're obliged to make all sorts of inquiries before we can take any further action.'

'I see,' said Desdemona, nodding owlishly. 'Yes, I see. Go on.'

'To put it baldly, do you yourself think there is any truth in the suggestion made by the anonymous letter-writer?'

Desdemona pressed the palms of her hands carefully against her eyes. 'If I *could* dismiss it,' she cried. 'If I could!'

'You have no idea, I suppose, who could have written the letters?' She shook her head. Alleyn wondered if she had glanced at him through her fingers.

'Have any of you been up to London since your father's funeral?'

'How frightful!' she said, dropping her hands and gazing at him. 'I was afraid of this. How frightful!'

'What?'

'You think one of us wrote the letter? Someone at Ancreton?'

'Well, really,' said Alleyn, stifling his exasperation, 'it's not a preposterous conjecture, is it?'

'No, no. I suppose not. But what a disturbing thought.'

'Well, did any of you go to London – '

'Let me think, let me think,' Desdemona muttered, again covering her eyes. 'In the evening. After we had – had – after Papa's funeral, and after Mr Rattisbon had – ' She made another little helpless gesture.

' – had read the Will?' Alleyn suggested.

'Yes. That evening, by the seven-thirty. Thomas and Jenetta (my sister-in-law) and Fenella (her daughter) and Paul (my nephew, Paul Kentish) all went up to London.'

'And returned? When?'

'Not at all. Jenetta doesn't live here and Fenella and Paul, because of – However, Fenella has joined her mother in a flat and I think Paul's staying with them. My brother Thomas, as you know, lives in London.'

'And nobody else has left Ancreton?'

Yes, it seemed that the following day Millamant and Cedric and Desdemona herself had gone up to London by the early morning train. There was a certain amount of business to be done. They returned in the evening. It was by that evening's post, the Wednesday's, Alleyn reflected, that the anonymous letter reached the Yard. He found by dint of cautious questioning that they had all separated in London and gone their several ways to meet in the evening train.

'And Miss Orrincourt?' Alleyn asked.

'I'm afraid,' said Desdemona grandly, 'that I've really no knowledge at all of Miss Orrincourt's movements. She was away all day yesterday; I imagine in London.'

'She's staying on here?'

'You may well look astonished,' said Desdemona, though Alleyn, to his belief, had looked nothing of the sort. 'After everything, Mr Alleyn. After working against us with Papa! After humiliating and wounding us in every possible way. In the teeth, you might say, of the Family's feelings, she stays on. T'uh!'

'Does Sir Cedric – ?'

'Cedric,' said Desdemona, 'is now the head of the Family, but I have no hesitation in saying that I think his attitude to a good many things inexplicable and revolting. Particularly where Sonia Orrincourt (you'll never get me to believe she was born Orrincourt) is concerned. What he's up to, what both of them – However!'

Alleyn did not press for an exposition of Cedric's behaviour. At the moment he was fascinated by Desdemona's. On the wall opposite her hung a looking-glass in a Georgian frame. He saw that Desdemona was keeping an eye on herself. Even as she moved her palms from before her eyes, her fingers touched her hair and she slightly turned her head while her abstracted yet watchful gaze noted, he thought, the effect. And as often as she directed her melting glance upon him, so often did it return to the mirror to affirm with a satisfaction barely veiled its own limpid quality. He felt as if he interviewed a mannequin.

'I understand,' he said, 'that it was you who found the tin of rat-bane in Miss Orrincourt's suitcase?'

'Wasn't it awful? Well, it was three of us, actually. My sister Pauline (Mrs Kentish), my sister-in-law, and Cedric and I. In her box-room, you know. A very common-looking suitcase smothered in Number Three Company touring labels. As I've pointed out to Thomas a thousand times, the woman is simply a squalid little ham actress. Well, *not* an actress. All eyes and teeth in the third row of the chorus when she's lucky.'

'Did you yourself handle it?'

'Oh, we all handled it. Naturally. Cedric tried to prise up the lid, but it wouldn't come. So he tapped the tin, and said he could tell from the sound that it wasn't full.' She lowered her voice. ' "Only half-full," he said. And Milly (my sister-in-law, Mrs Henry Ancred) said – ' She paused.

'Yes?' Alleyn prompted, tired of these genealogical parentheses. 'Mrs Henry Ancred said?'

'She said that to the best of her knowledge it had never been used.' She changed her position a little and added: 'I don't understand Milly. She's so off-hand. Of course I know she's frightfully capable but – well, she's not an Ancred and doesn't feel as we do. She's – well, let's face it, she's a bit MC, do you know?'

Alleyn did not respond to this appeal from blue blood to blue blood. He said: 'Was the suitcase locked?'

'We wouldn't have broken anything open, Mr Alleyn.'

'Wouldn't you?' he said vaguely. Desdemona glanced in the mirror. 'Well – Pauline might,' she admitted after a pause.

Alleyn waited for a moment, caught Fox's eye and stood up. He said: 'Now, Miss Ancred, I wonder if we may see your father's room?'

'Papa's *room?*'

'If we may.'

'I couldn't – you won't mind if I – ? I'll ask Barker – '

'If he'd just show us in the general direction we could find our own way.'

Desdemona stretched out her hands impulsively. 'You *do* understand,' she said. 'You do understand how one feels. Thank you.'

Alleyn smiled vaguely, dodged the outstretched hands and made for the door. 'Perhaps Barker,' he suggested, 'could show us the room.'

Desdemona swept to the bell-push and in a moment or two Barker came in. With enormous aplomb she explained what he was to do. She contrived to turn Barker into the very quintessence of family retainers. The atmosphere in the little sitting-room grew more and more feudal. 'These gentlemen,' she ended, 'have come to help us, Barker. We, in our turn, must help them, mustn't we? You will help them, won't you?'

'Certainly, miss,' said Barker. 'If you would come this way, sir?'

How well Troy had described the great stairs and the gallery and the yards and yards of dead canvas in heavy frames. And the smell. The Victorian smell of varnish, carpet, wax, and mysteriously, paste. A yellow smell, she had said. Here was the first long corridor, and there, branching from it, the passage to Troy's tower. This was where she had lost herself that first night and these were the rooms with their ridiculous names. On his right, *Bancroft* and *Bernhardt;* on his left, *Terry* and *Bracegirdle;* then an open linen closet and bathrooms. Barker's coattails jigged steadily ahead of them. His head was stooped, and one saw only a thin fringe of grey hair and a little dandruff on his back collar. Here was the cross-corridor, corresponding with the picture gallery, and facing them a closed door, with the legend, in gothic lettering, *'Irving.'*

'This is the room, sir,' said Barker's faded and breathless voice.

'We'll go in, if you please.'

The door opened on darkness and the smell of disinfectant. A momentary fumbling, and then a bedside lamp threw a pool of light upon a table and a crimson counterpane. With a clatter of rings Barker pulled aside the window curtains and then let up the blinds.

The aspect of the room that struck Alleyn most forcibly was the extraordinary number of prints and photographs upon the walls. They were so lavishly distributed that almost all the paper, a red flock powdered with stars, was concealed by them. Next he noticed the heavy richness of the appointments; the enormous looking-glass, the brocades and velvets, the massive and forbidding furniture.

Suspended above the bed was a long cord. He saw that it ended, not in a bell-push, but in raw strands of wire.

'Will that be all, sir?' said Barker, behind them.

'Stop for a minute, will you?' Alleyn said. 'I want you to help us, Barker.'

II

He was indeed very old. His eyes were filmy and expressed nothing but a remote sadness. His hands seemed to have shrunk away from their own empurpled veins, and were tremulous. But all these witnesses of age were in part disguised by a lifetime's habit of attentiveness to other people's wants. There was the shadow of alacrity still about Barker.

'I don't think,' Alleyn said, 'that Miss Ancred quite explained why we are here. It's at Mr Thomas Ancred's suggestion. He wants us to make fuller inquiries into the cause of Sir Henry's death.'

'Indeed, sir?'

'Some of his family believe that the diagnosis was too hastily given.'

'Quite so, sir.'

'Had you any such misgivings yourself?'

Barker closed and unclosed his hands. 'I can't say I had, sir. Not at first.'

'Not at first?'

'Knowing what he took to eat and drink at dinner, sir, and the way he was worked up, and had been over and over again. Dr Withers had warned him of it, sir.'

'But later? After the funeral? And now?'

'I really can't say, sir. What with Mrs Kentish and Mrs Henry and Miss Desdemona asking me over and over again about a certain missing article and what with us all being very put about in the servants' hall, I can't really say.'

'A tin of rat-bane was the missing article?'

'Yes, sir. I understand they've found it now.'

'And the question they want settled is whether it was an opened or unopened tin before it was lost. Is that it?'

'I understand that's it, sir. But we've had that stuff on the premises these last ten years and more. Two tins there were, sir, in one of the outside store-rooms and there was one opened and used up and thrown out. That I do know. About this one that's turned up, I can't say. Mrs Henry Ancred recollects, sir, that it was there about a year ago, unopened, and Mrs Bullivant, the cook, says it's been partly used since then, and Mrs Henry doesn't fancy so, and that's all I can say, sir.'

'Do you know if rat poison has ever been used in Miss Orrincourt's room?'

Barker's manner became glazed with displeasure.

'Never to my knowledge, sir,' he said.

'Are there no rats there?'

'The lady in question complained of them, I understand, to one of the housemaids, who set traps and caught several. I believe the lady said she didn't fancy the idea of poison, and for that reason it was not employed.'

'I see. Now, Barker, if you will, I should like you to tell me exactly what this room looked like when you entered it on the morning after Sir Henry's death.'

Barker's sunken hand moved to his lips and covered their trembling. A film of tears spread over his eyes.

'I know it's distressing for you,' Alleyn said, 'and I'm sorry. Sit down. No, please sit down.'

Barker stooped his head a little and sat on the only high chair in the room.

'I'm sure,' Alleyn said, 'that if there was anything gravely amiss you'd want to see it remedied.'

Barker seemed to struggle between his professional reticence and his personal distress. Finally, in a sudden flood of garrulity, he produced the classical reaction: 'I wouldn't want to see this house mixed up in anything scandalous, sir. My father was butler here to the former baronet, Sir Henry's second cousin – Sir William Ancred, that was – I was knife-boy and then footman under him. He was not,' said Barker, 'anything to do with theatricals, sir, the old gentleman wasn't. This would have been a great blow to him.'

'You mean the manner of Sir Henry's death?'

'I mean' – Barker tightened his unsteady lips – 'I mean the way things were conducted lately.'

'Miss Orrincourt?'

'T'uh!' said Barker, and thus established his life-long service to the Ancreds.

'Look here,' Alleyn said suddenly, 'do you know what the family have got into their heads about this business?'

There was a long pause before the old voice whispered: 'I don't like to think. I don't encourage gossip below stairs, sir, and I don't take part in it myself.'

'Well,' Alleyn suggested, 'suppose you tell me about this room.'

It was, after all, only a slow enlargement of what he had already heard. The darkened room, the figure hunched on the bed, 'as if,' Barker said fearfully, 'he'd been trying to crawl down to the floor,' the stench and disorder and the broken bell-cord.

'Where was the end?' Alleyn asked. 'The bell-push itself?'

'In his hand, sir. Tight clenched round it, his hand was. We didn't discover it at first.'

'Have you still got it?'

'It's in his dressing-table drawer, sir. I put it there, meaning to get it mended.'

'Did you unscrew it or examine it in any way?'

'Oh, no, sir. No. I just put it away and disconnected the circuit on the board.'

'Right! And now, Barker, about the night before, when Sir Henry went to bed. Did you see anything of him?'

'Oh, yes, indeed, sir. He rang for me as usual. It was midnight when the bell went, and I came up to his room. I'd valeted him, sir, since his own man left.'

'Did he ring his room bell?'

'No, sir. He always rang the bell in the hall as he went through. By the time he reached his room, you see, I had gone up the servants' stairs and was waiting for him.'

'How did he seem?'

'Terrible. In one of his tantrums and talking very wild and angry.'

'Against his family?'

'Very hot against them.'

'Go on.'

'I got him into his pyjamas and gown and him raging all the while and troubled with his indigestion pain as well. I put out the medicine he took for it. He said he wouldn't take it just then so I left the bottle and glass by his bed. I was offering to help him into bed when he says he must see Mr Rattisbon. He's the family solicitor, sir, and always comes to us for The Birthday. Well, sir, I tried to put Sir Henry off, seeing he was tired and upset, but he wouldn't hear of it. When I took him by the arm he got quite violent. I was alarmed and tried to hold him but he broke away.'

Alleyn had a sudden vision of the two old men struggling together in this grandiose bedroom.

'Seeing there was nothing for it,' Barker went on, 'I did as he ordered, and took Mr Rattisbon up to his room. He called me back and told me to find the two extra helps we always get in for The Birthday. A Mr and Mrs Candy, sir, formerly on the staff here and now in a small business in the village. I understood from what Sir Henry said that he wished them to witness his Will. I showed them up, and he then told me to inform Miss Orrincourt that he would be ready for his hot drink in half an hour. He said he would not require me again. So I left him.'

'And went to give this message?'

'After I had switched over the mechanism of his bell, sir, so that if he required anything in the night it would sound in the passage outside Mrs Henry's door. It has been specially arranged like this, in case of an emergency, and, of course, sir, it must have broke off in his hand before it sounded, because even if Mrs Henry had slept through it, Miss Dessy was sharing her room and must have heard. Miss Dessy sleeps very light, I understand.'

'Isn't it strange that he didn't call out?'

'He wouldn't be heard, sir. The walls in this part of the house are very thick, being part of the original outer walls. The previous baronet, sir, added this wing to Ancreton.'

'I see. At this time where was Miss Orrincourt?'

'She had left the company, sir. They had all moved into the drawing-room.'

'*All* of them?'

'Yes, sir. Except her and Mr Rattisbon. And Mrs Alleyn, who was a guest. They were all there. Mrs Kentish said the young lady had gone to her room and that's where I found her. Mr Rattisbon was in the hall.'

'What was the business with the hot drink?'

The old man described it carefully. Until the rise of Sonia Orrincourt, Millamant had always prepared the drink. Miss Orrincourt had taken over this routine. The milk and ingredients were left in her room by the housemaid, who turned down her bed. She brewed the drink over a heater, put it in a Thermos flask, and, half an hour after he had retired, took it to his room. He slept badly and sometimes would not drink it until much later in the night.

'What happened to the Thermos flask and the cup and saucer?'

'They were taken away and washed up, sir. They've been in use since.'

'Had he drunk any of it?'

'It had been poured into the cup, sir, at all events, and into the saucer for that cat, as was always done, and the saucer set on the floor. But the cup and the flask and the medicine bottle had been overturned and there was milk and medicine soaked into the carpet.'

'Had he taken his medicine?'

'The glass was dirty. It had fallen into the saucer.'

'And has, of course, been washed,' said Alleyn. 'What about the bottle?'

'It had been knocked over, sir, as I mentioned. It was a new bottle. I was very much put out, sir, but I tried to tidy the room a bit, not knowing exactly what I was doing. I remember I took the dirty china and the bottle and Thermos downstairs with me. The bottle was thrown out, and the other things cleared up. The medicine cupboard has been cleaned out thoroughly. It's in the bathroom, sir, through that door. The whole suite,' said Barker conscientiously, 'has been turned out and cleaned.'

Fox mumbled inarticulately.

'Well,' said Alleyn. 'To go back to the message you took to Miss Orrincourt that night. Did you actually see her?'

'No, sir. I tapped on the door and she answered.' He moved uneasily.

'Was there anything else?'

'It was a queer thing – ' His voice faded.

'What was a queer thing?'

'She must have been alone,' Barker mused, 'because, as I've said, sir, the others were downstairs, and afterwards, *just* afterwards, when I took in the grog-tray, there they all were. But before I knocked on her door, sir, I could have sworn that she was laughing.'

III

When Barker had gone, Fox sighed gustily, put on his spectacles and looked quizzically through them at the naked end of the bell-cord.

'Yes, Br'er Fox, exactly,' said Alleyn, and went to the dressing-table. 'That'll be the lady,' he said.

A huge photograph of Sonia Orrincourt stood in the middle of the dressing-table.

Fox joined Alleyn. 'Very taking,' he said. 'Funny, you know, Mr Alleyn. That's what they call a pin-up girl. Plenty of teeth and hair and limbs. Sir Henry put it in a silver frame, but that, you might say, is the only difference. Very taking.'

Alleyn opened the top drawer on the left.

'First pop,' Fox remarked.

Alleyn pulled on a glove and gingerly took out a pear-shaped wooden bell-push. 'One takes these pathetic precautions,' he said, 'and a hell of a lot of use they are. Now then.' He unscrewed the end of the bell-push and looked into it.

'See here, Fox. Look at the two points. Nothing broken. One of the holding-screws and its washer are tight. No bits of wire. The other screw and washer are loose. Got your lens? Have a look at that cord again.'

Fox took out a pocket lens and returned to the bed. 'One of the wires is unbroken,' he said presently. 'No shiny end, and it's blackened like they do get with time. The other's different, though. Been dragged through and scraped, I'd say. That's what must have happened. He put his weight on it and they pulled through.'

'In that case,' Alleyn said, 'why is one of the screws so tight, and only one wire shiny? We'll keep this bell-push, Fox.'

He had wrapped his handkerchief round it and dropped it in his pocket, when the door was opened and Sonia Orrincourt walked in.

IV

She was dressed in black, but so dashingly that mourning was not much suggested. Her curtain of ashen hair and her heavy fringe were glossy, her eyelids were blue, her lashes incredible and her skin sleek. She wore a diamond clasp and bracelet and ear-rings. She stood just inside the room.

'Pardon the intrusion,' she said, 'but am I addressing the police?'

'You are,' said Alleyn. 'Miss Orrincourt?'

'That's the name.'

'How do you do? This is Inspector Fox.'

'Now listen!' said Miss Orrincourt, advancing upon them with a professional gait. 'I want to know what's cooking in this icehouse. I've got my rights to look after, same as anybody else, haven't I?'

'Undoubtedly.'

'Thank you. Very kind I'm sure. Then perhaps you'll tell me who asked you into my late fiance's room and just what you're doing now you've got there.'

'We were asked by his family and we're doing a job of work.'

'*Work?* What sort of work? Don't tell me the answer to that one,' said Miss Orrincourt angrily. 'I seem to know it. They're trying to swing something across me. Is that right? Trying to pack me up. *What is it?* That's what I want to know. Come on. *What is it?*'

'Will you first of all tell me how you knew we were here and why you thought we were police officers?'

She sat on the bed, leaning back on her hands, her hair falling vertically from her scalp. Behind her was spread the crimson counterpane. Alleyn wondered why she had ever attempted to be an actress while there were magazine artists who needed models. She looked in a leisurely manner at Fox's feet. 'How do I know you're police? That's a scream! Take a look at your boy friend's boots.'

'Yours, partner,' Alleyn murmured, catching Fox's eye.

Fox cleared his throat. 'Er – *touché,*' he said carefully. 'Not much good me trying to get by with a sharp-eyed young lady, is it, sir?'

'Well, come on,' Miss Orrincourt demanded. 'What's the big idea? Are they trying to make out there's something funny in the Will? Or what? What are you doing, opening my late fiance's drawers? Come on!'

'I'm afraid,' said Alleyn, 'you've got this situation the wrong way round. We're on a job, and part of that job is asking questions. And since you're here, Miss Orrincourt, I wonder if you'd mind answering one or two?'

She looked at him, he thought, as an animal or a completely unselfconscious child might look at a stranger. It was difficult to expect anything but perfect sounds from her. He experienced a shock each time he heard the Cockney voice with its bronchial overtones, and the phrases whose very idiom seemed shoddy, as if she had abandoned her native dialect for something she had half-digested at the cinema.

'All upstage and county!' she said. 'Fancy! And what were you wanting to know?'

'About the Will, for instance.'

'The Will's all right,' she said quickly. 'You can turn the place inside out. Crawl up the chimney if you like. You won't find another Will. I'm telling you, and I know.'

'Why are you so positive?'

She had slipped back until she rested easily on her forearm. 'I don't mind,' she said. 'I'll tell you. When I came in here last thing that night, my fiancé showed it to me. He'd had old Rattisbon up and a couple of witnesses and he'd signed it. He showed me. The ink was still wet. He'd burnt the old one in the fireplace there.'

'I see.'

'And he couldn't have written another one even if he'd wanted to. Because he was tired and his pain was bad and he said he was going to take his medicine and go to sleep.'

'He was in bed when you visited him?'

'Yes.' She waited for a moment, looking at her enamelled finger-nails. 'People seem to think I've got no feelings, but I've been very upset. Honestly. Well, he was sweet. And when a girl's going to be married and everything's marvellous it's a terrible thing for this to happen, I don't care what any one says.'

'Did he seem very ill?'

'That's what everybody keeps asking. The doctor and old Pauline and Milly. On and on. Honestly, I could scream. He just had one of his turns and he felt queer. And with the way he'd eaten and thrown a temperament on top of it, no wonder. I gave him his hot drink and kissed him nighty-nighty and he seemed all right and that's all I know.'

'He drank his hot milk while you were with him?'

She swung over a little with a luxurious movement and looked at him through narrowed eyes. 'That's right,' she said. 'Drank it and liked it.'

'And his medicine?'

'He poured that out for himself. I told him to drink up like a good boy, but he said he'd wait a bit and see if his tummy wouldn't settle down without it. So I went.'

'Right. Now, Miss Orrincourt,' said Alleyn, facing her with his hands in his pockets, 'you've been very frank. I shall follow your example. You want to know what we're doing here. I'll tell you. Our job, or a major part of it, is to find out why you played a string of rather infantile practical jokes on Sir Henry Ancred and let it be thought that his granddaughter was responsible.'

She was on her feet so quickly that he actually felt his nerves jump. She was close to him now; her under-lip jutted out and her brows, thin hairy lines, were drawn together in a scowl. She resembled some drawing in a man's magazine of an infuriated baggage in a bedroom. One almost expected some dubious caption to issue in a balloon from her lips.

'Who says I did it?' she demanded.

'I do, at the moment,' Alleyn said. 'Come now. Let's start at Mr Juniper's shop. You bought the Raspberry there, you know.'

'The dirty little so-and-so,' she said meditatively. 'What a pal! *And* what a gentleman, I don't suppose.'

Alleyn ignored these strictures upon Mr Juniper. 'Then,' he said, 'there's that business about the paint on the banisters.'

Obviously this astonished her. Her face was suddenly bereft of expression, a mask with slightly dilated eyes. 'Wait a bit,' she said. 'That's funny!'

Alleyn waited.

'Here!' she said. 'Have you been talking to young Ceddie?'

'No.'

'That's what you say,' she muttered, and turned on Fox. 'What about you, then?'

'No, Miss Orrincourt,' said Fox blandly. 'Not me or the Chief Inspector.'

'Chief Inspector?' she said. 'Coo!'

Alleyn saw that she was looking at him with a new interest and had a premonition of what was to come.

'That'd be one of the high-ups, wouldn't it? Chief Inspector who? I don't seem to have caught the name.'

Any hopes he may have entertained that his connection with Troy was unknown to her vanished when she repeated his name, clapped her hand over her mouth and ejaculating 'Coo! That's a good one,' burst into fits of uncontrollable laughter.

'Pardon me,' she said presently, 'but when you come to think of it it's funny. You can't get away from it, you know, it's funny. Seeing it was her that – Well, of course! That's how you knew about the paint on the banisters.'

'And what,' Alleyn asked, 'is the connection between Sir Cedric Ancred and the paint on the banisters?'

'I'm not going to give myself away,' said Miss Orrincourt, 'nor Ceddie either, if it comes to that. Ceddie's pretty well up the spout anyway. If he's let me down he's crazy. There's a whole lot of things I want to know first. What's all this stuff about a book? What's the idea? Is it me, or is it everybody else in this dump that's gone hay-wire? Look! Somebody puts a dirty little book in a cheese-dish and serves it up for lunch. And when they find it, what do these half-wits do? Look at me as if I was the original hoodunit. Well, I mean to say, it's silly. And what a book! Written by somebody with a lisp and what about? Keeping people fresh after they're dead. Give you the willies. And when I say I never put it in the cheese-dish what do they do? Pauline starts tearing herself to shreds and Dessy says, "We're not so foolish as to suppose you'd want to run your head in a noose," and Milly says she happens to know I've read it, and they all go out as if I was something the cat'd brought in, and I sit there wondering if it's me or all of them who ought to be locked up.'

'And had you ever seen the book before?'

'I seem to remember,' she began, and then looking from Alleyn to Fox with a new wariness, she said sharply: 'Not to notice. Not to know what it was about.' And after a pause she added dully: 'I'm not much of a one for reading.'

Alleyn said: 'Miss Orrincourt, will you without prejudice tell me if you personally were responsible for any of the practical jokes other than the ones already under discussion?'

'I'm not answering any questions. I don't know what's going on here. A girl's got to look after herself. I thought I had one friend in this crazy-gang, now I'm beginning to think *he's* let me down.'

'I suppose,' said Alleyn, wearily, 'you mean Sir Cedric Ancred?'

'*Sir* Cedric Ancred,' Miss Orrincourt repeated with a shrill laugh. 'The bloody little baronet. Excuse my smile, but honestly it's a scream.' She turned her back on them and walked out, leaving the door open.

They could still hear her laughing with unconvincing virtuosity as she walked away down the corridor.

V

'Have we,' Fox asked blandly, 'got anywhere with that young lady? Or have we not?'

'Not very far, if anywhere at all,' Alleyn said, morosely. 'I don't know about you, Fox, but I found her performance tolerably convincing. Not that impressions of that sort amount to very much. Suppose she did put arsenic in the old man's hot milk, wouldn't this be the only line she could reasonably take? And at this stage of the proceedings, when I still have a very faint hope that we may come across something that blows their damn' suspicions to smithereens, I couldn't very well insist on anything. We'll just have to go mousing along.'

'Where to?' Fox asked.

'For the moment, in different directions. I've been carrying you about like a broody hen, Foxkin, and it's time you brought forth. Down you go and exercise the famous technique on Barker and his retinue of elderly maids. Find out all about the milk, trace its whole insipid history from cow to Thermos. Inspire gossip. Prattle. Seek out the paper-dump, the bottle-dump, the mops and the pails. Let us go clanking back to London like a dry canteen. Salvage the Thermos flask. We'll have to try for an analysis but what a hope! Get along with you, Fox. Do your stuff.'

'And where may I ask, Mr Alleyn, are you going?'

'Oh,' said Alleyn, 'I'm a snob. I'm going to see the baronet.'

Fox paused at the doorway. 'Taking it by and large, sir,' he said, 'and on the face of it as it stands, do you reckon there'll be an exhumation?'

'There'll be one exhumation at all events. Tomorrow, if Dr Curtis can manage it.'

'Tomorrow!' said Fox, startled. 'Dr Curtis? Sir Henry Ancred?'

'No,' Alleyn said, 'the cat, Carabbas.'

CHAPTER 13

Spotlight on Cedric

Alleyn interviewed Cedric in the library. It was a place without character or life. Rows of uniform editions stood coldly behind glass doors. There was no smell of tobacco, or memory of fires, only the darkness of an unused room.

Cedric's manner was both effusive and uneasy. He made a little dart at Alleyn and flapped at his hand. He began at once to talk about Troy. 'She was too marvellous, a perfect darling. So thrilling to watch her at work: that *magical* directness, almost intimidating, one felt. You must be madly proud of her, of course.'

His mouth opened and shut, his teeth glinted, his pale eyes stared and his voice gabbled on and on. He was restless too, and wandered about the room aimlessly, lifting lids of empty cigarette boxes and moving ornaments. He recalled acquaintance with Alleyn's nephews, with whom, he said, he had been at school. He professed a passionate interest in Alleyn's work. He returned again to Troy, suggesting that he alone among the Philistines had spoken her language. There was a disquieting element in all this, and Alleyn, when an opportunity came, cut across it.

'One moment,' he said. 'Our visit is an official one. I'm sure you will agree that we should keep it so. May we simply think the fact of my wife having been commissioned to paint Sir Henry a sort of freakish coincidence and nothing to do with the matter in hand? Except, of course, in so far as her job may turn out to have any bearing on the circumstances.'

Cedric's mouth had remained slightly open. He turned pink, touched his hair, and said: 'Of course if you feel like that about it. I merely thought that a friendly atmosphere – '

'That was extremely kind,' said Alleyn.

'Unless your somewhat muscular sense of the official proprieties forbids it,' Cedric suggested acidly, 'shall we at least sit down?'

'Thank you,' said Alleyn tranquilly, 'that would be much more comfortable.'

He sat in a vast armchair, crossed his knees, joined his hands, and with what Troy called his donnish manner, prepared to tackle Cedric.

'Mr Thomas Ancred tells me you share the feeling that further inquiries should be made into the circumstances of Sir Henry's death.'

'Well, I suppose I do,' Cedric agreed fretfully. 'I mean, it's all pretty vexing, isn't it? Well, I mean one would like to know. All sorts of things depend . . . And yet again it's not very delicious . . . Of course, when one considers that I'm the one who's most involved . . . Well, *look* at me. *Incarcerated*, in this frightful house! And the entail a pittance. All those taxes too, and *rapacious* death duties. Never, never will anybody be found mad enough to rent it, and as for schools, Carol Able does nothing but exclaim how inconvenient and how damp. And now the war's over the problem children will be hurried away. One will be left to wander in rags down whispering corridors. So that you see,' he added, waving his hands, 'one does rather wonder – '

'Quite so.'

'And they *will* keep talking about me as Head of the Family. Before I know where I am I shall have turned into another Old Person.'

'There are one or two points,' Alleyn began, and immediately Cedric leant forward with an ineffable air of concentration, 'that we'd like to clear up. The first is the authorship of these anonymous letters.'

'Well, I didn't write them.'

'Have you any idea who did?'

'Personally I favour my Aunt Pauline.'

'Really? Why?'

'She prefaces almost every remark she makes with the phrase: "I have reason to believe." '

'Have you asked Mrs Kentish if she wrote the letters?'

'Yes, indeed. She denies it hotly. Then there's Aunt Dessy. Quite capable, in a way, but more likely, one would have thought, to tell us flatly what she suspected. I mean, why go in for all this hush-hush letter-writing? That leaves my cousins Paul and Fenella, who are, one imagines, too pleasurably engrossed in their amorous martyrdom for any outside activities; my Mama, who is much too common-sensical; my aunt-in-law, Jenetta, who is too grand; and all the servants led by the Ancient of Days. That, as they say in sporting circles, is the field. Unless you feel inclined to take in the squire and the parson and dear old Rattlebones himself. It couldn't be more baffling. No, on the whole I plump for Pauline. She's about some-where. Have you encountered her? Since the Tragedy she is almost indistinguishable from Lady Macduff. Or perhaps that frightful Shakespearian dowager who curses her way up hill and down dale through one of the historical dramas. Constance? Yes, Pauline is now all compact of tragedy. Dessy's pretty bad, but wait till you meet Pauline.'

'Do you know if there's any paper in the house of the kind used for these letters?'

'Gracious, no! Exercise-book paper! The servants wouldn't have had it at any price. By the way, talking of exercise books, *do* you think Caroline Able might have done it? I mean, she's so wrapped up in id and isms and tracing everything back to the Oedipus Complex. Might it perhaps have all snapped back at her and made her a weeny bit odd? It's only an idea, of course. I merely throw it out for what it's worth.'

'About this tin of rat-bane,' Alleyn began. Cedric interrupted him with a shrill cry.

'My dear, what a party! Imagine! Milly, the complete hausfrau (my mama, you know)' – Cedric added the inevitable parentheses – 'and Dessy steaming up the stairs and Pauline tramping at her heels like one of the Fates, and poor little me panting in the rear. We didn't know what we were looking for, really. Partly rat poison and partly they thought there might be compromising papers some-where because Sonia's quite lovely, don't you think, and *really* – the

Old Person! *Hardly* adequate, one couldn't help feeling. I pointed out
that, constant or flighty, a Will was a Will, but nothing would stay
them. I said in fun: "You don't expect, darlings, to find phials of poison in her luggage, do you?" and that put the idea of luggage into
their heads. So up into the box-room they hounded me, and there,
to use the language of the chase, we "found".'

'You yourself took the tin out of the suitcase?'

'Yes, indeed. I was petrified.'

'What was it like?'

'Like? But didn't dear Uncle Tom give it to you?'

'Was it clean or dirty?'

'My dear, *filthy*. They wanted me to prise open the lid, and such a
struggle as I had. Little bits of rat-bane flying up and hitting me. I
was terrified. And then it wouldn't come out.'

'Who first suggested this search?'

'Now, that *is* difficult. Did we, thinking of that beastly little
brochure in the cheese-dish (and there, I must tell you, I see the
hand of Panty), did we with one accord cry: "rat-bane" and let loose
the dogs of war? I fancy Pauline, after coining the phrase "no
smoke" (or is it "reek"?) "without heat," said: "But where would she
get any arsenic?" and that Milly (my Mama), or it might have been
me, remembered the missing rat-bane. Anyway, no sooner was it
mentioned than Pauline and Dessy were in full cry for the guilty
apartment. If you could see it, too. Darling Sonia! Well, "darling"
with reservations. The bed-chamber a welter of piercing pink frills
and tortured satin and dolls peering from behind cushions or squatting on telephones, do you know?'

'I would be very glad,' said Alleyn, 'if the suitcase could be
produced.'

'Really? You wish, no doubt, to explore it for fingerprints? But of
course you shall have it. Unbeknown, I suppose, to darling Sonia?'

'If possible.'

'I'll trip upstairs and get it myself. If she's there, I'll tell her there's
a telephone call.'

'Thank you.'

'Shall I go now?'

'One moment, Sir Cedric,' Alleyn began, and again Cedric, with
that winsome trick of anxiety, leant towards him. 'Why did you,

with Miss Sonia Orrincourt, plan a series of practical jokes on your grandfather?'

It was not pleasant to watch the blood sink from Cedric's face. The process left his eyelids and the pouches under his eyes mauvish. Small grooves appeared beside his nostrils. His colourless lips pouted and then widened into an unlovely smile.

'Well, really!' he tittered. 'That just shows you, doesn't it? So darling Sonia has confided in you.' And after a moment's hesitation he added: 'As far as I'm concerned, dear Mr Alleyn, that's the end of darling Sonia.'

II

'Perhaps I should explain,' Alleyn said after a pause, 'that Miss Orrincourt has not made any statement about the practical jokes.'

'She *hasn't?*' The ejaculation was so incisive that it was difficult to believe Cedric had uttered it. He now lowered his head and appeared to look at the carpet between his feet. Alleyn saw his hands slide over each other. 'How perfectly futile,' Cedric's voice said. 'Such a *very* old gag. Such an ancient wheeze! I didn't know but you've just told me! And in I go, as they say, boots and all.' He raised his face. Its pinkness had returned and its expression suggested a kind of boyish ruefulness. 'Now *do* promise you won't be lividly angry. It sounds too childish, I know. But I implore you, dear Mr Alleyn, to look about you. Observe the peculiar flavour of Katzenjammer Castle. The façade now. The utterly unnerving inequalities of the façade. The terrifying Victoriana within. The gloom. Note particularly the gloom.'

'I'm afraid,' Alleyn said, 'that I don't follow this. Unless you're going to tell me you hoped to enliven the architecture and decor of Ancreton by painting spectacles and flying cows on your grandfather's portrait.'

'But I didn't!' Cedric protested shrilly. 'That *miraculous* portrait! No, believe me, I didn't.'

'And the paint on the banister?'

'I didn't do that either. Darling Mrs Alleyn! I wouldn't have dreamed of it.'

'But at least you seem to have known about it.'

'I didn't do it,' he repeated.

'The message written in grease-paint on the mirror? And the grease-paint on the cat?'

Cedric gave a nervous giggle. 'Well – '

'Come,' said Alleyn. 'You had dark red grease-paint under your finger-nail, you know.'

'*What* sharp eyes!' cried Cedric. 'Dearest Mrs Alleyn! *Such* a help she must be to you.'

'You did, in fact – '

'The Old Person,' Cedric interrupted, 'had been particularly roco-co. I couldn't resist. The cat, too. It was a kind of practical pun. The cat's whiskers!'

'And had you anything to do with the squeaking cushion in his chair?'

'Wasn't it too robust and Rabelaisian? Sonia bought it and I – I can't deny it – I placed it there. But why not? If I might make a tiny squeak of protest, dear Mr Alleyn, *has* all this got *anything* to do with the business in hand?'

'I think it might well have been designed to influence Sir Henry's Will, and with both his Wills we are, as I think you'll agree, very definitely concerned.'

'This is too subtle for my poor wits, I'm afraid.'

'It was common knowledge, wasn't it, that his youngest grand-daughter was, at this time, his principal heir?'

'But one never knew. We bounced in and out of favour from day to day.'

'If this is true, wouldn't these tricks, if attributed to her, very much affect her position?' Alleyn waited but was given no answer. 'Why, in fact, did you allow him to believe she was the culprit?'

'That devilish child,' Cedric said, 'gets away with innumerable hideous offences. A sense of injured innocence must have been quite a change for her.'

'You see,' Alleyn went on steadily, 'the flying cow was the last trick of five, and, as far as we know, was the final reason for Sir Henry's changing his Will that night. It was fairly conclusively proved to him that Panty did not do it, and it's possible that Sir Henry, not knowing which of his family to suspect, took his revenge on all.'

'Yes, but – '

'Now whoever was a party to these tricks – '

'At least you'll admit that I wouldn't be very likely to try and cut myself out of the Will – '

'I think that result was unforeseen. You hoped, perhaps, to return to your former position with Panty out of the picture. To something, in fact, on the lines of the Will read at the dinner party, but rather better. You have told me that you and Miss Orrincourt were partners in one of these practical jokes. Indeed you've suggested to me that you at least had knowledge of them all.'

Cedric began to speak very rapidly. 'I resent all this talk of partnership. I resent the implication and deny it. You force me into an intolerable position with your hints and mysteries. I suppose there's nothing left but for me to admit I knew what she was doing and why she did it. It amused me and it enlivened the ghastly boredom of these wretched festivities. Panty I consider an abomination, and I don't in the least regret that she was suspected or that she was cut out of the Will. She probably wallowed in her borrowed glory. There!'

'Thank you,' said Alleyn. 'That clears up quite a lot of the fog. And now, Sir Cedric, are you quite sure you don't know who wrote the letters?'

'Absolutely.'

'And are you equally sure you didn't put the book on embalming in the cheese-dish?'

Cedric gaped at him. 'I?' he said. 'Why should I? Oh, no! I don't want Sonia to turn out to be a murderess. Or I didn't, then. I'd rather thought . . . I . . . we'd . . . it doesn't matter. But I must say I'd like to *know*.'

Looking at him, Alleyn was visited by a notion so extravagant that he found himself incapable of pressing Cedric any further on the subject of his relationship with Miss Orrincourt.

He was, in any case, prevented from doing so by the entrance of Pauline Kentish.

Pauline entered weeping: not loudly, but with the suggestion of welling tears held bravely back. She seemed to Alleyn to be an older and woollier version of her sister, Desdemona. She took the uncomfortable line of expressing thankfulness that Alleyn was his wife's husband. 'Like having a *friend* to help us.' Italicized words and even phrases surged about in her conversation. There was much talk of Panty. Alleyn had been so kind, the child had taken a tremendous fancy to him. 'And I always think,' Pauline said, gazing at him, 'that they KNOW.' From here they were soon involved in Panty's misdoings. Pauline, if he had now wanted them, supplied good enough alibis for the practical jokes. 'How could she when the poor child was being watched; closely, anxiously watched? Dr Withers had given explicit orders.'

'And much good they've done, by the way!' Cedric interrupted. 'Look at Panty!'

'Dr Withers is extremely clever, Cedric. It's not his fault if Juniper's drugs have deteriorated. Your grandfather's medicines were always a great help to him.'

'Including rat-bane?'

'That,' said Pauline in her deepest voice, 'was not prescribed, Cedric, by Dr Withers.'

Cedric giggled.

Pauline ignored him and turned appealingly to Alleyn. 'Mr Alleyn, what are we to think? Isn't it all too tragically dreadful? The suspense! The haunting suspicion! The feeling that here in our midst . . . ! What are we to do?'

Alleyn asked her about the events following Sir Henry's exit from the little theatre on the night of his death. It appeared that Pauline herself had led the way to the drawing-room, leaving Troy, Paul and Fenella behind. Miss Orrincourt had only remained a very short time in the drawing-room where, Alleyn gathered, a lively discussion had taken place as to the authorship of the flying cow. To this family wrangle the three guests had listened uncomfortably until Barker arrived, with Sir Henry's summons for Mr Rattisbon. The squire and the rector seized upon this opportunity to make their escape. Paul and Fenella came in on their way to bed. Troy had already gone upstairs. After a little more desultory haggling the Birthday party broke up.

Pauline, Millamant and Desdemona had forgathered in Pauline's room, *Bernhardt,* and had talked exhaustively. They went together to the bathrooms at the end of the passage and encountered Mr Rattisbon, who had evidently come out of Sir Henry's rooms. Alleyn, who knew him, guessed that Mr Rattisbon, skipped, with late Victorian coyness, past the three ladies in their dressing-gowns and hurriedly down the passage to his own wing. The ladies performed their nightly rites together and together returned to their adjacent rooms. At this juncture Pauline began to look martyred.

'Originally,' she said, '*Bernhardt* and *Bancroft* were one large room, a nursery, I think. The wall between is the merest partition. Milly and Dessy shared *Bancroft*. Of course, I know there was a great deal to be talked about and for a time I joined in. Milly's bed was just through the wall from mine, and Dessy's quite close. But it had been a long day and one *was exhausted*. They went on and on. I became quite frantic with sleeplessness. Really it *was* thoughtless.'

'Dearest Aunt Pauline, why didn't you beat on the wall and scream at them?' Cedric asked, with some show of interest.

'I wasn't going to do that,' Pauline rejoined with grandeur and immediately contradicted herself. 'As a matter of fact I did at last tap. I said wasn't it getting rather late. Dessy asked what time it was, and Milly said it couldn't be more than one. There was quite an argument, and at last Dessy said: "Well, if you're so certain, Pauline, look at your watch and see." And in the end I did, and it was five minutes to three. So at last they stopped and then it was only to snore. Your mother snores, Cedric.'

'I'm so sorry.'

'And to *think* that only a little way away, while Dessy and Milly gossiped and snored, a frightful tragedy was being enacted. To think that if only I had obeyed my instinct to go to Papa and tell him –'

'To tell him what, Aunt Pauline?'

Pauline shook her head slowly from side to side and boggled a little. 'Everything was so sad and dreadful. One seemed to see him rushing to his doom.'

'One also saw Paul and Panty rushing to theirs, didn't one?' Cedric put in. 'You could have pleaded with him for them perhaps?'

'I cannot expect, Cedric, that you would understand or sympathize with disinterested impulses.'

'No,' Cedric agreed with perfect candour. 'I don't think they exist.'

'T'uh!'

'And if Mr Alleyn has no further absorbing questions to ask me I think I should like to leave the library. I find the atmosphere of unread silent friends in half-morocco exceedingly gloomy. Mr Alleyn?'

'No, thank you, Sir Cedric,' Alleyn said cheerfully. 'No more questions. If I may go ahead with my job?'

'Oh, do. Please consider this house your own. Perhaps you would like to buy it. In any case I do hope you'll stay to dinner. And your own particular silent friend. What is his name?'

'Thank you so much, but Fox and I,' Alleyn said, 'are dining out.'

'Then in that case,' Cedric murmured, sidling towards the door, 'I shall leave Aunt Pauline to divert you with tales of Panty's innocence in the matter of cheese-dishes, and her own incapability of writing anonymous letters.'

He was prevented from getting to the door by Pauline. With a movement of whose swiftness Alleyn would have thought her incapable, she got there first, and there she stood in a splendid attitude, the palms of her hands against the door, her head thrown back. 'Wait!' she said breathlessly. 'Wait!'

Cedric turned with a smile to Alleyn. 'As I hinted,' he said, 'Lady Macduff. With all her pretty chickens concentrated in the persons of Panty and Paul. The hen (or isn't it oddly enough "dam"?) at bay.'

'Mr Alleyn,' said Pauline, 'I was going to say nothing of this to anybody. We are an ancient family – '

'On my knees,' said Cedric, 'on my knees, Aunt Pauline, not the Sieur d'Ancred.'

' – and perhaps wrongly, we take some pride in our antiquity. Until today no breath of dishonour has ever smirched our name. Cedric is now Head of the Family. For that reason and for the sake of my father's memory I would have spared him. But now, when he does nothing but hurt and insult me and try to throw suspicion on my child, now when I have no one to protect me – ' Pauline stopped as if for some important petoration. But something happened to her. Her face crinkled and reminded Alleyn instantly of her daughter's. Tears gathered in her eyes. 'I have reason to believe,' she began and stopped short, looking terrified. 'I don't care,' she said, and her voice cracked piteously. 'I never could bear people to be unkind to me.' She nodded her head at Cedric. 'Ask him,' she said, 'what he was doing in Sonia Orrincourt's rooms that night. Ask him.'

She burst into tears and stumbled out of the room.

'Oh, *bloody* hell!' Cedric ejaculated shrilly and darted after her.

III

Alleyn, left alone, whistled disconsolately, and after wandering about the cold and darkening room went to the windows and there made a series of notes in his pocket-book. He was still at this employment when Fox came in.

'They said I'd find you here,' Fox said. 'Have you done any good, Mr Alleyn?'

'If stirring up a hive and finding foul-brood can be called good. What about you?'

'I've got the medicine bottle and three of the envelopes. I've had a cup of tea in Mr Barker's room.'

'That's more than I've had in the library.'

'The cook and the maids came in and we had quite a nice little chat. Elderly party, it was. Mary, Isabel and Muriel, the maids are. The cook's Mrs Bullivant.'

'And what did you and Mary, Isabel and Muriel talk about?'

'We passed the time of day and listened to the wireless. Mrs Bullivant showed me photographs of her nephews in the fighting forces.'

'Come *on*, Fox,' said Alleyn, grinning.

'By gradual degrees,' said Fox, enjoying himself, 'we got round to the late baronet. He must have been a card, the late old gentleman.'

'I believe you.'

'Yes. The maids wouldn't say much while Mr Barker was there, but he went out after a bit and then it was, as you might say, plain sailing.'

'You and your methods!'

'Well, we were quite cosy. Naturally, they were dead against Miss Orrincourt, except Isabel, and she said you couldn't blame the old gentleman for wanting a change from his family. It came as a bit of a surprise from Isabel, who's the oldest of the maids, I should say. She's the one who looks after Miss Orrincourt's rooms, and it seems Miss Orrincourt got quite friendly with her. Indiscreet, really, but you know the type.'

'It's evident, at least, that you do.'

'They seemed to be as thick as thieves, Miss O. and Isabel, and yet, you know, Isabel didn't mind repeating most of it. The garrulous sort, she is, and Mrs Bullivant egging her on.'

'Did you get anywhere with the history of the milk?'

'Isabel took it out of a jug in the refrigerator and left it in Miss Orrincourt's room. The rest of the milk in the jug was used for general purposes next day. Miss O. was in her room and undressing when Isabel brought it. It couldn't have been more than ten minutes or so later that Miss O. took it to the old gentleman. It was heated by Isabel in the kitchen and some patent food put in. The old gentleman fancied Miss O. did it, and said nobody else could make it to suit him. It was quite a joke between Isabel and Miss O.'

'So there's no chance of anybody having got at it?'

'Only if they doped the tin of patent food, and I've got that.'

'Good.'

'And I don't know if you're thinking she might have tampered with the medicine, sir, but it doesn't seem likely. The old gentleman never let anybody touch the bottle on account of Miss Desdemona Ancred having once given him embrocation in error. It was a new bottle, Isabel says, I've got it from the dump. Cork gone, but there's enough left for analysis.'

'Another job for Dr Curtis. What about the Thermos?'

'Nicely washed and sterilized and put away. I've taken it, but there's not a chance.'

'And the same goes, I imagine, for the pails and cloths?'

'The pails are no good, but I found some tag-ends of rag.'

'Where have you put these delicious exhibits?'

'Isabel,' said Fox primly, 'hunted out a case. I told her I had to buy pyjamas in the village, being obliged unexpectedly to stay the night, and I mentioned that a man doesn't like to be seen carrying parcels. I've promised to return it.'

'Didn't they spot you were taking these things?'

'Only the patent food. I let on that the police were a bit suspicious about the makers and it might have disagreed. I dare say they didn't believe me. Owing to the behaviour of the family I think they know what's up.'

'They'd be pretty dumb if they didn't.'

'Two other points came out that might be useful,' said Fox.

Alleyn had a clear picture of the tea-party. Fox, no doubt, had sipped and complimented, had joked and sympathized, had scarcely asked a question, yet had continually received answers. He was a pastmaster at the game. He indulged his hostesses with a few innocuous hints and was rewarded with a spate of gossip.

'It seems, Mr Alleyn, that the young lady was, as Isabel put it, leading Sir Henry on and no more.'

'D'you mean – '

'Relationship,' said Fox sedately, 'according to Isabel, had not taken place. It was matrimony or nothing.'

'I see.'

'Isabel reckons that before this business with the letters came out, there was quite an understanding between Miss O. and Sir Cedric.'

'What sort of understanding, in the name of decency?'

'Well, sir, from hints Miss O. dropped, Isabel works it out that after a discreet time had elapsed Miss O. would have turned into Lady A. after all. So that what she lost on the swings she would, in a manner of speaking, have picked up on the roundabouts.'

'Good Lord!' said Alleyn. ' "What a piece of work is man!" That, if it's true, would explain quite a number of the young and unlovely baronet's antics.'

'Supposing Miss Orrincourt did monkey with the Thermos, Mr Alleyn, we might have to consider whether Sir Cedric knew what she was up to.'

'We might indeed.'

'I know it's silly,' Fox went on, rubbing his nose, 'but when a case gets to this stage I always seem to get round to asking myself whether such-and-such a character is a likely type for homicide. I know it's silly, because there isn't a type, but I ask myself the question just the same.'

'And at the moment you ask it about Sonia Orrincourt?'

'That's right, sir.'

'I don't see why you shouldn't. It's quite true, that beyond the quality of conceit, nobody's found a nice handy trait common to all murderers. But I'm not so sure that you should sniff at yourself for saying: "That man or woman seems to me to have characteristics that are inconceivable in a murderer!" They needn't be admirable characteristics either.'

'D'you remember what Mr Barker said about the rats in Miss Orrincourt's rooms?'

'I do.'

'He mentioned that Miss Orrincourt was quite put-about by the idea of using poison, and refused to have it at any price. Now, sir, would a young woman who was at least, as you might say, toying with the idea of poison, behave like that? Would she? She wouldn't do it by accident. She might do it to suggest she had a dread of poison, though that'd be a very far-fetched kind of notion too. And would she have owned up as readily to those practical jokes? Mind, you caught her nicely, but she gave me the impression she was upset more on account of being found out for these pranks themselves than because she thought they'd lead us to suspect something else.'

'She was more worried about the Will than anything else,' Alleyn said. 'She and Master Cedric planned those damned stunts with the object of setting the old man against Panty. I fancy she was responsible for the portrait vandalism, Cedric having possibly told her to confine her daubs to dry canvas. We know she bought the Raspberry, and he admits he placed it. I *think* she started the ball rolling by painting the banister. They plotted the whole thing together. He practically admitted as much. Now, all that worries her may be merely an idea that the publication of these goings-on could upset the Will.'

'And yet – '

'I know. I know. That damn bell-push. All right, Fox. Good work. And now, I suppose, we'd better see Mrs Henry Ancred.'

IV

Millamant was at least a change from her relations-by-marriage in that she was not histrionic, answered his questions directly, and stuck to the point. She received them in the drawing-room. In her sensible blouse and skirt she was an incongruous figure there. While she talked she stitched that same hideously involved piece of embroidery which Troy had noticed with horror and which Panty had been accused of unpicking. Alleyn heard nothing either to contradict or greatly to substantiate the evidence they had already collected.

'I wish,' he said, after a minute or two, 'that you would tell me your own opinion about this business.'

'About my father-in-law's death? I thought at first that he died as a result of his dinner and his temperament.'

'And what did you think when these letters arrived?'

'I didn't know what to think. I don't now. And I must say that with everybody so excited and foolish about it one can't think very clearly.'

'About the book that turned up in the cheese-dish . . .' he began.

Millamant jerked her head in the direction of the glass case. 'It's over there. Someone replaced it.'

He walked over to the case and raised the lid. 'If you don't mind, I'll take charge of it presently. You saw her reading it?'

'Looking at it. It was one evening before dinner. Some weeks ago, I think.'

'Can you describe her position and behaviour? Was she alone?'

'Yes. I came in and she was standing as you are now, with the lid open. She seemed to be turning over the leaves of the book as it lay there. When she saw me she let the lid fall. I was afraid it might have smashed, but it hadn't.'

Alleyn moved away to the cold hearth, his hands in his pockets, 'I wonder,' said Milly, 'if you'd mind putting a match to the fire. We light it at four-thirty, always.'

Glad of the fire, for the crimson and white room was piercingly cold, and faintly amused by her air of domesticity, he did as she asked. She moved, with her embroidery, to a chair before the hearth. Alleyn and Fox sat one on each side of her.

'Mrs Ancred,' Alleyn said, 'do you think any one in the house knew about this second Will?'

'She knew. She says he showed it to her that night.'

'Apart from Miss Orrincourt?'

'They were all afraid he might do something of the sort. He was always changing his Will. But I don't think any of them knew he'd done it.'

'I wondered if Sir Cedric – '

The impression that with Millamant all would be plain speaking was immediately dispelled. Her short hands closed on her work like traps. She said harshly: 'My son knew nothing about it. Nothing.'

'I thought that as Sir Henry's successor – '

'If he had known he would have told me. He knew nothing. It was a great shock to both of us. My son,' Millamant added, looking straight before her, 'tells me everything – everything.'

'Splendid,' murmured Alleyn after a pause. Her truculent silence appeared to demand comment. 'It's only that I should like to know whether this second Will was made that night when Sir Henry went to his room. Mr Rattisbon, of course, can tell us.'

'I suppose so,' said Millamant, selecting a strand of mustard-coloured silk.

'Who discovered the writing on Sir Henry's looking-glass?'

'I did. I'd gone in to see that his room was properly done. He was very particular and the maids are old and forget things. I saw it at once. Before I could wipe it away he came in. I don't think,' she said meditatively, 'that I'd ever before seen him so angry. For a moment he actually thought I'd done it, and then, of course, he realized it was Panty.'

'It was not Panty,' Alleyn said.

He and Fox had once agreed that if, after twenty years of experience, an investigating officer has learned to recognize any one manifestation, it is that of genuine astonishment. He recognized it now in Millamant Ancred.

'What are you suggesting?' she said at last. 'Do you mean – ?'

'Sir Cedric has told me he was involved in one of the other practical jokes that were played on Sir Henry, and knew about all of them. He's responsible for this one.'

She took up her embroidery again. 'He's trying to shield somebody,' she said. 'Panty, I suppose.'

'I think not.'

'It was very naughty of him,' she said in her dull voice. 'If he played one of these jokes, and I don't believe he did, it was naughty. But I can't see – I may be very stupid, but I can't see why you, Mr Alleyn, should concern yourself with any of these rather foolish tricks.'

'Believe me, we shouldn't do so if we thought they were irrelevant.'

'No doubt,' she said, and after a pause, 'you've been influenced by your wife. She would have it that Panty was all innocence.'

'I'm influenced,' Alleyn said, 'by what Sir Cedric and Miss Orrincourt have told me.'

She turned to look at him, moving her torso stiffly. For the first time her alarm, if she felt alarm, coloured her voice. 'Cedric? And that woman? Why do you speak of them together like that?'

'It appears that they planned the practical jokes together.'

'I don't believe it. She's told you that. I can see it now,' said Millamant on a rising note. 'I've been a fool.'

'What can you see, Mrs Ancred?'

'She planned it all. Of course she did. She knew Panty was his favourite. She planned it, and when he'd altered the Will she killed him. She's trying to drag my boy down with her. I've watched her. She's a diabolical, scheming woman, and she's trying to entrap my boy. He's generous and unsuspecting and kind. He's been too kind. He's at her mercy,' Millamant cried sharply and twisted her hands together.

Confronted by this violence and with the memory of Cedric fresh in his mind, Alleyn was hard put to it to answer her. Before he could frame a sentence she had recovered something of her composure. 'That settles it,' she said woodenly. 'I've kept out of all this, as far as one can keep out of their perpetual scenes and idiotic chattering. I've thought all along that they were probably right but I left it to them. I've even felt sorry for her. Now I hope she suffers. If I can tell you anything that will help you, I'll do so. Gladly.'

'Oh, damn!' thought Alleyn. 'Oh, Freud! Oh, hell!' And he said: 'There may still be no case, you know. Have you any theory as to the writer of the anonymous letters?'

'Certainly,' she said with unexpected alacrity.

'You have?'

'They're written on the paper those children use for their work. She asked me some time ago to re-order it for them when I was in the village. I recognized it at once. Caroline Able wrote the letters.'

And while Alleyn was still digesting this, she added: 'Or Thomas. They're very thick. He spent half his time in the school wing.'

CHAPTER 14

Psychiatry and a Churchyard

There was something firmly coarse about Milly Ancred. After performances by Pauline, Desdemona and Cedric, this quality was inescapable. It was incorporate in her solid body, her short hands, the dullness of her voice and her choice of phrase. Alleyn wondered if the late Henry Irving Ancred, surfeited with ancestry, fine feeling and sensibility, had chosen his wife for her lack of these qualities – for her normality. Yet was Milly, with her adoration of an impossible son, normal?

'But there is no norm,' he thought, 'in human behaviour; who should know this better than Fox and I?'

He began to ask her routine questions, the set of questions that crop up in every case and of which the investigating officer grows tired. The history of the hot drink was traced again with no amendments, but with clear evidence that Milly had resented her dethronement in favour of Miss Orrincourt. He went on to the medicine. It was a fresh bottle. Dr Withers had suggested an alteration and had left the prescription at the chemist. Miss Orrincourt had picked it up at Mr Juniper's on the day she collected the children's medicine, and Milly herself had sent Isabel with it to Sir Henry's room. He was only to use it in the event of a severe attack, and until that night had not done so.

'She wouldn't put it in that,' said Milly. 'She wouldn't be sure of his taking a dose. He hated taking medicine and only used it when he was really very bad. It doesn't seem to have been much good, anyway. I've no faith in Dr Withers.'

'No?'

'I think he's careless. I thought at the time he ought to have asked more questions about my father-in-law's death. He's too much wrapped up in his horse racing and bridge and not interested enough in his patients. However,' she added, with a short laugh, 'my father-in-law liked him well enough to leave more to him than to some of his own flesh and blood.'

'About the medicine,' Alleyn prompted.

'She wouldn't have interfered with it. Why should she use it when she had the Thermos in her own hands?'

'Have you any idea where she could have found the tin of rat-bane?'

'She complained of rats when she first came here. I asked Barker to set poison and told him there was a tin in the storeroom. She made a great outcry and said she had a horror of poison.'

Alleyn glanced at Fox, who instantly looked extremely bland.

'So,' Milly went on, 'I told Barker to set traps. When we wanted rat-bane, weeks afterwards, for *Bracegirdle,* the tin had gone. It was an unopened tin, to the best of my knowledge. It had been in the store-room for years.'

'It must have been an old brand,' Alleyn agreed. 'I don't think arsenical rat-bane is much used nowadays.'

He stood up and Fox rose with him. 'I think that's all,' he said.

'No,' said Millamant strongly, 'it's not all. I want to know what the woman has said about my son.'

'She suggested they were partners in the practical jokes and he admitted it.'

'I warn you,' she said, and for the first time her voice was unsteady. 'I warn you, she's trying to victimize him. She's worked on his kindness and good nature and his love of fun. I warn you – '

The door at the far end of the room opened and Cedric looked in. His mother's back was turned to him, and, unconscious of his presence, she went on talking. Her shaking voice repeated over and over again that he had been victimized. Cedric's gaze moved from her to Alleyn, who was watching him. He sketched a brief grimace, deprecating, rueful, but his lips were colourless and the effect was of a distortion. He came in and shut the door with great delicacy. He carried a much be-labelled suitcase, presumably Miss Orrincourt's, which, after a further grimace at Alleyn, he placed behind a chair. He then minced across the carpet.

'Darling Milly,' he said, and his hands closed on his mother's shoulders. She gave a startled cry. 'There now! I made you jump. *So* sorry.'

Millamant covered his hands with her own. He waited for a moment, submissive to her restless and possessive touch. 'What is it, Milly?' he asked. 'Who's been victimizing little Me? Is it Sonia?'

'*Ceddie?*'

'I've been such a goose, you can't think. I've come to "fess up," like a good boy,' he said nauseatingly, and slid round to his familiar position on the floor, leaning against her knees. She held him there, strongly.

'Mr Alleyn,' Cedric began, opening his eyes very wide, 'I couldn't be more sorry about rushing away just now after Aunt Pauline. Really, it was too stupid. But one does like to tell people things in one's own way, and there she was, huffing and puffing and going on as if I'd been trying to conceal some dire skeleton in my, I assure you, too drearily barren cupboard.'

Alleyn waited.

'You see – (Milly, my sweet, this is going to be a faint shock to you, but never mind) – you see, Mr Alleyn, there's been a – what shall I call it? – a – well, an *understanding*, of sorts, between Sonia and me. It only really developed quite lately. After dearest Mrs Alleyn came here. She seems to have noticed quite a number of things; perhaps she noticed that.'

'If I understand you,' Alleyn said, 'she, I am sure, did not.'

'Really?'

'Are you trying to tell me why you visited Miss Orrincourt's rooms on the night of your grandfather's death?'

'Well,' Cedric muttered petulantly, 'after Aunt Pauline's announcement – and, by the way, she gleaned her information through a nocturnal visit to the *archaic* offices at the end of the passage – after that there seems to be nothing for it but an elaborate cleaning of the breast, does there?'

'Cedric,' Millamant said, 'what has this woman done to you?'

'My sweet, nothing, thank God. I'm trying to tell you. She really is too beautiful, Mr Alleyn, don't you think? I know you didn't like her, Milly dear, and how right you seem to have been. But I really was quite intrigued and she was so bored and it was only the teeniest flutter, truly. I merely popped in on my way to bed and had a good giggle with her about the *frightful* doings down below.'

'Incidentally,' Alleyn suggested, 'you may have hoped to hear the latest news about Sir Henry's Will.'

'Well, that among other things. You see, I did rather wonder if the flying cow hadn't been sort of once too often, as it were. Sonia did it before dinner, you know. And then at the dinner the Old Person announced a Will that was really quite satisfactory from both our points of view, and with the insufferable Panty not even a starter, one rather wished Sonia had left well alone.'

'Cedric,' said his mother suddenly, 'I don't think, dear, you should go on. Mr Alleyn won't understand. Stop.'

'But, Milly, my sweet, don't you see dear old Pauline has already planted a horrid little seed of suspicion, and one simply must tweak it up before it sprouts. Mustn't one, Mr Alleyn?'

'I think,' Alleyn said, 'you'll be well advised to make a complete statement.'

'There! Now, where was I? Oh, yes. Now, all would have been well if Carol Able, who is so scientific and "un-thing" that she's a sort of monster, hadn't made out a water-tight alibi for that septic child. This, of course, turned the Old Person's suspicious glare upon all of us equally, and so he wrote the second Will and so we were all done in the eye except Sonia. And to be *quite* frank, Milly and Mr Alleyn, I should so like to have it settled whether she's a murderess or not, rather quickly.'

'Of course she is,' Millamant said.

'Yes, but are you *positive*? It really is of mountainous significance for me.'

'What do you mean, Cedric? I don't understand – '

'Well – well, never mind.'

'I think I know what Sir Cedric means,' Alleyn said. 'Isn't it a question of marriage at some time in the future with Miss Orrincourt?'

Millamant, with a tightening of her hold on Cedric's shoulder, said, 'No!' loudly and flatly.

'Oh, Milly darling,' he protested, wriggling under her hand, 'please let's be civilized.'

'It's all nonsense,' she said. 'Tell him it's all nonsense. A disgusting idea! Tell him.'

'What's the use when Sonia will certainly tell him something
else.' He appealed to Alleyn. 'You do understand, don't you? I mean,
one can't deny she's decorative and in a way it would have been
quite fun. Don't you think it would have worked, Mr Alleyn? I do.'

His mother again began to protest. He freed himself with ugly
petulance and scrambled to his feet. 'You're idiotic, Milly. What's the
good of hiding things.'

'You'll do yourself harm.'

'What harm? I'm in the same position, after all, as you. I don't
know the truth about Sonia but I want to find out.' He turned to
Alleyn with a smile. 'When I saw her that night she told me about
the new Will. I knew then that if he died I'd be practically ruined.
There's no collaboration where I'm concerned, Mr Alleyn. I didn't
murder the Old Person. *Pas si bête!*'

II

' *"Pas si bête,"* ' Fox quoted as they made their way to the school
wing. 'Meaning, "not such a fool." I shouldn't say he was, either,
would you, Mr Alleyn?'

'Oh, no. There are no flies on the egregious Cedric. But what a
cold-blooded little worm it is, Fox! Grandpapa dies, leaving him
encumbered with a large unwanted estate and an insufficient
income to keep it up. Grandpapa, on the other hand, dies leaving his
extremely dubious fiancée a fortune. What more simple than for the
financially embarrassed Cedric to marry the opulent Miss O.? I could
kick that young man,' said Alleyn thoughtfully, 'in fourteen completely different positions and still feel half-starved.'

'I reckon,' said Fox, 'it's going to be a case for the Home
Secretary.'

'Oh, yes, yes, I'm afraid you're right. Down this passage, didn't
they say? And there's the green baize door. I think we'll separate
here, Fox. You to collect your unconsidered trifles in Isabel's case
and, by the way, you might take charge of Miss Orrincourt's. Here it
is. Then, secretly, Foxkin, exhume Carabbas, deceased, and enclose

him in a boot-box. By the way, do we know who destroyed poor Carabbas?'

'Mr Barker,' said Fox, 'got Mr Juniper to come up and give him an injection. Strychnine, I fancy.'

'I hope, whatever it was, it doesn't interfere with the autopsy. I'll meet you on the second terrace.'

Beyond the green baize door the whole atmosphere of Ancreton was charged. Coir runners replaced the heavy carpets, passages were draughty and smelt of disinfectant, and where Victorian prints may have hung there were pictures of determined modernity that had been executed with a bright disdain for comfortable, but doubtless undesirable, prettiness.

Led by a terrific rumpus, Alleyn found his way to a large room where Miss Able's charges were assembled, with building games, with modelling clay, with paints, hammers, sheets of paper, scissors and paste. Panty, he saw, was conducting a game with scales, weights and bags of sand, and appeared to be in hot dispute with a small boy. When she saw Alleyn she flung herself into a strange attitude and screamed with affected laughter. He waved to her and she at once did a comedy fall to the floor, where she remained, apeing violent astonishment.

Miss Caroline Able detached herself from a distant group and came towards him.

'We're rather noisy in here,' she said crisply. 'Shall we go to my office? Miss Watson, will you carry on?'

'Certainly, Miss Able,' said an older lady, rising from behind a mass of children.

'Come along, then,' said Caroline Able.

Her office was near at hand and was hung with charts and diagrams. She seated herself behind an orderly desk, upon which he at once noticed a pile of essays written on paper with yellow lines and ruled margin.

'I suppose you know what all this is about,' he said.

Miss Able replied cheerfully that she thought she did. 'I see,' she said frankly, 'quite a lot of Thomas Ancred and he's told me about all the trouble. It's been a pretty balanced account, as a matter of fact. He's fairly well adjusted, and has been able to deal with it quite satisfactorily so far.'

Alleyn understood this to be a professional opinion on Thomas, and wondered if a courtship had developed and if it was conducted on these lines. Miss Able was pretty. She had a clear skin, large eyes and good teeth. She also had an intimidating air of utter sanity.

'I'd like to know,' he said, 'what you think about it all.'

'It's impossible to give an opinion that's worth much,' she replied, 'without a pretty thorough analysis of one if not all of them. Obviously the relationship with their father was unsatisfactory. I should have liked to know about his marriage. One suspected, of course, that there was a fear of impotency, not altogether sublimated. The daughter's violent antagonism to his proposed second marriage suggests a rather bad father-fixation.'

'Does it? But it wasn't a particularly suitable alliance from – from the ordinary point of view, was it?'

'If the relationship with the father,' Miss Able said firmly, 'had been properly adjusted, the children should not have been profoundly disturbed.'

'Not even,' Alleyn ventured, 'by the prospect of Miss O. as a mother-in-law and principal beneficiary in the Will?'

'Those may have been the reasons advanced to explain their antagonism. They may represent an attempt to rationalize a basic and essentially sexual repulsion.'

'Oh, dear!'

'But, as I said before,' she added, with a candid laugh, 'one shouldn't pronounce on mere observation. Deep analysis might lead to a much more complex state of affairs.'

'You know,' Alleyn said, taking out his pipe and nursing it in his palm, 'you and I, Miss Able, represent two aspects of investigation. Your professional training teaches you that behaviour is a sort of code or cryptogram disguising the pathological truth from the uninformed, but revealing it to the expert. Mine teaches me to regard behaviour as something infinitely variable *after* the fact and often at complete loggerheads *with* the fact. A policeman watches behaviour, of course, but his deductions would seem completely superficial to you.' He opened his hand. 'I see a man turning a dead pipe about in his hand and I think that, perhaps unconsciously, he's longing to smoke it. May he?'

'Do,' said Miss Able. 'It's a good illustration. I see a man caressing his pipe and I recognize a very familiar piece of fetishism.'

'Well, don't tell me what it is,' Alleyn said hurriedly.

Miss Able gave a short professional laugh.

'Now, look here,' he said, 'how do you account for these anonymous letters we're all so tired of? What sort of being perpetrated them and why?'

'They probably represent an attempt to make an effect and are done by someone whose normal creative impulses have taken the wrong turning. The desire to be mysterious and omnipotent may be an additional factor. In Patricia's case for instance – '

'Patricia? Oh, I see. That's Panty, of course.'

'We don't use her nickname over here. We don't think it a good idea. We think nicknames can have a very definite effect, particularly when they are of a rather humiliating character.'

'I see. Well, then, in Patricia's case?'

'She formed the habit of perpetrating rather silly jokes on people. This was an attempt to command attention. She used to let her performances remain anonymous. Now she usually brags about them. That, of course, is a good sign.'

'It's an indication, at least, that she's not the author of the more recent practical jokes on her grandfather.'

'I agree.'

'Or the author of the anonymous letters.'

'That, I should have thought,' said Miss Able patiently, 'was perfectly obvious.'

'Who do you think is responsible for the letters?'

'I've told you, I can't make snap decisions or guesses.'

'Couldn't you just unbend far enough to have one little potshot?' he said persuasively. Miss Able opened her mouth, shut it again, looked at him with somewhat diminished composure and finally blushed. 'Come!' he thought, 'she hasn't analysed herself into an iceberg, at least.' And he said aloud: 'Without prejudice, now, who among the grown-ups would you back as the letter-writer?' He leant forward, smiling at her, and thought: 'Troy would grin if she saw this exhibition.' As Miss Able still hesitated, he repeated: 'Come on; who would you back?'

'You're very silly,' Miss Able said, and her manner, if not coy, was at least very much less impersonal.

'Would you say,' Alleyn went on, 'that the person who wrote them is by any chance the practical joker?'

'Quite possible.'

He reached a long arm over the desk and touched the top sheet of the exercises. 'They were written,' he said, 'on this paper.'

Her face was crimson. With a curious and unexpected gesture she covered the paper with her hands. 'I don't believe you,' she said.

'Will you let me look at it?' He drew the sheet out from under her hands and held it to the light. 'Yes,' he said. 'Rather an unusual type with a margin. It's the same watermark.'

'He didn't do it.'

'He?'

'Tom,' she said, and the diminutive cast a new light upon Thomas. 'He's incapable of it.'

'Good,' Alleyn said. 'Then why bring him up?'

'Patricia,' said Miss Able, turning a deeper red, 'must have taken some of this exercise paper over to the other side. Or . . .' She paused, frowning.

'Yes?'

'Her mother comes over here a great deal. Too often, I sometimes think. She's not very wise with children.'

'Where is the paper kept?'

'In that cupboard. The top one. Out of reach of the children.'

'Do you keep it locked?'

She turned on him quickly. 'You're not going to suggest that I would write anonymous letters? I?'

'But you do keep it locked, don't you?' said Alleyn.

'Certainly. I haven't denied that.'

'And the key?'

'On my ring and in my pocket.'

'Has the cupboard been left open at all? Or the keys left out of your pocket?'

'Never.'

'The paper comes from a village shop, doesn't it?'

'Of course it does. Any one could buy it.'

'So they could,' he agreed cheerfully, 'and we can find out if they have. There's no need, you see, to fly into a huff with me.'

'I do not,' said Miss Able mulishly, 'fly into huffs.'

'Splendid! Now look here. About this medicine your kids had. I want to trace its travels. Not inside the wretched kids, but *en route* to them.'

'I really don't see why – '

'Of course you don't and I'll tell you. A bottle of medicine for Sir Henry came up at the same time and its history is therefore bound up with theirs. Now, as the pudding said to the shop assistant, can you help me, Moddom?'

This laborious pun was not immediately absorbed by Miss Able. She looked at him with wonder but finally produced a tolerably indulgent smile.

'I suppose I can. Miss Orrincourt and Mrs Alleyn . . .'

Here came the now familiar pause and its inevitable explanation. 'Fancy!' said Miss Able. 'I know,' said Alleyn, 'about the medicine?'

'I was really very annoyed with Miss Orrincourt. It seems that she asked Mrs Alleyn to drive the trap round to the stables and she herself brought in the medicine. Instead of leaving it in the hall, or as you would think she might have done, bringing it in here to me, she simply dumped the whole lot in the flower-room. It seems that Sir Henry had given her some flowers out of the conservatory and she'd left them there. She's abnormally egocentric, of course. I waited and waited, and finally, at about seven o'clock, went over to the other side to ask about it. Mrs Ancred and I hunted everywhere. Finally, it was Fenella who told us where they were.'

'Was Sir Henry's medicine with theirs?'

'Oh, yes. Mrs Ancred sent it up at once.'

'Were the bottles alike?'

'We made no mistake, if that's what you're wondering. They were the same sort of bottles, but ours was much larger and they were both clearly labelled. Ours had the instructions attached. Unnecessarily, as it turned out, because Dr Withers came up himself that evening and he weighed the children again and measured out their doses himself. It was odd, because he'd left it that I should give the medicine and I could have managed perfectly well; but evidently,' said Miss Able with a short laugh, 'he'd decided I was not to be trusted.'

'It's a fault on the right side, I suppose,' Alleyn said vaguely. 'They have to be careful.'

Miss Able looked unconvinced. 'No doubt,' she said. 'But I still can't understand why he wanted to come up to Ancreton, when he was supposed to be so busy. And after all that fuss, we've had to go back to the ointment.'

'By the way,' Alleyn asked, 'did you happen to see the cat Carabbas before it died?'

Instantly she was away on her professional hobby-horse. He listened to an exposition on Panty's fondness for the cat, and the strange deductions which Miss Able drew, with perfect virtuosity, from this not unusual relationship.

'At this stage of her development, it was really a bad disturbance when the link was broken.'

'But,' Alleyn ventured, 'if the cat had ringworm . . .'

'It wasn't ringworm,' said Miss Able firmly. 'I ought to know. It might have been mange.'

Upon that pronouncement he left her, apparently in two minds about himself. She shook hands with an air of finality, but when he reached the door he thought he heard an indeterminate sound, and turned to find her looking anxiously at him.

'Is there anything else?' he asked.

'It's only that I'm worried about Tom Ancred. They're dragging him in and making him do all their dirty work. He's quite different. He's too good for them. I'm afraid this will upset him.'

And then with a rather strenuous resumption of her professional manner: 'Psychologically, I mean,' said Miss Able.

'I quite understand,' said Alleyn, and left her.

He found Fox waiting for him on the second terrace. Fox was sitting on the steps with his greatcoat drawn closely round him and his spectacles on his nose. He was reading from the manual on poisons which Alleyn had lent him in the train. By his side were two suitcases. One of these Alleyn recognized as Miss Orrincourt's. The other, he presumed, was Isabel's. Near by was a boot-box tied up with string. As Alleyn bent over Fox he noticed an unpleasant smell.

'Carabbas?' he asked, edging the box away with his foot.

Fox nodded. 'I've been asking myself,' he said, and placed a square finger under a line of print. Alleyn read over his shoulder. 'Arsenic. Symptoms. Manifested as progressive cachexia and loss of flesh; falling out of hair . . .'

Fox glanced up and jerked a thumb at the boot-box.

'Falling out of hair,' he said. 'Wait till you've had a look at Carabbas deceased.'

III

'You know, Fox,' Alleyn said as they walked back to the village, 'if Thomas Ancred can stand having his lightest cares implacably laid at the door of some infantile impropriety, he and Miss Able will probably get along together very nicely. Obviously, she's in love with him, or should I say that obviously she finds herself adjusted to a condition of rationalized eroticism in relation to poor old Thomas?'

'Courting, do you reckon?'

'I think so. Fox, I think we've had Ancreton for the moment, but I'm going to ask you to stay behind and warn the parson about an exhumation. Return to Katzenjammer Castle in the morning and ask the inmates if they've any objection to having their prints taken. They won't have any if they're not completely dotty. Bailey can come down by the morning train and work round the house for the stuff we want there. Get him to check prints on any relevant surfaces. It'll all be utterly useless no doubt, but it had better be done. I'll go back to the Yard. I want to learn Messrs Mortimer and Loame's recipe for tasteful embalming. As soon as we get the exhumation order through we'll come down and meet you here. There's a train this evening. Let's have a meal at the pub and then I'll catch it. I was going to see Dr Withers again, but I fancy that particular interview had better wait. I want to get the medicine bottle and poor old Carabbas up to London.'

'What's the betting, Mr Alleyn? Arsenic in the medicine or not?'

'I'm betting *not.*'

'Routine job. It'll be a nuisance if they don't find anything, though. Not a hope with the Thermos.'

'No, damn it.'

They walked in silence. Frost tingled in the dusk and hardened the ground under their feet. A pleasant smell of burning wood laced the air and from Ancreton woods came the sound of wings.

'What a job!' Alleyn said suddenly.

'Ours, sir?'

'Yes, ours. Walking down a country lane with a dead cat in a boot-box and working out procedure for disentombing the body of an old man.'

'Somebody's got to do it.'

'Certainly. But the details are unlovely.'

'Not much doubt about it, sir, is there? Homicide?'

'Not much doubt, old thing. No.'

'Well,' said Fox, after a pause, 'as it stands, the evidence all points one way. It's not one of those funny affairs where you have to clear up half a dozen suspects.'

'But *why* kill him? She knew the Will was in her favour. She wanted to be Lady Ancred. She knew he wasn't likely to live much longer. Why incur the appalling risk when all she had to do was marry him and wait?'

'He was always changing his Will. Perhaps she thought he might do it again.'

'She seems to have had him pretty well where she wanted him.'

'Might she be all that keen on the present baronet?'

'Not she,' said Alleyn. 'Not she.'

'Hard to imagine, I must say. Suppose, though, that Miss O. is not the party we'll be after, and suppose we know the old gentleman was done away with. Who's left? Not Sir Cedric, because he knew about the second Will.'

'Unless,' said Alleyn, 'he gambled on marrying the heiress.'

'By gum, yes, there's that, but what a gamble! With that fortune she could have hoped for better, wouldn't you say?'

'She could hardly hope for worse, in my opinion.'

'Well, then,' Fox reasoned, 'suppose we count those two out. Look at the rest of the field.'

'I do so without enthusiasm. They all thought the Will announced at the Birthday Dinner was valid. Desdemona, Millamant, Dr Withers and the servants expected to do moderately well; Thomas's expectations were handsome. The Kentish family, and the Claude Ancreds got damn all. In the "haves" the only motive is cupidity, in the "have-nots," revenge.'

'Opportunity?' Fox speculated.

'If an analysis of the medicine bottle proves negative, we're left with the Thermos flask, now sterilized, and as far as we can see, Miss O. Unless you entertain a notion of delayed action with Barker inserting arsenic in the crayfish.'

'You will have your joke, Mr Alleyn.'

'You should have heard me trifling with Miss Able,' Alleyn grunted. 'That was pretty ghastly, if you like.'

'And the exhumation's on,' Fox ruminated after another long silence. 'When?'

'As soon as we've got the order and Dr Curtis can manage it. By the way, Ancreton Church is above the village over there. We'll have a look at the churchyard while the light still holds.'

And presently they climbed a gentle lane, now deep in shadow, and pushed open a lych-gate into the churchyard of St Stephen's, Ancreton.

It was pleasant after the dubious grandeurs of the manor house to encircle this church, tranquil, ancient, and steadfastly built. Their feet crunched loudly on the gravelled path, and from the hedges came a faint stir of sleepy birds. The grass was well kept. When they came upon a quiet company of headstones and crosses they found that the mounds and plots before them were also carefully tended. It was possible in the fading light to read inscriptions. 'Susan Gascoigne of this parish. Here rests one who in her life rested not in well-doing.' 'To the Memory of Miles Chitty Bream who for fifty years tended this churchyard and now sleeps with those he faithfully served.' Presently they came upon Ancred graves. 'Henry Gaisbrook Ancreton Ancred, fourth baronet, and Margaret Mirabel, his wife.' 'Percival Gaisbrook Ancred,' and many others, decently and properly bestowed. But such plain harbourage was not for the later generations, and towering over this sober company of stone rose a marble tomb topped by three angels. Here, immortalized in gold inscriptions, rested Sir Henry's predecessor, his wife, his son Henry Irving Ancred, and himself. The tomb, Alleyn read, had been erected by Sir Henry. It had a teak and iron door, emblazoned in the Ancred arms, and with a great keyhole.

'It'll be one of these affairs with shelves,' Fox speculated. 'Not room enough for the doctor, and no light. It'll have to be a canvas enclosure, don't you reckon, Mr Alleyn?'

'Yes.'

The lid of Fox's large silver watch clicked. 'It's five o'clock, sir,' he said. 'Time we moved on if you're to have tea at the pub and catch that train.'

'Come along, then,' said Alleyn quietly, and they retraced their steps to the village.

CHAPTER 15

New System

As Troy waited for Alleyn's return her thoughts moved back through the brief period of their reunion. She examined one event, then another; a phrase, a gesture, an emotion. She was astonished by the simplicity of her happiness; amused to find herself expectant, even a little sleek. She was desired, she was loved, and she loved again. That there were hazards ahead she made no doubt, but for the moment all was well; she could relax and find a perspective.

Yet, like a rough strand in the texture of her happiness, there was an imperfection. Her thoughts, questing fingers, continually and reluctantly sought it out. This was Alleyn's refusal to allow his work a place in their relationship. It was founded, she knew, in her own attitude during their earliest encounters which had taken place against a terrible background; in her shrinking from the part he played at that time and in her expressed horror of capital punishment.

Troy knew very well that Alleyn accepted these reactions as fundamental and implicit in her nature. She knew he did not believe that for her, in love, an ethic unrelated to that love could not impede it. It seemed to him that if his work occasionally brought murderers to execution, then surely, to her, he must at those times be of the same company as the hangman. Only by some miracle of love, he thought, did she overcome her repulsion.

But the bald truth, she told herself helplessly, was that her ideas were remote from her emotions. 'I'm less sensitive than he thinks,' she said. 'What he does is of no importance. I love him.' And although she disliked such generalities, she added: 'I am a woman.'

It seemed to her that while this withdrawal existed they could not be completely happy. 'Perhaps,' she thought, 'this business with the Ancreds will, after all, change everything. Perhaps it's a kind of beastly object lesson. I'm in it. He can't keep me out. I'm in on a homicide case.' And with a sensation of panic she realized that she had been taking it for granted that the old man she had painted was murdered.

As soon as Alleyn came in and stood before her she knew that she had made no mistake. 'Well, Rory,' she said, going to him, 'we're for it, aren't we, darling?'

'It looks a bit like it.' He walked past her, saying quickly: 'I'll see the AC in the morning. He'll let me hand over to someone else. Much better.'

'No,' Troy said, and he turned quickly and looked at her. She was aware, as if she had never before fully appreciated it, of the difference in their heights. She thought: 'That's how he looks when he's taking statements,' and became nervous.

'No?' he said. 'Why not?'

'Because it would be high-falutin, because it would make me feel an ass.'

'I'm sorry.'

'I look upon this case,' Troy said, and wished her voice would sound more normal, 'as a sort of test. Perhaps it's been sent to larn us like acts-of-God; only I must say I always think it's so unfair to call earthquakes and tidal-waves acts-of-God and not bumper harvests and people like Leonardo and Cézanne.'

'What the devil,' Alleyn asked in a mild voice, 'are you talking about?'

'Don't snap at me,' said Troy. He made a quick movement towards her. 'No. Please listen. I want, I really do want you to take this case as long as the AC lets you. I really want you to keep me with you this time. We've got in a muddle about me and your job. When I say I don't mind your job you think I'm not telling the truth, and if I ask you questions about these kinds of cases you think I'm being a brave little woman and biting on the bullet.'

She saw his mouth twist in an involuntary smile.

'Whereas,' she hurried on, 'I'm not. I know I didn't relish having our courtship all muddled up with murder on the premises, and I know I don't think people ought to hang other people. But you do, and you're the policeman, not me. And it doesn't do any good trying to pretend you're dodging out to pinch a petty larcener when I know jolly well what you are up to, and, to be perfectly honest, am often dying to hear about it.'

'That's not quite true, is it – the last bit?'

'I'd infinitely rather talk about it. I'd infinitely rather feel honestly shocked and upset with you, than vaguely worried all by myself.'

He held out a hand and she went to him. 'That's why I said I think this case has been sent to larn you.'

'Troy,' Alleyn said, 'do you know what they say to their best girls in the antipodes?'

'No.'

'You'll do me.'

'Oh!'

'You'll do me, Troy.'

'I thought perhaps you'd prefer me to remain a shrinking violet.'

'The truth is, I've been a bloody fool and never did and never will deserve you.'

'Don't,' said Troy, 'let's talk about deserving.'

'I've only one excuse and logically you'll say it's no excuse. Books about CID men will tell you that running a murderer to earth is just a job to us, as copping a pickpocket is to the ordinary PC. It's not. Because of its termination it's unlike any other job in existence. When I was twenty-two I faced its implications and took it on, but I don't think I fully realized them for another fifteen years and that was when I fell most deeply in love, my love, with you.'

'I've faced its implications, too, and once for all, over this Ancred business. Before you came in I even decided that it would be good for both of us if, by some freak, it turned out that I had a piece of information somewhere in the back of my memory that's of vital importance.'

'You'd got as far as that?'

'Yes. And the queer thing is,' Troy said, driving her fingers through her hair, 'I've got the most extraordinary conviction that somewhere in the back of my memory it is there, waiting to come out.'

II

'I want you,' Alleyn said, 'to tell me again, as fully as you possibly can, about your conversation with Sir Henry after he'd found the writing on the looking-glass and the grease-paint on the cat's whiskers. If you've forgotten how it went at any particular stage, say so. But, for the love of Mike, darling, don't elaborate. Can you remember?'

'I think so. Quite a lot, anyway. He was furious with Panty, of course.'

'He hadn't a suspicion of the egregious Cedric?'

'None. Did Cedric – ?'

'He did. He's lisped out an admission.'

'Little devil,' said Troy. 'So it *was* grease-paint on his fingernail.'

'And Sir Henry – ?'

'He just went on and on about how much he'd doted on Panty and how she'd grieved him. I tried to persuade him she hadn't done it, but he only made their family noise at me: "T'uh!" you know?'

'Yes, indeed.'

'Then he started to talk about marriages between first cousins and how he disapproved of them, and this got mixed up in no time with a most depressing account of how he was' – Troy swallowed and went on quickly – 'was going to be embalmed. We actually mentioned the book. Then I think he sniffed a bit at Cedric as his heir, and said he'd never have children and that poor Thomas wouldn't marry.'

'He was wrong there, I fancy.'

'No! Who?'

'The psychiatrist, or should it be "psychiatriste"?'

'Miss Able?'

'She thinks he's quite satisfactorily sublimated his libido or something.'

'Oh, good! Well, and then as he would keep talking about when he was Gone, I tried to buck him up a bit and had quite a success. He turned mysterious and talked about there being surprises in store for everybody. And upon that Sonia Orrincourt burst in and said they were all plotting against her and she was frightened.'

'And that's all?' Alleyn said after a pause.

'No – no, it isn't. There was something else he said. Rory, I can't remember what it was, but there was something else.'

'That was on Saturday the seventeenth, wasn't it?'

'Let me see. I got there on the sixteenth. Yes. Yes, it was the next day. But I wish,' Troy said slowly, 'I do wish I could remember the other thing he talked about.'

'Don't try. It may come back suddenly.'

'Perhaps Miss Able could screw it out of me,' said Troy with a grin. 'In any case we'll call it a day.'

As they moved away she linked her arm through his. 'First instalment of the new system,' she said. 'It's gone off tolerably quietly, hasn't it?'

'It has, my love. Thank you.'

'One of the things I like about you,' Troy said, 'is your nice manners.'

III

The next day was a busy one. The Assistant Commissioner after a brisk interview with Alleyn, decided to apply for an exhumation order. 'Sooner the better, I suppose. I was talking to the Home Secretary yesterday and told him we might be on his tracks. You'd better go right ahead.'

'Tomorrow then, sir, if possible,' Alleyn said. 'I'll see Dr Curtis.'

'Do.' And as Alleyn turned away: 'By the way, Rory, if it's at all difficult for Mrs Alleyn – '

'Thank you very much sir, but at the moment she's taking it in her stride.'

'Splendid. Damn' rum go – what?'

'Damn' rum,' Alleyn agreed politely, and went to call on Mr Rattisbon.

Mr Rattisbon's offices in the Strand had survived the pressure of the years, the blitz and the flying bomb. They were, as Alleyn remembered them on the occasion of his first official visit before the war, a discreetly active memorial to the style of Charles Dickens, with the character of Mr Rattisbon himself written across them like an inscription. Here was the same clerk with his trick of slowly raising his head and looking dimly at the inquirer, the same break-neck stairs, the same dark smell of antiquity. And here, at last, shrined in leather, varnish and age was Mr Rattisbon, that elderly legal bird, perched at his desk.

'Ah, yes, Chief Inspector,' Mr Rattisbon gabbled, extending a claw at a modish angle, 'come in, come in, sit down, sit down. Glad to see yer. M-m-maah!' And when Alleyn was seated Mr Rattisbon darted the old glance at him, sharp as the point of a fine nib. 'No trouble, I hope?' he said.

'The truth is,' Alleyn rejoined, 'my visits only arise, I'm afraid, out of some sort of trouble.'

Mr Rattisbon instantly hunched himself, placed his elbows on his desk and joined his finger-dps in front of his chin.

'I've come to ask about certain circumstances that relate to the late Sir Henry Ancred's Will. Or Wills.'

Mr Rattisbon vibrated the tip of his tongue between his lips, rather as if he had scalded it and hoped in this manner to cool it off. He said nothing.

'Without more ado,' Alleyn went on, 'I must tell you that we are going to ask for an exhumation.'

After a considerable pause Mr Rattisbon said: 'This is exceedingly perturbing.'

'May I, before we go any further, say I do think that instead of coming to us with the story I'm about to relate, Sir Henry's successors might have seen fit to consult their solicitor.'

'Thank yer.'

'I don't know, sir, of course, how you would have advised them, but I believe that this visit must sooner or later have taken place. Here is the story.'

Twenty minutes later Mr Rattisbon tipped himself back in his chair and gave a preparatory bay at the ceiling.

'Ma-m-ah!' he said. 'Extraordinary. Disquieting. Very.'

'You will see that all this rigmarole seems to turn about two factors, (a) It was common knowledge in his household that Sir Henry Ancred was to be embalmed, (b) He repeatedly altered his Will, and on the eve of his death appears to have done so in favour of his intended wife, largely to the exclusion of his family and in direct contradiction to an announcement he made a couple of hours earlier. It's here, I hope, Mr Rattisbon, that you can help us.'

'I am,' said Mr Rattisbon, 'in an unusual, not to say equivocal, position. Um. As you have very properly noted, Chief Inspector, the correct procedure on the part of the family, particularly on the part of Sir Cedric Gaisbrooke Percival Ancred, would have been to consult this office. He has elected not to do so. In the event of a criminal action he will scarcely be able to avoid doing so. It appears that the general intention of the family is to discredit the position of the chief beneficiary and further to suggest that there is a case for a criminal charge against her. I refer, of course, to Miss Gladys Clark.'

'To *whom?*'

' – known professionally as Miss Sonia Orrincourt.'

' "Gladys Clark," ' Alleyn said thoughtfully. 'Well!'

'Now, as the solicitor for the estate, I am concerned in the matter. On consideration, I find no objection to giving you such information as you require. Indeed, I conceive it to be my professional duty to do so.'

'I'm extremely glad,' said Alleyn, who had known perfectly well that Mr Rattisbon, given time, would arrive at precisely this decision. 'Our principal concern at the moment is to discover whether Sir Henry Ancred actually concocted his last Will after he left the party on the eve of his death.'

'Emphatically no. It was drawn up, in this office, on Sir Henry's instruction, on Thursday, the twenty-second of November of this year, together with a second document, which was the one quoted by Sir Henry as his last Will and Testament at his Birthday dinner.'

'This all sounds rather erratic.'

Mr Rattisbon rapidly scratched his nose with the nail of his first finger. 'The procedure,' he said, 'was extraordinary, I ventured to say so at the time. Let me take these events in their order. On Tuesday, the twentieth November, Mrs Henry Irving Ancred telephoned this office to the effect that Sir Henry Ancred wished me to call upon him immediately. It was most inconvenient, but the following day I went down to Ancreton. I found him in a state of considerable agitation and clothed – m-m-m-ah – in a theatrical costume. I understood that he had been posing for his portrait. May I add, in parentheses,' said Mr Rattisbon with a bird-like dip of his head, 'that although your wife was at Ancreton, I had not the pleasure of meeting her on that occasion. I enjoyed this privilege upon my later visit.'

'Troy told me.'

'It was the greatest pleasure. To return. On this first visit of Wednesday the twenty-first of November, Sir Henry Ancred showed me his rough drafts of two Wills. One moment.'

With darting movements, Mr Rattisbon drew from his filing cabinet two sheafs of paper covered in a somewhat flamboyant script. He handed them to Alleyn. A glance showed him their nature. 'Those are the drafts,' said Mr Rattisbon. 'He required me to engross two separate Wills based on these notes. I remarked that this procedure was unusual. He put it to me that he was unable to come to a decision regarding the – ah – the merits of his immediate relatives, and was, at the same time, contemplating a second marriage. His previous Will, in my opinion a reasonable disposition, he had already destroyed. He instructed me to bring these two new documents to Ancreton when I returned for the annual Birthday observances. The first was the Will witnessed and signed before the dinner and quoted by Sir Henry *at* dinner as his last Will and Testament. It was destroyed late that evening. The second is the document upon which we are at present empowered to act. It was signed and witnessed in Sir Henry Ancred's bedroom at twelve-twenty that night – against, may I add, *against* my most earnest representations.'

'Two Wills,' Alleyn said, 'in readiness for a final decision.'

'Precisely. He believed that his health was precarious. Without making any specific accusations he suggested that certain members of his family were acting separately or in collusion against him. I believe, in view of your own exceedingly lucid account,' Mr Rattisbon dipped his head again, 'that he referred, in fact, to these practical jokes. Mrs Alleyn will have described fully the extraordinary incident of the portrait. An admirable likeness, if I may say so. She will have related how Sir Henry left the theatre in anger.'

'Yes.'

'Subsequently the butler came to me with a request from Sir Henry that I should wait upon him in his room. I found him still greatly perturbed. In my presence, and with considerable violence, he tore up the, as I considered, more reasonable of the two drafts, and, in short, threw it on the fire. A Mr and Mrs Candy were shown in and witnessed his signature to the second document. Sir Henry then informed me that he proposed to marry Miss Clark in a

week's time and would require my services in the drawing up of a
marriage settlement. I persuaded him to postpone this matter until
the morning and left him, still agitated and inflamed. That, in effect,
is all I can tell you.'

'It's been enormously helpful,' Alleyn said. 'One other point if
you don't mind. Sir Henry's two drafts are not dated. He didn't by
any chance tell you when he wrote them?'

'No. His behaviour and manner on this point were curious. He
stated that he would enjoy no moment's peace until both Wills had
been drawn up in my office. But no. Except that the drafts were
made before Tuesday, the twentieth, I cannot help you here.'

'I'd be grateful if they might be put away and left untouched.'

'Of course,' said Mr Rattisbon, greatly flustered, 'by all means.'

Alleyn placed the papers between two clean sheets and returned
them to their drawer.

That done, he rose, and Mr Rattisbon at once became very lively.
He escorted Alleyn to the door, shook hands and uttered a string of
valedictory phrases. 'Quite so, quite so,' he gabbled. 'Disquieting.
Trust no foundation but nevertheless disquieting. Always depend
upon your discretion. Extraordinary. In many ways, I fear, an unpre-
dictable family. No doubt if counsel is required . . . Well, goodbye.
Thank yer. Kindly remember me to Mrs Alleyn. Thank yer.'

But as Alleyn moved, Mr Rattisbon laid a claw on his arm. 'I shall
always remember him that night,' he said. 'He stopped me as I
reached the door and I turned and saw him, sitting upright in bed
with his gown spread about him. He was a fine-looking old fellow. I
was quite arrested by his appearance. He made an unaccountable
remark, too, I recollect. He said: "I expect to be very well attended,
in future, Rattisbon. Opposition to my marriage may not be as strong
in some quarters as you anticipate. Goodnight." That was all. It was,
of course, the last time I ever saw him.'

IV

The Hon Mrs Claude Ancred had a small house in Chelsea. As a
dwelling-place it presented a startling antithesis to Ancreton. Here
all was lightness and simplicity. Alleyn was shown into a white

drawing-room, modern in treatment, its end wall one huge window overlooking the river. The curtains were pale yellow, powdered with silver stars, and this colour, with accents of clear cerise, appeared throughout the room. There were three pictures – a Matisse, a Christopher Wood, and, to his pleasure, an Agatha Troy. 'So you still stick around, do you?' he said, winking at it, and at that moment Jenetta Ancred came in.

An intelligent looking woman, he thought. She greeted him as if he was a normal visitor, and, with a glance at the painting, said: 'You see that we've got a friend in common,' and began to talk to him about Troy and their meeting at Ancreton.

He noticed that her manner was faintly and recurrently ironic. Nothing, she seemed to say, must be insisted upon or underlined. Nothing really matters very much. Over-statement is stupid and uncomfortable. This impression was conveyed by the crispness of her voice, its avoidance of stresses, and by her eyes and lips, which constantly erected little smiling barriers that half-discredited the frankness of her conversation. She talked intelligently about painting, but always with an air of self-deprecation. He had a notion she was warding off the interview for which he had asked.

At last he said: 'You've guessed, of course, why I wanted you to let me come?'

'Thomas came in last night and told me he'd seen you and that you'd gone down to Ancreton. This is an extremely unpleasant development, isn't it?'

'I'd very much like to hear your views.'

'Mine?' she said, with an air of distaste. 'They can't possibly be of the smallest help, I'm afraid. I'm always a complete onlooker at Ancreton. And please don't tell me the onlooker sees most of the game. In this instance she sees as little as possible.'

'Well,' said Alleyn cheerfully, 'what does she think?'

She waited for a moment, looking past him to the great window. 'I think,' she murmured, 'that it's almost certain to be a tarradiddle. The whole story.'

'Convince us of that,' Alleyn said, 'and we're your slaves for ever in the CID.'

'No, but really. They're so absurd, you know, my in-laws. I'm very attracted to them, but you can't imagine how absurd they can be.'

Her voice died away. After a moment's reflection she said: 'But Mrs Alleyn saw them. She must have told you.'

'A little.'

'At one time it was fifth columnists. Pauline suspected such a nice little Austrian doctor who's since taken a very important job at a big clinic. At that time he was helping with the children. She said something told her. And then it was poor Miss Able who was supposed to be undermining her influence with Panty. I wonder if, having left the stage, Pauline's obliged to find some channel for her histrionic instincts. They all do it. Naturally, they resented Miss Orrincourt, and resentment and suspicion are inseparable with the Ancreds.'

'What did you think of Miss Orrincourt?'

'I? She's too lovely, isn't she? In her way, quite flawless.'

'Apart from her beauty?'

'There didn't seem to be anything else. Except a very robust vulgarity.'

'But does she really think as objectively as all that?' Alleyn wondered. 'Her daughter stood to lose a good deal through Sonia Orrincourt. Could she have achieved such complete detachment?' He said: 'You were there, weren't you, when the book on embalming appeared in the cheese-dish?'

She made a slight grimace. 'Oh, yes.'

'Have you any idea who could have put it there?'

'I'm afraid I rather suspected Cedric. Though why . . . For no reason except that I can't believe any of the others would do it. It was quite horrible.'

'And the anonymous letters?'

'I feel it must have been the same person. I can't imagine how any of the Ancreds – after all they're not – However.'

She had a trick of letting her voice fade out as if she had lost faith in the virtue of her sentences. Alleyn felt that she pushed the suggestion of murder away from her, with both hands, not so much for its dreadfulness as for its offence against taste.

'You think, then,' he said, 'that their suspicion of Miss Orrincourt is unfounded and that Sir Henry died naturally?'

'That's it. I'm quite sure it's all a make-up. They think it's true. They've just got one of their "things" about it.'

'That explanation doesn't quite cover the discovery of a tin of rat-bane in her suitcase, does it?'

'Then there must be some other explanation.'

'The only one that occurs to me,' Alleyn said, 'is that the tin was deliberately planted, and if you accept that you accept something equally serious: an attempt to place suspicion of murder upon an innocent person. That in itself constitutes – '

'No, no,' she cried out. 'No, you don't understand the Ancreds. They plunge into fantasies of their own making, without thinking of the consequences. This wretched tin must have been put in the suitcase by a maid or have got there by some other freakish accident. It may have been in the attic for years. None of their alarms ever means anything. Mr Alleyn, may I implore you to dismiss the whole thing as nonsense? Dangerous and idiotic nonsense, but, believe me, utter nonsense.'

She had leant forward, and her hands were pressed together. There was a vehemence and an intensity in her manner that had not appeared before.

'If it's nonsense,' he said, 'it's malevolent nonsense.'

'Stupid,' she insisted, 'spiteful, too, perhaps, but only childishly so.'

'I shall be very glad if it turns out to be no more.'

'Yes, but you don't think it will.'

'I'm wide open to conviction,' he said lightly.

'If I could convince you!'

'You can at least help by filling in some of the gaps. For instance, can you tell me anything about the party in the drawing-room when you all returned from the little theatre? What happened?'

Instead of answering him directly she said, with a return to her earlier manner, 'Please forgive me for being so insistent. It's silly to try and ram one's convictions down other people's throats. They merely feel that one protests too much. But, you see, I know my Ancreds.'

'And I'm learning mine. About the aftermath of the Birthday Party?'

'Well, two of our visitors, the rector and a local squire, said good-night in the hall. Very thankfully, poor darlings, I'm sure. Miss Orrincourt had already gone up. Mrs Alleyn had stayed behind in the theatre with Paul and Fenella. The rest of us went into the drawing-room and there the usual family arguments started, this time on the subject of that abominable disfigurement of the portrait. Paul and Fenella came in and told us that no damage had been done. Naturally, they were very angry. I may tell you that my daughter, who has not quite grown out of the hero-worship state-of-affairs, admires your wife enormously. These two children planned what they fondly imagined to be a piece of detective work. Did Mrs Alleyn tell you?'

Troy had told Alleyn, but he listened again to the tale of the paintbrush and finger-prints. She dwelt at some length on this, inviting his laughter, making, he thought, a little too much of a slight incident. When he asked her for further details of the discussion in the drawing-room she became vague. They had talked about Sir Henry's fury, about his indiscretions at dinner.

Mr Rattisbon had been sent for by Sir Henry. 'It was just one more of the interminable emotional parties,' she said. 'Everyone, except Cedric and Milly, terrifically hurt and grand because of the Will he told us about at dinner.'

'Every one? Your daughter and Mr Paul Ancred too?'

She said much too lightly: 'My poor Fen does go in a little for the Ancred temperament, but not, I'm glad to say, to excess. Paul, thank goodness, seems to have escaped it, which is such a very good thing, as it appears he's to be my son-in-law.'

'Would you say that during this discussion any of them displayed singular vindictiveness against Miss Orrincourt?'

'They were all perfectly livid about her. Except Cedric. But they're lividly angry with somebody or another a dozen times a month. It means nothing.'

'Mrs Ancred,' Alleyn said, 'if you've been suddenly done out of a very pretty fortune your anger isn't altogether meaningless. You yourself must surely have resented a little your daughter's position.'

'No,' she said quickly. 'I knew, as soon as she told me of her engagement to Paul, that her grandfather would disapprove. Marriage between cousins was one of his bugbears. I knew he'd take it out of them both. He was a vindictive old man. And Fen hadn't bothered to hide her dislike of Miss Orrincourt. She'd said . . .' She stopped short. He saw her hands move convulsively.

'Yes?'

'She was perfectly frank. The association offended her taste. That was all.'

'What are her views of all this business – the letters and so on?'

'She agrees with me.'

'That the whole story is simply a flight of fancy on the part of the more imaginative members of the family?'

'Yes.'

'I should like to see her if I may?'

The silence that fell between them was momentary, a brief check in the even flow of their voices, but he found it illuminating. It was as if she winced from an expected hurt, and poised herself to counter it. She leant forward, and with an air of great frankness made a direct appeal.

'Mr Alleyn,' she said, 'I'm going to ask a favour. Please let Fenella off. She's highly strung and sensitive. Really sensitive. It's not the rather bogus Ancred sensibility. All the unhappy wrangling over her engagement and the shock of her grandfather's death and then – this horrid and really dreadful business: it's fussed her rather badly. She overheard me speaking to you when you rang up for this talk and even that upset her. I've sent them both out. Please, will you be very understanding and let her off?'

He hesitated, wondering how to frame his refusal, and if her anxiety was based on some much graver reason than the one she gave him.

'Believe me,' she said, 'Fenella can be of no help to you.'

Before he could reply Fenella herself walked in, followed by Paul.

'I'm sorry, Mummy,' she said rapidly and in a high voice. 'I know you didn't want me to come. I had to. There's something Mr Alleyn doesn't know, and I've got to tell him.'

CHAPTER 16

Positively the Last Appearance of Sir Henry Ancred

Afterwards, when he told Troy about Fenella's entrance, Alleyn said the thing that struck him most at the time was Jenetta Ancred's command of *savoir-faire*. Obviously this was a development she had not foreseen and one which filled her with dismay. Yet her quiet assurance never wavered, nor did she neglect the tinge of irony that was implicit in her good manners.

She said: 'Darling, how dramatic and alarming. This is my girl, Fenella, Mr Alleyn. And this is my nephew, Paul Ancred.'

'I'm sorry to burst in,' said Fenella. 'How do you do? Please may we talk to you?' She held out her hand.

'*Not* just at this moment,' said her mother. 'Mr Alleyn and I really are rather busy. Do you mind, darling?'

Fenella's grip on his hand had been urgent and nervous. She had whispered: 'Please.' Alleyn said: 'May we just hear what this is about, Mrs Ancred?'

'Mummy, it's important. Really.'

'Paul,' said her mother, 'can't you manage this firebrand of yours?'

'I think it's important too, Aunt Jen.'

'My dearest children, I honestly don't think you know – '

'But Aunt Jen, we do. We've talked it over quite cold-bloodedly. We know that what we've got to say may bring a lot of publicity and scandal on the family,' said Paul with something very like relish. 'We don't enjoy the prospect, but we think any other course would be dishonest.'

446

'We accept the protection of the law,' said Fenella rather loudly. 'It'd be illogical and dishonest to try and circumvent justice to save the family face. We know we're up against something pretty horrible. We accept the responsibility, don't we, Paul?'

'Yes,' said Paul. 'We don't like it, but we do it.'

'Oh,' Jenetta cried out vehemently, 'for pity's sake don't be so heroic! Ancreds, Ancreds, both of you!'

'Mummy, we're *not*. You don't even know what we're going to say. This isn't a matter of theatre; it's a matter of principle, and, if you like, of sacrifice.'

'And you both see yourselves being sacrificial and high-principled. Mr Alleyn,' Jenetta said, and it was as if she added: 'After all, we speak the same language, you and I. I do most earnestly beg you to take whatever these ridiculous children have to say with a colossal pinch of salt.'

'Mummy, it's important.'

'Then,' said Alleyn, 'let's have it.'

She gave in, as he had expected, lightly and with grace. 'Well, then, if we must be instructed . . . Do at least sit down, both of you, and let poor Mr Alleyn sit down too.'

Fenella obeyed, with the charm of movement that was characteristic of all the female Ancreds. She was, as Troy had told him, a vivid girl. Her mother's spareness was joined in Fenella with the spectacular Ancred beauty and lent it delicacy. 'Nevertheless,' Alleyn thought, 'she can make an entrance with the best of them.'

'Paul and I,' she began at once, speaking very rapidly, 'have talked and talked about it. Ever since those letters came. We said at first that we wouldn't have anything to do with it. We thought people who wrote that kind of letter were beyond everything, and it made us feel perfectly beastly to think there was any one in the house who could do such a thing. We were absolutely certain that what the letter said was an odious, malicious lie.'

'Which is precisely,' her mother said without emphasis, 'what I have been telling Mr Alleyn. I really do think, darling – '

'Yes, but that's not all,' Fenella interrupted vehemently. 'You can't just shrug your shoulders and say it's horrid. If you don't mind my saying so, Mummy dear, that's your generation all over. It's muddled thinking. In its way it's the kind of attitude that leads to wars. That's what Paul and I think anyway. Don't we, Paul?'

Paul, with a red determined face, said: 'What Fen means, I think, Aunt Jenetta, is that one can't just say "Jolly bad form and all bally-hoo," and let it go at that. Because of the implications. If Sonia Orrincourt didn't poison Grandfather, there's somebody in the house who's trying to get her hanged for something she didn't do, and that's as much as to say there's somebody in the house who's as good as a murderer.' He turned to Alleyn: 'Isn't that right, sir?'

'Not necessarily right,' Alleyn said. 'A false accusation may be made in good faith.'

'Not,' Fenella objected, 'by the kind of person who writes anonymous letters. And anyway, even if it was in good faith, we know it's a false accusation, and the realistic thing to do is to say so and, and . . .' She stumbled, shook her head angrily and ended with childish lameness, 'and jolly well make them admit it and pay the penalty.'

'Let's take things in their order?' Alleyn suggested. 'You say you know the suggestion made in the letters is untrue. How do you know this?'

Fenella glanced at Paul with an air of achievement and then turned to Alleyn and eagerly poured out her story.

'It was that evening when she and Mrs Alleyn drove down to the chemist's and brought back the children's medicine. Cedric and Paul and Aunt Pauline were dining out, I'd got a cold and cried off. I'd been doing the drawing-room flowers for Aunt Milly and I was tidying up in a sink-room where the vases are kept. It's down some steps off the passage from the hall to the library. Grandfather had had some orchids sent for Sonia and she came to get them. I must say she looked lovely. Sort of sparkling, with furs pulled up round her face. She swept in and asked in that ghastly voice for what she called her bokay, and when she saw it was a spray of absolutely heavenly orchids she said: "Quite small, isn't it? Not reely much like flowers, are they?" Everything she'd done and everything she meant at Ancreton seemed to sort of ooze out of her and everything I felt about her suddenly boiled over in me. I'd got a cold and was feeling pretty ghastly, anyway. I absolutely blazed. I said some pretty frightful things about even a common little gold-digger having the decency to be grateful. I said I thought her presence in the house was an insult to all of us, and I supposed that when she'd bamboozled Grandfather into marrying her she'd amuse herself with her frightful boy-friends until he was obliging enough to die and leave her his money. Yes, Mummy, I know it was awful, but it just *steamed* out of me and I couldn't stop it.'

'Oh, my poor Fen!' Jenetta Ancred murmured.

'It's the way she took it that's important,' Fenella continued, still gazing at Alleyn. 'I must admit she took it pretty well. She said, quite calmly, that it was all very fine for me to talk, but I didn't know what it was like to be on my beamends with no chance of getting anywhere in my job. She said she knew she wasn't any good for the stage except as a showgirl, and that didn't last long. I can remember the actual words she used. Fifth-rate theatrical slang. She said: "I know what you all think. You think I'm playing Noddy up for what I can get out of him. You think that when we're married I'll begin to work in some of the funny business. Look, I've had all that, and I reckon I'll be as good a judge as anybody of what's due to my position." And then she said she'd always thought she was the Cinderella type. She said she didn't expect me to understand what a kick she'd get out of being Lady Ancred. She was extraordinarily frank and completely childish about it. She told me she used to lie in bed imagining how she'd give her name and address to people in shops, and what it would sound like when they called her m'lady. "Gee," she said, "will that sound good! Boy, oh boy!" I really think she'd almost forgotten I was there, and the queer thing is that I didn't feel angry with her any longer. She asked me all sorts of questions about precedence; about whether at a dinner-party she'd go in before Lady Baumstein. Benny Baumstein is the frightful little man who owns the Sunshine Circuit shows. She was in one of his No. 3 companies. When I said she would, she said "Yip-ee" like a cow-girl. It was frightful, of course, but it was so completely real that in a way I respected it. She actually said she knew what she called her "accent" wasn't so hot, but she was going to ask "Noddy" to teach her to speak more refined.' Fenella looked from her mother to Paul and shook her head helplessly. 'It was no good,' she said, 'I just succumbed. It was awful, and it was funny, and most of all it was somehow genuinely pathetic.' She turned back to Alleyn: 'I don't know if you can believe that,' she said.

'Very easily,' Alleyn returned. 'She was on the defensive and angry when I saw her, but I noticed something of the same quality myself. Toughness, naivety, and candour all rolled into one. Always very disarming. One meets it occasionally in pickpockets.'

'But in a funny sort of way,' Fenella said, 'I felt that she was honest and had got standards. And much as I loathed the thought of her marriage to Grandfather, I felt sure that according to her lights she'd play fair. And most important of all, I felt that the title meant much more to her than the money. She was grateful and affectionate because he was going to give her the title, and never would she have done anything to prevent him doing so. While I was still gaping at her she took my arm, and believe it or not, we went upstairs together like a couple of schoolgirls. She asked me into her frightful rooms, and I actually sat on the bed while she drenched herself in pre-war scent, repainted her face and dressed for dinner. Then she came along to my room and sat on my bed while I changed. She never left off talking, and I suffered it all in a trance. It really was most peculiar. Down we went, together still, and there was Aunt Milly, howling for the kids' and Grandfather's medicine. We'd left it, of course, in the flower-room, and the queerest thing of all,' Fenella slowly wound up, 'was that, although I still took the gloomiest possible view of her relationship with Grandfather, I simply could *not* continue to loathe her guts. And, Mr Alleyn, I swear she never did anything to harm him. Do you believe me? Is all this as important as Paul and I think it is?'

Alleyn, who had been watching Jenetta Ancred's hands relax and the colour return to her face, roused himself and said: 'It may be of enormous importance. I think you may have tidied up a very messy corner.'

'A messy corner,' she repeated. 'Do you mean – ?'

'Is there anything else?'

'The next part really belongs to Paul. Go on, Paul.'

'Darling,' said Jenetta Ancred, and the two syllables, in her deepish voice, sounded like a reiterated warning. 'Don't you think you've made your point? Must we?'

'Yes, Mummy, we must. Now then, Paul.'

Paul began rather stiffly and with a deprecatory air: 'I'm afraid, sir, that all this is going to sound extremely obvious and perhaps a bit high-falutin, but Fen and I have talked it over pretty thoroughly and we've come to a definite conclusion. Of course it was obvious from the beginning that the letters meant Sonia Orrincourt. She was the only person who didn't get one, and she's the one who benefit-ed most by Grandfather's death. But those letters were written before they found the rat-bane in her suitcase, and, in fact, before there was a shred of evidence against her. So that if she's innocent, and I agree with Fenella that she is, it means one of two things. Either the letter-writer knew something that he or she genuinely thought suspicious, and none of us did know anything of the sort; or, the letter was written out of pure spite, and not to mince matters, with the intention of getting her hanged. If that's so, it seems to me that the tin of rat-bane was deliberately planted. And it seems to me – to Fen and me – that the same person put that book on embalm-ing in the cheese-dish because he was afraid nobody would ever remember it, and was shoving it under our noses in the most start-ling form he could think of.'

He paused and glanced nervously at Alleyn, who said: 'That sounds like perfectly sound reasoning to me.'

'Well, then, sir,' said Paul quickly, 'I think you'll agree that the next point is important. It's about this same damn' silly business with the book in the cheese-dish, and I may as well say at the out-set it casts a pretty murky light on my cousin Cedric. In fact, if we're right, we've got to face the responsibility of practically accusing Cedric of attempted murder.'

'Paul!'

'I'm sorry, Aunt Jen, but we've decided.'

'If you're right, and I'm sure you're wrong, have you thought of the sequel? The newspapers. The beastliness. Have you thought of poor Milly, who dotes on the little wretch?'

'We're sorry,' Paul repeated stubbornly.

'You're inhuman,' cried his aunt and threw up her hands.

'Well,' said Alleyn peaceably, 'let's tackle this luncheon-party while we're at it. What was everybody doing before the book on embalming made its appearance?'

This seemed to nonplus them. Fenella said impatiently: 'Just sit-ting. Waiting for someone to break it up. Aunt Milly does hostess at Ancreton, but Aunt Pauline (Paul's mother) rather feels she ought to when in residence. She – you don't mind my mentioning it Paul, darling? – she huffs and puffs about it a bit, and makes a point of waiting for Aunt Milly to give the imperceptible signal to rise. I rather fancied Aunt Milly kept us sitting for pure devilment. Anyway, there we stuck.'

'Sonia fidgeted,' said Paul, 'and sort of groaned.'

'Aunt Dessy said she thought it would be nice if we could escape having luncheon dishes that looked like the village pond when the floods had subsided. That was maddening for Aunt Milly. She said with a short laugh that Dessy wasn't obliged to stay on at Ancreton.'

'And Dessy,' Paul continued, 'said that to her certain knowledge Milly and Pauline were holding back some tins of whitebait.'

'Everybody began talking at once, and Sonia said: "Pardon me, but how does the chorus go?" Cedric tittered and got up and wandered to the sideboard.'

'And this is our point, sir,' Paul cut in with determination. 'The cheese was found by my cousin Cedric. He went to the sideboard and came back with a book, and dropped it over my mother's shoulder on to her plate. It gave her a shock as you can imagine.'

'She gave a screech and fainted, actually,' Fenella added.

'My Mama,' said Paul unhappily, 'was a bit wrought up by the funeral and so on. She really fainted, Aunt Jen.'

'My dear boy, I'm sure she did.'

'It gave her a fright.'

'Naturally,' Alleyn murmured, 'books on embalming don't fall out of cheese-dishes every day in the week.'

'We'd all,' Paul went on, 'just about *had* Cedric. Nobody paid any attention to the book itself. We merely suggested that it wasn't amazingly funny to frighten people, and that anyway he stank.'

'I was watching Cedric, then,' Fenella said. 'There was something queer about him. He never took his eyes off Sonia. And then, just as we were all herding Aunt Pauline out of the room, he gave one of his yelps and said he'd remembered something in the book. He ran to the door and began reading out of it about arsenic.'

'And then somebody remembered that Sonia had been seen looking at the book.'

'And I'll swear,' Fenella cut in, 'she didn't know what he was driving at. I don't believe she ever really understood. Aunt Dessy did her stuff and wailed and said: "No, no, don't go on! I can't bear it!" and Cedric purred: "But, Dessy, my sweet, what have I said? Why shouldn't darling Sonia read about her fiance's coming embalment?" and Sonia burst into tears and said we were all plotting against her and rushed out of the room.'

'The point is, sir, if Cedric hadn't behaved as he did, nobody would have thought of connecting the book with the suggestion in the letters. You see?'

Alleyn said: 'It's a point.'

'There's something else,' Paul added, again with that tinge of satisfaction in his voice. '*Why* did Cedric look in the cheese-dish?'

'Presumably because he wanted some cheese?'

'No!' Paul said triumphantly. 'That's just where we've got him, sir. He never touches cheese. He detests it.'

'So you see,' said Fenella.

II

When Alleyn left, Paul showed him into the hall, and, after some hesitation, asked if he might walk with him a little way. They went together, head-down against a blustering wind, along Cheyne Walk. Ragged clouds scurried across the sky, and the sounds of river traffic were blown intermittently against their chilled ears. Paul, using his stick, limped along at a round pace, and for some minutes in silence.

At last he said: 'I suppose it's true that you can't escape your heredity.' And as Alleyn turned his head to look at him, he went on slowly: 'I meant to tell you that story quite differently. Without any build-up. Fen did, too. But somehow when we got going something happened to us. Perhaps it was Aunt Jen's opposition. Or perhaps when there's anything like a crisis we can't escape a sense of audience. I heard myself doing the same sort of thing over there.' He jerked his head vaguely towards the east. 'The gay young officer rallying his men. It went down quite well with them, too, but it makes me feel pretty hot under the collar when I think about it now. And about the way we strutted our stuff back there at Aunt Jen's.'

'You made your points very neatly,' said Alleyn.

'A damn' sight too neatly,' Paul rejoined, grimly. 'That's why I did think I'd like to try and say without any flourishes that we do honestly believe that all this stuff about poison has simply been concocted by Cedric to try and upset the Will. And we think it would be a pretty poor show to let him get away with it. On all counts.'

Alleyn didn't reply immediately, and Paul said, nervously: 'I suppose it'd be quite out of order for me to ask whether you think we're right.'

'Ethically,' said Alleyn, 'yes. But I don't think you realized the implications. Your aunt did.'

'I know, Aunt Jen's very fastidious. It's the dirty linen in public that she hates.'

'And with reason,' said Alleyn.

'Well, we'll all have to lump it. But what I meant really was, were we right in our deductions?'

'I ought to return an official and ambiguous answer to that,' Alleyn said. 'But I won't. I may be wrong, but on the evidence that we've got up to date I should say your deductions were ingenious and almost entirely wrong.'

A sharp gust carried away the sound of his voice.

'What?' said Paul, distantly and without emphasis. 'I didn't quite hear – '

'Wrong,' Alleyn repeated, strongly. 'As far as I can judge, you know, quite wrong.'

Paul stopped short, and, dipping his head to meet the wind, stared at Alleyn with an expression not of dismay, but of doubt, as if he still thought he must have misunderstood.

'But I don't see . . . we thought. . . it all hangs together – '

'As an isolated group of facts, perhaps it does.'

They resumed their walk, and Alleyn heard him say fretfully: 'I wish you'd explain.' And after another pause he peered rather anxiously at Alleyn. 'Perhaps it wouldn't do, though,' he added.

Alleyn thought for a moment, and then, taking Paul by the elbow, steered him into the shelter of a side street. 'We can't go on bawling at each other in a gale,' he said, 'but I don't see that it can do any harm to explain this much. It's quite possible that if all this dust had not been raised after your grandfather's death, Miss Orrincourt might still have become Lady Ancred.'

Paul's jaw dropped. 'I don't get that.'

'You don't?'

'Good God,' Paul roared out suddenly, 'you can't mean Cedric?'

'Sir Cedric,' said Alleyn, dryly, 'is my authority. He tells me he has seriously considered marrying her.'

After a long silence Paul said slowly: 'They're as thick as thieves, of course. But I never guessed . . . No, it'd be too much . . . I'm sorry, sir, but you're sure – ?'

'Unless he invented the story.'

'To cover up his tracks,' said Paul instantly.

'Extremely elaborate and she could deny it. As a matter of fact her manner suggested some sort of understanding between them.'

Paul raised his clasped hands to his mouth and thoughtfully blew into them. 'Suppose,' he said, 'he suspected her, and wanted to make sure?'

'That would be an entirely different story.'

'Is that your theory, sir?'

'Theory?' Alleyn repeated vaguely. 'I haven't got a theory. I haven't sorted things out. Mustn't keep you standing here in the cold.' He held out his hand. Paul's was like ice. 'Goodbye,' said Alleyn.

'One minute, sir. Will you tell me this? I give you my word it'll go no further. Was my Grandfather murdered?'

'Oh, yes,' said Alleyn. 'Yes. I'm afraid we may be sure of that. He was murdered.' He walked down the street, leaving Paul, still blowing on his frozen knuckles, to stare after him.

III

The canvas walls were faintly luminous. They were laced to their poles with ropes and glowed in the darkness. Blobs of light from hurricane lanterns suspended within formed a globular pattern across the surface. One of these lanterns must have been touching the wall, for the village constable on duty outside could clearly make out shadows of wire and the precise source of light.

He glanced uneasily at the motionless figure of his companion, a police officer from London, wearing a short cape. 'Bitter cold,' he said.

'That's right.'

'Be long, d'yew reckon?'

'Can't say.'

The constable would have enjoyed a walk. He was a moralist and a philosopher, well known in Ancreton for his pronouncements upon the conduct of politicians and for his independent views in the matter of religion. But his companion's taciturnity, and the uncomfortable knowledge that anything he said would be audible on the other side of the canvas, put a damper on conversation. He stamped once or twice, finding reassurance in the crunch of gravel under his feet. There were noises within the enclosure: voices, soft thumps. At the far end and high above them, as if suspended in the night, and lit theatrically from below, knelt three angels. 'Through the long night watches,' the constable said to himself, 'may Thine angels spread their white wings above me, watching round my head.'

Within the enclosure, but, close beside him, the voice of the Chief Inspector from the Yard said: 'Are we ready, Curtis?' His shadowy figure suddenly loomed up inside the canvas wall. 'Quite ready,' somebody else said. 'Then if I may have the key, Mr Ancred?' 'Oh – oh – er – yes.' That was poor Mr Thomas Ancred.

The constable listened, yet desired not to listen, to the next too-lucid train of sounds. He had heard them before, on the day of the funeral, when he came down early to have a look while his cousin, the sexton, got things fixed up. Very heavy lock. They'd had to give it a drop of oil. Seldom used. His flesh leapt on his bones as a screech rent the cold air. 'Them ruddy hinges,' he thought. The blobs of light were withdrawn and the voices with them. He could still hear them, however, though now they sounded hollow. Beyond the hedge a match flared up in the dark. That would be the driver of the long black car, of course, waiting in the lane. The constable wouldn't have minded a pipe himself.

The Chief Inspector's voice, reflected from stone walls, said distinctly: 'Get those acetylene lamps going, Bailey.' 'Yes, sir,' someone answered, so close to the constable that he jumped again. With a hissing noise, a new brilliance sprang up behind the canvas. Strange distorted shadows leapt among the trees about the cemetery.

Now came sounds to which he had looked forward with squeamish relish. A drag of wood on stone followed by the uneven scuffles of boots and heavy breathing. He cleared his throat and glanced stealthily at his companion.

The enclosure was again full of invisible men. 'Straight down on the trestles. Right.' The squeak of wood and then silence.

The constable drove his hands deep into his pockets and looked up at the three angels and at the shape of St Stephen's spire against the stars. 'Bats in that belfry,' he thought. 'Funny how a chap'll say it, not thinking.' An owl hooted up in Ancreton woods.

Beyond the canvas there was movement. A light voice said jerkily: 'I think, if it doesn't make any difference, I'd like to wait outside. I won't go away. You can call me, you know.'

'Yes, of course.'

A canvas flap was pulled aside, letting out a triangle of light on the grass. A man came out. He wore a heavy overcoat and muffler and his hat was pulled over his face, but the constable had recognized his voice and shifted uneasily.

'Oh, it's you, Bream,' said Thomas Ancred.

'Yes, Mr Thomas.'

'Cold, isn't it?'

'Hard frost before dawn, sir.'

Above them the church clock gave a preparatory whirr and with a sweet voice told two in the morning.

'I don't like this much, Bream.'

'Very upsetting, sir, I'm sure.'

'Terribly upsetting, yes.'

'And yet, sir,' said Bream with a didactic air, 'I been thinking: this here poor remains beant a matter to scare a chap, if rightly considered. It beant your respected father hisself as you might put it, sir. He's well away receiving his reward by now, and what you are called to look upon is a harmless enough affair. No more, if you'll excuse me, than a left-off garment. As has been preached at us souls regular in this very church.'

'I dare say,' said Thomas. 'Nevertheless . . . Well, thank you.'

He moved away down the gravel path. The London officer turned to watch him. Thomas did not move quite out of range of the veiled light. He stood, with his head bent, near the dim shape of a gravestone and seemed to be rubbing his hands together.

'Cold and nervous, poor chap,' Bream said to himself.

'Before we go any further' (that was Chief Inspector Alleyn again), 'will you make a formal examination, Mr Mortimer? We'd like your identification of the name-plate and your assurance that everything is as it was at the time of the funeral.'

A clearing of the throat, a pause and then a muffled voice. 'Perfectly in order. Our own workmanship, Mr Alleyn. Casket and plate.'

'Thank you. All right, Thompson.'

The click of metal and the faint grind of disengaging screws. This seemed to Bream to continue an unconscionable time. Nobody spoke. From his mouth and nostrils and those of the London constable, little jets of breath drifted out and condensed on the frozen air. The London man switched on his flash-lamp. Its beam illuminated Thomas Ancred, who looked up and blinked.

'I'm just waiting,' he said. 'I won't go away.'

'Quite all right, sir.'

'Now,' ordered the voice in the enclosure, 'everything free? Right!'

'Just ease a little, it's a precision fit. That's right. Slide.'

'*Oh, cripes!*' Bream said to himself.

Wood whispered along wood. This sound was followed by complete silence. Thomas Ancred turned away from grass to gravel path and walked aimlessly to and fro.

'Curtis? Will you and Dr Withers – ?'

'Yes. Thanks. Move that light a little this way, Thompson. Will you come here, Dr Withers?'

'The – ah – the process is quite satisfactory, don't you consider, Doctor? Only a short time, of course, but I can assure you there would be no deterioration.'

'Indeed? Remarkable.'

'One is gratified.'

'I think we'll have that bandage taken away, if you please. Fox, will you tell Mr Ancred we're ready for him?'

Bream watched the thick-set Inspector Fox emerge and walk over towards Thomas. Before he had gone more than a few paces there was a sudden and violent ejaculation inside the enclosure. '*Good God, look at that!*' Inspector Fox paused. The Chief Inspector's voice said, very sharply, 'Quiet, Dr Withers, please,' and there followed a rapid whispering.

Inspector Fox moved away and joined Thomas Ancred. 'If you'll come this way, Mr Ancred.' 'Oh! yes, of course. Very good. Right ho!' said Thomas in a high voice, and followed him back to the enclosure. 'If I moved a bit,' Bream thought, 'when they opened the flaps I'd see in.' But he did not move. The London constable held the doorway open, glancing impassively into the tent before he let the canvas fall. The voices began again.

'Now, this is not going to be a very big ordeal, Mr Ancred.'

'Oh, isn't it? Oh, good.'

'Will you – ?'

Bream heard Thomas move. 'There, you see. Quite peaceful.'

'I – yes – I identify him.'

'That's all right, then. Thank you.'

'No,' said Thomas, and his voice rose hysterically, 'it's not all right. There's something all wrong, in fact. Papa had a fine head of hair. Hadn't he, Dr Withers? He was very proud of it, wasn't he? And his moustache. This is bald. *What have they done with his hair?*'

'Steady! Put your head down. You'll be all right. Give me that brandy, Fox, will you? Damn, he's fainted.'

IV

'Well, Curtis,' Alleyn said as the car slid between rows of sleeping houses, 'I hope you'll be able to give us something definite.'

'Hope so,' said Dr Curtis, stifling a heavy yawn.

'I'd like to ask you, Doctor,' said Fox, 'whether you'd expect one fatal dose of arsenic to have that effect.'

'What effect? Oh, the hair. No. I wouldn't. It's more often a symptom of chronic poisoning.'

'In for one of those messes, are we?' Fox grumbled. 'That will be nice. Fields of suspects opened up wide, with the possibility of Miss O. being framed.'

'There are objections to chronic poisoning, Br'er Fox,' Alleyn said. 'He might die when he'd concocted a Will unfavourable to the poisoner. And moreover, you'd expect a progressive loss of hair, not a sudden post-mortem moult. Is that right, Curtis?'

'Certainly.'

'Well, then,' Fox persisted heavily, 'how about the embalming process? Would that account for it?'

'Emphatically not,' Mr Mortimer interjected. 'I've given the Chief Inspector our own formula. An unusual step, but in the circumstances desirable. No doubt, Doctor, he has made you conversant – '

'Oh, yes,' sighed Dr Curtis. 'Formalin. Glycerine. Boric Acid. Menthol. Potassium nitrate. Sodium citrate. Oil of cloves. Water.'

'Precisely.'

'Hey!' said Fox. 'No arsenic?'

'You're two days late with the news, Br'er Fox. Things have moved while you were at Ancreton. Arsenic went out some time ago, didn't it, Mr Mortimer?'

'Formalin,' Mr Mortimer agreed with hauteur, 'is infinitely superior.'

'There now,' Fox rumbled with great satisfaction. 'That does clear things up a bit, doesn't it, Mr Alleyn? If arsenic's found it's got no business to be there. That's something definite. And what's more, any individual who banked on its being used by the embalmer made the mistake of his or her life. Nothing for counsel to muddle the jury with, either. Mr Mortimer's evidence would settle that. Well.'

Alleyn said: 'Mr Mortimer, had Sir Henry any notion of the method used?'

In a voice so drowsy that it reminded Alleyn of the dormouse's, Mr Mortimer said: 'It's very curious, Chief Inspector, that you should ask that question. Oh, very curious. Because, between you and I, the deceased gentleman showed quite an unusual interest. He sent for me and discussed the arrangements for the interment. Two years ago, that was.'

'Good Lord!'

'That is not so unusual in itself. Gentlemen of his position do occasionally give detailed instructions. But the deceased was so very particular. He – well, really,' Mr Mortimer said, coughing slightly, 'he quite read me a little lecture on embalming. He had a little book. Yes,' said Mr Mortimer, swallowing a yawn, 'rather a quaint little book. Very old. It seemed an ancestor of his had been embalmed by the method, *quate* outdated, I may say, outlined in this tainy tome. Sir Henry wished to ascertain if our method was similar. When I ventured to suggest the book was somewhat demode, he became – well, *so* annoyed that it was rather awkward. Very awkward, in fact. He was insistent that we should use the same process on – ah – for – ah – himself. He quate *ordered* me to do it.'

'But you didn't consent?'

'I must confess, Chief Inspector, I – I – the situation was most awkward. I feared he would upset himself seriously. I must confess that I compromaysed. In point of fact, I – '

'You consented?'

'I would have gladly refused the commission altogether but he would take no refusal. He forced me to take the book away with me. I returned it with compliments, and without comment through the registered post. He replied that when the time came I was to understand my instructions. The – ah – the time came and – and – '

'You followed your own method, and said nothing to anybody?'

'It seemed the only thing to do. Anything else was impossible from the point of view of technique. Ridiculous, in fact. Such preposterous ingredients! You can't imagine.'

'Well,' said Fox, 'as long as you can testify there was no arsenic. Eh, Mr Alleyn?'

'I must say,' said Mr Mortimer, 'I don't at all care for the idea of giving evidence in an affair of this sort. Ours is a delicate, and you might say exclusive, profession, Chief Inspector. Publicity of this kind is most undesirable.'

'You may not be subpoenaed, after all,' said Alleyn.

'Not? But I understood Inspector Fox to say – '

'You never know. Cheer up, Mr Mortimer.'

Mr Mortimer muttered to himself disconsolately and fell into a doze.

'What about the cat?' Fox asked. 'And the bottle of medicine?'

'No report yet.'

'We've been busy,' Dr Curtis complained. 'You and your cats! The report should be in some time today. What's all this about a cat anyway?'

'Never you mind,' Alleyn grunted, 'you do your Marsh-Berzelius tests with a nice open mind. And your Fresenius process later on, I shouldn't wonder.'

Dr Curtis paused in the act of lighting his pipe. '*Fresenius* process?' he said.

'Yes, and your ammonium chloride and your potassium iodide and your Bunsen flame and your platinum wire. And look for the pretty green line, blast you!'

After a long silence Dr Curtis said: it's like that, is it?' and glanced at Mr Mortimer.

'It may be like that.'

'Having regard to the general lay-out?'

'That's the burden of our song.'

Fox said suddenly: 'Was he bald when they laid him out?'

'Not he. Mrs Henry Ancred and Mrs Kentish were both present. They'd have noticed. Besides, the hair was there, Fox. We collected it while you were ministering to Thomas.'

'Oh!' Fox ruminated for a time and then said loudly: 'Mr Mortimer! Mr Mortimer!'

'Wha – ?'

'Did you notice Sir Henry's hair when you were working on him?'

'Eh? Oh, yes,' said Mr Mortimer, hurriedly, but in a voice slurred with sleep. 'Yes, indeed. We all remarked on it. A magnificent head of hair.' He yawned hideously. 'A magnificent head of hair,' he repeated.

Alleyn looked at Dr Curtis. 'Consistent?' he asked.

'With your green line? Yes.'

'Pardon?' said Mr Mortimer anxiously.

'All right, Mr Mortimer. Nothing. We're in London. You'll be in bed by daybreak.'

CHAPTER 17

Escape of Miss O.

At breakfast Alleyn said: 'This case of ours is doing the usual snow-ball business, Troy.'

'Gathering up complications as it goes?'

'A mass of murky stuff in this instance. Grubby stuff, and a lot of it waste matter. Do you want an interim report?'

'Only if you feel like making one. And is there enough time?'

'Actually there's not. I can answer a crisp question or two, though, if you care to rap them out at me.'

'You know, I expect, what they'll be.'

'Was Ancred murdered? I think so. Did Sonia Orrincourt do it? I don't know. I shall know, I believe, when the analyst sends in his report.'

'If he finds the arsenic?'

'If he finds it in one place, then I'm afraid it's Sonia Orrincourt. If he finds it in three places, it's Sonia Orrincourt or one other. If he doesn't find it at all, then I *think* it's that other. I'm not positive.'

'And – the one other?'

'I suppose it's no more unpleasant for you to speculate about one than about several.'

'I'd rather know, if it's all right to tell me.'

'Very well,' Alleyn said, and told her.

After a long silence she said: 'But it seems completely unreal. I can't possibly believe it.'

'Didn't everything they did at Ancreton seem a bit unreal?'

463

'Yes, of course. But to imagine that underneath all the showings-off and temperaments *this* could be happening . . . I can't. Of all of them . . . that one!'

'Remember, I may be wrong.'

'You've a habit of not being wrong, though, haven't you?'

'The Yard,' said Alleyn, 'is littered with my blunders. Ask Fox. Troy, is this very beastly for you?'

'No,' said Troy, 'it's mostly bewildering. I didn't form any attachments at Ancreton. I can't give it a personal application.'

'Thank God for that,' he said and went to the Yard.

Here he found Fox in, waiting with the tin of rat-bane. 'I haven't had a chance to hear your further adventures at Ancreton, Foxkin. The presence of Mr Mortimer rather cramped our style last night. How did you get on?'

'Quite nicely, sir. No trouble really about getting the prints. Well, when I say no trouble, there was quite a bit of high-striking in some quarters as was to be expected in that family. Miss O. made trouble, and, for a while, stuck out she wouldn't have it, but I talked her round. Nobody else actually objected, though you'd have thought Mrs Kentish and Miss Desdemona Ancred were being asked to walk into the condemned cell, the way they carried on. Bailey got down by the early train in the morning and worked through the prints you asked for. We found a good enough impression in paint on the wall of Mrs Alleyn's tower. Miss O. all right. *And* her prints are in the book. Lots of others too, of course. Prints all over the cover, from when they looked at it after it turned up in the cheese-dish, no doubt. I've checked up on the letters, but there's nothing in it. They handed them round and there you are. Same thing in the flower-room. Regular mess of prints and some odds and ends where they'd missed sweeping. Coloured tape off florist's boxes, leaves and stalks, scraps of sealing-wax, fancy paper and so on. I've kept all of it in case there was anything. I took a chance to slip into Miss O.'s room. Nothing beyond some skittish literature and a few letters from men written before Sir Henry's day. One, more recent, from a young lady. I memorized it. "Dear S. Good for you, kid, stick to it, and don't forget your old pals when you're Lady A. Think the boy friend'd do anything for me in the business? God knows, I'm not so hot on this Shakespeare, but he must know other managements. Does he wear bed-socks? Regards Clarrie."'

'No mention of the egregious Cedric?'

'Not a word. We looked at Miss Abie's cupboard Only her own prints. I called in at Mr Juniper's. He says the last lot of that paper was taken up with some stuff for the rest of the house a fortnight ago. Two sets of prints on the bell-push from Sir Henry's room – his own and old Barker's. Looks as if Sir Henry had grabbed at it, tried to use it and dragged it off.'

'As we thought.'

'Mr Juniper got in a great way when I started asking questions. I went very easy with him, but he made me a regular speech about how careful he is and showed me his books. He reckons he always double-checks everything he makes up. He's particularly careful, he says, because of Dr Withers being uncommonly fussy. It seems they had a bit of a row. The doctor reckoned the kids' medicine wasn't right, and Juniper took it for an insult. He says the doctor must have made the mistake himself and tried to save his face by turning round on him. He let on the doctor's a bit of a lad and a great betting man, and he thinks he'd been losing pretty solidly and was worried, and made a mistake weighing the kids or something. But that wouldn't apply to Sir Henry's medicine, because it was the mixture as before. And I found out that at the time he made it up he was out of arsenic and hasn't got any yet.'

'Good for Mr Juniper,' said Alleyn dryly.

'Which brings us,' Fox continued, 'to this tin.' He laid his great hand beside it on the desk. 'Bailey's gone over it for dabs. And here we have got something, Mr Alleyn, and about time too, you'll be thinking. Now this tin has got the usual set of prints. Some of the search party's, in fact. Latent, but Bailey brought them up and got some good photographs. There's Mrs Kentish's. She must have just touched it. Miss Desdemona Ancred seems to have picked it up by the edge. Mr Thomas Ancred grasped it more solidly round the sides and handled it again when he took it out of his bag. Mrs Henry Ancred held it firmly towards the bottom. Sir Cedric's prints are all over it, and there, you'll notice, are the marks round the lid where he had a shot at opening it.'

'Not a very determined shot.'

'No. Probably scared of getting rat-bane on his manicure,' said Fox. 'But the point is, you see – '

'No Orrincourt?'

'Not a sign of her. Not a sign of glove-marks either. It was a dusty affair, and the dust, except for the prints we got, wasn't disturbed.'

'It's a point. Well, Fox, now Bailey's finished with it we can open it.'

The lid was firm and it took a penny and considerable force to prise it up. An accretion of the contents had sealed it. The tin was three-parts full, and the greyish paste bore traces of the implement that had been used to scoop it out.

'We'll have a photo-micrograph of this,' Alleyn said.

'If Orrincourt's our bird, sir, it looks as if we'll have to hand the tin over to the defence, doesn't it?'

'We'll have to get an expert's opinion, Fox. Curtis's boys can speak up when they've finished the job in hand. Pray continue, as the Immortal used to say, with your most interesting narrative.'

'There's not much more. I took a little peep at the young baronet's room, too. Dunning letters, lawyer's letters, letters from his stock-broker. I should say he was in deep. I've made a note of the princi-pal creditors.'

'For an officer without a search warrant you seem to have got on very comfortably.'

'Isabel helped. She's taken quite a fancy for investigation. She kept a lookout in the passage.'

'With parlour-maids,' Alleyn said, 'you're out on your own. A masterly technique.'

'I called on Dr Withers yesterday afternoon and told him you'd decided on the exhumation.'

'How did he take it?'

'He didn't say much but he went a queer colour. Well, naturally. They never like it. Reflection on their professional standing and so on. He thought a bit and then said he'd prefer to be present. I said we'd expect that, anyway. I was just going when he called me back. "Here!" he said, kind of hurriedly and as if he wasn't sure he might not be making a fool of himself; "you don't want to pay too much attention to anything that idiot Juniper may have told you. The man's an ass." As soon as I was out of the house,' said Fox, 'I made a note of that to be sure the words were correct. The maid was show-ing me out at the time.'

'Curtis asked him last night, after we'd tithed up in the cemetery, if he'd like to come up and watch the analysis. He agreed. He's sticking to it that the embalmers must have used something that caused the hair to fall out. Mr Mortimer was touched to the professional quick, of course.'

'It's a line defending counsel may fancy,' said Fox gloomily.

The telephone rang and Fox answered it.

'It's Mr Mortimer,' he said.

'Oh, Lord! You take it, Fox.'

'He's engaged at the moment, Mr Mortimer. Can I help you?'

The telephone cackled lengthily and Fox looked at Alleyn with bland astonishment. 'Just a moment.' He laid down the receiver. 'I don't follow this. Mr Alleyn hasn't got a secretary.'

'What's all this?' said Alleyn sharply.

Fox clapped his hand over the receiver. 'He says your secretary rang up their office half an hour ago and asked them to repeat the formula for embalming. His partner, Mr Loame, answered. He wants to know if it was all right.'

'Did Loame give the formula?'

'Yes.'

'Bloody fool,' Alleyn said violently. 'Tell him it's all wrong and ring off.'

'I'll let Mr Alleyn know,' said Fox, and hung up the receiver. Alleyn reached for it and pulled the telephone towards him.

'Ancreton, 2A,' he said. 'Priority. Quick as you can.' And while he waited: 'We may want a car at once, Fox. Ring down, will you? We'll take Thompson with us. And we'll need a search warrant.' Fox went into the next room and telephoned. When he returned Alleyn was speaking. 'Hallo. May I speak to Miss Orrincourt? . . . Out? . . . When will she be in? . . . I see. Get me Miss Able, Barker, will you? . . . It's Scotland Yard here.' He looked round at Fox. 'We'll be going.' he said. 'She came up to London last night and is expected back for lunch. Damn! Why the hell doesn't the Home Office come to light with that report? We need it now, and badly. What's the time?'

'Ten to twelve, sir.'

'Her train gets in at twelve. We haven't an earthly . . . Hallo! Hallo! Is that you, Miss Able? . . . Alleyn here. Don't answer anything but yes or no, please. I want you to do something that is urgent and important. Miss Orrincourt is returning by the train that arrives at midday. Please find out if any one has left to meet her. If not, make some excuse for going yourself in the pony-cart. If it's too late for that, meet it when it arrives at the house. Take Miss Orrincourt into your part of the house and keep her there. Tell her I said so and take no refusal. It's urgent. She's not to go into the other part of the house. Got that? . . . Sure? . . . Right. Splendid. Goodbye.'

He rang off, and found Fox waiting with his overcoat and hat. 'Wait a bit,' he said. 'That's not good enough.' And turned back to the telephone. 'Get me Camber Cross Police Station. They're the nearest to Ancreton, aren't they, Fox?'

'Three miles. The local PC lives in Ancreton parish, though. On duty last night.'

'That's the chap, Bream . . . Hallo! . . . Chief Inspector Alleyn, Scotland Yard. Is your chap Bream in the station? . . . Can you find him?. . . Good! The Ancreton pub. I'd be much obliged if you'd ring through. Tell him to go at once to Ancreton Halt. A Miss Orrincourt will get off the midday train. She'll be met from the Manor House. He's to let the trap go away without her, take her to the pub, and wait there for me. Right! Thanks.'

'Will he make it?' Fox asked.

'He has his dinner at the pub and he's got a bike. It's no more than a mile and a half. Here we go, Fox. If, in the ripeness of time, Mr Loame is embalmed by his own firm, I hope they make a mess of him. What precisely did this bogus secretary say?'

'Just that you'd told him to get a confirmation of the formula. It was a toll-call, but, of course, Loame thought you were back at Ancreton.'

'And so he tells poor old Ancred's killer that there was no arsenic used in the embalming and blows our smoke-screen to hell. As Miss O. would say, what a pal! Where's my bag? Come on.'

But as they reached the door the telephone rang again.

'I'll go,' Alleyn said. 'With any luck it's Curtis.'

It was Dr Curtis. 'I don't know whether you'll like this,' he said. 'It's the Home Office report on the cat, the medicine and the deceased. First analysis completed. No arsenic anywhere.'

'Good!' said Alleyn. 'Now tell them to try for thallium acetate, and ring me at Ancreton when they've found it.'

II

They were to encounter yet another interruption. As they went out to the waiting car, they found Thomas, very white and pinched, on the bottom step.

'Oh, hallo,' he said. 'I was coming to see you. I want to see you awfully.'

'Important?' Alleyn said.

'To me,' Thomas rejoined with the air of innocence, 'it's as important as anything. You see, I came in by the morning train on purpose. I felt I had to. I'm going back this evening.'

'We're on our way to Ancreton now.'

'Really? Then I suppose you wouldn't . . . ? Or shouldn't one suggest it?'

'We can take you with us. Certainly,' said Alleyn after a fractional pause.

'Isn't that lucky?' said Thomas wistfully and got into the back seat with them. Detective-Sergeant Thompson was already seated *by* the driver. They drove away in a silence lasting so long that Alleyn began to wonder if Thomas, after all, had nothing to say. At last, however, he plunged into conversation with an abruptness that startled his hearers.

'First of all,' said Thomas loudly, 'I want to apologize for my behaviour last night. Fainting! Well! I thought I left that kind of thing to Pauline. Everybody was so nice, too. The doctors and you,' he said, smiling wanly at Fox, 'driving me home and everything. I couldn't be more sorry.'

'Very understandable, I'm sure,' said Fox comfortably. 'You'd had a nasty shock.'

'Well, I had. Frightful, really. And the worst of it is, you know, I can't shake it off. When I *did* go to sleep it was so beastly. The dreams. And this morning with the family asking questions.'

'You said nothing, of course,' said Alleyn.

'You'd asked me not to, so I didn't, but they took it awfully badly. Cedric was quite furious, and Pauline said I was siding against the family. The point is, Alleyn, I honestly don't think I can stand any more. It's unlike me,' said Thomas. 'I must have a temperament after all. Fancy!'

'What exactly do you want to see us about?'

'I want to know. It's the uncertainty. I want to know why Papa's hair had fallen out. I want to know if he was poisoned and if you think Sonia did it. I'm quite discreet, really, and if you tell me I'll give you my solemn word of honour not to say anything. Not even to Caroline Able, though I dare say she could explain why I feel so peculiar. I want to know.'

'Everything from the beginning?'

'Yes, if you don't mind. Everything.'

'That's a tall order. We don't know everything. We're trying, very laboriously, to piece things together, and we've got, I think, almost the whole pattern. We believe your father was poisoned.'

Thomas rubbed the palms of his hands across the back of the driver's seat. 'Are you certain? That's horrible.'

'The bell-push in his room had been manipulated in such a way that it wouldn't ring. One of the wires had been released. The bell-push hung by the other wire and when he grasped it the wooden end came away in his hand. We started from there.'

'That seems a simple little thing.'

'There are lots of more complicated things. Your father made two Wills, and signed neither of them until the day of his Birthday party. The first he signed, as I think he told you, before the dinner. The second and valid one he signed late that night. We believe that Miss Orrincourt and your nephew Cedric were the only two people, apart from his solicitor, who knew of this action. She benefited greatly by the valid Will. He lost heavily.'

'Then why bring him into the picture?' Thomas asked instantly.

'He won't stay out. He hovers. For one thing, he and Miss Orrincourt planned all the practical jokes.'

'Goodness! But Papa's death wasn't a practical joke. Or was it?'

'Indirectly, it's just possible that it was caused by one. The final practical joke, the flying cow on the picture, probably caused Sir Henry to fix on the second draft.'

'I don't know anything about all that,' Thomas said dismally. 'I don't understand. I hoped you'd just tell me if Sonia did it.'

'We're still waiting for one bit of the pattern. Without it we can't be positive. It would be against one of our most stringent rules for me to name a suspect to an interested person when the case is still incomplete.'

'Well, couldn't you behave like they do in books? Give me a pointer or two?'

Alleyn raised an eyebrow and glanced at Fox. 'I'm afraid,' he said, 'that without a full knowledge of the information our pointers wouldn't mean very much.'

'Oh, dear! Still, I may as well hear them. Anything's better than this awful blank worrying. I'm not quite such a fool,' Thomas added, 'as I dare say I seem. I'm a good producer of plays. I'm used to analysing character and I've got a great eye for a situation. When I read the script of a murder play I always know who did it.'

'Well,' Alleyn said dubiously, 'here, for what they're worth, are some relative bits of fact. The bell-push. The children's ringworm. The fact that the anonymous letters were written on the children's school paper. The fact that only Sir Cedric and Miss Orrincourt knew your father signed the second Will. The book on embalming. The nature of arsenical poisoning, and the fact that none has been found in his body, his medicine, or in the body of his cat.'

'Carabbas? Does he come in? That *is* surprising. Go on.'

'His fur fell out, he was suspected of ringworm and destroyed. He had not got ringworm. The children had. They were dosed with a medicine that acts as a depilatory and their fur did *not* fall out. The cat was in your father's room on the night of his death.'

'And Papa gave him some hot milk as usual. I see.'

'The milk was cleared away and the Thermos scalded out and used afterwards. No chemical analysis was possible. Now, for the tin of rat-bane. It was sealed with an accretion of its content and had not been opened for a very long time.'

'So Sonia didn't put arsenic in the Thermos?'

'Not out of the tin, at any rate.'

'Not at all, if it wasn't – if – '

'Not at all, it seems.'

'And you think that somehow or another he took the Dr Withers ringworm poison.'

'If he did, analysis will show it. We've yet to find out if it does.'

'But,' said Thomas. 'Sonia brought it back from the chemist's. I remember hearing something about that.'

'She brought it, yes, together with Sir Henry's medicine. She put the bottles in the flower-room. Miss Fenella Ancred was there and left the room with her.'

'And Dr Withers,' Thomas went on, rather in the manner of a child continuing a narrative, 'came up that night and gave the children the medicine. Caroline was rather annoyed because he'd said she could do it. She felt,' Thomas said thoughtfully, 'that it rather reflected on her capability. But he quite insisted and wouldn't let her touch it. And then, you know, it didn't work. They should have been as bald as eggs, but they were not. As bald as eggs,' Thomas repeated with a shudder. 'Oh, yes, I see. Papa *was*, of course.'

He remained sitting very upright, with his hands on his knees, for some twenty minutes. The car had left London behind and slipped through a frozen landscape. Alleyn, with a deliberate effort, retraced the history of the case: Troy's long and detailed account, the turgid statements of the Ancreds, the visit to Dr Withers, the scene in the churchyard. What could it have been that Troy knew she had forgotten and believed to be important?

Thomas, with that disconcerting air of switching himself on, broke the long silence.

'Then I suppose,' he said very abruptly and in a high voice, 'that you think either Sonia gave him the children's medicine or one of us did. But we are not at all murderous people. But I suppose you'll say that lots of murderers have been otherwise quite nice quiet people, like the Dusseldorf Monster. But what about motive? You say Cedric knew Papa had signed the Will that cut him out of almost everything, so Cedric wouldn't. On the other hand, Milly didn't know he'd signed a second Will, and she was quite pleased about the first one, really, so *she* wouldn't. And that goes for Dessy too. She wasn't best pleased, but she wasn't much surprised or worried. And I hope you don't think . . . However,' Thomas hurried on, 'we come to Pauline. Pauline might have been very hurt about Paul and Panty and herself, but it was quite true what Papa said. Her husband left her very nicely off and she's not at all revengeful. It's not as if Dessy and Milly or I *wanted* money desperately, and it's not as if Pauline or Panty or Fenella (I'd forgotten Fenella and Jen) are vindictive slayers. They just aren't. And Cedric thought he was all right. And *honestly*,' Thomas ended, 'you can't suspect Barker and the maids.'

'No,' said Alleyn, 'we don't.'

'So it seems you must suspect a person who wanted money very badly and was left some in the first Will. And, of course, didn't much care for Papa. And Cedric, who's the only one who fits, won't do.'

He turned, after making this profound understatement, to fix upon Alleyn a most troubled and searching gaze.

'I think that's a pretty accurate summing up,' Alleyn said.

'Who could it be!' Thomas mused distractedly and added with a sidelong glance: 'But, then, you've picked up all sorts of information which you haven't mentioned.'

'Which I haven't time to mention,' Alleyn rejoined. 'There are Ancreton woods above that hill. We'll stop at the pub.'

PC Bream was standing outside the pub and stepped forward to open the door of the car. He was scarlet in the face.

'Well, Bream,' Alleyn said, 'carried out your job?'

'In a manner of speaking, sir,' said Bream, 'no. Good afternoon, Mr Thomas.'

Alleyn stopped short in the act of getting out. 'What? Isn't she there?'

'Circumstances,' Bream said indistinctly, 'over which I 'ad no control, intervened, sir.' He waved an arm at a bicycle leaning against the pub. The front tyre hung in a deflated festoon about the axle. 'Rubber being not of the best – '

'Where is she?'

'On my arrival, having run one mile and a quarter – '

'Where is she?'

'Hup,' said Bream miserably, 'at the 'ouse.'

'Get in here and tell us on the way.'

Bream wedged himself into one of the tip-up seats and the driver turned the car. 'Quick as you can,' Alleyn said. 'Now, Bream.'

'Having received instructions, sir, by telephone, from the Super at Camber Cross, me having my dinner at the pub, I proceeded upon my bicycle in the direction of Ancreton 'Alt at eleven-fifty a.m.'

'All right, all right,' said Fox. 'And your tyre blew out.'

'At eleven-fifty-one, sir, she blew on me. I inspected the damage, and formed the opinion it was impossible to proceed on my bicycle. Accordingly I ran.'

'You didn't run fast enough, seemingly. Don't you know you're supposed to keep yourself fit in the force?' said Fox severely.

'I ran, sir,' Bream rejoined with dignity, 'at the rate of one mile in ten minutes and arrived at the 'Alt at twelve-four, the train 'aving departed at twelve-one, and the ladies in the pony-carriage being still in view on the road to the Manor.'

'The ladies?' said Alleyn.

'There was two of them. I attempted to attract their attention by raising my voice, but without success. I then returned to the pub, picking up that there cantankerous bike ong rowt.'

Fox muttered to himself.

'I reported by phone to the Super. He give me a blast, and said he would ring the Manor and request the lady in question to return. She 'as not done so.'

'No,' Alleyn said. 'I imagine she'd see him damned first.'

The car turned in at the great entrance and climbed through the woods. Half-way up the drive they met what appeared to be the entire school, marching and singing under the leadership of Miss Caroline Able's assistant. They stood aside to let the car pass. Alleyn could not see Panty among them.

'Not their usual time for a walk,' said Thomas.

The car drew up at last into the shadow of the enormous house.

'If nothing else has gone cock-eyed,' Alleyn said, 'she'll be in the school.'

Thomas cried out in alarm: 'Are you talking about Caroline Able?'

'No. See here, Ancred. We're going into the school. There's a separate entrance back there, and we'll use it. Will you go into this part of the house and please say nothing about our arrival?'

'Well, all right,' said Thomas, 'though I must say I don't quite see – '

'It's all very confusing. Away you go.'

They watched Thomas walk slowly up the steps, push open the great door, and pause for a second in the shadowy lobby. Then he turned and the door closed between them.

'Now, Fox,' Alleyn said, 'you and I will go into the school. I think the best thing we can do is to ask her to come back with us to London and make a statement. Awkward if she refuses, but if she does we'll have to take the next step. Drive back to the end of the building there.'

The car was turned, and stopped again at a smaller door in the west wing. 'Thompson, you and Bream wait back there in the car. If we want you, we'll get you. Come on, Fox.'

They got out. The car moved away. They had turned to the doorway when Alleyn heard his name called. Thomas was coming down the steps from the main entrance. He ran towards them, his coat flapping, and waved his arm.

'Alleyn! *Alleyn!* Stop!'

'*Now* what?' Alleyn said.

Thomas was breathless when he reached them. He laid his hands on the lapels of Alleyn's coat. His face was colourless and his lips shook. 'You've got to come,' he said. 'It's frightful. Something frightful's happened. Sonia's in there, horribly ill. Withers says she's been poisoned. He says she's going to die.'

CHAPTER 18

The Last Appearance of Miss O.

They had carried her into a small bedroom in the school.

When Alleyn and Fox, accompanied as far as the door by Thomas, walked unheralded into the room, they found Dr Withers in the act of turning Pauline and Desdemona out of it. Pauline appeared to be in an advanced state of hysteria.

'*Out*, both of you. At once, please. Mrs Ancred and I can do all that is necessary. And Miss Able.'

'A curse. That's what I feel. There's a curse upon this house. That's what it is, Dessy.'

'Out, I say. Miss Ancred, take this note. I've written it clearly. Ring up my surgery and tell them to send the things up immediately the car arrives. Can your brother drive my car? Very well.'

'There's a man and a car outside,' Alleyn said. 'Fox, take the note, will you?'

Pauline and Desdemona, who had backed before the doctor to the door, turned at the sound of Alleyn's voice, uttered incoherent cries, and darted past him into the passage. Fox, having secured the note, followed them.

'What the hell are you doing here!' Dr Withers demanded. 'Get out!' He glared at Alleyn and turned back to the bed. Millamant Ancred and Caroline Able were stooped above it, working, it seemed with difficulty, over something that struggled and made harsh inhuman noises. A heavy stench hung in the air.

'Get the clothes away, but put that other thing on her. Keep her covered as far as possible. That's right. Take my coat, Mrs Ancred,

476

please; I can't do with it. Now, we'll try the emetic again. Careful! Don't let me break the glass.'

Miss Able moved away with an armful of clothes. Millamant stood back a little, holding the doctor's jacket, her hands working nervously.

There, on a child's bed with a gay counterpane, Sonia Orrincourt strained and agonized, the grace of her body distorted by revolt and the beauty of her face obliterated in pain. As Alleyn looked at her, she arched herself and seemed to stare at him. Her eyes were blood-shot; one lid drooped and fluttered and winked. One arm, like that of a mechanical toy, repeatedly jerked up its hand to her forehead in a reiterated salaam.

He waited, at the end of the room, and watched. Dr Withers seemed to have forgotten him. The two women after a startled glance turned again to their task. The harsh cries, the straining and agonizing, rose in an intolerable crescendo.

'I'm going to give a second injection. Keep the arm still, if you can. Very well, then, get that thing out of the way. Now.'

The door opened a fraction. Alleyn moved to it, saw Fox and slipped through.

'Our chap ought to be back any minute with the doctor's gear,' Fox muttered.

'Have you rung for Dr Curtis and Co.?'

'They're on the way.'

'Thompson and Bream still on the premises?'

'Yes, sir.'

'Bring them in. Keep the servants in their own quarters. Shut up any rooms she's been in since she got here. Herd the family togeth-er and keep them together.'

'That's all been fixed, Mr Alleyn. They're in the drawing-room.'

'Good. I don't want to leave her yet.'

Fox jerked his thumb. 'Any chance of a statement?'

'None at the moment, far as I can see. Have you got anything, Fox?'

Fox moved closer to him, and in a toneless bass began to mutter rap-idly: 'She and the doctor and Miss Able had tea together in Miss Able's room. He'd come up to see the kids. She sent the little Kentish girl through to order it. Didn't fancy schoolroom tea. Tea set out for the rest of the family in the dining-room. Second tray brought from the pantry by Barker with tea for one. Second pot brewed by Mrs Kentish in the dining-room. Miss Desdemona put some biscuits on the tray. It was handed over to Miss Panty by Mrs Ancred. Miss Panty brought it back here. Miss O. was taken bad straight away before the other two had touched anything. The little girl was there and noticed everything.'

'Got the tea things?'

'Thompson's got them. Mrs Ancred kept her head and said they ought to be locked up, but in the fluster of getting the patient out the tray was knocked over. She left Mrs Kentish to carry on, but Mrs Kentish took hysterics and Isabel swept it up in the finish. Tea and hot water and broken china all over the shop. We ought to get a trace, though, somewhere, if there's anything. That little girl's sharp, by gum she is.'

Alleyn laid his hand swiftly on Fox's arm. In the room the broken sounds changed into a loud and rapid babbling – 'Ba-ba-ba-ba' – and stopped abruptly. At the same moment the uniformed driver appeared at the far end of the passage carrying a small case. Alleyn met him, took the case, and, motioning to Fox to come after, re-entered the room.

'Here's your case, Dr Withers.'

'All right. Put it down. When you go out, tell those women to get in touch with her people if she's got any. If they want to see her, they'll have to be quick.'

'Fox, will you – ?'

Fox slipped away.

'I said: When you go out,' Dr Withers repeated angrily.

'I'm afraid I must stay. This is a police matter, Dr Withers.'

'I'm perfectly well aware of what's happened. My duty is to my patient, and I insist on the room being cleared.'

'If she should become conscious . . .' Alleyn began, looking at the terrible face with its half-open eyes and mouth.

'If she regains consciousness, which she won't, I'll inform you.' Dr Withers opened the case, glanced up at Alleyn and said fiercely: 'If you don't clear out I'll take the matter up with the Chief Constable.'

Alleyn said briskly: 'That won't do at all, you know. We're both on duty here and here we both stay. Your patient's been given thallium acetate. I suggest that you carry on with the treatment, Dr Withers.'

There was a violent ejaculation from Caroline Able. Millamant said: 'That's the ringworm stuff! What nonsense!'

'How the hell . . .' Dr Withers began, and then: 'Very well. Very well. Sorry. I'm worried. Now, Mrs Ancred, I'll want your help here. Lay the patient – '

Forty minutes later, without regaining consciousness, Sonia Orrincourt died.

II

'The room,' Alleyn said, 'will be left exactly as it is. The police surgeon is on his way and will take charge. In the meantime, you'll all please join the others in the drawing-room. Mrs Ancred, will you and Miss Able go ahead with Inspector Fox?'

'At least, Alleyn,' said Dr Withers, struggling into his jacket, 'you'll allow us to wash up.'

'Certainly. I'll come with you.'

Millamant and Caroline Able, after exchanging glances, raised a subdued outcry. 'You must see . . .' Dr Withers protested.

'If you'll come out, I'll explain.'

He led the way and they followed in silence. Fox came out last and nodded severely to Bream, who was in the passage. Bream moved forward and stationed himself before the door.

Alleyn said: 'It's perfectly clear, I'm sure, to all of you that this is a police matter. She was poisoned, and we've no reason to suppose she poisoned herself. I may be obliged to make a search of the house (here is the warrant), and I must have a search of the persons in it. Until this has been done none of you may be alone. There is a wardress coming by car from London, and you may, of course, wait for her if you wish.'

He looked at the three faces, all of them marked by the same signs of exhaustion, all turned resentfully towards him. There was a long silence.

'Well,' Millamant said at last, with an echo of her old short laugh, 'you *can* search me. The thing I want to do most is sit down. I'm tired.'

'I must say,' Caroline Able began, 'I don't quite – '

'Here!' Dr Withers cut in. 'Will this suit you? I'm these ladies' medical man. Search me and then let them search each other in my presence. Any good?'

'That will do admirably. This room here is vacant, I see. Fox, will you take Dr Withers in?' Without further ado, Dr Withers turned on his heel and made for the open door. Fox followed him in and shut it.

Alleyn turned to the two women. 'We shan't keep you long,' he said, 'but if, in the meantime, you would like to join the others, I can take you to them.'

'Where are they?' Millamant demanded.

'In the drawing-room.'

'Personally,' she said, 'I'm beyond minding who searches me and who looks on.' Bream gave a self-conscious cough. 'If you and Miss Able like to take me into the children's play-room, which I believe is vacant, I shall be glad to get it over.'

'Well, really,' said Miss Able, 'well, of course, that is an extremely sane point of view, Mrs Ancred. Well, if *you* don't object.'

'Good,' Alleyn said. 'Shall we go?'

There was a screen, with Italian primitives pasted over it, in the play-room. The two women, at Alleyn's suggestion, retired behind it. First Millamant's extremely sensible garments were thrown out one by one, examined by Alleyn, collected again by Miss Able, and then, after an interval, the process was reversed. Nothing was discovered, and Alleyn, walking between them, escorted the two ladies to the bathroom, and finally through the green baize door and across the hall to the drawing-room.

Here they found Desdemona, Pauline, Panty, Thomas and Cedric, assembled under the eye of Detective-Sergeant Thompson. Pauline and Desdemona were in tears. Pauline's tears were real and ugly. They had left little traces, like those of a snail, down her carefully restrained make-up. Her eyes were red and swollen and she looked frightened. Desdemona, however, was misty, tragic and still beautiful. Thomas sat with his eyebrows raised to their limit and his hair ruffled, gazing in alarm at nothing in particular. Cedric, white and starded, seemed to be checked, by Alleyn's arrival, in a restless prowl round the room. A paperknife fell from his hands and clattered on the glass top of the curio cabinet.

Panty said: 'Hallo! Is Sonia dead? Why?'

'Ssh, darling! Darling, ssh!' Pauline moaned, and attempted vainly to clasp her daughter in her arms. Panty advanced into the centre of the room and faced Alleyn squarely. 'Cedric,' she said loudly, 'says Sonia's been murdered. Has she? Has she, Miss Able?'

'Goodness,' said Caroline Able in an uneven voice, 'I call that rather a stupid thing to say, Patricia, don't you?'

Thomas suddenly walked up to her and put his arm about her shoulders.

'Has she, Mr Alleyn?' Panty insisted.

'You cut off and don't worry about it,' Alleyn said. 'Are you at all hungry?'

'You bet.'

'Well, ask Barker from me to give you something rather special, and then put your coat on and see if you can meet the others coming home. Is that all right, Mrs Kentish?'

Pauline waved her hands and he turned to Caroline Able.

'An excellent idea,' she said more firmly. Thomas's hand still rested on her shoulder.

Alleyn led Panty to the door. 'I won't go,' she announced, 'unless you tell me if Sonia's dead.'

'All right, old girl, she is.' A multiple ejaculation sounded behind him. 'Like Carabbas?'

'No!' said her Aunt Millamant strongly, and added: 'Pauline, must your child behave like this?'

'They've both gone away,' Alleyn said. 'Now cut along and don't worry about it.'

'I'm not worrying,' Panty said, 'particularly. I dare say they're in Heaven, and Mummy says I can have a kitten. But a person likes to know.' She went out.

Alleyn turned and found himself face to face with Thomas.

Behind Thomas he saw Caroline Able stooping over Millamant, who sat fetching her breath in dry sobs, while Cedric bit his nails and looked on. 'I'm sorry,' Millamant stammered: 'it's just reaction, I suppose. Thank you, Miss Able.'

'You've been perfectly splendid, Mrs Ancred.'

'Oh, Milly, Milly!' wailed Pauline. 'Even you! Even your iron reserve. Oh, Milly!'

'Oh, *God!*' Cedric muttered savagely. 'I'm so *sick* of all this.'

'You,' Desdemona said, and laughed with professional bitterness. 'In less tragic circumstances, Cedric, that would be funny.'

'Please, all of you *stop*.'

Thomas's voice rang out with authority, and the dolorous buzz of reproach and impatience was instantly hushed.

'I dare say you're all upset,' he said. 'So are other people. Caroline is, and I am. Who wouldn't be? But you can't go on flinging temperaments right and left. It's very trying for other people and it gets us nowhere. So I'm afraid I'm going to ask you all to shut up, because I've got something to say to Alleyn, and if I'm right, and he says I'm right, you can all have hysterics and get on with the big scene. But I've got to know.'

He paused, still facing Alleyn squarely, and in his voice and his manner Alleyn heard an echo of Panty. 'A person likes to know,' Panty had said.

'Caroline's just told me,' Thomas said, 'that you think somebody gave Sonia the medicine Dr Withers prescribed for those kids. She says Sonia had tea with her. Well, it seems to me that means somebody's got to look after Caroline, and I'm the person to do it, because I'm going to marry her. I dare say that's a surprise to all of you, but I am, so that's that, and nobody need bother to say anything, please.'

With his back still turned to his dumbfounded family, Thomas, looking at once astonished and determined, grasped himself by the lapels of his coat and continued. 'You've told me you think Papa was poisoned with this stuff and I suppose you think the same person killed Sonia. Well, there's one person who ordered the stuff for the kids and wouldn't let Caroline touch it, and who ordered the medicine for Papa, and who is pretty well known to be in debt, and who was left quite a lot of money by Papa, and who had tea with Sonia. He's not in the room, now,' said Thomas, 'and I want to know where he is, and whether he's a murderer. That's all.'

Before Alleyn could answer, there was a tap on the door and Thompson came in. 'A call from London, for you, sir,' he said. 'Will you take it out here?'

Alleyn went out, leaving Thompson on guard, and the Ancreds still gaping. He found the small telephone-room across the hall, and, expecting a voice from the Yard, was astonished to hear Troy's.

'I wouldn't have done this if it mightn't be important,' said Troy's voice, twenty miles away. 'I telephoned the Yard and they told me you were at Ancreton.'

'Nothing wrong?'

'Not here. It's just that I've remembered what Sir Henry said that morning. When he'd found the writing on his looking-glass.'

'Bless you. What was it?'

'He said he was particularly angry because Panty, he insisted it was Panty, had disturbed two important documents that were on his dressing-table. He said that if she'd been able to understand them she would have realized they concerned her very closely. That's all. Is it anything?'

'It's almost everything.'

'I'm sorry I didn't remember before, Rory.'

'It wouldn't have fitted before. I'll be home tonight. I love you very much.'

'Goodbye.'

'Goodbye.'

When Alleyn came out into the hall, Fox was there waiting for him.

'I've been having a bit of a time with the doctor,' Fox said. 'Bream and our chap are with him now. I thought I'd better let you know, Mr Alleyn.'

'What happened?'

'When I searched him I found this in his left-hand side pocket.' Fox laid his handkerchief on the hall table and opened it out, disclosing a very small bottle with a screw top. It was almost empty. A little colourless fluid lay at the bottom.

'He swears,' said Fox, 'that he's never seen it before, but it was on him all right.'

Alleyn stood looking at the little phial for a long moment. Then he said: 'I think this settles it, Fox. I think we'll have to take a risk.'

'Ask a certain party to come up to the Yard?'

'Yes. And hold a certain party while this stuff is analysed. But there's no doubt in my mind about it, Fox. It'll be thallium acetate.'

'I'll be glad to make this arrest,' said Fox heavily, 'and that's a fact.'

Alleyn did not answer, and after another pause Fox jerked his head at the drawing-room door. 'Shall I – ?'

'Yes.'

Fox went away and Alleyn waited alone in the hall. Behind the great expanse of stained-glass windows there was sunlight. A patchwork of primary colours lay across the wall where Henry Ancred's portrait was to have hung. The staircase mounted into shadows, and out of sight, on the landing, a clock ticked. Above the enormous fireplace, the fifth baronet pointed his sword complacently at a perpetual cloudburst. A smouldering log settled with a whisper on the hearth, and somewhere, away in the servants' quarters, a voice was raised and placidly answered.

The drawing-room door opened, and with a firm step, and a faint meaningless smile on her lips, Millamant Ancred came out and crossed the hall to Alleyn.

'I believe you wanted me,' she said.

CHAPTER 19

Final Curtain

'It was the mass of detail,' Troy said slowly, 'that muddled me at first. I kept trying to fit the practical jokes into the pattern and they wouldn't go.'

'They fit,' Alleyn rejoined, 'but only because she used them after the event.'

'I'd be glad if you'd sort out the essentials, Rory.'

'I'll try. It's a case of maternal obsession. A cold, hard woman, with a son for whom she has a morbid adoration. Miss Able would tell you all about that. The son is heavily in debt, loves luxury, and is intensely unpopular with his relations. She hates them for that. One day, in the ordinary course of her duties, she goes up to her father-in-law's room. The drafts of two Wills are lying on the dressing-table. One of them leaves her son, who is his heir, more than generous means to support his title and property. The other cuts him down to the bare bones of the entailed estate. Across the looking-glass someone has scrawled "Grandfather is a bloody old fool." As she stands there, and before she can rearrange the papers, her father-in-law walks in. He immediately supposes, and you may be sure she shares and encourages the belief that his small granddaughter, with a reputation for practical jokes, is responsible for the insulting legend. Millamant is a familiar figure in his room, and he has no cause to suspect her of such an idiotic prank. Still less does he suspect the real perpetrator, her son Cedric Ancred, who has since admitted that this was one of a series of stunts designed by himself and Sonia Orrincourt to set the old man against Panty, hitherto his favourite.

'Millamant Ancred leaves the room with the memory of those two drafts rankling in her extremely tortuous mind. She knows the old man changes his Will as often as he loses his temper. Already Cedric is unpopular. Some time during the next few days, perhaps gradually, perhaps in an abrupt access of resentment, an idea is born to Millamant. The Will is to be made public at the Birthday dinner. Suppose the one that is favourable to Cedric is read, how fortunate if Sir Henry should die before he changes his mind! And if the dinner is rich, and he, as is most probable, eats and drinks unwisely, what more likely than he should have one of his attacks and the that very night? If, for instance, there was tinned crayfish? She orders tinned crayfish.'

'Just – hoping?'

'Perhaps no more than that. What do you think, Fox?'

Fox, who was sitting by the fire with his hands on his knees, said: 'Isabel reckons she ordered it on the previous Sunday when they talked over the dinner.'

'The day after the looking-glass incident. And on the following Monday evening, the Monday before the Birthday when Cedric and Paul and his mother were all out, Millamant Ancred went into the flower-room and found a large bottle of medicine marked "Poison" for the school children, and another smaller bottle for Sir Henry. The bottles had been left on the bench by Sonia Orrincourt, who had joined Fenella Ancred there and had gone upstairs with her and had never been alone in the flower-room.'

'And I,' Troy said, 'was putting the trap away and coming in by the east wing door. If . . . Suppose I'd let Sonia do that and taken the medicine into the school – '

'If you'll excuse my interrupting you, Mrs Alleyn,' Fox said, 'it's our experience that, when a woman makes up her mind to turn poisoner, nothing will stop her.'

'He's right, Troy.'

'Well,' said Troy, 'go on.'

'She had to chip away the chemist's sealing-wax before she got the corks out, and Fox found bits of it on the floor and some burnt matches. She had to find another bottle for her purpose. She emptied Sir Henry's bottle, filled it up with thallium, and in case of failure, poured the remainder into her own small phial. Then she filled the children's bottle with water and re-corked and re-sealed both Mr Juniper's bottles. When Miss Able came in for the children's medicine she and Millamant hunted everywhere for it. It was not found until Fenella came downstairs, and who was more astonished than Millamant to learn that Sonia had so carelessly left the medicine in the flower-room?'

'But suppose,' Troy said, 'he'd wanted the medicine before she knew about the Will?'

'There was the old bottle with a dose still in it. I fancy she removed that one some time during the Birthday. If a Will unfavourable to Cedric had been made public, that bottle would have been replaced and the other kept for a more propitious occasion. As it was, she saw to it that she was never alone from dinner until the next morning. Barker beat on the door of the room she shared with Desdemona. She had talked to Desdemona, you remember, until three o'clock – well after the time of Sir Henry's death. She built herself up a sort of emergency alibi with the same elaborate attention which she gives to that aimless embroidery of hers. In a way this led to her downfall. If she'd risked a solitary trip along those passages that night to Cedric's room she would have heard, no doubt, that Sir Henry had signed the second Will, and she would have made a desperate attempt to stop him taking his medicine.'

'Then she didn't mean at that time to throw suspicion on Sonia?'

'No, indeed. His death would appear to be the natural result of rash eating and pure temper. It was only when the terms of his last Will were made known that she got her second idea.'

'An atrocious idea.'

'It was all of that. It was also completely in character – tortuous and elaborate. Sonia had come between Cedric and the money. Very well, Sonia must go and the second Will be set aside. She remembered that she had found Sonia reading it. She remembered the rat-bane with its printed antidote to arsenical poisoning. So, the anonymous letters printed on the kids' paper she herself fetched from the village, appeared on the breakfast table. A little later, as nobody seemed to have caught on the right idea, the book on embalming appeared on the cheese-dish, and finally the tin of rat-bane appeared in Sonia's suitcase. At about this time she got a horrible jolt.'

'The cat,' said Fox.

'Carabbas!' Troy ejaculated.

'Carabbas had been in Sir Henry's room. Sir Henry had poured out milk for him. But the bottle of medicine had overturned into the saucer and presently Carabbas began to lose his fur. No wonder. He'd lapped up thallium acetate, poor chap. Millamant couldn't stand the sight of him about the house. He was one too much for her iron nerve. Accusing him of ringworm, and with the hearty consent of every one but Panty, she had him destroyed.

'She sat back awaiting events and unobtrusively jogging them along. She put the tin of arsenical rat-bane in Sonia Orrincourt's suitcase and joined in the search for it. She declared that it had been a full tin, but the servants disagreed. She forgot, however, to ease the lid, which was cemented in with the accretion of years.'

'But to risk everything and plan everything on the chance that arsenic was used by the embalmers!' Troy exclaimed.

'It didn't seem like a chance. Sir Henry had ordered Mortimer and Loame to use it, and Mr Mortimer had let him suppose they would do so. Her nerve went a bit, though, after the exhumation. She rang up the embalmers, using, no doubt, the deepest notes of her masculine voice, and said she was my secretary. Loame, the unspeakable ass, gave her their formula. That must have been a bitter moment for Millamant. Cedric's only means of avoiding financial ruin was by marrying the woman she loathed and against whom she had plotted; and now she knew that the frame-up against Sonia Orrincourt was no go. She didn't know, however, that we considered thallium acetate a possible agent and would look for it. She'd kept the surplus over from the amount she could not get into Sir Henry's bottle and she waited her chance. Sonia could still be disposed of; Cedric could still get the money.'

'She must be mad.'

'They're like that, Mrs Alleyn,' Fox said. 'Female poisoners behave like that. Always come at it a second time, and a third and fourth, too, if they get the chance.'

'Her last idea,' Alleyn said, 'was to throw suspicion on Dr Withers, who's a considerable beneficiary in both Wills. She put thallium in the milk when the tea-tray was sent in to Miss Able, knowing Withers and Sonia Orrincourt were there and knowing Sonia was the only one who took milk. A little later she slipped the bottle into Withers's jacket. With Sonia dead, she thought, the money would revert after all to Cedric.'

'Very nasty, you know,' Fox said mildly. 'Very nasty case indeed, wouldn't you say?'

'Horrible,' Troy said under her breath.

'And yet, you know,' Fox went on, 'it's a guinea to a gooseberry she only gets a lifer. What do you reckon, sir?'

'Oh, yes,' Alleyn said, looking at Troy. 'It'll be that if it's not an acquittal.'

'But surely – ' Troy began.

'We haven't got an eye-witness, Mrs Alleyn, to a single action that would clinch the case. Not one.' Fox got up slowly. 'Well, if you'll excuse me. It's been a long day.'

Alleyn saw him out. When he returned, Troy was in her accustomed place on the hearthrug. He sat down and after a moment she leant towards him, resting her arm across his knees.

'Nothing is clear-cut,' she said, 'when it comes to one's views. Nothing.' He waited. 'But we're together,' she said. 'Quite together now. Aren't we?'

'Quite together,' Alleyn said.

Swing, Brother, Swing

For Bet who asked for it
And now gets it with my love

Contents

1 Letters   495
2 The Persons Assemble   501
3 Pre-Prandial   516
4 They Dine   534
5 A Wreath for Rivera   551
6 Dope   578
7 Dawn   611
8 Morning   637
9 The Yard   657
10 The Revolver, the Stiletto and his Lordship   680
11 Episodes in Two Flats and an Office   702
12 GPF   721

Cast of Characters

Lord Pastern and Bagott	
Lady Pastern and Bagott	
Félicité de Suze	*Her daughter*
The Hon Edward Manx	*Lord Pastern's second cousin*
Carlisle Wayne	*Lord Pastern's niece*
Miss Henderson	*Companion-Secretary to Lady Pastern*

Spence
Miss Parker
William } *Domestic*
Mary } *staff at*
Myrtle } *Duke's Gate*
Hortense

Breezy Bellairs		
Happy Hart	*Pianist*	*of Breezy*
Sydney Skelton	*Tympanist*	*Bellairs'*
Carlos Rivera	*Piano accordionist*	*Boys*
Caesar Bonn	*Maître de café at* The Metronome	
David Hahn	*His secretary*	
Nigel Bathgate	*Of the Evening Chronicle*	

Dr Allington
Mrs Roderick Alleyn

Chief Detective-Inspector Alleyn		*Of the*
Detective-Inspector Fox		*Criminal*
Dr Curtis		*Investigation*
Detective-Sergeant Bailey	*Fingerprint expert*	*Department,*
Detective-Sergeant Thompson	*Photographer*	*New*
Detective-Sergeants Gibson, Marks, Scott and Sallis		*Scotland Yard*

Sundry policemen, waiters, bandsmen, etc.

CHAPTER 1

Letters

From Lady Pastern and Bagott to her niece by marriage, Miss Carlisle Wayne:

3 DUKE'S GATE,
EATON PLACE,
LONDON. SW1

MY DEAREST CARLISLE, – I am informed with that air of inconsequence which characterizes all your uncle's utterances, of your arrival in England. Welcome Home. You may be interested to learn that I have rejoined your uncle. My motive is that of expediency. Your uncle proposes to give Clochemere to the nation and has returned to Duke's Gate, where, as you may have heard, I have been living for the last five years. During the immediate post-war period I shared its dubious amenities with members of an esoteric Central European sect. Your uncle granted them what I believe colonials would call squatters' rights, hoping no doubt to force me back upon the Cromwell Road or the society of my sister Desirée with whom I have quarrelled since we were first able to comprehend each other's motives.

Other aliens were repatriated, but the sect remained. It will be a sufficient indication of their activities if I tell you that they caused a number of boulders to be set up in the principal

reception room, that their ceremonies began at midnight and
were conducted in antiphonal screams, that their dogma
appeared to prohibit the use of soap and water and that they
were forbidden to cut their hair. Six months ago they
returned to Central Europe (I have never inquired the precise
habitat) and I was left mistress of this house. I had it cleaned
and prepared myself for tranquillity. Judge of my dismay! I
found tranquillity intolerable. I had, it seems, acclimatized
myself to nightly pandemonium. I had become accustomed to
frequent encounters with persons who resembled the minor
and dirtier prophets. I was unable to endure silence, and the
unremarkable presence of servants. In fine, I was lonely.
When one is I lonely, one thinks of one's mistakes. I thought
of your uncle. Is one ever entirely bored by the incomprehensible? I doubt it. When I married your uncle (you will recollect that he was an attaché at your Embassy in Paris and a
frequent caller at my parents' house), I was already a widow,
I was not, therefore, *jeune fille.* I did not demand Elysium.
Equally I did not anticipate the ridiculous. It is understood
that after a certain time one should not expect the impossible
of one's husband. If he is tactful, one remains ignorant. So
much the better. One is reconciled. But your uncle is not tactful. On the contrary, had there been liaisons of the sort which
I trust I have indicated, I should have immediately become
aware of them. Instead of second or possibly third establish-
ments I found myself confronted in turn by Salvation Army
Citadels, by retreats for Indian yogis, by apartments devoted
to the study of Voodoo; by a hundred and one ephemeral and
ludicrous obsessions. Your uncle has turned with appalling
virtuosity from the tenets of Christadelphians, to the practice
of nudism. He has perpetrated antics which, with his increasing years, have become the more intolerable. Had he been
content to play the pantaloon by himself and leave me to
deplore, I should have perhaps been reconciled. On the contrary, he demanded my collaboration.

For example, in the matter of nudism. Imagine me, a de
Fouteaux, suffering a proposal that I should promenade

without costume, behind laurel hedges in the Weald of Kent. It was at this juncture and upon this provocation that I first left your uncle. I have returned at intervals only to be driven away again by further imbecilities. I have said nothing of his temper, of his passion for scenes, of his minor but distressing idiosyncrasies. These failings have, alas, become public property.

Yet, my dearest Carlisle, as I have indicated, we are together again at Duke's Gate. I decided that silence had become intolerable and that I should be forced to seek a flat. Upon this decision came a letter from your uncle. He is now interested in music and has associated himself with a band in which he performs upon the percussion instruments. He wished to use the largest of the reception rooms for practice; in short he proposed to rejoin me at Duke's Gate. I am attached to this house. Where your uncle is, there also is noise and noise has become a necessity for me. I consented.

Félicité, also, has rejoined me. I regret to say I am deeply perturbed on account of Félicité. If your uncle realized, in the smallest degree, his duty as a stepfather, he might exert some influence. On the contrary he ignores, or regards with complacency, an attachment so undesirable that I, her mother, cannot bring myself to write more explicitly of it. I can only beg, my dearest Carlisle, that you make time to visit us. Félicité has always respected your judgement. I hope most earnestly that you will come to us for the first weekend in next month. Your uncle, I believe, intends to write to you himself. 1 join my request to his. It will be delightful to see you again, my dearest Carlisle, and I long to talk to you.

Your affectionate aunt,
CECILE DE FOUTEAUX PASTERN AND BAGOTT

From Lord Pastern and Bagott to his niece, Miss Carlisle Wayne:

> 3 DUKES GATE,
> EATON PLACE,
> LONDON, SW1

DEAR 'LISLE, – I hear you've come back. Your aunt tells me she's asked you to visit us. Come on the third and we'll give you some music.

> Your aunt's living with me again.
>> Your affectionate uncle,
>> GEORGE

From 'The Helping Hand', GPF's page in *Harmony*:

DEAR GPF, – I am eighteen and unofficially engaged to be married. My fiancé is madly jealous and behaves in a manner that I consider more than queer and terribly alarming. I enclose details under separate cover because after all he might read this and then we *should* be in the soup. Also five shillings for a special Personal Chat letter. Please help me.

> 'TOOTS'

Poor Child in Distress, let me help you if I can. Remember I shall speak as a man and that is perhaps well, for the masculine mind is able to understand this strange self-torture that is clouding your fiancé's love for you and making you so unhappy. Believe me, there is only *one* way. You must be patient. You must prove your love by your candour. Do not tire of reassuring him that his suspicions are groundless. Remain tranquil. *Go on loving him*. Try a little gentle laughter but if it is unsuccessful *do not continue*. Never let him think you impatient. A thought. *There are some natures so delicate and sensitive that they must be handled like flowers. They need sun. They must be tended. Otherwise their spiritual growth is checked*. Your Personal Chat letter will reach you tomorrow.

Footnote to GPF's Page. – GPF will write you a very special Personal Chat if you send postal order to 'Personal Chat, *Harmony*, 5 Materfamilias Lane, EC2'

From Miss Carlisle Wayne to Miss Félicité de Suze.

> FRIAR'S PARDON,
> BENHAM,
> BUCKS.

DEAR FÉE, – I've had rather a queer letter from Aunt 'Cile who wants me to come up on the third. What have you been up to?
> LOVE,
> LISLE

From The Hon. Edward Manx to Miss Carlisle Wayne:

> HARROW FLATS,
> SLOANE SQUARE,
> LONDON, SW1

DEAREST LISLE, – Cousin Cecile says you are invited to Duke's Gate for the weekend on Saturday the third. I shall come down to Benham in order to drive you back. Did you know she wants to marry me to Félicité? I'm not at all keen and neither, luckily, is Fée. She's fallen in a big way for an extremely dubious number who plays a piano accordion in Cousin George's band. I imagine there's a full-dress row in the offing *à cause,* as Cousin Cecile would say, *de* the band and particularly *de* the dubious number whose name is Carlos something. They aren't 'alf cups-of-tea are they? Why do you go away to foreign parts? I shall arrive at about 5 p.m. on the Saturday.
> Love,
> NED

From the *Monogram* gossip column:

Rumour hath it that Lord Pastern and Bagott, who is a keen exponent of boogie-woogie, will soon be heard at a certain restaurant 'not a hundred miles from Piccadilly'. Lord Pastern and Bagott who, of course, married Madame de Suze (*née* de Fouteaux), plays the tympani with enormous zest. His band includes such well-known exponents as Carlos Rivera and is conducted by

none other than the inimitable Breezy Bellairs, both of the
Metronome. By the way, I saw lovely Miss Félicité (Fée) de Suze,
Lady Pastern and Bagott's daughter by her first marriage, lunch-
ing the other day at the Tarmarc *à deux* with the Hon Edward
Manx who is, of course, her second cousin on the distaff side.

From Mr Carlos Rivera to Miss Félicité de Suze:

> 102 BEDFORD MANSIONS,
> AUSTERLY SQUARE,
> LONDON, SW 1

LISTEN GLAMOROUS, – You cannot do this thing to me. I am not
an English Honourable This or Lord That to sit complacent
while my woman makes a fool of me. No. With me it is all or
nothing. I am a scion of an ancient house. I do not permit tres-
passers and I am tired. I am very tired indeed, of waiting. I wait
no longer. You announce immediately our engagement or –
finish! It is understood? Adios.
> CARLOS DA RIVERA

Telegram from Miss Félicité de Suze to Miss Carlisle Wayne:

Darling for pity's sake come everything too tricky and peculiar
honestly do come genuine cri de coeur tons of love darling Fée.

Telegram from Miss Carlisle Wayne to Lady Pastern and Bagott:

Thank you so much love to come arriving
about six Saturday 3rd Carlisle.

CHAPTER 2

The Persons Assemble

At precisely 11 o'clock in the morning GPF walked in at a side door of the *Harmony* offices in 5 Materfamilias Lane, EC2. He went at once to his own room. PRIVATE GPF was written in white letters on the door. He unwound the scarf with which he was careful to protect his nose and mouth from the fog, and hung it, together with his felt hat and overcoat, on a peg behind his desk. He then assumed a green eyeshade and shot a bolt in his door. By so doing he caused a notice, ENGAGED, to appear on the outside.

His gas fire was burning brightly and the tin saucer of water set before it to humidify the air, sent up a little drift of steam. The window was blanketed outside by fog. It was as if a yellow curtain had been hung on the wrong side of the glass. The footsteps of passers-by sounded close and dead and one could hear the muffled coughs and shut-in voices of people in a narrow street on a foggy morning. GPF rubbed his hands together, hummed a lively air, seated himself at his desk and switched on his green-shaded lamp. 'Cosy,' he thought. The light glinted on his dark glasses, which he took off and replaced with reading spectacles.

'One, two. Button your boot,' sang GPF in a shrill falsetto and pulled a wire basket of unopened letters towards him. 'Three four, knock on the gate,' he sang facetiously and slit open the top letter. A postal order for five shillings fell out on the desk.

'Dear GPF (he read), – I feel I simply must write and thank you for your *lush* Private Chat letter – which I may as well confess

has rocked me to my foundations. You couldn't be more right
to call yourself Guide, Philosopher and Friend, honestly you
couldn't. I've thought so much about what you've told me and
I can't help wondering what you're *like*. To look at and listen to,
I mean. I think your voice must be rather deep ('Oh, Crumbs!'
GPF murmured), and I'm sure you are tall. I wish – '

He skipped restlessly through the next two pages and
arrived at the peroration: 'I've tried madly to follow your
advice but my young man really is! I can't help thinking that
it would be immensely energizing to talk to you. I mean really *talk*. But I suppose that's hopelessly out of bounds, so I'm
having another five bob's worth of Private Chat.' GPF followed
the large flamboyant script and dropped the pages, one by one,
into a second wire basket. Here at last, was the end. 'I suppose
he would be madly jealous if he knew I had written to you like
this but I just felt I had to.

　　　　'Yours gratefully,
　　　　　"Toots" '

GPF reached for his pad of copy paper, gazed for a moment in a
benign, absent manner at the fog-blinded window and then fell to.
He wrote with great fluency, sighing and muttering under his breath.
　'Of course I am happy,' he began, 'to think that I have helped.' The
phrases ran out from his pencil '– you must think of GPF as a friendly
ghost – write again if you will – more than usually interested – best
of luck and my blessing –' When it was finished he pinned the postal
note to the top sheet and dropped the whole in a further basket
which bore the legend 'Personal Chat'.
　The next letter was written in a firm hand on good notepaper.
GPF contemplated it with his head on one side, whistling between
his teeth.

'The writer (it said) is fifty years old and has recently consented
to rejoin her husband who is fifty-one. He is eccentric to the
verge of lunacy but, it is understood, not actually certifiable. A
domestic crisis has arisen in which he refuses to take the one
course compatible with his responsibilities as a stepfather. In a
word, my daughter contemplates a marriage that from every

point of view, but that of unbridled infatuation, is disastrous. If further details are required I am prepared to supply them, but the enclosed cuttings from newspapers covering a period of sixteen years will, I believe, speak for themselves. I do not wish this communication to be published, but enclose a five shilling postal order which I understand will cover a letter of personal advice.

    'I am , etc.,

      'CECILE DE FOUTEAUX PASTERN AND BAGOTT'

GPF dropped the letter deliberately and turned over the sheaf of paper clippings. 'PEER SUED FOR KIDNAPPING STEPDAUGHTER,' he read. 'PEER PRACTISES NUDISM.' 'SCENE IN MAYFAIR COURTROOM.' 'LORD PASTERN AGAIN.' LADY PASTERN AND BAGOTT SEEKS DIVORCE.' 'PEER PREACHES FREE LOVE.' 'REBUKE FROM JUDGE.' 'LORD PASTERN NOW GOES YOGI.' ' "BOOGIE-WOOGIE PEER." ' 'INFINITE VARIETY.'

GPF glanced through the letterpress beneath these headlines, made a small impatient sound and began to write very rapidly indeed. He was still at this employment when, glancing up at the blinded window, he saw, as if on a half-developed negative, a shoulder emerge through the fog. A face peered, a hand was pressed against the glass and then closed to tap twice. GPF unlocked his door and returned to his desk. A moment later the visitor came coughing down the passage. 'Entrez!' called GPF modishly and his visitor walked into the room.

'Sorry to harry you,' he said. 'I thought you'd be in this morning. It's the monthly subscription to that relief fund. Your signature to the cheque.'

GPF swivelled round in his chair and held out Lady Pastern's letter. His visitor took it, whistled, read it through and burst out laughing. 'Well!' he said. 'Well, honestly.'

'Press cuttings,' said GPF and handed them to him.

'She must be in a fizz! That it should come to this!'

'Damned if I know why you say that.'

'I'm sorry. Of course there's no reason, but . . . How have you replied?'

'A stinger.'

'May I see it?'

'By all means. There it is. Give me the cheque.'

The visitor lent over the desk, at the same time reading the copy-sheets and groping in his breast pocket for his wallet. He found a cheque and, still reading, laid it on the desk. Once he looked up quickly as if to speak but GPF was bent over the cheque so he finished the letter.

'Strong,' he said.

'Here's the cheque,' said GPF.

'Thank you.' He glanced at it. The signature was written in a small, fat and incredibly neat calligraphy: 'G. P. Friend.'

'Don't you ever sicken of all this?' the visitor asked abruptly with a gesture towards the wire basket.

'Plenty of interest. Plenty of variety.'

'You might land yourself in a hell of a complication one of these days. This letter, for instance – '

'Oh, fiddle,' said GPF, crisply.

II

'Listen,' said Mr Breezy Bellairs, surveying his band. 'Listen, boys, I know he's dire but he's improving. And listen, it doesn't matter if he's dire. What matters is this, like I've told you: he's George Settinjer, Marquis of Pastern and Bagott, and he's Noise Number One for publicity. From the angle of news-value, not to mention snob-value, he's got all the rest of the big shots fighting to buy him a drink.'

'So what?' asked the tympanist morosely.

' "So what!" Ask yourself, what. Look, Syd, I'm keeping you on with the Boys, first, last and all the while. I'm paying you full-time same as if you played full-time.'

'That's not the point,' said the tympanist. 'The point is I look silly, stepping down half-way through the bill on a gala night. Me! I tell you straight, I don't like it.'

'Now, listen Syd. Listen boy. You're featured, aren't you? What am I going to do for you? I'm going to give you a special feature appearance. I'm going to fetch you out on the floor by me to take a star-call, aren't I? That's more than I've ever done, boy. It's good, isn't it? With that coming to you, you should worry if the old bee likes to tear himself to shreds in your corner for half an hour, on Saturday night.'

'I remind you,' said Mr Carlos Rivera, 'that you speak of a gentleman who shall be my father-in-law.'

'OK, OK, OK Take it easy, Carlos, take it easy, boy! That's fine,' Mr Bellairs gabbled, flashing his celebrated smile. 'That's all hunky-dory by us. This is in committee, Carlos. And didn't I say he was improving? He'll be good, pretty soon. Not as good as Syd. That'd be a laughable notion. But good.'

'As you say,' said the pianist. 'But what's all this about his own number?'

Mr Bellairs spread his hands. 'Well, now, it's this way, boys. Lord Pastern's got a little idea. It's a little idea that came to him about this new number he's written.'

'Hot Guy, Hot Gunner?' said the pianist, and plugged out a phrase in the treble. 'What a number!' he said without expression.

'Take it easy now, Happy. This little number his lordship's written will be quite a little hit when we've hotted it up.'

'As you say.'

'That's right. I've orchestrated it and it's snappy. Now, listen. This little idea he's got about putting it across is quite a notion, boys. In its way. It seems Lord Pastern's got round to thinking he might go places as a soloist with this number. You know. A spot of hot drumming and loosing off a six-shooter.'

'For chris-sake!' the tympanist said idly.

'The idea is that Carlos steps out in a spotlight and gives. Hot and crazy, Carlos. Burning the air. Sky the limit.'

Mr Rivera passed the palm of his hand over his hair. 'Very well. And then?'

'Lord Pastern's idea is that you get right on your scooter and take it away. And when you've got to your craziest, another spot picks him out and he's sitting in tin-can corner wearing a cowboy hat and he gets up and yells "yippi-yi-dee" and shoots off a gun at you and you do a trick fall – '

'I am not an acrobat – '

'Well, anyway, you fall and his lordship goes to market and then we switch to a cod funeral march and swing it to the limit. And some of the Boys carry Carlos off and I lay a funny wreath on his breast.

Well,' said Mr Bellairs after a silence, 'I'm not saying it's dynamic, but it might get by. It's crazy and it might be kind of good, at that.'

'Did you say,' asked the tympanist, 'that we finish up with a funeral march? Was that what you said?'

'Played in the Breezy Bellairs Manner, Syd.'

'It was what he said, boys,' said the pianist. 'We sign ourselves off with a corpse and muffled drums. Come to the Metronome for a gay evening.'

'I disagree entirely,' Mr Rivera interposed. He rose gracefully. His suit was dove-grey with a widish pink stripe. Its shoulders seemed actually to curve upwards. He was bronzed. His hair swept back from his forehead and ears in thick brilliant waves. He had flawless teeth, a slight moustache and large eyes and he was tall. 'I like the idea,' he said. 'It appeals to me. A little macabre, a little odd, perhaps, but it has something. I suggest, however, a slight alteration. It will be an improvement if, on the conclusion of Lord Pastern's solo, I draw the rod and shoot *him*. He is then carried out and I go into my hot number. It will be a great improvement.'

'Listen, Carlos – '

'I repeat, a great improvement.'

The pianist laughed pointedly and the other grinned.

'You make the suggestion to Lord Pastern,' said the tympanist. 'He's going to be your ruddy father-in-law. Make it and see how it goes.'

'I think we better do it like he says, Carl,' said Mr Bellairs. 'I think we better.'

The two men faced each other. Mr Bellairs' expression of geniality had become habitual. He might have been a cleverly made ventriloquist's doll with a pale rubber face that was constantly and arbitrarily creased in a roguish grimace. His expressionless eyes with their large pale irises and enormous pupils might have been painted. Wherever he went, whenever he spoke, his lips parted and disclosed his teeth. Two dimples grooved his full cheeks, the flesh creased at the corners of his eyes. Thus, hour after hour, he smiled at the couples who danced slowly past his stand; smiled and bowed and beat the air and undulated and smiled. He sweated profusely from these exertions and at times would mop his face with a snowy handkerchief. And behind him every night his Boys, dressed in soft shirts and sculptured dinner-jackets with steel pointed buttons and silver revers, flexed their muscles and inflated their lungs in obedience to the pulse of his celebrated miniature baton of chromium-tipped ebony, presented to him by a lady of title. Great use was made of chromium at the Metronome by Breezy's Boys. Their instruments glittered with it, they wore wrist-watches on chromium bracelets, the band-title appeared in chromium letters on the piano which was painted in aluminium to resemble chromium. Above the Boys, a giant metronome, outlined in coloured lights, swung its chromium-tipped pendulum in the same measure. 'Hi-dee-ho-dee-oh,' Mr Bellairs would moan. 'Gloomp-gloomp, giddy-iddy, hody-oh-do.' For this and for the way he smiled and conducted his band he was paid three hundred pounds a week by the management of the Metronome, and out of that he paid his Boys. He was engaged with an augmented band for charity balls, and sometimes for private dances. 'It was a grand party,' people would say, 'they had Breezy Bellairs and every-thing.' In his world he was a big noise.

His Boys were big noises. They were all specialists. He had select-ed them with infinite pains. They were chosen for their ability to make the hideous and extremely difficult rumpus known as The Breezy Bellairs Manner and for the way they looked while they made it. They were chosen because of their sex appeal and their endurance. Breezy said: 'The better they like you the more you got to give.' Some of his players he could replace fairly easily; the second and third saxophonists and the double-bass, for instance, but Happy Hart, the pianist and Syd Skelton the tympanist and Carlos Rivera the piano accordionist, were, he said and believed, the Tops. It was a constant nagging anxiety to Breezy that some day, before his public had *had* Happy or Syd or Carlos, one or all of them might get hostile or fed up or something, and leave him for The Royal Flush Swingsters or Bones Flannagan and His Merry Mixers or The Percy Personalities. So he was always careful how he handled these three.

He was being careful now, with Carlos Rivera. Carlos was good. His piano accordion talked in The Big Way. When his engagement to Félicité de Suze was announced it'd be A Big Build-up for Breezy and the Boys. Carlos was as good as they come.

'Listen, Carlos,' Breezy urged feverishly. 'I got an idea. Listen, how about we work it this way? How about letting his lordship fire at you like what he wants and miss you. See? He looks surprised and goes right ahead pulling the trigger and firing and you go right ahead in your hot number and every time he fires, one of the other boys acts like *he's* been hit and plays a queer note and how about these boys playing a note each down the scale? And you just smile and sign off and bow kind of sardonically and leave him flat? How about that, boys?'

'We-ell,' said the Boys judicially.

'It is a possibility,' Mr Rivera conceded.

'He might even wind up by shooting himself and getting carried off with the wreath on his breast.'

'If somebody else doesn't get in first,' grunted the tympanist.

'Or he might hand the gun to me and I might fire it at him and it might be empty, and he might go into his act and end up with a funny faint and get carried out.'

'I repeat,' Rivera said, 'it is a possibility. We shall not quarrel in this matter. Perhaps I may speak to Lord Pastern myself.'

'Fine!' Breezy cried, and raised his tiny baton. 'That's fine. Come on, boys. What are we waiting for? Is this a practice or is it a practice? Where's this new number? Fine! On your marks. Everybody happy? Swell. Let's go.'

III

' "Carlisle Wayne," said Edward Manx, ' "was thirty years old, but she retained something of the air of adolescence, not in her speech, for that was tranquil and assured, but in her looks and manner. Her movements were fluid; boyish perhaps. She had long legs, slim hands and a thin beautiful face. Her clothes were wisely chosen and gallantly worn but she took no great trouble with them and seemed to be well-dressed rather by accident than design. She liked travel but dreaded sight-seeing and would retain memories as sharp as pencil drawings of unimportant details; a waiter, a group of sailors, a woman in a bookstall. The names of the streets or even the towns where these persons had been encountered would often be lost to her; it was people in whom she was really interested. For people she had an eye as sharp as a needle and she was extremely tolerant." '

' "Her remote cousin, The Honourable Edward Manx," ' Carlisle interrupted, ' "was a dramatic critic. He was thirty-seven years old and of romantic appearance but not oppressively so. His profession-al reputation for rudeness was cultivated with some pains for, although cursed with a violent temper, he was by instinct of a courteous disposition!" '

'Gatcha!' said Edward Manx, turning the car into the Uxbridge Road.

' "He was something of a snob but sufficiently adroit to disguise this circumstance under a show of social indiscrimination. He was unmarried – " '

' "having a profound mistrust of those women who obviously admired him – " '

' " – and a dread of being rebuffed by those of whom he was not quite sure." '

'You *are* as sharp as a needle you know,' said Manx, uncomfort-ably.

'Which is probably why I, too, have remained unmarried.'

'I wouldn't be surprised. All the same I've often wondered – '

'I invariably click with such frightful men.'

'Lisle, how old were we when we invented this game?'

' "Novelettes?" Wasn't it in the train when we came back from our first school holidays with Uncle George? He wasn't married then so it must have been over sixteen years ago. Félicité was only two when Aunt Cecile married him and she's eighteen now.'

'It was then. I remember you began by saying: "There was once a very conceited, bad-tempered boy called Edward Manx. His elderly cousin, a peculiar peer – " '

'Even in those days, Uncle George was prime material, wasn't he?'

'Lord, yes! Do you remember – '

They told each other anecdotes, familiar to both, of Lord Pastern and Bagott. They recalled his first formidable row with his wife, a distinguished Frenchwoman of great composure who came to him as a widow with a baby daughter. Lord Pastern, three years after their marriage, became an adherent of a sect that practised baptism by total immersion. He wished his stepdaughter to be rechristened by this method in a sluggish and eel-infested stream that ran

through his country estate. Upon his wife's refusal he sulked for a
month and then, without warning, took ship to India where he
immediately succumbed to the more painful austerities of the yogi.
He returned to England, loudly proclaiming that almost everything
was an illusion and, going by stealth to his stepdaughter's nursery,
attempted to fold her infant limbs into esoteric postures, exhorting
her, at the same time, to bend her gaze upon her navel and say 'Om'.
Her nurse objected, was given notice by Lord Pastern and reinstated
by his wife. A formidable scene ensued.

'My Mama was there, you know,' said Carlisle. 'She was supposed
to be Uncle George's favourite sister but she made no headway at all.
She and Aunt Cecile held an indignation meeting with the nanny in
the boudoir, and Uncle George sneaked down the servants' stairs
with Félicité and drove her thirty miles in his car to some sort of yogi
boarding-house. They had to get the police to find them. Aunt 'Cile
laid a charge of kidnapping.'

'That was the first time Cousin George became banner headlines
in the press,' Edward observed.

'The second time was the nudist colony.'

'True. And the third was the near-divorce.'

'I was away for that,' Carlisle observed.

'You're always going away. Here I am, a hard-working pressman
who ought to be in constant transit to foreign parts, and you're the
one to go away. He was taken with the doctrine of free love, you
remember, and asked a number of rather odd women down to
Clochemere. Cousin Cecile at once removed with Félicité, who was
by now twelve years old, to Duke's Gate, and began divorce proceedings. But it turned out that Cousin George's love was only free in the
sense that he delivered innumerable lectures without charge to his
guests and then told them to go away and get on with it. So the
divorce fell through, but not before counsel and bench had enjoyed
an orgy of wisecracks and the press had exhausted itself.'

'Ned,' Carlisle asked, 'do you imagine that it's at all hereditary?'

'His dottiness? No, all the other Settinjers seem to be tolerably
sane. No, I fancy Cousin George is a sport. A sort of monster, in the
nicest sense of the word.'

'That's a comfort. After all I'm his blood-niece, if that's the way to
put it. You're only a collateral on the distaff side.'

'Is that a cheap sneer, darling?'

'I wish you'd put me wise to the current set-up. I've had some very queer letters and telegrams. What's Félicité up to? Are you going to marry her?'

'I'll be damned if I do,' said Edward with some heat. 'It's Cousin Cecile who thought that one up. She offered to house me at Duke's Gate when my flat was wrested from me. I was there for three weeks before I found a new one and naturally I took Fée out a bit and so on. It now appears that the invitation was all part of a deep-laid plot of Cousin Cecile's. She really is excessively French, you know. It seems that she went into a sort of state-huddle with my mama and talked about Félicité's *dot* and the desirability of the old families standing firm. It was all terrifically Proustian. My mama, who was born in the colonies and doesn't like Félicité, anyway, kept her head and preserved an air of impenetrable grandeur until the last second when she suddenly remarked that she never interfered in my affairs and wouldn't mind betting I'd marry an organizing secretary in the Society for Closer Relations with Soviet Russia.'

'Was Aunt Cile at all rocked?'

'She let it pass as a joke in poor taste.'

'What about Fée, herself?'

'She's in a great to-do about her young man. He, I don't mind telling you, is easily the nastiest job of work in an unreal sort of way that you are ever likely to encounter. He glistens from head to foot and is called Carlos Rivera.'

'One mustn't be insular.'

'No doubt, but wait till you see him. He goes in for jealousy in a big way and says he's the scion of a noble Spanish-American family. I don't believe a word of it and I think Félicité has her doubts.'

'Didn't you say in your letter that he played the piano accordion?'

'At the Metronome, in Breezy Bellairs' Band. He walks out in a spotlight, and undulates. Cousin George is going to pay Breezy some fabulous sum to let him, Cousin George, play the tympani. That's how Félicité met Carlos.'

'Is she really in love with him?'

'Madly, she says, but she's beginning to take a poor view of his jealousy. He can't go dancing with her himself, because of his work. If she goes to the Metronome with anyone else he looks daggers over

his piano accordion and comes across and sneers at them during the
solo number. If she goes to other places he finds out from other
bandsmen. They appear to be a very close corporation. Of course,
being Cousin George's step-daughter, she's used to scenes, but she's
getting a bit rattled nevertheless. It seems that Cousin Cecile, after
her interview with my mama, asked Félicité if she thought she could
love me. Fée telephoned at once to know if I was up to any nonsense
and asked me to lunch with her. So we did and some fool put it in
the paper. Carlos read it and went into his act with unparalleled
vigour. He talked about knives and what his family do with their
women when they are flighty.'

'Fée *is* a donkey,' said Carlisle after a pause.

'You, my dearest Lisle, are telling me.'

IV

Three, Duke's Gate, Eaton Place, was a pleasant Georgian house of
elegant though discreet proportions. Its front had an air of reticence
which was modified by a fan-light, a couple of depressed arches and
beautifully designed doors. One might have hazarded a guess that
this was the town house of some tranquil, wealthy family who in
pre-war days had occupied it at appropriate times and punctually left
it in the charge of caretakers during the late summer and the shooting seasons. A house for orderly, leisured and unremarkable people,
one might have ventured.

Edward Manx dropped his cousin there, handing her luggage
over to a mild elderly manservant and reminding her that they
would meet again at dinner. She entered the hall and noticed with
pleasure that it was unchanged.

'Her ladyship is in the drawing-room, miss,' said the butler.
'Would you prefer – ?'

'I'll go straight in, Spence.'

'Thank you miss. You are in the yellow room, miss. I'll have your
luggage taken up.'

Carlisle followed him to the drawing-room on the first floor. As
they reached the landing a terrific rumpus broke out beyond a doorway on their left.

A saxophone climbed through a series of lewd dissonances into a prolonged shriek; a whistle was blown and cymbals clashed. 'A wireless, at last, Spence?' Carlisle ejaculated. 'I thought they were forbidden.'

'That is his lordship's band, miss. They practise in the ballroom.'

'The band,' Carlisle muttered. 'I'd forgotten. Good heavens!'

'Miss Wayne, my lady,' said Spence, in the doorway.

Lady Pastern and Bagott advanced from the far end of a long room. She was fifty and tall for a Frenchwoman. Her figure was impressive, her hair rigidly groomed, her dress admirable. She had the air of being encased in a transparent, closely-fitting film that covered her head as well as her clothes and permitted no disturbance of her surface. Her voice had edge. She used the faultless diction and balanced phraseology of the foreigner who has perfect command but no love of the English language.

'My dearest Carlisle,' she said crisply, and kissed her niece with precision, on both cheeks.

'Dear Aunt Cile, how nice to see you.'

'It is charming of you to come.'

Carlisle thought that they had uttered these greetings like characters in a somewhat dated comedy, but their pleasure, nevertheless, was real. They had an affection for each other, an unexacting enjoyment of each other's company. 'What I like about Aunt Cecile,' she had said to Edward, 'is her refusal to be rattled about anything.' He had reminded her of Lady Pastern's occasional rages and Carlisle retorted that these outbursts acted like safety-valves and had probably saved her aunt many times from committing some act of physical violence upon Lord Pastern.

They sat together by the large window. Carlisle, responding punctually to the interchange of inquiries and observations which Lady Pastern introduced, allowed her gaze to dwell with pleasure on the modest cornices and well-proportioned panels; on chairs, tables and cabinets which, while they had no rigid correspondence of period, achieved an agreeable harmony born of long association. 'I've always liked this room,' she said presently. 'I'm glad you don't change it.'

'I have defended it,' Lady Pastern said, 'in the teeth of your uncle's most determined assaults.'

'Ah,' thought Carlisle, 'the preliminaries are concluded. Now, we're off.'

'Your uncle,' Lady Pastern continued, 'has, during the last sixteen years, made periodic attempts to introduce prayer-wheels, brass Buddhas, a totem-pole, and the worst excesses of the surrealists. I have withstood them all. On one occasion I reduced to molten silver an image of some Aztec deity. Your uncle purchased it in Mexico City. Apart from its repellent appearance I had every reason to believe it spurious.'

'He doesn't change,' Carlisle murmured.

'It would be more correct, my dear child, to say that he is constant in inconstancy.' Lady Pastern made a sudden and vigorous gesture with both her hands. 'He is ridiculous to contemplate,' she said strongly, 'and entirely impossible to live with. A madman, except in a few unimportant technicalities. He is not, alas, certifiable. If he were, I should know what to do.'

'Oh, come!'

'I repeat, Carlisle, I should know what to do. Do not misunderstand me. For myself, I am resigned. I have acquired armour. I can suffer perpetual humiliation. I can shrug my shoulders at unparalleled buffooneries. But when my daughter is involved,' said Lady Pastern with uplifted bust, 'complaisance is out of the question. I assert myself. I give battle.'

'What's Uncle George up to, exactly?'

'He is conniving, where Félicité is concerned, at disaster. I cannot hope that you are unaware of her attachment.'

'Well – '

'Evidently you are aware of it. A professional bandsman who, as no doubt you heard on your arrival, is here, now, at your uncle's invitation, in the ballroom. It is almost certain that Félicité is listening to him. An utterly impossible young man of a vulgarity – ' Lady Pastern paused and her lips trembled, 'I have seen them together at the theatre,' she said. 'He is beyond everything. One cannot begin to describe. I am desperate.'

'I'm so sorry, Aunt Cile,' Carlisle said uneasily.

'I knew I should have your sympathy, dearest child. I hope I shall enlist your help. Félicité admires and loves you. She will naturally make you her confidante.'

'Yes, but Aunt Cile – '

A clamour of voices broke out in some distant part of the house. 'They are going,' said Lady Pastern, hurriedly. 'It is the end of the *repetition*. In a moment, your uncle and Félicité will appear. Carlisle, may I implore you – '

'I don't suppose – ' Carlisle began dubiously, and at that juncture, hearing her uncle's voice on the landing, rose nervously to her feet. Lady Pastern, with a grimace of profound significance, laid her hand on her niece's arm. Carlisle felt a hysterical giggle rise in her throat. The door opened and Lord Pastern and Bagott came trippingly into the room.

CHAPTER 3
Pre-Prandial

He was short, not more than five foot seven, but so compactly built that he did not give the impression of low stature. Everything about him was dapper, though not obtrusively so; his clothes, the flower in his coat, his well-brushed hair and moustache. His eyes, light grey with pinkish rims, had a hot impertinent look, his underlip jutting out and there were clearly defined spots of local colour over his cheek-bones. He came briskly into the room, bestowed a restless kiss upon his niece and confronted his wife.

'Who's dinin'?' he said.

'Ourselves, Félicité, Carlisle, of course, and Edward Manx. And I have asked Miss Henderson to join us, tonight.'

'Two more,' said Lord Pastern. 'I've asked Bellairs and Rivera.'

'That is quite impossible, George,' said Lady Pastern, calmly.

'Why?'

'Apart from other unanswerable considerations, there is not enough food for two extra guests.'

'Tell 'em to open a tin.'

'I cannot receive these persons for dinner.'

Lord Pastern grinned savagely. 'All right. Rivera can take Félicité to a restaurant and Bellairs can come here. Same numbers as before. How are you, Lisle?'

'I'm very well, Uncle George.'

'Félicité will not dine out with this individual, George. I shall not permit it.'

'You can't stop 'em.'

'Félicité will respect my wishes.'

'Don't be an ass,' said Lord Pastern. 'You're thirty years behind the times, m'dear. Give a gel her head and she'll find her feet.' He paused, evidently delighted with the aphorism. 'Way you're goin', you'll have an elopement on your hands. Comes to that, I don't see the objection.'

'Are you demented, George?'

'Half the women in London'd give anything to be in Fée's boots.'

'A Mexican bandsman.'

'Fine well set-up young feller. Inoculate your old stock. That's Shakespeare, ain't it, Lisle? I understand he comes of a perfectly good Spanish family. Hidalgo, or whatever it is,' he added vaguely. 'A feller of good family happens to be an artist and you go and condemn him. Sort of thing that makes you sick.' He turned to his niece: 'I've been thinkin' seriously of givin' up the title, Lisle.'

'George!'

'About dinner, Cile. Can you find something for them to eat or can't you? Speak up.'

Lady Pastern's shoulders rose with a shudder. She glanced at Carlisle who thought she detected a glint of cunning in her aunt's eye. 'Very well, George,' Lady Pastern said, 'I shall speak to the servants. I shall speak to Dupont. Very well.'

Lord Pastern darted an extremely suspicious glance at his wife and sat down. 'Nice to see you, Lisle,' he said. 'What have you been doin' with yourself?'

'I've been in Greece. Famine relief.'

'If people understood dietetics there wouldn't be all this starvation,' said Lord Pastern, darkly. 'Are you keen on music?'

Carlisle returned a guarded answer. Her aunt, she realized, was attempting to convey by means of a fixed stare and raised eyebrows, some message of significance.

'I've taken it up, seriously,' Lord Pastern continued. 'Swing. Boogie-woogie. Jive. Find it keeps me up to the mark.' He thumped with his heel on the carpet, beat his hands together and in a strange nasal voice. intoned: ' "Shoo-shoo-shoo, Baby. Bye-bye, Bye, Baby." '

The door opened and Félicité de Suze came in. She was a striking young woman with large black eyes, a wide mouth, and an air of being equal to anything. She cried: 'Darling – you're Heaven its very self,' and kissed Carlisle with enthusiasm. Lord Pastern was still clapping and chanting. His step-daughter took up the burden of his song, raised a finger and jerked rhythmically before him. They grinned at each other. 'You're coming along very prettily indeed, George,' she said.

Carlisle wondered what her impression would have been if she were a complete stranger. Would she, like Lady Pastern, have decided that her uncle was eccentric to the point of derangement? 'No,' she thought, 'probably not. There's really a kind of terrifying sanity about him. He's overloaded with energy, he says exactly what he thinks and he does exactly what he wants to do. But he's an oversimplification of type, and he's got no perspective. He's never mildly interested in anything. But which of us,' Carlisle reflected, 'has not, at some time, longed to play the big drum?'

Félicité, with an abandon that Carlisle found unconvincing, flung herself into the sofa beside her mother. 'Angel!' she said richly, 'don't be so *grande dame*. George and I are having fun!'

Lady Pastern disengaged herself and rose: 'I must see Dupont.'

'Ring for Spence,' said her husband. 'Why d'you want to go burrowin' about in the servants' quarters?'

Lady Pastern pointed out, with great coldness, that in the present food shortage one did not, if one wished to retain the services of one's cook, send a message at seven in the evening to the effect that there would be two extra for dinner. In any case, she added, however great her tact, Dupont would almost certainly give notice.

'He'll give us the same dinner as usual,' her husband rejoined. ' "The Three Courses of Monsieur Dupont!" '

'Extremely witty,' said Lady Pastern coldly. She then withdrew.

'George!' said Félicité. 'Have you won?'

'I should damn' well think so. Never heard anything so preposterous in me life. Ask a couple of people to dine and your mother behaves like Lady Macbeth. I'm going to have a bath.'

When he had gone, Félicité turned to Carlisle and made a wide helpless gesture. 'Darling, *what* a life! Honestly! One prances about from moment to moment on the edge of a volcano, *never* knowing when there'll be a major eruption. I suppose you've heard all about ME.'

'A certain amount.'

'He's madly attractive.'

in what sort of way?'

Félicité smiled and shook her head. 'My dear Lisle, he just does things for me.'

'He's not by any chance a bounder?'

'He can bound like a ping-pong ball and I won't bat an eyelid. To me he's Heaven; *but* just plain Heaven.'

'Come off it, Fée,' said Carlisle. 'I've heard all this before. What's the catch in it?'

Félicité looked sideways at her. 'How do you mean, the catch?'

'There's always a catch in your young men, darling, when you rave like this about them.'

Félicité began to walk showily about the room. She had lit a cigarette and wafted it to-and-fro between two fingers, nursing her right elbow in the palm of the left hand. Her manner became remote. 'When English people talk about a bounder,' she said, 'they invariably refer to someone who has more charm and less *gaucherie* than the average Englishman.'

'I couldn't disagree more; but go on.'

Félicité said loftily: 'Of course I knew from the first, Mama would kick like the devil. *C'la va sans dire*. And I don't deny Carlos is a bit tricky. In fact, "It's Hell but it's worth it" is a fairly accurate summing-up of the situation at the moment. I'm adoring it, really. I think.'

'I don't think.'

'Yes, I am,' said Félicité violently. 'I adore a situation. I've been brought up on situations. Think of George. You know, I honestly believe I've got more in common with George than I would have had with my own father. From all accounts, Papa was excessively *rangé*.'

'You'd do with a bit more orderliness yourself, old girl. In what way is Carlos tricky?'

'Well, he's just *so* jealous he's like a Spanish novel.'

'I've never read a Spanish novel unless you count *Don Quixote* and I'm certain you haven't. What's he do?'

'My dear, everything. Rages and despairs and sends frightful letters by special messenger. I got a stinker this morning, *à cause de* – Well, *à cause de* something that really is a bit diffy.'

She halted and inhaled deeply. Carlisle remembered the confidences that Félicité had poured out in her convent days, concerning what she called her 'raves'. There had been the music master who had fortunately snubbed Félicité and the medical student who hadn't. There had been the brothers of the other girls and an actor whom she attempted to waylay at a charity matinée. There had been a male medium, engaged by Lord Pastern during his spiritualistic period, and a dietician. Carlisle pulled herself together and listened to the present recital. It appeared that there was a crisis: a *'crise'* as Félicité called it. She used far more occasional French than her mother and was fond of laying her major calamities at the door of Gallic temperament.

' – And as a matter of fact,' Félicité was saying, 'I hadn't so much as smirked at another *soul*, and there he was seizing me by the wrists and giving me that shattering sort of look that begins at your boots and travels up to your face and then makes the return trip. And, breathing loudly, don't you know, through the nose. I don't deny that the first time was rather fun. But after he got wind of old Edward it really was, and I may say still is, beyond a joke. And now to crown everything, there's the *crise*.'

'But what crisis. You haven't said – '

For the first time Félicité looked faintly embarrassed.

'He found a letter,' she said. 'In my bag. Yesterday.'

'You aren't going to tell me he goes fossicking in your bag? And what letter, for pity's sake? Honestly, Fée!'

'I don't expect you to understand,' Félicité said grandly. 'We were lunching and he hadn't got a cigarette. I was doing my face at the time and I told him to help himself to my case. The letter came out of the bag with the case.'

'And he – well, never mind, *what* letter?'

'I know you're going to say I'm mad. It was a sort of rough draft of a letter I sent to somebody. It had a bit in it about Carlos. When I saw it in his hand I was pretty violently rocked. I said something like "Hi-hi you can't read that," and of course Carlos with that tore everything wide open. He said "So." '

' "So what?" '

' "So," all by itself. He does that. He's Latin-American.'

'I thought that sort of "so" was German.'

'Whatever it is I find it terrifying. I began to fluff and puff and tried to pass it off with a jolly laugh but he said that either he could trust me or he couldn't and if he could, how come I wouldn't let him read a letter? I completely lost my head and grabbed it and he began to hiss. We were in a restaurant.'

'Good lord!'

'Well, I know. Obviously he was going to react in a really big way. So in the end the only thing seemed to be to let him have the letter. So I gave it to him on condition he wouldn't read it till we got back to the car. The drive home was hideous. But hideous.'

'But what was in the letter, if one may ask, and who was it written to? You are confusing, Fée.'

There followed a long uneasy silence. Félicité lit another cigarette. 'Come on,' said Carlisle at last.

'It happened,' said Félicité haughtily, 'to be written to a man whom I don't actually know, asking for advice about Carlos and me. Professional advice.'

'What can you mean! A clergyman? Or a lawyer?'

'I don't think so. He'd written me rather a marvellous letter and this was thanking him. Carlos, of course, thought it was for Edward. The worst bit, from Carlos's point of view was where I said: "I suppose he'd be madly jealous if he knew I'd written to you like this." Carlos really got weaving after he read that. He – '

Félicité's lips trembled. She turned away and began to speak rapidly, in a high voice. 'He roared and stormed and wouldn't listen to anything. It was devastating. You can't conceive what it was like. He said I was to announce our engagement at once. He said if I didn't he'd – he said he'd go off and just simply end it all. He's given me a week. I've got till next Tuesday. That's all. I've got to announce it before next Tuesday.'

'And you don't want to?' Carlisle asked gently. She saw Félicité's shoulders quiver and went to her. 'Is that it, Fée?'

The voice quavered and broke. Félicité drove her hands through her hair. 'I don't know *what* I want,' she sobbed. 'Lisle, I'm in such a muddle. I'm terrified, Lisle. It's so damned awful, Lisle. I'm terrified.'

II

Lady Pastern had preserved throughout the war and its exhausted aftermath, an unbroken formality. Her rare dinner parties had, for this reason, acquired the air of period pieces. The more so since, by a feat of superb domestic strategy she had contrived to retain at Duke's Gate a staff of trained servants, though a depleted one. As she climbed into a long dress, six years old, Carlisle reflected that if the food shortage persisted, her aunt would soon qualify for the same class as that legendary Russian nobleman who presided with perfect equanimity at an interminable banquet of dry bread and water.

She had parted with Félicité, who was still shaking and incoherent, on the landing. 'You'll see him at dinner,' Félicité had said. 'You'll see what I mean.' And with a spurt of defiance: 'And anyway, I don't care what anyone thinks. If I'm in a mess, it's a thrilling mess. And if I want to get out of it, it's not for other people's reasons. It's only because – Oh, God, what's it *matter!*'

Félicité had then gone into her own room and slammed the door. It was perfectly obvious, Carlisle reflected, as she finished her face and lit a cigarette, that the wretched girl was terrified and that she herself would, during the weekend, be a sort of buffer-state between Félicité, her mother and her stepfather. 'And the worst of it is,' Carlisle thought crossly, 'I'm fond of them and will probably end by involving myself in a major row with all three at once.'

She went down to the drawing-room. Finding nobody there, she wandered disconsolately across the landing and, opening a pair of magnificent double-doors, looked into the ballroom.

Gilt chairs and music stands stood in a semi-circle like an island in the vast bare floor. A grand piano stood in their midst. On its closed lid, with surrealistic inconsequence, was scattered a number of umbrellas and parasols. She looked more closely at them and recognized a black and white, exceedingly Parisian, affair, which ten years ago or more her aunt had flourished at Ascot. It had been an outstanding phenomenon, she remembered, in the Royal Enclosure and had been photographed. Lady Pastern had been presented with it by some Indian plenipotentiary on the occasion of her first marriage and had clung to it ever since. Its handle represented a bird and had ruby eyes. Its shaft was preposterously thin and was jointed and bound with platinum. The spring catch and the dark bronze section that held it were uncomfortably encrusted with jewels and had ruined many a pair of gloves. As a child, Félicité had occasionally been permitted to unscrew the head and the end section of the shaft and this, for some reason, had always afforded her extreme pleasure. Carlisle picked it up, opened it, and, jeering at herself for being superstitious, hurriedly shut it again. There was a pile of band-parts on the piano seat and on the top of this a scribbled programme.

'Floor Show,' she read. '(1) A New Way with Old Tunes. (2) Skelton. (3) Sandra. (4) Hot Guy.'

At the extreme end of the group of chairs and a little isolated, was the paraphernalia of a dance-band tympanist – drums, rattles, a tambourine, cymbals, a wire whisk and coconut shells. Carlisle gingerly touched a pedal with her foot and jumped nervously when a pair of cymbals clashed. 'It would be fun,' she thought, 'to sit down and have a whack at everything. What can Uncle George be like in action!'

She looked round. Her coming-out ball had been here; her parents had borrowed the house for it. Utterly remote, those years before the war! Carlisle repeopled the hollow room and felt again the curious fresh gaiety of that night. She felt the cord of her programme grow flossy under the nervous pressure of her gloved fingers. She saw the names written there and read them again in the choked print of casualty lists. The cross against the supper dances had been for Edward. 'I don't approve,' he had said, guiding her with precision, and speaking so lightly that, as usual, she doubted his intention. 'We've no business to do ourselves as well as all this.' 'Well, if you're not having fun – ' 'But I am, I am.' And he had started one of their 'novelettes': 'in the magnificent ballroom at Duke's Gate, the London House of Lord Pastern and Bagott, amid the strains of music and the scent of hot-house blooms – ' And she had cut in: 'Young Edward Manx swept his cousin into the vortex of the dance.' 'Lovely,' she thought. Lovely it had been. They had had the last dance together and she had been tired yet buoyant, moving without conscious volition; *really* floating, she thought. 'Goodnight, goodnight, it's been perfect.' Later, as the clocks struck four, up the stairs to bed, light-headed with fatigue, drugged with gratitude to all the world for her complete happiness.

'How young,' thought Carlisle, looking at the walls and floor of the ballroom, 'and how remote. The Spectre of the Rose,' she thought, and a phrase of music ended her recollections on a sigh.

There had been no real sequel. More balls, with the dances planned beforehand, an affair or two and letters from Edward who was doing special articles in Russia. And then the war.

She turned away and recrossed the landing to the drawing-room. It was still unoccupied. 'If I don't talk to somebody soon,' Carlisle thought, 'I shall get a black dog on my back.' She found a collection of illustrated papers and turned them over, thinking how strange it was that photographs of people eating, dancing, or looking at something that did not appear in the picture, should command attention.

'Lady Dartmoor and Mr Jeremy Thringle enjoyed a joke at the opening night of *Fewer and Dearer*.' 'Miss Penelope Santon-Clarke takes a serious view of the situation at Sandown. With her, intent on his racing-card, is Captain Anthony Barr-Barr.' 'At the Tarmac: Miss Félicité de Suze in earnest conversation with Mr Edward Manx.' 'I don't wonder,' thought Carlisle, 'that Aunt Cecile thinks it would be a good match,' and put the paper away from her. Another magazine lay in her lap: a glossy publication with a cover-illustration depicting a hill-top liberally endowed with flowers and a young man and woman of remarkable physique gazing with every expression of delight and well-being at something indistinguishable in an extremely blue sky. The title *Harmony* was streamlined across the top of the cover.

Carlisle turned the pages. Here was Edward's monthly review of the shows. Much too good, it was, mordant and penetrating, for a freak publication like this. He had told her they paid very well. Here, an article on genetics by 'The Harmony Consultant', here something a bit over-emotional about famine relief, which Carlisle, an expert in her way, skimmed through with disapproval. Next an article: 'Radiant Living', which she passed by with a shudder. Then a two-page article headed: 'Crime Pays', which proved to be a highly flavoured but extremely outspoken and well-informed article on the drug-racket. Two Latin American business firms with extensive connections in Great Britain were boldly named. An editorial note truculently courted information backed by full protection. It also invited a libel action and promised a further article. Next came a serial by a Big Name and then, on the centre double-page with a banner headline:

'The Helping Hand'
Ask GPF about it
(Guide, Philosopher, Friend)

Carlisle glanced through it. Here were letters from young women asking for advice on the conduct of their engagements and from young men seeking guidance in their choice of wives and jobs. Here was a married woman prepared, it seemed, to follow the instructions of an unknown pundit in matters of the strictest personal concern, and here a widower who requested an expert report on remarriage with someone twenty years his junior. Carlisle was about to turn the page when a sentence caught her eye:

'I am nineteen and unofficially engaged to be married. My fiancé is madly jealous and behaves – '

She read it through to the end. The style was vividly familiar. The magazine had the look of having been frequently opened here. There was cigarette ash in the groove between the pages. Was it possible that Félicité – ? But the signature: 'Toots!' Could Félicité adopt a nom-de-plume like Toots? Could her unknown correspondent – ? Carlisle lost herself in a maze of speculation from which she was aroused by some faint noise; a metallic click. She looked up. Nobody had entered the room. The sound was repeated and she realized it had come from her uncle's study, a small room that opened off the far end of the drawing-room. She saw that the door was ajar and that the lights were on in the study. She remembered that it was Lord Pastern's unaltered habit to sit in this room for half an hour before dinner, meditating upon whatever obsession at the moment enthralled him, and that he had always liked her to join him there.

She walked down the long deep carpet to the door and looked in.

Lord Pastern sat before the fire. He had a revolver in his hands and appeared to be loading it.

III

For a few moments Carlisle hesitated. Then, in a voice that struck her as being pitched too high, she said: 'What *are* you up to, Uncle George?'

He started and the revolver slipped in his hands and almost fell.

'Hallo,' he said. 'Thought you'd forgotten me.'

She crossed the room and sat opposite him. 'Are you preparing for burglars?' she asked.

'No.' He gave her what Edward had once called one of his leery looks and added: 'Although you might put it that way. I'm gettin' ready for my big moment.' He jerked his hand towards a small table that stood at his elbow. Carlisle saw that a number of cartridges lay there. 'Just goin' to draw the bullets,' said Lord Pastern, 'to make 'em into blanks, you know. I like to attend to things myself.'

'But what is your big moment?'

'You'll see tonight. You and Fée are to come. It ought to be a party. Who's your best young man?'

'I haven't got one.'

'Why not?'

'Ask yourself.'

'You're too damn' standoffish, me gel. Wouldn't be surprised if you had one of those things – Oedipus and all that. I looked into psychology when I was interested in companionate marriage.'

Lord Pastern inserted his eyeglass, went to his desk, and rummaged in one of the drawers.

'What's happening tonight?'

'Special extension night at the Metronome. I'm playin'. Floor show at 11 o'clock. My first appearance in public. Breezy engaged me. Nice of him, wasn't it? You'll enjoy yourself, Lisle.'

He returned with a drawer filled with a strange collection of objects: pieces of wire, a fret-saw, razor blades, candle-ends, wood-carving knives, old photographs, electrical gear, plastic wood, a number of tools and quantities of putty in greasy paper. How well Carlisle remembered that drawer. It had been a wet-day solace of her childhood visits. From its contents, Lord Pastern, who was dexterous in such matters, had concocted mannikins, fly-traps and tiny ships.

'I believe,' she said, 'I recognize almost everything in the collection.'

'Y' father gave me that revolver,' Lord Pastern remarked. 'It's one of a pair. He had 'em made by his gunsmith to take special target ammunition. Couldn't be bored having to reload with every shot like you do with target pistols, y'know. Cost him a packet these did. We were always at it, he and I. He scratched his initials one day on the butt of this one. We'd had a bit of a row about differences in performance in the two guns, and shot it out. Have a look.'

She picked up the revolver gingerly. 'I can't see anything.'

'There's a magnifying glass somewhere. Look underneath near the trigger-guard.'

Carlisle rummaged in the drawer and found a lens. 'Yes,' she said. 'I can make them out now, CDW'

'We were crack shots. He left me the pair. The other's in the case, somewhere in that drawer.'

Lord Pastern took out a pair of pliers and picked up one of the cartridges. 'Well, if you haven't got a young man,' he said, 'we'll have Ned Manx. That'll please your aunt. No good asking anyone else for Fée. Carlos cuts up rough.'

'Uncle George,' Carlisle ventured as he busied himself over his task, 'do you approve of Carlos? Really?'

He muttered and grunted. She caught disjointed phrases: ' – take their course – own destiny – goin' the wrong way to work. He's a damn' fine piano accordionist,' he said loudly and added, more obscurely: 'They'd much better leave things to me.'

'What's he like?'

'You'll see him in a minute. I know what I'm about,' said Lord Pastern crimping the end of a cartridge from which he had extracted the bullet.

'Nobody else seems to. Is he jealous?'

'She's had things too much her own way. Make her sit up a bit and a good job, too.'

'Aren't you making a great number of blank cartridges?' Carlisle asked idly.

'I rather like making them. You never know. I shall probably be asked to repeat my number lots of times. I like to be prepared.'

He glanced up and saw the journal which Carlisle still held in her lap. 'Thought you had a mind above that sort of stuff,' said Lord Pastern, grinning.

'Are you a subscriber, darling?'

'Y' aunt is. It's got a lot of sound stuff in it. They're not afraid to speak their minds, b'God. See that thing on drug-runnin'? Names and everything and if they don't like it they can damn' well lump it. The police,' Lord Pastern said obscurely, 'are no good. Pompous incompetent lot. Hidebound. Ned,' he added, 'does the reviews.'

'Perhaps,' Carlisle said lightly, 'he's GPF too.'

'Chap's got brains,' Lord Pastern grunted bewilderingly. 'Hog-sense in that feller.'

'Uncle George,' Carlisle demanded suddenly, 'you don't know by any chance, if Fée's ever consulted GPF?'

'Wouldn't let on if I did, m'dear. Naturally.'

Carlisle reddened. 'No, of course you wouldn't if she'd told you in confidence. Only usually Fée can't keep anything to herself.'

'Well, ask her. She might do a damn' sight worse.'

Lord Pastern dropped the two bullets he had extracted into the waste-paper basket and returned to his desk. 'I've been doin' a bit of writin' myself,' he said. 'Look at this, Lisle.'

He handed his niece a sheet of music manuscript. An air had been set down, with many rubbings out, it seemed, and words had been written under the appropriate notes. 'This Hot Guy,' Carlisle read, 'does he get mean? This Hot Gunner with his accord-een. Shoots like he plays an' he tops the bill. Plays like he shoots an' he shoots to kill. Hide oh hi. Yip. Ho de oh do. Yip. Shoot buddy, shoot and we'll sure come clean. Hot Guy, Hot Gunner and your accord-een. Bo. Bo. Bo.'

'Neat,' said Lord Pastern complacently. 'Ain't it?'

'It's astonishing,' Carlisle murmured and was spared the necessity of further comment by the sound of voices in the drawing-room.

'That's the Boys,' said Lord Pastern briskly. 'Come on.'

The Boys were dressed in their professional dinner suits. These were distinctive garments, the jackets being double-breasted with steel buttons and silver revers. The sleeves were extremely narrow and displayed a great deal of cuff. The taller of the two, a man whose rotundity was emphasized by his pallor, advanced, beaming upon his host.

'Well, well, well,' he said. 'Look who's here.'

It was upon his companion that Carlisle fixed her attention. Memories of tango experts, of cinema near-stars with cigarette holders and parti-coloured shoes, of armoured women moving doggedly round dance floors in the grasp of younger men; all these memories jostled together in her brain.

' – and Mr Rivera – ' her uncle was saying. Carlisle withdrew her hand from Mr Bellairs' encompassing grasp and it was at once bowed over by Mr Rivera.

'Miss Wayne,' said Félicité's Carlos.

He rose from his bow with grace and gave her a look of automatic homage. 'So we meet, at last,' he said. 'I have heard so much.' He had, she noticed, a very slight lisp.

Lord Pastern gave them all sherry. The two visitors made loud conversation: 'That's very fine,' Mr Breezy Bellairs pronounced and pointed to a small Fragonard above the fireplace. 'My God, that's beautiful, you know, Carlos. Exquisite.'

'In my father's hacienda,' said Mr Rivera, 'there is a picture of which 1 am vividly reminded. This picture to which I refer, is a portrait of one of my paternal ancestors. It is an original Goya.' And while she was still wondering how a Fragonard could remind Mr Rivera of a Goya, he turned to Carlisle. 'You have visited the Argentine, Miss Wayne, of course?'

'No,' said Carlisle.

'But you must. It would appeal to you enormously. It is a little difficult, by the way, for a visitor to see us, as it were from the inside. The Spanish families are very exclusive.'

'Oh.'

'Oh, yes. An aunt of mine, Donna Isabella da Manuelos-Rivera used to say ours was the only remaining aristocracy.' He inclined towards Lord Pastern and laughed musically. 'But, of course, she had not visited a certain charming house in Duke's Gate, London.'

'What? I wasn't listening,' said Lord Pastern. 'Look here, Bellairs, about tonight – '

'Tonight,' Mr Bellairs interrupted, smiling from ear to ear, 'is in the bag. We'll rock them, Lord Pastern. Now, don't you worry about tonight. It's going to be wonderful. You'll be there, of course, Miss Wayne?'

'I wouldn't miss it,' Carlisle murmured, wishing they were not so zealous in their attentions.

'I've got the gun fixed up,' her uncle said eagerly. 'Five rounds of blanks, you know. What about those umbrellas, now – '

'You are fond of music, Miss Wayne? But of course you are. You would be enchanted by the music of my own country.'

'Tangos and rhumbas?' Carlisle ventured. Mr Rivera inclined towards her. 'At midnight,' he said, 'with the scent of magnolias in the air – those wonderful nights of music. You will think it strange, of course, that I should be' – he shrugged up his shoulders and lowered his voice –'performing in a dance band. Wearing these appalling clothes! Here, in London! It is terrible, isn't it?'

'I don't see why.'

'I suppose,' Mr Rivera sighed, 'I am what you call a snob. There are times when I find it almost unendurable. But I must not say so.' He glanced at Mr Bellairs who was very deep in conversation with his host. 'A heart of gold,' he whispered. 'One of nature's gentlemen. I should not complain. How serious we have become,' he added gaily. 'We meet and in two minutes I confide in you. You are *simpatica*, Miss Wayne. But of course, you have been told that before.'

'Never,' said Carlisle firmly, and was glad to see Edward Manx come in.

'Evenin', Ned,' said Lord Pastern, blinking at him. 'Glad to see you. Have you met – '

Carlisle heard Mr Rivera draw in his breath with a formidable hiss. Manx, having saluted Mr Bellairs, advanced with a pleasant smile and extended hand. 'We haven't met, Rivera,' he said, 'but at least I'm one of your devotés at the Metronome. If anything could teach me how to dance I'm persuaded it would be your piano accordion.'

'How do you do,' said Mr Rivera, and turned his back. 'As I was saying, Miss Wayne,' he continued. 'I believe entirely in first impressions. As soon as we were introduced – '

Carlisle looked past him at Manx who had remained perfectly still. At the first opportunity, she walked round Mr Rivera and joined him. Mr Rivera moved to the fireplace before which he stood with an air of detachment, humming under his breath. Lord Pastern instantly buttonholed him. Mr Bellairs joined them with every manifestation of uneasy geniality. 'About my number, Carlos,' said Lord Pastern, 'I've been tellin' Breezy – '

'Of all the filthy rude – ' Manx began to mutter.

Carlisle linked her arm in his and walked him away. 'He's just plain frightful, Ned. Félicité must be out of her mind,' she whispered hastily.

'If Cousin George thinks I'm going to stand round letting a bloody fancy-dress dago insult me – '

'For *pity's* sake don't fly into one of your rages. Laugh it off.'

'Heh-heh-heh – '

'That's better.'

'He'll probably throw his sherry in my face. Why the devil was I asked if he was coming? What's Cousin Cecile thinking of?'

'It's Uncle George – shut up. Here come the girls.'

Lady Pastern, encased in black, entered with Félicité at her heels. She suffered the introductions with terrifying courtesy. Mr Bellairs redoubled his geniality. Mr Rivera had the air of a man who never blossoms but in the presence of the great.

'I am so pleased to have the honour, at last, of being presented,' he said. 'From Félicité I have heard so much of her mother. I feel, too, that we may have friends in common. Perhaps, Lady Pastern, you will remember an uncle of mine who had, I think, some post at our Embassy in Paris many years ago. Señor Alonza da Manuelos-Rivera.'

Lady Pastern contemplated him without any change of expression. 'I do not remember,' she said.

'After all it was much too long ago,' he rejoined gallantly. Lady Pastern glanced at him with cold astonishment, and advanced upon Manx. 'Dearest Edward,' she said, offering her cheek, 'we see you far too seldom. This is delightful.'

'Thank you, Cousin Cecile. For me, too.'

'I want to consult you. You will forgive us, George. I am determined to have Edward's opinion on my *petit-point*.'

'Let me alone,' Manx boasted, 'with *petit-point*.'

Lady Pastern put her arm through his and led him apart. Carlisle saw Félicité go to Rivera. Evidently she had herself well in hand: her greeting was prettily formal. She turned with an air of comradeship from Rivera to Bellairs and her stepfather. 'Will anyone bet me,' she said, 'that I can't guess what you chaps have been talking about?'

Mr Bellairs was immediately very gay. 'Now, Miss de Suze, that's making it just a little tough. I'm afraid you know much too much about us. Isn't that the case, Lord Pastern?'

'I'm worried about those umbrellas,' said Lord Pastern moodily and Bellairs and Félicité began to talk at once.

Carlisle was trying to make up her mind about Rivera and failing to do so. Was he in love with Félicité? If so, was his jealousy of Ned Manx a genuine and therefore an alarming passion? Was he, on the other hand, a complete adventurer? Could he conceivably be that to which he pretended? Could any human being be as patently bogus as Mr Rivera or was it within the bounds of possibility that the scions of noble Spanish-American families behave in a manner altogether too faithful to their Hollywood opposites? Was it her fancy or had his olive-coloured cheeks turned paler as he stood and watched Félicité? Was the slight tic under his left eye, that smallest possible muscular twitch really involuntary or, as everything else about him seemed to be, part of an impersonation along stereotyped lines? And as these speculations chased each other through her mind, Rivera himself came up to her.

'But you are so serious,' he said. 'I wonder why. In my country we have a proverb: a woman is serious for one of two reasons; she is about to fall in love or already she loves without success. The alternative being unthinkable, I ask myself: to whom is this lovely lady about to lose her heart?'

Carlisle thought: 'I wonder if this is the line of chat that Félicité has fallen for.' She said: 'I'm afraid your proverb doesn't apply out of South America.'

He laughed as if she had uttered some brilliant equivocation and began to protest that he knew better, indeed he did. Carlisle saw Félicité stare blankly at them and, turning quickly, surprised just such another expression on Edward Manx's face. She began to feel acutely uncomfortable. There was no getting away from Mr Rivera. His raillery and archness mounted with indecent emphasis. He admired Carlisle's dress, her modest jewel, her hair. His lightest remark was pronounced with such a killing air that it immediately assumed the character of an impropriety. Her embarrassment at these excesses quickly gave way to irritation when she saw that while Mr Rivera bent upon her any number of melting glances he also kept a sharp watch upon Félicité. 'And I'll be damned,' thought Carlisle, 'if I let him get away with that little game.' She chose her moment and joined her aunt who had withdrawn Edward Manx to the other end of the room and, while she exhibited her embroidery, muttered anathemas upon her other guests. As Carlisle came up, Edward was in the middle of some kind of uneasy protestation. ' – but, Cousin Cecile, 1 don't honestly think I can do much about it. I mean – Oh, hallo, Lisle, enjoying your Latin-American petting party?'

'Not enormously,' said Carlisle, and bent over her aunt's embroidery. 'It's lovely, darling,' she said. 'How do you do it?'

'You shall have it for an evening bag. I have been telling Edward that I fling myself on his charity, and, Lady Pastern added in a stormy undertone, 'and on yours, my dearest child.' She raised her needlework as if to examine it and they saw her fingers fumble aimlessly across its surface.

'You see, both of you, this atrocious person. I implore you – ' Her voice faltered. 'Look,' she whispered, 'look now. Look at him.'

Carlisle and Edward glanced furtively at Mr Rivera who was in the act of introducing a cigarette into a jade holder. He caught Carlisle's eye. He did not smile but glossed himself over with appraisement. His eyes widened. 'Somewhere or another,' she thought, 'he has read about the gentlemen who undress ladies with a glance.' She heard Manx swear under his breath and noted with surprise her own gratification at this circumstance. Mr Rivera advanced upon her.

'Oh, lord!' Edward muttered.

'Here,' said Lady Pastern loudly, 'is Hendy. She is dining with us. I had forgotten.'

The door at the far end of the drawing-room had opened and a woman plainly dressed came quietly in.

'Hendy!' Carlisle echoed. 'I had forgotten Hendy,' and went swiftly towards her.

CHAPTER 4

They Dine

Miss Henderson had been Félicité's governess and had remained with the family after she grew up, occupying a post that was half-way between that of companion and secretary to both Félicité and her mother. Carlisle called her controller-of-the-household and knew that many a time she had literally performed the impossible task this title implied. She was a greyish-haired woman of forty-five; her appearance was tranquil but unremarkable, her voice pleasant. Carlisle, who liked her, had often wondered at her faithfulness to this turbulent household. To Lady Pastern, who regarded all persons as neatly graded types, Miss Henderson was no doubt an employee of good address and perfect manners whose presence at Duke's Gate was essential to her own piece of mind. Miss Henderson had her private room where usually she ate in solitude. Sometimes, however, she was asked to lunch or dine with the family; either because a woman guest had slipped them up, or because her employer felt it was suitable that her position should be defined by such occasional invitations. She seldom left the house and if she had any outside ties, Carlisle had never heard of them. She was perfectly adjusted to her isolation and if she was ever lonely, gave no evidence of being so. Carlisle believed Miss Henderson to have more influence than anyone else with Félicité, and it struck her now as odd that Lady Pastern should not have mentioned Hendy as a possible check to Mr Rivera. But then the family did not often remember Hendy until they actually wanted her for something. 'And I myself,' Carlisle thought guiltily, 'although I like her so much, had forgotten to ask after her.' And she made her greeting the warmer because of this omission.

'Hendy,' she said, 'how lovely to see you. How long is it? Four years?'

'A little over three, I think.' That was like her. She was always quietly accurate.

'You look just the same,' said Carlisle, nervously aware of Mr Rivera close behind her.

Lady Pastern icily performed the introductions. Mr Bellairs bowed and smiled expansively from the hearthrug. Mr Rivera, standing beside Carlisle, said: 'Ah, yes, of course. Miss Henderson.' And might as well have added: 'The governess, I believe.' Miss Henderson bowed composedly and Spence announced dinner.

They sat at a round table; a pool of candlelight in the shadowed dining-room. Carlisle found herself between her uncle and Rivera. Opposite her, between Edward and Bellairs, sat Félicité. Lady Pastern, on Rivera's right, at first suffered his conversation with awful courtesy, presumably, thought Carlisle, in order to give Edward Manx, her other neighbour, a clear run with Félicité. But as Mr Bellairs completely ignored Miss Henderson, who was on his right, and lavished all his attention on Félicité herself, this manoeuvre was unproductive. After a few minutes Lady Pastern engaged Edward in what Carlisle felt to be an extremely ominous conversation. She caught only fragments of it as Rivera had resumed his crash tactics with herself. His was a simple technique. He merely turned his shoulders on Lady Pastern, leant so close to Carlisle that she could see the pores of his skin, looked into her eyes, and, with rich insinuation, contradicted everything she said. Lord Pastern was no refuge, as he had sunk into a reverie from which he roused himself from time to time only to throw disjointed remarks at no one in particular, and to attack his food with a primitive gusto which dated from his Back-to-Nature period. His table-manners were defiantly and deliberately atrocious. He chewed with parted lips, glaring about him like a threatened carnivore, and as he chewed he talked. To Spence and the man who assisted him and to Miss Henderson who accepted her isolation with her usual composure, the conversation must have come through like the dialogue in a boldly surrealistic broadcast.

'. . . such a good photograph, we thought, Edward, of you and Félicité at the Tarmac. She so much enjoyed her party with you . . . '

'. . . but I'm not at all musical . . . '

'. . . you must not say so. You are musical. There is music in your eyes – your voice . . . '

'. . . now that's quite a nifty little idea, Miss de Suze. We'll have to pull you in with the boys . . . '

'. . . so it is arranged, my dear Edward.'

'. . . thank you, Cousin Cecile, but . . . '

'. . . you and Félicité have always done things together, haven't you? We were laughing yesterday over some old photographs. Do you remember at Clochemere . . .?'

'. . . C, where's my sombrero?'

'. . . with this dress you should wear flowers. A cascade of orchids. Just here. Let me show you . . . '

'. . . I beg your pardon, Cousin Cecile, I'm afraid I didn't hear what you said . . . '

'Uncle George, it's time you talked to me . . . '

'Eh? Sorry, Lisle, I'm wondering where my sombrero . . . '

'Lord Pastern is very kind in letting me keep you to myself. Don't turn away. Look. Your handkerchief is falling.'

'*Damn!*'

'Edward!'

'I beg your pardon, Cousin Cecile, I don't know what I'm thinking of.'

'Carlos.'

'. . . in my country, Miss Wayne . . . no, I cannot call you Miss Wayne. Car-r-r-lisle! What a strange name. Strange and captivating.'

'Carlos!'

'Forgive me. You spoke?'

'About those umbrellas, Breezy.'

'Yes, I did speak.'

'A thousand pardons, I was talking to Carrlisle.'

'I've engaged a table for three, Fée. You and Carlisle and Ned. Don't be late.'

'My music tonight shall be for you.'

'I am coming, also, George.'

'*What!*'

'Kindly see that it is a table for four.'

'Maman! But I thought . . . '

'You won't like it, C.'

'I propose to come.'

'Damn it, you'll sit and glare at me and make me nervous.'

'Nonsense, George,' Lady Pastern said crisply. 'Be good enough to order the table.'

Her husband glowered at her, seemed to contemplate giving further battle, appeared suddenly to change his mind and launched an unexpected attack at Rivera.

'About your being carried out, Carlos,' he said importantly, 'it seems a pity I can't be carried out, too. Why can't the stretcher party come back for me?'

'Now, now, now,' Mr Bellairs interrupted in a great hurry. 'We've got everything fixed, Lord Pastern, now, haven't we? The first routine. You shoot Carlos. Carlos falls. Carlos is carried out. You take the show away. Big climax. Finish. Now don't you get me bustled,' he added playfully. 'It's good and it's fixed. Fine. That's right, isn't it?'

'It is what has been decided,' Mr Rivera conceded grandly. 'For myself, I am perhaps a little dubious. Under other circumstances I would undoubtedly insist upon the second routine. I am shot at but I do not fall. Lord Pastern misses me. The others fall. Breezy fires at Lord Pastern and nothing happens. Lord Pastern plays, faints, is removed. I finish the number. Upon this routine under other circumstances, I should insist.' He executed a sort of comprehensive bow, taking in Lord Pastern, Félicité, Carlisle and Lady Pastern. 'But under these exclusive and most charming circumstances, I yield. I am shot. I fall. Possibly I hurt myself. No matter.'

Bellairs eyed him. 'Good old Carlos,' he said uneasily.

'I still don't see why I can't be carried out, too,' said Lord Pastern fretfully.

Carlisle heard Mr Bellairs whisper under his breath: 'For the love of Pete!' Rivera said loudly: 'No, no, no, no. Unless we adopt completely the second routine, we perform the first as we rehearsed. It is settled.'

'Carlisle,' said Lady Pastern, rising, 'shall we . . .?'

She swept her ladies into the drawing-room.

II

Félicité was puzzled, resentful and uneasy. She moved restlessly about the room, eyeing her mother and Carlisle. Lady Pastern paid no attention to her daughter. She questioned Carlisle about her experiences in Greece and received her somewhat distracted answers with perfect equanimity. Miss Henderson, who had taken up Lady Pastern's box of embroidery threads, sorted them with quiet movements of her hands and seemed to listen with interest.

Suddenly Félicité said: 'I don't see much future in us all behaving as if we'd had the Archbishop of Canterbury to dinner. If you've got anything to say about Carlos, all of you, I'd be very much obliged if you'd say it.'

Miss Henderson, her hands still for a moment, glanced up at Félicité and then bent again over her task. Lady Pastern having crossed her ankles and wrists, slightly moved her shoulders and said: 'I do not consider this a suitable occasion, my dear child, for any such discussion.'

'Why?' Félicité demanded.

'It would make a scene, and under the circumstances,' said Lady Pastern with an air of reasonableness, 'there's no time for a scene.'

'If you think the men are coming in, Maman, they are not. George has arranged to go over the programme again in the ballroom.'

A servant came in and collected the coffee cups. Lady Pastern made conversation with Carlisle until the door had closed behind him.

'So I repeat,' Félicité said loudly. 'I want to hear, Maman, what you've got to say against Carlos.'

Lady Pastern slightly raised her eyes and lifted her shoulders. Her daughter stamped. 'Blast and hell!' she said.

'Félicité!' said Miss Henderson. It was neither a remonstrance nor a warning. The name fell like an unstressed comment. Miss Henderson held an embroidery stiletto firmly between her finger and thumb and examined it placidly.

Félicité made an impatient movement. 'If you think,' she said violently, 'anybody's going to be at their best in a strange house with a hostess who looks at them as if they smelt!'

'If it comes to that, dearest child, he does smell. Of a particularly heavy kind of scent, I fancy,' Lady Pastern added thoughtfully.

From the ballroom came a distant syncopated roll of drums ending in a crash of cymbals and a loud report. Carlisle jumped nervously. The stiletto fell from Miss Henderson's fingers to the carpet. Félicité, bearing witness in her agitation to the efficacy of her governess's long training, stooped and picked it up.

'It is your uncle, merely,' said Lady Pastern.

'I ought to go straight out and apologize to Carlos for the hideous way he's been treated,' Félicité stormed, but her voice held an overtone of uncertainty and she looked resentfully at Carlisle.

'If there are to be apologies,' her mother rejoined, 'it is Carlisle who should receive them. I am so sorry, Carlisle, that you should have been subjected to these – ' she made a fastidious gesture – 'to these really insufferable attentions.'

'Good lord, Aunt Cile,' Carlisle began in acute embarrassment, and was rescued by Félicité who burst into tears and rushed out of the room.

'I think, perhaps . . .?' said Miss Henderson, rising.

'Yes, please go to her.'

But before Miss Henderson reached the door, which Félicité had left open, Rivera's voice sounded in the hall. 'What is the matter?' it said distinctly and Félicité, breathless, answered, 'I've got to talk to you.' 'But certainly, if you wish it.' 'In here, then.' The voices faded, were heard again, indistinctly, in the study. The connecting door between the study and the drawing-room was slammed-to from the far side. 'You had better leave them, I think,' said Lady Pastern.

'If I go to my sitting-room, she may come to me when this is over.'

'Then go,' said Lady Pastern, drearily. 'Thank you, Miss Henderson.'

'Aunt,' said Carlisle when Miss Henderson had left them, 'what are you up to?'

Lady Pastern, shielding her face from the fire, said: 'I have made a decision. I believe that my policy in this affair has been a mistaken one. Anticipating my inevitable opposition, Félicité has met this person in his own setting and has, as I think you would say, lost her eye. I cannot believe that when she has seen him here, and has observed his atrocious antics, his immense vulgarity, she will not come to her senses. Already one can see, she is shaken. After all, I remind myself, she is a de Fouteaux and a de Suze. Am I not right?'

'It's an old trick, darling, you know. It doesn't always work.'

'It is working, however,' said Lady Pastern, setting her mouth. 'She sees him, for example, beside dear Edward to whom she has always been devoted. Of your uncle as a desirable contrast, I say nothing, but at least his clothes are unexceptionable. And though I deeply resent, dearest child, that you should have been forced, in my house, to suffer the attentions of this animal, they have assuredly impressed themselves disagreeably upon Félicité.'

'Disagreeably – yes,' said Carlisle turning pink. 'But look here, Aunt Cecile, he's shooting this nauseating little line with me to – well, to make Fée sit up and take notice.' Lady Pastern momentarily closed her eyes. This, Carlisle remembered, was her habitual reaction to slang. 'And, I'm not sure,' Carlisle added, 'that she hasn't fallen for it.'

'She cannot be anything but disgusted.'

'I wouldn't be astonished if she refuses to come to the Metronome tonight.'

'That is what I hope. But I am afraid she will come. She will not give way so readily, I think.' Lady Pastern rose. 'Whatever happens,' she said, 'I shall break this affair. Do you hear me Carlisle? I shall break it.'

Beyond the door at the far end of the room, Félicité's voice rose, in a sharp crescendo, but the words were indistinguishable.

'They are quarrelling,' said Lady Pastern with satisfaction.

III

As Edward Manx sat silent in his chair, a glass of port and a cup of coffee before him, his thoughts moved out in widening circles from the candle-lit table. Removed from him, Bellairs and Rivera had drawn close to Lord Pastern. Bellairs' voice, loud but edgeless, uttered phrase after phrase. 'Sure, that's right. Don't worry, it's in the bag. It's going to be a world-breaker. OK, we'll run it through. Fine.' Lord Pastern fidgeted, stuttered, chuckled, complained.

Rivera, leaning back in his chair, smiled, said nothing and turned his glass. Manx, who had noticed how frequently it had been refilled, wondered if he was tight.

There they sat, wreathed in cigar-smoke, candle-lit, an unreal group. He saw them as three dissonant figures at the centre of an intolerable design. 'Bellairs,' he told himself, 'is a gaiety merchant. Gaiety!' How fashionable, he reflected, the word had been before the war. Let's be gay, they had all said, and glumly embracing each other had tramped and shuffled, while men like Breezy Bellairs made their noises and did their smiling for them. They christened their children 'Gay,' they used the word in their drawing-room comedies and in their dismal, dismal songs. 'Gaiety!' muttered the disgruntled and angry Edward. 'A lovely word, but the thing itself, when enjoyed is unnamed. There's Cousin George, who is undoubtedly a little mad, sitting, like a mouth-piece for his kind, between a jive-merchant and a cad. And here's Fée antic-ing inside the unholy circle while Cousin Cecile solemnly gyrates against the beat. In an outer ring, I hope unwillingly, is Lisle, and here I sit, as sore as hell, on the perimeter.' He glanced up and found that Rivera was looking at him, not directly, but out of the corners of his eyes. 'Sneering,' thought Edward, 'like an infernal caricature of himself.'

'Buck up, Ned,' Lord Pastern said, grinning at him. 'We haven't had a word from you. You want takin' out of yourself. Bit of gaiety, what?'

'By all means, sir,' said Edward. A white carnation had fallen out of the vase in the middle of the table. He took it up and put it in his coat. 'The blameless life,' he said.

Lord Pastern cackled and turned to Bellairs. 'Well, Breezy, if you think it's right, we'll order the taxis for a quarter past ten. Think you can amuse yourselves till then?' He pushed the decanter towards Bellairs.

'Sure, sure,' Bellairs said. 'No, thanks a lot, no more. A lovely wine, mind you, but I've got to be a good boy.'

Edward slid the port on to Rivera, who, smiling a little more broadly, refilled his glass.

'I'll show you the blanks and the revolver, when we move,' said Lord Pastern. 'They're in the study.' He glanced fretfully at Rivera who slowly pulled his glass towards him. Lord Pastern hated to be kept waiting. 'Ned, you look after Carlos, will you? D'you mind, Carlos? I want to show Breezy the blanks. Come on, Breezy.'

Manx opened the door for his uncle and returned to the table. He sat down and waited for Rivera to make the first move. Spence came in, lingered for a moment, and withdrew. There followed a long silence.

At last Rivera stretched out his legs and held his port to the light. 'I am a man,' he said, 'who likes to come to the point. You are Félicité's cousin, yes?'

'No.'

'No?'

'I'm related to her stepfather.'

'She has spoken of you as her cousin.'

'A courtesy title,' said Edward.

'You are attached to her, I believe?'

Edward paused for three seconds and then said, 'Why not?'

'It is not at all surprising,' Rivera said, and drank half his port. 'Carlisle also speaks of you as her cousin. Is that too a courtesy title?'

Edward pushed back his chair. 'I'm afraid I don't see the point of all this,' he said.

'The point? Certainly. I am a man,' Rivera repeated, 'who likes to come to the point. I am also a man who does not care to be cold-shouldered or to be – what is the expression – taken down a garden path. I find my reception in this house unsympathetic. This is displeasing to me. I meet, at the same time, a lady who is not displeasing to me. Quite on the contrary. I am interested. I make a tactful inquiry. I ask, for example, what is the relationship of this lady to my host. Why not?'

'Because it's a singularly offensive question,' Edward said and thought: 'My God, I'm going to lose my temper.'

Rivera made a convulsive movement of his hand and knocked his glass to the floor. They rose simultaneously.

'In my country,' Rivera said thickly, 'one does not use such expressions without a sequel.'

'Be damned to your country.'

Rivera gripped the back of his chair and moistened his lips. He emitted a shrill belch. Edward laughed. Rivera walked towards him, paused, and raised his hand with the tips of the thumb and middle finger daintily pressed together. He advanced his hand until it was close to Edward's nose and, without marked success, attempted to snap his finger. 'Bastard,' he said cautiously. From the distant ball-room came a syncopated roll of drums ending in a crash of cymbals and a deafening report.

Edward said: 'Don't be a fool, Rivera.'

'I laugh at you till I make myself vomit.'

'Laugh yourself into a coma if you like.'

Rivera laid the palm of his hand against his waist. 'In my country this affair would answer itself with a knife,' he said.

'Make yourself scarce or it'll answer itself with a kick in the pants,' said Edward. 'And if you worry Miss Wayne again I'll give you a damn' sound hiding.'

'Aha!' cried Rivera, 'so it is not Félicité but the cousin. It is the enchanting little Carlisle. And I am to be warned off, ha? No, no, my friend.' He backed away to the door. 'No, no, no, no.'

'*Get out.*'

Rivera laughed with great virtuosity and made an effective exit into the hall. He left the door open. Edward heard his voice on the next landing. 'What is the matter?' and after a pause, 'But certainly if you wish it.'

A door slammed.

Edward walked once round the table in an irresolute manner. He then wandered to the sideboard and drove his hands through his hair. 'This is incredible,' he muttered. 'It's extraordinary. I never dreamt of it.' He noticed that his hand was shaking and poured himself a stiff jorum of whisky. 'I suppose,' he thought, 'it's been there all the time and I simply didn't recognize it.'

Spence and his assistant came in. 'I beg your pardon, sir,' said Spence. 'I thought the gentlemen had left.'

'It's all right, Spence. Clear, if you want to. Pay no attention to me.'

'Are you not feeling well, Mr Edward?'

'I'm all right, I think. I've had a great surprise.'

'Indeed, sir? Pleasant, I trust.'

'In its way, wonderful, Spence. Wonderful.'

IV

'There y'are,' said Lord Pastern complacently. 'Five rounds and five extras. Neat, aren't they?'

'Look good to me,' said Bellairs, returning him the blank cartridges. 'But I wouldn't know.' Lord Pastern broke open his revolver and began to fill the chamber. 'We'll try 'em,' he said.

'Not in here, for Pete's sake, Lord Pastern.'

'In the ballroom.'

'It'll rock the ladies a bit, won't it?'

'What of it?' said Lord Pastern simply. He snapped the revolver shut and gave the drawer a shove back on the desk. 'I can't be bothered puttin' that thing away,' he said. 'You go to the ballroom. I've got a job to do. I'll join you in a minute.'

Obediently, Breezy left him and went into the ballroom where he wandered about restlessly, sighing and yawning and glancing towards the door.

Presently his host came in looking preoccupied.

'Where's Carlos?' Lord Pastern demanded.

'Still in the dining-room, I think,' said Bellairs with his loud laugh. 'Wonderful port you've turned on for us, you know, Lord Pastern.'

'Hope he can hold it. We don't want him playin' the fool with the show.'

'He can hold it.'

Lord Pastern clapped his revolver down on the floor near the tympani. Bellairs eyed it uneasily.

'I wanted to ask you,' said Lord Pastern sitting behind the drums. 'Have you spoken to Sydney Skelton?'

Bellairs smiled extensively: 'Well, I just haven't got round . . . ' he began.

Lord Pastern cut him short. 'If you don't want to tell him,' he said, 'I will.'

'No, no!' cried Bellairs in a hurry. 'No. I don't think that'd be quite desirable, Lord Pastern, if you can understand.' He looked anxiously at his host who had turned away to the piano and with an air of restless preoccupation, examined the black-and-white parasol. Breezy continued: 'I mean to say, Syd's funny. He's very temperamental, if you know what I mean. He's quite a tough guy to handle, Syd. You have to pick your moment with Syd, if you can understand.'

'Don't keep on asking if I can understand things that are as simple as falling off a log,' Lord Pastern rejoined irritably. 'You think I'm good on the drums, you've said so.'

'Sure, sure.'

'You said if I'd made it my profession I'd have been as good as they come. You said any band'd be proud to have me. Right. I am going to make it my profession and I'm prepared to be your full-time tympanist. Good. Tell Skelton and let him go. Perfectly simple.'

'Yes, but – '

'He'll get a job elsewhere fast enough, won't he?'

'Yes. Sure. Easy. But . . . '

'Very well, then,' said Lord Pastern conclusively. He had unscrewed the handle from the parasol and was now busy with the top end of the shaft. 'This comes to bits,' he said. 'Rather clever, what? French.'

'Look!' said Bellairs winningly. He laid his soft white hand on Lord Pastern's coat. 'I'm going to speak very frankly, Lord Pastern. You know. It's a hard old world in our game, if you under – I mean, I have to think all round a proposition like this, don't I?'

'You've said you wished you had me permanently,' Lord Pastern reminded him. He spoke with a certain amount of truculence but rather absent-mindedly. He had unscrewed a small section from the top end of the parasol shaft. Breezy watched him mesmerized, as he took up his revolver and, with the restless concentration of a small boy in mischief, poked this section a short way up the muzzle, at the same time holding down with his thumb the spring catch that served to keep the parasol closed. 'This,' he said, 'would fit.'

'Hi!' Breezy said, 'is that gun loaded?'

'Of course,' Lord Pastern muttered. He put down the piece of shaft and glanced up. 'You said it to me and Rivera,' he added. He had Hotspur's trick of reverting to the last remark but four.

'I know, I know,' Bellairs gabbled, smiling to the full extent of his mouth, 'but listen. I'm going to put this very crudely . . . '

'Why the hell shouldn't you!'

'Well then. You're very keen and you're good. Sure, you're good! But, excuse my frankness, will you stay keen? That's my point, Lord Pastern. Suppose, to put it crudely, you died on it.'

'I'm fifty-five and as fit as a flea.'

'I mean, suppose you kind of lost interest. Where,' asked Mr Bellairs passionately, 'would I be then?'

'I've told you perfectly plainly . . .'

'Yes, but . . .'

'Do you call me a liar, you bloody fellow?' shouted Lord Pastern, two brilliant patches of scarlet flaming over his cheekbones. He clapped the dismembered parts of the parasol on the piano and turned on his conductor who began to stammer.

'Now, listen, Lord Pastern, I – I'm nervy tonight. I'm all upset. Don't get me flustered, now.'

Lord Pastern bared his teeth at him. 'You're a fool,' he said. 'I've been watchin' you.' He appeared to cogitate and come to a decision. 'Ever read a magazine called *Harmony?*' he demanded.

Breezy shied violently. 'Why yes. Why – I don't know what your idea is, Lord Pastern, bringing that up.'

'I've half a mind,' Lord Pastern said darkly, 'to write to that paper. I know a chap on the staff.' He brooded for a moment, whistling between his teeth and then barked abruptly: 'If you don't speak to Skelton tonight, I'll talk to him myself.'

'OK, OK I'll have a wee chat with Syd. OK.'

Lord Pastern looked fixedly at him. 'You'd better pull y'self together,' he said. He took up his drumsticks and without more ado beat out a deafening crescendo, crashed his cymbals and snatching up his revolver pointed it at Bellairs and fired. The report echoed madly in the empty ballroom. The piano, the cymbals and the double-bass zoomed in protest and Bellairs, white to the lips, danced sideways.

'For chrissake!' he said violently and broke into a profuse sweat.

Lord Pastern laughed delightedly and laid his revolver on the piano. 'Good, isn't it?' he said. 'Let's just run through the programme. First, there's "A New Way With Old Tunes." "Any Ice Today?" "I Got Everythin'," "The Peanut Vendor", and "The Umbrella Man". That's a damn' good idea of mine about the umbrellas.'

Bellairs eyed the collection on the piano and nodded.

'The Black and White parasol's m'wife's. She doesn't know I've taken it. You might put it together and hide it under the others will you? We'll smuggle 'em out when she's not lookin'.'

Bellairs fumbled with the umbrellas and Lord Pastern continued: 'Then Skelton does his thing. I find it a bit dull, that number. And then the Sandra woman does her songs. And then,' he said with an affectation of carelessness, 'then you say somethin' to introduce me, don't you?'

'That's right.'

'Yes. Somethin' to the effect that I happened to show you a thing I'd written, you know, and you were taken with it and that I've decided that my métier lies in this direction and all that. What?'

'Quite.'

'I come out and we play it once through and then we swing it, and then there's shootin', and then, by God, I go into my solo. Yes.'

Lord Pastern took up his drumsticks, held them poised for a moment and appeared to go into a brief trance. 'I'm still not so sure the other routine wasn't the best after all,' he said.

'Listen! Listen!' Breezy began in a panic.

Lord Pastern said absently: 'Now, you keep your hair on. I'm thinkin'.' He appeared to think for some moments and then, ejaculating: 'Sombrero!' darted out of the room.

Breezy Bellairs wiped his face with his handkerchief, sank on to the piano stool and held his head in his hands.

After a considerable interval the ballroom doors were opened and Rivera came in. Bellairs eyed him. 'How's tricks, Carlos?' he asked dolefully.

'Not good.' Rivera stroking his moustache with his forefinger, walked stiffly to the piano. 'I have quarrelled with Félicité.'

'You asked for it, didn't you? Your little line with Miss Wayne . . .'

'It is well to show women that they are not irreplaceable. They become anxious and, in a little while, they are docile.'

'Has it worked out that way?'

'Not yet, perhaps. I am angry with her.' He made a florid and violent gesture. 'With them all! I have been treated like a dog. I Carlos de . . .'

'Listen,' said Breezy, 'I can't face a temperament from you, old boy. I'm nearly crazy with worry myself. I just can't face it. God, I wish I'd never taken the old fool on! God, I'm in a mess! Give me a cigarette, Carlos.'

'I am sorry. I have none.'

'I asked you to get me cigarettes,' said Breezy and his voice rose shrilly.

'It was not convenient. You smoke too much.'

'Go to hell.'

'Everywhere,' Rivera shouted, 'I am treated with impertinence. Everywhere I am insulted.' He advanced upon Bellairs, his head thrust forward. 'I am sick of it all,' he said. 'I have humbled myself too much. I am a man of quick decisions. No longer shall I cheapen myself by playing in a common dance band . . . '

'Here, here, here!'

'I give you, now, my notice.'

'You're under contract. Listen, old man . . . '

'I spit on your contract. No longer shall I be your little errand boy. "Get me some cigarettes." Bah!'

'Carlos!'

'I shall return to my own country.'

'Listen, old boy . . . I – I'll raise your screw . . . ' His voice faltered.

Rivera looked at him and smiled. 'Indeed? By how much? It would be by perhaps five pounds?'

'Have a heart, Carlos.'

'Or if, for instance, you would care to advance me five hundred . . . '

'You're crazy! Carlos, for Pete's sake . . . Honestly, I haven't got it.'

'Then,' said Rivera magnificently, 'you must look for another to bring you your cigarettes. For me it is . . . finish.'

Breezy wailed loudly: 'And where will I be? What about me?'

Rivera smiled and moved away. With an elaborate display of non-chalance, he surveyed himself in a wall-glass, fingering his tie. 'You will be in a position of great discomfort, my friend,' he said. 'You will be unable to replace me. I am quite irreplaceable.' He examined his moustache closely in the glass and caught sight of Breezy's reflection. 'Don't look like that,' he said, 'you are extremely ugly when you look like that. Quite revolting.'

'It's a breach of contract. I can . . . ' Breezy wetted his lips. 'There's the law,' he mumbled. 'Suppose . . . '

Rivera turned and faced him.

'The law?' he said. 'I am obliged to you. Of course, one can call upon the law, can one not? That is a wise step for a band leader to take, no doubt. I find the suggestion amusing. I shall enjoy repeating it to the ladies who smile at you so kindly, and ask you so anxiously for their favourite numbers. When I no longer play in your band their smiles will become infrequent and they will go elsewhere for their favourite numbers.'

'You wouldn't do that, Carlos.'

'Let me tell you, my good Breezy, that if the law is to be invoked, it is I who invoke it.'

'Damn and blast you,' Breezy shouted in a frenzy.

'What the devil's all the row about?' asked Lord Pastern. He had entered unobserved. A wide-brimmed sombrero decorated his head, its strap supporting his double-chin. 'I thought I'd wear this,' he said. It goes with the shootin' don't you think? Yipee!'

V

When Rivera left her, Félicité had sat on in the study, her hands clenched between her knees, trying to bury quickly and forever the memory of the scene they had just ended. She looked aimlessly about her, at the litter of tools in the open drawer at her elbow, at the typewriter, at familiar prints, ornaments and books. Her throat was dry. She was filled with nausea and an arid hatred. She wished ardently to rid herself of all memory of Rivera and in doing so to humiliate and injure him. She was still for so long that when at last she moved, her right leg was numb and her foot pricked and tingled. As she rose stiffly and cautiously, she heard someone cross the landing, pass the study and go into the drawing-room next door.

'I'll go up to Hendy,' she thought. 'I'll ask Hendy to tell them I'm not coming to the Metronome.'

She went out on the landing. Somewhere on the second floor her stepfather's voice shouted: 'My sombrero, you silly chap – somebody's taken it. That's all. Somebody's collared it.' Spence came through the drawing-room door, carrying an envelope on a salver.

'It's for you, Miss,' he said. 'It was left on the hall table. I'm sure I'm very sorry it was not noticed before.'

She took it. It was addressed in typescript. Across the top was printed a large 'Urgent' with 'by District Messenger' underneath. Félicité returned to the study and tore it open.

Three minutes later Miss Henderson's door was flung open and she, lifting her gaze from her book, saw Félicité, glowing before her.

'Hendy – Hendy, come and help me dress. Hendy, come and make me lovely. Something marvellous has happened. Hendy, darling, it's going to be a wonderful party.'

CHAPTER 5

A Wreath for Rivera

Against a deep blue background the arm of a giant metronome kept up its inane and constant gesture. It was outlined in miniature lights, and to those patrons who had drunk enough, it left in its wake a formal ghost-pattern of itself in colour. It was mounted on part of the wall overhanging the band alcove. The ingenious young man responsible for the décor had so designed this alcove that the band platform itself appeared as a projection from the skeleton tower of the metronome. The tip of the arm swept to and fro above the bandsmen's heads in a maddening reiterative arc, pointing them out, insisting on their noise. This idea had been considered 'great fun' by the ingenious young man but it had been found advisable to switch off the mechanism from time to time and when this was done the indicator pointed downwards. Either Breezy Bellairs or a favoured soloist was careful to place himself directly beneath the light-studded pointer at its tip.

On their semi-circular rostrum the seven performers of the dance band crouched; blowing, scraping and hitting at their instruments. This was the band that worked on extension nights, from dinner-time to eleven o'clock, at the Metronome: it was known as The Jivesters, and was not as highly paid or as securely established as Breezy Bellairs and His Boys. But of course it was a good band, carefully selected by Caesar Bonn, the manager and *maître de café*, who was also a big shareholder in the Metronome.

Caesar himself, glossy, immeasurably smart, in full control of his accurately graded cordiality, moved, with a light waggle of his hips, from the vestibule into the restaurant and surveyed his guests. He bowed roguishly as his head-waiter, with raised hand, preceded a party of five to their table. 'Hallo, Caesar. Evenin',' said Lord Pastern. 'Brought my family, you see.'

Caesar flourished his hands. 'It is a great evening for the Metronome, my lady. A gala of galas.'

'No doubt,' said her ladyship.

She seated her guests. Herself, with erect bust, faced the dance floor, her back to the wall. She raised her lorgnette. Caesar and the head-waiter hovered. Lord Pastern ordered hock.

'We are much too close, George,' Lady Pastern shouted above The Jivesters who had just broken out in a frenzy. And indeed their table had been crammed in alongside the band dais and hard by the tympanist. Félicité could have touched his foot. 'I had it put here specially,' Lord Pastern yelled. 'I knew you'd want to watch me.'

Carlisle, sitting between her uncle and Edward Manx, nervously clutched her evening bag and wondered if they were all perhaps a little mad. What, for instance, had come over Félicité? Why, whenever she looked at Edward, did she blush? Why did she look so often and so queerly at him, like a bewildered and – yes – a besotted schoolgirl? And why, on the landing at Duke's Gate, after a certain atrocious scene with Rivera (Carlisle closed her memory on the scene) had Ned behaved with such ferocity? And why, after all, was she, in the middle of a complicated and disagreeable crisis, so happy?

Edward Manx, seated between Félicité and Carlisle, was also bewildered. A great many things had happened to him that evening. He had had a row with Rivera in the dining-room. He had made an astonishing discovery. Later (and, unlike Carlisle, he found this recollection entirely agreeable) he had come on to the landing at the precise moment when Rivera was making a determined effort to embrace Carlisle and had hit Rivera very hard on the left ear. While they were still, all three of them, staring at each other, Félicité had appeared with a letter in her hands. She had taken one look at Edward and going first white under her make-up and then scarlet, had fled upstairs. From that moment she had behaved in the most singular manner imaginable. She kept catching his eye and as often as this happened she smiled and blushed. Once she gave a mad little laugh. Edward shook his head and asked Lady Pastern to dance. She consented. He rose, and placing his right hand behind her iron waist, walked her cautiously down the dance floor. It was formidable, dancing with Cousin Cecile.

'If anything,' she said when they had reached the spot farthest away from the band, 'could compensate for my humiliation in appearing at this lamentable affair, my dearest boy, it is the change your presence has wrought in Félicité.'

'Really?' said Edward nervously.

'Indeed, yes. From her childhood, you have exerted a profound influence.'

'Look here, Cousin Cecile – ' Edward began in extreme discomfort, but at that moment the dance band which had for some time contented itself with the emission of syncopated grunts and pants, suddenly flared into an elaborate rumpus. Edward was silenced.

Lord Pastern put his head on one side and contemplated the band with an air of critical patronage. 'They're not bad, you know,' he said, 'but they haven't got enough guts. Wait till you hear us, Lisle. What?'

'I know,' Carlisle said encouragingly. At the moment his naïveté touched her. She was inclined to praise him as one would a child. Her eyes followed Edward who now guided Lady Pastern gingerly past the band-dais. Carlisle watched them go by and in so doing caught the eye of a man who sat at the next table. He was a monkish-looking person with a fastidious mouth and well-shaped head. A woman with short dark hair was with him. They had an air of comradeship. 'They look nice,' Carlisle thought. She felt suddenly uplifted and kindly disposed to all the world, and, on this impulse, turned to Félicité. She found that Félicité, also, was watching Edward and still with that doting and inexplicable attention.

'Fée,' she said softly, 'what's up? What's happened?' Félicité, without changing the direction of her gaze, said: 'Something too shattering, darling. I'm all *bouleversée* but I'm in Heaven.'

Edward and Lady Pastern, after two gyrations, came to a halt by their table. She disengaged herself and resumed her seat. Edward slipped in between Carlisle and Félicité. Félicité leant towards him and drew the white carnation from his coat. 'There's nobody else here with a white flower,' she said softly.

'I'm very *vieux jeu* in my ways,' Edward rejoined.

'Let's dance, shall we?'

'Yes, of course.'

'Want to dance, C?' asked Lord Pastern.

'No, thank you, George.'

'Mind if Lisle and I trip a measure? It's a quarter to eleven, I'll have to go round and join the Boys in five minutes. Come on, Lisle.'

You had, thought Carlisle, to keep your wits about you when you danced with Uncle George. He had a fine sense of rhythm and tremendous vigour. No stickler for the conventions, he improvised steps as the spirit moved him, merely tightening his grip upon her as an indication of further variations and eccentricities. She noticed other couples glancing at them with more animation than usually appears on the faces of British revellers.

'D'you jitter-bug?' he asked.

'No, darling.'

'Pity. They think 'emselves too grand for it in this place. Sickenin' lot of snobs people are, by and large, Lisle. Did I tell you I'm seriously considerin' givin' up the title?'

He swung her round with some violence. At the far end of the room she caught a glimpse of her cousin and his partner. Ned's back was towards her. Félicité gazed into his eyes. Her hand moved farther across his shoulders. He stooped his head.

'Let's rejoin Aunt Cile, shall we?' said Carlisle in a flat voice.

II

Breezy Bellairs hung up his overcoat on the wall and sat down, without much show of enthusiasm, at a small table in the inner room behind the office. The tympanist, Syd Skelton, threw a pack of cards on the table and glanced at his watch. 'Quarter-to,' he said. 'Time for a brief gamble.'

He dealt two poker hands. Breezy and Skelton played show poker on most nights at about this time. They would leave the Boys in their room behind the band dais and wander across to the office. They would exchange a word with Caesar or David Hahn, the secretary, in the main office, and then repair to the inner room for their gamble. It was an agreeable prelude to the long night's business.

'Hear you've been dining in exalted places,' said Skelton acidly.

Breezy smiled automatically and with trembling hands picked up his cards. They played in a scarcely broken silence. Once or twice Skelton invited conversation, but without success.

At last he said irritably: 'What's the trouble? Why the great big silence?'

Breezy fiddled with his cards and said: 'I'm licked all to hell, Syd.'

'For the love of Mike! What's the tragedy this time?'

'Everything. I'll crack if it goes on. Honest, I'm shot to pieces.'

'It's your own show. I've warned you. You look terrible.'

'And how do I feel! Listen, Syd, it's this stunt, tonight. It's his lordship. It's been a big mistake.'

'I could have told you that, too. I did tell you.'

'I know. I know. But we're booked to capacity, Syd.'

'It's cheap publicity. Nothing more nor less and you know it. Pandering to a silly dope, just because he's got a title.'

'He's not all that bad. As an artist.'

'He's terrible,' said Skelton briefly.

'I know the number's crazy and full of corn but it'll get by. It's not that, old boy, it's him. Honest, Syd, I think he's crackers.' Breezy threw his cards face down on the table. 'He's got me that *nervy*,' he said. 'Listen, Syd, he's – he hasn't said anything to you, has he?'

'What about?'

'So he hasn't. All right. Fine. Don't take any notice if he does, old man.'

Skelton leant back in his chair. 'What the hell are you trying to tell me?' he demanded.

'Now, don't make me nervous,' Breezy implored him. 'You know how nervy I get. It's just a crazy notion he's got. I'll stall him off, you bet.' He paused. Skelton said ominously, 'It wouldn't be anything about wanting to repeat this fiasco, would it?'

'In a way it would, Syd. Mind, it's laughable.'

'Now, you get this,' Skelton said, and leant across the table. 'I've stood down once, tonight, to oblige you, and I don't like it and I won't do it again. What's more it's given me a kind of unpleasant feeling that I'm doing myself no good, working with an outfit that goes in for cheap sensationalism. You know me. I'm quick tempered and I make quick decisions. There's other bands.'

'Now, Syd, Syd, Syd! Take it easy,' Breezy gabbled. 'Forget it, old boy. I wouldn't have mentioned anything only he talked about chatting to you, himself.'

'By God,' Skelton said, staring at him, 'are you trying to tell me, by any chance, that this old so-and-so thinks he'd like my job? Have you got the flaming nerve to . . . '

'For chrissake, Syd! Listen, Syd, I said it was crazy. Listen, it's going to be all right. It's not my fault, Syd. Be fair, now, it's not my fault.'

'Whose fault is it then?'

'Carlos,' said Breezy, lowering his voice to a whisper. 'Take it easy, now. He's next door, having a drink with Caesar. It's Carlos. He's put the idea into the old bee's head. He wants to keep in with him on account of the girl can't make up her mind and him wanting the old bee to encourage her. It's all Carlos, Syd. He told him he was wonderful.'

Skelton said briefly what he thought of Rivera. Breezy looked nervously towards the door. 'This settles it,' Skelton said, and rose. 'I'll talk to Carlos, by God.' Breezy clawed at him. 'No, Syd, not now. Not before the show. Keep your voice down, Syd, there's a pal. He's in there. You know how he is. He's thrown a temperament once tonight. Geeze,' cried Breezy, springing to his feet, 'I nearly forgot! He wants us to use the other routine in the new number, after all. Can you beat it? First it's this way and then it's what-have-you. He's got me so's I'm liable to give an imitation of a maestro doing two numbers at once. Gawd knows how his lordship'll take it. I got to tell the boys. I as near as damn it forgot, I'm that nervy. Listen, you haven't heard what's really got me so worried. You know what I am. It's that gun. It's such a hell of a thing, Syd, and his lordship's made those blanks himself and, by God, I'm nervous. He's dopey enough to mix the real things up with the phoney ones. They were all mucked up together in a bloody drawer, Syd, and there you are. And he really points the thing at Carlos, old boy, and fires it. Doesn't he now?'

'I wouldn't lose any sleep if he plugged him,' said Skelton with violence.

'Don't talk that way, Syd,' Breezy whispered irritably. 'It's a hell of a situation. I hoped you'd help me, Syd.'

'Why don't you have a look at the gun?'

'Me? I wouldn't know. He wouldn't let me near it. I tell you straight, I'm scared to go near him for fear I start him up bawling me out.'

After a long pause, Skelton said: 'Are you serious about this gun?'

'Do I look as if I was kidding?'

'It's eight minutes to eleven. We'd better go across. If I get a chance I'll ask him to show me the ammunition.'

'Fine, Syd. That'd be swell,' said Breezy, mopping his forehead. 'It'd be marvellous. You're a pal, Syd. Come on. Let's go.'

'Mind,' Skelton said, 'I'm not passing up the other business. I've just about had Mr Carlos Rivera. He's going to find something out before he's much older. Come on.'

They passed through the office. Rivera, who was sitting there with Caesar Bonn, disregarded them. Breezy looked timidly at him. 'I'm just going to fix it up with the Boys, old man,' he said. 'You'll enter by the end door, won't you?'

'Why not?' Rivera said acidly. 'It is my usual entrance. I perform as I rehearse. Naturally.'

'That's right. Naturally. Excuse my fussiness. Let's go, Syd.'

Caesar rose. 'It is time? Then I must felicitate our new artist.'

He preceded them across the vestibule where crowds of late arrivals still streamed in. Here they encountered Félicité, Carlisle and Edward. 'We're going in to wish George luck,' said Félicité. 'Hallo, Syd. Nice of you to let him have his fling. Come on, chaps.'

They all entered the bandroom which was immediately behind the dais end of the restaurant and led into the band alcove. Here they found the boys assembled with their instruments. Breezy held up his hand and, sweating copiously, beamed at them. 'Listen, boys. Get this. We'll use the other routine, if it's all the same with the composer. Carlos doesn't feel happy about the fall. He's afraid he may hurt himself on account he's holding his instrument.'

'Here!' said Lord Pastern.

'It's the way you wanted it, Lord Pastern, isn't it!' Breezy gabbled. 'That's fine, isn't it! Better egzzit altogether.'

'I faint and get carried out?'

'That's right. The other routine. I persuaded Carlos. Everybody happy? Swell.'

The Boys began to warm up their instruments. The room was filled with slight anticipatory noises. The double-bass muttered and zoomed.

Skelton strolled over to Lord Pastern. 'I had to come in and wish the new sensation all the best,' he said, looking hard at him.

'Thank yer.'

'A great night,' Caesar Bonn muttered. 'It will be long remembered.'

'Would this be a loaded gun?' Skelton asked, and laughed unpleasantly.

The revolver lay, together with the sombrero, near the drums. Lord Pastern took it up. Skelton raised his hands above his head. 'I confess everything,' he said. '*Is* it loaded?'

'With blanks.'

'By cripes,' said Skelton with a loud laugh, 'I hope they *are* blanks.'

'George made them himself,' said Félicité.

Skelton lowered his right hand and held it out towards Lord Pastern who put the revolver into it.

Breezy, at a distance, sighed heavily. Skelton broke the revolver, slipped a finger nail behind the rim of a cartridge and drew it out.

'Very nice work, Lord Pastern,' he said. He spun the cylinder, drawing out and replacing one blank after the other. 'Very nice work, indeed,' he said.

Lord Pastern, obviously gratified, embarked on a history of the revolver, of his own prowess as a marksman, and of the circumstances under which his brother-in-law had presented it to him. He pointed out the initials scratched under the butt. Skelton made a show of squinting down the barrel, snapped the revolver shut, and returned the weapon to Lord Pastern. He turned away and glanced at Breezy. 'OK,' he said. 'What are we waiting for?' He began to heighten the tension of his drums. 'Good luck to the new act,' he said, and the drums throbbed.

'Thanks, Syd,' said Breezy.

His fingers were in his waistcoat pocket. He looked anxiously at Skelton. He felt in one pocket after another. Sweat hung in fine beads over his eyebrows.

'What's up, boy?' said Happy Hart.

'I can't find my tablet.'

He began pulling his pocket linings out. 'I'm all to pieces without it,' he said. 'God, I know I've got one somewhere!'

The door leading to the restaurant opened and The Jivesters came through with their instruments. They grinned at Breezy's Boys and looked sideways at Lord Pastern. The room was full of oiled heads, black figures and the strange shapes of saxophones, double-basses, piano accordions and drums.

'We'd better make ourselves scarce, Fée,' Edward said. 'Come on, Lisle. Good luck, Cousin George.'

'Good luck.'

'Good luck.'

They went out. Breezy still searched his pockets. The others watched him nervously.

'You shouldn't let yourself get this way,' said Skelton.

Lord Pastern pointed an accusing finger at Breezy: 'Now perhaps you'll see the value of what I was tellin' you,' he admonished. Breezy shot a venomous glance at him.

'For Heaven's sake, boy,' said Happy Hart. 'We're *on*.'

'I've got to have it. I'm all shaky. I can't look. One of you . . . '

'What *is* all this!' Lord Pastern cried with extreme irritation. He darted at Breezy.

'It's only a tablet,' Breezy said. 'I always take one. For my nerves.'

Lord Pastern said accusingly, 'Tablet be damned!'

'For chrissake, I *got* to have it, blast you.'

'Put your hands up.'

Lord Pastern began with ruthless efficiency to search Breezy. He hit him all over and turned out his pockets, allowing various objects to fall about his feet. He opened his cigarette case and wallet and explored their contents. He patted and prodded. Breezy giggled. 'I'm ticklish,' he said foolishly. Finally Lord Pastern jerked a handkerchief out of Breezy's breast pocket. A small white object fell from it. Breezy swooped on it, clapped his hand to his mouth and swallowed. 'Thanks a lot. All set, boys? Let's go.'

They went out ahead of him. The lights on the walls had been switched off. Only the pink table-lamps glowed. A floodlight, hidden in the alcove ceiling, drove down its pool of amber on the gleaming dais; the restaurant was a swimming cave filled with dim faces, occasional jewels, many colours. The waiters flickered about inside it.

Little drifts of cigarette smoke hung above the tables. From the restaurant the band dais glowed romantically in its alcove. The players and their instruments looked hard and glossy. Above them the arm of the giant metronome pointed motionless at the floor. The Boys, smiling as if in great delight, seated themselves. The umbrellas, the sombrero and the tympani were carried in by waiters.

In the band room Lord Pastern, standing beside Breezy, fiddled with his revolver, whistled under his breath, and peered sideways through the door. Beyond the tympani, he could see the dimly glowing faces of his wife, his stepdaughter, his niece and his cousin. Félicité's face was inclined up to Ned Manx's. Lord Pastern suddenly gave a shrill cackle of laughter.

Breezy Bellairs glanced at him in dismay, passed his hand over his head, pulled down his waistcoat, assumed his ventriloquist's doll smile and made his entrance. The Boys played him on with their signature tune. A patter of clapping filled the restaurant like a mild shower. Breezy smiled, bowed, turned and, using finicking sharp gestures that were expressly his own, conducted.

Syd Skelton bounced slightly in his seat. His foot moved against the floor, not tapping but flexing and relaxing in a constant beat and against the syncopated, precise, illogic of the noises he made. The four saxophonists swayed together, their faces all looking alike, expressionless because of their compressed lips and puffed cheeks. When they had passages of rest they at once smiled. The band was playing tunes that Carlisle knew; very old tunes. They were recognizable at first and then a bedevilment known as the Breezy Bellairs Manner sent them screeching and thudding into a jungle of obscurity. 'All swing bandsmen,' Carlisle thought, 'ought to be Negroes. There's something wrong about their not being Negroes.'

Now three of them were singing. They had walked forward with long easy steps and stood with their heads close together, rocking in unison. They made ineffable grimaces. 'Peea-nuts,' they wailed. But they didn't let the song about peanuts, which Carlisle rather liked, speak for itself. They bedevilled and twisted and screwed it and then went beaming back to their instruments. There was another old song: 'The Umbrella Man'. She had a simple taste and its quiet monotony pleased her. They did it once, quietly and monotonously. The floodlight dimmed and a brilliant spotlight found the pianist.

He was playing by himself and singing. That was all right, thought Carlisle. She could mildly enjoy it. But a piercing shriek cut across the naïve tune. The spotlight switched to a doorway at the far end of the restaurant. Carlos Rivera stood there, his hands crawling over the keys of his piano accordion. He advanced between the tables and mounted the dais. Breezy turned to Rivera. He hardly moved his baton. His flesh seemed to jump about on his submerged skeleton. This was his Manner. Rivera, without accompaniment, squeezed trickles, blasts and moans from his piano accordion. He was a master of his medium. He looked straight at Carlisle, widening his eyes and bowing himself towards her. The sounds he made were frankly lewd, thought Edward Manx. It was monstrous and ridiculous that people in evening clothes should sit idly in a restaurant, mildly diverted, while Rivera directed his lascivious virtuosity at Carlisle.

Now the spotlight was in the centre of the dais and only the tympanist played, while the double-bass slapped his instrument. The others moved one by one through the spotlight, holding opened umbrellas and turning them like wheels.

It was an old trick and they did it, Carlisle thought, sillily. They underdid it. Lady Pastern during a quieter passage said clearly: 'Félicité, that is my Ascot parasol.'

'Well, Maman, I believe it is.'

'Your stepfather had no right whatsoever. It was a wedding present of great value. The handle is jewelled.'

'Never mind.'

'I object categorically and emphatically.'

'He's having difficulty with it. Look, they've stopped turning their parasols.'

The players were all back in their seats. The noise broadened and then faded out in an unanticipated wail and they were silent.

Breezy bowed and smiled and bowed. Rivera looked at Carlisle.

A young woman in a beautiful dress and with hair like blonde seaweed came out of a side door and stood in the spotlight, twisting a length of scarlet chiffon in her hands. She contemplated her audience as if she was a sort of willing sacrifice and began to moo very earnestly: 'Yeoo knee-oo it was onlee summer lightning.' Carlisle and Edward both detested her.

Next Syd Skelton and a saxophonist played a duet which was a *tour de force* of acrobatics, and earned a solid round of applause.

When it was over Skelton bowed and with an expression of huffy condescension walked into the band room.

In the ensuing pause, Breezy advanced to the edge of the dais. His smile was broad and winning. He said in a weak voice that he wanted to thank them all very very much for the wonderful reception his Boys had been given and that he had a little announcement to make. He felt sure that when he told them what was in store for them, they would agree with him that this was a very, very special occasion. (Lady Pastern hissed under her breath.) Some weeks ago, Breezy said, he had been privileged to hear a wonderful little performance on the tympani by a distinguished – well, he wouldn't say amateur. He had prevailed upon this remarkable performer to join the Boys tonight and as an additional attraction the number given would be this performer's own composition. Breezy stepped back, pronounced Lord Pastern's names and title with emphasis and looked expectantly towards the door at the rear of the alcove.

Carlisle, like all other relations, distant or close, of Lord Pastern, had often suffered acute embarrassment at his hands. Tonight she had fully expected to endure again that all too familiar wave of discomfort. When, however, he came through the door and stood before them with pink cheeks and a nervous smile, she was suddenly filled with compassion. It was silly, futile and immensely touching that he should make a fool of himself in this particular way. Her heart went out to him.

He walked to the tympani, made a polite little bow, and with an anxious expression, took his seat. They saw him, with a furtive air, lay his revolver on the dais close to Félicité's chair and place his sombrero over it. Breezy pointed his baton at him and said, 'Ladies and Gentlemen: "Hot Guy. Hot Gunner." ' He gave the initial down-beat and they were off.

It sounded, really, much like all the other numbers they had heard that night, Carlisle thought. Lord Pastern banged, and rattled, and zinged much in the same way as Syd Skelton. The words, when the three singers came out, were no sillier than those of the other songs. The tune was rather catchy. But, 'Oh,' she thought, 'how vulnerable he is among his tympani!'

Edward thought: 'There he sits, catsmeat to any satirist who feels as I do about the social set-up. You might make a cartoon of this or a parable. A cartoon, certainly. Cousin George, thumping and banging away under Breezy's baton and in the background a stream of displaced persons. The metronome is Time . . . finger of scorn . . . making its inane gesture to society. A bit too obvious, of course,' he thought, dismissing it, 'false, because of its partial truth.' And he turned his head to watch Carlisle.

Félicité thought: 'There goes George. He has fun, anyway.' Her glance strayed to Lord Pastern's sombrero. She touched Edward's knee. He bent towards her and she said in his ear: 'Shall I pinch George's gun? I could. Look!' She reached out towards the edge of the dais and slipped her hand under the sombrero.

'Fée, don't!' he ejaculated.

'Do you dare me?'

He shook his head violently.

'Poor George,' said Félicité, 'what *would* he do?' She withdrew her hand and leant back in her chair turning the white carnation in her fingers. 'Shall I put it in my hair?' she wondered. 'It would probably look silly and fall out but it might be a good idea. I wish he'd say something – just one thing – to show we understand each other. After this we can't just go on for ever, pretending.'

Lady Pastern thought: 'There is no end to one's capacity for humiliation. He discredits me and he discredits his class. It's the same story. There will be the same gossip, the same impertinences in the paper, the same mortification. Nevertheless,' she thought, 'I did well to come. I did well to suffer this torment tonight. My instinct was correct.' She looked steadily at Rivera who was advancing into the centre of the stage. 'I have disposed of you,' she thought triumphantly.

Lord Pastern thought: 'No mistakes so far. And one, bang and two bang and one crash bang zing. One two and three with his accordeen and wait for it. This is perfectly splendid. I *am* this noise. Look out. Here he comes. Hi-de oh hi. Yip. Here he comes. It's going to work. Hot gunner with his accord-een.'

He crashed his cymbal, silenced it and leant back in his seat.

Rivera had advanced in the spotlight. The rest of the band was tacit. The great motionless arm of the metronome stabbed its pointer down at his head. He seemed rapt: at once tormented and exalted. He swayed and jerked and ogled. Although he was not by any means ridiculous, he was the puppet of his own music. The performance was a protracted crescendo, and as it rocketed up to its climax he swayed backwards at a preposterous angle, his instrument raised, the pointer menacing it as it undulated across his chest. A screaming dissonance abruptly tore loose from the general din, the spotlight switched abruptly to the tympani. Lord Pastern, wearing his sombrero, had risen. Advancing to within five feet of Rivera he pointed his revolver at him and fired.

The accordion blared grotesquely down a scale. Rivera sagged at the knees and fell. The accordion crashed a final chord and was silent. At the same moment as the shot was fired the tenor saxophonist played a single shrill note and sat down. Lord Pastern, apparently bewildered, looked from the recumbent Rivera to the saxophonist, paused for a second and then fired three more blanks. The pianist, the trombone, and finally the double-bass each played a note in a descending scale and each imitated a collapse.

There was a further second's pause. Lord Pastern, looking very much taken aback, suddenly handed the revolver to Bellairs, who pointed it at him and pulled the trigger. The hammer clicked but there was no discharge. Bellairs aped disgust, shrugged his shoulders, looked at the revolver and broke it open. It discharged its shells in a little spurt. Breezy scratched his head, dropped the revolver in his pocket and made a crisp gesture with his baton-hand.

'Yipee,' Lord Pastern shouted. The band launched itself into a welter of noise. He darted back and flung himself at his tympani. The spotlight concentrated upon him. The metronome, which had been motionless until now, suddenly swung its long arm. Tick-tack, tick-tack, it clacked. A kaleidoscopic welter of coloured lights winked and flickered along its surface and frame. Lord Pastern went madly to work on the drums.

'Hell!' Edward ejaculated, 'at this pace he'll kill himself.'

Breezy Bellairs had got a large artificial wreath. Dabbing his eyes with his handkerchief he knelt by Rivera, placed the wreath on his chest and felt his heart. He bent his head, groped frantically inside the wreath and then looked up with a startled expression in the direction of the tympani, where the spotlight revealed Lord Pastern in an ecstatic fury, wading into his drums. His solo lasted about eighty seconds. During this time four waiters had come in with a stretcher. Bellairs spoke to them excitedly. Rivera was carried off while the saxophones made a grotesque lugubrious sobbing and Lord Pastern, by hitting the big drum and immediately releasing the tension, produced a series of muffled groans.

The metronome clacked to a standstill, the restaurant lights went up and the audience applauded generously. Breezy, white to the lips and trembling, indicated Lord Pastern who joined him, glistening with sweat, and bowed. Breezy said something inaudible to him and to the pianist and went out followed by Lord Pastern. The pianist, the double-bass and the three saxophonists began to play a dance tune.

'Good old George!' cried Félicité, 'I think he was superb, Maman darling, don't you? Ned, wasn't he Heaven?'

Edward smiled at her: 'He's astonishing,' he said, and added: 'Cousin C, do you mind if Lisle and I dance? You will, won't you, Lisle?'

Carlisle put her hand on his shoulder and they moved away. The head-waiter slid past them and stooped for a moment over a man at a table further down the room. The man rose, let his eyeglass fall and with a preoccupied look passed Carlisle and Edward on his way to the vestibule.

They danced in silence, companionably. At last Edward said: 'What will he do next, do you suppose? Is there anything left?'

'I thought it dreadfully pathetic.'

'Quintessence of foolery. Lisle, I haven't had a chance to talk to you about that business before we left. I suppose I oughtn't to have hit the fellow, considering the set-up with Fée, but really it was a bit too much. I'm sorry if I made an unnecessary scene, but I must say I enjoyed it.' When she didn't answer, he said uncertainly: 'Are you seriously annoyed? Lisle, you didn't by any chance . . .'

'No,' she said. 'No, I didn't. I may as well confess I was extremely gratified.' His hand tightened on hers. 'I stood,' she added, 'in the door of my cave and preened myself.'

'Did you notice his ear? Not a cauliflower, but distinctly puffy, and a little trickle of blood. And then the unspeakable creature had the infernal nerve to goggle at you over his hurdy-gurdy.'

'It's all just meant to be one in the eye for Fée.'

'I'm not so sure.'

'If it is, he's not having much success.'

'How do you mean?' Edward asked sharply.

'Arst yourself, dearie.'

'You mean Fée . . .' He stopped short and turned very red. 'Lisle,' he said, 'about Fée . . . Something very odd has occurred. It's astonishing and well, it's damned awkward. I can't explain but I'd like to think you understood.'

Carlisle looked up at him. 'You're not very lucid,' she said.

'Lisle, my dear . . . Lisle, see here . . .'

They had danced round to the band dais. Carlisle said: 'Our waiter's standing over there, watching us. I think he's trying to catch your eye.'

'Be blowed to him.'

'Yes, he is. Here he comes.'

'It'll be some blasted paper on my tracks. Yes, do you want me?'

The waiter had touched Edward's arm. 'Excuse me, sir. An urgent call.'

'Thank you. Come with me, Lisle. Where's the telephone?'

The waiter hesitated, glanced at Carlisle, and said: 'If Madame will excuse me, sir . . .' His voice sank to a murmur.

'Good lord!' Edward said and took Carlisle by the elbow. 'There's been some sort of trouble. Cousin George wants me to go in. I'll drop you at the table, Lisle.'

'What's he up to now, for pity's sake?'

'I'll come as soon as I can. Make my excuses.'

As he went out Carlisle saw, with astonishment, that he was very pale.

In the vestibule, which was almost deserted, Edward stopped the waiter. 'How bad is it?' he asked. 'Is he badly hurt?'

The man raised his clasped hands in front of his mouth. 'They say he's dead,' said the waiter.

<h2 style="text-align:center">III</h2>

Breezy Bellairs sat at the little table in the inner office where he had played poker. When Edward came through the outer office he had heard scuffling and expostulations and he had opened the door upon a violent struggle. Breezy was being lugged to his feet from a squatting position on the floor and hustled across the room. He was slack now, and unresisting. His soft hands scratched at the surface of the table. He was dishevelled and breathless; tears ran out of his eyes, and his mouth was open. David Hahn, the secretary, stood behind him and patted his shoulder. 'You shouldn't have done it, old boy,' he said. 'Honest. You shouldn't have done a thing like that.'

'Keep off me,' Breezy whispered. Caesar Bonn, wringing his hands in the conventional gesture of distress, looked past Edward into the main office. The man with the eyeglass sat at the desk there, speaking inaudibly into the telephone.

'How did it happen?' Edward asked.

'Look,' Lord Pastern said.

Edward crossed the room. 'You must not touch him,' Caesar Bonn gabbled. 'Excuse me, sir, forgive me. Doctor Allington has said at once, he must not be touched.'

'I'm not going to touch him.'

He bent down. Rivera lay on the floor. His long figure was stretched out tidily against the far wall. Near the feet lay the comic wreath of flowers and a little farther off his piano accordion. Rivera's eyes were open. His upper lip was retracted and the teeth showed. His coat was thrown open and the surface of his soft shirt was blotted with red. Near the top of the blot a short dark object stuck out ridiculously from his chest.

'What is it? It looks like a dart.'

'Shut that door,' Bonn whispered angrily. Hahn darted to the communicating door and shut it. Just before he did so, Edward heard the man at the telephone say: 'In the office. I'll wait for you, of course.'

'This will ruin us. We are ruined,' said Bonn.

'They will think it an after-hours investigation, that is all,' said Hahn. 'If we keep our heads.'

'It will all come out. I insist we are ruined.'

In a voice that rose to a weak falsetto, Breezy said: 'Listen boys. Listen, Caesar, I didn't know it was that bad. I couldn't see. I wasn't sure. I can't be blamed for that, can I? I passed the word something was wrong to the boys. It wouldn't have made any difference if I'd acted different, would it, Dave? They can't say anything to me, can they?'

'Take it easy, old man.'

'You did right,' Bonn said, vigorously. 'If you had done otherwise
– what a scene! What a débâcle! And to no purpose. No, no, it was
correct.'

'Yes, but look, Caesar, it's terrible, the way we carried on. A cod
funeral march and everything. I knew it was unlucky. I said so when
he told me he wanted the other routine. All the boys said so!' He
pointed a quivering finger at Lord Pastern. 'It was your big idea. You
wished it on us. Look where it's landed us. What a notion, a cod
funeral march!'

His mouth sagged and he began to laugh, fetching his breath in
gasps and beating on the table.

'Shut up,' said Lord Pastern, irritably. 'You're a fool.' The door
opened and the man with the eyeglass came in. 'What's all this
noise?' He asked. He stood over Breezy. 'If you can't pull yourself
together, Mr Bellairs,' he said, 'we shall have to take drastic steps to
make you.' He glanced at Bonn. 'He'd better have brandy. Can you
beat up some aspirin?'

Hahn went out. Breezy sobbed and whispered.

'The police,' said the man, 'will be here in a moment. I shall, of
course, be required to make a statement.' He looked hard at Edward.
'Who is this?'

'I sent for him,' said Lord Pastern. 'He's with my party. My cousin,
Ned Manx – Dr Allington.'

'I see.'

'I thought I'd like to have Ned,' Lord Pastern added wistfully.

Dr Allington turned back to Breezy and picked up his wrist. He
looked sharply at him. 'You're in a bit of a mess, my friend,' he
remarked.

'It's not my fault. Don't look at me like that. I can't be held
responsible, my God.'

'I don't suggest anything of the sort. Is brandy any good to you?
Ah, here it is.'

Hahn brought it in. 'Here's the aspirin,' he said. 'How many?' He
shook out two tablets. Breezy snatched the bottle and spilt half a
dozen on the table. Dr Allington intervened and gave him three. He
gulped them down with the brandy, wiped his face over with his
handkerchief, yawned broadly and shivered.

Voices sounded in the outer office. Bonn and Hahn moved towards Breezy. Lord Pastern planted his feet apart and lightly flexed his arms. This posture was familiar to Edward. It usually meant trouble. Dr Allington put his glass in his eye. Breezy made a faint whimpering.

Somebody tapped on the door. It opened and a thickset man with grizzled hair came in. He wore a dark overcoat, neat, hard and unsmart, and carried a bowler hat. His eyes were bright and he looked longer and more fixedly than is the common habit at those he newly encountered. His sharp impersonal glance dwelt in turn upon the men in the room and upon the body of Rivera, from which they had stepped aside. Dr Allington moved out from the group.

'Trouble here?' said the newcomer. 'Are you Dr Allington, sir? My chaps are outside. Inspector Fox.'

He walked over to the body. The doctor followed him and they stood together, looking down at it. Fox gave a slight grunt and turned back to the others. 'And these gentlemen?' he said. Caesar Bonn made a dart at him and began to talk very rapidly.

'If I could just have the names,' said Fox and took out his notebook. He wrote down their names, his glance resting longer on Breezy than upon the others. Breezy lay back in his chair and gaped at Fox. His dinner jacket with its steel buttons sagged on one side. The pocket was dragged down.

'Excuse me, sir,' Fox said, 'are you feeling unwell?' He stooped over Breezy.

'I'm shot all to hell,' Breezy whimpered.

'Well, now, if you'll just allow me . . . ' He made a neat unobtrusive movement and stood up with the revolver in his large gloved hand.

Breezy gaped at it and then pointed a quivering hand at Lord Pastern.

'That's not my gun,' he chattered. 'Don't you think it is. It's his lordship's. He fired it at poor old Carlos and poor old Carlos fell down like he wasn't meant to. That's right, isn't it, chaps? Isn't it, Caesar? God, won't somebody speak up for me and tell the Inspector? His lordship handed me that gun.'

'Don't you fret,' Fox said comfortably. 'We'll have a chat about it presently.' He dropped the revolver into his pocket. His sharp glance travelled again over the group of men. 'Well, thank you, gentlemen,' he said, and opened the door. 'We'll need to trouble you a little further, Doctor, but I'll ask the others to wait in here, if you please.'

They filed into the main office. Four men already waited there. Fox nodded and three of them joined him in the inner room. They carried black cases and a tripod.

'This is Dr Curtis, Dr Allington,' said Fox. He unbuttoned his overcoat and laid his bowler on the table. 'Will you two gentlemen take a look? We'll get some shots when you're ready, Thompson.'

One of the men set up a tripod and camera. The doctors behaved like simultaneous comedians. They hitched up their trousers, knelt on their right knees and rested their forearms on their left thighs.

'I was supping here,' said Dr Allington. 'He was dead when I got to him, which must have been about three to five minutes after this' – he jabbed a forefinger at the blotch on Rivera's shirt – 'had happened. When I got here they had him where he is now. I made a superficial examination and rang the Yard.'

'Nobody tried to withdraw the weapon?' said Dr Curtis, and added: 'Unusual, that.'

'It seems that one of them, Lord Pastern it was, said it shouldn't be touched. Some vague idea of an effusion of blood following the withdrawal. They realized almost at once that he was dead. At a guess, would you say there'd been considerable penetration of the right ventricle? I haven't touched a thing, by the way. Can't make out what it is.'

'We'll take a look in a minute,' said Dr Curtis. 'All right, Fox.'

'All right, Thompson,' said Fox.

They moved away. Their shadows momentarily blotted the wall as Thompson's lamp flashed. Whistling under his breath he manoeuvred his camera, flashed and clicked.

'OK, Mr Fox,' he said at last.

'Dabs,' said Fox. 'Do what you can about the weapon, Bailey.'

The fingerprint expert, a thin dark man, squatted by the body.

Fox said, 'I'd like to get a statement about the actual event. You can help us there, Dr Allington? What exactly was the set-up? I understand a gun was used against the deceased in the course of the entertainment.'

He had folded his overcoat neatly over the back of his chair. He now sat down, his knees apart, his spectacles adjusted, his note-book flattened out on the table. 'If I may trouble you, Doctor,' he said. 'In your own words, as we say.'

Dr Allington fitted his glass in position and looked apologetic. 'I'm afraid I'm not going to be a success,' he said. 'To be quite frank, Inspector, I was more interested in my guest than in the entertainment. And, by the way, I'd like to make my apologies to her as soon as possible. She must be wondering where the devil I've got to.'

'If you care to write a note, sir, we'll give it to one of the waiters.'

'What? Oh, all right,' said Dr Allington fretfully. A note was taken out by Thompson. Through the opened door they caught a glimpse of a dejected group in the main office. Lord Pastern's voice, caught mid-way in a sentence, said shrilly: '. . . entirely wrong way about it. Making a mess, as usual . . . ' and was shut off by the door.

'Yes, Doctor?' said Fox placidly.

'Oh, God, they were doing some kind of idiotic turn. We were talking and I didn't pay much attention except to say it was a pretty poor show, old Pastern making an ass of himself. This chap, here,' he looked distastefully at the body, 'came out from the far end of the restaurant and made a hell of a noise on his concertina or whatever it is, and there was a terrific bang. I looked up and saw old Pastern with a gun of some sort in his hand. This chap did a fall, the conductor dropped a wreath on him and then he was carried out. About three minutes later they sent for me.'

'I'll just get that down, if you please,' said Fox. With raised eyebrows and breathing through his mouth, he wrote at a steady pace. 'Yes,' he said comfortably, 'and how far, Doctor, would you say his lordship was from the deceased when he fired?'

'Quite close. I don't know. Between five and seven feet. I don't know.'

'Did you notice the deceased's behaviour, sir, immediately after the shot was fired? I mean, did it strike you there was anything wrong?'

Dr Allington looked impatiently at the door. 'Strike me!' he repeated. 'I wasn't struck by anything in particular. I looked up when the gun went off. I think it occurred to me that he did a very clever fall. He was a pretty ghastly looking job of work, all hair-oil and teeth.'

'Would you say . . . ' Fox began and was interrupted.

'I really wouldn't say anything, Inspector. I've given you my opinion from the time I examined the poor devil. To go any further would be unprofessional and stupid. I simply wasn't watching and therefore don't remember. You'd better find somebody who did watch and does remember.'

Fox had raised his head and now looked beyond Dr Allington to the door. His hand was poised motionless over his note-book. His jaw had dropped. Dr Allington slewed round and was confronted with a very tall dark man in evening dress.

'I was watching,' said this person, 'and I think I remember. Shall I try, Inspector?'

IV

'Good lor'!' Fox said heavily and rose. 'Well, thank you, Doctor Allington,' he said. 'I'll have a typed statement sent round to you tomorrow. Would you be good enough to read it through and sign it if it's in order? We'll want you for the inquest, if you please.'

'All right. Thanks,' said Dr Allington, making for the door which the newcomer opened. 'Thanks,' he repeated. 'Hope you make a better fist of it than I did, what?'

'Most unlikely, I'm afraid,' the other rejoined pleasantly, and closed the door after him. 'You're in for a party, Fox,' he said, and walked over to the body. Bailey, the fingerprint expert said: 'Good-evening, sir,' and moved away, grinning.

'*If* I may ask, sir,' said Fox, 'how do you come to be in on it?'

'May I not take mine ease in mine restaurant with mine wife? Shall there be no more cakes and ale? None for you, at all events, you poor chap,' he said, bending over Rivera. 'You haven't got the thing out yet, I see, Fox.'

'It's been dabbed and photographed. It can come out.'

Fox knelt down. His hand wrapped in his handkerchief closed round the object that protruded from Rivera's chest. It turned with difficulty. 'Tight,' he said.

'Let me look, may I?'

Fox drew back. The other knelt beside him. 'But what is it?' he said. 'Not an orthodox dart. There's a thread at the top. It's been unscrewed from something. Black. Silver mounted. Ebony, I fancy. Or a dark bronze. What the devil is it? Try again, Fox.'

Fox tried again. He twisted. Under the wet silk the wound opened slightly. He pulled steadily. With a jerk and a slight but horrible sound, the weapon was released. Fox laid it on the floor and opened out his handkerchief. Bailey clicked his tongue.

Fox said: 'Will you look at that. Good lord, what a set-up! It's a bit of an umbrella shaft, turned into a dart or bolt.'

'A black and white parasol,' said his companion. Fox looked up quickly but said nothing. 'Yes. There's the spring clip, you see. That's why it wouldn't come out readily. An elaborate affair, almost a museum piece. The clip's got tiny jewels in it. And look, Fox.'

He pointed a long finger. Protruding from one end was a steel, about two inches long, wide at the base and tapering sharply to a point. 'It looks like some sort of awl or stiletto. Probably it was originally sunk in a short handle. It's been driven into one end of this bit of parasol shaft and sealed up somehow. Plastic wood, I fancy. The end of the piece of shaft you see was hollow. Probably the longer section of the parasol screwed into it and a knob or handle of some kind, in turn, was screwed on the opposite end.' He took out his note-book and made a rapid sketch which he showed to Fox. 'Like this,' he said. 'It'll be a freak of a parasol. French, I should think. I remember seeing them in the enclosure at Longchamps when I was a boy. The shaft's so thin that they have to put a separate section in to take the clip and groove. This is the section. But why in the name of high fantasy use a bit of parasol shaft as a sort of dagger?'

'We'll have another shot of this, Thompson.' Fox rose stiffly and after a long pause said: 'Where were you sitting, Mr Alleyn?'

'Next door to the Pastern party. A few yards off the dais.'

'What a bit of luck,' said Fox simply.

'Don't be too sure,' rejoined Chief-Inspector Alleyn. He sat on the table and lit a cigarette. 'This is no doubt a delicate situation, Br'er Fox. I mustn't butt in on your job, you know.'

Fox made a short derisive noise. 'You'll take over, sir, of course.'

'I can at least make my report. I'd better warn you at the outset, I was watching that extraordinary chap Pastern most of the time. What a queer cup of tea it is, to be sure.'

'I suppose,' said Fox stolidly, 'you'll be telling me, sir, that you were his fag at Eton.'

Alleyn grinned at this jibe. 'If I had been I should probably have spent the rest of my life in a lunatic asylum. No, I was going to say that I watched him to the exclusion of the others. I noticed, for instance, that he really pointed his gun – a revolver of some sort – at this man and that he stood not more than seven feet off him when he did it.'

'This is more like it,' Fox said and reopened his book. 'You don't mind, Mr Alleyn?' he added primly.

Alleyn said, 'You're gloating over this, aren't you? Very well. They did a damn' silly turn, revolving umbrellas and parasols like a bunch of superannuated chorus girls and I noticed that one parasol, a very pansy Frenchified affair of black and white lace, seemed to be giving trouble. The chap had to shove his hand up to hold it.'

'Is that so?' Fox looked at Thompson. 'You might get hold of the umbrella.' Thompson went out. Bailey moved forward with an insufflator and bent over the weapon.

'I'd better describe the final turn, I suppose,' said Alleyn, and did so. His voice moved on quietly and slowly. Thompson returned with the black and white parasol. 'This is it, sure enough, sir,' he said. 'A section of the shaft's gone. Look here! No clip anywhere to keep it shut.' He laid it beside the dart.

'Good enough,' Fox said. 'Get your shots, will you.'

Thompson, having taken three further photographs of the weapon, folded it in the handkerchief and put it in Fox's case. 'I'll fix it up with proper protection when we're finished, Mr Fox,' he said. On a nod from Fox, he and Bailey went out with their gear.

' . . . when the shot was fired,' Alleyn was saying, 'he had swung round, facing Lord Pastern, with his back half-turned to the audience and fully turned to the conductor. He was inclined backwards at a grotesque angle, with the instrument raised. He was directly under the point of the metronome which was motionless. After the report he swung round still further and straightened up a bit. The piano accordion, if that's what it is, ran down the scale and let out an infernal bleat. His knees doubled and he went down on them, sat on his heels and then rolled over, fetching up on his back with his instrument between himself and the audience. At the same time one of the bandsmen aped being hit. I couldn't see Rivera clearly because the spotlight had switched to old Pastern who, after a moment's hesitation, loosed off the other rounds. Three more of the band chaps did comic staggers as if he'd hit them. Something seemed a bit out of joint here. They all looked as if they weren't sure what came next. However, Pastern gave his gun to Bellairs, who pointed it at him and pulled the trigger. The last round had been used, so there was only a click. Bellairs registered disgust, broke the revolver, pocketed it and gestured as much as to say: "I've had it. Carry on," and Lord Pastern then went to market in a big way and generally raised hell. He looked extraordinary. Glazed eyes, sweating, half-smiling and jerking about over his drums. An unnerving exhibition from a middle-aged peer but of course he's as mad as a March hare. Troy and I were snobbishly horrified. It was then that the metronome went into action in a blaze of winking lights. It'd been pointing straight down at Rivera before. A waiter chucked a wreath to the conductor who knelt down by this chap Rivera and dumped it on his chest. He felt his heart and then looked closely at Rivera and bent over his body, groping inside the wreath. He turned in a startled sort of way to old Pastern. He said something to the blokes with the stretcher. The wreath hid the face and the accordion was half across the stomach. Bellairs spoke to the pianist and then to Lord Pastern who went out with him when they finished their infernal din. I smelt trouble, saw a waiter speak to Allington and stop a chap in Lady Pastern's party. I had a long argument with myself, lost it and came out here. That's all. Have you looked at the revolver?'

'I've taken it off Bellairs. It's in my pocket.' Fox put his glove on, produced the revolver and laid it on the table. 'No known make,' he said.

'Probably been used for target-shooting,' Alleyn muttered. He laid the dart beside it. 'It'd fit, Fox. Look. Had you noticed?'

'We haven't got very far.'

'Of course not.'

'I don't know quite what line to take about all the folk in there.' Fox jerked his head in the direction of the restaurant.

'Better get names and addresses. The waiters can do it. They'll know a lot of them already. They can say it's a new police procedure on extension nights. It's our good fortune, Br'er Fox, that the public

will believe any foolishness if they are told we are the authors of it.
The Pastern party had better be held.'

'I'll fix it,' Fox said. He went out, revealing for a moment the
assembly in the outer office. '. . . hang about kickin' my heels all
night . . .' Lord Pastern's voice protested and was shut off abruptly.

Alleyn knelt by the body and began to search it. The coat was turned
and the breast pocket had been pulled out. Four letters and a gold cigarette case had slipped down between the body and the coat. The case
was half-filled and bore an inscription: 'From Félicité.' He searched the
other pockets. A jade holder. Two handkerchiefs. A wallet with three
pound notes. He laid these objects out in a row and turned to the piano
accordion. It was a large, heavily ornamental affair. He remembered
how it had glittered as Rivera swung it across his chest in the last
cacophony before he fell. As Alleyn lifted it, it raised a metallic wail. He
put it down hastily on the table and returned to his contemplation of
the body. Fox came back. 'That's all fixed up,' he said.

'Good.'

Alleyn stood up. 'He was a startling fellow to look at,' he said.
'One felt one had seen him in innumerable Hollywood band-
features, ogling the cameraman against an exotic background. We
might cover him up, don't you think? The management can produce
a clean tablecloth.'

'The mortuary van will be outside now, Mr Alleyn,' said Fox. He
glanced down at the little collection on the floor. 'Much obliged, sir,'
he said. 'Anything useful?'

'The letters are written in Spanish. Postmark. He'll have to be
dusted, of course.'

'I rang the Yard, Mr Alleyn. The ASM's compliments and he'll be
glad if you'll take over.'

'That's a thumping great lie,' said Alleyn mildly. 'He's in
Godalming.'

'He's come back, sir, and happened to be in the office. Quite a
coincidence.'

'You go to hell, Fox. Damn it, I'm out with my wife.'

'I sent a message in to Mrs Alleyn. The waiter brought back a
note.'

Alleyn opened the folded paper and disclosed a lively drawing of
a lady asleep in bed. Above her, encircled by a balloon, Alleyn and

Fox crawled on all fours inspecting, through a huge lens, a nest from which protruded the head of a foal, broadly winking. 'A very stupid woman, I'm afraid, poor thing,' Alleyn muttered, grinning, and showed it to Fox. 'Come on,' he said. 'We'll take another look at the revolver and then get down to statements.'

CHAPTER 16

Done

CHAPTER 6

Dope

Above the door leading from the foyer of the Metronome to the office was a clock with chromium hands and figures. As the night wore on, the attention of those persons who were congregated there became increasingly drawn to this clock, so that when at one in the morning the long hand jumped to the hour, everyone observed it. A faint sigh, and a dreary restlessness stirred them momentarily.

The members of the band, who were assembled at the end of the foyer, sat in dejected attitudes on gilded chairs that had been brought in from the restaurant. Syd Skelton's hands dangled between his knees, tapping each other flaccidly. Happy Hart was stretched back with his legs extended. The light found out patches on his trousers, worn shiny by the pressure of his thighs against the under-surface of his piano. The four saxophonists sat with their heads together, but they had not spoken for some time and inertia, not interest, held them in these postures of intimacy. The double-bass, a thin man, rested his elbows on his knees and his head on his hands. Breezy Bellairs, in the centre of his Boys, fidgeted, yawned, wiped his hands over his face, and bit feverishly at his nails. Near the band stood four waiters and the spotlight operator, whose interrogation has just ended, quite fruitlessly.

At the opposite end of the foyer, in a muster of easier chairs, sat Lady Pastern and her guests. Alone of the whole assembly, she held an upright posture. The muscles of her face sagged a little; its lines were clogged with powder and there were greyish marks under her eyes, but her wrists and ankles were crossed composedly, her hair was rigidly in order. On her right and left the two girls drooped in their chairs. Félicité, chain-smoking, gave her attention fitfully to the matter in hand and often took a glass from her bag and looked resentfully at herself, repainting her lips with irritable gestures.

Carlisle, absorbed as usual with detail, watched the mannerisms of her companions through an increasing haze of sleepiness and was only half-aware of what they said. Ned Manx listened sharply as if he tried to memorize all that he heard. Lord Pastern was never still. He would throw himself into a chair with an air of abandon and in a moment spring from it and walk aimlessly about the room. He looked with distaste at the speaker of the moment. He grimaced and interjected. At one side, removed from the two main groups, stood Caesar Bonn and the secretary, David Hahn. These two were watchful and pallid. Out of sight, in the main office, Dr Curtis, having seen to the removal of Rivera's body, jotted down notes for his report.

In the centre of the foyer, Inspector Fox sat at a small table with his note-book open before him and his spectacles on his nose. His feet rested side by side on the carpet and his large knees were pressed together. He contemplated his notes with raised eyebrows.

Behind Fox stood Chief Detective-Inspector Alleyn, and to him the attention of the company, in some cases fitfully, in others constantly, was drawn. He had been speaking for about a minute. Carlisle, though she tried to listen to the sense of his words, caught herself thinking how deep his voice was and how free from mannerisms his habit of speech. 'A pleasant chap,' she thought, and knew by the small affirmative noise Ned Manx made when Alleyn paused that he agreed with her.

' . . . so you see,' Alleyn was saying now, 'that a certain amount of ground must be covered here and that we must ask you to stay until it *has* been covered. That can't be helped.'

'Damned if I see . . . ' Lord Pastern began and fetched up short. 'What's your name?' he said. Alleyn told him. 'I thought so,' said Lord Pastern with an air of having found him out in something. 'Point is: are you suggestin' I dug a dart in the chap or aren't you? Come on.'

'It doesn't, at the moment, seem to be a question, as far as you are concerned, sir, of digging.'

'Well, shootin' then. Don't split straws.'

'One may as well,' Alleyn said mildly, 'be accurate.'

He turned aside to Fox's case which lay on a table. From it he took an open box containing the weapon that had killed Rivera. He held the box up, tilting it towards them.

'Will you look at this?' They looked at it. 'Do any of you recognize it? Lady Pastern?'

She had made an inarticulate sound, but now she said indifferently: 'It looks like part of a parasol handle.'

'A black and white parasol?' Alleyn suggested, and one of the saxophonists looked up quickly.

'Possibly,' said Lady Pastern. 'I don't know.'

'Don't be an ass, C,' said her husband. 'Obviously it's off that French thing of yours. We borrowed it.'

'You had no right whatever, George . . . '

Alleyn interrupted. 'We've found that one of the parasols used in the "Umbrella Man" number is minus a few inches of its shaft.' He glanced at the second saxophonist. 'I think you had some difficulty in managing it?'

'That's right,' the second saxophonist said. 'You couldn't shut it properly, I noticed. There wasn't a clip or anything.'

'This is it: five inches of the shaft containing the clip. Notice that spring catch. It is jewelled. Originally, of course, it kept the parasol closed. The actual handle or knob on its own piece of shaft has been engaged with the main shaft of the parasol. Can you describe it?' He looked at Lady Pastern, who said nothing. Lord Pastern said: 'Of course you can, C. A damn-fool thing like a bird with emeralds for eyes. French.'

'You're sure of that, sir?'

'Of course, I'm sure. Damn it, I took the thing to bits when I was in the ballroom.'

Fox raised his head and stared at Lord Pastern with a sort of incredulous satisfaction. Edward Manx swore under his breath, the women were rigidly horrified.

'I see,' Alleyn said. 'When was this?'

'After dinner. Breezy was with me. Weren't you, Breezy.'

Breezy shied violently and then nodded.

'Where did you leave the bits, sir?'

'On the piano. Last I saw of 'em.'

'Why,' Alleyn asked, 'did you dismember the parasol?'

'For fun.'

'*Mon Dieu, mon Dieu,*' Lady Pastern moaned.

'I knew it'd unscrew and I unscrewed it.'

'Thank you,' Alleyn said. 'For the benefit of those of you who haven't examined the parasol closely, I'd better describe it a little more fully. Both ends of this piece of shaft are threaded, one on the outer surface to engage with the top section, the other on the inner surface to receive the main shaft of the parasol. It has been removed and the outer sections screwed together. Now look again at this weapon made from the section that has been removed. You will see that a steel tool has been introduced into this end and sunk in plastic wood. Do any of you recognize this tool? I'll hold it a little closer. It's encrusted with blood and a little difficult to see.'

He saw Carlisle's fingers move on the arms of her chair. He saw Breezy rub the back of his hand across his mouth, and Lord Pastern blow out his cheeks. 'Rather unusual,' he said, 'isn't it? Wide at the base and tapering. Keen pointed. It might be an embroidery stiletto. I don't know. Do you recognize it, Lady Pastern?'

'No.'

'Anybody?' Lord Pastern opened his mouth and shut it again. 'Well,' Alleyn murmured after a pause. He replaced the box containing the weapon and took up Lord Pastern's revolver. He turned it over in his hands.

'If that's the way you chaps go to work,' said Lord Pastern, 'I don't think much of it. That thing may be smothered with fingerprints, for all you know, and you go pawin' it about.'

'It's been printed,' Alleyn said without emphasis. He produced a pocket-lens and squinted through it down the barrel. 'You seem to have given it some rough usage,' he said.

'No, I haven't,' Lord Pastern countered instantly. 'Perfect condition. Always has been.'

'When did you last look down the barrel, sir?'

'Before we came here. In my study, and again in the ballroom. Why?'

'George,' said Lady Pastern, 'I suggest for the last time that you send for your solicitor and refuse to answer any questions until he is here.'

'Yes, Cousin George,' Edward murmured, 'I honestly think . . . '

'My solicitor,' Lord Pastern rejoined, 'is a snufflin' old ass. I'm perfectly well able to look after myself, C. What's all this about my gun?'

'The barrel,' Alleyn said, 'is, of course, fouled. That's from the blank rounds. But under the stain left by the discharges there are some curious marks. Irregular scratches, they seem to be. We'll have it photographed but I wonder if in the meantime you can offer an explanation?'

'Here,' Lord Pastern ejaculated. 'Let me see.'

Alleyn gave him the revolver and lens. Grimacing hideously he pointed the barrel to the light and squinted down it. He made angry noises and little puffing sounds through his lips. He examined the butt through the lens and muttered indistinguishable anathemas. Most unexpectedly, he giggled. Finally he dumped it on the table and blew loudly. 'Hanky-panky,' he said briefly and returned to his chair.

'I beg your pardon?'

'When I examined the gun in my study,' Lord Pastern said forcibly, 'it was as clean as a whistle. As clean, I repeat, as a whistle. I fired one blank from it in my own house and looked down the barrel afterwards. It was a bit fouled and that was all. All right. There y'are!'

Carlisle, Félicité, Manx and Lady Pastern stirred uneasily. 'Uncle George,' Carlisle said. 'Please.'

Lord Pastern glared at her. 'Therefore,' he said, 'I repeat, hanky-panky. The barrel was unmarked when I brought the thing here. I ought to know. It was unmarked when I took it into the restaurant.'

Lady Pastern looked steadily at her husband. 'You *fool*, George,' she said.

'George.'

'Cousin George.'

'Uncle George . . . '

The shocked voices overlapped and faded out.

Alleyn began again. 'Obviously you realize the significance of all this. When I tell you that the weapon – it is, in effect, a dart, or bolt, isn't it? – is half an inch shorter than the barrel of the revolver and somewhat less in diameter . . . '

'All right, all right,' Lord Pastern interjected.

'I think,' said Alleyn, 'I should point out . . . '

'You needn't point anything out. And you,' Lord Pastern added, turning on his relatives 'can all shut up. I know what you're gettin' at. The barrel was unscratched. By God, I ought to know. And what's more, I noticed when Breezy and I were in the ballroom, that this bit of shaft would fit in the barrel. I pointed it out to him.'

'Here, here, here!' Breezy expostulated, 'I don't like the way this is going. Look here – '

'Did anyone else examine the revolver?' Alleyn interposed adroitly.

Lord Pastern pointed at Skelton. 'He did,' he said. 'Ask him.'

Skelton moved forward, wetting his lips.

'Did you look down the barrel?' Alleyn asked.

'Glanced,' said Skelton reluctantly.

'Did you notice anything unusual?'

'No.'

'Was the barrel quite unscarred?'

There was a long silence. 'Yes,' said Skelton at last.

'There y' are,' said Lord Pastern.

'It would be,' Skelton added brutally, 'seeing his lordship hadn't put his funny weapon in it yet.'

Lord Pastern uttered a short, rude and incredulous word. 'Thanks,' said Skelton and turned to Alleyn.

Edward Manx said: 'May I butt in, Alleyn?'

'Of course.'

'It's obvious that you think this thing was fired from the revolver. It's obvious, in my opinion, that you are right. How else could he have been killed? But isn't it equally obvious that the person who used the revolver could have known nothing about it? If he had wanted to shoot Rivera he could have used a bullet. If, for some extraordinary reason, he preferred a sort of rifle grenade or dart or what-not, he would surely have used something less fantastic than the affair you have just shown us. The only object in using the piece of parasol shaft, if it has in fact been so used, would have been this: the spring catch, which is jewelled, by the way, would keep the weapon fixed in the barrel and it wouldn't fall out if the revolver was pointed downwards and the person who fired the revolver would therefore be unaware of the weapon in the barrel. You wouldn't,' Edward said with great energy, 'fix up an elaborate sort of thing like this unless there was a reason for it and there would be no reason if you yourself had full control of the revolver and could load it at the last moment. Only an abnormally eccentric . . . ' He stopped short, floundered for a moment, and then said: 'That's the point I wanted to make.'

'It's well taken,' Alleyn said. 'Thank you.'

'Hi!' said Lord Pastern.

Alleyn turned to him.

'Look here,' he said. 'You think these scratches were made by the jewels on that spring thing. Skelton says they weren't there when he looked at the gun. If anyone was fool enough to try and shoot a feller with a thing like this, he'd fire it off first of all to see how it worked. In private. Follow me?'

'I think so, sir.'

'All right, then,' said Lord Pastern with a shrill cackle, 'why waste time jabberin' about scratches?'

He flung himself into his chair.

'Did any of you who were there,' Alleyn said, 'take particular notice when Mr Skelton examined the revolver?'

Nobody spoke. Skelton's face was very white. 'Breezy watched,' he said, and added quickly: 'I was close to Lord Pastern. I couldn't have . . . I mean . . . '

Alleyn said: 'Why did you examine it, Mr Skelton?'

Skelton wetted his lips. His eyes shifted their gaze from Lord Pastern to Breezy Bellairs. 'I – was sort of interested. Lord Pastern had fixed up the blanks himself and I thought I'd like to take a look. I'd gone in to wish him luck. I mean . . . '

'*Why don't you tell him!*'

Breezy was on his feet. He had been yawning and fidgeting in his chair. His face was stained with tears. He had seemed to pay little attention to what was said but rather to be in the grip of some intolerable restlessness. His interruption shocked them all by its unexpectedness. He came forward with a shambling movement and grinned at Alleyn.

'I'll tell you,' he said rapidly. 'Syd did it because I asked him to. He's a pal. I told him. I told him I didn't trust his lordship. I'm a nervous man where firearms are concerned. I'm a nervous man altogether if you can understand.' His fingers plucked at his smiling lips. 'Don't look at me like that,' he said, and his voice broke into a shrill falsetto. 'Everybody's staring as if I'd done something. Eyes. Eyes. Eyes. Oh, God, give me a smoke!'

Alleyn held out his cigarette case. Breezy struck it out of his hand and began to sob. 'Bloody sadist,' he said.

'I know what's wrong with you, you silly chap,' Lord Pastern said accusingly.

Breezy shook a finger at him. 'You *know!*' he said. 'You started it. You're as good as a murderer. You *are* a murderer, by God!'

'Say that again, my good Bellairs,' Lord Pastern rejoined with relish, 'and I'll have you in the libel court. Action for slander, b'George.'

Breezy looked wildly around the assembly. His light eyes with their enormous pupils fixed their gaze on Félicité. He pointed a trembling hand at her. 'Look at that girl,' he said, 'doing her face and sitting up like Jackie with the man she was supposed to love lying stiff and bloody in the morgue. It's disgusting.'

Caesar Bonn came forward, wringing his hands. 'I can keep silent no longer,' he said. 'If I am ruined, I am ruined. If I do not speak, there are others who will.' He looked at Lord Pastern, at Edward Manx and at Hahn.

Edward said: 'It's got to come out, certainly. In common fairness.'

'Certainly. Certainly.'

'What,' Alleyn asked, 'has got to come out?'

'Please, Mr Manx. You will speak.'

'All right, Caesar. I think,' Edward said slowly, turning to Alleyn, 'that you should know what happened before any of you arrived. I myself had only just walked into the room. The body was where you saw it.' He paused for a moment. Breezy watched him, but Manx did not look at Breezy. 'There was a sort of struggle going on,' he said. 'Bellairs was on the floor by Rivera and the others were pulling him off.'

'Damned indecent thing,' said Lord Pastern virtuously, 'trying to go through the poor devil's pockets.'

Breezy whimpered.

'I'd like a closer account of this, if you can give it to me. When exactly did this happen?' Alleyn asked.

Caesar and Hahn began talking at once. Alleyn stopped them. 'Suppose,' he said, 'we trace events through from the point where Mr Rivera was carried out of the restaurant!' He began to question the four waiters who had carried Rivera. The waiters hadn't noticed anything wrong with him. They were a bit flustered anyway because of the confusion about which routine was to be followed. There had been so many contradictory orders that in the end they just watched to see who fell down and then picked up the stretcher and carried him out. The wreath covered his chest. As they lifted him on to the stretcher, Breezy had said quickly: 'He's hurt. Get him out.' They had carried him straight to the office. As they put the stretcher down they heard him make a noise, a harsh rattling noise, it had been. When they looked closer they found he was dead. They fetched Caesar Bonn and Hahn and then carried the body into the inner room. Then Caesar ordered them back to the restaurant and told one of them to fetch Dr Allington.

Lord Pastern, taking up the tale, said that while they were still on the dais, after the removal of Rivera, Breezy had gone to him and muttered urgently: 'For God's sake come out. Something's happened to Carlos.' The pianist, Happy Hart, said that Breezy had stopped at the piano on his way out and had told him in an aside to keep going.

Caesar took up the story. Breezy and Lord Pastern came to the inner office. Breezy was in a fearful state, saying he'd seen blood on Rivera when he put the wreath on his chest. They were still gathered round Rivera's body, laying him out tidily on the floor. Breezy kept gibbering about the blood and then he caught sight of the body and turned away to the wall, retching and scrabbling in his overcoat pockets for one of his tablets and complaining because he had none. Nobody did anything for him and he went into the lavatory off the inner office and was heard vomiting in there. When he came back he looked terrible and stood gabbling about how he felt. At this point Breezy interrupted Caesar. 'I told them,' he said shrilly. 'I told them. It was a terrible shock to me when he fell. It was a shock to all of us, wasn't it, boys?'

The Boys stirred themselves and muttered in unison, that it had been a great shock.

'When he fell?' Alleyn said quickly. 'Then, definitely, he wasn't supposed to fall?'

They all began to explain at once with great eagerness. Two routines had been rehearsed. There had been a lot of argument about which should be followed. Right up to the last neither Lord Pastern nor Rivera could make up his mind which he preferred. In the one routine Lord Pastern was to have fired the revolver four times at Rivera, who should have smiled and gone on playing. At each of the shots a member of the band was to have played a note in a descending scale and aped having been hit. Then Rivera was to have made his exit and the whole turn continued as they had seen it done, except that it would have ended with Lord Pastern doing a comic fall. Breezy would have then placed the wreath on him and he would have been carried out. In the alternative routine, Rivera was to do the fall. Carlos, the Boys explained, hadn't liked the idea of falling with his instrument so the original plan had been adopted at the last moment.

'When I saw him drop,' Breezy chattered, 'I was rocked all to hell. I thought he'd done it to put one across us. He was like that, poor old Carlos. He was a bit that way. He didn't fancy the idea of falling, yet he didn't fancy his lordship getting the big exit. He was funny that way. It was a shock to all of us.'

'So the end was an improvisation?'

'Not exactly,' Lord Pastern said. 'I kept my head, of course, and followed the correct routine. It was a bit of a facer but there you were, what? The waiters saw Carlos fall and luckily had the sense to bring the stretcher. It would've been awkward if they hadn't as things turned out. Damn' awkward. I emptied the magazine as we'd arranged and these other fellers did their staggers. Then I handed the gun to Breezy and he snapped it and then broke it open. I always thought my first idea of Carlos getting shot was best. Though of course I did rather see that it ought to be me who was carried out.'

'And I thought,' Breezy said, 'I'd better drop that ruddy wreath on Carlos, like we first said. So I did.' His voice jumped into falsetto. 'When I saw the blood I thought at first he'd coughed it up. I thought he'd had one of those things – you know – a haemorrhage. At first. And then the wreath stuck on something. You'd scarcely credit it, would you, but I thought: for chrisake I'm hanging it on a peg. And then I saw. I told you that, all of you. You can't say I didn't.'

'Certainly you told us,' Caesar agreed, eyeing him nervously. 'In the office.' Breezy made a petulant sound and crouched back in his chair. Caesar went on quickly to relate that just before they heard Dr Allington's voice in the main office, Breezy had darted over to the body and had crouched down beside it, throwing back the coat and thrusting his hand into the breast pocket. He had said: 'I've got to get it. He's got it on him,' or something like that. They had been greatly shocked by this behaviour. He and Caesar and Hahn had pulled Breezy off and he had collapsed. It was during this scene that Edward Manx had arrived.

'Do you agree that this is a fair account of what happened, Mr Bellairs?' Alleyn asked after a pause.

For a moment or two it seemed as if he would get some kind of answer. Breezy looked at him with extraordinary concentration. Then he turned his head as if his neck was stiff. After a moment he nodded.

'What did you hope to find in the deceased's pockets?' Alleyn said.

Breezy's mouth stretched in its mannikin-grin. His eyes were blank. He raised his hands and the fingers trembled.

'Come,' Alleyn said, 'what did you hope to find?'

'Oh, God!' said Lord Pastern fretfully. 'Now he's goin' to blub again.'

This was an understatement. Hysteria took possession of Breezy. He screamed out some unintelligible protest or appeal, broke into a storm of sobbing laughter and stumbled to the entrance. A uniformed policeman came through the door and held him. 'Now, now,' said the policeman. 'Easy does it, sir, easy does it.'

Dr Curtis came out of the office and stood looking at Breezy thoughtfully. Alleyn nodded to him and he went to Breezy.

Breezy sobbed: 'Doctor! Doctor! Listen!' He put his heavy arm about Dr Curtis's shoulders and with an air of mystery whimpered in his ear. 'I think, Alleyn . . . ? said Dr Curtis. 'Yes,' Alleyn said, 'in the office, will you?'

When the door had shut behind them, Alleyn looked at Breezy's Boys.

'Can any of you tell me,' he said, 'how long he's been taking drugs?'

II

Lord Pastern, bunching his cheeks, said to nobody in particular, 'Six months.'

'You knew about it, my lord, did you?' Fox demanded and Lord Pastern grinned savagely at him. 'Not bein' a detective-inspector,' he said, 'I don't have to wait until a dope-fiend throws fits and passes out before I know what's wrong with him.'

He balanced complacently, toe and heel, and stroked the back of his head. 'I've been lookin' into the dope racket,' he volunteered. 'Disgraceful show. Runnin' sore in the body politic and nobody with the guts to tackle it.' He glared upon Breezy's Boys. 'You chaps!' he said, jabbing a finger at them, 'what did you do about it? Damn all.'

Breezy's Boys were embarrassed and shocked. They fidgeted, cleared their throats, and eyed one another. 'Surely,' Alleyn said, 'you must have guessed. He's in a bad way, you know.'

They hadn't been sure, it appeared. Happy Hart said they knew Breezy took some kind of stuff for his nerves. It was some special kind of dope. Breezy used to get people to buy it for him in Paris. He said it was some kind of bromide, Hart added vaguely. The double-bass said Breezy was a very nervous type. The first saxophone muttered something about hitting the high spots and corpse-revivers. Lord Pastern loudly pronounced a succinct but unprintable comment and they eyed him resentfully, 'I told him what it'd come to,' he announced. 'I threatened the chap. Only way. if you don't take a pull, by God,' I said, 'I'll give the whole story to the papers. *Harmony* f'r instance. I told him so, tonight.'

Edward Manx uttered a sharp ejaculation and looked as if he wished he'd held his tongue.

'Who searched him for his bloody tablet? Skelton demanded, glaring at Lord Pastern.

'The show,' Lord Pastern countered virtuously, 'had to go on, didn't it? Don't split straws, my good ass.'

Alleyn intervened. The incident of the lost tablet was related. Lord Pastern described how he went through Breezy's pockets and boasted of his efficiency. 'You fellers call it fannin' a chap,' he explained kindly, to Alleyn.

'This was immediately after Mr Skelton had inspected the revolver and handed it back to Lord Pastern?' Alleyn asked.

'That's right,' said one or two of the Boys.

'Lord Pastern, did you at any time after he'd done this lose sight of the revolver or put it down?'

'Certainly not. I kept it in my hip pocket from the time Skelton gave it to me until I went on the stage.'

'Did you look down the barrel after Mr Skelton returned it to you?'

'No.'

'I won't have this,' said Skelton loudly.

Alleyn glanced thoughtfully at him and returned to Lord Pastern. 'Did you, by the way,' he said, 'find anything in Mr Bellairs' pockets?'

'A wallet, a cigarette-case and his handkerchief,' Lord Pastern rejoined importantly. 'The pill was in the handerkchief.'

Alleyn asked for a closer description of this scene and Lord Pastern related with gusto how Breezy had stood with his hands up, holding his baton as if he were about to give his first down-beat and how he himself had explored every pocket with the utmost despatch and thoroughness. 'If,' he added, 'you're thinkin' that he might have had the dart on him, you're wrong. He hadn't. And he couldn't have got at the gun if he had, what's more. And he didn't pick anything up afterwards. I'll swear to that.'

Ned Manx said with some violence, 'For God's sake, Cousin George, think what you're saying.'

'It is useless, Edward,' said Lady Pastern. 'He will destroy himself out of sheer complacency.' She addressed herself to Alleyn. 'I must inform you that in my opinion and that of many of his acquaintances, my husband's eccentricity is of a degree that renders his statements completely unreliable.'

'That be damned!' shouted Lord Pastern. 'I'm the most truthful man I know. C, you're an ass.'

'So be it,' said Lady Pastern in her deepest voice, and folded her hands.

'When you came out on the dais,' Alleyn went on, disregarding this interlude, 'you brought the revolver with you and put it on the floor under a hat. It was near your right foot, I think, and behind the drums. Quite near the edge of the dais.'

Félicité had opened her bag and for the fourth time had taken out her lipstick and mirror. She made an involuntary movement of her hands, jerking the lipstick away as if she threw it. The mirror fell at her feet. She half rose. Her open bag dropped to the floor, and the glass splintered under her heel. The carpet was littered with the contents of her bag and blotted with powder. Alleyn moved forward quickly. He picked up the lipstick and a folded paper with typewriting on it. Félicité snatched the paper from his hand. 'Thank you. Don't bother. What a fool I am,' she said breathlessly.

She crushed the paper in her hand and held it while, with the other hand, she gathered up the contents of her bag. One of the waiters came forward, like an automaton, to help her.

'Quite near the edge of the dais,' Alleyn repeated. 'So that, for the sake of argument, you, Miss de Suze, or Miss Wayne, or Mr Manx, could have reached out to the sombrero. In fact, while some of your party were dancing, anyone who was left at the table could also have done this. Do you all agree?'

Carlisle was acutely aware of the muscles of her face. She was conscious of Alleyn's gaze, impersonal and deliberate, resting on her eyes and her mouth and her hands. She remembered noticing him, how many hours ago? when he sat at the next table. 'I mustn't look at Fée or at Ned,' she thought. She heard Edward move stealthily in his chair. The paper in Félicité's hand rustled. There was a sharp click and Carlisle jumped galvanically. Lady Pastern had flicked open her lorgnette and was now staring through it at Alleyn.

Manx said: 'You were next to our table, I think, weren't you, Alleyn?'

'By an odd coincidence,' Alleyn rejoined pleasantly.

'I think it better for us to postpone our answers.'

'Do you?' Alleyn said lightly. 'Why?'

'Obviously, the question about whether we could have touched this hat, or whatever it was . . . '

'You know perfectly well that it was, Ned,' Lord Pastern interjected. 'It was my sombrero, and the gun was under it. We've had all that.'

' . . . this sombrero,' Edward amended, 'is a question that has dangerous implications for all of us. I'd like to say that quite apart from the possibility, which we have not admitted, of any of us touching it, there is surely no possibility at all that any of us could have taken a revolver from underneath it, shoved a bit of a parasol up the barrel and replaced the gun, without anything being noticed. If you don't mind my saying so, the suggestion of any such manoeuvre is obviously ridiculous.'

'Oh, I don't know,' said Lord Pastern with an air of judicial impartiality. 'All that switchin' about of the light and the metronome waggin' and everybody naturally watchin' me, you know, I should say, in point of fact, it was quite possible. I wouldn't have noticed, I promise you.'

'George,' Félicité whispered fiercely, 'do you *want* to do us in?'

'I want the truth,' her stepfather shouted crossly. 'I was a Theosophist, once,' he added.

'You are and have been and always will be an imbecile,' said his wife, shutting her lorgnette.

'Well,' Alleyn said, and the attention of the band, the employees of the restaurant, and its guests, having been diverted to this domestic interchange, swung back to him, 'ridiculous or not, I shall put the question. You are, of course, under no compulsion to answer it. Did any of you handle Lord Pastern's sombrero?'

They were silent. The waiter, who had gathered up the pieces of broken mirror, faced Alleyn with an anxious smile. 'Excuse me, sir,' he said.

'Yes?'

'The young lady,' said the waiter, bowing towards Félicité, 'did put her hand under the hat. I was the waiter for that table, sir, and I happened to notice. I hope you will excuse me, Miss, but I did happen to notice.'

Fox's pencil whispered over the paper.

'Thank you,' said Alleyn.

Félicité cried out: 'This is the absolute *end*. Suppose I said it's not true.'

'I shouldn't,' Alleyn said. 'As Mr Manx has pointed out, I was sitting next to your table.'

'Then why ask?'

'To see if you would frankly admit that you did, in fact, put your hand under the sombrero.'

'People,' said Carlisle suddenly, 'think twice about making frank statements all over the place when a capital crime is involved.'

She looked up at Alleyn and found him smiling at her. 'How right you are,' he said. 'That's what makes homicide cases so tiresome.'

'Are we to hang about all night,' Lord Pastern demanded, 'while you sit gossipin'? Never saw such a damned amateur set-up in all m'life. Makes you sick.'

'Let us get on by all means, sir. We haven't very much more ground to cover here. It will be necessary, I'm afraid, for us to search you before we can let you off.'

'All of us?' Félicité said quickly.

They looked, with something like awe, at Lady Pastern.

'There is a wardress in the ladies' cloakroom,' Alleyn said, 'and a detective-sergeant in the men's. We shall also need your finger-prints, if you please. Sergeant Bailey will attend to that. Shall we set about it? Perhaps you, Lady Pastern, will go in first?'

Lady Pastern rose. Her figure, tightly encased, seemed to enlarge itself. Everybody stole uneasy glances at it. She faced her husband. 'Of the many indignities you have forced upon me,' she said, 'this is the most intolerable. For this I shall never forgive you.'

'Good lord, C,' he rejoined, 'what's the matter with being searched. Trouble with you is you've got a dirty mind. If you'd listened to my talks on the Body Beautiful that time in Kent . . .'

'*Silence!*' she said (in French) and swept into the ladies' cloakroom. Félicité giggled nervously.

'Anybody may search *me*,' Lord Pastern said, generously. 'Come on.'

He led the way to the men's cloakroom.

Alleyn said: 'Perhaps, Miss de Suze, you would like to go with your mother. It's perfectly in order, if you think she'd prefer it.'

Félicité was sitting in her chair with her left hand clutching her bag and her right hand out of sight. 'I expect she'd rather have a private martyrdom, Mr Alleyn,' she said.

'Suppose you go and ask her? You can get your part of the programme over when she is free.'

He stood close to Félicité, smiling down at her. She said: 'Oh, all right. If you like.' Without enthusiasm, and with a backward glance at Manx, she followed her mother.

Alleyn immediately took her chair and addressed himself to Manx and Carlisle.

'I wonder,' he said, 'if you can help me with one or two routine jobs that will have to be tidied up. I believe you were both at the dinner party at Lord Pastern's house – it's in Duke's Gate, isn't it? – before this show tonight.'

'Yes,' Edward said. 'We were there.'

'And the rest of the party? Bellairs and Rivera and of course Lord and Lady Pastern. Anyone else?'

'No,' Carlisle said, and immediately corrected herself: 'I'd forgotten. Miss Henderson.'

'Miss Henderson?'

'She used to be Félicité's governess and stayed on as a sort of general prop and stay to everybody.'

'What is her full name?'

'I – I really don't know. Ned, have you ever heard Hendy's Christian name?'

'No,' Edward said. 'Never. She's simply Hendy. I should think it might be Edith. Wait a moment, though,' he added after a moment, 'I do know. Fée told me years ago. She saw it on an electoral roll or something. It's Petronella Xantippe.'

'I don't believe you.'

'People so seldom have the names you expect,' Alleyn murmured vaguely. 'Can you give me a detailed description of your evening at Duke's Gate? You see, as Rivera was there, the dinner party assumes a kind of importance.'

Carlisle thought: 'We're waiting too long. One of us ought to have replied at once.'

'I want,' Alleyn said at last, 'if you can give it to me, an account of the whole thing. When everybody arrived. What you talked about. Whether you were all together most of the time or whether you split up, for instance, after dinner and were in different rooms. That kind of thing.'

They began to speak together and stopped short. They laughed uncomfortably, apologized and invited each other to proceed.

At last Carlisle embarked alone on a colourless narrative. She had arrived at Duke's Gate at about five and had seen her aunt and uncle and Félicité. Naturally there had been a good deal of talk about the evening performance. Her uncle had been in very good spirits.

'And Lady Pastern and Miss de Suze?' Alleyn said. Carlisle replied carefully that they were in much their usual form.

'And how is that?' he asked. 'Cheerful? Happy family atmosphere, would you say?'

Manx said lightly: 'My dear Alleyn, like most families they rub along together without – without – '

'Were you going to say "without actually bursting up"?'

'Well – well – '

'Ned,' Carlisle interjected, 'it's no good pretending Uncle George and Aunt Cecile represent the dead norm of British family life. Presumably Mr Alleyn reads the papers. If I say they were much as usual it means they were much as usual on their own lines.' She turned to Alleyn. 'On their own lines, Mr Alleyn, they were perfectly normal.'

'If you'll allow me to say so, Miss Wayne,' Alleyn rejoined warmly, 'you are evidently an extremely sensible person. May I implore you to keep it up.'

'Not to the extent of letting you think a routine argument to them is matter for suspicion to you.'

'They argue,' Manx added, 'perpetually and vehemently. It means nothing. Well, you've heard them.'

'And did they, for example, argue about Lord Pastern's performance in the band?'

'Oh, yes,' they said together.

'And about Bellairs or Rivera?'

'A bit,' said Carlisle, after a pause.

'Boogie-woogie merchants,' Manx said, 'are not, in the nature of things, my cousin Cecile's cups-of-tea. She is, as you may have noticed, a little in the *grande dame* line of business.'

Alleyn leant forward in his chair and rubbed his nose. He looked, Carlisle thought, like a bookish man considering some point that had been raised in an interminable argument.

'Yes,' he said at last. 'That's all right, of course. One can see the obvious and rather eccentric *mise en scène*. Everything you've told me is no doubt quite true. But the devil of it is, you know, that you're going to use the palpable eccentricities as a sort of smoke-screen for the more profound disturbances.'

They were astonished and disconcerted. Carlisle said tentatively that she didn't understand. 'Don't you?' Alleyn murmured. 'Oh, well! Shall we get on with it? Bellairs has suggested an engagement between Rivera and Miss de Suze. Was there an engagement, if you please?'

'No, I don't think so. Was there, Lisle?'

Carlisle said that she didn't think so, either. Nothing had been announced.

'An understanding?'

'He wanted her to marry him, I think. I mean,' Carlisle amended with heightened colour, 'I know he did. I don't think she was going to. I'm sure she wasn't.'

'How did Lord Pastern feel about it?'

'Who can tell?' Edward muttered.

'I don't think it bothered him much one way or the other,' Carlisle said. 'He was too busy planning his debut.'

But into her memory came the figure of Lord Pastern, bent over his task of drawing bullets from cartridges, and she heard again his grunted, 'much better leave things to me.'

Alleyn began to lead them step by step through the evening at Duke's Gate. What had they talked about before dinner? How had the party been divided, and into which rooms? What had they themselves done and said? Carlisle found herself landed with an account of her arrival. It was easy to say that her aunt and uncle had argued about whether there should be extra guests for dinner. It was not so easy when he led her back to the likelihood of an engagement between Rivera and Félicité, asking if it had been discussed and by whom, and whether Félicité had confided in her. 'These seem impertinent questions,' Alleyn said, and anticipated her attempt to suggest as much. 'But, believe me, they are entirely impersonal. Irrelevant matters will be most thankfully rejected and forgotten. We want to tidy up the field of enquiry; that's all.' And then it seemed to Carlisle that evasions would be silly and wrong and she said that Félicité had been worried and unhappy about Rivera.

She sensed Edward's uneasiness and added that there had been nothing in the Félicité-Rivera situation, nothing at all. 'Félicité makes emotional mountains out of sentimental molehills,' she said. 'I think she enjoys it.' But she knew while she said this that Félicité's outburst had been more serious than she suggested and she heard her voice lose its integrity and guessed that Alleyn heard this too. She began to be oppressed by his quiet insistence and yet her taste for detail made her a little pleased with her own accuracy, and she felt something like an artist's reluctance to slur or distort. It was easy again to recall her solitary time before dinner in the ball-room. As soon as she began to speak of it the sensation of nostalgia flashed up in her memory and she found herself telling Alleyn that her coming-out ball had been there, that the room had a host of associations for her and that she had stood there, recollecting them.

'Did you notice if the umbrellas and parasols were there?'

'Yes,' she said quickly. 'I did. They were there on the piano. I remembered the French parasol. It was Aunt Cile's. I remembered Félicité playing with it as a child. It takes to pieces.' She caught her breath. 'But you know it does that,' she said.

'And it was intact then, when you saw it? No bits gone out of the shaft?'

'No, no.'

'Sure?'

'Yes. I picked it up and opened it. That's supposed to be unlucky, isn't it? It was all right then.'

'Good. And after this you went into the drawing-room. I know this sounds aimlessly exacting but what happened next, do you remember?'

Before she knew where she was she had told him about the magazine, *Harmony*, and there seemed no harm in repeating her notion that Félicité had written one of the letters on GPF's page. Alleyn gave no sign that this was of interest. It was Edward who, unaccountably, made a stifled ejaculation. Carlisle thought: 'Have I blundered? and hurried on to an account of her visit to her uncle's study when he drew the bullets from the cartridges. Alleyn asked casually how he had set about this and seemed to be diverted from the matter in hand, amused at Lord Pastern's neatness and dexterity.

Carlisle was accustomed to being questioned about Lord Pastern's eccentricities. She considered him fair game and normally enjoyed trying to make sharp, not unkindly, little word-sketches of him for her friends. His notoriety was so gross that she had always felt it would be ridiculous to hesitate. She slipped into this habit now.

Then the picture of the drawer, pulled out and laid on the desk at his elbow, suddenly presented itself. She felt a kind of shrinking in her midriff and stopped short.

But Alleyn had turned to Ned Manx and Ned, drily and slowly, answered his questions about his own arrival in the drawing-room.

What impression did he get of Bellairs and Rivera? He hadn't spoken to them very much. Lady Pastern had taken him apart to show him her embroidery.

'*Gros-point?* Alleyn asked.

'And *petit-point.* Like most Frenchwomen of her period, she's pretty good. I really didn't notice the others, much.'

The dinner party itself came next. The conversation, Ned was saying, had been fragmentary, about all sorts of things. He couldn't remember in detail.

'Miss Wayne has an observer's eye and ear,' Alleyn said, turning to her. 'Perhaps you can remember, can you? What did you talk about? You sat, where?'

'On Uncle George's right.'

'And on your other hand?'

'Mr Rivera.'

'Can you remember what he spoke about, Miss Wayne?' Alleyn offered his cigarette case to her. As he lit her cigarette Carlisle looked past him at Ned who shook his head very slightly.

'I thought him rather awful, I'm afraid,' she said. 'He really was a bit too thick. All flowery compliments and too Spanish-grandee for anyone to swallow.'

'Do you agree, Mr Manx?'

'Oh, yes. He was quite unreal and rather ridiculous, I thought.'

'Offensively so, would you say?'

They did not look at each other. Edward said: 'He just bounded sky-high, if you call that offensive.'

'Did you speak of the performance tonight?'

'Oh, yes,' Edward said. 'And I must say I'm not surprised that the waiters were muddled about who they were to carry out. It struck me that both Uncle George and Rivera wanted all the fat and that neither of them could make up his mind to letting the other have the stretcher. Bellairs was clearly at the end of his professional tether about it.'

Alleyn asked how long the men had stayed behind in the dining-room. Reluctantly – too reluctantly Carlisle thought, with a rising sense of danger – Ned told them that Lord Pastern had taken Breezy away to show him the blank cartridges. 'So you and Rivera were left with the port?' Alleyn said.

'Yes. Not for long.'

'Can you recall the conversation?'

'There was nothing that would be any help to you.'

'You never know.'

'I didn't encourage conversation. He asked all sorts of questions about our various relationships to each other and I snubbed him.'

'How did he take that?'

'Nobody enjoys being snubbed, I suppose, but I fancy he had a tolerably thick hide on him.'

'Was there actually a quarrel?'

Edward stood up. 'Look here, Alleyn,' he said, 'if I was in the slightest degree implicated in this business I should have followed my own advice and refused to answer any of your questions. I am not implicated. I did not monkey with the revolver. I did not bring about Rivera's death.'

'And now,' Carlisle thought in despair, 'Ned's going to give him a sample of the family temper. Oh God!' she thought, 'please don't let him.'

'Good,' Alleyn said, and waited.

'Very well, then,' Edward said grandly and sat down.

'So there was a quarrel.'

'I merely,' Edward shouted, 'showed the man I thought he was impertinent and he walked out of the room.'

'Did you speak to him again after this incident?'

Carlise remembered a scene in the hall. The two men facing each other, Rivera with his hand clapped to his ear. What was it Ned had said to him? Something ridiculous, like a perky schoolboy. 'Put that in your hurdy-gurdy and squeeze it,' he had shouted with evident relish.

'I merely ask these questions,' Alleyn said, 'because the bloke had a thick ear, and I wondered who gave it to him. The skin's broken and I noticed you wear a signet ring.'

III

In the main office, Dr Curtis contemplated Breezy Bellairs with the air of wary satisfaction. 'He'll do,' he said, and stepping neatly behind Breezy's chair, he winked at Alleyn.

'He must have got hold of something over and above the shot I gave him. But he'll do.'

Breezy looked up at Alleyn and gave him the celebrated smile. He was pallid and sweating slightly. His expression was one of relief, of well-being. Dr Curtis washed his syringe in a tumbler of water on the desk and then returned it to his case.

Alleyn opened the door into the foyer and nodded to Fox, who rose and joined him. Together they returned to the contemplation of Breezy.

Fox cleared his throat: 'Alors,' he said cautiously, and stopped. 'Evidemment,' he said, 'il y a un avancement, n'est ce pas?'

He paused, slightly flushed, and looked out of the corners of his eyes at Alleyn.

'Pas grand'chose,' Alleyn muttered. 'But as Curtis says, he'll do for our purpose. You go, by the way, Br'er Fox, from strength to strength. The accent improves.'

'I still don't get the practice though,' Fox complained. Breezy, who was looking with complete tranquillity at the opposite wall, laughed comfortably. 'I feel lovely, now,' he volunteered.

'He's had a pretty solid shot,' Dr Curtis said. 'I don't know what he'd been up to before but it seems to have packed him up a bit. But he's all right. He can answer questions, can't you, Bellairs?'

'I'm fine,' Breezy rejoined dreamily. 'Box of birds.'

'Well . . . ' Alleyn said dubiously. Fox added in a sepulchral under-tone: 'Faute de mieux.' 'Exactly,' Alleyn said and, drawing up a chair, placed himself in front of Breezy.

'I'd like you to tell me something,' he said. Breezy lazily withdrew his gaze from the opposite wall and Alleyn found himself staring into eyes that, because of the enormous size of their pupils, seemed mere structures and devoid of intelligence.

'Do you remember,' he said, 'what you did at Lord Pastern's house?'

He had to wait a long time for an answer. At last Breezy's voice, detached and remote, said: 'Don't let's talk. It's nice not talking.'

'Talking's nice too, though.'

Dr Curtis walked away from Breezy and murmured to no one in particular, 'Get him started and he may go on.'

'It must have been fun at the dinner party,' Alleyn suggested. 'Did Carlos enjoy himself?'

Breezy's arm lay curved along the desk. With a luxurious sigh, he slumped further into the chair and rested his cheek on his sleeve. In a moment or two his voice began again, independently, it seemed, with no conscious volition on his part. It trailed through his scarcely moving lips in a monotone.

'I told him it was silly but that made no difference at all. "Look," I said, "you're crazy". Well of course I was sore on account of he held back on me, not bringing me my cigarettes.'

'What cigarettes?'

'He never did anything I asked him. I was so good to him. I was as good as gold. I told him. I said, "Look," I said, "she won't take it from you, boy. She's as sore as hell," I said, "and so's he, and the other girl isn't falling so what's the point?" I knew there'd be trouble. "And the old bastard doesn't like it," I said. "He pretends it doesn't mean a thing to him, but that's all hooey because he just naturally wouldn't like it." No good. No notice taken.'

'When was this?' Alleyn asked.

'Off and on. Most of the time you might say. And when we were in the taxi and he said how the guy had hit him, I said: "There you are, what was I telling you?" '

'Who hit him?'

There was a longer pause. Breezy turned his head languidly.

'Who hit Carlos, Breezy?'

'I heard you the first time. What a gang, though! The Honourable Edward Manx in serious mood while lunching at the Tarmac with Miss Félicité de Suze who is, of course, connected with him on the distaff side. Her stepfather is Lord Pastern and Bagott, but if you ask me it's a punctured romance. Cherchez la femme.'

Fox glanced up from his notes with an air of bland interest.

'The woman in this case, 'Alleyn said, 'being . . . ?'

'Funny name for a girl.'

'Carlisle?'

'Sound dopey to me, but what of that? But that's the sort of thing they do. Imagine having two names. Pastern and Bagott. And I can look after both of them, don't you worry. Trying to swing one across

me. What a chance! Bawling me out. Saying he'll write to this
bloody paper. Him and his hot gunning and where is he now.'

'Swing one across you?' Alleyn repeated quietly. He had pitched
his voice on Breezy's level. Their voices ran into and away from each
other. They seemed to the two onlookers to speak as persons in a
dream, with tranquillity and secret understanding.

'He might have known,' Breezy was saying, 'that I wouldn't come
at it but you've got to admit it was awkward. A permanent engagement. Thanks a lot. How does the chorus go?'

He laughed faintly, yawned, whispered: 'Pardon me,' and closed
his eyes.

'He's going,' Dr Curtis said.

'Breezy,' Allen said loudly, *Breezy.*'

'What?'

'Did Lord Pastern want you to keep him on permanently?'

'I told you. Him and his blankety blankety blank cartridges.'

'Did he want you to sack Skelton?'

'It was all Carlos's fault,' Breezy said quite loudly and on a plaintive
note. 'He thought it up. God, was he angry!'

'Who was angry?'

With a suggestion of cunning the voice murmured: 'That's
telling.'

'Was it Lord Pastern?'

'Him? Don't make me laugh!'

'Syd Skelton?'

'When I told him' Breezy whispered faintly, 'he looked like murder. Honest, I *was* nervy.'

He rolled his face over on his arm and fell into a profound sleep.
'He won't come out of that for eight hours,' said Dr Curtis.

IV

At two o'clock the cleaners came in; five middle-aged women who
were admitted by the police and who walked through the foyer into
the restaurant with the tools of their trade. Caesar Bonn was greatly distressed by their arrival and complained that the pressmen,
who had been sent away with a meagre statement that Rivera had

collapsed and died, would lie in wait for these women and question them. He sent the secretary, David Hahn, after the cleaners. 'They are to be silenced at all costs. At all costs, you understand.' Presently the drone of vacuum cleaners arose in the restaurant. Two of Alleyn's men had been there for some time. They now returned to the foyer and, joining the policemen on duty there, glanced impassively at its inhabitants.

Most of the Boys were asleep. They were sprawled in ungainly postures on their small chairs. Trails of ash lay on their clothes. They had crushed out their cigarette butts on empty packets, on the soles of their shoes, on match boxes or had pitched them at the floor containers. The smell of dead butts seemed to hang over the entire room.

Lady Pastern appeared to sleep. She was inclined backwards in her armchair and her eyes were closed. Purplish shadows had appeared on her face and deep grooves ran from her nostrils to the corners of her mouth. Her cheeks sagged. She scarcely stirred when her husband, who had been silent for a considerable time, said: 'Hi, Ned!'

'Yes, Cousin George?' Manx responded guardedly.

'I've got to the bottom of this.'

'Indeed?'

'I know who did it.'

'Really? Who?'

'I disagree entirely and emphatically with capital punishment,' Lord Pastern said, puffing out his cheeks at the group of police officials. 'I shall therefore keep my knowledge to myself. Let 'em muddle on. Murder's a matter for the psychiatrist, not the hangman. As for judges they're a pack of conceited old sadists. Let 'em get on with it. They'll have no help from me. For God's sake, Fée, stop fidgetin'.'

Félicité was curled up in the chair she had used earlier in the evening. From time to time she thrust her hands out of sight, exploring, it seemed, the space between the upholstered arms and seat. She did this furtively with sidelong glances at the others.

Carlisle said: 'What *is* it, Fée? What have you lost?'

'My hanky.'

'Here, take mine for pity's sake,' said Lord Pastern, and threw it at her.

The searching had gone forward steadily. Carlisle, who liked her privacy, had found the experience galling and unpleasant. The wardress was a straw-coloured woman with large artificial teeth and firm pale hands. She had been extremely polite and uncompromising.

Now the last man to be searched, Syd Skelton, returned from the men's cloakroom and at the same time Alleyn and Fox came out of the office. The Boys woke up. Lady Pastern opened her eyes.

Alleyn said: 'As the result of these preliminary inquiries . . . ' ('Preliminary!' Lord Pastern snorted.) ' . . . I think we have got together enough information and may allow you to go home. I'm extremely sorry to have kept you here so long.'

They were all on their feet. Alleyn raised a hand. 'There's one restriction, I'm afraid. I think you'll all understand, and I hope, respect it. Those of you who were in immediate communication with Rivera or who had access to the revolver used by Lord Pastern, or who seem to us, for sufficient reasons, to be in any way concerned in the circumstances leading to Rivera's death, will be seen home by police officers. We shall provide ourselves with search warrants. If such action seems necessary, we shall use them.'

'Of all the footlin', pettifoggin'. . . ' Lord Pastern began, and was interrupted.

'Those of you who come under this heading,' Alleyn said, 'are Lord Pastern and the members of his party, Mr Bellairs and Mr Skelton. That's all, I think. Thank you, ladies and gentlemen.'

'I'm damned if I'll put up with this. Look here, Alleyn . . . '

'I'm sorry, sir. I must insist, I'm afraid.'

'George,' said Lady Pastern, 'you have tried conclusions with the law on more than one occasion and as often as you have done so you have made a fool of yourself. Come home.'

Lord Pastern studied his wife with an air of detachment.

'Your hair-net's loose,' he pointed out, 'and you're bulgin' above your waist. Comes of wearin' stays. I've always said . . . '

'I, at least,' Lady Pastern said directly to Alleyn, 'am prepared to accept your conditions. So, I am sure, are my daughter and my niece. Félicité! Carlisle!'

'Fox!' said Alleyn.

She walked with perfect composure to the door and waited there. Fox spoke to one of the plain-clothes men who detached himself from the group near the entrance. Félicité held out a hand towards Edward Manx. 'Ned, you'll come, won't you? You'll stay with us?'

After a moment's hesitation he took her hand. 'Dearest Edward,' said Lady Pastern from the door. 'We should be so grateful.'

'Certainly, Cousin Cecile. Of course.'

Félicité still held his hand. He looked at Carlisle. 'Coming?' he asked.

'Yes, of course. Goodnight Mr Alleyn,' said Carlisle.

'Goodnight, Miss Wayne.'

They went out, followed by the plain-clothes man.

'I should like to have a word with you, Mr Skelton,' Alleyn said. 'The rest of you,' he turned to the Boys, the waiters, and the spot-light man, 'may go. You will be given notice of the inquest. Sorry to have kept you up so late. Goodnight.'

The waiters and the electrician went at once. The band moved forward in a group. Happy Hart said: 'What about Breezy?'

'He's sound asleep and will need a bit of rousing. I shall see he's taken home.'

Hart shuffled his feet and looked at his hands. 'I don't know what you're thinking,' he said, 'but he's all right. Breezy's OK, really. I mean, he's just been making the pace a bit too hot for himself as you might say. He's a very nervy type, Breezy. He suffers from insomnia. He took the stuff for his nerves. But he's all right.'

'He and Rivera got on well, did they?'

Several of the Boys said quickly: 'That's right. Sure. They were all right.' Hart added that Breezy was very good to Carlos and gave him his big chance in London.

All the Boys agreed fervently with this statement except Skelton. He stood apart from his associates. They avoided looking at him. He was a tall darkish fellow with narrow eyes and a sharp nose. His mouth was small and thin-lipped. He stooped slightly.

'Well, if that's all,' Happy Hart said uneasily, 'we'll say goodnight.'

'We've got their addresses, haven't we, Fox? Good. Thank you. Goodnight.'

They filed out, carrying their instruments. In the old days when places like the Metronome and Quags and the Hungaria kept going up to two in the morning the Boys had worked through, sometimes going on to parties in private houses. They were Londoners who turned home-wards with pale faces and blue jaws at the time when fans of water from giant hose pipes strike across Piccadilly and Whitehall. They had been among the tag-ends of the night in those times, going soberly to their beds as the first milk carts jangled. In summer-time they had undressed in the dawn to the thin stir of sparrows. They shared with taxi-drivers, cloakroom attendants, waiters and commissionaires, a specialized disillusionment.

Alleyn watched them go and then nodded to Fox. Fox approached Caesar Bonn and David Hahn, who lounged gloomily near the office door. 'Perhaps you gentlemen wouldn't mind coming into the office,' he suggested. They followed him in. Alleyn turned to Skelton. 'Now, Mr Skelton.'

'What's the idea,' Skelton said, 'keeping me back? I've got a home, same as everybody else. Though how the hell I'm going to get there's nobody's business.'

'I'm sorry. It's a nuisance for you, I know, but it can't be helped.'

'I don't see why.'

The office door was opened from inside. Two constables came out with Breezy Bellairs hanging between them like a cumbersome puppet. His face was lividly pale, his eyes half open. He breathed stertorously and made a complaining noise like a wretched child. Dr Curtis followed. Bonn and Hahn watched from inside the office.

'All right?' Alleyn said.

'He'll do. We'll just get him into his coat.'

They held Breezy up while Curtis, with difficulty, crammed him into his tight-fitting overcoat. During this struggle Breezy's baton fell to the floor. Hahn came forward and picked it up. 'You wouldn't think.' Hahn said, contemplating it sadly, 'how good he was. Not to look at him now.'

Dr Curtis yawned. 'These chaps'll see him into his bed,' he said. 'I'll be off, if you don't want me, Rory.'

'Right.' The dragging procession disappeared. Fox returned to the office and shut the door.

'That's a nice way,' Skelton said angrily, 'for a first-class band leader to be seen going home. Between a couple of flatties.'

'They'll be very tactful,' Alleyn rejoined. 'Shall we sit down?'

Skelton said he'd sat down for so long that his bottom was numb. 'Let's get cracking, for God's sake. I've had it. What's the idea?'

Alleyn took out his note-book.

'The idea,' he said, 'is further information. I think you can give it to us. By all means let's get cracking.'

'Why pick on me? I know no more than the others.'

'Don't you?' Alleyn said vaguely. He glanced up. 'What's your opinion of Lord Pastern as a tympanist?'

'Dire. What of it?'

'Did the others hold this opinion?'

'They knew. Naturally. It was a cheap stunt. Playing up the snob-value.' He thrust his hands down in his pockets and began to walk to and fro, impelled, it seemed, by resentment. Alleyn waited.

'It's when something like this turns up,' Skelton announced loudly, 'that you see how rotten the whole setup really is. I'm not ashamed of my work. Why the hell should I be? It interests me. It's not easy. It takes doing and anybody that tells you there's nothing to the best type of our kind of music talks through his hat. It's got something. It's clever and there's a lot of hard thinking behind it.'

'I don't know about music,' Alleyn said, 'but I can imagine that from the technical point of view your sort can be almost purely intellectual. Or is that nonsense?'

Skelton glowered at him. 'You're not far out. A lot of the stuff we have to play is wet and corny, of course. They,' he jerked his head at the empty restaurant, 'like it that way. But there's other stuff that's different. If I could pick my work I'd be in an outfit that went for the real mackay. In a country where things were run decently I'd be able to do that. I'd be able to say: "This is what I can do and it's the best I can do," and I'd be directed into the right channels. I'm a Communist,' he said loudly.

Alleyn was suddenly and vividly reminded of Lord Pastern. He said nothing and after a pause Skelton went on.

'I realize I'm working for the rottenest section of a crazy society but what can I do? It's my job and I have to take it. But this affair? Walking out and letting a dopy old deadbeat of a lord make a fool of himself with my instruments, and a lot of deadbeat effects added to them! Looking as if I like it! Where's my self-respect?'

'How,' Alleyn asked, 'did it come about?'

'Breezy worked it because . . . '

He stopped short and advanced on Alleyn. 'Here!' he demanded. 'What's all this in aid of? What do you want?'

'Like Lord Pastern,' Alleyn said lightly, 'I want the truth. Bellairs, you were saying, worked it because – of what?'

'I've told you. Snob-value.'

'And the others agreed?'

'They haven't any principles. Oh, yes. They took it.'

'Rivera, for instance, didn't oppose the idea?'

Skelton flushed deeply. 'No,' he said.

Alleyn saw his pockets bulge as the hidden hands clenched. 'Why not?' he asked.

'Rivera was hanging his hat up to the girl. Pastern's step-daughter. He was all out to make himself a hero with the old man.'

'That made you very angry, didn't it?'

'Who says it made me angry?'

'Bellairs said so.'

'Him! Another product of our so-called civilization. Look at him.'

Alleyn asked him if he knew anything about Breezy's use of drugs. Skelton, caught, as it seemed, between the desire of a zealot to speak his mind and an undefined wariness, said that Breezy was the child of his age and circumstances. He was a by-product, Skelton said, of a cynical and disillusioned social set-up. The phrases fell from his lips with the precision of slogans. Alleyn listened and watched and felt his interest stirring. 'We all knew,' Skelton said, 'that he was taking some kind of dope to keep him going. Even *he* knew – old Pastern. He'd nosed it out all right and I reckon he knew where it came from. You could tell. Breezy's changed a hell of a lot. He used to be a nice sort of joker in a way. Bit of a wag. Always having us on. He got off-side with the dago for that.'

'Rivera?'

'That's right. Breezy used to be crazy on practical jokes. He'd fix a silly squeaker in one of the saxes or sneak a wee bell inside the piano. Childish. He got hold of Rivera's p.a. and fixed it with little bits of paper between the keys so's it wouldn't go. Only for rehearsal, of course. Rivera came out all glamour and hair oil and swung his p.a. Nothing happened. There was Breezy grinning like he'd split his face and the Boys all sniggering. You had to laugh. Rivera tore the place up; he went mad and howled out he'd quit. Breezy had a hell of a job fixing him. It was quite a party.'

'Practical jokes,' Alleyn said. 'A curious obsession, I always think.'

Skelton looked sharply at him. 'Here!' he said, 'you don't want to get ideas. Breezy's all right. Breezy wouldn't come at anything like this.' He laughed shortly, and added with an air of disgust: 'Breezy fix Rivera! Not likely.'

'About this drug habit – ' Alleyn began. Skelton said impatiently: 'Well, there you are! It's just one of those things. I told you: we all knew. He used to go to parties on Sundays with some gang.'

'Any idea who they were?'

'No, I never asked. I'm not interested. I tried to tell him he was heading for a crash. Once. He didn't like it. He's my boss and I shut up. I've had turned it up and gone over to another band but I'm used to working with these boys and they do better stuff than most.'

'You never heard where he got his drug, whatever it is?'

Skelton muttered, 'I never *heard*. Naturally.'

'But you formed an opinion, perhaps?'

'Perhaps.'

'Going to tell me about it?'

'I want to know what you're getting at. I've got to protect myself, haven't I? I like to get things straight. You've got some notion that because I looked at Pastern's gun I might have shoved this silly umbrella what-have-you up the muzzle. Why don't you come to the point?'

'I shall do so,' Alleyn said. 'I've kept you behind because of this circumstance and because you were alone with Lord Pastern for a short time after you left the platform and before he made his entrance. So far as I can see at the moment there is no connection between your possible complicity and the fact that Bellairs takes drugs. As a police officer I'm concerned with drug addicts and their source of supply. If you can help me with any information, I'll be grateful. Do you know, then, where Bellairs got whatever he took?'

Skelton deliberated, his brows drawn together, his lower lip thrust out. Alleyn found himself speculating about his background. What accumulation of circumstances, ill-adjustments or misfortunes had resulted in this particular case? What would Skelton have been if his history had been otherwise? Were his views, his truculence, his suspicions, rooted in honesty or in some indefinable sense of victimization?

To what lengths would they impel him? And finally Alleyn asked himself the inevitable question: could this be a killer?

Skelton wetted his lips. 'The drug-racket,' he said, 'is like any other racket in a capitalistic government. The real criminals are the bosses, the barons, the high-ups. They don't get pulled in. It's the little blokes that get caught. You have to think it out. Silly sentiment and big talk won't work. I've got no tickets on the police department in this country. A fairly efficient machine working for the wrong ideas. But drug-taking's no good from any point of view. All right. I'll co-operate this far. I'll tell you where Breezy got his dope.'

'And where,' said Alleyn patiently, 'did Breezy get his dope?'

'From Rivera,' said Skelton. 'Now! From Rivera.'

CHAPTER 7

Dawn

Skelton had gone home, and Caesar Bonn and David Hahn. The cleaners had retired into some remote part of the building. Only the police remained: Alleyn and Fox, Bailey, Thompson, the three men who had searched the restaurant and band room and the uniformed constable who would remain on duty until he was relieved after daybreak. The time was now twenty minutes to three.

'Well, Foxkin,' said Alleyn, 'where are we? You've been very mousey and discreet. Let's have your theory. Come on.'

Fox cleared his throat and placed the palms of his hands on his knees. 'A very peculiar case,' he said disapprovingly. 'Freakish, you might say. Silly. Except for the corpse. Corpses,' Mr Fox observed with severity, 'are never silly.'

Detective-Sergeants Bailey and Thompson exchanged winks.

'In the first place, Mr Alleyn,' Fox continued, 'I ask myself: why do it that way? Why fire a bit of an umbrella handle from a revolver when you might fire a bullet? This applies in particular to his lordship. And yet it seems it must have been done. You can't get away from it. Nobody had a chance of stabbing the chap while he was performing, did they now?'

'Nobody.'

'All right, then. Now, if anybody pushed this silly weapon up the gun after Skelton examined it, they had the thing concealed about their person. Not much bigger than a fountain-pen but sharp as hell. Which brings us to Bellairs, for one. If you consider Bellairs, you have to remember that his lordship seems to have searched him very thoroughly before he went out to perform.'

'Moreover his lordship in the full tide of his own alleged innocence declares that the wretched Breezy didn't get a chance to pocket anything after he had been searched – or to get at the gun.'

'Does he really?' said Fox. 'Fancy!'

'In fact his lordship, who, I submit, is no fool, has been at peculiar pains to clear everybody but himself.'

'No fool, perhaps,' Fox grunted, 'but would you say a bit off the plumb, mentally?'

'Everybody else says so, at all events. In any case, Fox, I'll give sworn evidence that nobody stabbed Rivera before or at the time he was shot at. He was a good six feet away from everybody except Lord Pastern, who was busy with his blasted gun.'

'There you are! And it wasn't planted among the music stands because they were used by the other band. And anyway none of the musicians went near his lordship's funny hat where the gun was, and being like that, I ask myself, isn't his lordship the most likely to use a silly fanciful method if he'd made up his mind to do a man in? It all points to his lordship. You can't get away from it. And yet he seems so pleased with himself and kind of unruffled. Of course you do find that attitude in homicidal mania.'

'You do. What about motive?'

'Do we know what he thought about his stepdaughter keeping company with the deceased? The other young lady suggested that he didn't seem to care one way or the other but you never know. Something else may turn up. Personally, as things stand at the moment, I favour his lordship. What about you, Mr Alleyn?'

Alleyn shook his head. 'I'm stumped,' he said. 'Perhaps Skelton could have got the thing into the revolver when he examined it but Lord Pastern, who undoubtedly is as sharp as a needle, swears he didn't. They were alone together for a minute while Breezy made his announcement, but Skelton says he didn't go near Lord Pastern, who had the gun in his hip pocket. It's not likely to be a lie because Pastern could deny it. You didn't hear Skelton. He's an odd chap. A truculent Communist. Australian, I should say. A hard, determined thinker. Nobody's fool and completely sincere. One-track minded. There's no doubt he detested Rivera, both on general principles and because Rivera backed up Lord Pastern's appearance tonight. Skelton bitterly resented this and says so. He felt he was prostituting what he is pleased to regard as his art and conniving at something entirely against his social principles. I believe him to be fanatically sincere in this. He looked on Rivera and Lord Pastern as parasites. Rivera, by the way, supplied Breezy Bellairs with his dope, whatever it is. Curtis says cocaine, and it looks as if he found himself something to go on with when he searched the body. We'll have to follow that one up, Fox.'

'Dope,' said Fox profoundly. 'There you are! When we do get a windfall it's a dead man. Still, there may be something in his rooms to give us a lead. South America, now. That may link up with the Snowy Santos gang. They operate through South America. It'd be nice,' said Mr Fox, whose talents for some time had been concerned with the sale of illicit drugs, 'it'd be lovely, in fact, to get the tabs on Snowy Santos.'

'Lovely, wouldn't it?' Alleyn agreed absently. 'Get on with your argument, Fox.'

'Well now, sir. Seeing Rivera wasn't meant to fall down and *did*, you can say he was struck at that moment. I know that sounds like a glimpse of the obvious, but it cuts out any idea that there was some kind of jiggery-pokery *after* he fell because nobody knew he was going to fall. And unless you feel like saying somebody threw the weapon like a dart at the same time as his lordship fired the first shot – well,' said Fox disgustedly, 'that would be a fat-headed sort of notion, wouldn't it? So we come back to the idea it was fired from the revolver. Which is supported by the scratches in the barrel. Mind, we'll have to get the experts going there.'

'We shall, indeed.'

'But saying, for the moment, that the little jewelled clip, acting as a sort of stop, did mark the barrel, we come to Skelton's statement that the scratches were not there when he examined it. And that looks like his lordship again. Look at it how you will, you get back to his lordship, you know.'

'Miss de Suze,' Alleyn said, rubbing his nose in vexation, 'did grope under that damned sombrero. I saw her and so did Manx and so did the waiter. Manx seemed to remonstrate and she laughed and withdrew her hand. She couldn't have got the weapon in then but it shows that it was possible for anyone sitting on her chair to get at the gun. Lady Pastern was left alone at their table while the others danced.'

Fox raised his eyebrows and looked puffy. 'Very icy,' he said. 'A haughty sort of lady and with a will and temper of her own. Look how she's stood up to his lordship in the past. Very masterful.'

Alleyn glanced at his old colleague and smiled. He turned to the group of waiting men. 'Well, Bailey,' he said, 'we've about got to you. Have you found anything new?'

Bailey said morosely: 'Nothing to write home about, Mr Alleyn. No prints on this dart affair. I've packed it up with protection and can have another go at it.'

'The revolver?'

'Very plain sailing there, Mr Alleyn. Not a chance for latents.'

'That's why I risked letting him handle it.'

'Yes, sir. Well now,' said Bailey with a certain professional relish, 'the revolver, Lord Pastern's prints on the revolver. And this band leader's – Breezy Bellairs or whatever he calls himself.'

'Yes. Lord Pastern handed the gun to Breezy.'

'That's right, sir. So I understand.'

'Thompson,' said Alleyn suddenly, 'did you get a good look at Mr Manx's left hand when you dabbed him?'

'Yes, sir. Knuckles a bit grazed. Very slight. Wears a signet ring.'

'How about the band platform, Bailey?'

Bailey looked at his boots and said he'd been over the floor space round the tympani and percussion stand. There were traces of four fingertips identifiable as Miss de Suze's. No others.

'And Rivera? On the body?'

'Not much there,' Bailey said, 'but they would probably bring up latent prints where Bellairs and the doctor had handled him. That was all, so far.'

'Thank you. What about you other chaps in the restaurant and band room? Find anything? Gibson?'

One of the plain-clothes men came forward. 'Not much, sir. Nothing out of the ordinary. Cigarette butts and so on. We picked up the wads and shells and Bellairs' handkerchief, marked, on the platform.'

'He mopped his unpleasant eyes with it when he did his stuff with the wreath,' Alleyn muttered. 'Anything else?'

'There was a cork,' said Detective-Sergeant Gibson apologetically, 'on the band platform. Might have been dropped by a waiter, sir.'

'Not up there. Let's see it.' Gibson produced an envelope from which he shook out a smallish cork on to the table. Alleyn looked at it without touching it. 'When was the band platform cleaned?'

'Polished in the early morning, Mr Alleyn, and mopped over before the evening clients came in.'

'Where exactly did you find this thing?'

'Half-way back and six feet to left of centre. I've marked the place.'

'Good. Not that it'll help much.' Alleyn used his lens. 'it's got a black mark on it.' He stopped and sniffed. 'Boot polish, I think. It was probably kicked about the place by bandsmen. But there's another smell. Not wine or spirit and anyway it's not that sort of cork. It's smaller and made with a narrow end and a wide top. No trade-mark. What *is* this smell? Try, Fox.'

Fox's sniff was stentorian. He rose, meditated and said: 'Now, what am I reminded of?' They waited. 'Citronella,' Fox pronounced gravely. 'Or something like it.'

'How about gun-oil?' said Alleyn.

Fox turned and contemplated his superior with something like indignation. 'Gun-oil? You're not going to tell me, Mr Alleyn, that in addition to stuffing jewelled parasol handles up a revolver somebody stopped it with a cork like a ruddy pop-gun?'

Alleyn grinned. 'The case is taking liberties with your credulity, Br'er Fox.' He used his lens again. 'The bottom surface has been broken, I fancy. It's a forlorn hope, Bailey, but we might try for dabs.'

Bailey put the cork away. Alleyn turned to the others. 'I think you can pack up,' he said. 'I'm afraid I'll have to keep you, Thompson, and you, Bailey, with us. It's a non-stop show. Gibson, you'll pick up a search warrant and go on to Rivera's rooms. Take someone with you. I want a complete search there. Stott and Watson are attending to Bellairs' rooms and Sallis has gone with Skelton. You'll all report back to me at the Yard at ten. Get people to relieve you when you've finished. Bellairs and Skelton will both have to be kept under observation, damn it, though I fancy that for the next eight hours Breezy won't give anybody a headache except himself. Inspector Fox and I will get extra men to attend to Duke's Gate. All right. We'll move.'

In the office a telephone bell rang. Fox went in to answer it and was heard uttering words of reproach. He came out looking scandalized.

'It's that new chap we sent back with his lordship's party, Marks. And what do you suppose he's done?' Fox glared round upon his audience and slapped the palm of his hand on the table. 'Silly young chump! When they get in they say they're all going to the drawing-room. "Oh," said Marks, "then it's my duty, if you please, to accompany you." The gentlemen say they want to retire first, and they go off to the downstairs cloakroom. The ladies have the same idea and they go upstairs and Sergeant Expeditious Marks tries to tear himself in halves which is nothing to what I'll do for him. And while he's exhausting himself running up and down keeping observation, what happens? One of the young ladies slips down the servants' stairs and lets herself out by the back door.'

'Which one?' Alleyn asked quickly.

'Don't,' said Mr Fox with bitter scorn, 'ask too much of Detective-Sergeant Marks, sir. Don't make it too rough. He wouldn't know which one. Oh, no. He comes bleating to the phone while I daresay the rest of 'em are lighting off wherever the fancy takes 'em. Sergeant ruddy Police-College Marks! What is it?'

A uniformed constable had come in from the front entrance. 'I thought I'd better report, sir,' he said, 'I'm on duty outside. There's an incident.'

'All right,' said Alleyn. 'What incident?'

'A taxi's pulled up some distance away, sir, and a lady got out.'

'A lady!' Fox demanded so peremptorily that the constable glanced nervously at him.

'Yes, Mr Fox. A young lady. She spoke to the driver. He's waiting. She looked round and hesitated. I was in the entrance, sir, well in the shadow, and I don't think she saw me.'

'Recognize her?' Alleyn asked.

'I wouldn't be sure, sir. The clothes are different but I reckon it's one of the ladies in Lord Pastern's party.'

'Have you locked the doors behind you?'

'Yes, sir.'

'Unlock them and make yourself scarce. Clear out, all of you. Scatter. Step lively.'

The foyer was emptied in five seconds. The doors into the office and the band room closed noiselessly. Alleyn darted to the light switches. A single lamp was left to glow pinkly against the wall. The foyer was filled with shadow. He slipped to his knees behind a chair in the corner farthest from the light.

The clock ticked discreetly. Somewhere in a distant basement a pail clanked and a door slammed. Innumerable tiny sounds closer at hand became evident; the tap of a blind cord somewhere in the restaurant, a stealthy movement and scuffle behind the walls, an indefinable humming from the main switchboard. Alleyn smelt carpet, upholstery, disinfectant, and stale tobacco. Entrance into the foyer from outside must be effected through two sets of doors; those giving on the street and those inside made of plate-glass and normally open but now swung-to. Through these he could see only a vague greyness crossed by reflections in the glass itself. The image of the one pink lamp floated midway up the right-hand pane. He fixed his gaze on this. Now, beyond the glass doors, there came a paleness. The street door had been opened.

The face appeared quite suddenly against the plate glass, obscuring the reflected lamp and distorted by pressure. One door squeaked faintly as it opened.

She stood for a moment, holding her head-scarf half across her face. Then she moved forward swiftly and was down on her knees before an armchair. Her fingernails scrabbled on its tapestry. So intent was she upon her search that she did not hear him cross the thick carpet behind her, but when he drew the envelope from his pocket it made a slight crackle. Still kneeling, she swung round, saw him and cried out sharply.

'Is this what you are hunting for, Miss Wayne?' Alleyn asked.

II

He crossed over to the wall and switched up the lights. Without moving, Carlisle watched him. When he returned he still held the envelope. She put her hand to her burning face and said unsteadily: 'You think I'm up to no good, I suppose. I suppose you want an explanation.'

'I should be glad of an answer to my question. Is this what you want?'

He held the envelope up, but did not give it to her. She looked at it doubtfully. 'I don't know – I don't think – '

'The envelope is mine. I'll tell you what it contains. A letter that had been thrust down between the seat and the arm of the chair you have been exploring.'

'Yes,' Carlisle said. 'Yes. That's it. May I have it, please?'

'Do sit down,' Alleyn rejoined. 'We'd better clear this up, don't you think?'

He waited while she rose. After a moment's hesitation, she sat in the chair.

'You won't believe me, of course,' she said, 'but that letter – I suppose you have read it, haven't you – has nothing whatever to do with this awful business tonight. Nothing in the wide world. It's entirely personal and rather important.'

'Have you even read it?' he asked. 'Can you repeat the contents? I should like you to do that, if you will.'

'But – not absolutely correctly – I mean – '

'Approximately.'

'It – it's got an important message. It concerns someone – I can't tell you in so many words – '

'And yet it's so important that you return here at three o'clock in the morning to try and find it.' He paused, but Carlisle said nothing. 'Why,' he said, 'didn't Miss de Suze come and collect her own correspondence?'

'Oh, dear!' she said. 'This is difficult.'

'Well, for pity's sake keep up your reputation and be honest about it.'

'I am being honest, damn you!' said Carlisle with spirit. 'The letter's a private affair and – and – extremely confidential. Félicité doesn't want anyone to see it. I don't know exactly what's in it.'

'She funked coming back herself?'

'She's a bit shattered. Everyone is.'

'I'd like you to see what the letter's about,' said Alleyn after a pause. She began to protest. Very patiently he repeated his usual argument. When someone had been killed the nicer points of behaviour had to be disregarded. He had to prove to his own satisfaction that the letter was immaterial, and then he would forget it. 'You remember,' he said, 'this letter dropped out of her bag. Did you notice how she snatched it away from me? I see you did. Did you notice what she did after I said you would all be searched? She shoved her hand down between the seat and arm of that chair. Then she went off to be searched and I sat in the chair. When she came back she spent a miserable half-hour fishing for the letter and trying to look as if she wasn't. All right.'

He drew the letter from the envelope and spread it out before her. 'It's been fingerprinted,' he said, 'but without any marked success. Too much rubbing against good solid chair-cover. Will you read it or – '

'Oh, all right,' Carlisle said angrily.

The letter was typed on a sheet of plain notepaper. There was no address and no date.

'MY DEAR:' Carlisle read, 'Your loveliness is my undoing. Because of it I break my deepest promise to myself and to others. We are closer than you have ever dreamed. I wear a white flower in my coat tonight. It is yours. But as you value our future happiness, make not the slightest sign – even to me. Destroy this note, my love, but keep my love. GPF'

Carlisle raised her head, met Alleyn's gaze and avoided it quickly. 'A white flower,' she whispered. 'GPF? *GPF?* I don't believe it.'

'Mr Edward Manx had a white carnation in his coat, I think.'

'I won't discuss this letter with you,' she said strongly. 'I should never have read it. I won't discuss it. Let me take it back to her. It's nothing to do with this other thing. Nothing. Give it to me.'

Alleyn said, 'You must know I can't do that. Think for a moment. There was some attachment, a strong attachment of one kind or another, between Rivera and your cousin – your step-cousin. After Rivera is murdered, she is at elaborate pains to conceal this letter, loses it, and is so anxious to retrieve it that she persuades you to return here in an attempt to recover it. How can I disregard such a sequence of events?'

'But you don't know Fée! She's always in and out of tight corners over her young men. It's nothing. You don't understand.'

'Well,' he said looking good-humouredly at her, 'help me to understand. I'll drive you home. You can tell me on the way. Fox.'

Fox came out of the office. Carlisle listened to Alleyn giving him instructions. The other men appeared from the cloakroom, held a brief indistinguishable conversation with Fox and went out through the main entrance. Alleyn and Fox collected their belongings and put on their coats. Carlisle stood up. Alleyn returned the letter to its envelope and put it in his pocket. She felt tears stinging under her eyelids. She tried to speak and produced only an indeterminate sound.

'What is it?' he said, glancing at her.

'It can't be true,' she stammered. 'I won't believe it. I won't.'

'What? That Edward Manx wrote this letter?'

'He couldn't. He couldn't write like that to her.'

'No?' Alleyn said casually. 'You think not? But she's quite good-looking, isn't she? Quite attractive, don't you think?'

'It's not that. It's not that at all. It's the letter itself. He couldn't write like that. It's so bogus.'

'Have you ever noticed love-letters that are read out in court and published in the papers? Don't they sound pretty bogus? Yet some of them have been written by extremely intelligent people. Shall we go?'

It was cold out in the street. A motionless pallor stood behind the rigid silhouette of roofs. 'Dawn's left hand,' Alleyn said to nobody in particular and shivered. Carlisle's taxi had gone but a large police car waited. A second man sat beside the driver. Fox opened the door and Carlisle got in. The two men followed. 'We'll call at the Yard,' Alleyn said.

She felt boxed-up in the corner of the seat and was conscious of the impersonal pressure of Alleyn's arm and shoulder. Mr Fox, on the farther side, was a bulky man. She turned and saw Alleyn's head silhouetted against the bluish window. An odd notion came into her head. 'If Fée happens to calm down and take a good look at him,' she thought, 'it'll be all up with GPF and the memory of Carlos and everybody.' And with that her heart gave a leaden thump or two. 'Oh, Ned,' she thought, 'how you *could!*' She tried to face the full implication of the letter but almost at once shied away from it. 'I'm miserable,' she thought, 'I'm unhappier than I've been for years and years.'

'What,' Alleyn's voice said close beside her, 'I wonder, is the precise interpretation of the initials: GPF? They seem to ring some bell in my atrocious memory but I haven't got there yet. Why do you imagine "GPF?" ' She didn't answer and after a moment he went on. 'Wait a bit, though. Didn't you say something about a magazine you were reading before you visited Lord Pastern in his study? *Harmony?* Was that it?' He turned his head to look at her and she nodded. 'And the editor of the tell-it-all-to-auntie page calls himself Guide, Philosopher and Friend? How does he sign his recipes for radiant living?'

Carlisle mumbled: 'Like that.'

'And you had wondered if Miss de Suze had written to him,' Alleyn said tranquilly. 'Yes. Now, does this get us anywhere, do you imagine?'

She made a non-committal sound. Unhappy recollections forced themselves upon her. Recollections of Félicité's story about a correspondence with someone she had never met who had written her a 'marvellous' letter. Of Rivera reading her answer to this letter and making a scene about it. Of Ned Manx's article in *Harmony.* Of Félicité's behaviour after they all met to go to the Metronome. Of her taking the flower from Ned's coat. And of his stooping his head to listen to her as they danced together.

'Was Mr Manx,' Alleyn's voice asked, close beside her, 'wearing his white carnation when he arrived for dinner?'

'No,' she said, too loudly. 'No. Not till afterwards. There were white carnations on the table at dinner.'

'Perhaps it was one of them.'

'Then,' she said quickly, 'it doesn't fit. The letter must have been written before he ever saw the carnation. It doesn't fit. She said the letter came by district messenger. Ned wouldn't have known.'

'By district messenger, did she? We'll have to check that. Perhaps we'll find the envelope. Would you say,' Alleyn continued, 'that he seemed to be very much attached to her?'

(Edward had said: 'About Fée. Something very odd has occurred. I can't explain but I'd like to think you understand.')

'Strongly attracted, would you think?' Alleyn said.

'I don't know. I don't know what to think.'

'Do they see much of each other?'

'I don't know. He – he stayed at Duke's Gate while he was flat
hunting.'

'Perhaps an attachment developed then. What do you think?'

She shook her head. Alleyn waited. Carlisle now found his
unstressed persistence intolerable. She felt her moorings go and was
adrift in the darkness. A wretchedness of spirit that she was unable
to control or understand took possession of her. 'I won't talk about
it,' she stammered. 'It's none of my business. I can't go on like this.
Let me go, please. Please let me go.'

'Of course,' Alleyn said. 'I'll take you home.'

III

When they arrived at Duke's Gate, dawn was so far established that
the houses with their blind windows and locked doors were clearly
distinguishable in a wan half-light.

The familiar street, emerging from night, had an air of emacia-
tion and secrecy, Carlisle thought, and she was vaguely relieved
when milk bottles jingled up a side alley, breaking across the blank
emptiness. 'Have you got a key?' Alleyn said. He and Fox and the
man from the front seat waited, while she groped in her bag. As
she opened the door a second car drew up and four men got out.
The men from the front seat joined them. She thought: 'This
makes us all seem very important. This is an important case. A case
of murder.'

In the old days she had come back from parties once or twice with
Ned Manx at this hour. The indefinable house-smell made itself felt
as they entered. She turned on a lamp and it was light in the silent
hall. She saw herself reflected in the inner glass doors, her face
stained with tears. Alleyn came in first. Standing there, in evening
dress, with his hat in his hand, he might have been seeing her home,
about to wish her goodbye. The other men followed quickly. 'What
happens now?' she wondered. 'Will he let me go now? What are
they going to do?'

Alleyn had drawn a paper from his pocket. 'This is a search warrant,' he said. 'I don't want to hunt Lord Pastern out of his bed. It
will do, I think, if – '

He broke off, moved quickly to the shadowed staircase and up half a dozen steps. Fox and the other men stood quiet inside the doors. A little French clock in the stairwell ticked flurriedly. Upstairs on the first floor a door was flung open. A faint reflected light shone on Alleyn's face. A voice, unmistakably Lord Pastern's, said loudly: 'I don't give a damn how upset you are. You can have kittens if you like but you don't go to bed till I've got my timetable worked out. Sit down.'

With a faint grin Alleyn moved upstairs and Carlisle, after a moment's hesitation, followed him.

They were all in the drawing-room. Lady Pastern, still in evening dress and now very grey about the eyes and mouth, sat in a chair near the door. Félicité, who had changed into a housecoat and reduced her make-up, looked frail and lovely. Edward had evidently been sitting near her and had risen on Alleyn's entrance. Lord Pastern, with his coat off and his sleeves turned up, sat at a table in the middle of the room. Sheets of paper lay before him and he had a pencil between his teeth. A little removed from this group, her hands folded in the lap of her woollen dressing-gown and her grey hair neatly braided down her back, sat Miss Henderson. A plain-clothes officer stood inside the door. Carlisle knew all about him. He was the man who had escorted them home: hours ago, it seemed, in another age. She had given him the slip when she returned to the Metronome and now wondered, for the first time, how dim a view the police would take of this manoeuvre. The man looked awkwardly at Alleyn, who seemed about to speak to him as Carlisle entered, but stood aside to let her pass. Edward came quickly towards her. 'Where have you been?' he said angrily. 'What's the matter? I – ' He looked into her face. 'Lisle,' he said. 'What is it?'

Lord Pastern glanced up. 'Hallo,' he said. 'Where the devil did you get to, Lisle? I want you. Sit down.'

'It's like a scene from a play,' she thought. 'All of them sitting about exhausted, in a grand drawing-room. The third act of a thriller.' She caught the eye of the plain-clothes officer who was looking at her with distaste.

'I'm sorry,' she said. 'I'm afraid I just walked out by the back door.'

'I realize that, Miss,' he said.

'We can't be in two places at once, can we?' Carlisle added brightly. She was trying to avoid Félicité. Félicité was looking at her anxiously, obviously, with inquiring eyebrows.

Lord Pastern said briskly: 'Glad you've come, Alleyn, though I must say you've taken your time about it. I've been doin' your job for you. Sit down.'

Lady Pastern's voice, sepulchral with fatigue, said: 'May I suggest, George, that as in all probability this gentleman is about to arrest you, your choice of phrase is inappropriate.'

'That's a damn' tiresome sort of thing to say, C,' her husband rejoined. 'Gets you nowhere. What you want,' he continued, darting his pencil at Alleyn, 'is a time-table. You want to know what we were all doin' with ourselves before we went to the Metronome. System. All right. I've worked it out for you.' He slapped the paper before him. 'It's incomplete without Breezy's evidence, of course, but we can get that tomorrow. Lisle, there are one or two things I want from you. Come here.'

Carlisle stood behind him and looked at Allyn. His face was politely attentive, his eyes were on Lord Pastern's notes. In her turn and in response to an impatient tattoo of the pencil, she too looked at them.

She saw a sort of table, drawn up with ruled lines. Across the top, one each at the head of nine columns, she read their names: her own, Lady Pastern's, Félicité's, Edward's, Lord Pastern's, Bellairs', Rivera's, Miss Henderson's, and Spence's. Down the left hand side, Lord Pastern had written a series of times, beginning at 8.45 and ending at 10.30. These were ruled off horizontally and in the spaces thus formed, under each name, were notes as to the owner's whereabouts. Thus, at '9.15 approx,' it appeared that she and Lady Pastern had been in the drawing-room, Miss Henderson on her way upstairs, Félicité in the study, Rivera in the hall, Lord Pastern and Breezy Bellairs in the ballroom, and Spence in the servants' quarters.

'The times,' Lord Pastern explained importantly, 'are mostly only approximate. We know some of them for certain but not all. Thing is: it shows you the groupin'. Who was with who and who was alone. Method. Here y'are, Lisle. Go over it carefully and check your entries.'

He flung himself back in his chair and ruffled his hair. He reeked of complacency. Carlisle took up the pencil and found that her hand trembled. Exhaustion had suddenly overwhelmed her. She was nauseated and fuddled with fatigue. Lord Pastern's time-table swam before her. She heard her voice saying, 'I think you've got it right,' and felt a hand under her arm. It was Alleyn's. 'Sit down,' he said from an enormous distance. She was sitting down and Ned, close beside her, was making some sort of angry protest. She leant forward, propping her head on her hands. Presently it cleared and she listened, with an extraordinary sense of detachment, to what Alleyn was now saying.

' . . . very helpful, thank you. And now, I'm sure, you'll all be glad to get to bed. We shall be here during what's left of the night: hardly anything, I'm afraid, but we shan't disturb you.'

They were on their feet. Carlisle, feeling very sick, wondered what would happen if she got to hers. She looked at the others through her fingers and thought that there was something a little wrong, a little misshapen, about all of them. Her aunt, for instance. Why had she not seen before that Lady Pastern's body was too long and her head too big? It was so. And surely Félicité was fantastically narrow. Her skeleton must be all wrong: a tiny pelvis with the hip-bones jutting out from it like rocks. Carlisle's eyes behind their sheltering fingers turned to Lord Pastern, and she thought how monstrous it was that his forehead should overhang the rest of his face: a blind over a shop-window; that his monkey's cheeks should bunch themselves up when he was angry. Even Hendy: Hendy's throat was like some bird's and now that her hair was braided one saw that it was thin on top. Her scalp showed. They were caricatures, really, all of them. Subtly off-pitch: instruments very slightly out of tune. And Ned? He was behind her, but if she turned to look at him, what, in the perceptiveness born of nervous exhaustion, would she see? Were not his eyes black and small? Didn't his mouth, when it smiled, twist and show canine teeth a little too long? But she would not look at Ned.

And now, thought the bemused Carlisle, here was Uncle George at it again, 'I've no intention of goin' to bed. People sleep too much. No need for it: look at the mystics. Workin' from this time-table I can show you . . .'

'That's extremely kind of you, sir.' Alleyn's voice was clear and pleasant. 'But I think not. We have to get through our routine jobs. They're dreary beyond words and we're best left to ourselves while we do them.'

'Routine,' shouted Lord Pastern. 'Official synonym for inefficiency. Things are straightened out for you by someone who takes the trouble to use his head and what do you do? Tell him to go to bed while you gallop about his house makin' lists like a bum-bailiff. Be damned if I'll go to bed. Now!'

'Oh, God!' Carlisle thought desperately. 'How's he going to cope with this.' She felt the pressure of a hand on her shoulder and heard Ned's voice.

'May I suggest that whatever Cousin George decides to do there's no reason why the rest of us should keep a watch of supererogation.'

'None at all,' Alleyn said.

'Carlisle, my dear,' Lady Pastern murmured as if she was giving the signal to rise from a dinner party, 'shall we?' Carlisle stood up. Edward was close by and it seemed to her that he still looked angry. 'Are you all right?' he asked.

'Perfectly,' she said. 'I don't know what possessed me. I got a bit run down in Greece and I suppose – ' Her voice died. She was thinking of the long flight of stairs up to her room.

'My dearest child,' her aunt said, 'I shall never forgive myself that you have been subjected to this ordeal.'

'But she's wondering,' Carlisle thought, 'what I've been up to. They're all wondering.'

'Perhaps some wine,' her aunt continued, 'or whisky. It is useless to suggest, George, that you . . .'

'I'll get it,' Edward said quickly.

But Miss Henderson had already gone and now returned with a glass in her hand. As she took it from her, Carlisle smelt Hendy's particular smell of soap and talcum powder. 'Like a baby,' she thought, and drank. The almost neat whisky made her shudder convulsively. 'Hendy!' she gasped. 'You do pack a punch. I'm all right. Really. It's you, Aunt Cecile, who should be given corpse revivers.'

Lady Pastern closed her eyes momentarily upon this vulgarism. Félicité, who had been perfectly silent ever since Alleyn and Carlisle came in, said: 'I'd like a drink, Ned. Let's have a pub crawl in the dining-room, shall we?'

'The decanter's here if you want it, dear.' Miss Henderson also spoke for the first time.

'In that case,' Edward said, 'if it's all right by you, Alleyn, I'll take myself off.'

'We've got your address, haven't we? Right.'

'Goodbye, Cousin Cile. If there's anything I can do . . . ' Ned stood in the doorway. Carlisle did not look at him

'Goodbye, Lisle,' he said. 'Goodbye, Fée.'

Félicité moved swiftly to him and with an abrupt compulsive moment put her arm round his neck and kissed him. He stood for a moment with his head stooped and his hand on her arm. Then he was gone.

Beneath the heavy mask of exhaustion that her aunt wore, Carlisle saw a faint glimmer of gratification. 'Come, my children,' Lady Pastern said, almost briskly. 'Bed.' She swept them past Alleyn, who opened the door for them. As Carlisle turned, with the others, to mount the stairs, she heard Lord Pastern.

'Here I am,' he shouted, 'and here I stick. You don't turf me off to bed or anywhere else, short of arresting me.'

'I'm not, at the moment, proposing to do that,' Alleyn said distinctly, 'though I think, sir, I should warn you . . . ' The door shut off the remainder of his sentence.

IV

Alleyn shut the door on the retiring ladies and looked thoughtfully at Lord Pastern, 'I think,' he repeated, 'I should warn you that if you do decide, against my advice, to stay with us, what you do and say will be noted and the notes may be used . . . '

'Oh, fiddle-faddle!' Lord Pastern interrupted shrilly. 'All this rigmarole. I didn't do it and you can't prove I did. Get on with your precious routine and don't twaddle so.'

Alleyn looked at him with a sort of astonishment. 'You bloody little old fellow,' he thought. Lord Pastern blinked and smirked and bunched up his cheeks.

'All right, sir,' Alleyn said. 'But you're going to be given the customary warning, twaddle or not, and what's more I'll have a witness to it.'

He crossed the landing, opened the ballroom door, said, 'Fox, can you give me a moment?' and returned to the drawing-room where he waited in silence until Inspector Fox came in. He then said: 'Fox, I've asked Lord Pastern to go to bed and he refuses. I want you to witness this. I warn him that from now onwards his words and behaviour will be noted and that the notes may later on be used in evidence. It's a nuisance, of course, but short of taking a much more drastic step, I don't see what else can be done about it. Have the extra men turned up?'

Fox, looking with marked disapproval at Lord Pastern, said that they had.

'Tell them to keep observation, will you? Thank you, Fox, I'll carry on here.'

'Thank you, Mr Alleyn,' said Fox. 'I'll get on with it in the study, then.'

He turned to the door. Lord Pastern said: 'Hi! Where're you goin'? What're you up to?'

'If you'll excuse me for passing the remark, my lord,' said Fox severely, 'you're acting very foolishly. Very ill-advised and foolish, what you're doing, if I may say so.' He went out.

'Great ham-fisted ass of a chap,' Lord Pastern remarked.

'On the contrary, sir,' Alleyn rejoined with perfect politeness, 'an extremely efficient officer and should have had his promotion long ago.'

He left Lord Pastern, walked to the centre of the long drawing-room and surveyed it for some minutes with his hands in his pockets. A clock on the landing struck five. Alleyn began a closer inspection of the room. He traversed it slowly, moving across and across it and examining any object that lay in his path. Lord Pastern watched him and sighed and groaned audibly. Presently Alleyn came to a chair beside which stood an occasional table. On the table was an embroidery frame and a work-box of elaborate and elegant design. He opened the lid delicately and stooped to examine the contents. Here, neatly disposed, were innumerable skeins of embroidery silks. The box was fitted with every kind of tool, each in its appointed slot:

needle-cases, scissors, bodkins, a thimble, an ivory measure, a tape in a cloisonne case, stilettos held in their places by silken sheaths. One slot was untenanted. Alleyn sat down and began, with scrupulous care, to explore the box.

'Pity you didn't bring your sewin',' said Lord Pastern, 'isn't it?'

Alleyn took out his note-book, glanced at his watch and wrote briefly.

'I'd thank you,' Lord Pastern added, 'to keep your hands out of m'wife's property.' He attempted to repress a yawn, shed a tear over the effort and barked suddenly: 'Where's your search warrant, b'God?'

Alleyn completed another note, rose and exhibited his warrant. 'Tscha!' said Lord Pastern.

Alleyn had turned to examine Lady Pastern's embroidery. It was stretched over a frame and was almost completed. A riot of cupids in postures of extreme insouciance circled about a fabulous nosegay. The work was exquisite. He gave a slight appreciative chuckle which Lord Pastern instantly parodied. Alleyn resumed his search. He moved steadily on at a snail's pace. Half-an-hour crawled by. Presently an odd little noise disturbed him. He glanced up. Lord Pastern, still on his feet, was swaying dangerously. His eyes were glazed and horrible and his mouth was open. He had snored.

Alleyn tiptoed to the door at the far end of the room, opened it and slipped into the study. He heard a sort of roaring noise behind him, shut the door and, finding a key in the lock, turned it.

Inspector Fox, in his shirt sleeves, was examining the contents of an open drawer on the top of the desk. Laid out in front of him were a tube of plastic wood, an empty bottle marked 'gun-oil', with no cork in it, and a white ivory handle into which some tool had once fitted.

V

Fox laid a broad finger on the desk beside these exhibits, not so much for an index, as to establish their presence and significance. Alleyn nodded and crossed quickly to the door that gave on the landing. He locked it and waited near it with his head cocked. 'Here he comes,' he said.

There was a patter of feet outside. The handle of the door was turned and then rattled angrily. A distant voice said: 'I'm sorry, my lord, but I'm afraid that room's under inspection just now.'

'Who the hell d'you think you are?'

'Sergeant Marks, my lord.'

'Then let me tell you . . .'

The voices faded out.

'He won't get into the ballroom either,' said Fox, 'unless he tries a knock-up with Sergeant Whitelaw.'

'How about the dining-room?'

'They've finished there, Mr Alleyn.'

'Anything?'

'Wine had been spilt on the carpet. Port, I'd say. And there's a bit of a mark on the table near the centre flower-bowl as if a drop or two of water had lain there. White carnations in the bowl. Nothing else. The table had been cleared, of course.'

Alleyn looked at the collection on the desk. 'Where did you beat this lot up, Foxkin?'

'In this drawer which was pulled out and left on top of the desk like it is now. Half a junk shop in it, isn't there, sir? These articles were lying on the surface of the other mess.'

'Bailey had a go at it?'

'Yes. No prints on any of 'em,' said Fox. 'Which is funny.'

'How about the typewriter?'

'We've printed it. Only his lordship's dabs, and they're very fresh.'

'No cap on the plastic wood tube.'

'It was on the floor.'

Alleyn examined the tube. 'It's set hard, of course, at the open end, but not very deep. Tube's three-quarters full.'

'There are crumbs of plastic wood in the drawer and on the desk and the carpet.'

Alleyn said absently: 'Are there, by gum!' and turned his attention to the small white handle. 'Exhibit B,' he said. 'Know what it is, Fox?'

'I can only make a healthy guess, I fancy, Mr Alleyn.'

'It's the fellow of a number of gadgets in a very elegant French work-box in the drawing-room. Crochet hooks, scissors and so on. They're fixed inside the lid, in slots. One slot's empty.'

'This is just a handle, you'll notice, sir.'

'Yes. Do you think it ought to have an embroidery stiletto fixed in the hollow end?'

'It's what I reckoned.'

'I think you're right.'

Fox opened his bag and took out a narrow cardboard box. In this, secured and protected by strings, was the dart. The jewels in the spring clip, tiny emeralds and brilliants, glittered cheerfully. Only a narrow platinum band near the top and the stiletto itself were dulled with Rivera's blood.

'Bailey'll have to go for latent prints,' Fox said.

'Yes, of course. We can't disturb it. Later on it can be dismembered, but on looks, Fox, we've got something.'

Alleyn held the ivory handle beside the stiletto, 'I'll swear they belong,' he said, and put it down. 'Here's exhibit C. An empty gun-oil bottle. Where's that cork?'

Fox produced it. 'It fits,' he said. 'I've tried. It fits and it has the same stink. Though why the hell it should turn up on the bandstand . . . '

'Ah, me,' Alleyn said. 'Why the hell indeed? Well, look what turns up in your particular fancy's very own drawer in his very own study! Could anything be more helpful?'

Fox shifted bulkily in his chair and contemplated his superior officer for some moments. 'I know it seems funny,' he said at last. 'Leaving evidence all over the place: making no attempt to clear himself: piling up a case against himself, you might say. But then he *is* funny. Would you say he was not responsible within the meaning of the act?'

'I'm never sure what is the precise meaning of the infernal act. Responsible. Not responsible. Who's to mark a crucial division in the stream of human behaviour running down from something we are pleased to call sanity into raving lunacy? Where's the point at which a human being ceases to be a responsible being? Oh, I know the definitions, and I know we do our best with them, but it seems to me it's here, over this business of the pathology of behaviour, that any system of corrective and coercive law shows at its dimmest. Is this decidedly rum peer so far south in the latitude of behaviour that he would publicly murder a man by a ridiculously elaborate method that points directly to himself, and then, in effect, do everything in his power to get himself arrested? There have been cases of the sort, but is this going to be one of them?'

'Well, sir,' said Fox stolidly, 'I must say I think it is. It's early days yet, but as far as we've got I think it looks like it. This gentleman's previous record and his general run of behaviour points to a mental set-up that, without going beyond the ordinary view, is eccentric. Everyone knows he's funny.'

'Yes. Everyone. Everyone knows,' Alleyn agreed. 'Everyone would say: "It's in character. It's just like him!"'

With as near an approach to exasperation as Alleyn had ever heard from him, Fox said: 'All right, Mr Alleyn, then. I know what you're getting at. But who could have planted it on him? Tell me that. Do you believe any of the party at the table could have got at the revolver when it was under the sombrero and shoved this silly dart or bolt or what-have-you up it? Do you think Bellairs could have planted the bolt and picked it up after his lordship searched him? Where could he have planted it? In a bare band room with nothing in it but musical instruments and other men? And how could he have got it into the revolver when his lordship had the revolver on his person and swears to it that it never left him? Skelton? Skelton handled the gun while a roomful of people watched him do it. Could Skelton have palmed this thing up the barrel? The idea's laughable. Well, then.'

'All right, old thing,' Alleyn said. 'Let's get on with it. The servants will be about soon. How far have you got in here?'

'Not much further than what you've seen, sir. The drawer was a daisy. The bullets he extracted when he made his dummies are in the waste-paper basket there.'

'Carlisle Wayne watched him at that. How about the ballroom?'

'Bailey and Thompson are in there.'

'Oh, well. Let's have another look at Lord Pastern's revolver, Fox.'

Fox lifted it from his bag and laid it on the desk. Alleyn sat down and produced his lens.

'There's a very nice lens here, in his lordship's drawer,' Fox remarked. Alleyn grunted. He was looking into the mouth of the barrel.

'We'll get a photomicrograph of this,' he muttered. 'Two longish scratches and some scrabbles.' He gave the revolver to Fox, who was sitting in the chair which, nine hours earlier, Carlisle had occupied. Like Carlisle, Fox used Lord Pastern's lens.

'Did you notice,' Alleyn said, 'that when I gave the thing to that old freak to look at, it was the underside of the butt near the trigger guard that seemed to interest him? I can't find anything there. The maker's plate's on the heel. What was he up to, do you suppose?'

'God knows,' Fox grunted crossly. He was sniffing at the muzzle. 'You look like an old maid with smelling salts,' Alleyn observed.

'So I may, sir, but I don't smell anything except gun-oil.'

'I know. That's another thing. Listen.'

In some distant part of the house there was movement. A door slammed, shutters were thrown back and a window opened.

'The servants are stirring,' Alleyn said. 'We'll seal this room, leave a man to watch it and come back to it later on. Let's collect everything we've picked up, find out what the others have got and catch three hours' sleep. Yard at ten o'clock, don't forget. Come on.'

But he himself did not move. Fox looked dubiously at him and began to pack away the revolver, the plastic wood, the empty bottle and the ivory handle.

'No, blast it.' Alleyn said, 'I'll work through. Take those things, Fox, and dispatch them off to the experts. Fix up adequate relief for surveillance here, and away you go. I'll see you at ten. What's the matter?'

'I'd as soon stay, Mr Alleyn.'

'I know all about that. Zealous young officer. Away you go.'

Fox passed his hand over his short grizzled hair and said: 'I keep very fit, really. Make a point of never thinking about the retiring age. Well, thank you very much, Mr Alleyn.'

'I might have another dig at the witnesses.'

'The party upstairs won't wake before ten.'

'I'll stir 'em up if I need 'em. Why should they have all the fun? I want to ring up my wife. Good-morning to you, Mr Fox.'

Fox unlocked the door on to the landing and turned the handle. The door flew inwards, striking his shoulder. He stepped back with an oath and Lord Pastern's body fell across his feet.

VI

It remained there for perhaps three seconds. Its eyes were open and glared furiously. Fox bent over it and the mouth also opened.

'What the hell d'you think you're doin'?' Lord Pastern demanded.

He rolled over neatly and got to his feet. His jaw and cheeks glistened with a sort of hoar-frost, his eyes were bloodshot and his evening-dress disordered. A window on the landing shed the cruel light of early morning upon him and he looked ghastly in it. His manner, however, had lost little of its native aggressiveness. 'What are you starin' at?' he added.

'We might fairly ask you,' Alleyn rejoined, 'what you were up to, sitting, it appears, on the landing with your back to the door.'

'I dozed off. Pretty state of affairs when a man's kept out of his own rooms at five o'clock in the morning.'

'All right, Fox,' Alleyn said wearily, 'you get along.'

'Very well, sir,' said Fox. 'Good-morning, my lord.' He side-stepped Lord Pastern and went out leaving the door ajar. Alleyn heard him admonishing Sergeant Marks on the landing: 'What sort of surveillance do you call this?'

'I was only told to keep observation, Mr Fox. His lordship fell asleep as soon as he touched the floor. I thought he might as well be there as anywhere.'

Fox growled majestically and passed out of hearing.

Alleyn shut the study door and went to the window. 'We haven't finished in this room,' he said, 'but I think I may disturb it so far.'

He drew back the curtains and opened the window. It was now quite light outside. A fresh breeze came in through the window, emphasizing, before it dismissed them, the dense enclosed odours of carpet, leather and stale smoke. The desk lamp still shed a raffish yellowness on the litter that surrounded it. Alleyn turned from the window to face Lord Pastern and found him rummaging with quick inquisitive fingers in the open drawer on the desk.

'I wonder if I can show you what you're hunting for,' Alleyn said. He opened Fox's bag and then took out his note-book. 'Don't touch anything please, but will you look in that case?'

He did look, but impatiently, and, as far as Alleyn could see, without any particular surprise.

'Where'd you find that?' Lord Pastern demanded, pointing a not very steady finger at the ivory handle.

'In the drawer. Can you identify it?'

'I might be able to,' he muttered.

Alleyn pointed to the weapon. 'The stiletto that's been sunk in the end with plastic wood might have belonged to this ivory handle. We shall try it. If it fits, it came originally from Lady Pastern's work-box in the drawing-room.'

'So you say,' said Lord Pastern insultingly. Alleyn made a note.

'Can you tell me if this stiletto was in your drawer, here, sir? Before last night?'

Lord Pastern was eyeing the revolver. He thrust out his under lip, shot a glance at Alleyn, and darted his hand towards it.

'All right,' Alleyn said, 'you may touch it, but please answer my questions about the stiletto.'

'How should I know?' he said indifferently. 'I don't know.' Without removing if from the case, he tipped the revolver over and, snatching up his lens, peered at the under side of the butt. He gave a shrill cackle of laughter.

'What did you expect to see?' Alleyn asked, casually.

'Hoity-toity,' Lord Pastern rejoined. *Wouldn't* you like to know!'

He stared at Alleyn. His bloodshot eyes twinkled insolently. 'It's devilish amusin',' he said. 'Look at it whatever way you like, it's damn' funny.'

He dropped into an armchair, and with an air of gloating relish rubbed his hands together.

Alleyn shut down the lid of Fox's case and succeeded in snatching back his temper. He stood in front of Lord Pastern and deliberately looked into his eyes. Lord Pastern immediately shut them very tight and bunched his cheeks.

'I'm sleepy,' he said.

'Listen to me,' Alleyn said. 'Have you any idea at all of the personal danger you are in? Do you know the consequences of withholding or refusing crucial information when a capital crime has been committed? It's my duty to tell you that you are under grave suspicion. You've had the formal warning. Confronted with the body of a man whom, one assumes, you were supposed to hold in some sort of regard, you've conducted yourself appallingly. I must tell you, sir, that if you continue in this silly affectation of frivolity, I shall ask you to come to Scotland Yard, where you will be questioned and, if necessary, detained.'

He waited. Lord Pastern's face had gradually relaxed during this speech. His mouth now pouted and expelled a puff of air that blew his moustache out. He was, apparently, asleep again.

Alleyn contemplated him for some moments. He then seated himself at the desk in a position that enabled him to keep Lord Pastern in sight. After a moment's cogitation, he pulled the typewriter towards him, took Félicité's letter from his pocket, found a sheet of paper and began to make a copy.

At the first rattle of the keys Lord Pastern's eyes opened, met Alleyn's gaze and shut again. He mumbled something indistinguishable and snored with greater emphasis. Alleyn completed his copy and laid it beside the original. They had been typed on the same machine.

On the floor, beside the chair Carlisle had used on the previous night, lay the magazine, *Harmony*. He took it up and ruffled the pages. A dozen or more flopped over and then the binding opened a little. He was confronted with GPF's page and noticed, as Carlisle had noticed, the cigarette ash in the groove. He read the letter signed Toots, turned a few more pages and came upon the antidrug racket article and a dramatic review signed by Edward Manx. He once more confronted that preposterous figure in the armchair.

'Lord Pastern,' he said loudly, 'wake up. Wake up.'

Lord Pastern jerked galvanically, made a tasting noise with his tongue and lips, and uttered a nightmarish sound.

'A-a-ah?'

'Come now, you're awake. Answer me this,' said Alleyn, and thrust the copy of *Harmony* under his nose. 'How long have you known that Edward Manx was GPF?'

CHAPTER 8

Morning

Lord Pastern blinked owlishly at the paper, swung round in his chair and eyed the desk. The letter and the copy lay conspicuously beside the typewriter.

'Yes,' Alleyn said, 'that's how I know. Will you give me an explanation of all this?'

Lord Pastern leant forward and, resting his forearm on his knees, seemed to stare at his clasped hands. When he spoke his voice was subdued and muffled.

'No,' he said, 'I'll be damned if I do. I'll answer no questions. Find out for yourself. I'm for bed.'

He pulled himself out of the chair and squared his shoulders. The air of truculence was still there but Alleyn thought it overlaid a kind of indecision. With the nearest approach to civility that he had yet exhibited, he added: 'I'm within my rights, aren't I?'

'Certainly,' Alleyn said at once. 'Your refusal will be noted. That's all. If you change your mind about sending for your solicitor, we shall be glad to call him in. In the meantime, I'm afraid, sir, I shall have to place you under very close observation.'

'D'you mean some damn' bobby's goin' to follow me about like a hulkin' great poodle?'

'If you care to put it that way. It's no use, I imagine, for me to repeat any warnings about your own most equivocal position?'

'None whatever.' He went to the door and stood with his back to Alleyn, holding the knob and leaning heavily on it.

'Get them to give you breakfast,' he said without looking round, and went slowly out and up the stairs. Alleyn called his thanks after him and nodded to Marks who was on the landing. Marks followed Lord Pastern upstairs.

Alleyn returned to the study, shut the window, had a last look round, packed Fox's bag, removed it to the landing and finally locked and sealed the door. Marks had been replaced on the landing by another plain-clothes man. 'Hallo, Jimson,' Alleyn said. 'Just come on?'

'Yes, sir. Relieving.'

'Have you seen any of the staff?'

'A maid came upstairs just now, Mr Alleyn. Mr Fox left instructions they were to be kept off this floor so I sent her down again. She seemed very much put about.'

'She would,' Alleyn said. 'All right. Tactful as you can, you know, but don't miss anything.'

'Very good, sir.'

He crossed the landing and entered the ballroom where he found Thompson and Bailey packing up. Alleyn looked at the group of chairs round the grand piano and at a sheet of notepaper Bailey had collected. On it was pencilled the band programme for the previous night. Bailey pointed out the light coating of dust on the piano top and showed Alleyn where they had found clear traces of the revolver and the parasol and umbrellas. It was odd, Bailey and Thompson thought, but it appeared that quantities of dust had fallen after these objects had rested in this place. Not so very odd, Alleyn suggested, as Lord Pastern had, on his own statement, fired off a blank round in the ballroom and that would probably have brought down quite a lot of dust from the charming but ornately moulded ceiling. 'Happy hunting ground,' he muttered. 'Whose are the prints round these traces of the parasol section and knob? Don't tell me,' he added wearily. 'His lordship's?'

'That's right,' Thompson and Bailey said together. 'His lordship's and Breezy's.' Alleyn saw them go and then came out and sealed the ballroom doors.

He returned to the drawing-room, collected Lady Pastern's work-box, debated with himself about locking this room up too and decided against it. He then left all his gear under the eye of the officer on

the landing and went down to the ground floor. It was now six
o'clock.

The dining-room was already prepared for breakfast. The bowl of
white carnations, he noticed, had been removed to a side-table. As
he halted before a portrait of some former Settinjer who bore a mild
resemblance to Lord Pastern, he heard a distant mingling of voices
beyond the service door. The servants, he thought, having their first
snack. He pushed open the door, found himself in a servery with a
further door which led, it appeared, into the servants' hall. The best
of all early morning smells, that of freshly brewed coffee, was clearly discernible. He was about to go forward when a voice, loud,
dogged and perceptibly anxious, said very slowly:

'Parlez, monsieur, je vous en prie, plus lentement, et peut être
je vous er er – comprendari – No, blast it, as you were, je vous
pouverai – '

Alleyn pushed open the door and discovered Mr Fox seated cosily before a steaming cup of coffee, flanked by Spence and a bevy of
attentive ladies and vis-à-vis with a dark imposing personage in full
chef's regalia.

There was only a fractional pause while Alleyn surveyed this
tableau. Fox then rose.

'Perhaps you'd like a cup of coffee, Mr Alleyn,' he suggested, and
addressing the chef, added carefully: 'C'est Monsieur – er – le chef –
Inspecteur Alleyn, monsieur. Mr Alleyn, this is Miss Parker, the
housekeeper, and Mademoiselle Hortense. And these girls are Mary
and Myrtle. This is Mr Spence and this is Monsieur Dupont and the
young chap over there is William. Well!' concluded Fox, beaming
upon the company, 'this is what I call cosy.'

Alleyn took the chair placed for him by William and stared fixedly
at his subordinate. Fox responded with a bland smile. 'I was just
leaving, sir,' he said, 'when I happened to run into Mr Spence. I
knew you'd want to inform these good people of our little contretemps so here, in point of fact, I am.'

'Fancy,' said Alleyn.

Fox's technique on the working side of the green baize doors was
legendary at the Yard. This was the first time Alleyn had witnessed
it in action. But even now, he realized, the fine bloom of the exotic
was rubbed off and it was his own entrance which had destroyed it.

The atmosphere of conviviality had stiffened. Spence had risen, the maids hovered uneasily on the edges of their chairs. He did his best and it was a good best, but evidently Fox, who was an innocent snob, had been bragging about him and they all called him 'sir'.

'Well,' he said cheerfully, 'if Mr Fox has been on this job there'll be no need for me to bother any of you. This is the best coffee I've drunk for years.'

'I am gratified,' said M Dupont in fluent English. 'At present, of course, one cannot obtain the fresh beans as readily as one desires.'

Mademoiselle Hortense said: 'Naturally,' and the others made small affirmative noises.

'I suppose,' Fox said genially, 'his lordship's very particular about his coffee. Particular about everything, I dare say?' he added, invitingly.

William, the footman, laughed sardonically and was checked by a glance from Spence. Fox prattled on. It would be her ladyship, of course, who was particular about coffee. Being of Mlle Hortense's and M Dupont's delightful nationality. He attempted this compliment in French, got bogged down, and told Alleyn that M Dupont had been giving him a lesson. Mr Alleyn, he informed the company, spoke French like a native. Looking up, Alleyn found Spence gazing at him with an expression of anxiety.

'I'm afraid this is a great nuisance for all of you,' Alleyn said.

'It's not that, sir,' Spence rejoined slowly, it does put us all about very much, I can't deny. Not being able to get things done in the usual way – '

'I'm sure,' Miss Parker intervened, 'I don't know what her ladyship's going to say about the first floor. Leaving everything. It's very awkward.'

'Exactly. But the worrying thing,' Spence went on, 'is not knowing what it's all about. Having the police in, sir, and everything. Just because the party from this house happens to be present when this Mr Rivera passes away in a restaurant.'

'Quite so,' said Miss Parker.

'The circumstances,' Alleyn said carefully, 'are extraordinary. I don't know if Inspector Fox has told you – ' Fox said that he had been anxious not to distress the ladies. Alleyn thought that the ladies looked as if they were half dead with curiosity, agreed that Fox had shown great delicacy but added that it would have to come out sometime.

'Mr Rivera,' he said, 'was killed.'

They stirred attentively. Myrtle, the younger of the maids, ejaculated 'Murdered?' clapped her hand over her mouth and suppressed a nervous giggle. Alleyn said it looked very much like it and added that he hoped they would all co-operate as far as they were able in helping to clear the ground. He had known, before he met it, what their response would be. People were all very much alike when it came to homicide cases. They wanted to be removed to a comfortable distance where curiosity could be assuaged, prestige maintained, and personal responsibility dissolved. With working people this wish was deepened by a heritage of insecurity and the necessity to maintain caste. They were filled with a kind of generic anxiety: at once disturbed by an indefinite threat and stimulated by a crude and potent assault on their imagination.

'It's a matter,' he said, 'of clearing innocent people, of tidying them up. I'm sure you would be glad to help us in this, if you can.'

He produced Lord Pastern's time-table, spread it out before Spence, and told them who had compiled it.

'If you can help us check these times, any of you, we shall be very grateful,' he said.

Spence put on his spectacles and with an air of slight embarrassment began to read the time-table. The others, at Alleyn's suggestion, collected round him, not altogether unwillingly.

'It's a bit elaborate, isn't it?' Alleyn said. 'Let's see if it can be simplified at all. You see that between half-past eight and nine the ladies left the dining-room and went to the drawing-room. So we get the two groups in the two rooms. Can any of you add to or confirm that?'

Spence could. It was a quarter to nine when the ladies went to the drawing-room. When he came away from serving their coffee he passed Lord Pastern and Mr Bellairs on the landing. They went into his lordship's study. Spence continued on through the dining-room, paused there to see that William had served coffee to the gentlemen and noticed that Mr Manx and Mr Rivera were still sitting over their wine. He then went into the servants' hall, where a few minutes later he heard the nine o'clock news on the wireless.

'So now,' Alleyn said, 'we have three groups. The ladies in the drawing-room, his lordship and Mr Bellairs in the study, and Mr Manx and Mr Rivera in the dining-room. Can anyone tell us when the next move came and who made it?'

Spence remembered coming back into the dining-room and finding Mr Manx there alone. His reticence at this point became more marked, but Alleyn got from him the news that Edward Manx had helped himself to a stiff whisky. He asked casually if there was anything about his manner which was at all remarkable, and got the surprising answer that Mr Edward seemed to be very pleased and said he'd had a wonderful surprise.

'And now,' Alleyn said, 'Mr Rivera has broken away from the other groups. Where has he gone? Mr Manx is in the dining-room, his lordship and Mr Bellairs in the study, the ladies in the drawing-room, and where is Mr Rivera?'

He looked round the group of faces with their guarded unwilling expressions until he saw William, and in William's eye he caught a zealous glint. William, he thought, with any luck read detective magazines and spent his day-dreams sleuthing.

'Got an idea?' he asked.

'Well sir,' William said, glancing at Spence, 'if you'll excuse me, I think his lordship and Mr Bellairs have parted company where you've got to. I was tidying the hall, sir, and I heard the other gentleman, Mr Bellairs, come out of the study. I glanced up at the landing, like. And I heard his lordship call out he'd join him in a minute and I saw the gentleman go into the ballroom. I went and got the coffee-tray from the drawing-room, sir. The ladies were all there. I put it down on the landing and was going to set the study to rights, when I heard the typewriter in there. His lordship doesn't like being disturbed when he's typing, sir, so I took the tray by the staff stairs to the kitchen and after a few minutes came back. And his lordship must have gone into the ballroom while I was downstairs because I could hear him talking very loudly to Mr Bellairs, sir.'

'What about, do you remember?'

William glanced again at Spence and said: 'Well, sir, it was something about his lordship telling somebody something if Mr Bellairs didn't want to. And then there was a terrible loud noise. Drums. A report like a gun. They all heard it down here in the hall, sir.'

Alleyn looked at the listening staff. Miss Parker said coldly that his lordshp was no doubt practising, as if Lord Pastern was in the habit of loosing off firearms indoors and there was nothing at all remarkable in the circumstances. Alleyn felt that both she and Spence were on the edge of giving William a piece of their minds and he hurried on.

'What did you do next?' he asked William.

He had been, it appeared, somewhat shattered by the report, but had remembered his duties. 'I crossed the landing, sir, thinking I'd get on with the study, but Miss de Suze came out of the drawing-room. And then – well, the murdered gentleman, he came from the dining-room and they met and she said she wanted to speak to him alone and they went into the study.'

'Sure of that?'

Yes, it appeared that William was perfectly certain. He had lingered evidently at the end of the landing. He even remembered that Miss de Suze had something in her hand. He wasn't sure what it was. Something bright, it might have been, he said doubtfully. After she and the gentleman had gone into the study and shut the door, Miss Henderson had come out of the drawing-room and gone upstairs.

Alleyn said: 'Now, that's a great help. You see it corresponds exactly so far with his lordship's time-table. I'll just check it over, Fox, if you . . . '

Fox took the tip neatly and, while Alleyn affected to study Lord Pastern's notes, continued what he liked to call the painless extraction method with William. It must, he said, have been awkward for William. You couldn't go barging in on a tête-à-tête, could you, and yet a chap liked to get his job done. Life, said Fox, was funny when you came to think of it. Here was this poor young lady happily engaged in conversation with, well, he supposed he wasn't giving any secrets away if he said with her fiancé, and little did she think that in a couple of hours or so he would be lying dead. Miss Parker and the maids were visibly moved by this. William turned extremely red in the face and shuffled his feet. 'She'll treasure every word of that last talk, I'll be bound,' said Fox. 'Every word of it.' He looked inquiringly at William, who, after a longish pause, blurted out very loud: 'I wouldn't go so far as to say that, Mr Fox.'

'That'll do, Will,' said Spence quietly, but Fox's voice over-rode him.

'Is that so?' Fox inquired blandly. 'You wouldn't? Why not?'

'Because,' William announced boldly, 'they was at it hammer-and-tongs.'

'*Will!*'

William turned to his superior, 'I ought to tell the truth, didn't I, Mr Spence? To the police?'

'You ought to mind your own business,' said Miss Parker with some emphasis, and Spence murmured his agreement.

'All right, then,' William said, huffily. 'I'm sure I don't want to push myself in where I'm not welcome.'

Fox was extremely genial and complimented William on his natural powers of observation and Miss Parker and Spence upon their loyalty and discretion. He suggested, without exactly stating as much and keeping well on the safe side of police procedure, that any statements anybody offered would, by some mysterious alchemy, free all concerned of any breath of suspicion. In a minute or two he had discovered that sharp-eared William, still hovering on the landing, had seen Rivera go into the ballroom and had overhead most of his quarrel with Breezy Bellairs. To this account Spence and Miss Parker raised no objections and it was tolerably obvious that they had already heard it. It became clear that Mlle Hortense was stifling with repressed information. But she had her eye on Alleyn and it was to him that she addressed herself. She had that particular knack, that peculiar talent commanded by so many of her countrywomen, of making evident, without the slightest emphasis, her awareness of her own attractions and those of the man to whom she was speaking. Alleyn, she seemed to assume, would understand perfectly that she was the confidante of Mademoiselle. M Dupont, who had remained aloof, now assumed an air of gloomy acquiescence. It was understood he said, that the relationship between a personal maid and her mistress was one of delicacy and confidence.

'About l'*affaire Rivera* . . . ?' suggested Fox, doggedly Gallic.

Hortense lifted her shoulders and rocked her head slightly. She addressed herself to Alleyn. Undoubtedly this M Rivera had been passionately attached. That was evident. And Mademoiselle had responded, being extremely impressionable. But an engagement?

Not precisely. He had urged it. There had been scenes. Reconciliations. Further scenes. But last night! She suddenly executed a complicated and vivid gesture with her right hand as if she wrote something off on the air. And against the unuttered but almost tangible disapproval of the English servants, Hortense, with a darting incisiveness, said: 'Last night everything was ended. But irrevocably *ended.*'

II

It appeared that at twenty to ten Hortense was summoned to Lady Pastern's bedroom, where she prepared her for the road, putting her into a cloak, and adding, Alleyn supposed, some kind of super-gloss to that already immaculate surface. Hortense kept an eye on the time as the car was ordered for 10.30 and Lady Pastern liked to have leisure. About ten minutes later Miss Henderson had come in with the news that Félicité was extremely excited and wished to make an elaborate change in her *toilette*. She herself was sent to Félicité's room.

'And conceive the scene, Monsieur!' said Hortense, breaking into her native tongue. 'The room is complete disarray and Mademoiselle is *déshabillée*. There must be a complete new *toilette*, you understand. Everything, from the foundation, is it not? And while I dress her she relates the whole story. With M Rivera it is as if he had never been. There has been a formidable quarrel. She had dismissed him forever and in the meantime a letter had arrived in romantic circumstances. It is a letter from a journalistic gentleman she has never seen but with whom she has corresponded frequently. He is about to reveal himself. He declares his passionate attachment. Yet secrecy must be observed. And for myself,' Hortense added with conscious rectitude, 'I would never, never have allowed myself to repeat one syllable of this matter if it had not become my duty to assure Monsieur that as far as Mademoiselle is concerned, she had no further interest in M Rivera and was happily released from him and that this is not therefore a *crime passionelle*.'

'I see,' Alleyn said. 'Yes, perfectly. It is understood.'

Hortense gave him a soubrettish glance and a hard smile.

'And do you know,' he said, 'who this person was? The letter writer?'

Félicité, it appeared, had shown her the letter. And as the party was leaving for the Metronome, Hortense had run downstairs with Lady Pastern's vinaigrette and had seen (with what emotion!) Mr Edward Manx wearing a white flower in his coat. All was revealed! And how great, Hortense had reflected as Spence closed the front door on their departure, how overwhelming would be the joy of her ladyship, who had always desired this union! Hortense had been quite unable to conceal her own gratification and had sung for pure joy as she rejoined her colleagues in the servants' hall. Her colleagues, with the exception of M Dupont, now cast black glances at her and refrained from comment.

Alleyn checked over the events related by Hortense and found that they corresponded as nearly as made no difference with the group movements suggested by Lord Pastern's notes. From the nucleus of persons, further individuals had broken away. Manx had been alone in the drawing-room. Lady Pastern had been alone in her room until Hortense arrived. Hortense herself, and William, had cruised about the house and so had Spence. Alleyn was about to lay down his pencil when he remembered Miss Henderson. She had gone to her room earlyish in the evening and had presumably stayed there until she was visited by Félicité and herself reported this incident to Lady Pastern. It was odd, he thought, that he should have forgotten Miss Henderson.

But there were still a good many threads to be caught up and introduced into the texture. He referred again to Lord Pastern's notes. At 9.26, the notes declared specifically, Lord Pastern, then in the ballroom, had suddenly recollected the sombrero which he desired to wear in his own number. He had glanced at his watch, perhaps, and taken alarm. The note merely said: '9.26. Self. Ballroom. Sombrero. Search for. All over house. William. Spence. Etc.'

Questioned on this matter the servants willingly recalled the characteristic hullaballoo that had been raised in this search. It set in immediately after the last event related by William. Félicité and Rivera were in the study, Miss Henderson was on her way upstairs and William himself was hovering on the landing, when Lord Pastern shot out of the ballroom, shouting: 'Where's my sombrero?'

In no time the hunt was in full cry. Spence, William and Lord Pastern scattered in various directions. The sombrero was finally discovered by Miss Henderson (she was no doubt the 'etc' of the notes) in a cupboard on the top landing. Lord Pastern appeared with the thing on his head and re-entered the ballroom in triumph. During this uproar Spence, questing in the hall, had found a letter on the table addressed to Miss de Suze.

Here the narrative was interrupted by a dignified passage-of-arms between Spence, William and the parlourmaid, Mary. Mr Spence, William said resentfully, had torn a strip off him for not taking the letter in to Miss Félicité as soon as it came. William had denied knowledge of the letter and had not opened the door to any district messenger. Nor had Mary. Nor had anyone else. Spence obviously considered that someone was lying. Alleyn asked if any of them had seen the envelope. Hortense, needlessly dramatic, cried out that she had tidied an envelope up from the floor of Mademoiselle's bedroom. Fox held a smothered colloquy about rubbish bins with William, who made an excited exit and returned, flushed with modest triumph, to lay a crushed and stained envelope on the table before Alleyn. Alleyn recognized the eccentricities of Lord Pastern's typewriter and pocketed the envelope.

'It's my belief, Mr Spence,' William announced boldly, 'that there never was a district messenger.'

Leaving them no time to digest this theory, Alleyn continued with the business of checking Lord Pastern's time-table. Spence, still very anxious, said that having discovered the letter on the hall table, he had come upstairs and taken it into the drawing-room, where he found only his mistress Miss Wayne, and Mr Manx, who, he thought, had not long arrived there from the dining-room. On returning to the landing Spence encountered Miss de Suze, coming out of the study, and gave her the letter. Sounds of the sombrero-hunt reached him from upstairs. He was about to join in when a cry of triumph from Lord Pastern reassured him, and he returned to the servants' quarters. He had noticed the time: 9.45.

'And at that time,' Alleyn said, 'Lady Pastern and Miss Wayne are about to leave Mr Manx alone in the drawing-room and go upstairs. Miss de Suze and Miss Henderson are already in their rooms and Lord Pastern is about to descend, wearing his sombrero. Mr Bellairs and Mr Rivera are in the ballroom. We have 45 minutes to go before the party leaves for the Metronome. What happens next?'

But he had struck a blank. Apart from Hortense's previous account of her visits to the ladies upstairs there was little to be learned from the servants. They had kept to their own quarters until a few minutes before the departure to the Metronome, Spence and William had gone into the hall, assisted the gentlemen into their overcoats, given them their hats and gloves, and seen them into their cars.

'Who,' Alleyn asked, 'helped Mr Rivera into his coat?'

William had done this.

'Did you notice anything about him? Anything at all out of the ordinary, however slight?'

William said sharply: 'The gentleman had a – well, a funny ear, sir. Red and bleeding a bit. A cauliflower ear, as you might say.'

'Had you noticed this earlier in the evening? When you leant over his chair, serving him, at dinner, for instance?'

'No, sir. It was all right then, sir.'

'Sure?'

'Swear to it,' said William crisply.

'You think carefully, Will, before you make statements,' Spence said uneasily.

'I know I'm right, Mr Spence.'

'How do you imagine he came by this injury?' Alleyn asked.

William grinned, pure Cockney. 'Well, sir, if you'll excuse the expression, I'd say somebody handed the gentleman a fourpenny one.'

'Who, at a guess?'

William rejoined promptly: 'Seeing he was holding his right hand, tender-like, in his left and seeing the way the murdered gentleman looked at him so fierce, I'd say it was Mr Edward Manx, sir.'

Hortense broke into a spate of excited and gratified comment. M Dupont made a wide, conclusive gesture and exclaimed: 'Perfectly! It explains itself!' Mary and Myrtle ejaculated incoherently while Spence and Miss Parker, in a single impulse, rose and shouted awfully: 'That WILL DO, William.'

Alleyn and Fox left them, still greatly excited, and retraced their steps to the downstairs hall.

'What have we got out of that little party,' Alleyn grunted, 'beyond confirmation of old Pastern's time-table up to half an hour before they all left the house?'

'Damn all, sir. And what does that teach us?' Fox grumbled. 'Only that every man-jack of them was alone at some time or another and might have got hold of the parasol handle, taken it to the study, fixed this silly little stiletto affair in the end with plastic wood and then done Gawd-knows what. Every man-jack of 'em.'

'And every woman-jill?'

'I suppose so. Wait a bit, though.'

Alleyn gave him the time-table and his own notes. They had moved into the entrance lobby, closing the inner glassdoors behind them. 'Mull it over in the car,' Alleyn said. 'I think there's a bit more to be got out of it, Fox. Come on.'

But as Alleyn was about to open the front door Fox gave a sort of grunt and he turned back to see Félicité de Suze on the stairs. She was dressed for the day and in the dim light of the hall looked pale and exhausted. For a moment they stared at each other through the glass panel and then tentatively, uncertainly, she made an incomplete gesture with one hand. Alleyn swore under his breath and re-entered the hall.

'Do you want to speak to me?' he said. 'You're up very early.'

'I couldn't sleep.'

'I'm sorry,' he said formally.

'I think I do want to speak to you.'

Alleyn nodded to Fox, who re-entered the hall.

'Alone,' said Félicité.

'Inspector Fox is acting with me in this case.'

She glanced discontentedly at Fox. 'All the same,' she said, and then as Alleyn made no answer: 'Oh, well!'

She was on the third step from the foot of the stairs, standing there boldly, aware of the picture she made. 'Lisle told me,' she said, 'about you and the letter. Getting it from her, I mean. I suppose you take rather a dim view of my sending Lisle to do my dirty work, don't you?'

'It doesn't arise.'

'I was all *bouleversée*. I know it was rather awful letting her go, but I think in a way she quite enjoyed it.' He noticed that her upper lip was fuller than the under one and that when she smiled it curved richly. 'Darling Lisle,' she said, 'doesn't have much fun and she's so madly interested always in other people's little flutters.' She watched Alleyn out of the corners of her eyes and added: 'We're all devoted to her.'

'What do you want to ask me, Miss de Suze?'

'Please may I have the letter back? Please!'

'In due course,' he said. 'Certainly.'

'Not now?'

'I'm afraid, not now.'

'That's rather a bore,' said Félicité. 'I suppose I'd better come clean in a big way.'

'If it's relevant to the matter in hand,' Alleyn agreed. 'I am only concerned with the death of Mr Carlos Rivera.'

She leant back against the banister, stretching her arms along it and looking downwards, arranging herself for him to look at. 'I'd suggest we went somewhere where we could sit down,' she said, 'but here seems to be the only place where there's no lurking minor detective.'

'Let it be here, then.'

'You are not,' Félicité said, 'making this very easy.'

'I'm sorry. I shall be glad to hear what you have to say, but to tell the truth, there's a heavy day's work in front of us.'

They stood there, disliking each other. Alleyn thought: 'She's going to be one of the tricky ones. She may have nothing to say; I know the signs but I can't be sure of them.' And Félicité thought: 'I didn't really notice him last night. If he'd known what Carlos was like he'd have despised me. He's taller than Ned. I'd like him to be on my side thinking how courageous and young and attractive I am. Younger than Lisle, for instance, with two men in love with me. I wonder what sort of women he likes. I suppose I'm frightened.'

She slid down into a sitting position on the stairs and clasped her hands about her knees; young and bit boyish, a touch of the *gamine*.

'It's about this wretched letter. Well, not wretched at all, really, because it's from a chap I'm very fond of. You've read it, of course.'

'I'm afraid so.'

'My dear, I don't *mind*. Only, as you've seen, it's by way of being number one secrecy and I'll feel a bit low if it all comes popping out, particularly as it's got utterly *no* connection with your little game. It just couldn't be less relevant.'

'Good.'

'But I suppose I've got to prove that, haven't I?'

'It would be an excellent move if you can.'

'Here we go, then,' said Félicité.

Alleyn listened wearily, pinning his attention down to the recital, shutting out the thought of time sliding away, and of his wife who would soon wake and look to see if he was there. Félicité told him that she had corresponded with GPF of *Harmony* and that his advice had been too marvellously understanding and that she had felt an urge like the kick of a mule to meet him but that although his replies had grown more and more come-to-ish he had insisted that his identity must remain hidden. 'All Cupid-and-Psycheish only definitely less rewarding,' she said. And then the letter had arrived and Edward Manx had appeared with a white flower in his coat and, suddenly, after never having gone much for old Ned, she had felt astronomically uplifted. Because, after all, it was rather bracing, wasn't it, to think that all the time Ned was GPF and writing these really gorgeous things and falling for one like a dray-load of bricks? Here Félicité paused and then added rather hurriedly and with an air of hauteur: 'You'll understand that by this time poor Carlos had, from my point of view, become comparatively a dim figure. I mean, to be as bald as an egg about it, he just faded out. I mean it couldn't have mattered less about Carlos because clearly I wasn't his cup-of-tea and we'd both gone tepid on it and I knew he wouldn't mind. You do see what I mean about that, don't you?'

'Are you trying to tell me that you and Rivera had parted as friends?'

Félicité shook her head vaguely and raised her eyebrows. 'Even that makes it sound too important,' she said. 'It all just came peacefully unstuck.'

'And there was no quarrel, for instance, when you and he were in the study between a quarter and half-past nine? Or later, between Mr Manx and Mr Rivera?'

There was a long pause. Félicité bent forward and jerked at the strap of her shoe. 'What in the world,' she said indistinctly, 'put these quaint little notions into your head?'

'Are they completely false?'

'I know,' she said loudly and cheerfully. She looked up into his face. 'You've been gossiping with the servants.' She appealed to Fox. 'Hasn't he?' she demanded playfully.

'I'm sure I couldn't say, Miss de Suze,' said Fox blandly.

'How could you!' she accused Alleyn. 'Which of them was it? Was it Hortense? My poor Mr Alleyn, you don't know Hortense. She's the world's most accomplished liar! She just can't help herself, poor thing. It's pathological.'

'So there was no quarrel?' Alleyn said. 'Between any of you?'

'My dear, haven't I told you?'

'Then why,' he asked, 'did Mr Manx punch Mr Rivera over the ear?'

Félicité's eyes and mouth opened. Then she hunched her shoulders and caught the tip of her tongue between her teeth. He could have sworn she was astonished and in a moment it was evident that she was gratified.

'No!' she said. 'Honestly? Ned did? Well, I must say I call that a handsome tribute. When did it happen? Before we went down to the Met? After dinner? When?'

Alleyn looked steadily at her: 'I thought,' he said, 'that perhaps you could tell me that.'

'I? But I promise you . . .'

'Had he got a trickle of blood on his ear when you talked to him in the study? On the occasion, you know, when you say there was no quarrel?'

'Let me think,' said Félicité, and rested her head on her crossed arms. But the movement was not swift enough. He had seen the blank look of panic in her eyes. 'No.' Her voice muffled by her arms said slowly, 'No, I'm sure . . .'

There was some change of light above, where the stairs ran up to the first landing. He looked up. Carlisle Wayne stood there in the shadow. Her figure and posture still retained the effect of movement, as if while she came downstairs, she had suddenly been held in suspension as the action of a motion picture may be suspended to give emphasis to a specific moment. Over Félicité's bent head, Alleyn with a slight movement of his hand arrested Carlisle's descent. Félicité had begun to speak again.

'After all,' she was saying, 'one is a bit uplifted. It's not every day in the week that people give other people cauliflower ears for love of one's bright eyes.' She raised her face and looked at him. 'How naughty of Ned, but how sweet of him. Darling Ned!'

'No, really!' said Carlisle strongly, 'this is too much!'

Félicité, with a stifled cry, was on her feet.

Alleyn said: 'Hallo, Miss Wayne. Good-morning to you. Have you any theory about why Mr Manx gave Rivera a clip over the ear? He did give him a clip, you know. Why?'

'If you must know,' Carlisle said in a high voice, 'it was because Rivera kissed me when we met on the landing.'

'Good lord!' Alleyn ejaculated, 'why didn't you say so before? Kissed *you*, did he? Did you like it?'

'Don't be a *bloody* fool!' Carlisle shouted and bolted upstairs.

'I must say,' Félicité said, 'I call that rather poor of darling Lisle.'

'If you'll excuse us,' Alleyn said. He and Fox left her staring thoughtfully at her fingernails.

III

'A shave,' Alleyn said in the car, 'a bath and with luck two hours' sleep. I'll take it out at home. We'll send the stuff on to the experts. What about you, Fox? Troy will be delighted to fix you up.'

'Thank you very much, sir, but I wouldn't think of troubling Mrs Alleyn. There's a little place – '

'I'll be damned to your little place. I've had enough insurbordina-tion from you, my lad. To hell with you. You're coming to us.'

Fox accepted this singular invitation in the spirit in which it was made. He took out his spectacles, Alleyn's note-book and Lord Pastern's time-table. Alleyn dragged his palm across his jaw, shud-dered, yawned and closed his eyes. 'A hideous curse on this case,' he murmured, and appeared to sleep. Fox began to whisper to himself. The car slipped down Cliveden Place, into Grosvenor Place, into Hyde Park Corner. 'T, t, t,' Fox whispered over the time-table.

'You sound,' Alleyn said without opening his eyes, 'like Dr Johnson on his way to Streatham. Can you crack your joints, Foxkin?'

'I see what you mean about this ruddy time-table.'

'What *did* I mean? Split me and sink me if I know what I meant.'

'Well, sir, our customer, whoever he or she may be, and you know my view on the point, had to be in the ballroom to pick up the bit of umbrella shaft, in the drawing-room to collect the stiletto and alone in the study to fix the stiletto to the bit of umbrella shaft with plastic wood.'

'You'll be coming round the mountain when you come.'

'It *is* a bit of a mountain and that's a fact. According to what the young lady, Miss Wayne, I mean, told you, sir, this perishing parasol was all right before dinner when she was in the ballroom and handled it, and according to her, his lordship was in the study drawing the bullets out of the cartridges. If that's correct he didn't get a chance to play the fool with the parasol before dinner. What's more it fits in with his lordship's own statement, which Bellairs can speak to, if he ever wakes up, that he took the parasol to bits on the piano *after* dinner. For fun.'

'Quite.'

'All right. Now where does this get us? If the time-table's correct, his lordship was never alone in the study after that.'

'And the only time he was alone at all, moreover, he was up and down the house, bellowing like a bull for his sombrero.'

'Doesn't that look like establishing an alibi?' Fox demanded.

'It looks a bit like the original alibi itself, Br'er Fox.'

'He might have carried the tube of plastic wood round in his pocket.'

'So he might. Together with the bit of parasol and the stiletto, pausing in mid-bellow to fix the job.'

'Gah! How about him just taking the stuff in his pocket to the Metronome and fixing everything there?'

'Oh, lord! When? How?'

'Lavatory?' Fox suggested hopefully.

'And when did he put the weapon in the gun? Skelton looked down the barrel just before they started playing, don't forget.'

The car stopped at traffic lights in Piccadilly. Fox contemplated the Green Park with disapproval. Alleyn still kept his eyes shut. Big Ben struck seven.

'By gum!' Fox said, bringing his palm down on his knee, 'by gum, how about this? How about his lordship in his damn-your-eyes fashion fitting the weapon into the gun while he sat there behind his drums? In front of everybody, while one of the other turns was on? It's amazing what you can do when you brazen it out. What's that yarn they're always quoting, sir? I've got it. *The Purloined Letter!* Proving that if you make a thing obvious enough nobody notices it?'

Alleyn opened one eye. '*The Purloined Letter,*' he said. He opened the other eye. 'Fox, my cabbage, my rare edition, my *objet d'art*, my own special bit of *bijouterie*, be damned if I don't think you've caught an idea. Come on. Let's further think of this.'

They talked intensively until the car pulled up, in a cul-de-sac off Coventry Street, before Alleyn's flat.

Early sunlight streamed into the little entrance hall. Beneath a Benozzo Gozzoli, a company of dahlias, paper-white in a blue bowl, cast translucent shadows on a white parchment wall. Alleyn looked about him contentedly.

'Troy's under orders not to get up till eight,' he said. 'You take first whack at the bath, Fox, while I have a word with her. Use my razor. Wait a bit.' He disappeared and returned with towels. 'There'll be something to eat at half-past nine,' he said. 'The visitor's room's all yours, Fox. Sleep well.'

'Very kind, I'm sure,' said Fox. 'May I send my compliments to Mrs Alleyn, sir?'

'She'll be delighted to receive them. See you later.'

Troy was awake in her white room, sitting up with her head aureoled in short locks of hair. 'Like a faun,' Alleyn said, 'or a bronze dahlia. Are you well this morning?'

'Bouncing, thanks. And you?'

'As you see. Unhoused, unannealed and un-everything that's civilized.'

'A poor state of affairs,' said Troy. 'You look like the gentleman in that twenty-foot canvas in the Luxembourg. Boiled shirt in dents and gazing out over Paris through lush curtains. I think it's called. "The Hopeless Dawn"! His floozy is still asleep in an elephantine bed, you remember.'

'I don't remember. Talking of floozies, oughtn't you to be asleep yourself?'

'God bless my soul!' Troy complained, 'I haven't been bitten by the tsetse-fly. It's getting on for nine hours since I went to bed, damn it.'

'OK OK.'

'What's happened, Rory?'

'One of the kind we don't fancy.'

'Oh, *no.*'

'You'll hear about it anyway, so I may as well tell you. It's that florid number we saw playing the piano accordion, the one with the teeth and hair.'

'You don't mean – '

'Somebody pinked him with a sort of dagger made out of a bit of a parasol and needlework stiletto.'

'Gatcha!'

He explained at some length.

'Well but . . . ' Troy stared at her husband. 'When have you got to be at the Yard?'

'Ten.'

'All right. You've got two hours and time for breakfast. Good morning, darling.'

'Fox is in the bathroom. I know I'm not fit for a lady's bed-chamber.'

'Who said?'

'If you didn't, nobody.' He put his arm across her and stooped his head. 'Troy,' he said, 'may I ask Fox this morning?'

'If you want to, my dearest.'

'I think I might. How much, at a rough guess, would you say I loved you?'

'*Words* fail me,' said Troy, imitating the late Harry Tate.

'And me.'

'There's Mr Fox coming out of the bathroom. Away with you.'

'I suppose so. Good-morning, Mrs Quiverful.'

On his way to the bathroom Alleyn looked in upon Fox. He found him lying on the visitor's room bed, without his jacket but incredibly neat; his hair damp, his jaw gleaming, his shirt stretched tight over this thick pectoral muscles. His eyes were closed but he opened them as Alleyn looked in.

'I'll call you at half-past nine,' Alleyn said. 'Did you know you were going to be a godfather, Br'er Fox?' And as Fox's eyes widened he shut the door and went whistling to the bathroom.

CHAPTER 9

The Yard

At ten-thirty in the Chief-Inspector's room at New Scotland Yard, routine procedure following a case of homicide was efficiently established.

Alleyn sat at his desk taking reports from Detective-Sergeants Gibson, Watson, Scott and Sallis. Mr Fox, with that air of good humour crossed with severity, which was his habitual reaction to reports following observation, listened critically to his juniors, each of whom held his official note-book. Six men going soberly about their day's work. Earlier that morning, in other parts of London, Captain Entwhistle, an expert on ballistics, had fitted a dart made from a piece of parasol into a revolver and had fired it into a bag of sand; Mr Carrick, a Government analyst, had submitted a small cork to various tests for certain oils; and Sir Grantly Morton, the famous pathologist, assisted by Curtis, had opened Carlos Rivera's thorax, and, with the greatest delicacy, removed his heart.

'All right,' Alleyn said. 'Get yourselves chairs and smoke if you want to. This is liable to be a session.'

When they were settled, he pointed the stem of his pipe at a heavy-jawed, straw-coloured, detective-sergeant with a habitually startled expression. 'You searched the deceased's rooms, didn't you, Gibson? Let's take you first.'

Gibson thumbed his note-book open, contemplated it in apparent astonishment and embarked on a high-pitched recital.

'*The deceased man. Carlos Rivera:* he said, '*lived at 102 Bedford Mansions, Austerly Square, SWI. Service Flat, Rental £500 a year.*'

'Why don't we all play piano accordions?' Fox asked of nobody in particular.

'*At 3 a.m. on the morning of June 1st,*' Gibson continued in a shrill-ish voice, '*having obtained a search warrant, I effected entrance to above premises by means of a key on a ring removed from the body of the deceased. The flat consists of an entrance lobby, six-by-eight feet, a sitting room twelve-by-fourteen, and a bedroom nine-by-eleven feet. Furnishings: – Sitting room: Carpet, purple, thick. Curtains, full length, purple satin.*'

'Stay with me with flagons!' Alleyn muttered. 'Purple.'

'You might call it morve, Mr Alleyn.'

'Well, go on.'

'*Couch, upholstered green velvet, three armchairs, ditto, dining-table, six dining-chairs, open fireplace. Walls painted fawn. Cushions: Seven. Green and purple satin.*' He glanced at Alleyn. 'I beg pardon, Mr Alleyn? Anything wrong?'

'Nothing. Nothing. Go on.'

'*Bookcase. Fourteen books. Foreign. Recognized four as on police lists. Pictures: four.*'

'What were *they* like?' Fox asked.

'Never you mind, you dirty old man,' said Alleyn.

'Two were nood studies, Mr Fox, what you might call heavy pin-ups. The others were a bit more so. *Cigarette boxes: four. Cigarettes, commercial product. Have taken one from each box. Wall safe. Combination lock but found note of number in deceased's pocket book. Contents: –* '

'Half a minute,' Alleyn said. 'Have all the flats got these safes?'

'I ascertained from inquiries, sir, that deceased had his installed.'

'Right. Go on.'

'*Contents. I removed a number of papers, two ledgers or account books and a locked cash box containing three hundred pounds in notes of low denomination, and thirteen shillings in silver.*' Here Gibson paused of his own accord.

'There now!' said Fox. 'Now we *may* be on to something.'

'*I left a note of the contents of the safe in the safe and I locked the safe,*' said Gibson, on a note of uncertainty, induced perhaps by misgivings about his prose style. 'Shall I produce the contents now, sir, or go on to the bedroom?'

'I doubt if I can take the bedroom,' Alleyn said. 'But go on.'

'It was done up in black, sir. Black satin.'

'Do you put all this in your notes?' Fox demanded suddenly. 'All this about colours and satin?'

'They tell us to be thorough, Mr Fox.'

'There's a medium to all things,' Fox pronounced sombrely. 'I beg pardon, Mr Alleyn.'

'Not at all, Br'er Fox. The bedroom, Gibson.'

But there wasn't anything much to the purpose in Gibson's meticulous account of Rivera's bedroom unless the revelation that he wore black satin pyjamas with embroidered initials could be called, as Alleyn suggested, damning and conclusive evidence as to character. Gibson produced the spoil of the wall-safe and they examined it. Alleyn took the ledgers and Fox the bundle of correspondence. For some time there was silence, broken only by the whisper of papers.

Presently, however, Fox brought his palm down on his knees and Alleyn, without looking up, said: 'Hallo?'

'Peculiar,' Fox grunted. 'Listen to this, sir.'

'Go ahead.'

' "How tender," ' Mr Fox began, ' "is the first burgeoning of love! How delicate the tiny bud, how easily cut with frost! Touch it with gentle fingers, dear lad, lest its fragrance be lost to you forever." '

'Cor!' whispered Detective-Sergeant Scott.

' "You say," ' Mr Fox continued, ' "that she is changeable. So is a day in spring. Be patient. Wait for the wee petals to unfold. If you would care for a very special, etc." ' Fox removed his spectacles and contemplated his superior.

'What do you mean by your "etc.," Fox? Why don't you go on?'

'That's what it says. Etc. Then it stops. Look.'

He flattened a piece of creased blue letter paper out on the desk before Alleyn. It was covered with typing, closely spaced. The Duke's Gate address was stamped on the top.

Alleyn said: 'What's that you're holding back?'

Fox laid his second exhibit before him. It was a press-cutting and printed on paper of the kind used in the more exotic magazines. Alleyn read aloud: ' "Dear GPF, I am engaged to a young lady who at times is very affectionate and then again goes cold on me. It's not halitosis because I asked her and she said it wasn't and wished I wouldn't harp on about it. I am twenty-two, five-foot eleven in my socks and well built. I drag down £550 per annum. I am an A grade motor mechanic and I have prospects of a rise. She reckons she loves me and yet she acts like this. What should be my attitude? Spark-plug." '

'I should advise a damn' good hiding,' Alleyn said. 'Poor old Spark-plug.'

'Go on, sir. Read the answer.'

Alleyn continued: ' "Dear Spark-plug. Yours is not as unusual a problem as perhaps you, in your distress of mind, incline to believe. How tender is the first burgeoning – " Yes, here we go again. Yes. All right. Fox. You've found apparently, a bit of the rough draft and the finished article. The draft, typed on Duke's Gate letter-paper, looks as if it had been crumpled up in somebody's pocket, doesn't it? Half a minute.'

He opened his own file and in a moment the letter Félicité had dropped from her bag at the Metronome had been placed beside the other. Alleyn bent over them. 'It's a potshot, of course,' he said, 'but I'm ready to bet it's the same machine. The "s" out of alignment. All the usual indications.'

'Where does this lead us?' Fox asked. Gibson, looking gratified, cleared his throat. Alleyn said: 'It leads us into a bit of a tangle. The letter to Miss de Suze was typed on the machine in Lord Pastern's study on the paper he uses for that purpose. The machine carried his dabs only. I took a chance and asked him, point-blank, how long he'd known that Edward Manx was GPF He wouldn't answer but I'll swear I rocked him. I'll undertake he typed the letter after he saw Manx put a white carnation in his coat, marked the envelope, "By District Messenger," and put it on the hall table where it was discovered by the butler. All right. Now, not so long ago, Manx stayed at Duke's Gate for three weeks and I suppose it's reasonable to assume that he may have used the typewriter and the blue letter-paper in the study when he was jotting down notes for his nauseating little GPF numbers in *Harmony*. So this draft may have been typed by Manx. But, as far as we know, Manx met Rivera for the first time last night and incidentally dotted him what William pleasingly called a fourpenny one, because Rivera kissed, *not* Miss de Suze but Miss Wayne. Now, if we're right so far, how and when the hell did Rivera get hold of Manx's rough draft of this sickening GPF stuff? Not last night, because we've got it from Rivera's safe, and he didn't go back to his rooms. Answer me that, Fox.'

'Gawd knows.'

'We don't, at all events. And if we find out, is it going to tie up with Rivera's murder? Well, press on, chaps, press on.'

He returned to the ledger and Fox to the bundle of papers. Presently Alleyn said: 'Isn't it extraordinary how business-like they are?'

'Who's that, Mr Alleyn?'

'Why, blackmailers to be sure. Mr Rivera was a man of parts, Fox. Piano accordions, drug-running, blackmail. Almost a pity we've got to nab his murderer. He was ripe for bumping off, was Mr Rivera. This is a neatly kept record of monies and goods received and disbursed. On the 3rd of February, for instance, we have an entry. "Cash, £150, 3rd instalment, SFF." A week later, a cryptic note on the debit side: "6 doz. per SS, £360," followed by a series of credits: "JCM, £10." "BB £100," and so on. These entries are in a group by themselves. He's totted them up and balanced the whole thing, showing a profit of £200 on the original outlay of £360.'

'That'll be his dope racket, by gum. SS, did you say, Mr Alleyn? By gum, I wonder if he *is* in with the Snowy Santos bunch.'

'And "BB" on the paying side. "BB" is quite a profitable number on the paying side.'

'Breezy Bellairs?'

'I shouldn't wonder. It looks to me, Fox, as if Rivera was a medium high-up in the drug racket. He was one of the boys we don't catch easily. It's long odds he never passed the stuff out direct to the small consumer. With the exception, no doubt, of the wretched Bellairs. No, I fancy Rivera's business was confined to his purple satin parlour. At the smallest sign of our getting anywhere near him, he'd have burnt his books and, if necessary, returned to his native hacienda or what have you.'

'Or got in first by laying information against the small man. That's the line they take as often as not.'

'Yes, indeed. As often as not. What else have you got in your lucky dip, Br'er Fox?'

'Letters,' said Fox. 'A sealed package. And the cash.'

'Anything that chimes in with his book-keeping. I wonder.'

'Wait a bit, sir. I wouldn't be surprised. Wait a bit.'

They hadn't long to wait. The too-familiar raw material of the blackmailer's trade was soon laid out on Alleyn's desk: the dingy, colourless letters, paid for again and again, yet never redeemed, the discoloured clips from dead newspapers, one or two desperate appeals for mercy, the inexorable entries on the credit side. Alleyn's fingers seemed to tarnish as he handled them but Fox rubbed his hands.

'This is something like,' Fox said, and after a minute or two: 'Look at this, Mr Alleyn.'

It was a letter signed 'Félicité' and was some four months old. Alleyn read it through and handed it back to Fox, who said: 'It establishes the relationship.'

'Apparently.'

'Funny,' said Fox. 'You'd have thought from the look of him, even when he was dead, that any girl in her senses would have picked him for what he was. There are two other letters. Much the same kind of thing.'

'Yes.'

'Yes. Well now,' said Fox slowly. 'Leaving the young lady aside for the moment, where, if anywhere, does this get us with his lordship?'

'Not very far, I fancy. Unless you find something revealing a hitherto unsuspected irregularity in his lordship's past and he doesn't strike me as one to hide his riotings.'

'All the same, sir, there may be something. What about his lordship encouraging this affair with his step-daughter? Doesn't that look as if Rivera had a hold on him?'

'It might,' Alleyn agreed, 'if his lordship was anybody but his lordship. But it might. So last night, having decided to liquidate Rivera, he types this letter purporting to come from GPF with the idea of throwing the all-too-impressionable Miss de Suze into Edward Manx's arms!'

'There you are!'

'How does Lord Pastern know Manx as GPF? And if Rivera used this GPF copy to blackmail Manx it wasn't a very hot instrument for his purpose, being typed. Anybody at Duke's Gate might have typed it. He would have to find it on Manx and try a bluff. And he hadn't met Manx. All right. For purposes of your argument we needn't pursue that one at the moment. All right. It fits. In a way. Only only . . . 'He rubbed his nose. 'I'm sorry, Fox, but I can't reconcile the flavour of Pastern and Manx with all this. A most untenable argument, I know. I won't try to justify it. What's in that box?'

Fox had already opened it and shoved it across the desk. 'It'll be the stuff itself,' he said. 'A nice little haul, Gibson.'

The box contained neat small packages, securely sealed and, in a separate carton, a number of cigarettes.

'That'll be it,' Alleyn agreed. 'He wasn't the direct receiver, evidently. This will have come in by the usual damned labyrinth.' He glanced up at Detective-Sergeant Scott, a young officer. 'You haven't worked on any of these cases, I think, Scott. This is probably cocaine or heroin, and has no doubt travelled long distances in bogus false teeth, fat men's navels, dummy aids to hearing, phoney bayonet fitments for electric light bulbs and God knows what else. As Mr Fox says, Gibson, it's a nice little haul. We'll leave Rivera for the moment, I think.' He turned to Scott and Watson. 'Let's hear how you got on with Breezy Bellairs.'

Breezy, it appeared, lived in a furnished flat in Pikestaff Row, off Ebury Street. To this address Scott and Watson had conveyed him, and with some difficulty put him to bed. Once there, he had slept stertorously through the rest of the night. They had combed out the flat which, unlike Rivera's, was slovenly and disordered. It looked, they said, as if Breezy had had a frantic search for something. The pockets of his suits had been pulled out, the drawers of his furniture disembowelled and the contents left where they lay. The only thing in the flat that was at all orderly was Breezy's pile of band-parts. Scott and Wilson had sorted out a bundle of correspondence consisting of bills, dunning reminders, and his fanmail, which turned out to be largish. At the back of a small bedside cupboard they had found a hypodermic syringe which they produced, and a number of torn and empty packages which were of the same sort as those found in Rivera's safe. 'Almost too easy,' said Fox with the liveliest satisfaction. 'We knew it already, of course, through Skelton, but here's positive proof Rivera supplied Bellairs with his dope. By gum,' he added deeply. 'I'd like to get this line on the dope racket followed in to one of the high-ups. Now, I wonder. Breezy'll be looking for this stuff and won't know where to find it. He'll be very upset. I ask myself if Breezy won't be in the mood to talk.'

'You'd better remind yourself of your police code, old boy.'

'It'll be the same story,' Fox muttered. 'Breezy won't know how Rivera got it. He won't know.'

'He hasn't been long on the injection method,' Alleyn said. 'Curtis had a look for needle-marks and didn't find so very many.'

'He'll be fretting for it, though,' said Fox, and after a moment's pondering: 'Oh, well. It's a homicide we're after.'

Nothing more of interest had been found in Breezy's flat and Alleyn turned to the last of the men. 'How did you get on with Skelton, Sallis?'

'Well, sir,' said Sallis, in a loud public-school voice, 'he didn't like me much to begin with. I picked up a search warrant on the way and he took a very poor view of that. However, we talked sociology for the rest of the journey and I offered to lend him *The Yogi and the Commissar*, which bent the barriers a little. He's Australian by birth, and I've been out there, so that helped to establish a more matey attitude.'

'Get on with your report now,' Fox said austerely. 'Don't meander. Mr Alleyn isn't concerned to know how much Syd Skelton loves you.'

'I'm sorry, sir.'

'Use your notes and get on with it,' Fox counselled.

Sallis opened his note-book and got on with it. Beyond a quantity of communistic literature there was little out of the ordinary to be found in Skelton's rooms, which were in the Pimlico Road. Alleyn gathered that Sallis had conducted his search during a lively exchange of ideas and could imagine Skelton's guarded response to Sallis's pinkish, facile and consciously ironical observations. Finally, Skelton, in spite of himself, had gone to sleep in his chair and Sallis then turned his attention stealthily to a table which was used as a desk.

'I'd noticed that he seemed rather uneasy about this table, sir. He stood by it when we first came in and shuffled the papers about. I had the feeling there was something there that he wanted to destroy. When he was safely off, I went through the stuff on the table, and I found this. I don't know if it's much cop, really, sir, but here it is.'

He gave a sheet of paper to Alleyn, who opened it up. It was an unfinished letter to Rivera, threatening him with exposure if he continued to supply Breezy Bellairs with drugs.

II

The other men had gone and Alleyn invited Fox to embark upon what he was in the habit of calling 'a hag'. This involved the ruthless taking to pieces of the case and a fresh attempt to put the bits together in their true pattern. They had been engaged upon this business for about half an hour when the telephone rang. Fox answered it and announced with a tolerant smile that Mr Nigel Bathgate would like to speak to Mr Alleyn.

'I was expecting this,' Alleyn said. 'Tell him that for once in a blue moon I want to see him. Where is he?'

'Down below.'

'Hail him up.'

Fox said sedately: 'The Chief would like to see you 'Mr Bathgate,' and in a few moments Nigel Bathgate of the *Evening Chronicle* appeared, looking mildly astonished.

'I must say,' he said, shaking hands, 'that this is uncommonly civil of you, Alleyn. Have you run out of invectives or do you at last realize where the brains lie?'

'If you think I asked you up with the idea of feeding you with banner headlines you're woefully mistaken. Sit down.'

'Willingly. How are you, Mr Fox?'

'Nicely, thank you, sir. And you?'

Alleyn said: 'Now, you attend to me. Can you tell me anything about a monthly called *Harmony?*'

'What sort of things? Have you been confiding in GPF, Alleyn?'

'I want to know who he is.'

'Has this got anything to do with the Rivera case?'

'Yes, it has.'

'I'll make a bargain with you. I want a nice meaty bit of stuff straight from the Yard's mouth. All about old Pastern and how you happened to be there and the shattered romance . . . '

'Who've you been talking to?'

'Charwomen, night porters, chaps in the band. And I ran into Ned Manx a quarter of an hour ago.'

'What had he got to say for himself?'

'He hung out on me, blast him. Wouldn't utter. And he's not on a daily, either. Uncooperative twerp.'

'You might remember he's the chief suspect's cousin.'

'Then there's no doubt about it being old Pastern?'

'I didn't say so and you won't suggest it.'

'Well, hell, give me a story.'

'About this paper. *Do* you know GPF? Come on.'

Nigel lit a cigarette and settled down. 'I don't know him,' he said. 'And I don't know anyone who does. He's a chap called G.P. Friend, I'm told, and he's supposed to own the show. If he does, he's on to a damn' useful thing. It's a mystery, that paper. It breaks all the rules and rings the bell. It first came out about two years ago with a great fanfare of trumpets. They bought out the old *Triple Mirror*, you know, and took over the plant and the paper and in less than no time trebled the sales. God knows why. The thing's a freak. It mixes sound criticism with girly-girly chat and runs top price serials alongside shorts that would bring a blush to the cheeks of *Peg's Weekly*. They tell me it's GPF's page that does the trick. And look at it! That particular racket blew out before the war and yet he gets by with it. I'm told the personal letters at five bob a time are a gold mine in themselves. He's said to have an uncanny knack of hitting on the things all these women want him to say. The types that write in are amazing. All the smarties. Nobody ever sees him. He doesn't get about with the boys and the chaps who free-lance for the rag never get past a sub who's always very bland and entirely uncommunicative. There you are. That's all I can tell you about GPF.'

'Ever heard what he looks like?'

'No. There's a legend he wears old clothes and dark glasses. They say he's got a lock on his office door and never sees anybody on account he doesn't want to be recognized. It's all part of an act. Publicity. They play it up in the paper itself – "Nobody knows who GPF is." '

'What would you think if I told you he was Edward Manx?'

'Manx! You're not serious.'

'Is it so incredible?'

Nigel raised his eyebrows. 'On the face of it, yes. Manx is a reputable and very able specialist. He's done some pretty solid stuff. Leftish and fairly authoritative. He's a coming man. He'd turn sick in his stomach at the sight of GPF, I'd have thought.'

'He does their dramatic reviews.'

'Yes, I know, but that's where they're freakish. Manx has got a sort of damn-your-eyes view about theatre. It's one of his things. He wants state-ownership and he'll scoop up any chance to plug it. And I imagine their anti-vice parties wouldn't be unpleasing to Manx. He wouldn't go much for the style, which is tough and coloured, but he'd like the policy. They give battle in a big way, you know. Names all over the place and a general invitation to come on and sue us for libel and see how you like it. Quite his cup of tea. Yes, I imagine *Harmony* runs Manx to give the paper *cachet* and Manx writes for *Harmony* to get at their public. They pay. Top prices.' Nigel paused and then said sharply: 'But Manx as GPF! That's different. Have you actually good reason to suspect it? Are you on to something?'

'The case is fluffy with doubts at the moment.'

'The Rivera case? It ties up with that?'

'Off the record, it does.'

'By God,' said Nigel profoundly, 'if Ned Manx spews up that page it explains the secrecy! By God, it does.'

'We'll have to ask him,' Alleyn said. 'But I'd have liked to have a little more to go on. Still, we can muscle in. Where's the *Harmony* office?'

'Materfamilias Lane. The old *Triple Mirror* place.'

'When does this blasted rag make its appearance? It's a monthly, isn't it?'

'Let's see. It's the 27th today. It comes out in the first week of the month. They'll be going to press any time now.'

'So GPF's likely to be on tap at the office?'

'You'd think so. Are you going to burst in on Manx with a brace of manacles?'

'Never you mind.'

'Come on,' Nigel said. 'What do I get for all this?'

Alleyn gave him a brief account of Rivera's death and a lively description of Lord Pastern's performance in the band.

'As far as it goes, it's good,' Nigel said, 'but I could get as much from the waiters.'

'Not if Caesar Bonn knows anything about it.'

'Are you going to pull old Pastern in?'

'Not just yet. You write your stuff and send it along to me.'

'It's pretty!' Nigel said. 'It's as pretty as paint. Pastern's good at any time but like this he's marvellous. May I use your typewriter?'

'For ten minutes.'

Nigel retired with the machine to a table at the far end of the room. 'I can say you were there, of course,' he said hurriedly.

'I'll be damned if you can.'

'Come, come, Alleyn, be big about this thing.'

'I know you. If we don't ring the bell you'll print some revolting photograph of me looking like a half-wit. Caption: "Chief Inspector who watched crime but doesn't know whodunit!" '

Nigel grinned. 'And would that be a story, and won't that be the day! Still, as it stands, it's pretty hot. Here we go, chaps.' He began to rattle the keys.

Alleyn said: 'There's one thing, Fox, that's sticking out of this mess like a road-sign and I can't read it. Why did that perishing old mountebank look at the gun and then laugh himself sick? Here! Wait a moment. Who was in the study with him when he concocted his dummies and loaded his gun? It's a thin chance but it might yield something.' He pulled the telephone towards him. 'We'll talk once more to Miss Carlisle Wayne.'

III

Carlisle was in her room when the call came through and she took it there, sitting on her bed and staring aimlessly at a flower print on the wall. A hammer knocked at her ribs and her throat constricted. In some remote part of her mind she thought: 'As if I was in love, instead of frightened sick.'

The unusually deep and clear voice said: 'Is that you, Miss Wayne? I'm sorry to bother you again so soon but I'd like to have another word with you.'

'Yes,' said Carlisle. 'Would you? Yes.'

'I can come to Duke's Gate or, if you would rather, can see you here at the Yard.' Carlisle didn't answer at once and he said: 'Which would suit you best?'

'I – I think – I'll come to your office.'

'It might be easier. Thank you so much. Can you come at once?'

'Yes. Yes, I can, of course.'

'Splendid.' He gave her explicit instructions about which entrance to use and where to ask for him. 'Is that clear? I shall see you in about twenty minutes, then.'

'In about twenty minutes,' she repeated, and her voice cracked into an absurd cheerful note as if she was gaily making a date with him. 'Right-ho,' she said and thought with horror: 'But I never say "right-ho." He'll think I'm demented.'

'Mr Alleyn,' she said loudly.

'Yes? Hallo?'

'I'm sorry I made such an ass of myself this morning. I don't know what happened. I seemed to have gone extremely peculiar.'

'Never mind,' said the deep voice easily.

'Well – all right. Thank you. I'll come straight away.'

He gave a small polite not unfriendly sound and she hung up the receiver.

'Booking a date with the attractive inspector, darling?' said Félicité from the door.

At the first sound of her voice Carlisle's body had jerked and she had cried out sharply.

'You *are* jumpy,' Félicité said, coming nearer.

'I didn't know you were there.'

'Obviously.'

Carlisle opened her wardrobe. 'He wants to see me. Lord knows why.'

'So you're popping off to the Yard. Exciting for you.'

'Marvellous isn't it?' Carlisle said, trying to make her voice ironical. Félicité watched her change into a suit. 'Your face wants a little attention,' she said.

'I know.' She went to the dressing-table. 'Not that it matters.'

When she looked in the glass she saw Félicité's face behind her shoulder. 'Stupidly unfriendly,' she thought, dabbing at her nose.

'You know, darling,' Félicité said, 'I'm drawn to the conclusion you're a dark horse.'

'Oh, Fée!' she said impatiently.

'Well, you appear to have done quite a little act with my late best young man, last night, and here you are having a sly assignation with the dynamic inspector.'

'He probably wants to know what kind of tooth-paste we all use.'

'Personally,' said Félicité, 'I always considered you were potty about Ned.'

Carlisle's hand shook as she pressed powder into the tear stains under her eyes.

'You *are* in a state, aren't you?' said Félicité.

Carlisle turned on her. 'Fée, for pity's sake come off it. As if things weren't bad enough without your starting these monstrous hares. You *must* have seen that I couldn't endure your poor wretched incredibly phoney young man. You *must* see that Mr Alleyn's summons to Scotland Yard has merely frightened seven bells out of me. How you *can!*'

'What about Ned?'

Carlisle picked up her bag and gloves. 'If Ned writes the monstrous bilge you've fallen for in *Harmony* I never want to speak to him again,' she said violently. 'For the love of Mike pipe down and let me go and be grilled.'

But she was not to leave without further incident. On the first-floor landing she encountered Miss Henderson. After her early-morning scene with Alleyn on the stairs, Carlisle had returned to her room and remained there, fighting down the storm of illogical weeping that had so suddenly overtaken her. So she had not met Miss Henderson until now.

'Hendy!' she cried out, 'what's the matter?'

'Good-morning, Carlisle. The matter, dear?'

'I thought you looked – I'm sorry. I expect we all look a bit odd. Are you hunting for something?'

'I've dropped my little silver pencil somewhere. It can't be here,' she said, as Carlisle began vaguely to look. 'Are you going out?'

'Mr Alleyn wants me to call and see him.'

'Why?' Miss Henderson said sharply.

'I don't know. Hendy, isn't this awful, this business? And to make matters worse I've had a sort of row with Fée.'

The light on the first landing was always rather strange, Carlisle told herself, a cold reflected light coming from a distant window making people look greenish. It must be that, because Henderson answered her quite tranquilly and with her usual lack of emphasis. 'Why, of all mornings, did you two want to have a row?'

'I suppose we're both scratchy. I told her I thought the unfortunate Rivera was ghastly and she thinks I'm shaking my curls at Mr Alleyn. It was too stupid for words.'

'I should think so, indeed.'

'I'd better go.'

Carlisle touched her lightly on the arm and crossed to the stairs. She hesitated there, without turning to face Miss Henderson, who had not moved. 'What is it?' Miss Henderson said. 'Have you forgotten something?'

'No. Hendy, you know, don't you, about the fantastic thing they say killed him? The piece of parasol with an embroidery stiletto in the end.'

'Yes.'

'Do you remember – I know this is ridiculous – but do you remember, last night when there was that devastating bang from the ballroom? Do you remember you and Aunt Cile and Fée and I were in the drawing-room and you were sorting Aunt Cile's work-box?'

'Was I?'

'Yes. And you jumped at the bang and dropped something.'

'Did I?'

'And Fée picked it up.'

'Did she?'

'Hendy, was it an embroidery stiletto?'

'I remember nothing about it. Nothing at all.'

'I didn't notice where she put it. I wondered if you had noticed.'

'If it was something from the work-box, I expect she put it back. Won't you be late, Carlisle?'

'Yes,' Carlisle said without turning. 'Yes, I'll go.'

She heard Miss Henderson walk away into the drawing-room. The door closed gently and Carlisle went downstairs. There was a man in a dark suit in the hall. He got up when he saw her and said: 'Excuse me, Miss, but are you Miss Wayne?'

'Yes, I am.'

'Thank you, Miss Wayne.'

He opened the glass doors for her and then the front door. Carlisle went quickly past him and out into the sunshine. She was quite unaware of the man who stepped out from the corner a little way down Duke's Gate and who, glancing impatiently at his watch, waited at the bus stop and journeyed with her to Scotland Yard. 'Keep observation on the whole damn' boiling,' Alleyn had said irritably at six o'clock that morning. 'We don't know *what* we want.'

She followed a constable who looked oddly domesticated without his helmet down a linoleumed corridor to the Chief Inspector's room. She thought: 'They invite people to come and make statements. It means something. Suppose they suspect me. Suppose they've found out some little thing that makes them think I've done it.' Her imagination galloped wildly. Suppose, when she went into the room, Alleyn said: 'I'm afraid this is serious. Carlisle Loveday Wayne I arrest you for the murder of Carlos Rivera and I warn you . . . ' They would telephone for any clothes she wanted. Hendy, perhaps, would pack a suitcase. Perhaps, secretly, they would all be a little lightened, almost pleasurably worried, because they would no longer be in fear for themselves. Perhaps Ned would come to see her.

'In here, if you please, Miss,' the constable was saying with his hand on the doorknob.

Alleyn rose quickly from his desk and came towards her. 'Punctilious,' she thought. 'He's got nice manners. Are his manners like this when he's going to arrest people?'

'I'm so sorry,' he was saying. 'This must be a nuisance for you.'

The solid grizzled detective was behind him. Fox. That was Inspector Fox. He had pulled up a chair for her and she sat in it, facing Alleyn. 'With the light on my face,' she thought. 'That's what they do.'

Fox moved away and sat behind a second desk. She could see his head and shoulders but his hands were hidden from her.

'You'll think my object in asking you to come very aimless, I expect,' Alleyn said, 'and my first question will no doubt strike you as being completely potty. However, here it is. You told us last night that you were with Lord Pastern when he made the dummies and loaded the revolver.'

'Yes.'

'Well, now, did anything happen, particularly in respect of the revolver, that struck you both as being at all comic?'

Carlisle gaped at him. '"Comic." '

'I told you it was a potty question,' he said.

'If you mean did we take one look at the revolver and then shake with uncontrollable laughter, we didn't.'

'No,' he said. 'I was afraid not.'

'The mood was sentimental if anything. The revolver was one of a pair given to Uncle George by my father and he told me so.'

'You were familiar with it, then?'

'Not in the least. My father died ten years ago, and when he lived was not in the habit of showing me his armoury. He and Uncle George were both crack shots, I believe. Uncle George told me my father had the revolvers made for target shooting.'

'You looked at the gun last night? Closely?'

'Yes – because – ' Beset by nervous and unreasoned caution she hesitated.

'Because?'

'My father's initials are scratched on it. Uncle George told me to look for them.'

There was a long pause. 'Yes, I see,' Alleyn said.

She found she had twisted her gloves tightly together and doubled them over. She felt a kind of impatience with herself and abruptly smoothed them out.

'It was one of a pair,' Alleyn said. 'Did you look at both of them?'

'No. The other was in a case in the drawer on his desk, I just saw it there. I noticed it because the drawer was under my nose, almost, and Uncle George kept putting the extra dummies, if that's what you call them, into it.'

'Ah, yes. I saw them there.'

'He made a lot more than he wanted, in case,' her voice faltered, 'in case he was asked to do his turn again some time.'

'I see.'

'Is that all?' she said.

'As you've been kind enough to come,' Alleyn said with a smile, 'perhaps we should think up something more.'

'You needn't bother, thank you.'

He smiled broadly. 'Fée was doing her stuff for him on the stairs this morning,' Carlisle thought. 'Was she actually showing the go-ahead signal or was she merely trying to stall him off?'

'It's about the steel end in this eccentric weapon. The bolt or dart,' Alleyn said, and her attention snapped taut again. 'We are almost certain that it's the business end of an embroidery stiletto from the work-box in the drawing-room. We found the discarded handle. I wonder if by any chance you remember when you last noticed the stiletto. If, of course, you happen to have noticed it?'

'So this is it,' she thought. 'The revolver was nothing, it was a red herring. He's really got me here to talk about the stiletto.'

She said: 'I don't think the work-box was open when I was in the drawing-room before dinner. At any rate I didn't notice it.'

'I remember you told me that Lady Pastern showed you and Manx her *petit-point*. That *was* when you were all in the drawing-room before dinner, wasn't it? We found the *petit-point*, by the way, beside the work-box.'

'Therefore,' she thought, 'Aunt Cile or Ned or I might have taken the stiletto.' She repeated: 'I'm sure the box wasn't open.'

She had tried not to think beyond that one time, that one safe time about which she could quickly speak the truth.

'And after dinner?' Alleyn said casually.

She saw again the small gleaming tool drop from Miss Henderson's fingers when the report sounded in the ballroom. She saw Félicité automatically stoop and pick it up and a second later burst into tears and run furiously from the room. She heard her loud voice on the landing: 'I've got to speak to you,' and Rivera's: 'But certainly, if you wish it.'

'After dinner?' she repeated flatly.

'You were in the drawing-room then. Before the men came in. Perhaps Lady Pastern took up her work. Did you, at any time, see the box open or notice the stiletto?'

How quick was thought? As quick as people said? Was her hesitation fatally long? Here she moved, on the brink of speech. She could hear the irrevocable denial, and yet she had not made it. And suppose he had already spoken to Félicité about the stiletto? 'What am I looking like?' she thought in a panic. 'I'm looking like a liar already.'

'Can you remember?' he asked. So she had waited too long.

'I – don't think I can.' Now, she had said it. Somehow it wasn't quite as shaming to lie about remembering as about the fact itself. If things went wrong she could say afterwards: 'Yes, I remember, now, but I had forgotten. It had no significance for me, at the time.'

'You don't *think* you can.' She had nothing to say but he went on almost at once: 'Miss Wayne, you will please try to look squarely at this business. Will you try to pretend that it's an affair that you have read about and in which you have no personal concern. Not easy. But try. Suppose, then, a group of complete strangers was concerned in Rivera's death and suppose one of them, not knowing much about it, unable to see the factual wood for the emotional trees, was asked a question to which she knew the answer. Perhaps the answer seems to implicate her. Perhaps it seems to implicate someone she is fond of. She doesn't in the least know, it may be, what the implications are but she refuses to take the responsibility of telling the truth about one detail that may fit in with the whole truth. She won't, in fact, speak the truth if by doing so she's remotely responsible for bringing an extraordinarily callous murderer to book. So she lies. At once she finds that it doesn't end there. She must get other people to tell corroborative lies. She finds herself, in effect, whizzing down a dangerous slope with her car out of control, steering round some obstacles, crashing into others, doing irreparable damage and landing herself and possibly other innocent people in disaster. You think I'm overstating her case, perhaps. Believe me, I've seen it happen very often.'

'Why do you say all this to me?'

'I'll tell you why. You said just now that you didn't remember noticing the stiletto at any time after dinner. Before you made this statement you hesitated. Your hands closed on your gloves and suddenly twisted them. Your hands behaved with violence and yet they trembled. After you had spoken they continued to have a sort of independent life of their own. Your left hand kneaded the gloves and your right hand moved rather aimlessly across your neck and over your face. You blushed deeply and stared very fixedly at the top of my head. You presented me, in fact, with Example A from any handbook on behaviour of the lying witness. You were a glowing demonstration of the bad liar. And now, if all this is nonsense, you can tell counsel for the defence, how I bullied you and he will treat me to as nasty a time as his talents suggest when I'm called to give evidence. Now I come to think of it, he'll be very unpleasant indeed. So, however, will prosecuting counsel if you stick to your lapse of memory.'

Carlisle said angrily: 'My hands feel tike feet. I'm going to sit on them. You don't play fair.'

'My God!' Alleyn said, 'this isn't a game! It's murder.'

'He was atrocious. He was much nastier than anyone else in the house.'

'He may have been the nastiest job of work in Christendom. He was murdered and you're dealing with the police. This is not a threat but it's a warning: we've only just started: a great deal more evidence may come our way. You were not alone in the drawing-room after dinner.'

She thought: 'But Hendy won't tell and nor will Aunt Cile. But William came in some time, about then. Suppose he saw Fée on the landing? Suppose he noticed the stiletto in her hand? And then she remembered the next time she had seen Félicité. Félicité had been on top of the world, in ecstasy, because of the letter from GPF She had changed into her most gala dress and her eyes were shining. She had already discarded Rivera as easily as she had discarded all her previous young men. It was fantastic to tell lies for Félicité. There was something futile about this scene with Alleyn. She had made a fool of herself for nothing.

He had taken an envelope from a drawer on his desk and now opened it and shook its contents out before her. She saw a small shining object with a sharp end.

'Do you recognize it?' he asked.

'The stiletto.'

'You say that because we've been talking about the stiletto. It's not a bit like it really. Look again.'

She leant over it. 'Why,' she said, 'it's a – pencil.'

'Do you know whose pencil?'

She hesitated. 'I think it's Hendy's. She wears it on a chain like an old-fashioned charm. She always wears it. She was hunting for it on the landing this morning.'

'This is it. Here are her initials. PXH. Very tiny. You almost need a magnifying glass. Like the initials you saw on the revolver. The ring at the end was probably softish silver and the gap in it may have opened with the weight of the pencil. I found the pencil in the work-box. Does Miss Henderson ever use Lady Pastern's work-box?'

This at least was plain sailing. 'Yes. She tidies it very often for Aunt Cile.' And immediately Carlisle thought: 'I'm no good at this. Here it comes again.'

'Was she tidying the box last night? After dinner?'

'Yes,' Carlisle said flatly. 'Oh, yes. Yes.'

'Did you notice, particularly? When exactly was it?'

'Before the men came in. Well, only Ned came in actually, Uncle George and the other two were in the ballroom.'

'Lord Pastern and Bellairs were at this time in the ballroom and Rivera and Manx in the dining-room. According to the time-table.' He opened a file on his desk.

'I only know that Fée had gone when Ned came in.'

'She had joined Rivera in the study by then. But to return to this incident in the drawing-room. Can you describe the scene with the work-box? What were you talking about?'

Félicité had been defending Rivera. She had been on edge in one of her moods. Carlisle had thought: 'She's *had* Rivera but she won't own up.' And Hendy, listening, had moved her fingers about inside the work-box. There was the stiletto in Hendy's fingers and, dangling from her neck, the pencil on its chain.

'They were talking about Rivera. Félicité considered he'd been snubbed a bit and was cross about it.'

'At about this time Lord Pastern must have fired off his gun in the ballroom,' Alleyn muttered. He had spread the time-table out on his desk. He glanced up at her. His glance, she noticed, was never vague or indirect, as other people's might be. It had the effect of immediately collecting your attention. 'Do you remember that?' he asked.

'Oh, yes.'

'It must have startled you, surely?'

What were her hands doing now? She was holding the side of her neck again.

'How did you all react to what must have been an infernal racket? What for instance did Miss Henderson do? Do you remember?'

Her lips parted drily. She closed them again, pressing them together.

'I think you do remember,' he said. 'What did she do?'

Carlisle said loudly: 'She let the lid of the box drop. Perhaps the pencil was caught and pulled off the chain.'

'Was anything in her hands?'

'The stiletto,' she said, feeling the words grind out.

'Good. And then?'

'She dropped it.'

Perhaps that would satisfy him. It fell to the carpet. Anyone might have picked it up. Anyone, she thought desperately. Perhaps he will think a servant might have picked it up. Or even Breezy Bellairs, much later.

'Did Miss Henderson pick it up?'

'No.'

'Did anyone?'

She said nothing.

'You? Lady Pastern? No. Miss de Suze?'

She said nothing.

'And a little while afterwards, a very little while, she went out of the room. Because it was immediately after the report that William saw her go into the study with Rivera. He noticed that she had something shiny in her hand.'

'She didn't even know she had it. She picked it up automatically. I expect she just put it down in the study and forgot all about it.'

'We found the ivory handle there,' Alleyn said, and Fox made a slight gratified sound in his throat.

'But you mustn't think there was any significance in all this.'

'We're glad to know how and when the stiletto got into the study, at least.'

'Yes,' she said. 'I suppose so. Yes.'

Someone tapped on the door. The bareheaded constable came in with a package and an envelope. He laid them on the desk. 'From Captain Entwhistle, sir. You asked to have them as soon as they came in.'

He went out without looking at Carlisle.

'Oh, yes,' Alleyn said. 'The report on the revolver, Fox. Good. Miss Wayne, before you go, I'll ask you to have a look at the revolver. It'll be one more identification check.'

She waited while Inspector Fox came out from behind his desk and unwrapped the parcel. It contained two separate packages. She knew the smaller one must be the dart and wondered if Rivera's blood was still encrusted on the stiletto. Fox opened the larger package and came to her with the revolver.

'Will you look at it?' Alleyn said. 'You may handle it. I would like your formal identification.'

Carlisle turned the heavy revolver in her hands. There was a strong light in the room. She bent her head and they waited. She looked up, bewildered. Alleyn gave her his pocket lens. There was a long silence.

'Well, Miss Wayne?'

'But. . . But it's extraordinary. I can't identify it. There are no initials. This isn't the same revolver.'

CHAPTER 10

The Revolver, the Stiletto and his Lordship

'And what,' Alleyn asked when Carlisle had left them, 'is the betting on the favourite now, Br'er Fox?'

'By gum,' Fox said, 'you always tell us that when a homicide case is full of fancy touches, it's not going to give much trouble. Do you stick to that, sir?'

'I'll be surprised if this turns out to be the exception, but I must say it looks like it at the moment. However, the latest development does at least cast another ray of light on your playmate. Do you remember how the old devil turned the gun over when we first let him see it at the Metronome? D'you remember how he squinted through the lens at the butt? And I told you how he took another look at it in the study and then had an attack of the dry grins and when I asked him what he expected to see, had the infernal nerve to come back at me with: "Hoity-toity" – yes "hoity-toity" – would-n't you like to know!'

'Ugh!'

'He'd realized all along, of course, that this wasn't the weapon he loaded in the study and took down to the Metronome. Yes,' Alleyn added as Fox opened his mouth, 'and don't forget he showed Skelton the gun a few minutes before it was fired. Miss Wayne says he pointed out the initials to Skelton.'

'*That* looks suspicious in itself,' Fox said instantly. 'Why go to the trouble of pointing out initials to two people? He was getting something fixed up for himself. So he could turn round and say: "That's not the gun I fired." '

'Then why didn't he say so at once?'

'Gawd knows.'

'If you ask me he was sitting pretty, watching us make fools of ourselves.'

Fox jabbed his finger at the revolver. 'If this isn't the original weapon,' he demanded, 'what the hell is it? It's the one this projectile-dart-bolt or what-have-you was fired from because it's got the scratches in the barrel. That means someone had this second gun all ready loaded with the dart and ammunition and substituted it for the original weapon. Here! What's the report say, Mr Alleyn?'

Alleyn was reading the report. 'Entwhistle,' he said, 'has had a ballistic orgy over the thing. The scratches could have been made by the brilliants in the parasol clip. In his opinion they were so made. He's sending photo-micrographs to prove it. He's fired the bolt – let's stick to calling this hybrid a bolt, shall we? – from another gun with an identical bore and it is "somewhat similarly scratched," which is a vile phrase. He pointed out that wavering, irregular scars were made when the bolt was shoved up the barrel. The spring-clip was pressed back with the thumb, while it was being inserted and then sprang out once it was inside the barrel, thus preventing the bolt from falling out if the weapon was pointed downwards. The bolt was turned slightly as it was shoved home. The second scar was made by the ejection of the bolt, the clip retaining its pressure while being expelled. He says that the scars in the revolver we submitted don't extend quite as deep up the barrel as those made by the bolt which he fired from his own gun, but he considers that they were made by the same kind of procedure and the same bolt. At a distance of four feet, the projectile shoots true. Over long distances there are "progressive divergences", caused by the weight of the clip on one side or by air-resistance. Entwhistle says he's very puzzled by the fouling from the bore, which is quite unlike anything in his experience. He removed it and sent it along for analysis. The analyst finds that the fouling consists of particles of carbon and of various hydro-carbons including members of the paraffin series, apparently condensed from vapour.'

'Funny.'

'That's all.'

'All right,' Fox said heavily. 'All right. That looks fair enough. The bolt that plugged Rivera *was* shot out of this weapon. This weapon is not the one his lordship showed Miss Wayne and Syd Skelton. But unless you entertain the idea of somebody shooting off another gun at the same instant, this is the one that killed Rivera. You accept that, sir?'

'I'll take it as a working premise. With reservations and remembering our conversation in the car.'

'All right. Well, after Skelton examined the gun with the initials, did his lordship get a chance to substitute this one and fire it off? Could he have had this one on him all the time?'

'Hobnobbing, cheek by jowl with a dozen or so people at close quarters? I should say definitely not. And, he didn't know Skelton would ask to see the gun. And what did he do with the gun afterwards? We searched him, remember.'

'Planted it? Anyway, where is it?'

'Somewhere at the Metronome if we're on the right track and we've searched the Metronome. But go on.'

'Well, sir, if his lordship didn't change the gun who did?'

'His stepdaughter could have done it. Or any other member of his party. They were close to the sombrero remember. They got up to dance and moved round between the table and the edge of the dais. Lady Pastern was alone at the table for some time. I didn't see her move but I wasn't watching her, of course. All the ladies had largish evening bags. The catch in that theory, Br'er Fox, is that they wouldn't have known they were going to be within reach of the sombrero and it's odds on they didn't know he was going to put his perishing gun under his sombrero anyway.'

Fox bit at his short grizzled moustache, planted the palms of his hands on his knees and appeared to go into a sort of trance. He interrupted it to mutter: 'Skelton, now. Syd Skelton. Could Syd Skelton have worked the substitution? You're going to remind me they were all watching him, but were they watching all that closely? Syd Skelton.'

'Go on, Fox.'

'Syd Skelton's on his own, in a manner of speaking. He left the band platform before his lordship came on for his turn. Syd walked out. Suppose he had substituted the gun for the other with the initials? Suppose he walked right out and dropped the other one down the first grating he came to? Syd knew he was going to get the chance, didn't he?'

'How, when and where did he convert the bit of parasol shaft and stiletto into the bolt and put it up the barrel of the second revolver? Where did he get his ammunition? And when did he get the gun? *He* wasn't at Duke's Gate.'

'Yes,' Fox said heavily, 'that's awkward. I wonder if you could get round that one. Well, leave it for the time being. Who else have we got? Breezy. From the substitution angle, can we do anything about Breezy?'

'He didn't get alongside Pastern, on either of their statements, from the time Skelton looked at the gun until after Rivera was killed. They were alone together in the bandroom before Breezy made his entrance but Pastern, with his usual passionate industry in clearing other people, says Breezy didn't go near him. And Pastern had his gun in his hip pocket, remember.'

Fox returned to his trance.

'I think,' Alleyn said, 'it's going to be one of those affairs where the whittling away of impossibilities leaves one face-to-face with a mere improbability which, as you would say, "faute de mieux," one is forced to accept. And I think, so far Fox, we haven't found my improbable notion an impossibility. At least it has the virtue of putting the fancy touches in a more credible light.'

'We'll never make a case of it, I reckon, if it does turn out to be the answer.'

'And we'll never make a case of it if we pull in his lordship and base the charge on the assumption that he substituted this gun for the one he loaded and says he fired. Skelton's put up by the defence and swears he examined the thing at his own request and saw the initials and that this is not the same weapon. Counsel points out that three minutes later Lord Pastern goes on for his turn.'

Fox snarled quietly to himself and presently broke out. 'We call this blasted thing a bolt. Be damned if I don't think we'll get round to calling it a dart. Be damned if I'm not beginning to wonder if it was used like one. Thrown at the chap from close by. After all it's not impossible.'

'Who by? Breezy?'

'No,' Fox said slowly. 'No. Not Breezy. His lordship cleared Breezy in advance by searching him. Would you swear Breezy didn't pick anything up from anywhere after he came out to conduct?'

'I believe I would. He walked rapidly through the open door and down an alley-way between the musicians. He stood in a spotlight a good six feet or more away from anything, conducting like a great jerking jellyfish. They all say he couldn't have picked anything up after Pastern searched him, and in any case I would certainly swear he didn't put his hands near his pockets and that up to the time Rivera fell he was conducting with both hands and that none of his extraordinary antics in the least resembled dart-throwing. I was watching him. They rather fascinated me, those antics. And if you want any more, Br'er Fox, Rivera had his back turned to Breezy when he fell.'

'All right. His lordship then. His lordship was facing Rivera. Close to him. *Blast.* Unless he's ambidextrous, how'd he fire off a gun and throw a dart all in a split second? This is getting me nowhere. Who else, then?'

'Do you fancy Lady Pastern as a dart queen?'

Fox chuckled. 'That *would* be the day, sir, wouldn't it? But how about Mr Manx? We've got a motive for Manx. Rivera had proof that Manx wrote these sissy articles in *Harmony*. Manx doesn't want that known. Blackmail,' said Fox without much conviction.

'Foxkin,' Alleyn said, 'let there be a truce to these barren speculations. May I remind you that up to the time he fell Rivera was raising hell with a piano accordion?'

Fox said, after another long pause: 'You know I like this case. It's got something. Yes. And may I remind *you*, sir, that he wasn't meant to fall. None of them expected him to fall. Therefore he fell because somebody planted a bloody little steel embroidery gadget on a parasol handle in his heart before he fell. So where, if you don't object to the inquiry, Mr Alleyn, do we go from here?'

'I think,' Alleyn said, 'that you institute a search for the missing gun and I pay a call on Miss Petronella Xantippe Henderson.' He got up and fetched his hat. 'And I think, moreover,' he added, 'that we've been making a couple of perishing fools of ourselves.'

'About the dart?' Fox demanded. 'Or the gun?'

'About *Harmony*. Think this one over while I call on Miss Henderson and then tell me what you make of it.'

Five minutes later he went out, leaving Fox in a concentrated trance.

II

Miss Henderson received him in her room. It had the curiously sep-arate, not quite congenial air that seems to be the characteristic of sitting-rooms that are permanently occupied by solitary women in other people's houses. There were photographs: of Félicité, as a child, as a schoolgirl and in her presentation dress; one intimidating portrait of Lady Pastern and one, enlarged, it would seem, from a snapshot, of Lord Pastern in knickerbockers and shooting boots with a gun under his arm, a spaniel at his heels, a large house at his back and an expression of impertinence on his face. Above the desk hung a group of women-undergraduates clad in the tube-like brevity of the nineteen-twenties. A portion of Lady Margaret Hall loomed in the background.

Miss Henderson was dressed with scrupulous neatness, in a dark suit that faintly resembled a uniform or habit. She received Alleyn with perfect composure. He looked at her hair, greyish, quietly fashionable in its controlled grooming, at her eyes, which were pale, and at her mouth, which was unexpectedly full.

'Well, Miss Henderson,' he said, 'I wonder if you will be able to throw any light on this very obscure business.'

'I'm afraid it's most unlikely,' she said tranquilly.

'You never know. There's one point, at least, where I hope you will help us. You were present at last night's party in this house, both before and after dinner, and you were in the drawing-room when Lord Pastern, with the help of all the people concerned, worked out and wrote down the time-table which he afterwards gave to me.'

'Yes,' she agreed, after he had waited for a second or two.

'Would you say that as far as your personal observations and recollections cover them, the movements set down in the time-table are accurate?'

'Oh, yes,' she said at once, 'I think so. But of course, they don't go very far – my recollections. I was the last to arrive in the drawing-room, you know, before dinner, and the first to leave after dinner.'

'Not quite the first, according to the time-table, surely?'

She drew her brows together as if perturbed at the suggestion of inaccuracy. 'Not?' she said.

'The time-table puts Miss de Suze's exit from the drawing-room a second or two before yours.'

'How stupid of me. Félicité did go out first but I followed almost at once. I forgot for the moment.'

'You were all agreed on this point, last night, when Lord Pastern compiled his time-table?'

'Yes. Perfectly.'

'Do you remember that just before this there was a great rumpus in the ballroom? It startled you and you dropped a little stiletto on the carpet. You were tidying Lady Pastern's work-box at the time. Do you remember?'

He had thought at first that she used no more make-up than a little powder but he saw now that the faint warmth of her cheeks was artificial. The colour became isolated as the skin beneath and about it bleached. Her voice was quite even and clear.

'It was certainly rather an alarming noise,' she said.

'Do you remember, too, that Miss de Suze picked up the stiletto? I expect she meant to return it to you or to the box but she was rather put out just then. She was annoyed, wasn't she, by the, as she considered, uncordial reception given to her fiancé?'

'He was not her fiancé. They were not engaged.'

'Not officially, I know.'

'Not unofficially. There was no engagement.'

'I see. In any case, do you remember that instead of replacing the stiletto, she still had it in her hand when, a moment later, she left the room?'

'I'm afraid I didn't notice.'

'What did you do?'

'Do?'

'At that moment? You had been tidying the box. It was exquisitely neat when we found it this morning. Was it on your knees? The table was a little too far from your chair for you to have used it, I think.'

'Then,' she said, with her first hint of impatience, 'the box was on my knees.'

'So that was how the miniature silver pencil you wear on a chain came to be in the box?'

Her hands went to the bosom of her dress, fingering it.

'Yes. I suppose so. Yes. I didn't realize . . . was that where it was?'

'Perhaps you dropped the lid and caught the pencil, dragging it off the chain.'

'Yes,' she repeated. 'Yes. I suppose so. Yes, I remember I did do that.'

'Then why did you hunt for it this morning on the landing?'

'I had forgotten about catching it in the box,' she said rapidly.

'Not,' Alleyn murmured apologetically, 'a frightfully good memory.'

'These are trivial things that you ask me to remember. In this house we are none of us at the moment concerned with trivial things.'

'Are you not? Then, I suggest that you searched the landing, not for your trinket, which you say was a trivial thing, but for something that you knew could not be in the work-box because you had seen Miss de Suze take it out with her when she left the drawing-room in a rage. The needlework stiletto.'

'But Inspector Alleyn, I told you I didn't notice anything of the sort.'

'Then what were you looking for?'

'You have apparently been told. My pencil.'

'A trivial thing but your own. Here it is.'

He opened his hand, showed her the pencil. She made no movement and he dropped it in her lap. 'You don't seem to me,' he remarked casually, 'to be an unobservant woman.'

'If that's a compliment,' she said, 'thank you.'

'Did you see Miss de Suze again, after she left the drawing-room with the stiletto in her hand and after she had quarrelled with Rivera when they were alone together in the study?'

'Why do you say they quarrelled?'

'I have it on pretty good authority.'

'Carlisle?' she said sharply.

'No. But if you cross-examine a policeman about this sort of job, you know, he's not likely to be very communicative.'

'One of the servants, I suppose,' she said, dismissing it and him without emphasis. He asked her again if she had seen Félicité later that evening and after watching him for a moment she said that she had. Félicité had come to this room and had been in the happiest possible mood. 'Excited?' he suggested, and she replied that Félicité had been pleasurably excited. She was glad to be going out with her cousin, Edward Manx, to whom she was attached, and was looking forward to the performance at the Metronome.

'After this encounter you went to Lady Pastern's room, didn't you? Lady Pastern's maid was with her. She was dismissed, but not before she had heard you say that Miss de Suze was very much excited and that you wanted to have a word with her mother about this.'

'Again, the servants.'

'Anybody,' Alleyn said, 'who is prepared to speak the truth. A man has been murdered.'

'I have spoken nothing but the truth.' Her lips trembled and she pressed them together.

'Good. Let's get on with it then, shall we?'

'There's nothing at all that I can tell you. Nothing at all.'

'But at least you can tell me about the family. You understand, don't you, that my job, at the moment, is not so much finding the guilty person as clearing persons who may have been associated with Rivera but are innocent of his murder. That may, indeed it does, take in certain members of this household. It takes in the inter-communications of the household, the detailed as well as the general set-up. Now, in your position . . . '

'My position!' she muttered, with a sort of repressed contempt. Almost inaudibly she added: 'What do you know of my position?'

Alleyn said pleasantly: 'I've heard you're called the Controller of the Household.' She didn't answer and he went on: 'In any case it has been a long association and I suppose, in any ways, an intimate one. With Miss de Suze, for instance. You have brought her up, really, haven't you?'

'Why do you keep speaking about Félicité? This has nothing to do with Félicité.' She got up, and stood with her back towards him, changing the position of an ornament on the mantelpiece. He could see her carefully kept and very white hand steady itself on the edge of the shelf. 'I'm afraid I'm not behaving very well, am I?' she murmured. 'But I find your insistence rather trying.'

'Is that because, at the moment, it's directed at Miss de Suze and the stiletto?'

'Naturally, I'm uneasy. It's disturbing to feel that she will be in the smallest degree involved.' She leant her head against her hand.

From where he stood, behind her, she looked like a woman who had come to rest for a moment and fallen into an idle speculation. Her voice came to him remotely from beyond her stooped shoulders as if her mouth was against her hand. 'I suppose she simply left it in the study. She didn't even realize she had it in her hand. It was not in her hand when she came upstairs. It had no importance for her at all.' She turned to face him. 'I shall tell you something,' she said. 'I don't want to. I'd made up my mind I'd have no hand in this. It's distasteful to me. But I see now that I must tell you.'

'Right.'

'It's this. Before dinner last night, and during dinner, I had opportunity to watch those – those two men.'

'Rivera and Bellairs?'

'Yes. They were extraordinary creatures and I suppose in a sort of way I was interested.'

'Naturally. In Rivera at all events.'

'I don't know what servants' gossip you have been listening to, Inspector Alleyn.'

'Miss Henderson, I've heard enough from Miss de Suze herself to tell me that there was an understanding between them.'

'I watched those two men,' she said exactly as if he hadn't spoken. 'And I saw at once there was bad blood between them. They looked at each other – I can't describe it – with enmity. They were both, of course, incredibly common and blatant. They scarcely spoke to each other but during dinner, over and over again, I saw the other one, the conductor, eyeing him. He talked a great deal to Félicité and to Lord Pastern but he listened to . . . '

'To Rivera?' Alleyn prompted. She seemed to be incapable of pronouncing his name.

'Yes. He listened to him as if he resented every word he spoke. That would have been natural enough from any of us.'

'Was Rivera so offensive?'

An expression of eagerness appeared on her face. Here was something, at last, about which she was ready to speak.

'Offensive?' she said. 'He was beyond everything. He sat next to Carlisle and even she was nonplussed. Evidently she attracted him. It was perfectly revolting.'

Alleyn thought distastefully: 'Now what's behind all this? Resentment? At Carlisle rather than Félicité attracting the atrocious Rivera? Or righteous indignation? Or what?'

She raised her head. Her arm still rested on the mantelpiece and she had stretched out her hand to a framed photograph of Félicité in presentation dress. He moved slightly and saw that her eyes were fixed on the photograph. Félicité's eyes, under her triple plumage, stared back with the glazed distaste (so suggestive of the unwitting influence of Mr John Gielgud) that characterizes the modish photograph. Miss Henderson began to speak again and it was as if she addressed herself to the photograph. 'Of course, Félicité didn't mind in the least. It was nothing to her. A relief, no doubt. Anything rather than suffer his odious attentions. But it was clear to me that the other creature and he had quarrelled. It was quite obvious.'

'But if they hardly spoke to each other how could . . . '

'I've told you. It was the way the other person, Bellairs, looked at him. He watched him perpetually.'

Alleyn now stood before her. They made a formal conversation piece with the length of the mantelpiece between them. He said: 'Miss Henderson, who was beside you at the dinner table?'

'I sat next to Lord Pastern. On his left.'

'And on your left?'

She made a fastidious movement with her shoulders. 'Mr Bellairs.'

'Do you remember what he talked to you about?'

Her mouth twisted. 'I don't remember that he spoke to me at all,' she said. 'He had evidently realized that I was a person of no importance. He devoted himself to Félicité who was on his other side. He gave me his shoulder.'

Her voice faded out almost before she had uttered the last word as if, too late, she had tried to stop herself.

'If he gave you his shoulder,' Alleyn said, 'how did it come about that you could see this inimical stare of his?'

The photograph of Félicité crashed on the hearth. Miss Henderson cried out and knelt. 'How clumsy of me,' she whispered.

'Let me do it. You may cut your fingers.'

'No,' she said sharply, 'don't touch it.'

She began to pick up the slivers of glass from the frame and drop them in the grate. 'There's a looking-glass on the wall of the dining-room,' she said. 'I could see him in that.' And in a flat voice that had lost all its urgency she repeated. 'He watched him perpetually.'

'Yes,' Alleyn said. 'I remember the looking-glass. I accept that.'

'Thank you,' she said ironically.

'One more question. Did you go into the ballroom at any time after dinner?'

She looked up at him warily and after a moment said: 'I believe I did. Yes. I did.'

'When?'

'Félicité had lost her cigarette-case. It was when they were changing and she called out from her room. She had been in the ballroom during the afternoon and thought she might have left it there.'

'Had she done so?'

'Yes. It was on the piano. Under some music.'

'What else was on the piano?'

'A bundle of parasols.'

'Anything else?'

'No,' she said. 'Nothing.'

'Or on the chairs or floor?'

'Nothing.'

'Are you sure?'

'Perfectly sure,' she said, and dropped a piece of glass with a little tinkle in the grate.

'Well,' Alleyn said, 'if I can't help you, perhaps I'd better take myself off.'

She seemed to examine the photograph. She peered at it as if to make certain there were no flaws or scratches on Félicité's image. 'Very well,' she said, and stood up, holding the face of the photograph against her flattish chest. 'I'm sorry if I haven't told you the kind of things you want to be told. The truth is so seldom what one really wants to hear, is it? But perhaps you don't think I have told you the truth.'

'I think I am nearer to it than I was before I visited you.'

He left her, with the broken photograph still pressed against the bosom of her dark suit. On the landing he encountered Hortense. Her ladyship, Hortense said, smiling knowledgeably at him, would be glad to see him before he left. She was in her boudoir.

III

It was a small, delicately appointed room on the same floor. Lady Pastern rose from her desk, a pretty Empire affair, as he came in. She was firmly encased in her morning-dress. Her hair was rigid, her hands ringed. A thin film of make-up had been carefully spread over the folds and shadows of her face. She looked ghastly but completely in order.

'It is so good of you to spare me a moment,' she said, and held out her hand. This was unexpected. Evidently she considered that her change of manner required an explanation, and without wasting time, she let him have it.

'I did not realize last night,' she said concisely, 'that you must be the younger son of an old friend of my father's. You are Sir George Alleyn's son, are you not?'

Alleyn bowed. This, he thought, is going to be tiresome.

'Your father,' she said, 'was a frequent visitor at my parents' house in the Faubourg St Germaine. He was, in those days, an attaché, I think, at your Embassy in Paris.' Her voice faded and an extraordinary look came over her face. He was unable to interpret it.

'What is it, Lady Pastern?' he asked.

'Nothing. I was reminded for a moment, of a former conversation. We were speaking of your father. I remember that he and your mother called upon one occasion, bringing their two boys with them. Perhaps you do not recollect the visit.'

'It is extremely kind of you to do so.'

'I had understood that you were to be entered in the British Diplomatic Service.'

'I was entirely unsuited for it, I'm afraid.'

'Of course,' she said, with a sort of creaking graciousness, 'young men after the first war began to find their vocation in unconventional fields. One understands and accepts these changes, doesn't one?'

'Since I am here as a policeman,' Alleyn said politely, 'I hope so.'

Lady Pastern examined him with that complete lack of reticence which is often the characteristic of royal personages. It occurred to him that she herself would also have shaped up well, in an intimidating way, as a policewoman.

'It is a relief to me,' she announced, after a pause, 'that we are in your hands. You will appreciate my difficulties. It will make an enormous difference.'

Alleyn was familiar enough with this point of view, and detested it. He thought it advisable, however, to say nothing. Lady Pastern, erecting her bust and settling her shoulders, continued:

'I need not remind you of my husband's eccentricities. They are public property. You have seen for yourself to what lengths of imbecility he will go. I can only assure you that though he may be, and indeed is, criminally stupid, he is perfectly incapable of crime as the word is understood in the profession you have elected to follow. He is not, in a word, a potential murderer. Or,' she added, apparently as an afterthought, 'an actual one. Of that you may be assured.' She looked affably at Alleyn. Evidently, he thought, she had been a dark woman. There was a tinge of sable in her hair. Her skin was sallow and he thought she probably used something to deal with a darkness of the upper lip. It was odd that she should have such pale eyes. 'I cannot blame you,' she said, as he was still silent, 'if you suspect my husband. He has done everything to invite suspicion. In this instance, however, I am perfectly satisfied that he is guiltless.'

'We shall be glad to find proof of his innocence,' Alleyn said.

Lady Pastern closed one hand over the other. 'Usually,' she said, 'I comprehend entirely his motives. But entirely. On this occasion, however, I find myself somewhat at a loss. It is obvious to me that he develops some scheme. But what? Yes: I confess myself at a loss. I merely warn you, Mr Alleyn, that to suspect my husband of this crime is to court acute embarrassment. You will gratify his unquenchable passion for self dramatization. He prepares a denouement.'

Alleyn took a quick decision. 'It's possible,' he said, 'that we've anticipated him there.'

'Indeed?' she said quickly. 'I'm glad to hear it.'

'It appears that the revolver produced last night was not the one Lord Pastern loaded and took to the platform. I think he knows this. Apparently it amuses him to say nothing.'

'Ah!' She breathed out a sound of immense satisfaction. 'As I thought. It amuses him. Perfectly! And his innocence is established, no doubt?'

Alleyn said carefully: 'If the revolver produced is the one he fired, and the scars in the barrel suggest that it is, then a very good case could be made out on the lines of substitution.'

'I'm afraid I do not understand. A good case?'

'To the effect that Lord Pastern's revolver was replaced by this other one which was loaded with the bolt that killed Rivera. That Lord Pastern fired it in ignorance of the substitution.'

She had a habit of immobility but her stillness now declared itself as if until this moment she had been restless. The creased lids came down like hoods over her eyes. She seemed to look at her hands. 'Naturally,' she said, 'I make no attempt to understand these assuredly very difficult complexities. It is enough, little as he deserves to escape, that my husband clears himself.'

'Nevertheless,' Alleyn said, 'it remains necessary to discover the guilty person.' And he thought: 'Damn it, I'm beginning to talk like a French phrase book myself!'

'No doubt,' she said.

'And the guilty person, it seems obvious, was one of the party who dined here last night.'

Lady Pastern now closed her eyes completely. 'A most distressing possibility,' she murmured.

'Hands,' Alleyn thought, 'Carlisle Wayne's hands fingering her neck. Miss Henderson's hand jerking the photograph off the mantelpiece. Lady Pastern's hands closing upon each other like vices. Hands.'

'Furthermore,' he said, 'if the substitution theory is right, the time-field is narrowed considerably. Lord Pastern put his revolver under his sombrero on the edge of the band dais, you remember.'

'I made a point of disregarding him,' his wife said instantly. 'The whole affair was entirely distasteful to me. I did not notice and therefore I do *not* remember.'

'That's what he did, however. The possibilities as far as substitution goes are therefore limited to the people who were within easy reach of his sombrero.'

'No doubt you will question the waiters. The man was of the type which makes itself insufferable to servants.'

'By gum!' Alleyn thought, 'you're almost one up on me there, old girl!' But he said: 'We must remember that the substituted weapon was charged with a bolt and blank cartridges. The bolt was made out of a section of your parasol handle and its point of a stiletto from your work-box.' He paused. Her fingers were more closely inter-locked, but she didn't move or speak. 'And the blanks,' he added, 'were, it is almost certain, made by Lord Pastern and left in his study. The waiters are ruled out, I think.'

Her lips parted and closed again. She said: 'Am I, perhaps, being stupid? It seems to me that this theory of substitution may embrace a wider field. Why could the change of weapons not have been effected before my husband appeared? He was later than the others in appearing. So, for example, was Mr Bellairs, I believe that is the conductor's name.'

'Lord Pastern insists that neither Bellairs nor anyone else had an opportunity to get at his revolver, which he says he carried in his hip pocket, until he put it under the sombrero. I am persuaded that the change-over was effected after Lord Pastern made his entrance on the band dais and it's obvious that the substituted revolver must have been prepared by someone who had access to your parasol . . .'

'In the restaurant,' she interrupted quickly. 'Before the perform-ance. The parasols must have been within reach of all of them.'

' . . . and also access to the study in this house.'

'Why?'

'To get the stiletto which was carried there.'

She drew in her breath sharply. 'It may have been an entirely dif-ferent stiletto, I imagine.'

'Then why has this particular one disappeared from the study? Your daughter took it away from the drawing-room when she left for her interview in the study with Rivera. Do you remember that?'

He could have sworn that she did if only because she made no sign whatsoever. She couldn't achieve the start of astonishment or dismay which this statement should have produced if she hadn't been prepared for it.

'I remember nothing of the sort,' she said.

'That is what happened, however,' Alleyn said, 'and it appears that the steel was removed in the study since we found the ivory handle there.'

After a moment she lifted her chin and looked directly at him. 'It is with the greatest reluctance that I remind you of the presence of

Mr Bellairs in this house last night. I believe he was in the study with my husband after dinner. He had ample opportunity to return there.'

'According to Lord Pastern's time-table to which you have all sub-scribed he had from about a quarter-to-ten until half-past when, with the exception of Rivera and Mr Edward Manx, the rest of the party was upstairs. Mr Manx, I remember, said he was in the drawing-room during this period. He had, by the way, punched Rivera on the ear shortly beforehand.'

'Ah!' Lady Pastern breathed out her small ejaculation. She took a moment or two over digesting this information and Alleyn thought she was very well pleased with it. She said: 'Dear Edward is immensely impulsive.'

'He was annoyed, I gather, because Rivera had taken it upon him-self to kiss Miss Wayne.'

Alleyn would have given a lot to have Lady Pastern's thoughts floating above her head in clear letters, encased by a balloon as in one of Troy's little drawings, or to have heard them through spectral earphones. Were there four elements? Desire that Manx should be concerned only with Félicité? Gratification that Manx should have gone for Rivera? Resentment that Carlisle and not Félicité had been the cause? And fear: fear that Manx should be more gravely involved? Or some deeper fear?

'Unfortunately,' she said, 'he was a totally impossible person. It is, I feel certain, an affair of no significance. Dear Edward.'

Alleyn said abruptly: 'Do you ever see a magazine called *Harmony*?' and was startled by her response. Her eyes widened. She looked at him as if he had uttered some startling impropriety.

'Never!' she said loudly. 'Certainly not. Never.'

'There is a copy in the house. I thought perhaps . . .'

'The servants may take it. I believe it is the kind of thing they read.'

'The copy I saw was in the study. It has a correspondence page, conducted by someone who calls himself GPF.'

'I have not seen it. I do not concern myself with this journal.'

'Then,' Alleyn said, 'there's not much point in my asking if you suspected that Edward Manx was GPF.'

It was not possible for Lady Pastern to leap to her feet: her corsets alone prevented such an exercise. But, with formidable energy and comparative speed, she achieved a standing position. He saw with astonishment that her bosom heaved and that her neck and face were suffused with a brickish red.

'Impossible!' she panted. 'Never! I shall never believe it. An insufferable suggestion.'

'I don't quite see . . . ' Alleyn began, but she shouted him down.

'Outrageous! He is utterly incapable.' She shot a fusillade of adjectives at him. 'I cannot discuss such a fantasy. Incredible! Monstrous! Libellous! Libel of the grossest kind! Never!'

'But why do you say that? On account of the literary style?'

Lady Pastern's mouth opened and shut. She stared at him with an air of furious indecision. 'You may say so.' she said at last. 'You may put it in that way. Certainly. On account of style.'

'And yet you have never read the magazine?'

'Obviously it is a vulgar publication. I have seen the cover.'

'Let me tell you,' Alleyn suggested, 'how the theory has arisen. I really should like you to understand that it's not based on guesswork. May we sit down?'

She sat down abruptly. He saw, and was bewildered to see, that she was trembling. He told her about the letter Félicité had received and showed her the copy he had made. He reminded her of the white flower in Manx's coat and of Félicité's change of manner after she had seen it. He said that Félicité believed Manx to be GPF and had admitted as much. He said they had discovered original drafts of articles that had subsequently appeared on GPF's page and that these drafts had been typed on the machine in the study. He reminded her that Manx had stayed at Duke's Gate for three weeks. Throughout this recital she sat bolt upright, pressing her lips together and staring, inexplicably, at the top right-hand drawer of her desk. In some incomprehensible fashion he was dealing her blow after shrewd blow, but he kept on and finished the whole story. 'So you see, don't you,' he ended, 'that, at least, it's a probability?'

'Have you asked him?' she said pallidly. 'What does he say?'

'I have not asked him yet. I shall do so. Of course, the whole question of his identity with GPF may be irrelevant as far as this case is concerned.'

'Irrelevant!' she ejaculated, as if the suggestion was wildly insane. She was looking again at her desk. Every muscle of her face was controlled but tears now began to form in her eyes and trickle over her cheeks.

'I'm sorry,' Alleyn said, 'that you find this distressing.'

'It distresses me,' she said, 'because I find it is true. I am in some confusion of mind. If there is nothing more . . . '

He got up at once. 'There's nothing more,' he said. 'Goodbye, Lady Pastern.'

She recalled him before he reached the door. 'One moment.'

'Yes?'

'Let me assure you, Mr Alleyn,' she said, pressing her handker-chief against her cheek, 'that my foolishness is entirely unimportant. It is a personal matter. What you have told me is quite irrelevant to this affair. It is of no consequence whatever, in fact.' She drew in her breath with a sound that quivered between a sigh and a sob. 'As for the identity of the person who has perpetrated this outrage, I mean the murder, not the journalism, I am persuaded it was one of his own kind. Yes, certainly,' she said more vigorously, 'one of his own kind. You may rest assured of that.' And finding himself dismissed, he left her.

IV

As Alleyn approached the first landing on his way down he was sur-prised to hear the ballroom piano. It was being played somewhat unhandily and the strains were those of hotly syncopated music taken at a funeral pace. Detective-Sergeant Jimson was on duty on the landing. Alleyn jerked his head at the ballroom doors, which were ajar. 'Who's that playing?' he asked. 'Is it Lord Pastern? Who the devil opened that room?'

Jimson, looking embarrassed and scandalized, replied that he thought it must be Lord Pastern. His manner was so odd that Alleyn walked past him and pushed open the double doors.

Inspector Fox was discovered seated at the piano with his specta-cles on his nose. He was inclined forward tensely, and followed with concentration a sheet of music in manuscript. Facing him, across the piano, was Lord Pastern who, as Alleyn entered, beat angrily, but rhythmically, upon the lid and shouted: 'No, no, my good ass, not a bit like it. N'yah – *yo*. Bo bo bo. Again.' He looked up and saw Alleyn. 'Here!' he said, 'can you play?'

Fox rose without embarrassment and removed his spectacles.

'Where have you come from?' Alleyn demanded.

'I had a little matter to report, sir, and as you were engaged for the moment I've been waiting in here. His lordship was looking for someone to try over a piece he's composing but I'm afraid . . .'

'I'll have to get one of these women,' Lord Pastern cut in impatiently. 'Where's Fée? This chap's no good.'

'I haven't sat down to the piano since I was a lad,' said Fox mildly.

Lord Pastern made for the door but Alleyn intercepted him.

'One moment, sir,' he said.

'It's no good worryin' me with any more questions,' Lord Pastern snapped at him. 'I'm busy.'

'Unless you'd prefer to come to the Yard you'll answer this one, if you please. When did you first realize that the revolver we produced after Rivera was killed was not the one you loaded in the study and carried on to the band platform?'

Lord Pastern smiled at him. 'Nosed that out for yourselves, have you?' he remarked. 'Fascinatin', the way our police work.'

'I still want to know when you made this discovery.'

'About eight hours before you did.'

'As soon as you were shown the substitute and noticed there were no initials?'

'Who told you about initials? Here!' Lord Pastern said with some excitement, 'have you found my other gun?'

'Where do you suggest we look for it?'

'If I knew where it was, my good fathead, I'd have got it for meself. I value that gun, by God!'

'You handed over the weapon you fired at Rivera to Breezy Bellairs,' Fox said suddenly. 'Was it that one, my lord? The one with the initials? The one you loaded in this house? The one that's missing?'

Lord Pastern swore loudly. 'What d'you think I am?' he shouted. 'A bloody juggler? Of course it was.'

'And Bellairs walked straight into the office with you and I took it off him a few minutes later and it *wasn't* the same gun. That won't wash, my lord,' said Fox, 'if you'll excuse my saying so. It won't wash.'

'In that case,' Lord Pastern said rudely, 'you can put up with it dirty.' Alleyn made a slight, irritated sound and Lord Pastern instantly turned on him. 'What are *you* snufflin' about?' he demanded, and before Alleyn could answer he renewed his attack on Fox. 'Why don't you ask Breezy about it?' he said. 'I should have thought even *you'd* have got at Breezy.'

'Are you suggesting, my lord, that Bellairs might have worked the substitution after the murder was committed?'

'I'm not suggestin' anything.'

'In which case,' Fox continued imperturbably, 'perhaps you'll tell me how Rivera was killed?'

Lord Pastern gave a short bark of laughter. 'No, really!' he said, 'it's beyond belief how bone-headed you are.'

Fox said: 'May I press this point a little further, Mr Alleyn?'

From behind Lord Pastern, Alleyn returned Fox's inquiring glance with a dubious one. 'Certainly, Fox,' he said.

'I'd like to ask his lordship if he'd be prepared to swear on oath that the weapon he handed Bellairs after the fatality was the one that is missing.'

'Well, Lord Pastern,' Alleyn said, 'will you answer Mr Fox?'

'How many times am I to tell you I won't answer any of your tom-fool questions. I gave you a time-table, and that's all the help you get from me.'

For a moment the three men were silent; Fox by the piano, Alleyn near the door and Lord Pastern midway between them like a truculent Pekinese, an animal, it occurred to Alleyn, he closely resembled.

'Don't forget, my lord,' Fox said, 'that last night you stated yourself that anybody could have got at the revolver while it was under the sombrero. Anybody, you remarked; for all you'd have noticed.'

'What of it?' he said, bunching his cheeks.

'There's this about it, my lord. It's a tenable theory that one of the party at your own table could have substituted the second gun, loaded with the bolt, and that you could have fired it at Rivera, without knowing anything about the substitution.'

'That cat won't jump,' Lord Pastern said, 'and you know it. I didn't tell anybody I was going to put the gun under my sombrero. Not a soul.'

'Well, my lord,' Fox said, 'we can make inquiries about that.'

'You can inquire till you're blue in the face and much good may it do you.'

'Look here, my lord,' Fox burst out, 'do you *want* us to arrest you?'

'Not sure I don't. It'd be enough to make a cat laugh.' He thrust his hands in his trousers pockets, walked round Fox, eyeing him, and fetched up in front of Alleyn. 'Skelton,' he said, 'saw the gun. He handled it just before he went on and when he came out while I waited for my entrance he handled it again. While Breezy did the speech about me, it was.'

'Why did he handle it this second time?' Alleyn asked.

'I was a bit excited. Nervy work, hangin' about for your entrance. I was takin' a last look at it and I dropped it and he picked it up and squinted down the barrel in a damn-your-eyes supercilious sort of way. Professional jealousy.'

'Why didn't you mention this before, my lord?' Fox demanded, and was ignored. Lord Pastern grinned savagely at Alleyn. 'Well,' he said with gloating relish, 'what about this arrest? I'll come quietly.'

Alleyn said: 'You know I do wish that for once in a blue moon you'd behave yourself.'

For the first time, he thought, Lord Pastern was giving him his full attention. He was suddenly quiet and wary. He eyed Alleyn with something of the air of a small boy who is not sure if he can bluff his way out of a misdemeanour.

'You really are making the most infernal nuisance of yourself, sir,' Alleyn went on, 'and, if you will allow me, the most appalling ass of yourself into the bargain.'

'See here, Alleyn,' Lord Pastern said with a not entirely convincing return to his former truculence. 'I'm damned if I'll take this. I know what I'm up to.'

'Then have the grace to suppose we know what we're up to, too. After all, sir, you're not the only one to remember that Rivera played the piano accordion.'

For a moment Lord Pastern stood quite still with his jaw dropped and his eyebrows half-way up his forehead. He then said rapidly: 'I'm late. Goin' to m'club,' and incontinently bolted from the room.

CHAPTER 11

Episodes in Two Flats and an Office

'Well, Mr Alleyn,' said Fox, 'that settles it, in my mind. It's going to turn out the way you said. Cut loose the trimmings and you come to the – well the *corpus delicti* as you might say.'

They were sitting in a police car outside the house in Duke's Gate. Both of them looked past the driver, and through the windscreen, at a jaunty and briskly moving figure, its hat a little to one side and swinging its walking stick.

There he goes,' Fox said, 'as cocksure and perky as you please, and there goes our chap after him. Say what you like, Mr Alleyn, the art of trailing your man isn't what it was in the service. These young fellows think they signed on for the sole purpose of tearing about the place with the Flying Squad.' And having delivered himself of his customary grumble, Fox, still contemplating the diminishing figure of Lord Pastern, added: 'Where do we go from here, sir?'

'Before we go anywhere you'll be good enough to explain why your duties led you back to Duke's Gate and more particularly, to playing that old antic's boogie-woogie on the piano.'

Fox smiled in a stately manner. 'Well, sir,' he said, 'as to what brought me, it was a bit of stale information, and another bit that's not so stale. Skelton rang up after you left, to say he had inspected his lordship's revolver the second time and was sorry he hadn't mentioned it last night. He said that he and our Mr Eton-and-Oxford Detective-Sergeant Sallis got into a discussion about the *petit bourgeoisie* or something and it went out of his head. I thought it better

702

not to ring you at Duke's Gate. Extension wires all over the shop in that house. So, as it seemed to settle the question about which gun his lordship took on the platform with him, I thought I'd pop along and tell you.'

'And Pastern saved you the trouble?'

'Quite so. And as to the piano, there was his lordship saying he'd been inspired, so to speak, with a new composition and wanted someone to try it over. He was making a great to-do over the ballroom being sealed. Our chaps have finished in there so there seemed no harm in obliging him. I thought it might establish friendly relations,' Fox added sadly, 'but I can't say it did in the end. Shall we tell this chap where we're going, sir?'

Alleyn said: 'We'll call at the Metronome, then we'll have a look at Breezy and see how the poor swine's shaping up this morning. Then we'll have a brief snack, Br'er Fox, and when that's over it'll be time to visit GPF in his den. If he's there, blast him.'

'Ah, by the way,' Fox said, as they moved off, 'that's the other bit of information. Mr Bathgate rang the Yard and said he'd got hold of someone who writes regularly for this paper *Harmony* and it seems that Mr Friend is generally supposed to be in the office on the afternoon and evening of the last Sunday in the month, on account of the paper going to press the following week. This gentleman told Mr Bathgate that nobody on the regular staff except the editor ever sees Mr Friend. The story is he deals direct with the proprietors of the paper but popular opinion in Fleet Street reckons he owns the show himself. They reckon the secrecy business is nothing but a build-up.'

'Silly enough to be incredible,' Alleyn muttered. 'But we're knee-deep in imbecility. I suppose we can take it. All the same, I fancy we'll turn up a better reason for Mr Friend's elaborate incognito before this interminable Sunday is out.'

Fox said, with an air of quiet satisfaction: 'I fancy we shall, sir. Mr Bathgate's done quite a nice little job for us. It seems he pressed this friend of his a bit further and got him on to the subject of Mr Manx's special articles for the paper and it came out that Mr Manx is often in their office.'

'Discussing his special articles. Picking up his galley-sheets or whatever they do.'

'Better than that, Mr Alleyn. This gentleman told Mr Bathgate
that Mr Manx had been noticed coming out of GPF's room on several occasions, one of them being a Sunday afternoon.'

'Oh.'

'Fits, doesn't it?'

'Like a glove. Good for Bathgate. We'll ask him to meet us at the
Harmony offices. This being the last Sunday in the month, Br'er Fox,
we'll see what we can see. But first – the Metronome.'

II

When Carlisle left the Yard, it was with a feeling of astonishment
and aimless boredom. So it wasn't Uncle George's revolver after all.
So there had been an intricate muddle that someone would have to
unravel. Alleyn would unravel it and someone else would be arrested and she ought to be alarmed and agitated because of this.
Perhaps, in the hinterland of her emotions, alarm and agitation
were already established and waited to pounce, but in the meantime she was only drearily miserable and tired. She was pestered by
all sorts of minor considerations. The thought of returning to Duke's
Gate and trying to cope with the situation there was intolerable. It
wasn't so much the idea that Uncle George or Aunt Cile or Fée
might have murdered Carlos Rivera that Carlisle found appalling: it
was the prospect of their several personalities forcing themselves
upon her own; their demands upon her attention and courtesy.
She had a private misery, a galling unhappiness, and she wanted to
be alone with it.

While she walked irresolutely towards the nearest bus stop, she
remembered that not far from here, in a cul-de-sac called Costers
Row, was Edward Manx's flat. If she walked to Duke's Gate she
would pass the entry into this blind street. She was persuaded that
she did not want to see Edward, that an encounter would, indeed, be
unbearable; yet, aimlessly, she began to walk on. Church-going people returning home with an air of circumspection made a pattering
sound in the empty streets. Groups of sparrows flustered and pecked.
The day was mildly sunny. The Yard man, detailed to keep observation on Carlisle, threaded his way through a trickle of pedestrians and

recalled the Sunday dinners of his boyhood. Beef, he thought, Yorkshire pudding, gravy, and afterwards a heavy hour or so in the front room. Carlisle gave him no trouble at all but he was hungry.

He saw her hesitate at the corner of Costers Row and himself halted to light a cigarette. She glanced along the file of housefronts and then, at a more rapid pace, crossed the end of the row and continued on her way. At the same time a dark young man came out of a house six doors down Costers Row and descended the steps in time to catch a glimpse of her. He shouted: 'Lisle!' and waved his arm. She hurried on, and once past the corner, out of his sight, broke into a run. 'Hi Lisle!' he shouted. 'Lisle!' and loped after her. The Yard man watched him go by, turn the corner, and overtake her. She spun round at the touch of his hand on her arm and they stood face to face.

A third man who had come out of some doorway farther up the cul-de-sac walked briskly down the path on the same side as the Yard man. They greeted each other like old friends and shook hands. The Yard man offered cigarettes and lit a match. 'How's it going, Bob?' he said softly. 'That your bird?'

'That's him. Who's the lady?'

'Mine,' said the first, whose back was turned to Carlisle.

'Not bad,' his colleague muttered, glancing at her.

'I'd just as soon it was my dinner, though.'

'Argument?'

'Looks like it.'

'Keeping their voices down.'

Their movements were slight and casual: acquaintances pausing for a rather aimless chat.

'What's the betting?' said the first.

'They'll separate. I never have the luck.'

'You're wrong, though.'

'Going back to his place?'

'Looks like it.'

'I'll toss you for it.'

'OK.' The other pulled his clenched hand out of his pocket. 'Your squeak,' he said.

'Heads.'

'It's tails.'

'I never get the luck.'

'I'll ring in then and get something to eat. Relieve you in half an hour, Bob.'

They shook hands again heartily as Carlisle and Edward Manx, walking glumly towards them, turned into Costers Row.

Carlisle had seen Edward Manx out of the corner of her eye as she crossed the end of the cul-de-sac. Unreasoned panic took hold of her. She lengthened her stride, making a show of looking at her watch, and when he called her name, broke into a run. Her heart pounded and her mouth was dry. She had the sensation of a fugitive in a dream. She was the pursued and, since even in her sudden alarm she was confusedly aware of something in herself that frightened her, she was also the pursuer. This nightmarish conviction was intensified by the sound of his feet clattering after her and of his voice, completely familiar but angry, calling her to stop.

Her feet were leaden, he was overtaking her quite easily. Her anticipation of his seizing her from behind was so vivid that when his hand actually closed on her arm it was something of a relief. He jerked her round to face him and she was glad to feel angry.

'What the hell do you think you're doing?' he said breathlessly.

'That's my business,' she panted, and added defiantly: 'I'm late. I'll be late for lunch. Aunt Cile will be furious.'

'Don't be an ass, Lisle. You ran when you saw me. You heard me call out and you kept on running. What the devil d'you mean by it?'

His heavy eyebrows were drawn together and his lower lip jutted out.

'Please let me go, Ned,' she said. 'I really am late.'

'That's utterly childish and you know it. I'm getting to the bottom of this. Come back to the flat. I want to talk to you.'

'Aunt Cile . . . '

Oh, for God's sake! I'll ring Duke's Gate and say you're lunching here.'

'No.'

For a moment he looked furious. He still held her arm and his fingers bit into it, hurting her. Then he said more gently: 'You can't expect me to let a thing like this pass: it's a monstrous state of affairs. I must know what's gone wrong. Last night, after we got back from the Metronome, I could tell there was something. Please, Lisle. Don't let's stand here snarling at each other. Come back to the flat.'

'I'd rather not. Honestly. I know I'm behaving queerly.'

He had slipped the palm of his hand inside her arm, pressing it against him. His hand was gentler now but she couldn't escape it. He began to speak persuasively and she remembered how, even when they were children, she had never been able to resist his persuasiveness. 'You will, Lisle, won't you? Don't be queer, I can't bear all this peculiarity. Come along.'

She looked helplessly at the two men on the opposite corner, thinking vaguely that she had seen one of them before. 'I wish I knew him,' she thought, 'I wish I could stop and speak to him.'

They turned into Costers Row. 'There's some food in the flat. It's quite a nice flat. I want you to see it. We'll have lunch together, shan't we? I'm sorry I was churlish, Lisle.'

His key clicked in the lock of the blue door. They were in a small lobby. 'It's a basement flat,' he said, 'but not at all bad. There's even a garden. Down those stairs.'

'You go first,' she said. She actually wondered if that would give her a chance to bolt and if she would have the nerve to do it. He looked fixedly at her.

'I don't believe I trust you,' he said lightly. 'On you go.'

He followed close on her heels down the steep stairs and took her arm again as he reached past her and unlocked the second door.

'Here we are,' he said, pushing it open. He gave her a little shove forward.

It was a large, low-ceilinged room, white-washed and oak-beamed. French windows opened on a little yard with potted flowers and plane-trees in tubes. The furniture was modern: steel chairs with rubber-foam upholstery, a carefully planned desk, a divan bed with a scarlet cover. A rigorous still-life hung above the fireplace, the only picture in the room. The bookshelves looked as if they had been stocked completely from a Left Book shop. It was a scrupulously tidy room.

'The oaken beams are strict stockbroker's Tudor,' he was saying. 'Completely functionless, of course, and pretty revolting. Otherwise not so bad, do you think? Sit down while I find a drink.'

She sat on the divan and only half-listened to him. His belated pretence that, after all, this was a pleasant and casual encounter did nothing to reassure her. He was still angry. She took the drink he brought and found her hand was shaking so much she couldn't carry the glass to her lips. The drink spilled. She bent her head down and took a quick gulp at it, hoping this would steady her. She rubbed furtively with her handkerchief at the splashes on the cover and knew, without looking, that he watched her.

'Shall we go in, boots and all, or wait till after lunch?' he said.

'There's nothing to talk about. I'm sorry to be such an ass, but after all it was a bit of a night. I suppose murder doesn't suit me.'

'Oh, no,' he said, 'that won't do. You don't bolt like a rabbit at the sight of me because somebody killed a piano accordionist.' And after a long pause he added smoothly, 'Unless, by any chance, you think I killed him. Do you?'

'Don't be a dolt,' she said, and by some fortuitous mischance, an accident quite beyond her control and unrelated to any recognizable impulse, her answer sounded unconvincing and too violent. It was the last question she had expected from him.

'Well, at least I'm glad of that,' he said. He sat on the table near to her. She did not look up at him but straight before her at his left hand, lying easily across his knee. 'Come on,' he said, 'what have I done? There *is* something I've done. What is it?'

She thought: 'I'll have to tell him something: part of it. Not the real thing itself but the other bit that doesn't matter so much.' She began to search for an approach, a line to take, some kind of credible presentation, but she was deadly tired and she astonished herself by saying abruptly and loudly: 'I've found out about GPF.'

His hand moved swiftly out of her range of sight. She looked up expecting to be confronted by his anger or astonishment but he had turned aside, skewing round to put his glass down on the table behind him.

'Have you?' he said. 'That's awkward, isn't it?' He moved quickly away from her and across the room to a wall cupboard which he opened. With his back turned to her he said: 'Who told you? Did Cousin George?'

'No,' she said wearily surprised. 'No, I saw the letter.'

'Which letter?' he asked, groping in the cupboard.

'The one to Félicité.'

'Oh,' said Manx slowly. 'That one.' He turned round. He had a packet of cigarettes in his hand and came towards her holding it out.

She shook her head and he lit one himself with steady hands. 'How did you come to see it?' he said.

'It was lost. It – I – oh, what *does* it matter? The whole thing was perfectly clear. Need we go on?'

'I still don't see why this discovery should inspire you to spring like an athlete at the sight of me.'

'I don't think I know myself.'

'What were you doing last night?' he demanded suddenly. 'Where did you go after we got back to Duke's Gate? Why did you turn up again with Alleyn? What were you up to?'

It was impossible to tell him that Félicité had lost the letter. That would lead at once to his discovering that Alleyn had read it: worse than that, it would lead inevitably to the admittance, perhaps the discussion, of his new attitude towards Félicité. 'He might,' she thought, 'tell me, point-blank, that he is in love with Fee and I'm in no shape to jump that hurdle.'

So she said: 'It doesn't matter what I was up to. I can't tell you. In a way it would be a breach of confidence.'

'Was it something to do with this GPF business?' Manx said sharply, and after a pause: 'You haven't told anybody about this discovery, have you?'

She hadn't told Alleyn. He had found out for himself. Miserably she shook her head.

He stooped over her. 'You mustn't tell anybody, Lisle. That's important. You realize how important, don't you?'

Isolated sentences, of an indescribable archness, flashed up in her memory of that abominable page. 'You don't need to tell me that,' she said, looking away from his intent and frowning eyes, and then suddenly burst out: 'It's such ghastly stuff, Ned. That magazine. It's like one of our novelettes gone hay-wire. How you could!'

'My articles are all right,' he said, after a pause: 'So that's it, is it? You *are* a purist, aren't you?'

She clasped her hands together and fixed her gaze on them. 'I must tell you,' she said, 'that if, in some hellish muddled way, entirely beyond my comprehension, this GPF business has anything to do with Rivera's death – '

'Well?'

'I mean, if it's going to – I mean – '

'You mean that if Alleyn asks you point-blank about it, you'll tell him?'

'Yes,' she said.

'I see.'

Carlisle's head ached. She had been unable to face her breakfast and the drink he had given her had taken effect. Their confused antagonism, the sense of being trapped in this alien room, her personal misery: all these circumstances were joined in a haze of uncertainty. The whole scene had become unreal and unendurable. When he put his hands on her shoulders and said loudly: 'There's more to it than this. Come on, what is it?' she seemed to hear him from a great distance. His hands were bearing down hard. 'I *will* know,' he was saying.

At the far end of the room a telephone bell began to ring. She watched him go to it and take the receiver off. His voice changed its quality and became the easy friendly voice she had known for so long.

'Hallo? Hallo, Fée darling. I'm terribly sorry, I should have rung up. They kept Lisle for hours grilling her at the Yard. Yes: I ran into her and she asked me to telephone and say she was so late she'd try for a meal somewhere at hand, so I asked her to have one with me. Please tell Cousin Cecile it's entirely my fault and not hers: I promised to ring for her.' He looked at Carlisle over the telephone. 'She's perfectly all right,' he said. 'I'm looking after her.'

III

If any painter, a surrealist for choice, attempted to set the figure of a working detective officer against an appropriate and composite background, he would turn his attention to rooms overlaid with films of dust, to objects suspended in unaccustomed dinginess, to ash-trays and tablecloths, unemptied waste bins, tables littered with powder, dirty glasses, disordered chairs, stale food, and garments that retained an unfresh smell of disuse.

When Alleyn and Fox entered the Metronome at 12.30 on this Sunday morning, it smelt of Saturday night. The restaurant, serveries and kitchens had been cleaned, but the vestibule and offices were

untouched and upon them the aftermath of festivity lay like a thin
pall of dust. Three men in shirt sleeves greeted Alleyn with that tinge
of gloomy satisfaction which marks an unsuccessful search.

'No luck?' Alleyn said.

'No luck yet, sir.'

'There's the passage that runs through from the foyer and behind
the offices to the back premises,' said Fox. 'That's the way the
deceased must have gone to make his entrance from the far end of
the restaurant.'

'We've been along there, Mr Fox.'

'Plumbing?'

'Not yet, Mr Alleyn.'

'I'd try that next.' Alleyn pointed through the two open doors of
Caesar Bonn's office into the inner room. 'Begin there,' he said.

He went alone into the restaurant. The table he and Troy had sat
at was the second on the right. The chairs were turned up on its surface. He replaced one of them and seated himself. 'For twenty years,'
he thought, 'I have trained my memory and trained it rigorously.
This is the first time I have been my own witness in a case of this
sort. Am I any good or am I rotten?'

Sitting alone there, he recreated his scene, beginning with small
things: the white cloth, the objects on the table, Troy's long hand close
to his own and just within his orbit of vision. He waited until these
details were firm in his memory and then reached out a little farther.
At the next table, her back towards him, sat Félicité de Suze in her red
dress. She turned a white carnation in her fingers and looked sidelong
at the man beside her. He was between Alleyn and the lamp on their
table. His profile was rimmed with light. His head was turned towards
the band dais. On his right, more clearly visible, more brilliantly lit,
was Carlisle Wayne. In order to watch the performance she had
swung round with her back half-turned to the table. Her hair curved
back from her temples. There was a look of compassion and bewilderment in her face. Beyond Carlisle, with her back to the wall, a heavy
shape almost obscured by the others, sat Lady Pastern. As they moved
he could see in turn her stony coiffure, her important shoulders, the
rigid silhouette of her bust; but never her face.

Raised above them, close to them, a figure gestured wildly among
the tympani. This was a vivid picture because it was contained by a

pool of light. Lord Pastern's baldish head darted and bobbed. Metallic highlights flashed among his instruments. The spotlight shifted and there, in the centre of the stage, was Rivera, bent backwards, hugging his piano accordion to his chest. Eyes, teeth, and steel and mother-of-pearl ornament glittered. The arm of the metronome pointed fixedly at his chest. Behind, half-shadowed, a plump hand jerked up and down, beating the air with its miniature baton. A wide smile glistened in a moon face. Now Lord Pastern faced Rivera on the perimeter of the light pool. His revolver pointed at the contorted figure, flashed, and Rivera fell. Then the further shots and comic falls and then . . . In the deserted restaurant Alleyn brought his hands down sharply on the table. It had been then, and not until then, that the lights began their infernal blinking. They popped in and out down the length of the metronome and about its frame, in and out, red, green, blue, green, red. Then, and not until then had the arm swung away from the prostrate figure and, with the rest of that winking stuttering bedazzlement, gone into action.

Alleyn got up and mounted the bandstand. He stood on the spot where Rivera had fallen. The skeleton tower of the metronome framed him. The reverse side of this structure revealed its electrical equipment. He looked up at the pointer of the giant arm which was suspended directly above his head. It was a hollow steel or plastic casting studded with miniature lights, and for a moment reminded him fantastically of the jewelled dart. To the right of the bandroom door and hidden from the audience by the piano, a small switchboard was sunk in the wall. Happy Hart, they had told Alleyn, was in charge of the lights. From where he sat at the piano and from where he fell to the floor he could reach out to the switches. Alleyn did so, now, pulling down the one marked 'Motor'. A hidden whirring sound prefaced the first loud 'clack'. The giant downward-pointing arm swept semi-circularly across, back, across and back to its own ratchet-like accompaniment. He switched on the lights and stood for a moment, an incongruous figure, motionless at the core of his kaleidoscopic setting. The point of the arm, flashing its lights, swept within four inches of his head and away and back and away again. 'If you watched the damn' thing for long enough, I believe it'd mesmerize you,' he thought, and turned off the switches.

Back in the offices he found Mr Fox in severe control of two plumbers who were removing their jackets in the lavatory.

'If we can't find anything fishing with wires, Mr Alleyn,' Fox said, 'it'll be a case of taking down the whole job.'

'I don't hold out ecstatic hopes,' Alleyn said, 'but get on with it.'

One of the plumbers pulled the chain and contemplated the ensuing phenomena.

'Well?' said Fox.

'I wouldn't say she was a sweetly running job,' the plumber diagnosed, 'and yet again she *works* if you can understand me.' He raised a finger, and glanced at his mate.

'Trap-trouble?' ventured his mate.

'Ar.'

'We'll leave you to it,' Alleyn said, and withdrew Fox into the office. 'Fox,' he said, 'let's remind ourselves of the key pieces in this jig-saw atrocity. What are they?'

Fox said promptly: 'The set-up at Duke's Gate. The drug racket. *Harmony.* The substitution. The piano accordion. The nature of the weapon.'

'Add one more. The metronome was motionless when Rivera played. It started its blasted tick-tack stuff after he fell and after the other rounds had been fired.'

'I get you, sir. Yes,' said Fox, placidly, 'there's that too. Add the metronome.'

'Now, let's mug over the rest of the material and see where we are.'

Sitting in Caesar Bonn's stale office, they sorted, discarded, correlated and dissociated the fragments of the case. Their voices droned on to the intermittent accompaniment of plumbers' aquatics. After twenty minutes Fox shut his note-book, removed his spectacles and looked steadily at his superior officer.

'It amounts to this,' he said. 'Setting aside a handful of insignificant details, we're short of only one piece.' He poised his hand, palm down, over the table. 'If we can lay hold of that and if, when we've got it, it fits; well, our little picture's complete.'

'If,' Alleyn said, 'and when.'

The door of the inner office opened and the senior plumber entered. With an air of false modesty he extended a naked arm and bleached hand. On the palm of the hand dripped a revolver. 'Would this,' he asked glumly, 'be what you was wanting?'

IV

Dr Curtis waited for them outside the main entrance to Breezy's flat.

'Sorry to drag you out, Curtis,' Alleyn said, 'but we may need your opinion about his fitness to make a statement. This is Fox's party. He's the drug baron.'

'How do you expect he'll be, Doctor?' Fox asked.

Dr Curtis stared at his shoes and said guardedly: 'Heavy hangover. Shaky. Depressed. May be resentful. May be placatory. Can't tell.'

'Suppose he decides to talk, is it likely to be truthful?'

'Not very. They usually lie.'

Fox said: 'What's the line to take? Tough or coaxing?'

'Use your own judgement.'

'You might tip us the wink, though, Doctor.'

'Well,' said Curtis, 'let's take a look at him.'

The flats were of the more dubious modern kind and brandished chromium steel almost in the Breezy Bellairs Manner – showily and without significance. Alleyn, Fox and Curtis approached the flat by way of a rococo lift and a tunnel-like passage. Fox pressed a bell and a plain-clothes officer answered the door. When he saw them he snibbed back the lock and closed the door behind him.

'How is he?' Alleyn asked.

'Awake, sir. Quiet enough, but restless.'

'Said anything?' Fox asked. 'To make sense, I mean.'

'Nothing much, Mr Fox. Very worried about the deceased, he seems to be. Say he doesn't know what he's going to do without him.'

'*That* makes sense at all events,' Fox grunted. 'Shall we go in, sir?'

It was an expensive and rather characterless flat, only remarkable for its high content of framed and signed photographs and its considerable disorder. Breezy, wearing a dressing-gown of unbelievable sumptuousness, sat in a deep chair into which he seemed to shrink a little further as they came in. His face was the colour of an uncooked fowl and as flabby. As soon as he saw Dr Curtis he raised a lamentable wail.

'Doc,' he whined, 'I'm all shot to heaps. Doc, for pete-sake take a look at me and tell them.'

Curtis picked up his wrist.

'Listen,' Breezy implored him, 'you know a sick man when you see one – listen – '

'Don't talk.'

Breezy pulled at his lower lip, blinked at Alleyn and, with the inconsequence of a ventriloquist's doll, flashed his celebrated smile.

'Excuse us,' he said.

Curtis tested his reflexes, turned up his eyelid and looked at his tongue.

'You're a bit of a mess,' he said, 'but there's no reason why you shouldn't answer any questions these gentlemen like to put to you.' He glanced at Fox. 'He's quite able to take in the usual warning,' he said.

Fox administered it and drew up a chair, facing Breezy, who shot out a quavering finger at Alleyn.

'What's the idea,' he said, 'shooting this chap on to me? What's wrong with talking to me yourself?'

'Inspector Fox,' Alleyn said, 'is concerned with investigations about the illicit drug trade. He wants some information from you.'

He turned away and Fox went into action.

'Well, now, Mr Bellairs,' Fox said, 'I think it's only fair to tell you what we've ascertained so far. Save quite a bit of time, won't it?'

'I can't tell you a thing. I don't know a thing.'

'We're aware that you're in the unfortunate position,' Fox said, 'of having formed the taste for one of these drugs. Gets a real hold on you, doesn't it, that sort of thing?'

Breezy said: 'It's only because I'm overworked. Give me a break and I'll cut it out. I swear I will. But gradually. You have to make it gradual. That's right, isn't it, Doc?'

'I believe,' Fox said comfortably, 'that's the case. That's what I understand. Now, about the supply. We've learnt on good authority that the deceased, in this instance, was the source of supply. Would you care to add anything to that statement, Mr Bellairs?'

'Was it the old bee told you?' Breezy demanded. 'I bet it was the old bee. Or Syd. Syd knew. Syd's had it in for me. Dirty bolshevik! Was it Syd Skelton?'

Fox said that the information had come from more than one
source and asked how Lord Pastern knew Rivera had provided the
drugs. Breezy replied that Lord Pastern nosed out all sorts of things.
He refused to be drawn further.

'I understand,' Fox went on, 'that his lordship tackled you in the
matter last evening.'

Breezy at once became hysterical. 'He'd ruin me! That's what he'd
do. Look! Whatever happens don't let him do it. He's crazy enough
to do it. Honest. Honest he is.'

'Do what?'

'Like what he said. Write to that bloody paper about me.'

'*Harmony*?' Fox asked, at a venture. 'Would that be the paper?'

'That's right. He said he knew someone – God, he's got a thing
about it. You know – the stuff. Damn and blast him,' Breezy
screamed out, 'he'll kill me. He killed Carlos and now what'll I do,
where'll I get it? Everybody watching and spying and I don't *know*.
Carlos never told me. I don't *know*.'

'Never told you?' Fox said peacefully. 'Fancy that now! Never let
on how he got it! And I bet he made it pretty hot when it came to
paying up. Um?'

'God, you're telling me!'

'And no reduction made, for instance, if you helped him out?'

Breezy shrank back in his chair. 'I don't know anything about
that. I don't get you at all.'

'Well, I mean to say,' Fox explained, 'there'd be opportunities,
wouldn't there? Ladies, or it might be their partners, asking the band
leader for a special number. A note changes hands and it might be a
tip or it might be payment in advance, and the goods delivered next
time. We've come across instances. I wondered if he got you to oblige
him. You don't have to say anything you don't want to, mind. We've
the names and addresses of all the guests last night and we've got our
records. People that are known to like it, you know. So I won't press
it. Don't let it worry you. But I thought that he might have had some
arrangement with you. Out of gratitude as you might put it – '

'Gratitude!' Breezy laughed shrilly. 'You think you know too
much,' he said profoundly, and drew in his breath. He was short of
breath and had broken into a sallow, profuse sweat. 'I don't know
what I'll do without Carlos,' he whispered. 'Someone'll have to help

me. It's all the old bee's fault. Him and the girl. If I could just have a smoke – ' He appealed to Dr Curtis. 'Not a prick. I know you won't give me a prick. Just one little smoke. I don't usually in the mornings but this is exceptional, Doc. Doc, couldn't you – '

'You'll have to hang on a bit longer,' Dr Curtis said, not unkindly. 'Wait a bit. We won't let it go longer than you can manage. Hang on.'

Suddenly and inanely Breezy yawned, a face-splitting yawn that bared his gums and showed his coated tongue. He rubbed his arms and neck. 'I keep feeling as if there's something under my skin. Worms or something,' he said, fretfully.

'About the weapon,' Fox began.

Breezy leant forward, his hands on his knees, aping Fox. 'About the weapon?' he mimicked savagely. 'You mind your business about the weapon. Coming here tormentin' a chap. Whose gun was it? Whose bloody sunshade was it? Whose bloody stepdaughter was it? Whose bloody business is it? Get out!' He threw himself back in his chair, panting. 'Get out. I'm within my rights. Get out.'

'Why not?' Fox agreed. 'We'll leave you to yourself. Unless Mr Alleyn . . . ?'

'No,' Alleyn said.

Dr Curtis turned at the door. 'Who's your doctor, Breezy?' he asked.

'I haven't got a doctor,' Breezy whispered. 'Nothing ever used to be wrong with me. Not a thing.'

'We'll find someone to look after you.'

'Can't *you*? Can't you look after me, Doc?'

'Well,' Dr Curtis said, 'I might.'

'Come on,' said Alleyn, and they went out.

V

One end of Materfamilias Lane had suffered a bomb and virtually disappeared, but the other stood intact, a narrow City street with ancient buildings, a watery smell, dark entries and impertinent charm.

The *Harmony* offices were in a tall building at a corner where Materfamilias Lane dived downhill and a cul-de-sac called Journeyman's Steps led off to the right. Both were deserted on this

Sunday afternoon. Alleyn's and Fox's feet rang loudly on the pavement as they walked down Materfamilias Lane. Before they reached the corner they came upon Nigel Bathgate standing in the arched entry to a brewer's yard.

'In me,' Nigel said, 'you see the detective's ready reckoner and pocket-guide to the City.'

'I hope you're right. What have you got for us?'

'His room's on the ground floor with the window in this street. The nearest entrance is round the corner. If he's there the door to his office'll be latched on the inside with an "Engaged" notice displayed. He locks himself in.

'He's there,' Alleyn said.

'How do you know?'

'He's been tailed. Our man rang through from a call-box and he should be back on the job by now.'

'Up the side street if he's got the gumption,' Fox muttered. 'Look out, sir!'

'Softly does it,' Alleyn murmured.

Nigel found himself neatly removed to the far end of the archway, engulfed in Fox's embrace and withdrawn into a recess. Alleyn seemed to arrive there at the same time.

'You cry mum and I'll cry budget!' Alleyn whispered. Someone was walking briskly down Materfamilias Lane. The approaching footsteps echoed in the archway as Edward Manx went by in the sunlight.

They leant motionless against the dark stone and clearly heard the bang of a door.

'Your sleuth-hound,' Nigel pointed out with some relish, 'would appear to be at fault. Whom do you suppose he's been shadowing? Obviously, not Manx.'

'Obviously,' Alleyn said, and Fox mumbled obscurely.

'Why are we waiting?' Nigel asked fretfully.

'Give him a few minutes,' Alleyn said. 'Let him settle down.'

'Am I coming in with you?'

'Do you want to?'

'Certainly. One merely,' Nigel said, 'rather wishes that one hadn't met him before.'

'May be a bit of trouble, you know,' Fox speculated.

'Extremely probable,' Alleyn agreed.

A bevy of sparrows fluttered and squabbled out in the sunny street, an eddy of dust rose inconsequently, and somewhere, out of sight, halliards rattled against an untenanted flagpole.

'Dull,' Fox said, 'doing your beat in the City on a Sunday afternoon. I had six months of it as a young chap. Catch yourself wondering why the blazes you were there and so on.'

'Hideous,' Alleyn said.

'I used to carry my Police Code and Procedure on me and try to memorize six pages a day. I was,' Fox said simply, 'an ambitious young chap in those days.'

Nigel glanced at his watch and lit a cigarette.

The minutes dragged by. A clock struck three and was followed by an untidy conclave of other clocks, overlapping each other. Alleyn walked to the far end of the archway and looked up and down Materfamilias Lane.

'We may as well get under way,' he said. He glanced again up the street and made a sign with his hand. Fox and Nigel followed him. A man in a dark suit came down the footpath. Alleyn spoke to him briefly and then led the way to the corner. The man remained in the archway.

They walked quickly by the window, which was uncurtained and had the legend *Harmony* painted across it, and turned into the cul-de-sac. There was a side door with a brass plate beside it. Alleyn turned the handle and the door opened. Fox and Nigel followed him into a dingy passage which evidently led back into a main corridor. On their right, scarcely discernible in the sudden twilight, was a door. The word 'Engaged', painted in white, showed clearly. From beyond it they heard the rattle of a typewriter.

Alleyn knocked. The rattle stopped short and a chair scraped on the boards. Someone walked towards the door and a voice, Edward Manx's, said: 'Hallo? Who is it?'

'Police,' Alleyn said.

In the stillness they looked speculatively at each other. Alleyn poised his knuckles at the door, waited, and said: 'May we have a word with you, Mr Manx?'

After a second's silence the voice said: 'One moment. I'll come out.'

Alleyn glanced at Fox, who moved in beside him. The word 'Engaged' shot out of sight noisily and was replaced by the letters 'GPF.' A latch clicked and the door opened inwards. Manx stood there with one hand on the jamb and the other on the door. There was a wooden screen behind him.

Fox's boot moved over the threshold.

'I'll come out,' Manx repeated.

'On the contrary, we'll come in, if you please,' Alleyn said.

Without any particular display of force or even brusqueness, but with great efficiency, they went past him and round the screen. He looked for a second at Nigel and seemed not to recognize him. Then he followed them and Nigel unobtrusively followed him.

There was a green-shaded lamp on a desk at which a figure was seated with its back towards them. As Nigel entered, the swivel-chair creaked and spun round. Dingily dressed and wearing a green eye-shade, Lord Pastern faced them with bunched cheeks.

CHAPTER 12

GPF

He made a high-pitched snarling noise as they closed round him and reached out his hand towards an ink-pot on the desk.

Fox said: 'Now, my lord, don't you do anything you'll be sorry for,' and moved the ink-pot.

Lord Pastern sank his head with a rapid movement between his shoulders. From behind them Edward Manx said: 'I don't know why you've done this, Alleyn. It'll get you no further.'

Lord Pastern said: 'Shut up, Ned,' and glared at Alleyn. 'I'll have you kicked out of the force,' he said. 'Kicked out, by God!' And after a silence: 'You don't get a word from me. Not a syllable.'

Alleyn pulled up a chair and sat down facing him. 'That will suit us very well,' he said. 'You are going to listen, and I advise you to do so with as good a grace as you can muster. When you've heard what I've got to say you may read the statement I've brought with me. You can sign it, alter it, dictate another or refuse to do any of these things. But in the meantime, Lord Pastern, you are going to listen.'

Lord Pastern folded his arms tightly across his chest, rested his chin on his tie and screwed up his eyes. Alleyn took a folded typescript from his breast pocket, opened it and crossed his knees.

'This statement was prepared,' he said, 'on the assumption that you are the man who calls himself G.P. Friend and writes the articles signed GPF in *Harmony*. It is a statement of what we believe to be fact and doesn't concern itself overmuch with motive. I, however, will deal rather more fully with motive. In launching this paper and in writing these articles, you found it necessary to observe complete anonymity. Your reputation as probably the most quarrelsome man in England, your loudly publicized domestic rows, and your notorious eccentricities would make an appearance in the role of Guide Philosopher and Friend a fantastically bad joke. We presume, therefore, that through a reliable agent you deposited adequate security in a convenient bank with the specimen signature of G.P. Friend as the negotiating instrument. You then set up the legend of your own anonymity and launched yourself in the role of oracle. With huge success.'

Lord Pastern did not stir but a film of complacency overspread his face.

'This success,' Alleyn went on, 'it must always be remembered, depends entirely upon the preservation of your anonymity. Once let Harmony's devotees learn that GPF is none other than the notoriously unharmonious peer whose public quarrels have been the punctual refuge of the penny-press during the silly season – once let that be known and GPF is sunk, and Lord Pastern loses a fortune. All right. Everything goes along swimmingly. You do a lot of your journalism at Duke's Gate, no doubt, but you also make regular visits to this office wearing dark glasses, the rather shabby hat and scarf which are hanging on the wall there, and the old jacket you have on at this moment. You work behind locked doors and Mr Edward Manx is possibly your only confidant. You enjoy yourself enormously and make a great deal of money. So, perhaps, in his degree, does Mr Manx.'

Manx said: 'I've no shares in the paper if that's what you mean. My articles are paid for at the usual rate.'

'Shut up, Ned,' said his cousin automatically.

'The paper,' Allen continued, 'is run on eccentric but profitable lines. It explodes bombs. It exposes rackets. It mingles soft-soap and cyanide. In particular it features an extremely efficient and daringly personal attack on the drug racket. It employs experts, it makes accusations, it defies and invites prosecution. Its information is accurate and if it occasionally frustrates its own professed aims by warning criminals before the police are in a position to arrest them, it is far too much inflated with crusaders' zeal and rising sales to worry its head about that.'

'Look here, Alleyn . . . ' Manx began angrily, and simultaneously Lord Pastern shouted: 'What the hell do you think you're getting at?'

'One moment,' Alleyn said. Manx thrust his hands in his pocket and began to move about the room. 'Better to hear this out, after all,' he muttered.

'Much better,' Alleyn agreed. 'I'll go on. Everything prospered in the *Harmony* set-up until you, Lord Pastern, discovered an urge to exploit your talents as a tympanist and allied yourself with Breezy Bellairs and His Boys. Almost immediately there were difficulties. First: your step-daughter, for whom I think you have a great affection, became attracted by Carlos Rivera, the piano accordionist in the band. You are an observant man: for a supreme egoist, surprisingly so. At some time of your association with the Boys, I don't know precisely when, you became aware that Breezy Bellairs was taking drugs and, more important, that Carlos Rivera was supplying them. Through your association with *Harmony*, you are well up in the methods of drug-distribution and you are far too sharp not to realize that the usual pattern was being followed. Bellairs was in a position to act as a minor distributing agent. He was introduced to the drug, acquired a habit for it, was forced to hand it out to clients at the Metronome, and as a reward was given as much as Rivera thought was good for him at the usual exorbitant rate.'

Alleyn looked curiously at Lord Pastern, who, at that moment, met his eye and blinked twice.

'It's an odd situation,' Alleyn said, 'isn't it? Here we have a man of eclectic, violent and short-lived enthusiasms suddenly confronted with a situation where his two reigning passions and his one enduring attachment are brought into violent opposition.'

He turned to Manx, who had stopped still and was looking fixedly at him.

'A situation of great possibilities from your professional point of view, I should imagine,' Alleyn said. 'The step-daughter whom Lord Pastern loves falls for Rivera, who is engaged in an infamous trade which Lord Pastern is zealous in fighting. At the same time Rivera's dupe is the conductor of the band in which Lord Pastern burns to perform. As a final twist in an already tricky situation, Rivera has discovered, perhaps amongst Lord Pastern's music during a band rehearsal, some rough drafts for GPF's page, typed on Duke's Gate letter-paper. He is using them, no doubt, to force on his engagement to Miss de Suze. "Either support my suit or . . . " For Rivera, in addition to running a drug racket, is an accomplished blackmailer. How is Lord Pastern to play the drums, break the engagement, preserve his anonymity as GPF and explode the drug racket?'

'You can't possibly,' Manx said, 'have proof of a quarter of all this. It's the most brazen guesswork.'

'A certain amount of guesswork. But we have enough information and hard fact to carry us some way. I think that between you, you are going to fill out the rest.'

Manx laughed shortly. 'What a hope!' he said.

'Well,' Alleyn murmured, 'let us go on and see. Lord Pastern's inspiration comes out of a clear sky while he is working on his copy for GPF's page in *Harmony*. Among the letters in his basket, seeking guidance, philosophy and friendship is one from his stepdaughter.' He stopped short. 'I wonder,' he said, 'if at some time or another there is also one from his wife? Asking perhaps for advice in her marital problems.'

Manx looked quickly at Lord Pastern and away again.

'It might explain,' Alleyn said thoughtfully, 'why Lady Pastern is so vehement in her disapproval of *Harmony*. If she *did* write to GPF, I imagine the answer was one of the five shilling Private Chat Letters and extremely displeasing to her.'

Lord Pastern gave a short bark of laughter and shot a glance at his cousin.

'However,' Alleyn went on, 'we are concerned, at this point, with the fact that Miss de Suze does write for guidance. Out of this coincidence, an idea is born. He answers the letter. She replies. The correspondence goes on, becoming, as Miss de Suze put it to me, more and more come-to-ish. Lord Pastern is an adept. He stages (again I quote Miss de Suze) a sort of Cupid-and-Psyche act at one remove. She asks if they may meet. He replies ardently but refuses. He has all the fun of watching her throughout in his own character. Meanwhile he appears to Rivera to be supporting his suit. But the ice gets thinner and thinner and his figure-skating increasingly hazardous. Moreover, here he is with a golden opportunity for a major journalistic scoop. He could expose Bellairs, represent himself as a brilliant investigator who has worked on his own in the band and now hands the whole story over to *Harmony*. And yet – and yet – there are those captivating drums, those entrancing cymbals, those stimulating wire whisks. There is his own composition. There is his debut. He skates on precariously but with exhilaration. He fiddles with the idea of weaning Bellairs from his vice and frightens him into fits by threatening to supplant Syd Skelton. He – '

'Did you,' Lord Pastern interrupted, 'go to that police school or whatever it is? Hendon?'

'No,' Alleyn said. 'I didn't.'

'Well, get on, get on,' he snapped.

'We come to the night of the début and of the great inspiration. Lady Pastern quite obviously desires a marriage between her daughter and Mr Edward Manx.'

Manx made an expostulatory sound. Alleyn waited for a moment. 'Look here, Alleyn,' Manx said, 'you can at least observe some kind of decency. I object most strongly – ' He glared at Nigel Bathgate.

'I'm afraid you'll have to lump it,' Alleyn said mildly. Nigel said: 'I'm sorry, Manx. I'll clear out if you like, but I'll hear it all, in any case.'

Manx turned on his heel, walked over to the window and stood there with his back to them.

'Lord Pastern,' Alleyn continued, 'seems to have shared this hope. And now, having built up a spurious but ardent mystery round GPF, he gets his big idea. Perhaps he notices Mr Manx's instant dislike of Rivera and perhaps he supposes this dislike to arise from an attachment to his stepdaughter. At all events he sees Mr Manx put a white carnation in his coat, he goes off to his study and he types a romantic note to Miss de Suze in which GPF reveals himself as the wearer of a white carnation. The note swears her to secrecy. Miss de Suze, coming straight from a violent quarrel with Rivera, sees the white flower in Mr Manx's jacket and reacts according to plan.'

Manx said: 'Oh, my *God!*' and drummed his fingers on the window-pane.

'The one thing that seems to have escaped Lord Pastern's notice,' Alleyn said, 'is the fact that Mr Manx is enormously attracted, not by Miss de Suze, but by Miss Carlisle Wayne.'

'Hell!' said Lord Pastern sharply, and slewed round in his swivel chair. 'Hi!' he shouted. 'Ned!'

'For pity's sake,' Manx said impatiently, 'let's forget it. It couldn't matter less.' He caught his breath. 'In the context,' he added.

Lord Pastern contemplated his cousin's back with extreme severity and then directed his attention once more upon Alleyn.

'Well?' he said.

'Well,' Alleyn repeated, 'so much for the great inspiration. But your activity hasn't exhausted itself. There is a scene with Bellairs in the ballroom, overheard by your footman and in part related to me by the wretched Breezy himself. During this scene you suggest yourself as a successor to Syd Skelton, and tick Bellairs off about his drug habit. You go so far, I think, as to talk about writing to *Harmony*. The idea, at this stage, would appear to be a comprehensive one. You will frighten Breezy into giving up cocaine, expose Rivera, and keep on with the band. It was during this interview that you behaved in a rather strange manner. You unscrewed the end section of Lady Pastern's parasol, removed the knob and absentmindedly pushed the bit of shaft a little way up the muzzle of your revolver, holding down the spring clip as you did so. You found that it fitted like a miniature ramrod or bolt. Or, if you like, a rifle grenade.'

'*I* told you that meself.'

'Exactly. Your policy throughout has been to pile up evidence against yourself. A sane man, and we are presuming you sane, doesn't do that sort of thing unless he believes he has an extra trick or two in hand, some conclusive bits of evidence that must clear him. It was obvious that you thought you could produce some such evidence and you took great glee in exhibiting the devastating frankness of complete innocence. Another form of figure-skating on thin ice. You would let us blunder about making clowns of ourselves, and, when the sport palled or the ice began to crack, you would, if you'll excuse the mixed metaphor, plank down the extra tricks.'

A web of thread-like veins started out on Lord Pastern's blanched cheek-bones. He brushed up his moustache and, finding his hand shook, looked quickly at it, and thrust it inside the breast of his coat.

'It seemed best,' Alleyn said, 'to let you go your own gait and see how far it would take you. You wanted us to believe that Mr Manx was GPF: there was nothing to be gained, we thought, and there might be something lost in letting you see we recognized the equal possibility of your being GPF yourself. This became a probability when the drafts of copy turned up amongst Rivera's blackmailing material. Because Rivera had never met Manx but was closely associated with you.'

Alleyn glanced up at his colleague. 'It was Inspector Fox,' he said, 'who first pointed out that you had every chance, during the performance, while the spotlight was on somebody else, to load the revolver with that fantastic bolt. All right. But there remained your first trump card – the substituted weapon. The apparently irrefutable evidence that the gun we recovered from Breezy was not the one you brought down to the Metronome. But when we found the original weapon in the lavatory beyond the inner office that difficulty, too, fell into place in the general design. We had got as far as abundant motive and damning circumstances. Opportunity began to appear.'

Alleyn stood up, and with him Lord Pastern, who pointed a quivering finger at him.

'You bloody fool!' he said drawing his lips back from his teeth. 'You can't arrest me – you – '

'I believe I could arrest you,' Alleyn rejoined, 'but not for murder. Your second trump card is unfortunately valid. You didn't kill Rivera because Rivera was not killed by the revolver.'

He looked at Manx. 'And now,' he said, 'we come to you.'

II

Edward Manx turned from the window and walked towards Alleyn with his hands in his pockets. 'All right,' he said, 'you come to me. What have you nosed out about me?'

'This and that,' Alleyn rejoined. 'On the face of it there's one evidence that you quarrelled with Rivera and clipped him over the ear. Nosing, as you would put it, beneath the surface, there's your association with *Harmony*. You, and perhaps you alone, knew that Lord Pastern was GPF. He told you Rivera was blackmailing him – '

'He didn't tell me.'

' – and if, in addition, you knew Rivera was a drug merchant – ' Alleyn waited for a moment but Manx said nothing.' – why then, remembering your expressed loathing for this abominable trade, something very like a motive began to appear.'

'Oh, nonsense,' Manx said lightly. 'I don't go about devising quaint deaths for everyone I happen to think a good or a bad lot.'

'One never knows. There have been cases. And you could have changed the revolvers.'

'You've just told us that he wasn't killed by the revolver.'

'Nevertheless the substitution was made by his murderer.' Manx laughed acidly. 'I give up,' he said, and threw out his hands. 'Get on with it.'

'The weapon that killed Rivera couldn't have been fired from the revolver because at the time Lord Pastern pulled the trigger, Rivera had his piano accordion across his chest and the piano accordion is uninjured.'

'I could have told you that,' said Lord Pastern, rallying.

'It was a patently bogus affair, in any case. How, for instance, could Lord Pastern be sure of shooting Rivera with such a footling tool? A stiletto in the end of a bit of stick? If he missed by a fraction of an inch Rivera might not die instantly and might not die at all. No. You have to be sure of getting the right spot and getting it good and proper, with a bare bodkin.'

Manx lit a cigarette with unsteady hands. 'Then in that case I can't for the life of me see' – he stopped – 'whodunit,' he said, 'and how.'

'Since it's obvious Rivera wasn't hurt when he fell,' Alleyn said, 'he was stabbed after he fell.'

'But he wasn't meant to fall. They'd altered the routine. We've had that till we're sick of the sound of it.'

'It will be our contention that Rivera did not know that the routine had been altered.'

'Bosh!' Lord Pastern shouted so unexpectedly that they all jumped. 'He wanted it changed. I didn't. It was Carlos wanted it.'

'We'll take that point a bit later,' Alleyn said. 'We're considering how, and when, he was killed. Do you remember the timing of the giant metronome? It was motionless, wasn't it, right up to the moment when Rivera fell; motionless and pointing straight down at him. As he leant backwards its steel tip was poised rather menacingly, straight at his heart.'

'Oh, for pity's sake!' Manx said disgustedly. 'Are you going to tell us somebody dropped the bolt out of the metronome?'

'No. I'm trying to dismiss the fancy touches, not add to them. Immediately after Rivera fell, the arm of the metronome went into action. Coloured lights winked and popped in and out along its entire surface and that of the surrounding tower frame. It swung to and fro with a rhythmic clack. The whole effect of course, carefully planned, was dazzling and unexpected. One's attention was drawn away from the prostrate figure and what actually happened during the next ten seconds or so was quite lost on the audience. To distract attention still further from the central figure, a spotlight played on the tympani where Lord Pastern could be seen in terrific action. But what seemed to happen during those ten confusing seconds?'

He waited again and then said: 'Of course you remember, both of you. A waiter threw Breezy a comic wreath of flowers. He knelt down and, pretending to weep, using his handkerchief, opened Rivera's coat and felt for his heart. He felt for his heart.'

III

Lord Pastern said: 'You're wrong, Alleyn, you're wrong. I searched him. I'll swear he had nothing on him then and I'll swear he didn't get a chance to pick anything up. Where the devil was the weapon? You're wrong. I searched him.'

'As I intended you to do. Yes. Did you notice his baton while you searched him?'

'I told you, damn it. He held it above his head. Good God!' Lord Pastern added, and again, 'Good God!'

'A short black rod. The pointed steel was held in his palm, protected by the cork out of an empty gun-oil bottle in your desk. Fox reminded me this morning of Poe's story *The Purloined Letter*. Show a thing boldly to unsuspecting observers and they will think it's what they expect it to be. Breezy conducted your programme last night with a piece of parasol handle and a stiletto. You saw the steel mounting glinting as usual at the tip of an ebony rod. The stiletto was concealed in his palm. It really was quite like his baton. Probably that gave him the idea when he handled the dismembered parasol in the ballroom. I think you asked him, didn't you, to put it together.'

'Why the hell,' Lord Pastern demanded, 'didn't you tell us this straight away? Tormentin' people. It's a damn' scandal. I'll take you up on this, Alleyn, by God I will.'

'Did you,' Alleyn asked mildly, 'go out of your way to confide in us? Or did you wilfully and dangerously play a silly lone hand? I think I may be forgiven, sir, for giving you a taste of your own tactics. I wish I could believe it had shaken you a bit: but that, I'm afraid, is too much to hope for.' Lord Pastern bunched up his cheeks and swore extensively, but Manx said with a grin: 'You know, Cousin George, I rather think we bought it. We've hindered the police in the execution of their duty.'

'Serve 'em damn' well right.'

'I'm still sceptical,' Manx said. 'Where's your motive? Why should he kill the man who supplied him with his dope?'

'One of the servants at Duke's Gate overheard a quarrel between Bellairs and Rivera when they were together in the ballroom. Breezy asked Rivera for cigarettes – drugged cigarettes, of course – and Rivera refused to give him any. He intimated that their association was ended and talked about writing to *Harmony*. Fox will tell you that sort of thing's quite a common gambit when these people fall out.'

'Oh, yes,' Fox said. 'They do it, you know. Rivera would have a cast-iron story ready to protect himself and get in first with the information. We'd pick Breezy up and be no further on. We might suspect Rivera but we wouldn't get on to anything. Not a thing.'

'Because,' Lord Pastern pointed out, 'you're too thick headed to get your man when he's screamin' for arrest under your great noses. That's why. Where's your initiative? Where's your push and drive? Why can't you – ' he gestured wildly – 'stir things up? Make a dust?'

'Well, my lord,' said Fox placidly 'we can safely leave that kind of thing to papers like *Harmony,* can't we?'

Manx muttered: 'But to kill him – no, I can't see it. And to think all that nonsense up in an hour – '

'He's a drug addict,' Alleyn said. 'He's been drawing near the end of his tether for some time, I fancy, with Rivera looming up bigger and bigger as his evil genius. It's a common characteristic for the addict to develop an intense hatred of the purveyor upon whom he is so slavishly dependent. This person becomes a sort of Mephistopheles-symbol for the addict. When the purveyor is also a blackmailer and for good measure in a position where he can terrify his victim by threats of withdrawal, you get an excruciating twist to the screw. I fancy the picture of you, Lord Pastern, firing point-blank at Rivera had begun to fascinate Bellairs long before he saw you fit the section into the barrel of the gun. I believe he had already played with the idea of frigging round with the ammunition. You added fuel to his fire.'

'That be damned – ' Lord Pastern began to shout, but Alleyn went on steadily.

'Breezy,' he said, 'was in an ugly state. He was frantic for cocaine, nervous about his show, terrified of what you would do. Don't forget, sir, you, too, had threatened him with exposure. He planned for a right-and-left coup. You were to hang, you know, for the murder. He has always had a passion for practical jokes.'

Manx gave a snort of nervous laughter. Lord Pastern said nothing.

'But,' Alleyn went on, 'it was all too Technicolor to be credible. His red-herrings were more like red whales. The whole set-up had the characteristic unreason and fantastic logic of the addict. A Coleridge creates Kubla Khan but a Breezy Bellairs creates a surrealistic dagger made of a parasol handle and a needlework stiletto. An Edgar Allan Poe writes *The Pit and the Pendulum* but a Breezy Bellairs steals a revolver and makes little scratches in the muzzle with a stiletto; he smokes it with a candle end and puts it in his overcoat pocket. Stung to an intolerable activity by his unsatisfied lust for cocaine he plans grotesquely but with frantic precision. He may crack at any moment, lose interest or break down, but for a crucial period he goes to work like a demon. Everything falls into place. He tells the band but *not* Rivera, that the other routine will be followed. Rivera had gone to the end of the restaurant to make his entrance. He persuades Skelton to look at Lord Pastern's revolver at the last minute. He causes himself to be searched, holding his dagger over his head, trembling with strangled laughter. He conducts. He kills. He finds Rivera's heart, and with his hands protected by a handkerchief and hidden from the audience by a comic wreath, he digs his stiletto in and grinds it round. He shows distress. He goes to the room where the body lies and shows greater distress. He changes carefully the scarred revolver in his overcoat pocket with the one Lord Pastern fired. He goes into the lavatory and makes loud retching noises while he disposes of Lord Pastern's unscarred gun. He returns, and being now at the end of his course, frantically searches

the body and probably finds the dope he needs so badly. He collaps-
es. That, as we see it, is the case against Breezy Bellairs.'

'Poor dope,' Manx said. 'If you're right.'

'Poor dope. Oh, yes,' Alleyn said. 'Poor dope.'

Nigel Bathgate murmured: 'Nobody else could have done it.'

Lord Pastern glared at him but said nothing.

'Nobody,' Fox said.

'But you'll never get a conviction, Alleyn.'

'That,' Alleyn said, 'may be. It won't ruin our lives if we don't.'

'How young,' Lord Pastern demanded suddenly, 'does a feller
have to be to get into detection?'

'If you'll excuse me, Alleyn,' Edward Manx said hurriedly, 'I
think I'll be off.'

'Where are you goin', Ned?'

'To see Lisle, Cousin George. We lunched,' he explained, 'at cross-
purposes. I thought she meant she knew it was you. I thought she
meant the letter was the one Fée got from *Harmony*. But I see now:
she thought it was me.'

'What the hell are you talkin' about?'

'It doesn't matter. Goodbye.'

'Hi, wait a minute. I'll come with you.' They went out into the
deserted twilight, Lord Pastern locking the door behind him.

'I'll be off too, Alleyn,' said Nigel as they stood watching the two
figures, one lean and loose-jointed, the other stocky and dapper,
walk briskly away up Materfamilias Lane. 'Unless – what are you
going to do?'

'Have you got the warrant, Fox?'

'Yes, Mr Alleyn.'

'Come on, then.'

IV

'The Judges' Rules,' Fox said, 'may be enlightened but there are
times when they give you the pip. I suppose you don't agree with
that, Mr Alleyn.'

'They keep you and me in our place, Br'er Fox, and I fancy that's
a good thing.'

'If we could confront him,' Fox burst out. 'If we could break him down.'

'Under pressure he might make a hysterical confession. It might not be true. That would appear to be the idea behind the Judges' Rules.'

Fox muttered something unprintable.

Nigel Bathgate said: 'Where are we heading?'

'We call on him,' Alleyn grunted. 'And with any luck we find he already has a visitor. Caesar Bonn of the Metronome.'

'How d'you know?'

'Information received,' said Fox. 'He made an arrangement over the telephone.'

'And so, what do you do about it?'

'We pull Bellairs in, Mr Bathgate, for receiving and distributing drugs.'

'Fox,' said Alleyn, 'thinks there's a case against him. Through the customers.'

'Once he's inside,' Fox speculated dismally, 'he *may* talk. In spite of the Usual Caution. Judges' Rules!'

'He's a glutton for limelight,' Alleyn said unexpectedly.

'So what?' Nigel demanded.

'Nothing. I don't know. He may break out somewhere. Here we go.'

It was rather dark in the tunnel-like passage that led to Breezy's flat. Nobody was about but a plain-clothes man on duty at the far end: a black figure against a mean window.

Walking silently on the heavy carpet, they came up to him. He made a movement of his head, murmured something that ended with the phrase: 'hammer and tongs'.

'Good,' Alleyn said, and nodded. The man stealthily opened the door into Breezy's flat.

They moved into an entrance lobby where they found a second man with a note-book pressed against the wall and a pencil poised over it. The four silent men almost filled the cramped lobby.

In the living-room beyond, Caesar Bonn was quarrelling with Breezy Bellairs.

'Publicity!' Caesar was saying. 'But of what a character! No, no! I am sorry. I regret this with all my heart. For me as for you it is a disaster.'

'Listen, Caesar, you're all wrong. My public won't let me down. They'd *want* to see me.' The voice rose steeply. 'They – love me,' Breezy cried out, and after a pause: 'You bloody swine, they *love* me.'

'I must go.'

'All right. You'll see. I'll ring Carmarelli. Carmarelli's been trying to get me for years. Or the Lotus Tree. They'll be fighting for me. And your bloody clientele'll follow me. They'll eat us. I'll ring Stein. There's not a restaurateur in Town – '

'One moment.' Caesar was closer to the door. 'To spare you discomfiture, I feel I must warn you. Already I have discussed this matter with these gentlemen. An informal meeting. We are all agreed. It will not be possible for you to appear at any first-class restaurant or club.'

They heard a falsetto whining. Caesar's voice intervened. 'Believe me,' he said, 'when I say I mean this kindly. After all, we are old friends. Take my advice. Retire. You can afford to do so, no doubt.' He gave a nervous giggle. Breezy had whispered. Evidently they were close together on the other side of the door. 'No, no!' Caesar said loudly. 'I can do nothing about it. Nothing! Nothing!'

Breezy screamed out abruptly: 'I'll ruin you!' and the pencil skidded across the plain-clothes officer's note-book.

'You have ruined yourself,' Caesar gabbled. 'You will keep silence. Understand me: there must be complete silence. For you there is no more spotlight. You are finished. *Keep off*!' There was a scuffle and a stifled ejaculation. Something thudded heavily against the door and slid down its surface. 'There now!' Caesar panted. He sounded scandalized and breathlessly triumphant. Unexpectedly, after a brief pause, he went on in a reflective voice. 'No, truly you are too stupid. This decides me. I am resolved. I inform the police of your activities. You will make a foolish appearance in court. Everyone will laugh a little and forget you. You will got to gaol or perhaps to a clinic. If you are of good behaviour you may, in a year or so, be permitted to conduct a little band.'

'*Christ!* Tell them, then! *Tell them!*' Beyond the door Breezy stumbled to his feet. His voice broke into falsetto. 'But it's me that'll tell the tale; me! If I go to the dock, by God, I'll wipe the grins off all your bloody faces. You haven't heard anything yet. Try any funny business with ME! Finished! By God, I've only just started. You're all going to hear how I slit up a bloody dago's heart for him.'

'This is it,' Alleyn said, and opened the door.

I Can Find My
Way Out

I Can Find My Way Out was first published in
Ellery Queen's Mystery Magazine (USA) in 1946.

At half past six on the night in question, Anthony Gill, unable to eat, keep still, think, speak or act coherently, walked from his rooms to the Jupiter Theatre. He knew that there would be nobody backstage, that there was nothing for him to do in the theatre, that he ought to stay quietly in his rooms and presently dress, dine and arrive at, say, a quarter to eight. But it was as if something shoved him into his clothes, thrust him into the street and compelled him to hurry through the West End to the Jupiter. His mind was overlaid with a thin film of inertia. Odd lines from the play occurred to him, but without any particular significance. He found himself busily reiterating a completely irrelevant sentence: 'She has a way of laughing that would make a man's heart turn over.'

Piccadilly, Shaftesbury Avenue. 'Here I go,' he thought, turning into Hawke Street, 'towards my play. It's one hour and twenty nine minutes away. A step a second. It's rushing towards me. Tony's first play. Poor young Tony Gill. Never mind. Try again.'

The Jupiter. Neon lights: I CAN FIND MY WAY OUT – *by Anthony Gill.* And in the entrance the bills and photographs. *Coralie Bourne with H. J. Bannington, Barry George and Canning Cumberland.*

Canning Cumberland. The film across his mind split and there was the Thing itself and he would have to think about it. How bad would Canning Cumberland be if he came down drunk? Brilliantly bad, they said. He would bring out all the tricks. Clever actor stuff, scoring off everybody, making a fool of the dramatic balance. 'In Mr Canning Cumberland's hands indifferent dialogue and unconvincing situations seemed almost real.' What can you do with a drunken actor?

He stood in the entrance feeling his heart pound and his inside deflate and sicken.

Because, of course, it was a bad play. He was at this moment and for the first time really convinced of it. It was terrible. Only one virtue in it and that was not his doing. It had been suggested to him by Coralie Bourne: 'I don't think the play you have sent me will do as it is but it has occurred to me – ' It was a brilliant idea. He had rewritten the play round it and almost immediately and quite innocently he had begun to think of it as his own although he had said shyly to Coralie Bourne: 'You should appear as joint author.' She had quickly, over emphatically, refused. 'It was nothing at all,' she said. 'If you're to become a dramatist you will learn to get ideas from everywhere. A single situation is nothing. Think of Shakespeare,' she added lightly. 'Entire plots! Don't be silly.' She had said later, and still with the same hurried, nervous air: 'Don't go talking to everyone about it. They will think there is more, instead of less, than meets the eye in my small suggestion. Please promise.' He promised, thinking he'd made an error in taste when he suggested that Coralie Bourne, so famous an actress, should appear as joint author with an unknown youth. And how right she was, he thought, because, of course, it's going to be a ghastly flop. She'll be sorry she consented to play in it.

Standing in front of the theatre he contemplated nightmare possibilities. What did audiences do when a first play flopped? Did they clap a little, enough to let the curtain rise and quickly fall again on a discomforted group of players? How scanty must the applause be for them to let him off his own appearance? And they were to go on to the Chelsea Arts Ball. A hideous prospect. Thinking he would give anything in the world if he could stop his play, he turned into the foyer. There were lights in the offices and he paused, irresolute, before a board of photographs. Among them, much smaller than the leading players, was Dendra Gay with the eyes looking straight into his. *She had a way of laughing that would make a man's heart turn over.* 'Well,' he thought, 'so I'm in love with her.' He turned away from the photograph. A man came out of the office. 'Mr Gill? Telegrams for you.'

Anthony took them and as he went out he heard the man call after him: 'Very good luck for tonight, sir.'

There were queues of people waiting in the side street for the early doors.

* * *

At six thirty Coralie Bourne dialled Canning Cumberland's number and waited.

She heard his voice. 'It's me,' she said.

'O God! darling, I've been thinking about you.' He spoke rapidly, too loudly. 'Coral, I've been thinking about Ben. You oughtn't to have given that situation to the boy.'

'We've been over it a dozen times, Cann. Why not give it to Tony? Ben will never know.' She waited and then said nervously, 'Ben's gone, Cann. We'll never see him again.'

'I've got a Thing about it. After all, he's your husband.'

'No, Cann, no.'

'Suppose he turns up. It'd be like him to turn up.'

'He won't turn up.'

She heard him laugh. 'I'm sick of all this,' she thought suddenly. 'I've had it once too often. I can't stand any more . . . Cann,' she said into the telephone. But he had hung up.

At twenty to seven, Barry George looked at himself in his bathroom mirror. 'I've got a better appearance,' he thought, 'than Cann Cumberland. My head's a good shape, my eyes are bigger and my jaw line's cleaner. I never let a show down. I don't drink. I'm a better actor.' He turned his head a little, slewing his eyes to watch the effect. 'In the big scene,' he thought, 'I'm the star. He's the feed. That's the way it's been produced and that's what the author wants. I ought to get the notices.'

Past notices came up in his memory. He saw the print, the size of the paragraphs; a long paragraph about Canning Cumberland, a line tacked on the end of it. 'Is it unkind to add that Mr Barry George trotted in the wake of Mr Cumberland's virtuosity with an air of breathless dependability?' And again: 'It is a little hard on Mr Barry George that he should be obliged to act as foil to this brilliant performance.' Worst of all: 'Mr Barry George succeeded in looking tolerably unlike a stooge, an achievement that evidently exhausted his resources.'

'Monstrous!' he said loudly to his own image, watching the fine glow of indignation in the eyes. Alcohol, he told himself, did two things to Cann Cumberland. He raised his finger. Nice, expressive hand. An actor's hand. Alcohol destroyed Cumberland's artistic integrity. It also invested him with devilish cunning. Drunk, he would burst the seams of a play, destroy its balance, ruin its form and himself emerge blazing with a showmanship that the audience mistook for genius. 'While I,' he said aloud, 'merely pay my author the compliment of faithful interpretation. Psha!'

He returned to his bedroom, completed his dressing and pulled his hat to the right angle. Once more he thrust his face close to the mirror and looked searchingly at its image. 'By God!' he told himself, 'he's done it once too often, old boy. Tonight we'll even the score, won't we? By God, we will.'

Partly satisfied, and partly ashamed, for the scene, after all, had smacked a little of ham, he took his stick in one hand and a case holding his costume for the Arts Ball in the other, and went down to the theatre.

At ten minutes to seven, H. J. Bannington passed through the gallery queue on his way to the stage door alley, raising his hat and saying: 'Thanks so much,' to the gratified ladies who let him through. He heard them murmur his name. He walked briskly along the alley, greeted the stage-doorkeeper, passed under a dingy lamp, through an entry and so to the stage. Only working lights were up. The walls of an interior set rose dimly into shadow. Bob Reynolds, the stage manager, came out through the prompt entrance. 'Hello, old boy,' he said, 'I've changed the dressing rooms. You're third on the right: they've moved your things in. Suit you?'

'Better, at least, than a black-hole the size of a WC but without its appointments,' HJ said acidly. 'I suppose the great Mr Cumberland still has the star room?'

'Well, yes, old boy.'

'And who pray, is next to him? In the room with the other gas fire?'

'We've put Barry George there, old boy. You know what he's like.'

'Only too well, old boy, and the public, I fear, is beginning to find out.' HJ turned into the dressing room passage.

The stage manager returned to the set where he encountered his assistant. 'What's biting *him?*' asked the assistant.

'He wanted a dressing room with a fire.'

'Only natural,' said the ASM nastily. 'He started life reading gas meters.'

On the right and left of the passage, nearest the stage end, were two doors, each with its star in tarnished paint. The door on the left was open. HJ looked in and was greeted with the smell of grease-paint, powder, wet white, and flowers. A gas fire droned comfortably. Coralie Bourne's dresser was spreading out towels. 'Good evening, Katie, my jewel,' said HJ. 'La Belle not down yet?'

'We're on our way,' she said.

HJ hummed stylishly: '*Bella filia del amore,*' and returned to the passage. The star room on the right was closed but he could hear Cumberland's dresser moving about inside. He went on to the next door, paused, read the card, 'Mr Barry George,' warbled a high derisive note, turned in at the third door and switched on the light.

Definitely not a second lead's room. No fire. A washbasin, however, and opposite mirrors. A stack of telegrams had been placed on the dressing table. Still singing he reached for them, disclosing a number of bills that had been tactfully laid underneath and a letter, addressed in a flamboyant script.

His voice might have been mechanically produced and arbitrarily switched off, so abruptly did his song end in the middle of a roulade. He let the telegrams fall on the table, took up the letter and tore it open. His face, wretchedly pale, was reflected and endlessly re-reflected in the mirrors.

At nine o'clock the telephone rang. Roderick Alleyn answered it. 'This is Sloane 84405. No, you're on the wrong number. *No.*' He hung up and returned to his wife and guest. 'That's the fifth time in two hours.'

'Do let's ask for a new number.'

'We might get next door to something worse.'

The telephone rang again. 'This is not 84406,' Alleyn warned it. 'No, I cannot take three large trunks to Victoria Station. No, I am not the Instant All Night Delivery. No.'

'They're 84406,' Mrs Alleyn explained to Lord Michael Lamprey. 'I suppose it's just faulty dialling, but you can't imagine how angry everyone gets. Why do you want to be a policeman?'

'It's a dull hard job, you know – ' Alleyn began.

'Oh,' Lord Mike said, stretching his legs and looking critically at his shoes, 'I don't for a moment imagine I'll leap immediately into false whiskers and plainclothes. No, no. But I'm revoltingly healthy, sir. Strong as a horse. And I don't think I'm as stupid as you might feel inclined to imagine – '

The telephone rang.

'I say, do let me answer it,' Mike suggested and did so.

'Hullo?' he said winningly. He listened, smiling at his hostess. 'I'm afraid – ' he began. 'Here, wait a bit – Yes, but – ' His expression became blank and complacent. 'May I,' he said presently, 'repeat your order, sir? Can't be too sure, can we? Call at 11 Harrow Gardens, Sloane Square, for one suitcase to be delivered immediately at the Jupiter Theatre to Mr Anthony Gill. Very good, sir. Thank you, sir. Collect. Quite.'

He replaced the receiver and beamed at the Alleyns.

'What the devil have you been up to?' Alleyn said.

'He just simply wouldn't listen to reason. I tried to tell him.'

'But it may be urgent,' Mrs Alleyn ejaculated.

'It couldn't be more urgent, really. It's a suitcase for Tony Gill at the Jupiter.'

'Well, then – '

'I was at Eton with the chap,' said Mike reminiscently. 'He's four years older than I am so of course he was madly important while I was less than the dust. This'll larn him.'

'I think you'd better put that order through at once,' said Alleyn firmly.

'I rather thought of executing it myself, do you know, sir. It'd be a frightfully neat way of gate-crashing the show, wouldn't it? I did try to get a ticket but the house was sold out.'

'If you're going to deliver this case you'd better get a bend on.'

'It's clearly an occasion for dressing up though, isn't it? I say,' said Mike modestly, 'would you think it most frightful cheek if I – well I'd promise to come back and return everything. I mean – '

'Are you suggesting that my clothes look more like a vanman's than yours?'

'I thought you'd have things – '

'For Heaven's sake, Rory,' said Mrs Alleyn, 'dress him up and let him go. The great thing is to get that wretched man's suitcase to him.'

'I know,' said Mike earnestly. 'It's most frightfully sweet of you. That's how I feel about it.'

Alleyn took him away and shoved him into an old and begrimed raincoat, a cloth cap and a muffler. 'You wouldn't deceive a village idiot in a total eclipse,' he said, 'but out you go .'

He watched Mike drive away and returned to his wife.

'What'll happen?' she asked.

'Knowing Mike, I should say he will end up in the front stalls and go on to supper with the leading lady. She, by the way, is Coralie Bourne. Very lovely and twenty years his senior so he'll probably fall in love with her.' Alleyn reached for his tobacco jar and paused. 'I wonder what's happened to her husband,' he said.

'Who was he?'

'An extraordinary chap. Benjamin Vlasnoff. Violent temper. Looked like a bandit. Wrote two very good plays and got run in three times for common assault. She tried to divorce him but it didn't go through. I think he afterwards lit off to Russia.' Alleyn yawned. 'I believe she had a hell of a time with him,' he said.

'All Night Delivery,' said Mike in a hoarse voice, touching his cap. 'Suitcase. One.'

'Here you are,' said the woman who had answered the door. 'Carry it carefully, now, it's not locked and the catch springs out.'

'Fanks,' said Mike. 'Much obliged. Chilly, ain't it?'

He took the suitcase out to the car.

It was a fresh spring night. Sloane Square was threaded with mist and all the lamps had halos round them. It was the kind of night when individual sounds separate themselves from the conglomerate voice of London; hollow sirens spoke imperatively down on the river and a bugle rang out over in Chelsea Barracks; a night, Mike thought, for adventure.

He opened the rear door of the car and heaved the case in. The catch flew open, the lid dropped back and the contents fell out. 'Damn!' said Mike and switched on the inside light.

Lying on the floor of the car was a false beard.

It was flaming red and bushy and was mounted on a chinpiece. With it was incorporated a stiffened moustache. There were wire hooks to attach the whole thing behind the ears. Mike laid it carefully on the seat. Next he picked up a wide black hat, then a vast overcoat with a fur collar, finally a pair of black gloves.

Mike whistled meditatively and thrust his hands into the pockets of Alleyn's mackintosh. His right hand fingers closed on a card. He pulled it out. 'Chief Detective-Inspector Alleyn,' he read, 'CID. New Scotland Yard.'

'Honestly,' thought Mike exultantly, 'this is a gift.'

Ten minutes later a car pulled into the kerb at the nearest parking place to the Jupiter Theatre. From it emerged a figure carrying a suitcase. It strode rapidly along Hawke Street and turned into the stage door alley. As it passed under the dirty lamp it paused, and thus murkily lit, resembled an illustration from some Edwardian spy story. The face was completely shadowed, a black cavern from which there projected a square of scarlet beard, which was the only note of colour.

The doorkeeper who was taking the air with a member of stage staff, moved forward, peering at the stranger.

'Was you wanting something?'

'I'm taking this case in for Mr Gill.'

'He's in front. You can leave it with me.'

'I'm so sorry,' said the voice behind the beard, 'but I promised I'd leave it backstage myself.'

'So you will be leaving it. Sorry, sir, but no one's admitted be'ind without a card.'

'A card? Very well. Here is a card.'

He held it out in his black-gloved hand. The stage doorkeeper, unwillingly removing his gaze from the beard, took the card and examined it under the light. 'Coo!' he said, 'what's up, governor?'

'No matter. Say nothing of this.'

The figure waved its hand and passed through the door.

' 'Ere!' said the doorkeeper excitedly to the stage hand, 'take a slant at this. That's a plainclothes flattie, that was.'

'*Plain* clothes!' said the stage hand. 'Them!'

' 'E's disguised,' said the doorkeeper. 'That's what it is. 'E's disguised 'isself.'

' 'E's bloody well lorst 'isself be'ind them whiskers if you arst me.'

Out on the stage someone was saying in a pitched and beautifully articulate voice: *'I've always loathed the view from these windows. However if that's the sort of thing you admire. Turn off the lights, damn you. Look at it.'*

'Watch it, now, watch it,' whispered a voice so close to Mike that he jumped.

'OK,' said a second voice somewhere above his head. The lights on the set turned blue.

'Kill that working light.'

'Working light gone.'

Curtains in the set were wrenched aside and a window flung open. An actor appeared, leaning out quite close to Mike, seeming to look into his face and saying very distinctly: 'God: it's frightful!' Mike backed away towards a passage, lit only from an open door. A great volume of sound broke out beyond the stage. 'House lights,' said the sharp voice. Mike turned into the passage. As he did so, someone came through the door. He found himself face to face with Coralie Bourne, beautifully dressed and heavily painted.

For a moment she stood quite still; then she made a curious gesture with her right hand, gave a small breathy sound and fell forward at his feet.

Anthony was tearing his programme into long strips and dropping them on the floor of the OP box. On his right hand, above and below, was the audience; sometimes laughing, sometimes still, sometimes as one corporate being, raising its hands and striking them together. As now; when down on the stage, Canning Cumberland, using a strange voice, and inspired by some inward devil, flung back the window and said: 'God: it's frightful!'

'Wrong! Wrong!' Anthony cried inwardly, hating Cumberland, hating Barry George because he let one speech of three words override him, hating the audience because they liked it. The curtain descended with a long sign on the second act and a sound like heavy rain filled the theatre, swelled prodigiously and continued after the house lights welled up.

'They seem,' said a voice behind him, 'to be liking your play.'

It was Gosset, who owned the Jupiter and had backed the show. Anthony turned on him stammering: 'He's destroying it. It should be the other man's scene. He's stealing.'

'My boy,' said Gosset, 'he's an actor.'

'He's drunk. It's intolerable.'

He felt Gosset's hand on his shoulder.

'People are watching us. You're on show. This is a big thing for you; a first play, and going enormously. Come and have a drink, old boy. I want to introduce you – '

Anthony got up and Gosset, with his arm across his shoulders, flashing smiles, patting him, led him to the back of the box.

'I'm sorry,' Anthony said. 'I can't. Please let me off. I'm going backstage.'

'Much better not, old son.' The hand tightened on his shoulder. 'Listen, old son – ' But Anthony had freed himself and slipped through the pass door from the box to the stage.

At the foot of the breakneck stairs Dendra Gay stood waiting. 'I thought you'd come,' she said.

Anthony said: 'He's drunk. He's murdering the play.'

'It's only one scene, Tony. He finishes early in the next act. It's going colossally.'

'But don't you understand – '

'I do. You *know* I do. But you're a success, Tony darling! You can hear it and smell it and feel it in your bones.'

'Dendra – ' he said uncertainly.

Someone came up and shook his hand and went on shaking it. Flats were being laced together with a slap of rope on canvas. A chandelier ascended into darkness. 'Lights,' said the stage manager, and the set was flooded with them. A distant voice began chanting. 'Last act, please. Last act.'

'Miss Bourne all right?' the stage manager suddenly demanded.

'She'll be all right. She's not on for ten minutes,' said a woman's voice.

'What's the matter with Miss Bourne?' Anthony asked.

'Tony, I must go and so must you. Tony, it's going to be grand. *Please* think so. *Please.*'

'Dendra – ' Tony began, but she had gone.

Beyond the curtain, horns and flutes announced the last act.

'Clear please.'

The stage hands came off.

'House lights.'

'House lights gone.'

'Stand by.'

And while Anthony still hesitated in the OP corner, the curtain rose. Canning Cumberland and H J Bannington opened the last act.

As Mike knelt by Coralie Bourne he heard someone enter the passage behind him. He turned and saw, silhouetted against the lighted stage, the actor who had looked at him through a window in the set. The silhouette seemed to repeat the gesture Coralie Bourne had used, and to flatten itself against the wall.

A woman in an apron came out of the open door.

'I say – here!' Mike said.

Three things happened almost simultaneously. The woman cried out and knelt beside him. The man disappeared through a door on the right.

The woman, holding Coralie Bourne in her arms, said violently: 'Why have you come back?' Then the passage lights came on.

Mike said: 'Look here, I'm most frightfully sorry,' and took off the broad black hat. The dresser gaped at him, Coralie Bourne made a crescendo sound in her throat and opened her eyes.

'Katie?' she said.

'It's all right, my lamb. It's not him, dear. You're all right.' The dresser jerked her head at Mike: 'Get out of it,' she said.

'Yes, of course, I'm most frightfully – ' He backed out of the passage, colliding with a youth who said: 'Five minutes, please.'

The dresser called out: 'Tell them she's not well. Tell them to hold the curtain.'

'No,' said Coralie Bourne strongly. 'I'm all right, Katie. Don't say anything. Katie, what was it?'

They disappeared into the room on the left.

Mike stood in the shadow of a stack of scenic flats by the entry into the passage. There was great activity on the stage. He caught a glimpse of Anthony Gill on the far side talking to a girl. The call boy was speaking to the stage manager who now shouted into space: 'Miss Bourne all right?'

The dresser came into the passage and called: 'She'll be all right. She's not on for ten minutes.'

The youth began chanting: 'Last act, please.'

The stage manager gave a series of orders. A man with an eyeglass and a florid beard came from further down the passage and stood outside the set, bracing his figure and giving little tweaks to his clothes. There was a sound of horns and flutes. Canning Cumberland emerged from the room on the right and on his way to the stage, passed close to Mike, leaving a strong smell of alcohol behind him. The curtain rose.

Behind his shelter, Mike stealthily removed his beard and stuffed it into the pocket of his overcoat.

A group of stage hands stood nearby. One of them said in a hoarse whisper:' 'E's squiffy.'

'Garn, 'e's going good.'

'So 'e may be going good. And for why? *Becos* 'e's squiffy.'

Ten minutes passed. Mike thought: 'This affair has definitely not gone according to plan.' He listened. Some kind of tension seemed to be building up on the stage. Canning Cumberland's voice rose on a loud but blurred note.

A door in the set opened. 'Don't bother to come,' Cumberland said. 'Goodbye. I can find my way out.' The door slammed. Cumberland was standing near Mike. Then, very close, there was a loud explosion. The scenic flats vibrated. Mike's flesh leapt on his bones and Cumberland went into his dressing rooms. Mike heard the key turn in the door. The smell of alcohol mingled with the smell of gunpowder. A stage hand moved to a trestle table and laid a pistol on it. The actor with the eyeglass made an exit. He spoke for a moment to the stage manager, passed Mike and disappeared in the passage.

Smells. There were all sorts of smells. Subconsciously, still listening to the play, he began to sort them out. Glue. Canvas. Greasepaint. The call boy tapped on the doors. 'Mr George, please. Miss Bourne, please.' They came out, Coralie Bourne with her dresser. Mike heard her turn a door handle and say something. An indistinguishable voice answered her. Then she and her dresser passed him. The others spoke to her and she nodded and then seemed to withdraw into herself, waiting with her head bent, ready to make her entrance. Presently she drew back, walked swiftly to the door in the set, flung it open and swept on, followed a minute later by Barry George.

Smells. Dust, stale paint, cloth. Gas. Increasingly, the smell of gas.

The group of stage hands moved away behind the set to the side of the stage. Mike edged out of cover. He could see the prompt corner. The stage manager stood there with folded arms, watching the action. Behind him were grouped the players who were not on. Two dressers stood apart, watching. The light from the set caught their faces. Coralie Bourne's voice sent phrases flying like birds into the auditorium.

Mike began peering at the floor. Had he kicked some gas fitting adrift? The call boy passed him, stared at him over his shoulder and went down the passage, tapping. 'Five minutes to the curtain, please. Five minutes.'

The actor with the elderly make-up followed the call boy out. 'God, what a stink of gas,' he whispered.

'Chronic, ain't it?' said the call boy. They stared at Mike and then crossed to the waiting group. The man said something to the stage manager who tipped his head up, sniffing. He made an impatient gesture and turned back to the prompt box, reaching over the prompter's head. A bell rang somewhere up in the flies and Mike saw a stage hand climb to the curtain platform.

The little group near the prompt corner was agitated. They looked back towards the passage entrance. The call boy nodded and came running back. He knocked on the first door on the right. '*Mr Cumberland! Mr Cumberland!* You're on for the call.' He rattled the door handle. '*Mr Cumberland! You're on.*'

Mike ran into the passage. The call boy coughed retchingly and jerked his hand at the door. 'Gas!'

'Break it in.'

'I'll get Mr Reynolds.'

He was gone. It was a narrow passage. From halfway across the opposite room Mike took a run, head down, shoulder forward, at the door. It gave a little and a sickening increase in the smell caught him in the lungs. A vast storm of noise had broken out and as he took another run he thought: 'It's hailing outside.'

'Just a minute *if you* please, sir.'

It was a stage hand. He'd got a hammer and screwdriver. He wedged the point of the screwdriver between the lock and the door-post, drove it home and wrenched. The screws squeaked, the wood splintered and gas poured into the passage. 'No winders,' coughed the stage hand.

Mike wound Alleyn's scarf over his mouth and nose. Half-forgotten instructions from anti-gas drill occurred to him. The room looked queer but he could see the man slumped down in the chair quite clearly. He stooped low and ran in.

He was knocking against things as he backed out, lugging the dead weight. His arms tingled. A high insistent voice hummed in his brain. He floated a short distance and came to earth on a concrete floor among several pairs of legs. A long way off, someone said loudly: 'I can only thank you for being so kind to what I know, too well, is a very imperfect play.' Then the sound of hail began again. There was a heavenly stream of clear air flowing into his mouth and nostrils. 'I could eat it,' he thought and sat up.

The telephone rang. 'Suppose,' Mrs Alleyn suggested, 'that this time you ignore it.'

'It might be the Yard,' Alleyn said, and answered it.

'Is that Chief Detective-Inspector Alleyn's flat? I'm speaking from the Jupiter Theatre. I've rung up to say that the Chief Inspector is here and that he's had a slight mishap. He's all right, but I think it might be as well for someone to drive him home. No need to worry.'

'What sort of mishap?' Alleyn asked.

'Er – well – er, he's been a bit gassed.'

'*Gassed!* All right. Thanks, I'll come.'

'*What* a bore for you, darling,' said Mrs Alleyn. 'What sort of case is it? Suicide?'

'Masquerading within the meaning of the act, by the sound of it. Mike's in trouble.'

'What trouble, for Heaven's sake?'

'Got himself gassed. He's all right. Goodnight, darling. Don't wait up.'

When he reached the theatre, the front of the house was in darkness. He made his way down the side alley to the stage door where he was held up.

'Yard,' he said, and produced his official card.

' 'Ere,' said the stage doorkeeper, "ow many more of you?'

'The man inside was working for me,' said Alleyn and walked in. The doorkeeper followed, protesting.

To the right of the entrance was a large scenic dock from which the double doors had been rolled back. Here Mike was sitting in an armchair, very white about the lips. Three men and two women, all with painted faces, stood near him and behind them a group of stage hands with Reynolds, the stage manager, and, apart from these, three men in evening dress. The men looked woodenly shocked. The women had been weeping.

'I'm most frightfully sorry, sir,' Mike said. 'I've tried to explain. This,' he added generally, 'is Inspector Alleyn.'

'I can't understand all this,' said the oldest of the men in evening dress irritably. He turned on the doorkeeper. 'You said – '

'I seen 'is card – '

'I know,' said Mike, 'but you see – '

'This is Lord Michael Lamprey,' Alleyn said. 'A recruit to the Police Department. What's happened here?'

'Doctor Rankin, would you – '

The second of the men in evening dress came forward. 'All right, Gosset. It's a bad business, Inspector. I've just been saying the police would have to be informed. If you'll come with me – '

Alleyn followed him through a door onto the stage proper. It was dimly lit. A trestle table had been set up in the centre and on it, covered with a sheet, was an unmistakable shape. The smell of gas, strong everywhere, hung heavily about the table.

'Who is it?'

'Canning Cumberland. He'd locked the door of his dressing room. There's a gas fire. Your young friend dragged him out, very pluckily, but it was no go. I was in front. Gosset, the manager, had asked me to supper. It's a perfectly clear case of suicide as you'll see.'

'I'd better look at the room. Anybody been in?'

'God, no. It was a job to clear it. They turned the gas off at the main. There's no window. They had to open the double doors at the back of the stage and a small outside door at the end of the passage. It may be possible to get in now.'

He led the way to the dressing room passage. 'Pretty thick, still,' he said. 'It's the first room on the right. They burst the lock. You'd better keep down near the floor.'

The powerful lights over the mirror were on and the room still had its look of occupation. The gas fire was against the left hand

wall. Alleyn squatted down by it. The tap was still turned on, its face
lying parallel with the floor. The top of the heater, the tap itself, and
the carpet near it, were covered with a creamish powder. On the end
of the dressing table shelf nearest to the stove was a box of this powder. Further along the shelf, greasepaints were set out in a row
beneath the mirror. Then came a wash basin and in front of this an
overturned chair. Alleyn could see the track of heels, across the pile
of the carpet, to the door immediately opposite. Beside the wash
basin was a quart bottle of whisky, three parts empty, and a tumbler.
Alleyn had had about enough and returned to the passage.

'Perfectly clear,' the hovering doctor said again, 'Isn't it?'

'I'll see the other rooms, I think.'

The one next to Cumberland's was like his in reverse, but smaller.
The heater was back to back with Cumberland's. The dressing shelf
was set out with much the same assortment of greasepaints. The tap
of this heater, too, was turned on. It was of precisely the same make
as the other and Alleyn, less embarrassed here by fumes, was able to
make a longer examination. It was a common enough type of gas fire.
The lead-in was from a pipe through a flexible metallic tube with a
rubber connection. There were two taps, one in the pipe and one at
the junction of the tube with the heater itself. Alleyn disconnected the
tube and examined the connection. It was perfectly sound, a close fit
and stained red at the end. Alleyn noticed a wiry thread of some red-
dish stuff resembling packing that still clung to it. The nozzle and tap
were brass, the tap pulling over when it was turned on, to lie in a parallel plane with the floor. No powder had been scattered about here.

He glanced round the room, returned to the door and read the
card: *'Mr Barry George.'*

The doctor followed him into the rooms opposite these, on the
left-hand side of the passage. They were a repetition in design of the
two he had already seen but were hung with women's clothes and
had a more elaborate assortment of greasepaint and cosmetics.

There was a mass of flowers in the star room. Alleyn read the
cards. One in particular caught his eye: *'From Anthony Gill to say a
most inadequate "thank you" for the great idea.'* A vase of red roses stood
before the mirror: *'To your greatest triumph, Coralie darling. C.C.'* In Miss
Gay's room there were only two bouquets, one from the management and one *'From Anthony, with love.'*

Again in each room he pulled off the lead-in to the heater and looked at the connection.

'All right, aren't they?' said the doctor.

'Quite all right. Tight fit. Good solid grey rubber.'

'Well, then – '

Next on the left was an unused room, and opposite it, 'Mr H J Bannington.' Neither of these rooms had gas fires. Mr Bannington's dressing table was littered with the usual array of greasepaint, the materials for his beard, a number of telegrams and letters, and several bills.

'About the body,' the doctor began.

'We'll get a mortuary van from the Yard.'

'But – Surely in a case of suicide – '

'I don't think this is suicide.'

'But, good God! – D'you mean there's been an accident?'

'No accident,' said Alleyn.

At midnight, the dressing room lights in the Jupiter Theatre were brilliant, and men were busy there with the tools of their trade. A constable stood at the stage door and a van waited in the yard. The front of the house was dimly lit and there, among the shrouded stalls, sat Coralie Bourne, Basil Gosset, H J Bannington, Dendra Gay, Anthony Gill, Reynolds, Katie the dresser, and the call boy. A constable sat behind them and another stood by the doors into the foyer. They stared across the backs of seats at the fire curtain. Spirals of smoke rose from their cigarettes and about their feet were discarded programmes. 'Basil Gosset presents I CAN FIND MY WAY OUT by Anthony Gill.'

In the manager's office Alleyn said: 'You're sure of your facts, Mike?'

'Yes, sir. Honestly. I was right up against the entrance into the passage. They didn't see me because I was in the shadow. It was very dark offstage.'

'You'll have to swear to it.'

'I know.'

'Good. All right, Thompson. Miss Gay and Mr Gosset may go home. Ask Miss Bourne to come in.'

When Sergeant Thompson had gone Mike said: 'I haven't had a chance to say I know I've made a perfect fool of myself. Using your card and everything.'

'Irresponsible gaiety doesn't go down very well in the service, Mike. You behaved like a clown.'

'I *am* a fool,' said Mike wretchedly.

The red beard was lying in front of Alleyn on Gosset's desk. He picked it up and held it out. 'Put it on,' he said.

'She might do another faint.'

'I think not. Now the hat: yes – yes, I see. Come in.'

Sergeant Thompson showed Coralie Bourne in and then sat at the end of the desk with his notebook.

Tears had traced their course through the powder on her face, carrying black cosmetic with them and leaving the greasepaint shining like snail tracks. She stood near the doorway looking dully at Michael. 'Is he back in England?' she said. 'Did he tell you to do this?' She made an impatient movement. 'Do take it off,' she said, 'it's a very bad beard. If Cann had only looked – ' Her lips trembled. 'Who told you to do it?'

'Nobody,' Mike stammered, pocketing the beard. 'I mean – As a matter of fact, Tony Gill – '

'*Tony?* But *he* didn't know. Tony wouldn't do it. Unless – '

'Unless?' Alleyn said.

She said frowning: 'Tony didn't want Cann to play the part that way. He was furious.'

'He says it was his dress for the Chelsea Arts Ball,' Mike mumbled. 'I brought it here. I just thought I'd put it on – it was idiotic, I know – for fun. I'd no idea you and Mr Cumberland would mind.'

'Ask Mr Gill to come in,' Alleyn said.

Anthony was white and seemed bewildered and helpless. 'I've told Mike,' he said. 'It was my dress for the ball. They sent it round from the costume hiring place this afternoon but I forgot it. Dendra reminded me and rang up the Delivery people – or Mike, as it turns out – in the interval.'

'Why,' Alleyn asked, 'did you choose that particular disguise?'

'I didn't. I didn't know what to wear and I was too rattled to think. They said they were hiring things for themselves and would get something for me. They said we'd all be characters out of a Russian melodrama.'

'Who said this?'

'Well – well, it was Barry George, actually.'

'*Barry,*' Coralie Bourne said. '*It was Barry.*'

'I don't understand,' Anthony said. 'Why should a fancy dress upset everybody?'

'It happened,' Alleyn said, 'to be a replica of the dress usually worn by Miss Bourne's husband who also had a red beard. That was it, wasn't it, Miss Bourne? I remember seeing him – '

'Oh, yes,' she said, 'you would. He was known to the police.' Suddenly she broke down completely. She was in an armchair near the desk but out of the range of its shaded lamp. She twisted and writhed, beating her hand against the padded arm of the chair. Sergeant Thompson sat with his head bent and his hand over his notes. Mike, after an agonized glance at Alleyn, turned his back. Anthony Gill leant over her: 'Don't,' he said violently. 'Don't! For God's sake, stop.'

She twisted away from him and, gripping the edge of the desk, began to speak to Alleyn; little by little gaining mastery of herself. 'I want to tell you. I want you to understand. Listen.' Her husband had been fantastically cruel, she said. 'It was a kind of slavery.' But when she sued for divorce he brought evidence of adultery with Cumberland. They had thought he knew nothing. 'There was an abominable scene. He told us he was going away. He said he'd keep track of us and if I tried again for divorce, he'd come home. He was very friendly with Barry in those days.' He had left behind him the first draft of a play he had meant to write for her and Cumberland. It had a wonderful scene for them. 'And now you will never have it,' he had said, 'because there is no other playwright who could make this play for you but I.' He was, she said, a melodramatic man but he was never ridiculous. He returned to the Ukraine where he was born and they had heard no more of him. In a little while she would have been able to presume death. But years of waiting did not agree with Canning Cumberland. He drank consistently and at his worst used to imagine her husband was about to return. 'He was really terrified of Ben,' she said. 'He seemed like a creature in a nightmare.'

Anthony Gill said: 'This play – was it – ?'

'Yes. There was an extraordinary similarity between your play and his. I saw at once that Ben's central scene would enormously strengthen your piece. Cann didn't want me to give it to you. Barry knew. He said: "Why not?" He wanted Cann's part and was furious when he didn't get it. So you see, when he suggested you should dress and make-up like Ben – ' She turned to Alleyn. 'You see?'

'What did Cumberland do when he saw you?' Alleyn asked Mike.

'He made a queer movement with his hands as if – well, as if he expected me to go for him. Then he just bolted into his room.'

'He thought Ben had come back,' she said.

'Were you alone at any time after you fainted?' Alleyn asked.

'I? No. No, I wasn't. Katie took me into my dressing room and stayed with me until I went on for the last scene.'

'One other question. Can you, by any chance, remember if the heater in your room behaved at all oddly?'

She looked wearily at him. 'Yes, it did give a sort of plop, I think. It made me jump. I was nervy.'

'You went straight from your room to the stage?'

'Yes. With Katie. I wanted to go to Cann. I tried the door when we came out. It was locked. He said: "Don't come in." I said: "It's all right. It wasn't Ben," and went on to the stage.'

'I heard Miss Bourne,' Mike said.

'He must have made up his mind by then. He was terribly drunk when he played his last scene.' She pushed her hair back from her forehead. 'May I go?' she asked Alleyn.

'I've sent for a taxi. Mr Gill, will you see if it's there? In the meantime, Miss Bourne, would you like to wait in the foyer?'

'May I take Katie home with me?'

'Certainly. Thompson will find her. Is there anyone else we can get?'

'No, thank you. Just old Katie.'

Alleyn opened the door for her and watched her walk into the foyer. 'Check up with the dresser, Thompson,' he murmured, 'and get Mr H. J. Bannington.'

He saw Coralie Bourne sit on the lower step of the dress-circle stairway and lean her head against the wall. Nearby, on a gilt easel, a huge photograph of Canning Cumberland smiled handsomely at her.

H. J. Bannington looked pretty ghastly. He had rubbed his hand across his face and smeared his makeup. Florid red paint from his lips had stained the crêpe hair that had been gummed on and shaped into a beard. His monocle was still in his left eye and gave him an extraordinarily rakish look. 'See here,' he complained, 'I've about *had* this party. When do we go home?'

Alleyn uttered placatory phrases and got him to sit down.

He checked over HJ's movements after Cumberland left the stage and found that his account tallied with Mike's. He asked if HJ had visited any of the other dressing rooms and was told acidly that HJ knew his place in the company. 'I remained in my unheated and squalid kennel, thank you very much.'

'Do you know if Mr Barry George followed your example?'

'Couldn't say, old boy. He didn't come near *me.*'

'Have you any theories at all about this unhappy business, Mr Bannington?'

'Do you mean, why did Cann do it? Well, speak no ill of the dead, but I'd have thought it was pretty obvious he was morbid-drunk. Tight as an owl when we finished the second act. Ask the great Mr Barry George. Cann took the big scene away from Barry with both hands and left him looking pathetic. All wrong artistically, but that's how Cann was in his cups.' HJ's wicked little eyes narrowed. 'The great Mr George,' he said, 'must be feeling very unpleasant by now. You might say he'd got a suicide on his mind, mightn't you? Or don't you know about that?'

'It was not suicide.'

The glass dropped from HJ's eye. 'God,' he said. 'God. I told Bob Reynolds! I told him the whole plant wanted overhauling.'

'The gas plant, you mean?'

'Certainly. I was in the gas business years ago. Might say I'm in it still with a difference, ha-ha!'

'Ha-ha!' Alleyn agreed politely. He leaned forward. 'Look here,' he said: 'We can't dig up a gas man at this time of night and may very likely need an expert opinion. You can help us.'

'Well, old boy, I was rather pining for a spot of shut-eye. But, of course – '

'I shan't keep you very long.'

'God, I hope not!' said HJ earnestly.

Barry George had been made up pale for the last act. Colourless lips and shadows under his cheek bones and eyes had skilfully underlined his character as a repatriated but broken prisoner-of-war. Now, in the glare of the office lamp, he looked like a grossly exaggerated figure of mourning. He began at once to tell Alleyn how grieved and horrified he was. Everybody, he said, had their faults, and poor old Cann was no exception but wasn't it terrible to think what could happen to a man who let himself go downhill? He, Barry George, was abnormally sensitive and he didn't think he'd ever really get over the awful shock this had been to him. What, he wondered, could be at the bottom of it? Why had poor old Cann decided to end it all?

'Miss Bourne's theory,' Alleyn began. Mr George laughed. 'Coralie?' he said. 'So she's got a theory! Oh, well. Never mind.'

'Her theory is this. Cumberland saw a man whom he mistook for her husband and, having a morbid dread of his return, drank the greater part of a bottle of whisky and gassed himself. The clothes and beard that deceived him had, I understand, been ordered by you for Mr Anthony Gill.'

This statement produced startling results. Barry George broke into a spate of expostulation and apology. There had been no thought in his mind of resurrecting poor old Ben, who was no doubt dead but had been, mind you, in many ways one of the best. They were all to go to the Ball as exaggerated characters from melodrama. Not for the world – he gesticulated and protested. A line of sweat broke out along the margin of his hair. 'I don't know what you're getting at,' he shouted. 'What are you suggesting?'

'I'm suggesting, among other things, that Cumberland was murdered.'

'You're mad! He'd locked himself in. They had to break down the door. There's no window. You're crazy!'

'Don't,' Alleyn said wearily, 'let us have any nonsense about sealed rooms. Now, Mr George, you knew Benjamin Vlasnoff pretty well. Are you going to tell us that when you suggested Mr Gill should wear a coat with a fur collar, a black sombrero, black gloves and a red beard, it never occurred to you that his appearance might be a shock to Miss Bourne and to Cumberland?'

'I wasn't the only one,' he blustered. 'HJ knew. And if it had scared him off, *she* wouldn't have been so sorry. She'd had about enough of him. Anyway if this is murder, the costume's got nothing to do with it.'

'That,' Alleyn said, getting up, 'is what we hope to find out.'

* * *

In Barry George's room, Detective Sergeant Bailey, a fingerprint expert, stood by the gas heater. Sergeant Gibson, a police photographer, and a uniformed constable were near the door. In the centre of the room stood Barry George, looking from one man to another and picking at his lips.

'I don't know why he wants me to watch all this,' he said. 'I'm exhausted. I'm emotionally used up. What's he doing? Where is he?'

Alleyn was next door in Cumberland's dressing room, with HJ, Mike and Sergeant Thompson. It was pretty clear now of fumes and the gas fire was burning comfortably. Sergeant Thompson sprawled in the armchair near the heater, his head sunk and his eyes shut.

'This is the theory, Mr Bannington,' Alleyn said. 'You and Cumberland have made your final exits; Miss Bourne and Mr George and Miss Gay are all on the stage. Lord Michael is standing just outside the entrance to the passage. The dressers and stage staff are watching the play from the side. Cumberland has locked himself in this room. There he is, dead drunk and sound asleep. The gas fire is burning, full pressure. Earlier in the evening he powdered himself and a thick layer of the powder lies undisturbed on the tap. Now.'

He tapped on the wall.

The fire blew out with a sharp explosion. This was followed by the hiss of escaping gas. Alleyn turned the taps off. 'You see,' he said, 'I've left an excellent print on the powdered surface. Now, come next door.'

Next door, Barry George appealed to him stammering: 'But I didn't know. I don't know anything about it. I don't *know.*'

'Just show Mr Bannington, will you, Bailey?'

Bailey knelt down. The lead-in was disconnected from the tap on the heater. He turned on the tap in the pipe and blew down the tube.

'An air lock, you see. It works perfectly.'

HJ was staring at Barry George. 'But I don't know about gas, HJ, HJ, tell them – '

'One moment.' Alleyn removed the towels that had been spread over the dressing shelf, revealing a sheet of clean paper on which lay the rubber push-on connection.

'Will you take this lens, Bannington, and look at it. You'll see that it's stained a florid red. It's a very slight stain but it's unmistakably greasepaint. And just above the stain you'll see a wiry hair. Rather like some sort of packing material, but it's not that. It's crêpe hair, isn't it?'

The lens wavered above the paper.

'Let me hold it for you,' Alleyn said. He put his hand over HJ's shoulder and, with a swift movement, plucked a tuft from his false moustache and dropped it on the paper. 'Identical, you see, ginger. It seems to be stuck to the connection with spirit gum.'

The lens fell. HJ twisted round, faced Alleyn for a second, and then struck him full in the face. He was a small man but it took three of them to hold him.

'In a way, sir, it's handy when they have a smack at you,' said Detective Sergeant Thompson half an hour later. 'You can pull them in nice and straightforward without any "will you come to the station and make a statement" business.'

'Quite,' said Alleyn, nursing his jaw.

Mike said: 'He must have gone to the room after Barry George and Miss Bourne were called.'

'That's it. He had to be quick. The call boy would be round in a minute and he had to be back in his own room.'

'But look here – what about motive?'

'That, my good Mike, is precisely why, at half past one in the morning, we're still in this miserable theatre. You're getting a view of the duller aspect of homicide. Want to go home?'

'No. Give me another job.'

'Very well. About ten feet from the prompt entrance, there's a sort of garbage tin. Go through it.'

At seventeen minutes to two, when the dressing rooms and passage had been combed clean and Alleyn had called a spell, Mike came to him with filthy hands. *'Eureka'* he said, 'I hope.'

They all went into Bannington's room. Alleyn spread out on the dressing table the fragments of paper that Mike had given him.

'They'd been pushed down to the bottom of the tin,' Mike said.

Alleyn moved the fragments about. Thompson whistled through his teeth. Bailey and Gibson mumbled together.

'There you are,' Alleyn said at last.

They collected round him. The letter that H. J. Bannington had opened at this same table six hours and forty five minutes earlier, was pieced together like a jigsaw puzzle.

DearHJ,

    Having seen the monthly statement of my account, I called at my bank this morning and was shown a cheque that is undoubtedly a forgery. Your histrionic versatility, my dear HJ, is only equalled by your audacity as a calligraphist. But fame has its disadvantages. The teller has recognized you. I propose to take action.

'Unsigned,' said Bailey.

'Look at the card on the red roses in Miss Bourne's room signed CC. It's a very distinctive hand.' Alleyn turned to Mike. 'Do you still want to be a policeman?'

'Yes.'

'Lord help you. Come and talk to me at the office tomorrow.'

'Thank you, sir.'

They went out, leaving a constable on duty. It was a cold morning. Mike looked up at the façade of the Jupiter. He could just make out the shape of the neon sign: I CAN FIND MY WAY OUT *by Anthony Gill.*